Hecate's Glory

Tor Books by Karen Michalson

Enemy Glory
Hecate's Glory

Hecate's Glory

Karen Michalson

TOR® **A Tom Doherty Associates Book** *New York*

HECATE'S GLORY

Edited by David G. Hartwell

A Tor Book
Published by Tom Doherty Associates, LLC
175 Fifth Avenue
New York, NY 10010

www.tor.com

Tor® is a registered trademark of Tom Doherty Associates, LLC.

Library of Congress Cataloging-in-Publication Data

Michalson, Karen.
    Hecate's glory / Karen Michalson.
        p. cm.
    "A Tom Doherty Associates book."
    ISBN 0-312-89060-5
    1. Young men—Fiction. 2. Wizards—Fiction. I. Title.

PS3563.I33123 H4 2003
813'.914—dc21

                                                    2002038759

First Edition: February 2003

0 9 8 7 6 5 4 3 2 1

For Bill
Again, for being there

Acknowledgments

Grateful acknowledgment is made to:

Jennie Dunham, my literary agent, for continuing belief in and support of this project.

David G. Hartwell of Tor Books for his peerless and patient editing. And to Moshe Feder of Tor for his enthusiasm, his copyediting ideas, and for suggesting the title of this volume. And to Sara Schwager for her copyediting. And to Jodi Rosoff of Tor for coordinating publicity for this volume and for its predecessor.

Tom Kidd of Pies Pak Public Relations for bookings and promotion.

Fellow writers Leah M. Hughes and Eva Wojcik-Obert for promotion, support, and friendship. May you both be darkly blessed.

One

I died before I woke, like the old prayer threatens.

I do not know how long I died. I do not know how long I lay dead and pulsing before my return. At some point in my waking it seemed that I had dreamt a good long death. Or rather, that I had died into a good long dream and found them both the same. There had been some sort of dream, for I remember my Goddess, Hecate, pulling my spirit into a questionable eternity and then my spirit making an equally questionable escape back into my body.

As I woke back into life, it seemed that my spirit had a strange downfall, that in my brief spell of dying I had risen and tripped through skies shifting storm clouds back and forth, and then that I had cut swiftly down through vanishing mountains of stars before I plopped and spread into something cold and wet. I subsided and felt like a thin dark shade flapping menace at the bottom of a dismal little pond. And then I was the pond and I knew my legs were coming soon.

I felt my thighs take shape first. They were like a distant kindhearted warmth forming itself into chaotic flesh and bone, and then they were only warm and prickly abstractions without the sensation of becoming a living body again, and then I lost them. I felt the inside of my face and eyes from somewhere in the back of my head, and then I felt my body emerge into a rough shape somewhere down below, and then I felt myself all through this new emergence for a long slow time. And then I lost all feeling again.

I lived and slept.

I think my sleep was long and purple, the still edge of a slow suspended dawn, but even there I felt or remembered something for I was sleeping now into life. I was a world away and falling, and Hecate was holding Her skirts to catch me into an eternity of bliss or damnation. But this time, before I reached Her, there were old colors in the wind that stopped my fall.

The colors told me who I was—told me how at first my spirit felt lighter than wave froth and then in spirit I was falling back into my North Country bed, and once again my body caught the weak charge of wakefulness.

First there were flimsy colors of shade which took long moments to come into yellows and browns, and then with effort I saw the old fisherman's nets and hooks hanging crazy from the ceiling above me, but their shapes blurred for a long time and I couldn't decide how far the ceiling was, or whether it was moving. I seemed to turn my head enough to hear something—a whisper of fish or a distant guess of wind still here and fading from the end of my dream. Purple sea flowers on the rough little table defined where I was and brought my long rest to rest. Their colors hurt me and so I slept in and out against them several times, lightly.

The slowly dying hurt of the colors suddenly tightened and jerked in quick painful tremors throughout my body. That is how I knew that their hurt was mine. But just as I succumbed to this new exquisite agony, the pain tore out of me and I went hollow and saw the heavy sword that Walworth, my self-appointed judge and enemy, was now holding steadily against my chest.

As I felt the unmistakable power in his magical weapon torturing me back into life, I devoutly wished that Walworth would find me guilty of the crimes he had come here to try me on, plunge his weapon through my heart, and make an end. It still wasn't clear to me why he was here, why he had found it in his interest to travel to the North Country, claim this old fisherman's hovel for Threle, and fulfill the niceties of Threlan law by listening to and scribing down the story I had spent this strange immeasurable night telling him.

What was clear to both of us was that it was a grave violation of all the laws of magic for me, a former student of Sunnashiven's Wizard School, to have entered this strange chaotic region and live to tell anybody about it.

That was Walworth's doing. The part about my still being somewhat alive, I mean. Walworth was aware that back in my youth, when I first began my formal studies in magic, my masters had placed a powerful wizard ban upon me and my fellow students against entering the North Country, so that should any of us ever do so, we would die in unimaginable agony from the slow wreck and heave of the Northern energies. He was also aware that I had come here to suffer and to die. Whether Walworth's decision to prolong my life and sickness so that I might tell my story for him to pronounce judgment upon is admirable or appalling, I do not pretend to say. Perhaps it is both.

I thought ruefully of my reasons for coming to the North Country, for choosing to die here of my ban. I had not yet shared these reasons with Walworth, but Walworth had not shared with me his reasons for coming here, nor why it was so damnably important to him to keep me alive for this makeshift trial, nor explained to me how he had become King of Threle in spite of losing the war.

He had informed me, as Threlan law demands, of the crimes of which I stood accused: of high treason against his person and his people, meaning against Threle itself; of using my priestly arts to aid his enemy, Emperor Roguehan, in his attempts to conquer Threle, and to influence the critical judgment of Walworth and his generals; and finally, of causing the death of his strange, god-touched cousin, Lord Cathe.

In matters in which a verdict of guilty would bring a sentence of death, which was in all of the above matters, Threlan law allows the accused to tell the court the story of his life, no matter how long the telling, for if a life might be taken, the full context of that life must be given due consideration. I had exercised my right under law to tell my story because I had hoped that Isulde, the dark fairy who invaded and tormented both of our dreams with her wild, melancholy beauty, would come for me as she had promised, or if not, one day read of it in the court record that Walworth had been tirelessly scribing. I wanted Isulde to know and remember my life, to remember me as one among an eternity of many who loved her. That was all I cared about before dying. I knew that this improbable hovel was her North Country home. The drunken old fisherman who snored and hooted through my telling was her foster father, as obsessed with her as Walworth and I were.

I despised both of them. The hovel was a physical emblem of the old man's slothfulness, and his slothfulness reminded me that for inscrutable reasons of her own, Isulde had come to him, in one of her multitude of fairy lives, to be fostered. He was not responsible for her existence, although throughout the night he had occasionally liked to give us that impression. Unearned glory disgusted me as much as it did Walworth, but he was too well bred to comment on it and I was too sick with the horror of my ban and of Hecate's sentence on me to bother.

I had come here not out of a sense of entitlement, but because I had hoped that Isulde would find and heal me, that her solemnly laughing fairy magic would brightly justify my decision to die. But Isulde had remained as cruelly distant as my ebbing life, as hidden as a cloud shadow vanishing under a cool clump of sea roots in the wide heat of the noon sun. I knew I was likely to die and never see or dream of her again. I knew she was likely to forget me. And I envied Walworth for the years he might have left to play with her in fairy dreams, should she continue to so choose.

Walworth kept his sword steady.

My thoughts of Isulde must have created yet another brief dying, because one of my heartbeats jerked me alive enough to once again feel the shock of knowing I was in body again and now had a physical life to hurt back into. Then I was getting rapidly used to my pulse again as Walworth put his sword aside and waited. When I woke to the energy of his sword, it was like my new pulse was bringing me somewhere and the sluggish blood rush to my head kept bobbing back down through my shoulders and neck to bring me somewhere else and so this particular return to life felt like the morning after a miserable drunk.

But I probably didn't breathe for a period of time after Walworth rushed life back into me from the sword, because I remember thinking that being alive I ought to breathe and it seems that I kept mentally preparing myself for doing so without hurrying things too much. There was a space where it seemed that I might live without breathing, or that my first new breath would commit me to my first new vulnerability and so there was strength in refusing to breathe. But air began to come and go in regular patterns and the patterns grounded me to living more securely than my freshly stinging blood and muscle.

"You have dried out your heart and tongue with speaking." Walworth said this matter-of-factly, in a voice that held neither mercy nor condemnation. Until he decided upon a verdict, he would not betray his thoughts.

I glanced dully at his sword arm and then at his hard, unrevealing eyes. "Dried and died from so much speaking. But there is much left to tell." My voice went hoarse and my words went invisible.

He glanced coolly at the snoring fisherman, who was drooling and chomping and wheezing low ugly whistle sounds. I wondered if we were both thinking of the injustice of a creature as beautiful as Isulde choosing that putrid mess of age and drunkenness as "father," of willingly coming to him in the childhood of her present incarnation to be fostered. The sources of the most exquisite beauty are laced with the most soul-killing ugliness.

Beauty knows no laws. Neither does justice.

As a priest of Hecate, and a devout votary of evil, I had a different perspective on justice than Walworth had. Hecate is evil, and insists that Her priests uphold all laws that restrain and restrict lives. Walworth, however, cherished law as an instrument of freedom, because the few laws that existed in Threle served only to augment that country's lack of restrictions. The fact that he was essentially violating a magical law by keeping me alive in order to fulfill the strict demands of Threlan justice was an interesting contradiction in his character that, were I not on my deathbed, I might have considered exploring. It surprised me, and reminded me that even back in my youth, when Walworth and I had been friends and comrades-in-arms fighting for Threle's defense, there was much about Walworth that no one, except possibly his tutor Mirand, was privy to.

Walworth spoke decisively. "As king and judge it is within my authority to call this court to recess."

"Perhaps you will let me die during the court's recess?" I asked dully, not caring whether he thought I was making a desperate joke.

"You are free to move about, although you are obviously incapable of doing so." Walworth spoke with an odd touch of geniality in his otherwise measured voice. While I was mulling over the implications of the distinction he had just made, cloudily attempting to decide whether it was a real distinction or merely a legal one, or perhaps just an inscrutable joke on his part, he destroyed my thoughts by saying, "The medicine I made to stave off your suffering is weakening. But there is a chance that I can keep life in you awhile longer by making more and magically charging it with my sword."

I nodded weakly, embarrassed at the offer, ashamed in any way to be beholden, and not entirely sure why it was worth feeling shame.

"Then we are recessed until my return." He stood up and left the hovel.

The door let in a pitch and fall of water waves, and then it closed and softened them. A soft racket of tides pulled all my hearing and awareness into the decrepit hovel where I was and I heard the steady sigh of an old strong lake wearing down the shore outside where the scarefisher Isulde had once made still creaked and wove kelp nets out of wind.

Then I plunged into my thoughts again to consider what I had told Walworth so far under this strange court proceeding. It is not exaggeration to say he had recorded a book's worth of my telling so far. And I knew that when I was finished with telling him the remainder of my tale, which stretched before me into uncertainty like the North Country night, I suspected that he would have yet another book's worth for the court records.

I had certainly been speaking a long time. But time runs differently here in the North Country than it does in the rest of the world, and so it was impossible to say how long I had been speaking my plea, whether for hours, or days, or strange broken pieces of centuries.

I wondered whether Walworth would decide that he was obligated to execute me at my story's end. Not that it mattered, I suppose, because even if he found me innocent, I still carried that horrific ban, and so chances were better than even that my fate would be worse than death. There seemed a fair chance that my ban would destroy me before I finished speaking and Walworth rendered his verdict, anyway.

Really this was all a knave's nonsense, but here we were, and there was nothing to say to it but to speak my life for the court.

So while Walworth absented himself into the night, and the fisherman snored and hooted, I considered the salient points of the tale I had told so far.

I was born in Sunnashiven, the capital of a redundantly poor and oppressive country called Sunna that I later cheerfully abandoned for the bright improbable freedom of Threle.

My earliest betrayal came from a witch called Mother Grana, who lived next to my parents' nervously empty and emotionally crippled house. When I was still young enough to puff under flattery without the ballast of cynicism, Grana dressed me in praise and played exciting magical games with me, and so I loved Grana. I loved her all the more so as my birth family abused and mocked my intellectual inclinations and taught me to be ashamed of wanting to study and become a great wizard.

Grana encouraged me by teaching me a wonderful and secret language, which I later learned was called Amara, a magical language known by very few wizards and spoken only by a few families in the Threlan duchy Walworth ruled before he became king. Grana also promised me magical and divine gifts that she claimed were made especially for me by the King of the Fairies and by all other manner of mythical creatures. And so I drew scintillating promises of a wonderful life from those promised gifts, but they were always blank disappointments that got "lost" or "destroyed" before she could deliver them.

One could argue I suppose that inextricably mixed with my first experience of betrayal was my first knowledge of Amara, that is, my first knowledge of something belonging to Walworth's duchy. In the map of divinity, that had to mean something, although I had no idea what.

Grana extracted a strange gift from me that has haunted me throughout my life. When I was still very young, and beginning to learn to sacrifice my true desires and longings to please Mother Grana, to destroy pieces of my young life every day to earn her approval, she led me through a spell of terrible and sickening power. The spell resulted in her pregnancy, even though she was very old, and her pregnancy resulted in the birth of a strange child that our temple priests adopted and named Lord Cathe. It would be years before I learned that through some nearly incomprehensible twist of genealogy, Cathe was Walworth's cousin. But what I learned throughout my youth was that Lord Cathe was a "child of the gods"—that he grew and aged more rapidly than nature allowed normal humans to. And then, to end the famine that was decimating Sunna, his growth was stopped by the temple priests and he was taken prisoner to be offered as a sacrifice.

Without intending to, I became instrumental in saving his life.

Walworth would surely have to consider this as he mulled over whether I was guilty of causing Cathe's death. He would have to remember that his loyal companion, Baniff the Gnome, rescued Cathe by working an exceptionally clever bit of magical illusion that resulted in me being placed in the cell and led out to be sacrificed in Cathe's place.

And then Baniff did the decent thing and rescued me. Although he did so at the insistence of my acquaintance Lady Aleta, a young fighter who would one day rule Clio, an independent county north of Sunna that belonged to no sovereign nation. Aleta hated studying in Sunnashiven and couldn't wait to return to her homeland, but she felt obligated to me because I had come into possession of a wizard's key that seemed important to some secret cause she and Baniff were working for.

Baniff put enough value on that key to take me to Threle, where I quickly became a member of Walworth's household and privy to the secret cause that concerned Aleta and Baniff. I learned that Baniff, Walworth, Walworth's tutor Master Wizard Mirand, and Walworth's twin sister Caethne, were planning a secret defense of Threle against agents of a rival warlord, Roguehan, who was conquering an empire.

I also learned that one of these agents was my teacher from Sunnashiven's Wizard School, a particularly incompetent master wizard called Grendel, whom I later had a cheerful hand in killing. All to defend Threle, of course. Would Walworth remember that when he thought about his verdict? Would it matter that I had once killed for him?

Or would he remember that Mirand had questioned my motivation in this act? That Mirand himself had died as an indirect result of that act? Mirand of course had been brought back to life by King Thoren's wizards, Thoren having been Threle's ruler at that time. Would Walworth remember how my actions on his behalf helped to destroy the entire border town we had been living in, and all the people in it? People Walworth had sworn by whatever gods he believed in to defend? Would he believe that I suffered over that horror as much as he suffered? That I suffered at all?

About my first foray into mass destruction, unintended though it was. Anyone who cares to can read the records for the sad details. Go to the Duchy of Helas, or what was the Duchy of Helas before Walworth was given control of it, and read the scars in the land. Listen to the wind weep blood for what once lived there.

I remember riding through all the destruction as it happened, experiencing the death throes of the town in my person because I had loved that town so much. I was being led through this torture by Lord Cathe, who, to my great surprise, had made another unexpected appearance in my miserable life. Cathe tricked me into separating from my friends and taking refuge in Kursen Monastery in the Duchy of Kant, where King Thoren couldn't punish me. My friends were riding to see Thoren, to explain about the town and the danger Threle was in, and it wasn't clear whether Thoren would believe them or hold them to account for the town's destruction. Then Thoren had Walworth and his companions arrested and put on trial for treason against Threle.

While I remained at Kursen Monastery, a place devoted to training students who felt they had a calling to become priests of evil deities, I became the scribe of El, Kursen's thoroughly evil and thoroughly self-divided high priest. That is how I learned that El was involved in forging letters and paying witnesses to lie in order to make it appear that Walworth was guilty of treason. Using the wizardry Mirand had taught me, I carefully collected as much evidence as I could and managed to save my friends' lives, and most likely save Threle, too, at their treason trial.

And my reward was to be consigned back to imprisonment in Kursen Monastery, in order to fulfill some bizarre detail of Threlan law. And no, Walworth did nothing to arrange for my escape. Thoren gave him command of the Threlan army and authority to fight openly against Roguehan. I suppose he was too busy defending his country to remember the friend who saved his life.

I must admit, however, that my own leaps into friendship after that experience were not particularly noble. Every year, in the dead of winter, Kursen Monastery chose a "Sun King," a student who was designated by various solar symbols to become a petty tyrant over his fellows for the next year. As an exercise in humility, everyone was bound to obey the Sun King's slightest whim or be turned out of Kursen without record of ever having studied there. The Sun King was led outside each winter as an offering to the killing cold and left there for a day. Should he survive, he ruled for the next year.

I befriended Devon, a young boy who was the designated Sun King, by magically forcing his affections to me. I secretly made sure that he lived through each winter, and through Devon I ruled Kursen as much I could considering El kept my spirit in thrall and had absolute power over me should he choose to exercise it. Devon and I shared rooms with a splendidly incompetent advanced clerical student named Cristo whose only discernible gift was his ability to annoy everyone in Kursen, El included. And so I had my own household, which I sometimes considered a sad foil to Walworth's.

After it became clear that Walworth was willing to abandon me, I bitterly made a decision to accept evil and to study under El to become a priest of Hecate, so I might learn the ways of evil and wreak revenge on the friends who had abandoned me.

One disappointment there was especially bitter. An illusionist named Welm, one of Roguehan's spies, was briefly held prisoner in the monastery for stealing a holy relic while posing as a wine keeper. For inexplicable reasons, I desperately wanted to believe that this illusionist was Baniff, disguising himself with magic and entering Kursen with the intent of escaping with me. For a while I blessed the fortunes of war. But when I learned beyond any distortion of reason that Welm was not Baniff, I was pleased to facilitate his escape and promised to use my priestly arts to do a favor for Roguehan in exchange for one day being given a position in Roguehan's court that would allow me to wreak revenge on Walworth.

The favor asked was to create enough psychic stresses in my master, El, that he would willingly choose to damn his spirit for eternity by turning from evil to good. I was to encourage El to reject his own evil deities and choose to suffer in eternity for betraying his calling to evil. El had his own psychic cracks and divisions. Every day of his life, whether he cared to admit it to himself or not, he violated a principal law of evil by loving his work. Evil demands self-sacrifice, but El made no such sacrifice. He liked what he did, and that was the lever I needed delicately to turn to widen this deadly contradiction in his heart.

And after I made this deal, Cathe showed up in my life with another deal. He wanted to be a god. To be immortal. And Caethne, Walworth's sister and Cathe's cousin, who Cathe claimed, improbably, was also his wife, had promised Cathe to accomplish this for him by bathing him in Walworth's blood. Although it sounded wildly out of character to me for Caethne to make such an offer, it was difficult to doubt her motivation. For as Cathe explained to me, she needed the help of a magician who was in a position to magically force Mirand to fall in love with her. She had loved him ever since he tutored her in magic, but he had not returned her passion. And because she was a student of his, he could easily defend himself against her magical advances. Of course I had once been a student of his, too, but my studies had been brief enough that any love spell I devised had a chance of working. Cathe assured me that if Mirand were to love her, Caethne would make Cathe a god. And if he were to become a god, I would be able to inherit Walworth's duchy and wreak revenge on the whole family.

I liked it.

And so I agreed to a second deal and found myself in a position of having to fulfill my professional obligations to each side.

I also struck up a strange, quasi friendship with a traveling minstrel called Ellisand. He played brilliant, beautiful elvish music, and he occasionally gave performances at Kursen Monastery in the course of his travels. The monks paid him well to make the students feel badly about themselves, especially those students who had strong musical proclivities but none of Ellisand's considerable gifts. And self-loathing is an important characteristic to encourage in many aspiring evil clerics. I loved and feared his music because it reminded me of the beauty and friendship and love that as an aspiring evil cleric I was now bound to destroy. It divided me. Fascinated me. And I felt that with Ellisand, for occasional odd moments of conversation, I could be honest.

The last thing I remember telling Walworth was how I had played a key role in destroying a military camp that was loyal to Roguehan. It was filled with Helan soldiers, Threlan ex-patriots who were angry with King Thoren for executing their former duke. So I was responsible once again, I suppose, for the deaths of a multitude of Threlans. As it was a camp posed against Walworth's army, I wondered if he would congratulate me. But as it was a camp full of Threlans, and I had used evil clerisy to destroy it, I also wondered if it would count against me.

"Strange to be so trusted. Strange to be so free and in the world once more." I had spoken these words to Walworth as a final comment on the story I had told him so far.

And then I had died briefly into the North Country night and returned at the blade of his sword.

Walworth returned through the door and gave me water to drink. It tasted like a dead star, but it opened my throat to speak.

He picked up his pen and positioned himself to resume recording my story.

I smiled. "You have taken down so much of my tale so far, my lord, that you may one day find yourself in danger of being considered a writer of tales."

He shrugged and so dismissed the implied compliment. "Flattery will have no effect on my final judgment." He said this graciously, however. The comparison clearly didn't offend him. "Do you wish to continue your plea?"

I considered. "I do not know yet, my lord."

He waited, as he had waited through my silences throughout the night. But then, so did Hecate, and eternity. Everything that mattered waited.

Two

*D*espite my enemy's skill at once more staving off my inevitable death, I did not resume. Not even my need to believe that Isulde might one day read the blood-drenched words of my tale in the record that Walworth now stood poised to resume transcribing compelled me to speak.

I no longer cared that Walworth, I mean, the new King of Threle, was trying me for high treason, or that he had purchased this North Country hovel from the strange old fisherman and declared it part of his kingdom in order to make his makeshift trial lawful. It was tiresome to be kept alive merely to fulfill my enemy's self-imposed legal obligation of holding a trial that we both knew could only end in my death, for once I had finished speaking my plea, Walworth would either pronounce me guilty or pronounce me innocent and be under no further obligation to prolong my life, leaving my ban to destroy me.

So I did not speak.

My silence opened into a sudden, wordless prayer to Hecate. It was a prayer of air and darkness, a deathbed petition to the hollow wane of Her womb. The prayer was speaking itself without my leave, slamming between my heartbeats and pulsing out in points of pain into the killing North Country night. The prayer began with all the secret names of Hecate that I was taught in Kursen Monastery, the ancient names that bless and strengthen my particular evil, but the names were carved in retreating spasms of pain from my last bout of death, not in words.

The North Country runs violent with so much primordial chaos that the clear clean force of cutting intellect that we evil clergy know as Hecate, the Goddess who calls us to destroy the comforts of the flesh, poison creativity, and carve up our minds into half-living mazes of blind sophistry, cannot be drawn upon there. And so I did not know if the prayer went to Her or just went out. But the prayer went, in a stream of uncontrolled energy, and ran patches of thought like this:

> *Hecate pale, Hecate ascetic, Hecate Lady of the Waning Moon. And now you are holding my hand in my prayer. And now we are dull. Lightly we harvest bloody asphodels on the border scenes of my life. You are telling me they are the wildflowers that died when I loved them for their*

beauty, that my love scared the fairies out of them and that is why you called me to your service. And now we are ghosts gliding through my childhood hell, and you solemnly nod as I am mocked and beaten for my intelligence. And now I am an older youth and you are guarding me in the cracks and shadows of a prison cell in the long night before I escape from the sacrificial evils of Sunnashiven. You are there as I enter Threle, and now you are silently tricking me into my youthful alliance with Walworth, watching me foolishly open my heart and taste the sweet fruits of an intense friendship that is doomed to betrayal, for you know that will inspire me to later open my heart to you. You laugh as I risk my life to save his at another treason trial, for you know he will leave me to rot in the pit of evil called Kursen Monastery, and there I will align my heart to your divine evil, and there you will ease my way to advance my revenge against Walworth. If I have transgressed against you, the sacred source of my evil, please have mercy and hold back your dogs from destroying my spirit when I die back into you. Hecate Lady Who Guards the Crossroads, all that I have told of my life tonight is yours to bless or destroy.

The prayer dissolved and there was hollow moonlight in my mouth. The moonlight had shredded itself through the walls of the hovel. It spread and bunched into fat wriggling moonfish that flapped their tails and softly dispersed themselves back into moony beams that snowed heavily from the crowded nets on the ceiling, for Northern moonlight is as chaotic and unpredictable as anything else the North Country offers. A solid wall won't necessarily block it, but an open sky is as likely to swallow it into invisibility as not. The old fisherman caught a moonfish and his teeth marked blood where he bit its back and noisily tried to suck down the light before it changed form again. The yellow candle on the table caught the falling moonlight and stretched like a young flower drinking life from a black sky. And then it held steady in its flame a burning lunar glow that made everything look as illusory as I felt.

It was Walworth who spoke, and as always, his voice conveyed the smooth, neutral tones of an experienced judge. "Have you finished your plea?"

"Death nearly finished it for me, my lord. I am tired and wish to die and take my chances with my deity's judgment. Pronounce your verdict and do your worst."

The old fisherman hooted, "Death! Hoo Hoo! As if things up here die so quickly! For so many strange years I have been dying and the North keeps me strong. Like a fairy and their songs! Like Isulde my sweet foster daughter."

The old man's mention of Isulde's name summoned back the need I had at the beginning to make my words available to her. Back behind the place in my life where Hecate corrupted my heart and made me evil there was Beauty, a flower opening to shadow and singing like a portal to the realm of fairy, the dream of a perfectly executed spell, a perfect execution, autumn nights in Helas where I briefly believed I mattered, and learned magic, and had such glorious friendships, and played with words and found them beautiful. And then didn't Isulde come to me in the dark of the woods in the dark of my heart like the fairy song I had always prayed to before I knew Hecate and then didn't I reluctantly open my heart to her for one brief fairy moment when the moon was on the edge of new and she was showing me something beautiful in my despair?

At the mention of Isulde's name, Walworth also went distant, as if try as he might, he could not reconcile the present justice demanded to a fairy beauty that transcended all justice. It took Walworth a moment to recover impassive neutrality, but once he did so, he said coolly, "You told of your role in the destruction of the Emperor Roguehan's military camp, and then you ceased speaking. Are you certain you want me to render a verdict or do you wish to continue your plea?"

"Yes," I replied, knowing how ambiguous my answer was. Perhaps I wanted both a verdict and to continue my tale. The Northern shadows were dancing with the lunar candle. The shadows were trying to kill the candle, but the darker they went, the brighter went the flame. *The fire I see by burns my eyes. Verdict and tale are one.* "And to keep my story pure, I shall continue to tell those portions of my tale touching yourself as if you are not here before me judging my words." He nodded assent. "Set this down."

The world was late. No matter how quickly I moved, the night moved faster. It was always somewhere ahead of me, somewhere down the road. I would not catch up to it. It would spin itself up into dawn long before I passed through. The road was colder than I wanted it to be. I saw no fellow travelers. When I spilled my head's blood upon the crossroads where I had earlier prayed to Hecate, my hand trembled a little as I opened my wound. I did not know why it trembled. I kept thinking that my blood shouldn't feel so warm. That is all I remember of my trek back to Kursen.

Maintaining invisibility for long periods of time and conjuring wizard fire had exhausted more energy than I realized. Most of my return journey was a struggle to think clearly and strategically about the mess I was in. First, the cook, my link with Roguehan, was dead from my master El's curse or soon would be. Although this was not my fault, it would not make Roguehan happy, and it closed off communicating with him. Second, since nearly a third of Kursen's students had died this night, I now had the job of reporting this happy news to my master. It was imperative that I use this event to somehow gain control over El's emotional state, which meant that above all, I needed to wake up and gather in my strength before arriving at the monastery—and I was so *very* tired. Third, Welm, the illusionist I once mistook for Baniff and freed from Kursen Monastery, might or might not tell Roguehan who helped raze his camp. And I couldn't just run to Threle for protection against Roguehan's anger, even if I didn't belong by law to the monastery, because Walworth's people would now be completely aware, via Baniff, that I had embraced evil. For all they knew, I was capable of drawing down incredible amounts of god fire if I chose—from the wrong gods. And of course, Mirand would now and always be extra guarded against me, making it more difficult to fulfill my agreement with Cathe.

Yes, it was all a mess, but I could do nothing with my jumbled thoughts now except wait for my fatigue to pass into a second alertness. If Roguehan discovered my treachery, there was a chance I could mitigate his anger by delivering up the prize I'd promised him. And, of course, El still kept my wretched spirit, which meant that I couldn't just remove myself from Kursen.

I let my eyes stick themselves shut and my upper body rest itself against my groaning thighs, and whatever thoughts I had were for forcing my legs into hard heavy strides against the road. *Only my legs, just make them move, nothing else exists or matters. Push push push and the rest will follow. Someday I'll wake up again but there is nothing else for now.*

I didn't notice it was already light until I dragged myself back through the monastery gates. The sight of Kursen woke me a little. Then I noticed how normal everything looked. Twisted branches, muddy ground, early sun cursing the walls, walls stiffening into the day's pressures. Who would think that nearly a third of Kursen's students had died last night? And here I was in superb condition for telling El all about it. I forced my legs to push their way down the path to the main building. Then I was leaning against the door and knocking weakly with my fist. And I remember the bronze felt cold and wet but that I felt this without caring.

I don't remember the doorkeeper letting me in, and I don't remember making my way through the hallways and up the stairs to El's apartments, but I do remember letting myself into El's rooms. His work area was empty with early morning. There was no sign of paperwork, for he had burned all paperwork with Riven, but there was no artwork either. The room was barren, so barren the feathery morning light felt sodden and full. I closed my eyes against the light and listened for El stirring in his private chambers, but heard nothing. I might have dozed off standing for a period of time.

I waited a sluggish half minute before opening the door to El's private chamber, and then I drew back in a shock of full wakefulness at the sight of his great staring eyes and outstretched arms. El was stiff and bloated across a great chair—the whites of his eyes red and runny, his skin ashy and sallow, his mouth open, and his breathing sporadic and irregular. There was a little, just a little, blood trickling from his mouth. There were blood flecks across his forehead.

"He's dying," said a doleful voice out of the corner. It was Cathe. Cathe was wearing traveling clothes and leaning on his staff. "Really I don't even like to look at him. Bit of nasty business over the border last night. Nasty for us, that is, if El here dies before you can deliver him in proper form to Roguehan." He was worried about what would happen to his aspirations to divinity if I should fail Roguehan and become a target of the emperor's wrath.

I swallowed. "Why is he dying?"

"Why is he dying? Really, Llewelyn, why *wouldn't* he be dying? Everybody else is. Or was. Kursen's warriors went on a death spree all over Roguehan's camp last night. Lovely as mud lice—for them. Lovelier than hot fish drowning in the moon's sweat—for them. Ugly as the underside of Habundia's broken births—for him. Do you know what it feels like for a high priest to suddenly have dozens of spirits simultaneously ripped out of his own? *Violent* spirits?"

"No."

"Have a gander. Take a ride." He pointed his rod insistently at El, whose body was coughing up something like a death rattle.

"I would prefer not to."

"Yes. Of course. Can't say as I blame you. Only a priest of Ares could derive real pleasure from riding this sort of death. But then, only a priest of Ares would dare to have such utter lack of aesthetics. May the Lady forgive them their sense of beauty. Ah, welladay. I did take on something of his pain a little while ago. 'Twas a bit too dry and salty and . . . *open* for my taste. So I gave it back." He sighed and leaned on his staff again. "He mustn't die. We don't need Roguehan knifing at your back to complicate things."

"You're a high priest. Can't you do something?"

"I already have. Come come come, take my hand." Habundia's force was immediately around us. "Now then. Breathe with me—good, rely on the Goddess for steadiness—down, down—Llewelyn," he whined my name and dropped my hand without releasing the goddess force. "You must work *with* me on this or all's lost. What do they teach you here, besides word work? Your personal power feels weaker than a sea fairy's fire. Come now."

"Cathe—I've been—I've been working most of the night and I need to recover. And with my ban against using my full individual powers, I'd rather not push myself any further right now."

"But that's the point—I'm about to release you of that wretched ban. It's more than time. Come then, sit with me." He dropped to the floor and hugged his knees to his chest, so I sat beside him and glanced at El. El was still breathing. Cathe appeared to ponder something. "This would be easier if you trusted me. Look, you *must* trust me. There's no help for it, but you must. I want you to feel your own ban, find the place where the Sunnashiven wizard collective fixed it in your being—you *can* do that, can't you?"

"Of course. I know where it is. It oozes like a scorpion's kiss between my aching joints and utter exhaustion." I sounded irritated.

"Like a scorpion's kiss? Really?" he asked excitedly. "I should think one of those would feel lighter—and—and—" He licked his lips. "—a tad *crunchier* than a wizard's ban. But then, I've never experienced a wizard's ban. Scorpions are a fine thing in the sunlight, aren't they, but there's a certain acid tang to kissing them on a grainy day, that's simply—"

"It was just an expression."

"Isn't everything? Now then, you're going to feel death. But if your master can stand it, you can. Consider it part of your training. And I'm going to catch you. You'll be fine, really. Perhaps even stronger for it. No different than falling off a cracked gallows when the rope breaks." He took my hand. "You should trust me—a little, even. I *do* know what I'm doing."

"I'll do better than trust you, Cathe. I won't even care." And really, I didn't. Life was all too exhausted and complicated to care.

"All right, come, there isn't time to quibble over the words. Sit by your master. At his feet now. Yes, perfect. And so, take both my hands against yours." He locked our fingers together and already I felt something like a death nausea beginning. I began to choke on rising waves of emptiness pulsing out of my stomach, and I couldn't control the wetness leaking from my shriveling eyes. "You feel that because I'm drawing on the last reserves of your energy. Follow me steady and push, push all your wakefulness and life force against the scorpion's kiss—good, it's stinging, stinging,—shudder, shudder and sweat—steady now, it's only death, we all feel it sometimes—steady, feel the Goddess—She's here—sweet learned Hecate for you, and over Her now is Habundia, Her source and Mother—for and from me." I felt somewhere all the queer sensations of all my body fluids being pressed out of me. I was an unwashed grape bursting with an ugly midsummer and running lax into the ground. "That's death you're feeling. Not so bad, not so bad. I'm keeping you. But I haven't got the ban yet. Is there enough life to push your ban into my hands here—wait—lean against the Girls, they are all my Girls and won't let you fall, their force pushes against yours—all right then—I've got you—squeeze out your ban, use your full powers now and die—call upon Hecate."

I don't know if I had the energy to call Her name. But something broke, and suddenly I did get a glimpse of Hecate, and Her dogs were the dogs I had feared in my mind as a child. She sang to me the way Grana used to sing. She gave me the moon and it crumbled into red powder when I tried to eat it, so I remained hungry. Then She gave me a vial of water. It tasted bad and ugly. As it coursed through my veins, it clogged my heart and slowed the time around me. I clawed at Her skirts because the drink was hurting me and there was nothing to wash it out with. She let Her dogs feed upon my spirit flesh and they howled with the pain of it and then withdrew. But there were now holes in my chest through which the air was able to enter and the wind sucked out something dull and oily which was not flesh or blood. I knew it was my ban against using my full individual powers, and that its removal was a gift of the Goddess and a sign of Her favor. I was then able to say the words. I asked Her to hold me forever. I asked to be Her child. I asked to never know anything. I asked to be Her Nothingness.

And I got the words right, for the Goddess I called Mother responded, "I cannot hold you unless I make you die."

"Make me die, then, Mother, for I am evil."

"Then come. Let Mother make you die. Die cold like the evil bit of living that you are. Come and fold into yourself. You are my child. You are my rat. You are my little frog. My fish. My worm in the womb. My ancient buzzing fly. My white canker. My deathless mold."

"Mother? Are you ending me?" I clung to Her skirt and a dog licked my mouth. For I thought somewhere I had come too close or gone too far and the Goddess was going to wipe out my spirit on the cold north wind that was now opening my chest cavity into a cave. "Please, Mother. Please don't end me yet. I love you."

"Your love is darkness. That is your phrase. The phrase with which you shall enter me at your time. Language is our binding. I name you my priest."

"Mother."

"I return your spirit to you for now it is mine."

"Mother."

"My powers are yours to draw down and use be the place and time proper for my energy."

"Mother."

"And know that to deviate from my law is now sickness and death to you. For you are Mother's little priest. And thus I ban you a second time against entering the North Country. For the North is not my place. Pass beyond the Drumuns and Mother takes back your life." I felt the holes in my flesh close and heal over my darkness, and then something like strength. "Sleep and decompose. Dream of the ground. Smell the animal remnants of life it sucks and spits. 'Tis ours, my broken bird. The place where your bones tumble out upon the north wind and break into fierceness upon dull rocks. Silly broken numbers that only Mother can sum together again."

" 'Tis ours, Mother. I shall dream heavy my belief in it."

And then there was a new sort of nausea abandoning me into nothing. When I came to, I saw that Cathe had turned El onto his side and was forcing his mouth to swallow a gray-black powder. And then I remember waking up in my bed but not getting there. It was much later. Evening. The day felt all wrong. Noise. Cristo was banging mugs. I was nervous first, shaking as sleep fled. Then I remembered why I was nervous. Then I felt a little sick, and despite my blankets, very cold. I did not want to move.

"El's sent for you twice," said Cristo. "Hey, you don't look so good. You tired? Did you go last night? Did you hear what happened?"

"Luvellun, you look all different." Devon bounced on my bed, and the motion echoed emptily in my head. "Where did you go last night? Did you get to see all the death? Cristo missed it."

"I went back to find you and when you weren't here, I didn't go," said Cristo sensibly. "Thought I'd wait."

I slowly sat up.

"Luvellun?" asked Devon. "Are you all right? Here, I found you a bat on a board. See? A clerical student pinned down its wings while it was still beating and struggling and gave it to me after it died." As he held the damn thing near my face, I started shuddering uncontrollably and vomiting all over the bedsheets, which made it impossible to speak. The bat's recent death was still echoing through the room, and the freshly killed flesh sent me out again without my even trying to feel it.

And then it was completely dark save for a little fire in the grate and Cristo was shaking me awake. I may have moaned a little. "Hey, El's still waiting to see you. I told him you were sick."

"Thanks, Cristo," I mumbled, my throat feeling sick over the words. I wanted to ask him about the bat but the thought of its pain sent gurgles of hot vomit up my throat and back down into my bowels. I coughed. "Whe heh—heh—where's Dev?"

"Sleepin' with the bat," said Cristo dumbly. And sure enough, Devon was curled up by the fire with arm outstretched over the board. I started coughing and hacking uncontrollably. "Get rid of it," I managed to spit out.

"Yeah, sure," said Cristo, puzzled. He threw it on the fire and my coughing got violent as its flesh wrinkled up and then passed with the smoke. "You sure you're all right?"

My coughing had roused Devon. "Luvellun, Luvellun, you're awake now." He looked desperately around the fireplace. "Where's the bat?" By suppressing memory, I suppressed sickness.

"I burned it," said Cristo.

Devon started to wail, "Cristo, you cud, that was special for Luvellun—"

"Hey—sssh! Come here, Devon," I said weakly. "I told him to burn it. It's all right. It was a fine ba—" I choked. "It was fine, really. But I—" I was so weak it was an effort to speak. I closed my eyes and leaned back in the pillows. "But no more—no more—"

"Bats?" Cristo finished my sentence.

I threw up burning saliva. "No more—anything. For now. 'Til I tell you differently. Understand? Promise, Dev? Dead and dying things make me sick now."

"I'm sorry, Luvellun," said Devon contritely. "I'll give them to Cristo."

"Yes, fine, but don't bring them here." I sighed and leaned back in my pillows again. I was weak but awake and alive.

The door opened. Slowly, carefully. It was El. Cathe was behind him. El was huffing with exertion and he spoke harshly. "Get out. Say nothing." Cristo and Devon both looked terrified and started to leave. "Cristo." El's voice stopped him at the door. "I hear of this elsewhere and you and Devon die. Twice over." Cristo stammered something and left with Devon. Cathe closed the door softly with his staff.

"Greetings from the other side," I said weakly.

El sat down heavily on Cristo's bed, ignoring my comment. He did not look particularly healthy himself. His breathing was labored and hard. "Hmmm." He settled himself with an effort, bent his head down, and rubbed the back of his neck. "Humm."

Cathe sat sharply on the end of my bed and leaned on his staff, and the motion sent me coughing. "Pretty pretty pretty. And so my blessed kinsman's come through it. Fine as faith. But then, why wouldn't he? Runs in the family, really it does. We all come from a long line of mystics. My dear—Luvellun here," he was speaking Botha but he used my Kantish name as if it were a courtesy to El, "does you much honor, Brother. Really I don't believe Kursen Monastery has ever had a direct initiation before."

I smiled weakly, glad to have an obvious physical excuse for not commenting right away.

"No, I don't believe we have," said El. He rubbed his neck again and looked at me. "So I suppose you are a natural priest now, Luvellun?"

"Praise Hecate." I coughed and coughed as I said it, so El did not insist that I speak further.

"Yes, praise Hecate." El smacked his lips and looked around tiredly. "Well."

"Well indeed," said Cathe cheerfully and enthusiastically. "I for one can't wait to tell the Sunnashiven clergy all about this most blessed event here at Kursen. It shall lend you and your monastery a great deal of well-deserved glory—and perhaps even buy you some protection against the unfortunate consequences of the recent little affair in Helas. I'm sure that the emperor's own priests would be loath to interfere with a place that has clearly been so—so, *blessed* by the Goddess Herself."

"I'm sure," said El dazedly. "The temple's done its own share of interfering recently. Damn them all into rotting grain." This was said without enthusiasm.

"Come come, your spirit will heal. And if it's your ban you're concerned about—really it's all for your own welfare. The Sunnan clergy feel that all the priesthood must be one—must be consolidated—united in the Goddess—and so what's a ban? If the more prominent high clergy cannot use their full powers in the Goddess, it makes it less likely for anyone to rebel against Sunnashiven—and there have been a few problems in the Helan monasteries."

"Good for the Helan monasteries," grumbled El.

"Brother," said Cathe in soft admonishment. "Really we evil brethren must stay together, and if that occasionally means giving over to the new empire—" El was glaring at him. "Consider your ban—a mark of prestige. Only the best and brightest members of our order get the privilege of being banned. It's all for the general welfare. To ensure that you stay close to Sunnashiven—no matter what happens. But really, with a direct initiation here, I'm quite sure that Kursen's sanctity will be respected. And, of course, the great sacrifice you've endured—the painful loss of so many students, surely that is worth something on the spiritual side, no matter what the emperor might think of it. Nothing in your daily activities should change. Take heart, and rest, and heal, and glory in the Lady's blessing." Cathe indicated me with his rod at the word *blessing*. I closed my eyes and pretended to faint to avoid speaking and saying something to destroy Cathe's intricate plot.

"Luvellun," said El, softly touching my shoulder.

"Yes." I rolled away from him on my side and pulled my soiled blankets over my head. This was Cathe's show.

"Yes, you're sick, poor boy, hmm. It is dangerous to be named priest without knowing anything of theory. Much that merely sickened you before is deadly to you now. You have the power to draw upon the Goddess, yes, hm—but should you use it in the wrong time or place, the rebound could kill you. You have a constant link to Her power but you have very little training in how to use Her power properly." There was a pause. "I suggest that you make yourself completely dependent on me and on my guidance for now. I shall work with you independently—no more classes." He said this as if he couldn't think of anything else to say. I made no response.

"Brother El is correct," hinted Cathe. "Stay close to him and all will be well. El, I should be quite happy to stay and witness the new brother's mundane initiation. Surely you must arrange something, some show to commemorate this event. Something grand and glorious I can report back to Sunnashiven."

"That is not how we do things here. Our initiation ceremonies always mark the last event of one's education. And even though my—disciple—has partaken of divine initiation—he still has much formal training to undergo. When he is ready, I shall do the proper thing."

"Of course, of course, wouldn't dream of interfering—but I suggest—for safety's sake, that you make this blessed event as public as possible."

"Yes, right. Hum. I'll call in witnesses tomorrow. That is," El raised his voice, "if you are up to it." I took it he meant me. I said nothing.

"Of course he will be up to it," said Cathe. "Let him alone to rest and pray and he'll be right as rhyme. The hard part is over. If the Goddess wanted him, She certainly had Her chance."

"All right then," said El. "Tomorrow." I heard him leave and once the door closed, I threw off my blanket.

Cathe went to the door, listened for the last sound of El's footsteps, and rekindled the nearly dead fire with his staff. "There now. You *will* be all right. Gave me a bit of a fright once or twice but that's all past. The story about Sunnashiven is all nonsense of course, but you know that."

"How did El recover so quickly?"

"My dear boy, I'm a high priest of Habundia Christus. I worked a healing on him in our Lady's name, and She consented. Oh, by the way, you *are* a priest now—thanks to me. No Hecate about it."

"Thanks. I guess."

"Well, I suppose there is Hecate about it because She is your deity and the sole source of your power and your sole authority now—but really it wasn't Her will to just have it happen like that—I had to beg and plead Her force for that one. Now—the rest should be easy as crushing tadpoles. El won't harm you—he's convinced your presence will deter even Roguehan from desecrating Kursen. A divine initiation is a sign of divine benevolence. Furthermore, his ban makes his powers considerably weaker—not so *you'd* notice, but over time he'll be easier to wear down, and when Roguehan finally arrives, El won't even think of fighting anybody."

"What ban?"

"Why, yours of course." I groaned. "Oh, come. *I* didn't want it. And the black powder it dribbled out in was burning my tender hands. And I needed my hands to save his life. By the way, it felt like no scorpion I ever kissed."

"Won't he know it was my ban?"

"That's quite impossible. As far as he knows, the Goddess took your ban. And the one he has really is from Sunnashiven. It will trace back there if it will trace anywhere. All that matters is that your power is no longer inhibited and his is. Your job is to prime him up for goodness and wait for word from the emperor. Study your love spells."

"Cathe—I won't be getting word from Roguehan anytime soon." And I explained about the cook.

"Ah welladay, that is a hitch, but at least his wrath can't fall on you over that one. I suppose I could offer myself as a courier for now. Create useful Sunnashiven tidbits for El as an excuse. Yes, it would not be a bad thing to become Roguehan's go-between with Kursen for now." He was starting to get up to leave. "Anything else I need to know?"

"Uh, Cathe—yes, sit down. You'd best be aware—about the Helan camp," and I explained my role in some detail, including that strange interlude with Welm and Baniff when they both saw me after I had led Kursen's students to destroy the camp. "So things are not—easy."

"So the gods answered your prayer. Delighted, I'm sure. Perhaps you were closer to initiation than I thought, although I really tend to doubt it. The circumstances had to be a great help. Hah, well and a spidery lick." He thought for a minute. "This is a fine cauldron of gasping geese. I can deal with Welm. That is, if I can find him. No, don't worry, I'll get to Roguehan first and fix it. Yes, don't worry about that. Just take care of El for now. And as to the other side." He sighed. "Lady lack it all but I'll see what I can do over there. Thanks for the warning." He sprang up lightly and went to the door. "Later, Brother."

"Yes, later." I slept and dreamt of nothing.

The following afternoon I was still bedridden, although I had managed to walk around my room a bit with Devon's help that morning. El brought in quite a crowd of witnesses shortly after midday, including Sister Elwyn and Brother Styrn and half a dozen senior clerical students. And El made quite a production out of the whole affair, by serving willow tea and biscuits to everyone as if this were all a grand party and he was the happy host. In fact, El was smiling and bobbing around more than twelve doorkeepers. He wanted credit. I was sitting up in bed and flashing my mug around. El had given me a beautifully engraved gold mug to drink from, I think it was one of his own. I was also boldly surveying the envy and fascination of the other students. Cristo was there, hunching his shoulders and looking quite uncomfortable.

I killed the subdued chatter by suddenly speaking. "Greetings, sons and daughters, bold children of the evil forces. So glad to see you all here." Then I looked at El with a mixture of respect and easy familiarity, and raised my mug to him. My words and gesture made it clear that El and I were now on near-equal terms and that my new status clearly superseded that of the other students.

I smiled over at El. He was now in the middle of pouring tea out of a large earthenware pitcher for Styrn. Styrn was shifting his weight from foot to foot and complaining that his mug felt too hot. I got an instant impression that El would like nothing better than to pour the hot tea down Styrn's shirt. Then my palms burned a little until Styrn's mug cooled.

Which reminded me that I really needed to ask El to show me a way to shield out all the sensations around me. I had no idea what a *sensitive* priest I would make. Before I met the Goddess, I had been able to open myself to feel selective sensations around me, and my study of wizardry had increased my skill in this area, but now everything came tumbling in without effort. A spider crawling across a wall three rooms away could send sensations across the back of my wrist. When I walked with Devon, the pain of the floorboards under my step became my own, which was partly why I was resting in bed. Surely the clergy didn't live like this. I wondered how many were like Cristo—initiated in name only but not in spirit.

When El finished pouring, he had to look in my direction because everyone else was. I caught his eyes briefly in a way that indicated that he was just another member of the crowd. "Greetings." I said this in a tone that loudly proclaimed, "Really you *might* notice me." He nodded and bowed. Twice. And with the earthenware pitcher in his hand, he looked very much like a Sunnan servant putting on airs. I drank my willow tea gingerly, as if the tea were more important to me in the moment than El's rare show of obeisance.

As soon as I finished drinking, everyone started murmuring and vying to kiss my hand, and they all called me "Brother" twice and three times over to impress everyone else with their humility. Which was only fitting, I suppose. Even El had to do it to prove to his colleagues he could be a sport about the whole thing. After all, I'd just beat his game plan for me by several years. And I didn't even have to ask him to release my spirit from his first. The Goddess had released it for me.

He kissed the back of my hand and released it. "Truly the Lady has blessed us in our loss," he intoned, and the energy level plummeted around me as everyone felt a homily coming on. "For as we remember our brave brothers and sisters who are now with Ares—" Everyone bowed their heads obediently. This was sort of sad, since most of the surviving students were quite content to have the field cleared a little, and their silence over the loss of their colleagues was shallower than El's pretense at health and joy. Only Cristo seemed genuinely disturbed, or impressed. I wasn't sure which. To me, sitting up in bed and idly receiving sensations, it felt like both. Perhaps Cristo was so rarely impressed with spiritual matters he found the sensation disturbing. He swayed uneasily back and forth. "—with Ares the Destroyer, yes, we also give joy and thanks for this sign of Hecate's favor. And now that we are fewer in number, it is fitting that we all remember that *we* are bound in evil, all of us one—"

"Taking orders and obedience from our high priest," I finished the sentence for him. "For let us remember to be ever humble, for if we were truly worthy, truly holy, we *all* of course would be dead—as the children of Ares are dead. Remember, evil as we are, and blessed as *I* might be in Her, we all still live, and that is something to be humble about."

"Yes," said El dourly. I had ended his homily for him.

There was a great deal of solemn silence and anxiously bowed heads now. No one who had remained behind from the peacemongers' last rampage could ever claim total seriousness again. After all, if you can't die for your deity one way or another, you'll never be accounted as worthy as someone who did. Even though it is certainly much easier to die for Ares than to die for say, Hecate. But then, I suppose one could always cut one's hands on the pages of a book and bleed to death. Or meet up with someone like Cathe.

The other students were all congratulating me again because their masters were there and they needed to impress them by acting enthusiastic. Devon asked me for a special blessing, being Sun King and all, and I graciously blessed him with Hecate's force, although in Devon's case, Her force didn't take. The power ran right through him and dispersed like badly colored smoke. And then all the clerical students asked for a blessing because they remembered they were supposed to, so I brought down Hecate's power again and blessed them all at once. Why not be generous? And the power came at my command, outside of myself but flowing through me, and taking nothing out of me. Just a reminder that the Goddess and I were now as one. That I had become a conduit of Her force. Clerical magic may be full of restrictions but at least it won't exhaust one like other magical practices do. That is, if you do it properly. You are the Goddess in the moment you pass Her power and you are infinite unto Her.

And then I blessed each member of the clergy, except for Cristo, who stayed awkwardly behind the crowd. I ended by blessing El twice over and several people declared they could see a pale yellow light around him when I brought down the Goddess force. And he rose and briefly took both my hands in his while he declared a close to the witnessing. And from that moment on, I was recognized as a natural priest and all my studies were private studies.

---

*I*t was two or three days after the witnessing before my heightened sensitivity receded into something manageable for daily life. And it was nearly a week before I could kiss Isulde in my dreams without the ecstasy being so intense that I instantly woke up away from her, the skin on my thighs burning and shriveling from my own semen. And so she refused all kisses, and teased that the fish her foster father caught made better lovers for the moon. And she bathed my thighs in cold brine water. And we ran together at a distance, which was dancing, for one touch of her own joy would flush tumbling along my bloodstream and spin me dizzy against the sun. And when the dizziness peaked with running in the brine, I'd wake up again in my dark little room and taste salt. She fed me clouds for grounding. And then in one dream, near the end of my recovery, there were no clouds, just an after-storm brassy sky, and Isulde was sitting on a rock outside a cave and offering me a large red-and-gold goblet. The goblet was warm and steaming and running over with four streams of golden liquid. She called it "the drink of the Northern sun." She named it "honey and gingercloves, peppers and saffron, the best summer days of years lost and worlds unseen, knights jousting at the raw midday, ruddy-red stallions charging fire, hooves igniting afternoon fields of ripening corn, peaches and oranges waiting heavy on gold plates, mead burning light in ruby pitchers, drink from the Northern sun's treasure chest and be strong—"

Yes, right. Well, the "Northern sun" woke me up to a god-splitting headache anyway, but once the pain faded, I *was* strong again. And fully aware of the power of my remaining ban against the North Country. But then my dreams were pure untrammeled delight once more.

I started my individual work with El as soon as I could walk without feeling the pain of the floor beneath me. The first thing I learned from him was that my heightened sensitivity was an aftereffect of my direct contact with the source of my own deity. I would only be that sensitive again at the point of death. Since he himself had nearly died, he had also experienced heightened sensations for a few days. I was to consider it tangible proof of my divine initiation, and, he smiled, I needn't say anything about his passing irritation with Styrn. Styrn could be irritating, but he was still a sincere and holy man.

He told me to take it as a warning that there would always be certain things I must avoid now, like meat and all things that reek of body and flesh, for Hecate denies the flesh for the mind. I must never permit myself to forget that the usual dietary restrictions were no longer a means of purifying and preparing myself for my deity's entrance into my being, restrictions that could be lapsed from occasionally without serious consequences. I was a priest now and could not break my Goddess's law without sickness or death. However, I would still need to learn to appreciate physical suffering, and there were ways to do this, but I must learn these ways with El's guidance and through using the proper precautions, which he would teach me in due time. A goddess is really a force like any other force, only purer and more intense, and I could, with a great deal of practice and concentration, protect myself against the natural consequences of violating Her law for short periods of time and in limited particular circumstances.

I was still expected to make some show of sacrificing something when I finally took my mundane initiation at the end of my studies, and El suggested an owl since it was customary at Kursen for all initiates into evil to kill Athena's bird to honor the place, no matter what else their personal deity demanded by way of sacrifice. Despite my restriction against flesh, Hecate would be pleased with the death of an owl under the circumstances of initiation. I did not remind El that I had already killed one owl for an initiation. I wondered if Hecate had noticed and counted that favorably toward my spiritual progress. I also never told El that despite my restrictions against flesh, once I recovered my strength and whenever I dreamed with Isulde, I had sexual experiences like singing rainbows, color-kissed orgasms like exploding sunstorms. But then, with the exception of Ellisand, I never told anyone about Isulde.

And on nights when I didn't need sleep, for I found that I had a higher stamina through my Lady Hecate than I ever had before, I sometimes wondered about my own weird progress in the magical arts. I was a wizard—of sorts. A wizard by training anyway, although I never became a master. I had practiced some witchcraft, and was fairly adept with the witchworkings I knew, but I could not call myself a witch in anything save the nominal sense. I knew no illusion, but I had gotten so skillful with my illusion ring that I could pass for a fair illusionist—which in itself was an illusion, I suppose. And finally, I was an alleged natural priest who had secretly been initiated through the interference of a still mortal high priest. And I had no papers or records to prove my priesthood at all until El decided it was time for a mundane initiation.

Yet for all my near successes in the various fields of serious magic, I was the absolute envy of Cristo, who never had any successes in anything. I remember reading a book of Sarana poetry in bed one evening near the end of my convalescence while Cristo was playing some game with Devon in front of the fireplace. Something that involved a stick and a bag of pebbles and all kinds of noise. I think Devon was winning, but I was trying to shut them both out of my consciousness in favor of reading, when Devon shrieked, "You're burning the stick, Cristo. You're burning the stick, you stupid cud! Make it stop or we can't play!"

"Burning whaaa—Damn, I dropped it!"

"You lose, Cristo!" whined Devon. "It's all in flames now. Luvelluuun." He ran over and jumped on my bed. "Make us another gaming stick. Use magic."

"I don't feel like conjuring anything right now, Dev. Why don't you both go outside and find one?" *And stay there*, I added silently because I was aware of Cristo's new sense of inferiority and didn't see the use in antagonizing it further. Devon, however, the Sun King of Destruction, did the job for me.

"Cristo's too lazy. He won't go anywhere. If he did he'd be dead like the peacemongers." Devon said this to me as if he were complaining that Cristo *wasn't* dead. Cristo stood up stiff and abashed. I felt a little sorry for him.

"Devon! Cristo isn't a peacemonger. He's a brother of Hecate. It was probably smart for him not to go." Then I teased Cristo in a tone of practiced affection. "Smartest thing you ever did, buddy. That is, if you *wanted* to live to enjoy our brilliant company." I really meant this as a friendly joke, to smooth down his pique. It was the worst thing I could have said.

"Yeah, what makes you think I *wanted* to live anyway? Hauuh, I could have been a martyr. I've got morals, ya know. I could have died in the violence. I was looking for *you*—where *were* you anyhow? Thought maybe you went after all—then some bizarre cleric in a traveling cloak wakes me up near dawn to throw you in bed—same guy that showed up here before—had to pacify Devon all night long too—he had *no* idea, man—next thing anyone knows, the Goddess is speaking to you personally and you're a goddamned priest!"

I chose not to enlighten him concerning my night's activities. "Well, Cristo, none of that was my fault." I looked at Devon. He was frozen in the awkward position of dribbling pebbles out of the bag. He was so startled by Cristo's burst of anger he didn't know how to respond, and he had temporarily forgotten how to move. "Hey, so we're brothers in fact now."

"Yeah, I ain't a brother. Never was. Really. Guess you know all about that now."

"Cristo, everybody's known all about that for a long time. But who cares? Half the priests in the world take initiation without taking on divinity. And some of them end up running monasteries and initiating others. At least you've got your papers in order. That's all anybody looks at. I won't have proper credentials for years, if ever."

"Proper credentials, yeah," spat Cristo, slightly mollified. Then, "But they ain't getting me a real job."

"Well, Cristo, there aren't a lot of real jobs to be gotten. Look, I'm sure the Goddess will speak to you in Her own time."

"Yeah, Cristo," Devon finally said, dropping the bag. "Don't be angry. Luvellun's always right. Why don't you bless him, Luvellun?"

"I don't want your goddamned blessing. I'm still a priest. I can bless myself. Damn, why didn't I go die with the peacemongers? One chance at glory and I blew it. I could have died for a *god*, man, any god. And I stayed back looking for *you*."

"Cristo, there will be other chances. There are chances for dying every single day if you care to look for them. Remember, the war's still going on, if you really want to chase it, and as a—*priest* in fine standing, you can certainly leave Kursen, dispensation or no, and follow the violence. Really I thought you were smarter, and more devoted to Hecate than that, but if martyrdom to a war god like Ares is what you *want*—"

"I'm a priest! I don't *want*! I can *be* Want! I know how to do it. I'm not stupid."

"Then do it," said Devon, settling himself down now as if to watch a performance.

"The gods damn you both for rotting grain—"

"Don't you mean, 'May we rot with the grain'?" asked Devon helpfully. He had heard the expression a lot and liked it.

"May you rot with—everything! May you rot!" Cristo bumbled out the door, tripped over the threshold, and loudly stamped down the hall.

And from that evening on, he said very little to either of us, or to anyone else as far as I could tell. It wasn't that he literally gave up talking altogether, but he restricted his utterances to the bare minimum needed for communicating basic needs, and he was almost wholly silent around me. And I would catch him reading occasionally—very occasionally, for his own studies. And I noticed he no longer ate as much as he used to. And once I saw him blanch a little at a massacre Devon found, so perhaps the Goddess had finally taken up within him. But he never did seem to find himself a job.

Oh, what else? Roguehan sent me flowers. Black orchids firm and dying. They stank of dead, rotting snakes, but it was two weeks after my initiation experience, so I managed to stomach the odor with only a twinge of nausea.

The flowers came stuffed in the cook's dead body, nearly an acre's worth packed tightly within his hollowed-out body cavity. The rest of the corpse was preserved and shielded in something like yellow wax, so it did not sicken me. The corpse arrived strapped to a bier dragged by the horse and the black-nettled donkey. Cathe had ridden the horse up from Sunnashiven. He sent the first servant he could collar to find me, and as soon as I arrived he greeted me with a singsong boasty complaint about the "sweet monotony of decaying orchids dwindling along the road, and really Roguehan ought to know that such death would just *sound* tangier had he waited until first harvest, and someday we would all get ourselves an emperor with real taste." Then he complimented me on my recovery while handing me a crumbly orchid. "For you, my priest."

The orchid was tied to a note which read:

> *Whatever it takes. What's a few Helans between friends?*
> *I trust then that El shall be amenable whenever I arrive.*
>> *Roguehan*

"And believe me, that one took Hermes's own skill, but you're all right on that end. Got Roguehan thinking that perhaps you're overeager and a bit ambitious, and needed to put El on the rack a little. Of course you knew nothing of the Threlans' little surprise, only intended the peacemongers to do enough damage to have propaganda value for the emperor—help him claim a need to take Kursen in hand that the Kantish locals could more than sympathize with. And as to the results of your little gesture—well, who can question the gods' blessing—you're a priest now and eager to serve with all your deity's might, the gods heard you and not even Roguehan can condemn you there. Besides, it's really the entertainment he lives for—he'd overlook almost anything for that. Keep El in hand for him and we're safe. By the way, I'm your new liaison. And as far as El's concerned, his link with the temple. How's he doing?"

"Quiet and steady. We're working together now."

"Excellent well. I'll tell you before Roguehan plans to arrive. If you need any help, you know who to ask." And he sauntered off on a high whistle, pointing his staff here and there as if he were calling his own attention to the hidden cracks in the world.

And that was that. I have no idea what Cathe told Baniff, if anything. He avoided the topic whenever I brought it up on his subsequent visits, admonishing me to learn my love spells and not concern myself with trivia. In fact, all I did learn from him about Walworth's friends and family came a few months later, around first harvest, when he informed me that the old duke and duchess had taken ill and died and so Walworth and Caethne were now joint rulers of the duchy. I wondered how Caethne liked being saddled with all the administrative chores while her brother ran a war. Then I wondered how Walworth liked his erratic twin being solely in charge of running the duchy with no one around to keep her in check. Then I decided they *both* deserved exactly what the gods had given them to work with.

Besides, I had plenty to work with myself. I needed to concentrate on my studies of Sarana and love spells and wizardry and all the theory that went along with my new priestly powers. I learned complicated methods for shielding myself against the sickness that came whenever I was exposed to bodily decay. I also learned that I could not maintain such a shield for more than a quarter-hour or so without sustaining great damage, as it involved reversing the current of Hecate's energy, that is, literally shaking hands with Athena. The trick was practicing a hearty neutrality in my mind while keeping up the shield, all the while knowing that one slip and Athena was likely to send me sicker than meat ever would. Once I could shield myself without El's direction, I was able to learn a critical appreciation of torture and physical suffering, and I really could ride other people's pain for short periods of time, although never with the fervor of a peacemonger. Then I learned how to work delicately with other people's emotions to bind them to Hecate's will without their knowledge.

El was mine to nurse along throughout this time, and I was fairly successful in fostering in him a spiritual and intellectual dependence on me, for I now had the advantage of being "specially chosen" by the Goddess and that gave me some authority in his eyes. Cathe did his best to convince El that my holy presence was the only thing keeping Roguehan *out* of Kursen. And El's ban did damp down his energy enough for me to feel confident about my emotional ascendancy over him, and confidence is crucial in these endeavors.

My intense study was broken only by Ellisand's music and my dreams of Isulde. For Ellisand did return several times to perform for us, and Isulde and I played together in his music like the sportive undines we were in those moments. When I opened my full sensitivity to his music—well, words would only insult the weird and lovely effects his music had. He transposed magical formulas into sounds. There was a pulse below the living surface that I hadn't heard before, but once I learned to reach and ride it—well, days or weeks would pass before the influence did.

I pestered him with flattery and gifts until he reluctantly condescended to have brief conversations with me after his performances, but he never seemed particularly eager to discuss his art with me. The art was there, he did it, he got paid for it, and the work allowed him to travel, that was all. He did tell me that he was half-elven, and that he had learned his craft in Gondal, as I had guessed.

Ellisand told me many curious things about Gondal. He said it was a large northern wasteland that had once been a glorious elvish kingdom, and that in the far south there were two cities that were now inhabited by humans. He was from an elf colony, and he assured me that there were several such colonies hidden in the wasteland. I didn't ask him how his human parent had found the colony, although I was curious about him being half-elven.

He also told me that in ancient times, before the elves retreated to their colonies, they left a gift upon the land, an energy that now existed as part of the structure of the world. "They used to tell me that whenever anything beautiful got created, the creator was drawing upon that elvish energy whether he knew it or not. That anytime a song or a painting or a story had emotional power, it was really a conduit for that elvish power, without which art couldn't exist."

"Do you believe that's true?" I asked him. I had never heard of this before.

"I believe it's a pretty story. I also believe it's true. What do I know? It works. I get paid." He laughed.

He was also a poet, and he knew all manner of languages for he traveled all the time. One time he read his poems to me and I heard music all through them, draining in and out of them in foreign keys. The words literally got lost in sweet, dreamy elvish music and emerged again as words. And—how can I describe this—it was like the words had different sides, and each side came from a different language, and together the sides made a universal word that spoke itself. And his voice was perfect—a perfect day, was how I thought of it. The only voice which could read the words properly and make them sing. And I saw visions in his words too. When I pressed him he said that the elves had not taught him poetry—the words simply came from himself. Although chaia helped, he hinted. I began bringing him lots of chaia, as much as I could grow or steal. I think it was the chaia that finally induced him to tolerate me with something like approachability if not friendliness.

But he usually said little to me, even under the influence of the weed. Although he did like to boast that he had lovers all over the civilized world—men and women, elves and gnomes and humans and various mixes. He seemed prouder of this than of his music. He despised monks as killers—all monks—but would play for anyone who paid—even sang for the new emperor once, which surprised me a little.

I asked him one summer afternoon when it was late enough in the day to be behind the worst of the heat why he had taken such an interest in the guy El had killed with his music if he truly despised all monks as killers.

"*Because* he killed him out of my music. The man's death was a response to my art." He took a long drag of chaia. "It was wild and different. Never had that happened before. Most monks hold back, do their best not to respond. But El couldn't hold back then and do what he did. Yeah, they're all killers."

"Yet when I respond, when I want to talk about your music, you never want to talk about it."

"That's because you do respond. What's to say? It's none of *my* business how."

"But I thought you'd like to know. It's your music doing it. It's your sensitivity, even if you like to pretend you're a different person when you're not playing. You even said your poetry comes from you. I can't believe you aren't your music, that you don't live your art—"

"Sensitivity—life," he spat. "I'm horny and I've got a girl to meet. You're the critic. Make sense of your own fantasies." He said this contemptuously, but when he saw how crushed I was by his distance, he added, "You know, playing music for you is worth all the rest, because you know *how* to love my music, if only you'd stop trying to make it die by questioning the reason behind every riff and chord."

"My questions are my responses."

"No they're not. Your sobs and smiles and shudders and cries of ecstasy are your responses. The only responses that count."

"Don't be absurd. If we clergy didn't question and analyze and strangle the meaning—"

"*Strangle* the meaning," said Ellisand slowly, cupping his hand around the chaia and dragging.

"If everyone just responded emotionally to art, half the clergy would be out of teaching jobs, certain orders of clerics would never find self-sacrificial paths to their own deities, monasteries would collapse—"

"Art provides an excuse for all that, man? Hey, I'm just a minstrel—what do I know? Look, I gotta go now. My girl's waiting, and she says she'll have some real food for me, not monk's peas and old grain. Despite the war shortages. Next time, Lew." He threw the stub of his chaia on the ground and walked jauntily away. In that one gesture I knew that he would always be happier than I.

I remember thinking that was the best thing anyone ever said to me, that line about playing music for me being worth all the rest. Really two people don't get much closer than that, do they? I cherished that tossed-off phrase for months. No, I still do cherish it. Had my life experiences been different I might have been able to believe in it as a sign of sincere friendship, coming from him. But of course, I had long ago ceased believing in friendship. I never brought up the topic of my responses again.

$\mathcal{I}$ paused here in my telling, and so did Walworth's pen.

"Beauty, my lord, is worth all the rest. Write it three times like a spell. Pray over it to whatever god you pray to."

"I do," he said solemnly, simply, and uncharacteristically. His sudden candor surprised me, but the intrusion of truth didn't last. "Will you continue?"

"Upon my life." I smiled weakly.

$\mathcal{I}$ should mention that it took Walworth about a year to lose all of southern Threle. Actually, Walworth never really *lost* the southern duchies. He just couldn't win them. And Roguehan, although he succeeded in nominally incorporating them into his empire, couldn't really win them either.

For Roguehan was constantly having to deal with unexpected, independent rebellions and random acts of war against his empire during all the time of his occupation, and the southern duchies became quite a liability—more trouble than the whole game was worth.

Which is a compliment to Walworth's brilliance as a strategist and skill as a fighter, for a lesser leader would have lost more quickly and decisively. Merchants as a rule are too independent-minded to make good soldiers, and Threlan merchants especially are not in the business of taking orders, unless it be orders for their wares. But

Walworth, with the help of Mirand's skill at rhetoric, managed for a while to use his soldier's love of independence as a spur toward fighting off their attackers. And to their credit, fight they did, often like Ares's own arms and legs.

*B*ut the details of the war, save as they touch my upon my life, can be read in other records, and you know them as well as anyone, my lord. Say I studied for a year and a day. Say others died better deaths."

Three

*I*t wasn't until well over a year since the destruction of Roguehan's camp that I had any living worth speaking of. Although I was now completely competent in using every aspect of my priestly powers, El was still refusing me a mundane initiation. This was mostly Cathe's fault. Cathe had El completely convinced, through various intricate lies, that my presence was the only thing deterring Roguehan from establishing his own people in Kursen, because the emperor was loath to interfere with a monastery that the Goddess had blessed with a natural priest. El feared that once I had the proper credentials on paper, I might leave Kursen for a job elsewhere and make the monastery vulnerable to a takeover by our esteemed emperor and so of course my credentials were not forthcoming.

Cathe, like me, was now an absolute master at keeping El's emotions stretched and thin and vulnerable. The ban helped of course, for the ban made it damn near impossible for El to run the monastery and defend himself against a fellow high priest like Cathe, who showed up unexpectedly in high good cheer to thrust thorny ideas into El's weakest heartbeats and scariest thoughts.

Whenever El tried to take advantage of my presence by complaining that his ban was gross interference on the part of Sunnashiven, Cathe would look sorrowfully sympathetic, gently clap El's shoulder, and praise his "dear brother" beyond the one lone moon for his patience and willingness to sacrifice untrammeled spiritual power for the welfare and safety of all, murmuring "in confidence" that "the emperor has recently had to relieve some crazy apostate administrators of Helan monasteries from their posts, and greatly prizes loyalty" and so on into the promises that the ban would be removed once southern Threle was secured for the empire, or a certain rebellion somewhere was put down, or some other future event came to pass.

One of my jobs was to pump up El's confidence and thus create in him an emotional dependency on me. So I would flatter El and create believable arguments for him to knife his hopes on concerning Cathe's benevolent intentions and my firm conviction that Kursen would always be El's to run. And whenever El appeared at all confident of his immunity from further interference, thanks to my stories and benign presence at Kursen, Cathe was sure to drop a few studied phrases in El's lap about the way theological opinions in Sunnashiven were liable to change with the roll of the hours, and how a few of Roguehan's advisors were now constructing arguments for the entire clergy having ownership rights in any monastery which housed a natural priest. And then Cathe would prance off and I would spend hours comforting El's fears and constructing easy paths between his heart and mine.

And so we kept him on the rack. And we waited for Roguehan to claim his promised entertainment so we could get on with our own plans.

Roguehan had sent word to El, via Cathe, that he and a few of his own chosen clerics desired to be present for this initiation. Not that he had any personal interest in the dedicant, but that he greatly desired to attend a religious ceremony at Kursen, as the Goddess had blessed the place, and he desired above all to meet me, the "beloved of Hecate." Anyway, it was in early fall that I finally received word from Roguehan that he expected to watch El freely embrace goodness at Sunreturn. Sunreturn is a common time for initiations, of course, and Kursen had one scheduled.

Cathe told me privately that Roguehan was expecting El to willingly embrace goodness *at* the initiation ceremony, and it was up to me to see that this conversion happened. I fully expected that Roguehan would then give me a fine position in his own court, and that I would then be free to help Cathe in his own aspirations and in doing so, help myself to a duchy. And so there was nothing to do but look forward to freedom.

The dedicant who was to be initiated at Sunreturn was the second initiate El had to coax and baby along into priesthood, just as he had solicitously coaxed and guided Jekan. She was aspiring to be a priestess of Venus Whose Beauty Enslaves. I believe she first entered Kursen Monastery during the spring preceding the Sunreturn of her initiation—a rather plain, unremarkable, sexless thing, with great glaring pimples and thick beetle-black brows that met over a hideous large nose indented with pockmarks. More beast than woman. She had no body, just a dollop of fat and two heavy legs that sort of supported it. Her breasts were well hidden in the noise. At least I never saw evidence of any. Her arms were rough and hairy, but she did have the good sense to keep them hidden in her flab as often as possible. It must be painful for someone like that to dedicate herself to beauty, but pain is the reason a lot of people come to Kursen.

I only noticed her because she quickly latched on to Cristo, who seemed embarrassed and then flattered by the attention. She had some unpronounceable name like Gogblgyn or Gbylgon. Devon called her the glob. Cristo shyly called her G and thought himself quite the man in doing so.

Cristo was always inviting her up to our rooms when he knew I was going to be returning from my work with El, just to make sure I was aware that he had a girlfriend, although he liked to insist they were "just friends." Well, "friends" are as friends do, of course, and all I know is that I entered the room many times when the two "just friends" were holding hands and kissing. The glob often had one leg in Cristo's lap and the rest of her body in a rickety chair, as Cristo was not large enough to support all of her. One time she and Cristo were both so startled by my entrance that the glob fell on the floor and knocked over the chair, breaking one of its legs. She looked up at me with her wide staring frog eyes as if I were going to flatten her with a stone. I merely assumed an air of politeness and fixed the chair leg through a bit of wizardry that was well beyond Cristo's skill with clerisy. That annoyed him to no end, because he now felt he had to justify to his lady friend why his magic couldn't mend a broken chair, but really he seemed to mind it more than she did. They were both splendidly unsuited to their callings and so, I suppose, more than a match for each other.

She didn't talk much herself. She just protruded her eyes until she prettified herself into something resembling a stuck frog, screwed up her mouth in a toothy smile, and mechanically picked pieces of skin off her lips when she got excited about something Cristo happened to say. I suppose this constituted listening. But that was all Cristo needed to inspire him to reach for his old heights of eloquence. So I got to hear all about him and his ladylove.

The story was that she had taken eight or nine years of monastic training somewhere in Medegard, which was why she spoke Kantish with such a horrible lisp. To my mind her training didn't show, unless she was aspiring to manifest some oddball deity of ugliness. I suspected that she was considered such an utter failure in the Medegardan monastery that they threw her out. I know *I* would have. But Cristo defended her elusive gifts up and down and asserted that G was unhappy with the course offerings in her first place of study. She was really a "sensitive soul" who felt "personally unfulfilled" by goodness. "Just like us," he insisted, except it took his "clever insightful" lady nearly a decade to figure out she was in the wrong place. The only goddess of love and beauty you could dedicate yourself to in the Medegardan cloisters was Aphrodite, and G was convinced she needed to change dedications and follow an evil deity for her own spiritual growth. Venus was calling her out of the darksome light and all that. Well, clerics of good alignment are usually easier about letting students go than we are, so she left. And ended up with Cristo. Praise Venus for her wit.

Since Roguehan now controlled all the Medegardan monasteries with his own people, I have no idea why she simply didn't stay where she was. It wasn't really clear to me that there *were* any monasteries of goodness still functioning in Medegard. But Cristo insisted that there had to be, or G couldn't have left one to come here. Never argue with logic.

To my surprise, though, Cristo's new lady was exceptionally dedicated to her improbable calling. She starved herself and exercised and cried a good deal to Venus until I must admit her body became healthy-looking, if not attractive. She learned herbal remedies to clear her face and she was faithful about using them, so her skin did become more supple, if never completely smooth and silken. And she learned potions to brighten her eyes and lips, and practiced walking as if time itself was heavy so her movements charmed all who watched. And she practiced talking in a smooth, seductive voice . . . and *listening* seductively, so that her responses became an irresistible means of attracting people to her. And she made herself beautiful clothes that really graced her form, and created captivating scents for herself, and learned quickly to love and draw strength from the admiration of other men and women. She gained beauty so quickly that I'm sure Venus Herself oversaw the transformation. I think everyone in the monastery had sex with her at least once, or claimed to have sex with her, except me, for my love for Isulde made me immune to anyone else's charms. And except for Cristo, for the more desirable G became, the less desirable Cristo became for her. Poor Cristo hinted around some that he had had her before she blossomed into beauty, but as no one seemed to believe him, he dropped the subject.

I heartily wished she had remained a glob, for I now had to put up with Cristo's sighs and loud silences and pacing. He was constantly annoying me by leaning over my head and casting a shadow over my papers while I was working, so he could stare out the window in the hopes of catching a glimpse of her. And he would always murmur something like, "Just checking the weather. Wonder if it's raining. Wouldn't want to get wet. Or cold. Or anything."

Devon didn't help matters, because he was constantly reporting G's latest conquests to Cristo. Just to see him squirm, presumably. Devon was not nearly as deft at torturing feelings as he was at torturing the bodies of already-dead animals, but long association had taught him how to get to Cristo. And Cristo, of course, helplessly encouraged Devon to report G's every move, because as much as Devon's tidbits of gossip stung, it stung Cristo more *not* to know about his love.

Cristo was lying on his bed and staring at the ceiling one afternoon when he should have been teaching. I was working out some clerical incantation or other on paper when Devon skipped lightly in.

"Hi, Luvellun, Brotherooo." He pummeled me playfully on my shoulders. "Hey, Cristo, I saw Madam G holding hands with Freffen and kissing him outside." Cristo despised Freffen. Rumor had it Freffen had a job.

"I don't care." He sat up. "Where outside?"

"Under the Sun King tree." This was the tree they had tied Devon to during the last two Sunreturns.

"Under the Sun King tree," he sneered and spat. "Who cares? Damn. Did they kiss a long time?"

"Not too long," chirped Devon. "There's a line." He sat down on my bed. "Oh, Luvellun, I need—"

"There's a *what*? Damn, all right, so *what* if there's a line? Am I supposed to care?"

"Probably," I offered. "Your Lady G there is probably staging a public event just to make you jealous."

"Yeah, well, it won't work," said Cristo. "Who's in the line?"

"I forgot," said Devon. "Everybody."

"Why don't you go down and wait in line yourself?" I asked Cristo.

"Wait in line *myself*," said Cristo. "Why? Wait in line. Heuuh! Who would want to?"

"I don't know. Devon says 'everybody.'"

"Not me," said Cristo. "No way." He sat there trying to convince himself he meant it. He was unsuccessful. "I, uh, should go to the library though." He stood up quickly and nervously went out the door.

"Luvellun, when can I make *my* dedication to Hecate? Master El says I'm not for that path. He thinks Hygeia Who Hurts. If anyone."

"Well, you certainly do like to torture things, Dev."

"I don't know if I like to torture things. It's just something to do."

He didn't sound bored exactly. Devon wasn't smart enough to be bored. His voice was matter-of-fact.

"You need to show El you're capable of studying. Hecate is a goddess for intellectuals."

"Then how did Cristo make it?" He sat back and waited for my answer. Devon wasn't being sarcastic, he was just temporarily confused and wanted to straighten it out.

"No one's ever been sure he did."

"Luvellun, I want to be a priest like you. I want to be clever with words and lies and stuff like you. I need you to write a paper for me. Two papers."

"Write a paper for you? Why?"

"To show Master El I can do work. To get dedicated. He wants proof of my commitment to Hecate."

"Look, Dev, if you were ready to be dedicated, you'd be writing papers yourself."

He bounced off my bed and playfully slapped me on the shoulder. "You'd do it if you loved me. If I were really special, and your best friend. Write it like I would and do something magical so El won't know."

"Devon, I can't." Disappointment wetted his eyes and face. "You *are* my friend, my best friend."

"More than Cristo?" He sounded faintly menacing.

"More than Cristo."

"More than Cousin Cathe?" Devon had taken to calling Cathe "cousin" because he heard me doing so. Cathe had not discouraged him.

"More than Cousin Cathe."

"More than—Ellisand?"

"Devon—when do I ever talk to Ellisand?"

"Whenever he comes. For hours. And you look all different when he plays." Even though Devon was now entering adolescence, he had the tightly screwed face of an upset child.

"Yes, Dev, more than Ellisand. And more than El. And more than anybody save Hecate Herself—"

"Then why can't I follow you and become Hecate Herself? She's only a goddess—"

"Only a—Dev, do you know what a goddess *is*?"

"A girl and a bitch and a queen and a love. That's what Cathe says."

I sighed. "It's really not that easy." Devon kept looking at me. "Cathe has a *special* way of putting things—he likes to boast—but there's a certain skill to using goddess energy—"

"So? You can use it for me. Then I can be a priest like you, and have Hecate, and you'll love me more." He nuzzled his head against my shoulder.

"Why don't you just be your lovable self and see what comes of it?" Devon flushed a little under what he perceived as a compliment. "There's bound to be some demigod or goddess who's paying attention. Those things come as they come. *I* don't care if you make a dedication or not."

"Really?"

"Really. There's more to life than monasticism."

"Oh." He paused. "Like what, Luvellun?"

"Like . . . like friendship, Dev." I smiled at him. "The kind of friendship that lasts forever and ever and never ends." *Like Walworth's betrayal that I will soon avenge*, I thought coldly.

"Yeah," he was grinning. "Like us." His eyes held a strange bright emptiness. "Screw El *and* Hecate." I winced a little. I wasn't sure whether it was his blasphemy or his unruffled ignorance that bothered me. "I love you too, Luvellun." At that moment Cristo returned, all hulked over in a barely suppressed rage. "As long as I'm the favorite, I don't need to be a stupid priest," he announced for Cristo's edification. Then he turned and crowed, "Hey, Cristo, how's G the pee?"

"I don't care. I don't know. I don't want to know. I was going to the library." He hulked himself over to his bed. "Really! Damn!" He shook his head. "I don't believe it. Do you? Do you believe what's going on?" The question was addressed to me.

"With you for a roommate, Cristo, I'm prepared to believe anything, including the possibility that in spite of all these interruptions, I'm going to get this incantation worked out today."

"Uh, man! Do you *know* what she's *doing*?"

"No, Cristo. And I *really* don't care."

"What's she doing?" asked Devon, just to be annoying.

I pushed back my chair. "Damn it! Shut up everyone! I need to work! Goddamned G isn't even here and she's irritating the hell out of me! Why don't you both get out?"

"She's—she's—she's screwing everyone in line," offered Cristo dolefully. "One at a time under the goddamn tree. Men, women, the goddamn stableboy is down there—goddamnit, she might as well charge for it."

"She is," reported Devon. "I saw her take a copper for a kiss. You want a copper, Cristo? Luvellun has some."

"Neuyah. No! I don't want a cuddy copper."

"You want to go to the tree and charge for coppers?" Devon pressed.

"Yeah, Cristo, go for it! Be almost like having a job," I added.

"Goddamn you!" Cristo sat down on his bed and started blubbering. "I don't want anything. This sucks all! Damn the Lady!"

"Damn *you*, Cristo! I'm busy. Up until three weeks ago your long-lost love looked like a piece of half-eaten dragon's get and nobody wanted her! Now she's Venus's favorite daughter. What can I say? She's probably getting ready for her initiation and learning to love her own beauty before she has to give it back up to Venus!"

"Yeah," snuffled Cristo, "I can't wait. And once she's ugly again, she'll crawl back to me."

"You mean she crawls?" asked Devon, awestruck.

"No, Goddess damn it!"

"You just said—"

"Shut up! I don't care what I just said!"

Devon looked at me and smiled. Then he sang, "Hey, Cristo, I hear she's got a job. Hear she's going back to Medegard to a new—"

"Shut up, would you?" choked Cristo. He coughed hard and sobbed and wheezed. "And there she is. Under a tree. Who cares? Who really cares what she does? I don't. Why doesn't she go screw—"

"You?" I finished the sentence for him.

"Yeah, screw you," said Devon.

"*Screw you!* Both of you rat cuds! Shut up!"

"Everyone shut up! I've got goddamned work to do! Here, Cristo, here's a whole bag of coppers for leaving me alone." I threw the bag in his lap. "Go buy out the line and have a whack or three." He blubbered and choked and didn't move. "Or *I* will!"

"You cud-sucking cud—" Cristo hurled the bag back at me and missed. It spattered and broke against the window, spurting ringing rolling coppers all over the floor. Devon was immediately clawing at Cristo's throat. Cristo stood to shake off his attacker but once he succeeded, Devon kicked him in the groin.

"You better leave Luvellun alone when he says." Cristo was crumpled up on the floor and groaning. "Luvellun says go! Now!" He kicked him again in his midsection and Cristo shuddered and spat.

"Oh, I can't—aehh, I can't get up! I can't walk now!"

"Damn it! *I'm* going to the library. Let up on him, Dev." Dev stepped back and nodded. I grabbed my work, stuffed it in a sack, and left. I couldn't wait until Sunreturn, when I would be out of this place and working in Roguehan's court.

My disgust and annoyance did not lift until I passed by the Sun

King tree. There was quite a crowd gathered under the tree. There was also a faint scent of blasted, overripe roses drifting toward me, a stale-sweet scent which cloyed and choked and grew heavier as I got nearer. Then I heard moans of delight, and various members of the audience were crying "Praise Venus." Then I saw the crowd applauding as a nude young man carrying a bundle of clothes pushed his way through to the back of the gathering with his staff and begin to silently dress himself. It was Cathe, which meant I was sure to hear a running commentary on the whole experience later. A young woman insisted on being next and everyone pushed her forward. G had to have Venus's own stamina to put up with all that.

I decided I had best give up on the library and approach Cathe for whatever news he was carrying but as I got close to him, he closed his eyes, delicately turned his head away, and breathed himself into a heavy trance. Then someone else in the crowd noticed me and called out, "Hey, G, there's the natural priest. May Venus take a natural priest!"

"Venus take a priest! Venus take a priest!" chanted the crowd, which parted so G could get a clear sight of who they meant. G raised one heavily braceleted arm to motion the eager young woman back. Then G gazed at me, or rather Venus Herself looked into my eyes, for I instantly recognized the goddess force which was manifest here. Unusual before initiation, but this really was Venus's power that G had pulled down. Once she was a priestess, G could draw on this power at will, but since G had not attained that status, I knew that Venus Herself was working with Her dedicant, that She was willing to use a willing G for some divine purpose of Her own.

G-Venus Whose Beauty Enslaves smiled, spread open her arms to me, and made little kissing motions with her mouth that I immediately felt against my neck. "Come to me," she called. "All are welcome." The crowd started whooping. "Take me, take a goddess." It sounded like a sales pitch.

"No thanks, I already have a goddess. And She abhors the body." Since Cathe was still in trance, I started to walk away, but G was full of Venus and not to be deterred. She ran to me through the opening the crowd had made, throwing herself against my body and pressing and rubbing her breasts against my chest. "Hecate and I are sisters. All evil deities are one. 'Tis no error for you to love Venus, Brother." She kissed me hard and the crowd turned to watch, whooping and howling. And I must admit my loins responded, although when I pushed her back to look at her, I knew she wasn't one fraction as beautiful as Isulde and so all desire fled.

"Put your tongue in my mouth and charm me with your words," she wheedled.

"No, Lady. You are beautiful, but I have other charms for my words."

I started to move away but the goddess force sharpened and Venus pulled my head down and licked my ear, whispering through G, "And I have charms for your charms, priest. Look upon the crowd who wets and hardens for Venus. Even though when you speak to me you speak as to the hem of my robe, or to the heel of my loosened sandal, or to the faintest stream of a river of an endless birthing ocean from which I come and come, it is to me you speak and I demand worship." I felt Cathe behind me. He was leaning on his staff with eyes closed, completely lost in trance and humming. I suddenly understood. Cathe was drawing down Venus Whose Beauty Enslaves through the most suitable vessel available.

"Would you like a vial of Venus blood such that the love-boy my son dips his arrows in? A shining lock of Venus hair? My own splendid girdle which draws all affection to the one who wears it?" She kissed me softly, and when She released Her kiss, I saw that the crowd was now surrounding us, and Venus and I and Cathe now occupied a clear space in the middle. "I can arm you for your conquest," She continued to whisper in my ear. "I play the game of the world, rolling dice from golden cups, matching chance against chance. Hear my voice through my dedicant. Take on the power my Mother's high priest commands. Take on my power and learn to slay with love. I am a force like any other. Use me well."

"All right, dearest Venus Whose Beauty Enslaves, and yet I love thee only for Hecate's sake and as Her sister, for first honors belong to my own Lady."

"You speak properly," she whispered, and as she buried me in a kiss, I ceased to hear the crowd and was only faintly aware of Cathe dropping to the ground as I gave myself up to the Goddess. We sank quickly into dry grass and crumbling leaves together. And then there was low steady clapping coming from the crowd as I pressed my mouth against Venus's and quickly ran my hands over Her neck and across Her bare responsive breasts. As I clasped and wrung Her light brown nipples, She moaned with delight and commanded, "Suck me, priest, suck my pap if you want my gifts" and so I obligingly let my mouth and tongue drop to Her left breast and began to softly suck and lick, only gradually increasing the rhythms until Her moans told me I could softly bite without Her feeling pain. And the scent of blasted roses came fast and thick. And I tasted rosewater all down my throat and drank an ocean's worth of roses out of the Goddess stream.

I continued sucking while I placed my left hand tight around the curve of her left breast, and I felt my old waning moon mark of evil pleasantly warm and tingle. Somewhere Cathe was muttering an incantation to keep the goddess energy steady, so I wasn't sure whether it was my skill or his that was producing Her softly seductive almost-sighs. As our energy peaked, I kissed one of those sighs into silence and as Cathe's murmuring stopped, I released my kiss, held my lips just above Hers, and whispered, "Where are my gifts, Goddess?"

"Can *you* give Venus such delight, oh son of my pale sister?" she whispered back close to my mouth.

"You know I can."

"And shall you use my gifts in delight?"

"Yes, *your* delight, Venus, for I shall use them to slay," I promised.

"Then I shall bless you in your undertaking. Take me—take my secrets." I pulled down my pants and lifted my shift, which was a little awkward in the circumstances, kissed her mouth hard while solidly clasping her breast, felt her body arch and tilt beneath me in anticipation, and drove my penis into an ocean of sticky singing wet roses, roses singing in cadence to the clapping crowd. And as I plunged, I tensed into a different ocean that was cold and stinging and unpleasant, climaxing at the instant she did, and for both of us it was brief. I rolled off her and She threw her arms about my neck, whispering close to my ear, "The vial of blood is in my womb, plunge your hand in and take it." I did so and removed a small black sealed bottle. "The lock of hair is loosened, place your hand in my tresses and receive it." I did so and withdrew a bright bundle of hair tied in black and pink ribbons. "My girdle is around my waist, take it." And there was a thin black silken string which I had not seen before. I untied and kept it. "My uses are yours."

And then Venus wasn't there. The crowd was whooping in awe over the gifts of favor I had received, and G the dedicant was looking at me wide-eyed and pleasantly confused with the novelty of her own beauty and her new ability to attract lovers. She was not aware of what had just happened. "And you, too, Brother," G cajoled. "You too wish to try Venus. Then come, for I am beautiful now in Her glory."

"I have." I hoisted my pants and wrapped my treasures in my shift, wondering at Cathe's priestly skill. He was sitting with eyes open now, nicely recovering from the effort. And right behind him was Cristo, standing openmouthed and sobbing great ugly tears for all the world to see.

G smiled up at Cristo in welcome, extending her hand. Cristo responded by trying to grab Cathe's rod so he could hit me or G or Cathe or anyone else at hand with it. Cathe responded by blasting Cristo, faster than a darting lizard's darting tongue, and as Cristo fell back shrieking, Cathe calmly extended his hand to me, and said, "The Lady is always generous with Her bounty. Come."

We walked in silence up to my rooms—a strange, puzzling, uneasy silence that was so unlike Cathe's usual wordy self-indulgent banter that I knew he had important news for me. Devon was sitting at my writing table and puzzling his way through papers he couldn't possibly understand. He turned to greet us and Cathe smiled wanly at him.

"Hey, Dev," I said with studied affection. "Our cousin here is a little tired right now and needs to be alone."

"So? Hi, Cathie."

"So it would greatly please me if you could leave him alone, Dev."

"All right, Luvie, let's you and me go for a walk and leave him here." Devon said this brightly, as if he had discovered a brilliant solution to Cathe's fatigue.

"Well, Dev, I'd like to, but my cousin here needs my priestly services right now. Why don't you—go find this book for me," I wrote down the title of something I knew would take him awhile to track down, "and when you come back, we'll—sup together. For as long as you like."

Devon surprised me by immediately acceding. "All right." He walked to the door in an exaggerated spider walk that was probably meant to be funny, so I laughed a little. "See you soon."

As soon as we were alone, Cathe said, "I can't stay much longer but here's the point of it now. G was sweetly necessary. Quite a conduit. She'll make a fine priestess. But now you're thoroughly armed, with tools and your own intelligence. Sunreturn is in eight weeks and you'll need papers. If El is still holding out on you by then, I'll initiate you into legal priesthood as soon as Roguehan gives me the monastery. I trust you'll be able to make full use of your prizes?"

"Sure."

"Will they be safe here?"

"I can protect them."

"I meant Devon. I really think the boy has outlived himself."

"I can deal with Devon. But if you feel better having them in your safekeeping—"

"No, no, no. I trust you. They'll be safer here than on the road. Well, then. After Sunreturn we proceed with our plans. You shall not see me again before. Swat my waggling nerves but I must know. You *are* prepared for everything—before and after, late and soon?"

"Of course."

"Any questions?"

"Have you and Roguehan spoken of my new position?"

"Yes, we have. But he's refusing to settle on anything until you deliver on your promise. And of course, it's crucial to get you into the right kind of position, so now is not the time to rattle things with the emperor by being too insistent. Of course, *I'd* like to see him use you as a spy, send you up to my cousins' duchy as an informant. With papers, you could claim to be a wandering cleric like me, concerned for the family's welfare, come to give aid and comfort to the people, selling cures for a living and such. I could fix your papers and make arrangements to get you accepted into the household—"

"Yes, fine. Go on."

"But I can't do anything about that until the emperor gives me something definite to work with. Look—turn El. It all hangs on that now, and once you do, Roguehan will be inclined to grant us anything. And make it a good show—a long-drawn-out one. Please him."

"I shall please him, Cathe. I shall please the living end out of him."

"Out of El, anyway—" He froze as if he heard something, went cautiously to the door, and opened it quickly. Then he sighed. "Clear."

"You are too nervous, coz. Relax, or I'll have Devon swat your nerves with a briar patch." Cathe looked mortified. "I have all the faith in the worlds that your deification and my duchy shall come to be. If my words don't make you a god, nothing will."

"Stay strong in the Goddess, then, Brother. See you at Sunreturn." Cathe bowed his head to me and left. I sat on my bed and savored the feeling of my life rushing against me and into my sole control, and I closed my eyes in the luxury of anticipation as Devon returned. He was noisy and bookless. He promptly informed me that El needed to see me.

"Something about G and Cristo." Great Goddess, would the issue never end? And it really wasn't even my issue. "Well, Dev," I said sorrowfully, "there goes our sup."

"Yeah," said Devon sourly. "Damn Cristo and all his cuddy rot."

"Well put."

"Thanks." Devon grinned. "Take a night walk later?"

"Yes, right." I knew by now the day was long ruined for work.

I strode through the halls, pushing my features into my accustomed mask of benevolent hero worship, concern, and loyalty to El and lightly pushed open the door into El's apartments. As soon as I entered the apartments, I realized that, as usual, Devon had gotten things wrong. G was there, Cristo was not, and El shot me a look that clearly meant I was not to intrude on their consultation. He was holding both of G's hands in his own and looking quite fatherly and supportive.

"Devon said you wanted to see me, Brother."

"Yes, Brother, wait outside." Standing by the door put me in a perfect position to eavesdrop. El was speaking.

"You have enormous potential, my daughter. I look in your eyes and traces of Venus look back, yes. I see the dried womb of an evil ocean. I see hundreds maiming themselves on the womb's jagged rocks, dying over and over of their own desires. Even your tears are cold and beautiful like the rose-colored ocean She constantly emerges from—"

"Master—I've never been beautiful before—never had lovers who desired me."

"Then bless the Goddess for Her gift. Give it back to Her at Sunreturn in all humility, acknowledging the beauty you tender is not your own but Hers. Have faith that She who gives will give back. When you are priestess, you can command Her beauty anytime. You know that."

Master," she sobbed. "I know Venus was with me today, I know the beauty comes, but it is a beauty that pierces hearts to break them. I want to keep my lovers forever. And not break them." She was weeping. "Ever since I was a child I was ugly. I have dreamt constantly of being beautiful and being loved."

"Yes, and so you want to own those who desire you lest your dream burst. Hold on to that desire, daughter, for it is an evil desire, pleasing to the Goddess, and it will pull you through your initiation. You never truly own a lover until you can destroy him."

Or an old false friend, I thought ruefully.

"Master—if Venus should reject me—should cast me from Herself—I should die of my own natural ugliness. I know that I should die."

"I doubt that Venus will reject you. You are already a vessel of Her power. You already draw on Her as She wills. Daughter—think hard. Why are you beautiful? You were a common ugly girl from Medegard with nothing to commend her. Has the Goddess blessed you through your intrinsic worth and value, of which you had none, or did She mysteriously choose you for Her own purposes?"

There was a pause. "I deserve nothing. She has blessed me for Herself. Yet I think beauty will buy me a love I've dreamt of deserving—"

"And it will. Even as a priestess it will. Evil is often loved and loved fiercely. You need only know that nothing you have is properly your own, not even your life, hmmm. Nothing. That is the highest lesson of evil. When I feel that your spirit knows this, I shall return it to you." El paused and sang softly, "Daughter—lovely, precious daughter. I will be with you as you make your sacrifice, holding your—*beautiful* spirit in beauty, restoring your spirit in tenderness. And the emperor himself will be there to watch. He's coming on a visit of state to Kursen and you are to be our model of how initiations are done. You have eight more weeks to charm with beauty and untold lifetimes to command Her power. Do not embarrass Kursen with your lack of faith. We are all counting on you."

"Do you really see Venus in me, Master?"

"Yes."

"Thank you. I shall—think about how to—rend my beauty." She had a hard time saying this. "I shall pray on it."

"And so shall I," El said earnestly.

The door opened and a sad little G walked slowly out. I stopped her as she passed me by taking one of her hands in mine. I kissed the back of her wrist long and slow. "Once loved always loved. Beauty is eternal, blessed of Venus. We all make our sacrifice and we all end up stronger for it."

"Thank you, Brother," she said softly, continuing on.

"I shall pray for you," I promised. I did feel a little for her and it seemed like a nice thing to say. Then I entered El's apartments. The high priest of Kursen Monastery no longer looked paternal or supportive. He looked haggard and pale and withdrawn, like an ill-fed, cranky child. Sitting with G had been an effort for him. I had grown intimate with these cracks and contrasts in El's energy, and expert in exploiting them. I softly closed the door behind me. "Beauty *is* eternal, Brother. G will be all right. She's already shattered one heart."

"Mhn. Yes? Whose?"

"Cristo's. Before her transformation. I'm sure the initiation will be all one and His Excellency will be pleased."

"Yes." El seemed far away, then he came back to me. "So my boy

Cristo has had his heart shattered. I hadn't noticed." El said this rue-fully. Much as he enjoyed torturing Cristo's pathetic career aspira-tions, he cared more for learning that he had missed something of emotional importance in Kursen.

"You've been busy, Brother. And tired. And Cristo is the next best thing to being a priest and so ought to be able to deal with his own heart." El was not to be jollied. "Brother High Priest, why should you have noticed? You must care for all of Kursen—the greater welfare of the monastery surpasses the heartbreak of any single member—surpasses anything."

"I came up to your rooms today to discuss your blessing the emperor at Sunreturn. Devon made it a point to let me know he was doing library business for you because you and Cathe were meeting to discuss 'priestly affairs.'" El said this without emotion, without exhaustion, and without accusation, so I made my face look bland and open. "I assumed I was to be included in any such discussions. When I arrived I discovered my assumption was wrong. How long have you two been plotting to take my job, MY LIFE, MY MONASTERY?" This last was said with such force the room vibrated. El could still command an impressive amount of energy, despite his ban.

"No, no, beloved Brother. Listen to me. Listen to my heart speak truth to yours." I could not get past his eyes, which had hardened into dull iron. "I'm plotting to save Kursen. Kursen—Kursen is—oh, in such danger—if only you knew what danger—but, of course, you can't know," I said half to myself. "Mustn't know, for your state of mind is crucial to everyone's health and well-being." I thought he was going to burst in the rage of one who feels his life is threatened, but he subsided into something like wishful fearfulness. I had suddenly become his last hope.

His voice was very tight and very old. "How are you plotting to save my monastery?" His hands tightly gripped his desk. I refused to answer. "Tell me or die. Natural priest or no, I'm still your better—"

"Beloved Brother, esteemed Master," I swallowed. "If you were not my better, I would not cherish Kursen as I do—seek to protect Kursen as I do. This is the hardest thing I have ever had to say to any-one. In all my lives." I took his gnarled, veined hands in mine, and they remained fixed in their clenched position. "Kursen is in grave danger. It is the last independent, non-state-owned monastery in the empire—thanks to—your work. I would not be here, in the position I'm in now, saved from goodness through Hecate, if not for you and the Goddess. I esteem you as the Goddess. I owe you everything. Natural priest or no, I owe you everything."

El began to sniffle a little like a child. He wanted to believe me, and he was struggling against his own desire. Emotionally this was exactly where I wanted him. He spoke stiffly, "I trusted you, my best and brightest. I brought you along and sought one day to make you archon, and then high priest, and—yes, turn everything I loved over to you with my last earth-breath. Someday *you* were to be my successor. And you repay me how—you you—*salamander slime*. There now." I knew from the thought in the words that this was a name he had called hated children when he was a child himself.

"Brother—High Priest—do you know why Roguehan wants Kursen?" I asked this as if I was asking a little boy if he wanted a bag of goodies. "The real reason?"

"Roguehan has cherished a grudge against you for years now, Master-Brother. Surely you know that." El nodded. "You held out on him when the other monasteries capitulated. He trusted *you* first— over that silly matter in Loudes, the treason trial I mean. He expected great things from you and you put your Goddess and your calling above his demands."

"Yes," said El sorrowfully. "I did."

"As you should have. As any high priest worthy of the name and calling would. For it is *your* calling." *There* was a light touch. "And why should the emperor or the state usurp *your* calling and play the Goddess to you? Does it not read in holy scripture that what is yours is yours?"

"No," said El. "You are mistaken. Nothing is ours. Ever."

"Kursen is yours. The Goddess Habundia Christus is yours. Spirituality is yours."

"Kursen is mine." His words were barely audible. "Mine! Yes, may I be damned! *My* one shortcoming. *My* one failure!" He muttered, "And so I am not perfect in Her keeping."

"And yet you could be. Perfect. Perfect in a way none of us could ever hope to achieve. And you—*you* could save Kursen. Listen to me—Roguehan only wants Kursen because he wants to watch you suffer. He's only coming here at Sunreturn to publicly give the shop away to Cathe, and when you cry out in torture over losing what you love, his priests will embarrass you and make you squirm for your weakness. The emperor only wants Kursen because it will pain *you* to lose it. Kursen is nothing to him without your pain."

"It *will* pain me to lose it."

"What if Roguehan didn't know that? What if he was wrong? What if we could get him believing that you were not in love with Kursen? I guarantee that under such conditions he wouldn't take it. It wouldn't mean anything to him. Pretend you hate it here and wish to go to Sunnashiven. Pretend you are leaving and placing Kursen in someone else's hands. Styrn's, maybe. Roguehan would insist you stay."

"Leave Kursen. Give away Kursen. I'd sooner turn to goodness and call myself Ceres." *Damn—here was the real turning.*

"So turn to goodness." I squeezed his hand and his shoulders, smiling supportively.

"What?" It wasn't so much a question as an expression of tiredness. "Turn to goodness. Only my wildest, most eccentric disciple would think of such madness."

"It would be the last thing anyone would expect." I breathed deeply and looked into his iron eyes. "Roguehan would be—would be—he wouldn't know what to do. Make a public spectacle out of declaring these grounds sacred to the deities of goodness, throw yourself on Ceres's mercy—leave the emperor with a monastery full of respirited evil priests in training on his hands, and Cathe—well, that will be one on Cathe—he'll have to content himself with his place in Sunnashiven or run a monastery dedicated to goodness."

"Sweet Christus, I'm tempted—" He started praying. "I am the Goddess. I am sacrifice, and want, and unfulfilled desire. I am Her. I am evil. No—don't tempt me. I cannot do it. I cannot throw away my life from Her—"

"But you are Her. Don't you understand?" I pleaded. "All of us, from Styrn right down to the stableboy, depend on you. To us you *are* Christus. You have led us to sacrifice everything—freedom, food, beauty, friendship, music, all the delights of life. In turn each initiate has ascended the dais and in turn each initiate has thrown away a life. Can our leader and Master do less? Save Kursen—save us all. Perhaps this is your ultimate test—Master High Priest. Sacrifice yourself and save us. Sacrifice yourself and save Kursen. Sacrifice yourself as Christus does in eternity."

"Sacrifice myself. Hhmm." He sounded wistful.

"What did you destroy to become a priest?"

"An owl and a little pet mouse. I made myself watch the owl eat my mouse and then I ate the owl. I loved them both."

"As much you now love Kursen?"

"No, hmm, I don't know. I was young. I thought I stopped all loving after that."

"No, you started loving Habundia Christus after that. Her daughter Hecate kept you for years and it was Her you loved, too. When you became an archon, what did you destroy for Her?"

"My love for beauty and learning. No, that was long given up. I gave up—I don't know—I worked and worked without feeling—I gave up my life—but you know, yes, I was never archon, never the fancy-titled workhorse of some other high priest. They gave me Kursen when I was still a priest."

"And you gave—" Silence. I could feel the struggle. "—And you gave—"

"I gave many initiates, I gave the Goddess the suffering and sacrifice of many new priests and priestesses."

"They gave themselves. You could not take them to their deities if they refused to go. Their sacrifices had to be freely given. You were here. What did you give?"

He exploded. "I GAVE NOTHING! I LOVED IT HERE!" And the insight I intended hit the mark. "And so perhaps the ultimate sacrifice is what She now demands. To become the very thing I loathe." He started shuddering and shaking like an old goat.

"Master, listen to Her words. 'Our only happiness comes from taking on the unhappiness of others. We are only worthy so far as we sacrifice ourselves to someone else.' You know the words?"

"Yes. For years I have taught them."

"Brother, this is not easy but answer this and act accordingly. Do you think that Habundia Christus would be pleased with your willingness to become the very thing you loathe? Do you think the Goddess of sacrifice would bless and crown the supreme sacrifice?"

"Yes," he swallowed. "It is all I have left to give."

"Then give to Her who demands all giving."

There were dried gouges across his face. "There's a certain poetry there, my boy. Remember when I first taught you to destroy poems?"

"Yes, I shall never forget, Master. You helped me destroy my first poem."

"Of course." He chuckled. "Loudes. I know. Well, then." Something both tender and hard broke behind his voice. "You know I shall die. It will take my full individual spiritual powers to turn to goodness, and with my ban—" His voice kissed silence. "—Hmmm, will you miss me—son?"

"Always."

"I shall return to you in future lives, perhaps. Well," he said with forced cheerfulness, "perhaps Habundia Christus shall even make me a god."

"Perhaps She will. Master." He suddenly seemed lighter. "It breaks my heart to see you turn, to lose you. But for Kursen we must all suffer. I shall be with you at Sunreturn, when you make your announcement."

"Yes, I wish you would. So." He looked tragically intent, an old man trying to remember the sun out of his first morning. The sun had gone all different now. "I must clear up my business here."

"I will help you."

"I must initiate G, hmm, the last of my little ducklings. She is hesitant."

"And you will pull her along like Jekan. For you are sensitive. And she shall always remember you."

"And you, do you want your papers?"

"No, I revile what Sunnashiven is doing to you. I wish to remain a natural priest forever. I don't need them." Actually, I needed Cathe to fix my papers into proclaiming me a votary of goodness.

He nodded. "You don't need anything. Yes. My best and brightest. May She keep you always." When I left him he was whistling. I saw him whistling several times after that, in the weeks before Sunreturn. And talking to the late-autumn birds. And playing dice with the doorkeeper. And telling all the stories of his life to the year's new snow and the dusty early-winter skies. He told me several times that when he was a child he fancied that birds carried invisible poems in their beaks. He wandered the grounds in perfect freedom, preparing, dismissing, dying into his very self, his heart becoming flawless as an old abandoned ghost.

It was awful, really. There were times when I felt sick observing El make his spiritual preparations to become the thing he loathed. El was so thoroughly evil, so illicitly happy in his service to Habundia Christus, that his willingness to sacrifice himself, to forgo the blissful eternity of evil he had earned through his work as a high priest for what would be for him the eternal torture of the goodness of Habundia Ceres, was too much too contemplate. He prepared to die with a nobility that was almost, well, terrifying. Roguehan should be highly pleased.

Four

*D*on't know *how* Roguehan will feel about that one," said Cathe, squinting and pointing his rod at the crippled morning sun. His arm was straight and steady—too steady, I thought, too stiff for the solar movement which, given his stance, Cathe's hand and eye should have been tracing. It was Sunreturn. The soiled light of Kursen was dragging along into the yearly wash of rebirth. Cathe was too intent on weighing my words to take into account the shaky movement of the sun's death throes. Even through my own nervous anticipation of the evening ritual, I could feel the day eluding him.

I looked at the ground and waited for Cathe to consider my plan. The snow was dull and lifeless. *Like everything else in Kursen,* I thought. Then I glanced over at the Sun King tree, where I had shielded Devon in warmth a few hours ago. Devon was straining against his tie to listen to us. Since we were speaking Botha, it didn't really matter whether he heard us or not, but the fact that we were having any sort of conversation at all greatly upset him.

I turned my back on the Sun King and considered that it was fitting that I should take my leave of the monastery as the sun returned, for I had first entered Kursen as the sun died. It was exactly three years since that day.

"Will you miss your life here, I wonder?" asked Cathe suddenly, as if in response to my thoughts.

"It seems I've always missed my life."

"Mmm." He sniffed and tasted the dirty scraps of sun which hung in the air, running his fingers lightly against his tongue without enjoyment. "A bit dry this year." He removed his fingers and smacked his lips. "Well. If it works, then famished birds on honeyed butterflies couldn't be better. I must say, it *is* a splendid piece of strategy on your part—absolutely splendid. I like it. I like it a lot. But—I don't know if the emperor will like it and so much depends on that. Well. If turning El means turning the whole monastery—" He let out a deep breath and looked at the main building, which oozed dead light. "—the old boy has more dedication to his calling in him than I'd thought. A rather twisty sort of nobility. A pinkling salmon's shame, really."

"Well, cousin, I suppose it's the strength of El's dedication that will make the show worthwhile. That's what Roguehan is paying for."

"Of course the emperor will understand it as El's last act of defiance, and there have been so many acts of defiance in the southern duchies lately he's become rather sensitive about such things. You know he executed a Helan advisor last week for wearing brown and blue to a council meeting—well, there was more to it than that, but there's his mood for you lately. We need him jolly and entertained, Llewelyn." Cathe was speaking in a slight whine. "We don't need him holding *you* accountable for any—unpleasantries."

"If Roguehan does mean to use me as a spy, he could do worse than hire a cleric who studied enough evil to turn his own high priest *and* his monastery to goodness. Roguehan may not like the gesture, but the way I see it, he really can't object too strenuously—not if he wants to convince the Midlanders that he leads a tolerant new empire in which Threle's southern duchies are happy and free. And he's smart enough to recognize it as exactly the sort of action which ought to buy me a deal of trust in the right places. Especially if you let the right places know about it, Brother."

"True enough," Cathe mused. "I'm sure Roguehan will see the value in that when he makes you a spy. So Kursen shifts. That's how worlds get born. Yes, fine. All right, then." He jabbed the ground with his rod, as if everything was now firmly decided. Then he said suddenly in a tone of nervous annoyance, "Does that boy ever stop howling?" Devon was whooping loudly to get my attention. "Whatever will he do when you're gone from here?"

"Destroy the place."

"Well, that certainly makes all the rest moot. Why don't you just freeze the damn thing out this year? We certainly don't need the liability of Kursen's mad puppy of a Sun King tracking you down to exact vengeance for friendship spurned now, do we?" Cathe sounded a little shrill. But then, his immortality was at stake.

"No." I grinned. "We don't need anything—of the sort."

"So." He looked around, searching for words for the sake of saying something. "And I suppose I could do worse with Walworth right now than be made high priest of a monastery in enemy territory dedicated to goodness."

It was my turn to sound alarmed. "He suspects your intentions?"

"No, don't be silly. There's never been a problem there. He's not refusing to take—and act on—the information I feed him. But some of his advisors are growing increasingly dependent on their own personal clerics now, and—well, as you know, the Threlans are going to have to rely more heavily on clerical magic to combat Roguehan's priests. Walworth would like me to attach myself more closely to the inner circle. Of course I can't do that yet. Not and work the other end for us."

"*Damn!* He *is* suspicious. He wants to keep you where you can be watched—"

"No no no—Llewelyn, lighten up. We're cousins—he wants to keep me where I won't be taken prisoner. He remembers the last time, and he's no longer in any position to spare a rescue party. It's all right, really it is. He thinks I'm spying for him—and of course, why wouldn't he think that, since I am? And he does rotate his spies frequently. Which is sensible. And, believe me, I *do* play the role of Habundia Ceres quite well. Been doing that one for years. Relax."

"Have you spoken to them about me, then?" My voice sounded purely professional; the rest of me was a gulp of tense curiousity.

"Of course not. How could I?"

"How *could* you? Cathe, I'm out of here tomorrow. I thought you were arranging things."

"Arranging things. Come to logic now, whatever on the gods' bloody earth would I say? I still don't know from Roguehan what your new position will be, and since arrangements must fall from that, and negotiations must be delicate—no, I haven't mentioned you yet." He paused and steadied his eyes against the light. "And of course since my kinsmen never ask—"

"Yes, of course, why would they? *Ask*, I mean."

"Well, actually they wouldn't. They have no reason to, you know, since I haven't exactly flaunted the fact of our—relationship."

"Perhaps we should let Roguehan in on our plans. Invite him to watch the destruction. You can't still be thinking about Zelar."

"Zelar is still thinking about Mirand," he snapped. "Unless you feel that Zelar is incapable of interfering with—"

"Yes, all right. Easy, Brother, after tonight all's one." I'd never seen him so agitated before. "Cathe, if Roguehan decides to give me work in Sevalas or Sunna, how do you plan to get me access to Walworth's household?"

"I had a plan. A marvelous plan." He looked affronted. "You see, I was sure I could convince the emperor to send you up there, that he would place you himself. And if it did fall on us to concoct a story, well, I thought Caethne would be our entry. I had a general idea that I could tell her about some wandering cleric I found on the road in the course of my travels who was looking for work like hundreds of other wandering clerics and speaks Sarana beautifully, and of course, knows his love spells. She'll accept you for the latter alone. As far as anyone else is concerned, well, yes he did take his training in Kursen but he went through a good deal of soul-searching, and found me by chance and the gods' goodwill on the road. I recognized my own kind immediately. After all, I became a high priest of evil in Sunnashiven before my horrible experience with the clergy there turned me to celebrate goodness in all things—"

"Yes, right."

"Well, yes, right, but the story works. And so I took a personal interest in this—other cleric—and initiated him into Athena at his request—which seemed appropriate—authorized the papers—and well, really I thought the commander of the Threlan army might greatly benefit from the services of a powerful cleric conversant with both sides of the equation. How was *I* to know there was some sort of history, bless the gods, and aren't wartime reunions fun?"

Now *I* sounded unconvinced. "Cathe—speaking of history, you never told me—what did you tell Baniff and the others after he saw me draw down evil god fire to destroy Roguehan's camp?"

He paused and studied the sky, then he looked at me and said mildly, "Absolutely nothing."

"Absolutely *nothing*?"

"Well, why bring it up? They didn't."

"*Damn*. So they know that I'm capable of working with evil deities and you never did anything to slant it? Never dropped any propaganda that might lead them to assume that my power does not derive from an evil source?"

"Well, really, Llewelyn, what could I say without giving away the game? It would be odd for me to bring the subject up because as far as my kin are concerned, I don't even know you. And as a high priest who adores Ceres's manifestations, it's not for me to appear to take an interest in such doings. Remember, I'm not *supposed* to be all that conversant with the actions of peacemongers and such."

"Didn't it occur to you that my own foray into peacemongering might make it difficult for me to earn the household's trust again? You've had over a year to smooth that business over and you did *nothing*?"

"Well, look, none of them should be *surprised* that you learned so much so quickly. What did they expect? That you'd cheerfully waste your life and mind scribbling papers in Kursen?"

"Damn it again, Cathe! I'm going to have enough problems gaining Mirand's trust without having to explain away the fact that I'm an evil cleric. I better damn well take credit for turning Kursen to the good. Thanks to you, I haven't anything else to establish my credibility on!"

"Yes, but when you think about it, what's to explain? Everyone knows Kursen is an evil place—I can't disguise that one for you. So, you found yourself here and you did what you had to do to survive. No blame there. And then you converted to Athena, so really what does it all matter? Look—your prayer and skill, evil or no, helped Threle destroy an enemy base. I would think with your intelligence and wit you'd use that fact to your advantage if the family makes your religion an issue—which I'm sure they won't. You can claim that even as a student of evil, your heart was in Threle and all that, and your studies have only made you stronger in the service of good, that you always found it in your nature to turn evil to good. So whatever Baniff saw is more likely to lend credibility to the conversion story than undercut it. And turning the monastery—well—" He clapped my shoulder. "—if something like that doesn't convince them of your good intentions, then nothing will and I might as well resign myself to my own mortality." Cathe said this last forcefully while squinting at me and driving his rod through the snow and into the frozen ground with a little eddy of goddess force. The ground layer of ice split and smoked. "Well, I suppose there's nothing for it now but a day's preparation." He swayed a little, balancing on his rod. "Shall I go sit with your master?"

"No. I sat up with him last night. He wishes to be alone today."

"Understandable. Lady, the sun does bite. Well, then I'm going to town to murder the time."

"Enjoy."

"Hehm. Why don't you go strengthen yourself for tonight's push?"

"I intend to strengthen myself, Brother. I'll be in my rooms saying my prayers. Until tonight."

"Until tonight." I watched him exit through the gate. He held his shoulders stiffly. Eternity—his eternity—balanced on tonight's success. Then I turned and walked back into the building, too intent on entering the rest of my life to do more than nod briefly in the general direction of Devon's cries and wails.

$\mathcal{I}$ spent the rest of the day sky-clad, lying still and solitary upon my hard bed, clenching and releasing my body's tension, falling in and out of trance. I was explaining to myself and to Lady Hecate that my intent was evil though my actions were nominally good. I was reminding my Goddess that I was about to work great harm upon Her high priest solely as a prelude to wreaking great harm against Walworth's entire household and accomplishing Cathe's deification. What was one high priest against a brand-new god? What was goodness against my heart's own revenge? It was vital to get my truest motivation straight and pure and tightly bound into my heart's darkest mind and then offer it unto the Goddess, lest Habundia condemn me through Hecate for influencing El into freely choosing to embrace Ceres. One slip in my own feelings and I was risking damnation as thoroughly as El was.

And yet I wasn't as clear about the issue as I needed to be, because every time I fell out of trance, I felt disturbing stabs of mild attachment for El.

For one thing, El had been damnably *kind* to me on the previous night, and silly as it sounds, it had been years since I'd experienced anything remotely resembling kindness from anyone.

El had invited me, Devon, and Cristo to join him for supper. I hadn't seen Cristo in the eight weeks since my sexual encounter with Venus through G, for he had moved out of our rooms that day and taken up residence with some other priest. I was therefore anticipating a wretched evening as I plodded down to El's apartments, and desired nothing more than to get the business over with quickly. But when I entered El's private rooms, I saw that everyone appeared to be in rare high cheer, so I supposed the meal would go smoothly. Devon and Cristo had no idea what was coming tomorrow, of course, and they both seemed highly pleased with the idea of being the high priest's honored guests.

It was only when their combined laughter peaked and faded that I noticed that El's mirth was all wrong. Something in his laughter was out of time and too soon. It struck me as the sort of laughter he should have decently saved for his stunning self-sacrifice to Ceres. His eyes brightened a little when he saw me.

"Blessed Sunreturn," I greeted him, smiling.

"Blessed Sunreturn, my son," said El grandly. "Be welcome. Be most welcome. Ah, yes, Cristo, have some more bread. You look hungry. There," he sounded satisfied as Cristo grabbed himself a fistful.

"Practicing, Master?" I said softly, as I settled myself next to him, knowing the strength of spirit it took for him to offer bread like Habundia Ceres offering sustenance.

"Hmm."

"Is it difficult for you?" I patted the back of his hand.

"Nothing done with love is difficult," he said stoically.

"I bless and admire your strength, Master." I kissed his hand respectfully and dropped it as Cristo hooted with crumbs and laughter. Apparently he had caught a few words out of El's last statement, because he crowed,

"Love, love—heh heh—we'll see love tomorrow all right and lots of it."

I decided that Cristo's weirdly joyful mood was due more to G giving up her beauty tomorrow than to El's presence. Perhaps if G were ugly again, all was forgiven, but I felt there was no reason to take up the subject directly. So I smiled at everyone around the table and extended my hand for the bread. "Wait," ordered El jovially, taking my hands in his like an old beggar woman looking for alms. I half-expected him to say, "Save my child." Instead, he intoned, "It would greatly please me to see you kill something tonight—"

"Yes, I shall kill," I said generously. "For Sunreturn and for everything the forces of evil bless." Cristo and Devon rattled their mugs loudly on the table to punctuate my words.

El dropped my hands and raised his empty chalice in a salute to me and the fading light, slowly chanting as the chalice filled with the darkness, "Excellent. A most excellent thing—to kill. To dream. To kill to honor the sun, yes." El slowly pulled a wooden cage containing a small owl down from a high bookshelf. "Athena's bird never lacked a home in Kursen Monastery, hm." He set the owl on the table, where it stretched its wings, *coowooed*, and hobbled over to Cristo's plate.

"Hey, I used to have an owl like that," announced Cristo, extending his finger. The owl bit it. Cristo drew back gasping and cursing and shaking drops of blood onto his plate as everyone laughed.

"Praise Hecate I'm at this end of the table," I joked. Actually, the blood of another priest of Hecate would not sicken me. But whether Cristo was a true priest on any given day, of course, was anyone's guess.

El chuckled indulgently before returning himself to solemnity. "It would mean lifetimes to me to see you honor the place properly this Sunreturn. I—greatly desire to—hmmm, feel that I've done some token initiation on you, papers or no. And I'm learning to embrace my own desires—so difficult a learning for me, yes." I was really touched. "And so I gathered witnesses." He said this loudly, as if he meant to please, gesturing toward Cristo and Devon. Devon looked up from Cristo's bloody finger and beamed at me. "And I truly desire to see you performing the rite—the last such rite Kursen will ever know," he added in a sad whisper.

"Kill it. Kill it now," crowed Devon. "Or let me."

Everyone laughed again. "All right, stand back," I ordered, smiling. The trance came quickly. The shield was more difficult for I wasn't exactly feeling neutral about anything right then, but slowly and painstakingly I dived into a hard aloofness and managed to carefully, carefully wrench my own goddess current against itself. When El sensed I was secure, he handed me the owl. I broke its neck cleanly, to some applause and cheers and more mug banging. El gave me a knife, and I carved out the meat to eat with my bread, knowing I'd have to keep the shield up for about fifteen minutes, which was my limit, and even after that, my body would feel slightly sick. But it really made El happy to see me do this rite. His eyes watered a little and Cristo and Devon pounded the table in approval as I swallowed some meat. El presented me a little bowl of cardamom pods and I sprinkled them on the rest of the meat as I ate.

El told us stories for the next hour. He drank and rambled on about the history of Kursen and the things that had happened here long before our time. And really, I must admit that the whole experience was rather sweet and nostalgic, for El himself was very much part of the history of the place, and I felt as he spoke of the monastery that he was speaking of his own life to me. At last, his voice trailed off and he smiled wanly. "Yes." Then he stood unsteadily, and announced, "And so, enough. To close the evening, I have a gift for you, Luvellun."

"Two gifts," said Devon. "We all got together and decided—"

"Ssh," said Cristo sharply. "The other gift is a surprise. It's for tomorrow when the emperor comes."

"You'll love it," crowed Devon. "It was our idea—mostly mine."

"Yes," said El mournfully, "tomorrow will be full of surprises. But now, for you." He handed me a plain wooden box. I shook it a little and smiled. El smiled back, a generous, paternal smile. "Please." I opened the box and there was a small silver brooch, designed for pinning riding cloaks, fashioned after the waning moon.

$\mathcal{T}$he same brooch which you see I still wear, my lord."

Walworth glanced at me but made no remark.

The brooch gleamed from my riding cloak through the North Country night like a beacon of energy, like an evil prayer to Beauty or a secret call to Isulde. Although I placed it on her altar at the beginning of the evening, and Walworth removed it and threw it on my chest, I didn't remember anyone present, including myself, pinning it back on my cloak. Perhaps the Northern shadows did it, playfully kissing this symbol of evil as Isulde used to kiss me.

Moon, waning, dead and soon to be. To continue my telling.

I pinned it to my shift and expressed admiration for its intricate artwork.

"My son," said El, "wear it always in Her name."

"I shall always wear the symbol of evil with pride, Father." El hugged me lightly around the shoulders. It was a fine evening, compared to all my other evenings in Kursen. Sometimes people have a nasty way of resembling friends once you know you have to leave them.

Anyway, my trance memories of El's kindness and the surprise he had thoughtfully arranged for tonight, a surprise he had troubled to consult my associates about, made it difficult for me to kill all compunction. But I prayed about it and that helped. And so I finally emerged from my trance strong and resolved.

I know I was strong and resolved because as soon as I pulled myself back into mundane consciousness, I went to my writing shelf to look at the brooch, to see if I could handle it without a twinge of regret. And I could. For me it was now Hecate's brooch, not El's. Then I began to dress myself, for it was getting close to evening and I needed to go out and release Devon's shield. And once I was dressed and collected in myself, I knew I was steady. I was prepared to see the job done, meet Roguehan, and get on with life.

It was then that I noticed that while I was in trance, someone had entered my room and stolen my illusion ring.

*O*ne . . . two . . . no, one . . . all right, two, then . . . three . . . no, two . . . three*eee* fine and prett*eeee* . . . two . . . one . . . dark, yes, as it should be . . . then down to the one again."

El was lighting candles and muttering to himself. I was watching him, and wishing that I hadn't been in such a damn hurry to unshield Devon and get to the ritual, for Roguehan hadn't arrived yet, and I could have been using the time to track my ring. As it was, I had to sit on the left side of the dais and look devout while El examined the height and shape and color of each flame from seventeen different angles and ask my opinion seventeen different times. Then, believe it or not, he would ask Devon's opinion, and Devon, bless his ugly little heart to a life's lasting horror, learned quickly that he need only express slight disapproval and the high priest would amuse him by extinguishing all the flames and starting his prayers and preparations over again. I sorely wanted to slap El into goodness myself and have an end. The candles were black and shaped like sea conches to honor Venus. They gave off a sweet, crusty, whorish sort of odor when they burned. The flames were a bright, horrific pink.

It was a flighty miserable business, this deathbed perfectionism, and I heartily wished it would end. When Brother Styrn wandered in to comment on the spacing of the silver vases of dead roses that El had probably spent hours arranging on a low table, I stood up, grabbed the brother's arm, and steered him directly off the dais. Too late. When I returned I saw El dumping the bouquets out all over the place and beginning again. I helped him with many compliments before resuming my seat, and I felt relieved to see him step back, admire the new arrangements, and nod.

"Devastating," called Styrn encouragingly from the front row.

"Yes," said El.

Devon started in, "I think—"

"They're Venus Herself," I interrupted, then whispered, "Another word from you and you get to live with Cristo from now on."

"They're beautiful," called Devon, but he pummeled my thigh, and added, "No I don't. Just you wait and see what you get, Luvie."

More clerics, including Elwyn, who was graciously bedecked with rose thorns, were filing into the front rows, and more students were filling in the back. From the snatches of conversation that reached me, it appeared that Roguehan still hadn't arrived. I did not see Cristo anywhere, but as the candlelight made it difficult to see faces in the dark of the back rows, I thought he might be out there waiting. Or too scared to come at last. I had not seen G anywhere, either, so I assumed she was still praying in seclusion. However, my attention was rudely drawn back to the dais, for the air around me was now beginning to stink like an old whore's back entrance. El had given G permission to create a special incense for the occasion, and G had come up with a blend that was so disgusting that Devon and I doubled over in hard painful gags as soon as El solemnly smudged us. Most of audience immediately retreated outside into the cold as soon as the scent hit them, where they would no doubt wait until the last possible moment to return to their seats.

El stood in the thick of it and sanctimoniously swung his censer to smudge the large, thronelike chair intended for Roguehan. "Yes, there now. Yes. She calls it 'The Back Side of Beauty.'" El was clearly satisfied with his assault upon the emperor's refined sensibilities.

But worse than the stink was the loss of precious minutes for tracking. I was not about to leave Kursen without my illusion ring. I considered the ring an indispensable magical item to have with me in Walworth's duchy, and it was only slightly comforting to know that since I had worn the ring for so long, it should be fairly easy for me to track it within Kursen, at least as easy as blasting the thief in and out of his next three lifetimes, which I also planned to do. With pleasure. But I had no desire to open up my sensitivities while sitting in this hideous cloud of incense and knowing that my concentration could be disrupted any second with the emperor's arrival. And if Zelar or another wizard were with him and happened to pick up on my signal, well, I really didn't want the world to know what magic I had at my disposal. Tracking through a shield was damn near impossible, of course. I'd have to track the ring later tonight. After the monastery turned to goodness, there'd be enough confusion to hide my probe.

But, really, who in Hecate's name even knew anything of the ring's uses besides El and Cathe? Even Devon and Cristo called the ring a "fire ring" because the only thing they had ever seen me do with it was light fires. And they only spoke of it when they wanted a fire lit. I couldn't imagine anyone stealing the ring as an attractive bauble and leaving all the other things on my desk—including the precious gifts of Venus that half the monastery had seen me receive. But what use did El have for the ring? And why would Cathe need to steal it? Where was Cathe, anyway?

"Devon, have you seen my fire ring?" I asked without breathing in too much.

"No." He choked through his shirt, which he was using to shield his face against the scent. "I can't see anything. Can't you make the smoke stop? For me?"

"No. Master High Priest?"

El had just lit the last candle. "Yes, Brother," he said thickly. The incense was getting to him too but he was so determined that nothing should mar his last initiation that he stalwartly refused to show any discomfort.

"I seem to have misplaced my ring. Have you seen it? Did I leave it in your apartments last night?" I knew I hadn't.

"No. I see nothing. I have no illusions." I looked in his eyes and knew he was telling me the truth. He studied the flame through two fingers. "Yes, hmm, twenty-four dull spots—"

At that moment the back doors burst open and the audience filed back in, coughing and covering their faces. Cathe was first among them. He strode jauntily toward us and swung himself easily up on the dais.

"Greetings from Sunnashiven, Brother," he said cheerily in Botha as he landed on his feet. "Fair greetings from the fair south on this wondrous eve of Venus. Where's the lucky initiate?" He clapped his hands expectantly and looked around, breathing deeply and ostentatiously as he bounced on his heels. "Aaaaaaah, what an absolutely perverse—mmm, ah—a perfume to charm a corpse to hardness, I'm sure—no, no, wetness, cold, used wetness—yes, delightful!"

El bowed stiffly. "Welcome. Brother." He used Kantish.

"Oh, well, I'm sure. I'm sure. Sun King." Cathe bowed to Devon, who acknowledged the bow by uncovering his face a little. "Brother Luvellun, Beloved of Hecate." Cathe bowed again to me. I waved my hand in annoyance and wondered what had changed since this morning. Cathe was positively joyful. He bounced over to the empty thronelike chair on the other side of the dais and half reclined in it. "Ah, yes."

"The throne is for the emperor," rebuked El.

"Yes, of course, and who do you think keeps it for him?" Cathe patted the arms. "Nice. Best seat in the house, I'm sure. I do like the fit of it."

"Never mind, Master," I whispered in Kantish, "He'll get his when you turn the place."

"Yes," said El. "Tonight we all get ours. Praise Habundia."

Cathe was still babbling in Botha and shifting his weight around in the throne. "Fine, fine—everything fine. Yes, praise Habundia, indeed." I heard the sound of footsteps approaching the platform. "His Excellency shall greatly enjoy this—trust me for a life." Cathe winked at El, who stood stiffly at attention. Then Cathe closed his eyes and listened intently to the footsteps. "There."

The instant Roguehan's party came close enough to view the dais, Cathe sprang out of his seat and bowed low. I took the hint and did likewise. Devon, of course, imitated me. El alone kept standing, fiercely standing in the garish pink light which rose and fell in uneven silences across the dais. Then the audience stood silently as Roguehan entered the platform. He was flanked by a little coterie of grinning clerics and grim-looking guards. Everything about the emperor was dark, a dark-spirited king dressed in dark clothes. His presence darkened the candles, that is, the candlelight seemed to fall short of touching him, even as the light made him visible. Nothing in his manner suggested that he stood upon our holy place of initiation, or that he stood anywhere at all, except in himself. He was what he wanted. There was a glowing sort of asceticism in his eyes that would have graced a high priest. He carried a huge white fluffy owl on his right arm. I wondered idly if Roguehan had ever been a monk. Then I decided he hadn't. The emperor was too strong in his own darkness to need the trappings of clerisy.

"My lord, I present to you Kursen Monastery." Cathe sounded like a jovial innkeeper who fully expected his patrons to enjoy themselves. He was taking credit for my work.

Roguehan smiled softly, ignoring Cathe to raise his arm and turn his face upward to admire his owl in the pink light, while the emperor's clerics respectfully ceased grinning and looked on in admiration. Roguehan stood in this pose for close to half a minute, making mock-kisses to his pet. I saw that the owl was attached to his wrist by a finely wrought gold chain. Then Roguehan motioned for his party to sit while he remained standing, gently lowering the bird to his chest. Then he slowly settled himself comfortably in the throne, all the while petting and focusing his attention on the owl. Then the audience sat, so Devon and I did the same. Cathe promptly took up a position standing behind the emperor's throne, from which he leaned down, spoke into Roguehan's ear, and gestured across the dais at me. Roguehan kept petting his owl, but he did glance briefly in my direction, so I inclined my head slightly. Then a severe coughing fit caused Roguehan to cover his face and set his owl on the throne's arm. The emperor's coughing freed up his guards and clerics to double over gagging.

"Nasty incense, my lord, quite nasty," said Cathe loudly and solicitously, fanning the air away from Roguehan. "Hold back on the smoke, Brother," he ordered harshly. "The candles alone should be sufficient." El swore softly and extinguished the burning incense with a wave of his arm. "Thank you. His Excellency is in a hurry to begin." El glared at Cathe's impudence. "*May* we begin, then?"

"Yes, of course," grumbled El in Kantish. "Wouldn't want to keep the cud waiting." I held back my laughter at this unexpected show of bravado but Devon giggled audibly. El swaggered ceremoniously over to Roguehan, bowed quickly and correctly, and addressed him in crisp Botha. "Your Excellency." Roguehan looked up idly and resumed petting his owl. "In *my* monastery—in Kursen Monastery, of which I am still high priest, we conduct initiations in Kantish. As you are ignorant—" El paused for several seconds. "—As you are ignorant of the language, you must find one among your own party to translate if you wish to follow our rite. I cannot be bothered." El's tone was deliberately insulting. Roguehan's clerics looked indignant. The emperor himself calmly gestured toward Cathe, apparently to indicate that Cathe was his translator.

"Well, Brother, let's get on with it then," said Cathe rudely in Botha. "None of us have the night."

El turned, gestured grandly toward Devon, and said in Kantish. "The Sun King."

Devon wasn't paying attention. He was kicking at my chair again. El waited and introduced him a second time but Roguehan was now engaged in low conversation with the cleric on his right. He and his advisor kept whispering and chuckling together as Devon crossed the dais, bowed, and welcomed the emperor to the monastery. The Sun King stood waiting for an acknowledgment until Cathe, who hadn't bothered to disrupt Roguehan's conversation with a translation, waved him back into his seat.

El then extended his hand in my direction, closed his eyes, and intoned, "The Goddess waits to destroy Her own. Come, Gogblgyn, who would be priestess to Venus Whose Beauty Enslaves, come and kiss your own destruction."

A few seconds drifted by in the candlelight. El looked anxious, as if he feared that G might refuse her beauty to the Goddess after all. But just as he opened his mouth to speak again, I heard a light step behind me and there was G, slowly and confidently entering the dais. She passed by my chair and stood still in the center of the stage, facing Roguehan. She was wearing layers of sheer pink veil wrapped around her head and body, leaving only her eyes and hands exposed. She was carrying a large copper basin, which she set at her feet. It made a sloshing noise as she set it down.

"My daughter," said El affectionately. "My lovely daughter who would break hearts." G made a long low graceful bow to the emperor, who was still engaged in whispered conversation. Roguehan did not respond, but he did study her for a few seconds as she rose before he pointedly resumed petting his owl. G's beauty seemed to bore him.

The audience, however, began clapping in unison and calling "Venus take us, Venus take us," just as her lovers had clapped and called out to her under the Sun King tree.

El raised one hand for silence. "Hear the words of our Mother Habundia. *'She who would be worthy of me must die unto me. She who would be my priestess must die unto her very self. She who would claim my power must kill the thing she loves. For that is what Habundia Christus and Her Children do and that is how you may know them. For the tree that is evil bears rotten fruit.'*" Cathe was not translating. Roguehan didn't seem to care. Then El faced his last initiate, took her hands in his, and asked, "Daughter, be thy fruit rotten?"

"Yes," she replied from under the folds of the veil. "Rend my veil and see." El gently removed the folds of pink, and as the material fell around her feet, a beautiful woman stood nude and fearless before a monastery of evil monks, her own high priest, and the emperor himself. If G was attractive eight weeks ago, she was ten times more attractive now, for the Goddess had clearly thrown Her mantle upon Her servant. G literally wore Venus all around her. Even Roguehan appeared to take notice, for as G looked steadily at him, he slightly inclined his head and kissed the back of his left hand to her. His clerics all nodded approval, and the guards, well, just sat there open-mouthed. I wondered how Cristo was faring. I was impressed by how closely G had entwined herself with Venus, closer than any other initiate had been entwined with a deity at Kursen. But I also felt a pang of pity for her. What was it like to be a glob who worshiped beauty, to be given the most sublime beauty any mortal could hold direct from beauty's source, to be allowed to love and enjoy this beauty, and to choose, to willingly choose, to destroy it? For G could take the gift and refuse priestesshood. That was the whole point of initiation.

"I see only beauty in and around you, daughter. And many would say that your fruit be whole and sweet."

"Yeah," cried several voices out of the audience.

"Listen to your lovers," El continued softly. "Do they hold your beauty as your own and love you for it?"

"No," said G softly. "My beauty is not my own. It belongs to Venus." G then faced Roguehan and continued seductively in Kantish, "In nature my legs are fat as bullocks, my stomach hangs around my knees and my skin is pocked and hairy and oily. In nature my face repulses, and my breath and body stink. In nature there are none to love me for myself."

Save Cristo, I thought.

"And in nature I am unable to earn the admiration of many. And so I came to the Goddess and She clothed my rottenness in Her own pretty deceits, and dressed my gruesome face in loveliness, and thus I am." The emperor seemed to enjoy the sound of her alluring voice, although he could not understand her words. Then she turned back to El. "I know the words and the truth, Father. '*I am not beautiful. Venus Whose Beauty Enslaves is beautiful through me.*'"

"Then slay the thing you love and go to Her." She looked up shyly and he squeezed her hand.

Then she walked determinedly up to me and said, "Kiss me for beauty's sake." I rose and did so, tenderly, as Roguehan watched, because I did pity G. Once I sat back down, I saw her sit before the copper basin and gaze quietly into its contents as if she were scrying. Then she prayed, softly, to herself, to Venus who was even now within her. Then she knelt, and said, "So beauty is washed away," and buried her face and hair and shoulders in the basin, splashing the rest of the contents all over her body, leaving no part untouched.

And when she rose, she was a horror. Even Devon gasped. Roguehan recoiled in dismay, and looked questioningly at Cathe, who was doing his best to explain matters. The emperor's clerics visibly shuddered and then tried to look professional and then just looked away. The guards looked sick. Here was a body, a living body, that would have made the original glob appear lovely. G was a wriggling lump of flesh covered with sharp, oozing spikes. Here and there the spikes broke for open sores, and I saw a rat dart out of a hole in her side. Her arms had become webbed like dragon wings, and the webbing covered great breasts which sprouted like cauliflower heads from under her arms. Her legs had become twisted and bent like a frog's and she had difficulty standing on them. Her face was lipless. The skin was like an old dragon's and where there wasn't skin the skull was exposed and her eyes—all three of them, rolled madly in their sockets. While the audience was applauding the sacrifice, El quietly did his job. He brought her a mirror.

"Behold your true form, Priestess." G could barely squeak her horror, but squeak she did, as El fearlessly placed his hand on her head and continued, "I return to you your spirit. For now you are one with the Goddess." And he lightly kissed her horrific face. Then G turned toward the audience, stretched her membraned arms, and called down Venus's force in the shrill voice of a skewered rat and lo and behold it came and she was as beautiful as before. Elwyn ran up on the dais, threw rose thorns around her neck, kissed her cheek, and quickly returned to her seat. Roguehan looked bright-eyed and smiling. He was clapping over a fine show and motioning G over to him. She skipped over, knelt, and kissed his hand. He plucked a white feather from his owl and gave it to her. She stood and ran over to El, flirtatiously kissed the feather, and smiled up at him. "Know, Sister, that so long as you keep the law of the Goddess, the law of Venus Whose Beauty Enslaves, you shall keep Her beauty. But should you in any way violate your deity's law, all beauty is forfeit and you shall return to the form you had even now. And so, the love you attract you must destroy."

"I know," she said shyly and sweetly. "Brother."

"I have a gift for you." El removed a long necklace of rose quartz pieces from his robe. They were barely visible in the pink light. "Wear these always in Her name." He placed them around her neck. "Go now, Sister, and be blessed." G bowed a final time to the emperor, picked up her veils, threw them playfully around her shoulders, and lightly pushed herself off the dais with one hand. She settled herself somewhere in the darkness of the audience.

Roguehan was now sitting up attentively. He was expecting the real entertainment to begin soon. El noticed his change in demeanor and looked pointedly at me. "Hum. The Beloved of Hecate." He indicated with his hand that I should stand. I strode over to Roguehan, bowed, and blessed him in Botha. When I brought down Hecate's force on him, his owl shrieked and Cathe waved me back so I let the force go before I finished speaking the blessing. His clerics laughed a little at the error, but Roguehan seemed to take it graciously. He was anticipating greater pleasures. He was smoothing down his bird's feathers when I resumed my seat. El strode officiously around the dais with his hands behind his back and the air of one who has important news to deliver.

"Here it comes," whispered Devon. "You're gonna love this."

"Tonight," said El sadly, "I have three gifts for the powers of evil. The first—was the gift of our beautiful sister." Applause and cries. He held up his hand, and turned his head away from the audience in a stunning gesture of humility. I saw the pale track of the flickering light on his face. Roguehan said something to Cathe and I heard Cathe begin to translate. The emperor looked quite pleased. "The second—the second is a surprise that I have planned in consultation with the Sun King—and others—for my favorite son here."

I thought I heard some hisses at the word "favorite."

"The Beloved of Hecate, our natural priest, our tangible evidence of the Goddess's blessing." I stood. "No, sit easy, son. This is for you. For never have you been publicly honored before the monastery with a gift. For being naturally a son of the Goddess, always have you refused legal initiation. You bear no papers."

"I bear nothing but Her blessing," I said humbly.

"'Tis blessing to bear Nothing," said El warmly. "And so—Sun King." Devon leapt to his feet, smiling. "Show the Brother how to bear Nothing."

"Bring in . . . Ellisand," crowed Devon, as if he were speaking a prearranged line. He was so excited he could hardly contain himself.

"Ellisand the minstrel?" asked Roguehan excitedly, recognizing the name and rising from his throne and turning to see Ellisand himself enter the dais and cross to center stage. Ellisand was escorted by the doorkeeper and two or three other servants, and he looked uncomfortable with the unusual attention until he saw them all drop to the floor in front of the emperor. Then Ellisand realized who he was about to play for and so made a long, theatrical bow. Roguehan looked positively delighted. He was clapping his hands and beaming while his clerics murmured in pleasant anticipation. I noticed El had left the dais.

I caught Roguehan's eyes, smiled, and gestured gracefully. "To my liege lord I tender my gift of music." Roguehan bowed his head in acknowledgment, and Cathe quietly nodded approval. El returned carrying a rather small chair, which he set in the center of the stage. The servants immediately stood around the chair like an honor guard while El indicated that it was for Ellisand. I wondered why the chair had arms. Ellisand glanced at the servants as if to say, "more monk nonsense," unslung his lyre, and sat. It was difficult for him to position himself and his instrument in the narrow space between the arms and as he shifted around, the doorkeeper pulled out a small knife and held it to Ellisand's throat. The other servants knocked his lyre to the floor and tied his arms to the chair's arms with bright scarfs.

The audience buzzed with excitement and Roguehan stood bolt upright, demanding from Cathe and everyone else, "What is this? Is this how Kursen treats musicians?"

"This is how Kursen treats everybody, my lord," Cathe said diplomatically. He had no idea what was up. Of course, neither did I. Ellisand looked more annoyed than alarmed. Since the emperor himself was objecting to this new bit of monkish rudeness, he probably thought he'd have nothing to fear. Maybe he'd even get a decent story out of it to impress his many lovers with. "Perhaps under different leadership—"

"Free him," commanded the emperor.

"Of course, my liege lord, your most Highest Excellency," said El obediently. "I intend to free him. Yes. My second gift. For my son. Who has always kept the *good* of the monastery at heart. Who has worked for years for the *good* of my own heart." He looked at me and I knew that El knew I had personal reasons for seeing him change alignments. I also knew that El felt trapped, that he himself saw nothing for it but to make the supreme sacrifice. "Sun King."

Devon jumped out of his chair. "Wait'll you see this one, Luvellun." He ran up to the doorkeeper and eagerly took his knife. The servants all stepped back, Devon bowed quickly to the emperor and then—and then—

He slowly cut off the musician's hands.

And with each plop of a severed hand against the lyre, a world died. And worlds die screaming. Ellisand was screaming, and Roguehan was screaming, and his clerics were screaming, and Cathe was screaming because Roguehan was, and I was screaming, screaming my life and soul out while El—the bastard—stood there laughing and Devon picked up a hand and looked puzzled by all the reaction. The audience was screaming and roaring and clapping and shouting El's name in wonderment, and stamping their feet and hooting and crying and singing and standing on their seats and screaming for more. You'd think they'd all just experienced a divine intervention. Devon picked up the other hand and ran over to me with them. I was appalled and outraged and didn't want to touch them. The blood and flesh sickened my stomach into making retching motions, but since I had eaten nothing all day, nothing came up.

"Don't you love them better than the finger? You once said that was the best gift I ever gave you. Love me?" El felt me draw down a blast to kill Devon and blocked it.

"There now." He raised his hand, looked most proud of himself, and intoned, "More, my friends. You want more sacrifice?" The audience cheered. "And for the third gift I return your spirits to you all." That quieted them down. Roguehan motioned his clerics to hold back their own fire. He looked emotionless and alert.

"What for evil are you doing?" called Styrn.

"Silence! Receive into yourselves your own life's path. I carry you in my heart no longer. Yes. I curse you all with freedom."

And he sent their spirits back, to mass confusion and plaintive cries of "Master Master. We need you, Master."

"And so—know that I also curse myself. I throw myself—" He was really wrenching his force here, for the candles died, and the darkness pulled in to itself. Out of the darkness came El's voice. "—*and* Kursen Monastery to the plentiful womb of Habundia Ceres, may Mother be merciful." And that was it. A beat of dark silence, a rousing emptiness of heat and wind, then the crashing of the roof over a screaming audience, then the rushing winter came, and then—well, the place didn't feel right anymore.

The piece of roof that sheltered the dais remained in place, but the rest of the roof had fallen and flattened the audience into the nauseating silence of sudden death. I found myself looking helplessly over the wreckage, and then up into the night sky from where winter kept descending in chill puffs of outrageous wind, feeling my own energy crash and shudder in response to the deadly fall of the roof.

It was of course only to be expected that the physical structures of Kursen would take some damage when El abruptly reversed the local energy from evil to good, and I should have been prepared for any damage I might have taken from the change, but I was still in such shock and disgust over the recent assault on Ellisand that I wasn't thinking clearly.

The proximity of all those mangled bodies and corpses in the audience as a result of the roof's collapse meant that I needed to put distance between myself and them. Of course the blood of another evil cleric would not cause me to sicken, but the the audience mostly consisted of students who had not been formally initiated into evil yet, and so my sickness rose with each expiring life. I was grateful that the roof did serve as something of a block against the sickening currents of death, but there was so much sudden dying before me I was feeling physically wretched.

As I stumbled in the dark over Ellisand's moans, I tripped into Cathe, who was quickly relighting the candles. The candles no longer gave off a scent, and their flames were now yellow, not pink. He thrust one in my hand and as the hot wax dripped and burned my skin, I saw a little pile of dust and bones where El had been standing. And on the pile was a small black-and-brown sparrow, with bright, defiant eyes. The sparrow was croaking in pain. It opened its wings and flew gracefully into the winter sky. Roguehan released his owl to follow it. I thought I heard him say, "Eat it."

Since Roguehan's clerics were clearly doing their best to draw upon their own evil deities for protection against the new spirit of the place, I did likewise. Hecate's force came weakly. However, with all of us pulling upon our deities, a sort of vortex against goodness formed on the dais until one of Roguehan's priestesses walked bravely upon the fallen ceiling, threw back her head, and screamed at the frigid sky. And the place felt different again, as if all energy was held in perfect balance, before settling out. She fainted with the effort, fainted before she could recover the place for evil. Roguehan sent two clerics to drag her back and revive her. The place was now neutral and nowhere. Roguehan sent a guard out to check the grounds.

Ellisand had lost enough blood to pass out, and while the vortex was forming and the priestess was working, I was ignoring my shuddery stomach sickness in a mad attempt to stop his bleeding. I made tourniquets out of the scarfs, I tried all the healing spells I knew from every branch of magic I'd ever studied, but my muscles sickened so much over the blood they all heaved in one direction, up my throat and pushing nausea out of the top of my head, so I couldn't swallow my spit or speak the words correctly. And when I did hit on a correct phrase and impulse, despite the conditions I was working under, the blood spurted faster. Roguehan ordered his guards to pull me away. "Let him die. He's worth nothing to me without his music."

Cathe said into my ear, "You can't heal him. Critics such as you are trained to destroy."

Another priestess spoke up eagerly, "My lord, I can save his music. I can attach his hands for you."

"Do it then," commanded Roguehan harshly.

Roguehan watched her intently as she ran to Devon and demanded the hands. He held out what was left of them. In his anger at failing to earn my praise, Devon had picked the flesh and muscle and bones apart with the knife, leaving nothing but a small lump of death which he had been cradling in his lap.

Roguehan blanched slightly at the loss. Then he turned to me in disgust.

"My lord—" expostulated Cathe.

"Bring me the hands." The priestess wrapped the mess Devon had created in a small black cloth and brought the bundle to her lord. Roguehan kept eye contact with me as he took the bundle from her. "Priest of Hecate. Eat them. Without a shield."

"You'd best," whispered Cathe. "Don't think about it. You'll feel better in a few days."

And so I didn't think about it. I swallowed the whole bloody mess as quickly as I could, the hands that had brought me beauty and joy, and then I promptly retched on them. The emperor made me eat the retch and ordered a guard to force my mouth closed so the stuff was forced all through my body and I was sure I would die. And worse than the sickness was the love I had felt for the music. I was forced to eat something I loved.

I don't know how long Roguehan would have allowed his clerics to feast on my pain if the guard he had sent out earlier hadn't returned to report, "There's a large fire out in front, Your Excellency. Think it's a suicide. Smells like flesh. There's a few servants gathered around it. My guess is most everyone who wasn't—" He glanced at the fallen ceiling. "—in here is out there. By the fire I mean, my lord."

"A suicide," said Roguehan. "All right, out." Cathe supported my shaking weight as all of us, except Ellisand, who was still unconscious, made our way outside. The Sun King tree was blazing, and there were a few servants trying to melt snow in basins to put out the blaze. They were not having much success. The doorkeeper and the servants who had flanked Ellisand went to join them. I smelled burning flesh and would have fainted if Cathe hadn't jerked me upright. He was muttering prayers to Habundia for me under his breath, and the prayers did seem to diminish the sickness a little, but there wasn't much he could do with the other clerics around.

I saw Devon go wide-eyed and indignant, and then he pushed forward through the crowd to the edge of the flames yelling, "Hey, that's not fair. That's my special tree, hey!" He picked up a basin of snow and hurled it into the middle of the blaze, from which came a loud cry and the words,

"You cud! You damn cuds all! Now I'm bruised and wet, you cud! Leave me alone!" It was Cristo. The servants couldn't melt the snow because the flames were illusion and snow does not have the human capacity of belief. Cristo had stolen my "fire ring" and because he was generating the illusion, he couldn't experience it. He had bungled his suicide. As soon as I realized this, the flames and the smell of burning flesh disappeared for me for I no longer believed in them. I pushed away from Cathe and started to stagger up to Cristo.

Cathe grabbed me. "What are you doing?" he whispered harshly.

"Saving our lives." I forced myself up to the blubbering Cristo amid cries of "He's burning himself." Two guards grabbed Devon to prevent him from going after me. I saw him struggle until one of the guards clubbed him into submission, and while the crowd was watching the altercation, I grabbed the illusion ring from Cristo's finger and put out the flames. Of course, because of my physical condition, I nearly fainted with the effort and Cathe, who now understood, ran forward to grab me.

"Make it a selling point," I hissed before violent gagging choked off my speech.

"Of course." He threw me reeling into the snow, spread his arms to the sky, held his staff aloft, and began a rapid prayer of thanks in Kantish to take up time while he thought of something to say. The guards and clerics were all openmouthed. Cristo was blubbering. Only Roguehan considered Cathe coolly. "My brothers and sisters. My lord," he said in Botha. "We have before us a miracle. A touch of Hecate Herself, who knows and protects Her own. For this Her natural priest, the 'Beloved of Hecate,' has withstood the flames of a would-be suicide and lived. For this is the Sun King tree," and he went to explain for an hour, while I lay shivering and freezing on the ground, all about Kursen's tradition of sacrificing the Sun King at Sunreturn, and how this very tree had been used for several years, and how Cristo, by choosing to sacrifice himself in this holy spot, had presumed to a worthiness he did not possess, and how yours truly had risked the flames to prevent even the memory of evil from being profaned, and surely I was a special son of the Goddess or I couldn't have lived and saved this spot.

I could see that the guards bought all of it, that the clerics looked at Roguehan and held their tongues, and that Roguehan looked on dispassionately. When Cathe finished his patter, Roguehan spoke quietly.

"Dispense with his suffering."

Cathe prayed loudly and freely over me, brought the sickness to an unbearable pitch for an agonizing half minute, and dispersed it. Hecate immediately felt cleansing to me. I stood and leaned against the Sun King tree, shielding myself in warmth.

"Saddle my horses. Oh, and take the Sun King with you. He has the makings of a torturer." The guards dragged him away to the stables. Roguehan turned to his coterie of clerics. "Is the story true?" His voice was even, impossible to read. No one answered. He repeated softly, "Answer or die. Priestess?" He was addressing the woman who had sought to save Ellisand's hands.

"I—I don't know, my lord. Perhaps it is true, perhaps not. I cannot tell without reading him through my deity."

Roguehan turned to the other clerics. "Kill her." They blasted her into infinity. Then he looked at the next priest in the group. "Answer or die."

"True," said the priest nervously, "definitely true, my lord."

Roguehan passed to the next priest, and then to the next two clerics. All said true. Then he passed back to the first. "And yet I know it is false as illusion. Kill your brother," he ordered the other three. They did so, with a blast that sent me reeling a little.

"We all knew it was false," said the next remaining cleric. Roguehan told him to step out before the other two. "Did you now?" he smiled.

The man nodded vigorously. "Yes, my lord, for Hermes the Liar told me so."

"Kill him for Hermes the Liar." The remaining two clerics, one of whom was the priestess who had tried to turn the monastery back to evil, were too frightened not to obey. "Now, you know what to do. The winner gets to be tortured at my pleasure." There was no winner, or rather, they both won, for they killed each other with a simultaneous blast. I don't think any of them were priests of Hecate, for their deaths reeked through my wizard shield and I had to hold the tree. Roguehan smiled at Cathe. "Looks like you won." Cathe made a low bow. "Come walk with me. The brother needn't expose himself to any more death."

I left Cristo clinging to the tree. He was stiff and openmouthed and immobilized by fright. Roguehan walked with us to a safe distance from the corpses, and then stopped, and said, "It seems I am in need of new advisors, Cathe."

"My lord."

"Clerics who aren't so—" He looked over at the bodies. "—narrowly specialized. Clerics who know something of the world. I like to reward cleverness, and I account your illusion trick clever. Clever enough to—fool the *right* people, shall we say? And so—"

"My lord," ventured Cathe with admirable monastic calmness, "my Brother Llewelyn here is quite adept fooling people, and I had thought he might be quite useful to you as a spy."

"A spy." He studied me. I bowed.

"He did get El to turn."

"Among other things." Roguehan glanced around Kursen's grounds. "And El's turning was a lamentably brief performance for the price it carried." Roguehan's owl returned out of the sky and landed on his arm. Its beak feathers were bloody. He petted it. "I shall never hear such music again," he said plaintively. He stared into the winter dark. "Well, there's still a war to fight." Roguehan looked at me. "I have punished you adequately for a poor job. You suffered the loss of the music too. And so I account us even." He extended his hand like a gentleman. I kissed it.

"I am eager to serve you, Your Excellency."

"I shall remember it. And your flame walking. 'Saving evil from being profaned by a worthiness the suicide did not possess.' Quite amusing." He lifted his owl to admire it in the winter moonlight. "For now, Brother Cathe, I trust you to take this mess in hand and do what you can to convince the public that Kursen has been turned to goodness. I wish to create comfort for the Midlanders. Llewelyn may remain here to help you, and for now he is imperial courier between here and Sunnashiven that the temple there might be kept informed of developments here. I'm a man of my word. Since your duties here will keep you from performing your old job, he might as well have it in payment for the night."

"Yes, lord," said Cathe, bowing.

"Thank you, lord Emperor," I echoed.

"Spy." He chuckled, walking off in the direction of the stables. The owl faded into darkness long after he did.

Five

*E*llisand lived the night, barely. Perhaps the tourniquets helped. Perhaps his incessant traveling had strengthened his body enough to withstand the shock of losing so much blood. Perhaps being of mixed race, he had inherited a hardier constitution than that of most pure elves or pure humans. Perhaps the cold winter wind had stanched the bleeding. Perhaps the gods intervened. I have no idea *how* he lived, but beyond all expectation, he lived.

It was a pair of servants who found him. The musician was nearly as dead as his audience, lying insensibly on the dais next to his lyre and partially obscured by his chair, which had toppled over him. His bloody arms were stretched in sleeping supplication toward the emperor's empty throne, exposed to the first pale light of the new sun. Everything on the dais was lightly wintered with the first snow of the new year. A strange snow. Warm and thin and melting into colors and airy blankness as soon as anyone looked at it. A shy, sparkly snow that lay all over Kursen without confronting anything more material than morning. I had felt the snow glowing along my chest a few hours earlier as it fell through the long swaying descent of the full moon. I imagined the dissipating glow around the dais, colored fractions of sunlight throwing themselves back out of blankness and into their newborn source, caressing and disappearing into the sun's best self like music. A hidden performance. A natural law just passing through.

And an audience of the dead for witness.

When the two servants came to dutifully report their find to the new high priest, Cathe was pawing through El's art collection and personal effects while airily discussing his "vision of the new Kursen" with me and Cristo and half a dozen servants who were waiting on other matters. Cathe had been spinning out the "vision" all night, and it was a fine vision, too, replete with higher pay and more promotions and better working conditions and plenty of good and healthful food worthy of Ceres Herself.

The new Kursen was all kinds of things at once. "A shining horn spilling freedom and abundance to all corners of the empire" and "a haven of fattening joy." The cooks liked the latter. It was also "a singing garden of Mother's own delights, where every sort of happiness takes wing with the baby birds." This Kursen was for the doorkeeper, and Cathe made deferential bird motions as he described it. The doorkeeper smiled in broad delight and repeated the motions with his hands. The stableboy was promised a "free horse and golden hay, for every growing thing blessed by Ceres is golden, my boy. You know, the Lady can be no other way save golden." The wine keeper heard Cathe ask absently, "Wouldn't it be a capital idea to open a public bar, now that evil needn't seclude us, and wouldn't the wine keeper enjoy being in charge of that, with many assistants, and the right to keep a hefty percentage of the profit for his trouble? The new Kursen must be a place of devout celebration, after all." And of whatever else popped into Cathe's mind as he rummaged around through El's drawers.

The servants who were now waiting had all heard bits and pieces of the "vision" earlier, for they had been shifting in and out of El's apartments all night, stealing whatever they could as they pledged loyalty to their new master and humbly asked him for instructions on their duties. Since Cathe was planning to dismiss them all anyway, he saw no reason not to use them to get the proper sort of image spread around the community, so he had been making them all wait on his pleasure that they might "overhear" useful tidbits of propaganda to take out into the world with them. Cathe was heightening their expectations as a prelude to dismissal, under the theory that it would make Kursen's new reputation more convincing if a lot of servants went around bragging that *they* would have been in charge of so and so had they been willing to compromise their allegiance to evil, and complaining that at least in the old Kursen you could get away with stealing, if you didn't touch the relics and were smart about it and so on.

To that end, Cathe had been amusing himself and Cristo by leaving piles of gold coins and small valuables in conspicuous places, closing his eyes in prayer, and pretending he didn't notice when the gold and valuables disappeared.

Cristo really seemed to get off on the whole thing, for even though he had tried to end his own life a few hours ago, he was now laughing great glaring barks of laughter under Cathe's steady encouragement. It was rather sad, and I have no idea why Cristo found this business funny, except that Cathe was conspicuously treating it like a practical joke so perhaps Cristo thought he was *supposed* to find it funny. And since there might be a permanent job for him too, he certainly wanted to please. But there was more than toadying in his laughter. Cristo found hypocrisy entertaining. He could feel superior to it, and I supposed that was worth living for.

When the servants finally saw their way to speak, Cathe was emptying a drawer of papers and telling Cristo for the third time that night, "which means, of course, that now there are ever so many teaching positions to be filled, permanent jobs, which—"

"The musician's still alive, Master. Thought you'd want to know about it. He's closer to death than life now, but he definitely *does* live. What about it?"

"What about what, my dear man?"

"Well, he's not too alive. Probably won't last the morning. We could just throw him in the hole when we do the rest of the corpses and no one need know about it. That is, if our new master high priest wishes to blast a burial hole for us in the frozen ground." Cathe dropped the papers and looked at the servants blankly, as if he had no idea of understanding their suggestion.

"I could help," said Cristo quickly, in an attempt to curry favor with the new high priest. Cathe and I stared at him incredulously. "Throw him in the hole, I mean," he mumbled. We kept staring. "If you make one . . ." Cristo coughed a little and looked away.

The other servant spoke, "Would it be like a profanity to push him under the roof until we can get a hole? Or until you decide what is to be done with the dead?"

Cathe then dropped his gaze, looked hurt and softly offended, and whispered in delicate studied shock, "*Decide* what is to be done with the dead. Yes, I suppose I must." He prayed with closed eyes and lost three gold pieces to the cook. The prayer was a masterful touch, but he really did the rest up, too, coming out of prayer and slowly making eye contact with both of the servants who had found Ellisand and finally, for the longest period of time, with Cristo. Then he sighed loudly, looked embarrassedly at the floor, raised his head with difficulty, and pretended to look gravely into the distance, as if his new position was a heaviness to his tender soul and he could see comfort somewhere on the other side of the exquisitely papered wall. Then he prayed again. Then he said helplessly, "Well."

"Master High Priest," I helped him out, "is something wrong? Is it something *I* did?"

"No, Brother, it's not you." He clapped my shoulder tenderly. "*You* shall make a fine devotee of goodness, and even now I thank the Lady for Her bountiful grace and your touching willingness to follow your old master over to Ceres." This was the fourth time Cathe had made this particular speech in the course of the night, but every time new servants entered, the performance had to be repeated for them. "Such strength of heart and mind and, well . . . I am truly ten leagues beyond the sky's delight that She accepted and preserved *you*—for Her own divine reasons, of course, but still—here we hail yet another miracle in your blessed life, I'm sure. No, no,—it is just—just—well—it seems there is so very much to do." He picked up an intricately carved god figure from El's dressing table and perused it, running his fingers over its face and then tightening his fists around its waist until his knuckles whitened. Cathe was now the tormented leader drawing strength and support from whatever was at hand. Wasn't the new master *sensitive* in his admiration and respect for the replica of an evil god? Surely he could see good in everything. Surely he was *serious*. "Fine copy," he choked. "But I suppose we shall now be looking for originals." He set it down quietly, lightly caressed it, and then turned to the hapless servants. "And so," he asked harshly, "the two of you think it is the business of the new Kursen Monastery to bury living musicians?"

The servants looked at each other. One spoke haltingly, "Uh, we could kill him first. If you want, Master. He might be dead now anyway."

"Oh, ye stray vipers!" This first and unexpected burst of anger out of the new master sent shock spiraling through the witnesses, which of course was Cathe's intent. "What has the sweet Lady given me to guide and endure? Kill him *first*?" Cathe spat. "Bury the *dead*, I tell you! Bury the collective corpse of evil that rots and stinks in the place of its final initiation! Bury your selves and your spotted spirits and bury your tongues for speaking such—oh, leave us be. Oh, sweet Habundia! Oh, Mother save us all from the spirit-killing tyranny of evil! Dear Mother, how deep and darkly has this place sunk." He wept a little, as if the apostasy of his new charges greatly pained him, then he let his voice fade into a quiet, steady clarity as he ordered, "Save the singer." He glanced earnestly through the knot of servants. "If any of you can."

"Uh, you want us to move him somewhere then?" asked the other servant uncertainly.

Cathe studied both of them with a brilliant look of contempt. "*Move* him? *Can* you? *Move* him? Can you *move* divinity? Is it not divinity that *moves*—in and through music—is it not—no, I want you to leave! Leave Kursen!" He punctuated this with his staff, which he rammed against the floor, producing scary whorls of fire. "Leave this poor injured musician to us and to our care! I am high priest here, and I myself shall tend to him! Cristo—" He waved his hand as if Cristo were now a dependable favorite. "—fetch bread and cheese and meat and good sweet wholesome water."

"Yes, Master High Priest." Cristo started to leave but one of the dismissed servants nudged the other, who spoke up quickly.

"Uh, before we leave, we want to know, do good monasteries have high priests?" Everyone held their breath. It was a damn good question, actually.

Cathe looked offended. Most offended. "Imperial ones do. It is an administrative title. Really, there is so much to do. Do you know," he announced, "I was once a high priest of evil, like your former master, until I—well, until Ceres gave me light and love." He cried great heavy tears. "I saw light and—and—love—love has such tender wings, you know, all brown and gold with perfume, and then—the sweetling sun sang my name, my *true* name—and so I came to Her, risked *death* to come to Her and so—Cristo—"

"Yes, Master High Priest."

"Cristo, dear Brother, on your way to the kitchen, spread the word that I want to cast forth all—" Cathe looked pointedly at the servants "—*all* belonging to evil, all whose words and attitudes bespeak lamentable allegiance to the enemies of good! It is our work and calling to hate evil here, Cristo! It is our job to hate, you understand! To hate!" Cathe turned to the servants, "And yet, you know, my dear Mother speaks to me of hate even now—speaks Her finest truth to me, She does—yes, my Lady, there is so very much to do." He froze with a look of utter horror on his face. "The cook *stole* what? The garden-girl stole *what*?" and on through a catalog of every servant in the place and his thieved loot, which Cathe finished by placing his hands on his chest and pretending to stagger around.

"A most sad day, Master High Priest." I helped him sit. The servants were already starting to accuse each other and exonerate themselves. Cathe waved them into silence.

"Keep your stolen dole as your final pay and leave these newly hallowed grounds. All of you! You and all servants who show themselves as bane to goodness. All servants of the old Kursen *are* bane!"

"Does that mean everyone is fired?" asked a nervous woman.

"Yes. We must begin the world anew." He said this as if it were difficult and it was solely his determination that was holding him up. The doorkeeper looked tragic. "Go, and may the Lady bless you." The moment they were gone, Cathe turned to Cristo. "Brother Cristo," said Cathe as if he were gaining control of himself, "it would be an immense relief to me if you would imprison Ellisand beneath the wine cellar. Give him his lyre, a loaf of bread, a pail of water—a wide pail, and, say nothing to anyone and—I believe I have the key somewhere in here." He shuffled through the drawer as I handed Cristo my key. "And come back here when you have done it."

If Cristo saw any incongruity here, he kept silent. He left.

"Ellisand's life may still have uses for us, that is, if he can keep his life beyond today," Cathe mused, tossing one of El's bejeweled baubles in his hand and smiling cockily at me. "I do like this job."

"You're wonderfully convincing."

"Yes, I am. You should see me around my cousin."

"Except that the servant has a point. Ceres has no high priests. Perhaps you should drop the title altogether."

"Yes, well, small detail. So I am—or was, depending on who I talk to, a high priest of Habundia Christus and I kept the title. After all, I am running a monastery, and this is the empire, where titles matter—and clerics who manage good monasteries are usually conversant with *all* the lower manifestations of goodness, which in a practical sense differs little from being a formal high priest on the evil side—and ah, welladay, what of it? I don't expect either of us will stay here for very long."

"Which brings up another issue. Imperial courier was not the sort of thing either of us had in mind."

"No, it wasn't—but sometimes what can you do? We didn't have execution in mind either, and mortality nearly came our way last night. Roguehan was impressed enough with our cleverness to let us live and you're no longer beholden to him. And really, the whole thing gives us both opportunity and imperial sanction to establish your new reputation for goodness, and once that happens—trust me, you'll get close to Walworth with Roguehan's blessing. The emperor likes you. Really he does."

"How can you tell?"

"You're still here. Well, I'm really quite satisfied—considering. Roguehan is in need of new advisors, and without his clerical guard around, I may get to work some influence. You'll be thick with the Threlans within a year *and* beyond suspicion. And who knows but that the emperor might have that in mind anyway. Trust me to work it." He picked up the god statue. "Ugly little image, actually. Don't suppose you want it for fun?"

"No."

He smashed it against the floor. "Got to show the gods who's in control once in a while." He kicked the pieces out of the way and opened a little cabinet of handsome, embroidered robes. "I don't suppose any of these will fit me, but we might hire ourselves a seamstress. Oh, and this one is—ah, nicely, touchingly scented with a packet of rotting grain—tipped with—" He held the packet to his nose. "—my favorite—a hint of mold—really El did have taste—"

"Uh, Master, you dropped something, let me help," said Cristo anxiously, entering the room and picking up pieces of the broken god. "Here's the key." He gave it to me.

"Oh, dear," said Cathe. "I should have offered the god to you— but now it's broken, and—"

"It's all right, Master, I've got a piece. Got several."

"A *piece* of the god, right here, Cristo. Fine morning's work. Did you bring all healthful and wholesome sustenance to Ellisand, as I asked?"

"I did as I was told, Master," said Cristo cheerfully, pocketing god pieces. "No one saw me."

"Would it matter if anyone did see you, Brother? It is not required to perform acts of healing kindness in secret, is it?"

"Uh, no. But you said—"

"To feed and care for the musician—if he still lived. He *does* still live, doesn't he?"

"Enough not to kill. He wasn't conscious and I had to carry him to the cell—"

"What cell?"

"You said to put him in the cell beneath the wine cellar." Cathe and I looked puzzled. "Didn't you? That's where he is—with bread and water—in the cell."

"Why did you imprison the man?" asked Cathe softly and apprehensively.

"Be—because you said. Didn't you?" Cristo looked to me for support. "Didn't he?"

Cathe also looked questioningly at me. The humble high priest was open to admitting a wrong if indeed he had committed one. "Did *I* ever order such an atrocity?"

"No, Master High Priest, you did not," I said solemnly.

Cathe looked at Cristo like this new shock was the worst of the morning. "I had high hopes for you here. Especially since it wasn't clear to me whether you were truly aligned to evil."

"Oh, I'm evil," said Cristo. Then he caught himself. "I mean—I'm good."

"You *mean* nothing. You're evil," said Cathe. "I see it now, plain as the Lady's own shining brow. And I fear that somehow your Goddess speaks to you through me. I ordered you to bring the musician here, where he might be cared for in all goodness, did I not, Brother?"

"Yes, Brother, you did," I said. "In all goodness."

"And yet you heard otherwise. Cristo—I know not what to say. Even here—even now—an evil power speaks to you."

Cristo stammered, "I heard you—I didn't hear—"

"Cristo, Cristo—I wanted so much to give you a permanent job here. To tell you your hard work had earned you the security of being employed here forever."

"I didn't hear you—"

"I even sought to overlook your failed suicide as an action belonging to the old Kursen—where you—well, I believe in faith that you've killed yourself out of a job. You attempted suicide and now you are the special recipient of the Goddess's own commands—thought you heard *me*." Cathe shook his head and shuddered. "You are evil and—and I fear I cannot keep you here."

"Master, I didn't mean anything. I'll go get him now." He said this weakly, as if the words were a form he had to follow.

"You must be turned free to find your way. Go in peace. Now. I—I shall draw up letters explaining it is not your fault."

So Cristo got burned after all.

But it struck me as a fairly comfortable burning. And Cristo seemed a little *brighter* for it. For one thing, he didn't linger, and his eyes showed no anger or resentment or pain, just a slow, almost grateful sloughing off of a tired mask which had thickened and stung with empty years. Cathe had truly blessed him with a gentle kind of evil, for Cristo had finally achieved, or received, the spiritual condition all evil aspires to: He had no choice. He *had* to leave Kursen. He *had* to face the expulsion every monk fears. He *had* to enter the world. And he *had* to accept his "punishment" as a reward and a validation of his intimacy with evil, an intimacy he had thought he was supposed to aspire to but which he never really achieved.

The high point of Cristo's career was when someone else took his life in hand and told him he could quit. It is a poor gift to be backstabbed with abundance, but Cristo seemed to be well-hiding a shadow of happiness with it. He could now be an evil cleric with no monastic responsibilities, no pressure to torture his mind into scholarly grinds, and no guilt. I knew he would brag about his dismissal for years—how the Goddess spoke to him special, how he was released to the world because he had perfected his evil nature, how he once had a "teaching position" in a monastery, and so on. Cathe was counting on this, of course, and just as he had "paid" the servants with their stolen loot, he was "paying" Cristo with a stolen status and the belief he had been made to suffer for his moral excellence. Cathe had made him an honorary martyr. No peacemonger ever had it so easy.

I believe he left Kursen immediately, for Cathe lost no time in fulfilling his word by writing a lengthy letter, reading it aloud to a dazed Cristo, and then sealing and handing it over to him with a flourish. Cristo shoved the paper next to his chest, nodded to me, and left. To my knowledge, his paper martyrdom was all he took with him into freedom.

*S*o Cathe and I had the monastery between us until we could take in a new group of servants from town. He sent me to town to solicit help for the new Kursen and in my absence he blasted all the corpses with fire and sent the smoke spiraling to all the various infinities of their lives. And we both dined in town that night, for as "good clerics" that was now permissible, and as propagandists that was now necessary, and we talked great storms throughout the evening about the new Kursen and its new mission, and promised gold and silver to anyone who wished to rebuild the fallen roof, and fine wages for all who wished to serve good by trying for other posts, and attracted much interest, although Cathe remained deliberately vague as to when Kursen would be restaffed with teachers. "We must put the dear place in working order again first," was all he'd say when asked.

We returned late, and it wasn't until midmorning next day that Cathe took me to the cell to see Ellisand. The poet was lying on the hard dirt floor and moaning into the darkness, but as soon as we entered the cell and the light from my sputtering candle fell on him, he turned his face away from us and all moaning stopped. Cathe touched him lightly with his staff and waited. Ellisand did not respond, but he was conscious, and his lack of response felt deliberate. After a few minutes it became clear that he was intentionally ignoring us.

"Would you like more bread?" Cathe finally asked solicitously.

No response.

"More water, perhaps? I *can* feel your thirst."

Silence.

"Ah, well. It *is* the sun's own pity, isn't it? Believe me, we are all *most* sorry—*most* sorry—in fact, the emperor himself was quite upset. Counts it a personal loss, I can assure you. And the proper parties *have* been thoroughly punished."

Still no response.

"Would you like to hear how?"

More silence, the silence of contempt.

"Well, I shall tell you, and perhaps you shall set it into a poem. The evil high priest of Kursen Monastery is worse than dead—turned himself and his grounds against his deity and got his sparrow soul devoured by Athena's bird for his troubles. Hideous end. And Devon—the Sun King Devon—well, Devon has been forcibly separated from Luvellun here, and, if you knew the depth and nature of his attachment to the good brother, you'd know he's experiencing a luscious amount of well-deserved pain. And Luvellun's old roommate Cristo—big fan of yours, by the way—well, Cristo was involved in the whole sordid affair, so as the new high priest of Kursen Monastery I turned him out. Do you know what it's like for a monk to be forced to earn his own living? Cristo has feared being set free for most of his life. Oh—and those cretins who applauded the—uh, unfortunate incident—they're all dead now, crushed by the ceiling."

Silence.

"Well really, what more can I do?" Cathe waited impatiently for an answer. "Look, the point of the day now is that you *can* still speak, and so you can still speak your poems, and so you can still write your way out of this dismal little cell and into something more comfortable—if you choose. We like to think of Kursen as a new monastery, dedicated to goodness now—a haven for the arts and all creative endeavors—a place for poets. And so—how's this for more comfortable board—we proclaim Ellisand of Gondal our new poet-in-residence—he speaks beauty for our scribes to catch—as soon as we get scribes, that is—and he tells the world of our new dedication to goodness—perhaps a little book—each poem dedicated to a different aspect of Ceres—and of course, we send a copy to the emperor, who deeply admires your artistic abilities." Minutes and minutes dragged by without response. "Well, think about it. Meat and wine and girls and boys and a warm room and anything else you care to ask for. Except freedom. You know we can't let you go, of course. It simply won't do at all to send a well-known musician like yourself maimed into the world. I shudder to think what poems your tongue could compose and how many people those poems could reach without our . . . management. But really, there are prisons and there are prisons and there's no reason yours can't be more comfortable than—this." Cathe nodded at me and we left. Ellisand had remained silent through all of Cathe's speech, but as soon as we were ascending the stairs, I heard him moaning again, more quietly now, more like sobs.

And because I became his jailer, I heard him moaning every time I approached his cell with bread and water, for Ellisand refused to speak his poems to us and so remained where he was. But every time he heard me enter his prison, the moaning stopped, for the poet would yield nothing but silence. I did my best to comfort him. I used wizardry to still his pain once or twice, but as I sensed this angered him more, I left him to feel whatever he felt. I spoke to him a great deal of the outside world and the changes occurring in Kursen and what joy it would give me to see him take up residence among us. And once or twice I begged him to speak. I even offered to run messages to his girlfriend, against my better judgment and without Cathe's knowledge. But as the only response he ever made to me was silence, I eventually gave up. He lived in darkness and emptiness, his back always to the door of his jail, his head always bowed and covered against my intrusive candlelight. And eventually he wasn't even there. That is, whenever I felt for his mind, it was somewhere else—constantly in a northern night staring through starry shadows, dreaming excruciating dreams at his still unspeaking lyre.

This state of affairs went on until the end of summer, and might have gone on forever, if Cathe hadn't finally managed to "work things." But let me say first that for eight months I ran back and forth to Sunnashiven at the emperor's whim, and that I greatly resented the fact that my reward for years of patient service was this miserable post as Roguehan's imperial message boy. It often occurred to me as I rode through the ruins of Helas that I had come full circle, for hadn't I begun my career at Kursen bearing messages in secret for another warlord? And now—well, the only difference I could find was that *those* messages were borne voluntarily, with good intent, and at great personal risk. These new messages were borne under orders, with great resentment, but with the emperor's own protection. As long as I wore the imperial insignia, nobody in Sunnashiven dared to accost me, and so long as I wore my clerical robe, nobody even thought about it.

As it happened, I was rarely sent to the temple. I was mostly sent to the bars in the city, where I drank foul stinky beer and met other couriers and spread the word among the people that Kursen Monastery in Kant was now changed to the good, and religious freedom was prevailing throughout the empire. For Roguehan had decided that I might as well spread as much propaganda as I could.

Which meant that when I wasn't traveling, Cathe had me writing deplorably convincing essays on Ceres and goodness for widespread publication. "Target them for Mirand," he advised, cocksure that Mirand would suddenly have the time and interest to read monkwork. "And I'll make sure he sees them. Can't hurt now to send up a copy in preparation for the grand reunion."

"You're sure there's going to be a reunion, then?" I looked wryly at my messenger pouch.

"Sure as sickness. Eternity depends on it. Roguehan's favorably impressed with your propaganda work in Sunnashiven. Keep it up."

I got quite adept at passing for a priest of Athena, and Hecate blessed me in my lie. With practice I could even fool other clerics, for I practiced holding my shield out against Cathe and managed to stretch my limit up to forty-five minutes. And I knew pretty much everything there was to know about wizardly defenses and love spells. And Cathe and I spent long days speaking Sarana, so my command of the language went from "quite good" to flawless. Not even a detectable accent, Cathe told me. And as I said, my new essays got distributed all over the place. I can't say in all it was an eight months ill spent, for I was in a much stronger position to enter the household than I had been at Sunreturn. But it was an eight months of wondering when and how Cathe would ever convince Roguehan to send me north.

So I was most relieved when Cathe told me at second harvest that my tenure as messenger had ended and that things had been "arranged." All I knew, and this was confirmed in a letter from the emperor, was that I was now to worm my way into Walworth's household using any means I wished and to do my best to influence Walworth's critical judgment and that of his generals. Should I succeed, then Cathe and I would become joint rulers of the duchy. Which meant, according to Cathe, that the whole thing would fall into my lap under his special divine protection once he became a god. And should Threle win the war, well, the family would still be destroyed, making Cathe (and therefore me) the lord of the land anyway, as we had discussed years ago.

I have no idea what magic Cathe used to sell Roguehan on the idea of finally sending me up into Threle, or if he used magic at all. To my knowledge he only met with Roguehan on two occasions, although he was in constant correspondence with the emperor. He did tell Roguehan all about my previous involvement with the family, although I'm quite sure the emperor already knew or suspected something of this, because of the role I played at Loudes. But Cathe filled him in on all the intimate details and assured me that Rogue-han was "mildly interested" in the aesthetic possibilities of bestowing the duchy on an old "friend of the family."

"But he's not going excite his aesthetic cravings too much over that one—considering what happened last time," Cathe said blithely. "If you're successful in misleading the Threlan commanders into an imperial victory, you can claim the duchy as a reward, and Rogue-han might find that pleasant to watch, a sweet aftertaste to victory, but it's his aftertaste. Just do your work properly, and the rest will follow."

"So he knows nothing of our intent."

"No, of course not." Cathe studied me. "Make them work for their defeat if you can. That's the point of it you know. Roguehan is terribly invested in watching them embrace and lick and kiss the destruction of Threle, or what remains of it, for they do love Threle so much."

"Yes, of course, which means I'll need all divine protection from you after Caethne—removes her brother."

"And you'll have it. Remember, the emperor is getting bored and impatient now. He's been laying siege to the southern Midland cities and burning the farmland for months, but with the exception of Ignothum and Threlanche, none of them have cracked. They've been storing and rationing food for months and there's no telling how long they'll hold out. And Walworth managed to disperse and do much damage to Roguehan's forces near Elasak—so things are not going as quickly as they might. The plains are a vasty tricky area and anybody's game right now. The cities could fall in weeks or years or never."

"Has your cousin made you privy to the extent of their supplies?"

"No, lately he hasn't made me privy to much." I glanced sharply at Cathe. "But that's not a concern—he likes what I'm doing to promote goodness here, and I gave him valuable information for taking back Elasak—he's just not interested in sending military messages to Kant right now, and really can you blame him? But look, your papers bear my name, and when you leave tomorrow, you may bear any message from me you find helpful. Manifest something appropriate, I don't care what—and I'm as confident as catfish livers that there'll be no problem." He breathed deeply and puffed up his chest. "I send you thoroughly prepared and trained for the work and in complete confidence of your success. I'll know you've succeeded when I get an invitation to the wedding. Which is probably when we'll meet again."

So I packed and made ready to leave that night, planning a route which would avoid the cities and therefore the armies and would take me directly into the Duchy of Walworth, the northernmost duchy of Threle. For Cathe and I had decided that my best point of entry was still Caethne, and Walworth was so busy running his army in the plains that getting access to him and Mirand might be difficult, and establishing some sort of trust and connection impossible. "Consult with her first," Cathe advised, and I concurred.

So it came down to the dawn of departure. I saddled and packed up my things on my horse, a fine broad-backed black stallion, and rode slowly past the wine cellar in the predawn darkness, thinking of Ellisand. I was reluctant to leave him to Cathe, although I saw no other option, for I was certain that Cathe would shut off all sustenance in my absence and let the prisoner die. It had long been clear that Ellisand was not going to break, and Cathe was getting concerned about a servant finding him. A few days ago he had mentioned walling up the cell with magic "and there an end," but the look on my face silenced his idea into the pretense of a weak joke. Sometimes I brought Ellisand better food without Cathe's knowledge but Ellisand seemed to view it as a bribe, for he never touched it. Beyond bread and water he ate nothing. Sometimes I left him soap and extra water, and he did manage to use that, but he would take of nothing else. He never spoke.

I had to let him know I was leaving for good and forever, and that his life was forfeit soon. And what harm in telling him how his music gave me life in Kursen's dark lean years and in expressing to him once more that, well, his fate was really his own if he would only consent to write for Cathe. Anyway, I knew I would dream better if I made the attempt.

So I hitched up my horse in the shadows, took a candle out of a saddlebag, and crept with the absolute silence of near dawn down to his cell.

And promptly fell into the sucking rushing golden whirl of an elvish dream.

Ellisand's dream was sprayed and flat and pulsing all over the cell and pummeling out of the door that I gingerly unlocked. I slipped and fell into pure dream, stood in a wind of violets and rose effortlessly on a nightingale's song. I stood steady in the sky—I held myself against the firm door and locked myself inside the golden whirl—yes, there's music here and—should I think so slightly—one thought and I rip the fabric—one move and he sees me in the center and wakes—one move and I dance into—I never saw such warmth and humming—so I do not think, but dance gingerly like a foreign wind and press my palms against a new number system swelling into a world structure like a bursting running mushroom with legs—I'm gone, eating the mushroom and my hands sweat oceans like cool streams of airless moonlight—elvish dreams rush through mine— another elf's dream, not even this one—a rush light into the rushing cold and light, and I was larger than a fiery oak's reflection of its own green spirit—I was the spirit of the oak whom the sun made sacrifice to and I swayed with song—my blood swayed with it—if I had blood—more like a pulse and rhythm and that was all my life and so I had to sing—had to because I was song—but sing of everything *else* and elsewhere—everything outside everything coming down the road all fiery living and gracious glances of time at once and still light *maybes* sprang in the distance.

And there in the distance Ellisand woke in anger and pulled the waves into himself and out of existence and so I stood silent and awkward in the cell and in the darkness, feeling like the trespasser I was. And when all was dark and void, he spoke to me out of the floor, spoke in his native language which to my ears sounded like oddly accented Sarana,

"Fuck you, monk."

And so in Sarana I answered. "And so you've decided to speak." I noticed a faint, very faint, will-o'-the-wisp glow around his lyre, but as soon as I noticed, the glow ended itself. I lit my candle. He was huddled on his side near his lyre, covering his face. "We're making progress, then. Shall I set that one down as your first line?"

No answer.

"I'm leaving, Ellisand. For all and ever. Going north into Threle and freedom."

The stiffening line of his back suggested, "So go."

I sat on the dirt floor, and said softly, "You won't live of course. You can't fight Cathe with dreams. You see, he's not amused anymore and you're getting to be a liability. Nosy servants—how to explain so many months of silence even if you were to start writing now, every-one believes in Kursen's goodness without your help, and everyone's convinced you died at Sunreturn when the roof caved in and surely if you lived it didn't take eight months to recover, so I'm sure you understand the problem we've got. I've done what I could for you, but I'm afraid you've closed the door on your own life. Was silence worth the loss?"

No response.

"I'm only asking out of intellectual curiosity, of course. Anyway, I leave and the bread and water will stop, and the air too, for Cathe will wall over the door with a few words and a shake of his staff and well,—and then you'll dream, shortly—until the dreams go bad— until the dreams go—and then—shall I leave you with Hecate's blessing?"

He sat up heavily and looked intently at his lyre, and as he did so his shadow fell across the candlelight and the instrument glowed slightly in the dark.

"Are you dreaming even now then, poet? I could take your dreams, you know, and let you feel death's claw without them."

He picked up the lyre between the stumps of his wrists, cradling it.

"Or I could tell Cathe you're going to cooperate, bring him a few lines for show, and persuade him it's not too late to treat you kindly. Which is it?"

The lyre glowed brighter.

"Yes, right. And I thought music was just a job like anything else, you pretentiously humble ass—and here you cling to your instrument—sorry—'tool of trade' as if it were your last living friend, as if it were alive, and you could dream me out of existence." Then I whispered, "I should take your lyre and sell it to a Sunnashiven barkeeper for memory's sake, to the bidder with the highest price, remembering your lofty insistence that art is just a business. I'll take instruction from you, Ellisand. I'll remember your practiced disdain for any critic who dares to love the beauty you create and maybe my doltish heart will stop whimpering for your perfection every time it hears someone ruffle an inferior chord or riff. Stupid us—stupid me! I believed in your work and survived hell through it and forgot once or twice it was all just a business and only a fool would feel anything!"

The lyre was a still-bright green with hazy blue edges. I couldn't see the lyre for the dream anymore.

"You're always so damn distant and casual—and really should your audience be likewise? Everyone so bloody cold and emotionless? Oh, please, then why not take up a living as a fishmonger and why bother creating art at all? None of us were supposed to miss it anyway! Play for whoever pays! Yes, and you won't even knock together a ragged line or two for your own sup, or capture something of your music in your poetry for me who once loved your music. Let all your art die then. Close your last chance out in dreams. *Fuck you!*"

Then I reached out through the now piercing blue for his instrument and knew instantly that the light wasn't coming from a dream. It was coming from Ellisand's own fierce protectiveness. The lyre was so much a part of his self that his own thoughts gripped and smothered the lyre in sweet elvish light. But there, inside the defensively cool light I touched, I felt a softer light like a bumpy summer rain. I did not see this light, I felt it, a difference, like a soft thin spirit in the strings which loved him fiercely.

His instrument was a living thing. The lyre could experience illusion.

I slowly withdrew my hand. It had to be dawn and passing by now. I thought of Cathe. Ellisand was still ignoring me. I didn't care. I heard the quiet of the dirt floor and slowly dying stone walls. I thought of the night I had once spent in another dark cell and what the thought of execution felt like. And I still didn't care. And I thought of his music and I spoke against all wisdom. "Ellisand. If by the name of Hecate I can restore your hands as they were, will you come north and play for me?"

He looked up. The light wavered into pale red.

"You play for me. I decide where and how and to whom else you perform. The money you earn will be for your traveling expenses, as I've only supplies for one. And your tongue shall be bound through my magic from speaking anything of Kursen. As far as anyone knows, I'm a charitable priest of Athena you met on the road. I'm doing this at great risk, for Cathe fears for what you can do to Kursen's new reputation, and he'll howl to the high moon when he finds you missing, but of course, you know that." He was studying me, not quite impassive, not quite hopeful. "Speak."

He put one stump against his lips, as if to say, "You first."

I took his stumps in my hands and instantly relaxed him into a trance, which was very easy thanks to his physical weakness. Then I set the binding spell on his tongue along with a control word, *lyre*, to strengthen the spell again as it weakened. Then I pulled him up and muttered a prayer to Hecate, which I told him was a cure, and at the end of the prayer I worked through my illusion ring and told him to behold and believe in his hands for they lived again through the Goddess.

And by the look on his face I knew the illusion was working for him, although of course I could only see stumps. And he repaid me by stroking the lyre with what he believed were his fingers, although I could hear no music because I had worked the illusion. But Ellisand did speak, and he said, "Needs tuning," so I knew for him the music played and that was a beginning. The lyre believed. And some-day, against all the laws of magic, I would find a way to make the illu-sion real for me too. It was something to live for. Besides revenge, I mean.

So I helped him to his feet and I helped him strap the lyre over his shoulder, reminding myself that I must never let him handle insensate objects lest the illusion die for him, and of course that would be the day's own difficulty, but I didn't care. And I didn't care for Cathe's ire either, which I postponed by magically walling up the cell behind us and manifesting a note which read, "Job's done." Cathe would hear about it all eventually but by then—well, the job would be done and over, so to speak. And so he'd have to "trust me" and get used to it.

After all, it's a poor deal of a god who can't take a joke.

Six

$\mathcal{W}$e rode swiftly through softly lurching disasters. That is how I remember our journey through what used to be southern Threle. Every lurch of the stallion we shared was a disaster, every border crossing a potential end. The afterdawn broke gray and fuzzy all over the little town near Kursen Monastery as we left it all behind us, and then the fuzziness broke into autumn drizzle, and then the drizzle broke into the attention I was giving the horse, who was giving me every indication that he'd rather be mare-chasing than galloping a straight pure line out of the empire. The drizzle was important because I needed to keep focused on the illusion I had created for my companion. I had to keep making sure that his own belief in his hands was strong enough right now for him to feel the rain against his palms and wrists, just as he had felt the hardness of our large saddle and the twitchy warmth of the stallion's neck as he mounted. For much to my relief he had remarked upon both with the joy of feeling through his hands again.

Of course, mounting was our first potential disaster, for I had to keep up the illusion spell while helping to physically lift his weight onto the horse so I could be as close to him as possible while working the complex magic. The horse would feel hands, of course, but the horse could not "choose" whether or not to support their imagined weight. That was indifferent physics. So I kept close oversight, and told Ellisand he was too weak from eight months of poor diet and dreams to mount by himself. But he was so convinced that he really could push his weight through his hands and pull himself up that he practically did it himself, for I noticed it didn't take all that much energy on my part to work the magic to get him up there. The small amount of power I needed to draw was another welcome indication of my illusion spell's strength.

For illusion is the most precarious and unpredictable of the magical arts. In theory, every living thing that does not "know better" is subject to illusion, that is, only illusionists can see through dreams to whatever is. But in fact, belief is such a chancy thing that not everyone responds to illusion spells in the same way. I'm not really an illusionist, but I do know, for example, that a dullard who is absolutely convinced that there are no exceptions to the world of his deeply narrow experience, that frogs never sprout feathers and pigs never fly and the gods never speak and poems never get written and magic never happens to him, is harder to convince of some things. One might make him believe he's shoveling manure instead of hay, or filling his maw on a common potato stew, or suffering unbearable physical pain, but it would take the gods' own work to make him think a fairy was digging new suns out of his garden, or his sickliest hen laid diamond dragon eggs, or a rainbow had just squirted solemn music on his plate. I'm not saying that sort of thing couldn't be done, and a truly expert illusionist is adept at discovering just what it takes to induce a difficult subject into believing in beautiful exceptions to his life, but intelligent subjects are far easier to work illusion on. Intelligence already knows that nothing is impossible. And highly creative subjects already believe, devoutly believe, in impossibilities. They sort of have to. And so I guessed that a musician like Ellisand would likely be more susceptible to illusion than most people. And so far I was right.

It was raining quite steadily once we got a mile or two northwest of town, and so I steadily remarked on the coolness of the raindrops, and how they tightened and stung and exploded against my taut knuckles until finally my skin sagged with moisture. I spoke the words by way of conversation but directed them into the illusion to strengthen the bond between his belief and my words. I was satisfied when he told me he didn't mind the wet chill in his fingers and never would again, but I kept up my own patter because it was precisely during these times of strongest belief that I needed to speak to him of sensations. If I could constantly create in him an association with my words when he did feel things in his hands, then I could use this association as an extra safeguard in moments when the illusion was in danger of slipping. I knew I needed as much control over his belief as I could get, because there was no telling what sort of event could kick his realization against the spell and then, well—even if wizardry held him dumb against speaking of Kursen, someone else was bound to see his stumps, recognize him, remember hearing rumors that Ellisand died during his last performance in Kursen and—well, truth had a way of coming out even in spite of the best-intentioned magic.

As long as Ellisand believed in his hands, everyone else would too, except illusionists, of course, which meant I had to scrutinize everyone we encountered. I wasn't worried about dullards, because

even the dullest dullards should have no problem in believing that a
man had hands. And as long as Ellisand believed he could feel the
saddle as he mounted, or feel the rain and wind against the back of
his own wrists as we rode, he would. And as long as the lyre believed
music was possible, music was, and their combined belief would
charm living audiences. But if Ellisand should try to pick up a mush
bowl or untie my traveling bags or open a lousy door—it was all a
softly dangerous chance. Belief is a funny thing, and for all I knew
his belief might be strong enough for small objects to respond as if
they were being handled—as I said, he nearly lifted himself on the
horse through the strength of his own belief—but there was no way
of knowing, and no inanimate object would respond of itself. Perhaps he could handle a spoon, or some spoons. Perhaps he could
dress himself in darkness but not in early dawn light. Perhaps he
could lift a dead feather but not in a heavy wind. I had to make sure
his hands only played with living things until I knew what would
hold the illusion and what wouldn't. I had to watch his every move,
and be quick with wizardry if he tried to unharness a saddle or pull
out a chair.

In effect, I thought ruefully as the increasing rain and coolness
sent the stallion into a rough uneasy canter, *by freeing Ellisand I've
become his prisoner. I am a prisoner of my own longing for a
beauty that will never exist for me again. And I'm riding in freedom to bring murder and lovely destruction upon a set of old illusions . . . of friends, I mean. And I shall murder by forcing sweet
love into their midst. And I have studied for years all the deadly
ways in which to become an illusion of a friend myself. I shall be a
distant audience to murder. I shall receive power like applause—
and yet—I've bound myself over to a poet in a moment of madness
for the sake of his music—music now dead to me forever. Is madness necessary to my task? If I couldn't feel to risk my life over a
memory of music, could I feel to take vengeance on a friendship
spurned years ago?*

I desperately wished to follow this line of thought, but a preposterous lurch of the horse interrupted everything important. The stallion had suddenly gone skittish over a pair of squirrels who were
scampering for cover from the quickly hardening rain, and he reared
up without warning, nearly throwing Ellisand out of the saddle.
Ellisand grabbed me for balance while squeezing his legs against the
horse's flanks in an attempt to keep from falling, which sent the poor
beast into a panicked rollicking gallop. I could have stopped the animal instantly with magic, of course, but I needed all that part of my

concentration for my passenger. Of course I couldn't feel Ellisand's hands against my sides, but I realized as I shortened and pulled on the reins and slowly got the horse under control that Ellisand's belief in his hands had kept him balanced. Ellisand was completely convinced he was holding to my sides. Well and excellent, another good sign, but I wasn't willing to take unnecessary chances that another pair of chattering squirrels could ruin all. "Grip me as close as you can with your arms. Lock your elbows around me and stay that way until I tell you differently," I ordered in Sarana, as I jerked harshly on the reins and made the horse completely halt.

"Why?" asked Ellisand reasonably, as the raindrops swelled and stung with morning chill. "We're not moving now." The horse shook and coughed, and then bucked forward a little as it tried to rub its face in the muddy ground. I jerked up its head. Hard. "Well, don't get angry with me, man. What do I know? I thought you were in a hurry to get up to Threle. Haven't sat on a horse at a dead stop in the middle of a rainstorm in a long time."

We were sitting in the fierce downpour and a cold little wind was kicking up, the kind of wind that made me feel that I was truly in a new place now, that the monastery was another past in my life. Then the horse was a black mat of water. Rain was seeping down my neck, inside my riding clothes, and along my back. It was puddling coldly in my boots under the arches of my feet. Rain was falling in my eyes and weighting my eyelids. The rushing sound of rain was shuddering all over the woods. I magically felt rain all over Ellisand too, in all the same places I felt it in myself. And then I probed for his emotions, and I knew that he was not exactly curious or impatient concerning our standstill—he was just waiting for whatever was next. Waiting not in a stupidly passive way, but in an easy, whatever-you-say, it's-your-life-who-am-I-to-argue, take-it-as-it-comes way. His attitude read, "After all, if my traveling companion has suddenly up and decided to sit on a mad stallion stopped dead in the middle of a rainstorm on a deserted road and get us both drenched with cold and fever, what the hell? It's an experience." This was an attitude I found strangely nerve-wracking under the circumstances. It felt like he was throwing something like a judgment over me, and I suddenly felt an old unwelcome need to prove that there was a clever reason for everything I did. And yet my magic told me all judgment was from me, not him. Ellisand really intended no judgment. I'm not entirely sure he even knew what judgment was. Which somehow made his attitude feel worse.

Anyway, the horse was really a madman. The crazy beast was

liable to throw us both and ruin the illusion for Ellisand. I sat for a few minutes in the windy downpour trying to think of how best to avoid another potential disaster.

"Hey, Lew, are you saying a prayer or something?" The question was an impersonal tease. Ellisand didn't much care what I was doing, he simply felt like talking.

"Or something." The horse shuddered and coughed again, and then walked a few paces of its own volition before I harshly jerked on the bit again to make him stop. "Here." I manifested my rain cloak from out of a saddlebag and threw it over Ellisand, adjusting the hood over his rain-matted hair.

"Hey, neat conjuring, Lew."

"It wasn't conjured. It was manifested. It's mine. There." I pulled the sleeves around his arms and straightened out the cloak. "It was in one of my bags and I magically removed it and you're going to wear it. Now." I sent dry warmth scurrying in the thin air pockets between the rain cloak and his drenched clothes, between his clothes and skin, and around his would-be hands and fingers for good measure. "You should be feeling dry now. Keep your face covered. Let's put as much distance between ourselves and Cathe as we possibly can before we excite gossip. There's bound to be other travelers on the road soon."

"What about you?"

I ignored the question. "The horse is easily spooked and unused to two riders. The saddle, large as it is, was not meant to seat two people. You have no stirrups for balance, and it's plain to me even without magic that you're not in peak physical condition. I don't want you exerting yourself. And I don't trust the horse to give us a smooth ride. So you're going to hold me tightly with your arms and lean into my back—as if we were one. Got it?"

"Why don't you conjure up a second pair of stirrups?"

Because I can't create reality and illusion at the same time, damn you. I do not say this. "Because the saddle's too small."

"Why don't you magically lengthen out the saddle?"

"Because my witch sense tells me the horse will be happier if he thinks he's only got one rider to contend with—so it behooves us to sit as close together as possible."

"I didn't know you were a witch."

"There's a lot you don't know. Now be silent and hold on. I'd like to make the Medegard border by nightfall." Ellisand grabbed me with his arms and I kicked the stallion hard, which sent him immediately into a rapid, heady canter. I decided if I could get the stallion into an even rhythm, however fast, I could steady myself enough to perhaps risk magically controlling the horse without dropping my attention from the illusion. Ellisand's incredible belief in his hands could sustain the illusion for hours without my help, but I wasn't comfortable dropping my attention yet. It was too soon.

And then I realized that if the illusion ever broke, I'd have to kill the poet, and kill him in such a way that his body would never be found. And since it was only a matter of time before people recognized who I was traveling with, if it came to killing I might have to create a story about us taking separate roads somewhere and how I didn't really know what his next destination was. We just happened to meet up for a while, that's all. Maybe he went back to Gondal.

I don't know how I felt about this. As I said before, I had no strong emotional attachment to Ellisand as a person. His music was a tool for reaching the better, most beautiful places of my mind, just as my stallion was a tool for reaching the Duchy of Walworth. But Ellisand? I don't even know if I liked him, and now that I think about it, I can't even honestly say that I *disliked* him. I don't know what I felt about him. I was certainly jealous of his untroubled naturalness, his take-things-as-they-come simplicity. I had thought eight months in prison would have worn and fractured his easy self-assurance into something less annoying, but now that he believed he had his hands and music back and knew he only had me to contend with, prison didn't exist anywhere in or about him. I guess I felt mostly chagrined, but with a chagrin which felt worse than jealousy. His life had a way of rebuking mine. He could remark on the simple autumn rain and make all sophistry and commentary feel dirty and sweaty.

I kept thinking of my years of study, and the rain kept falling, and the horse kept bouncing and pounding, and I kept seeing a vision of rows and rows of guilty children standing unwashed in each raindrop—like poisonous billowing flowers—and then my mind was dangerously off, for in my vision one child stood straight and open and crossed her legs and clasped her little hands behind her back. She was pleading innocent to stealing a candied plum. She was hastily swallowing melting candy under her practiced words. She had a dirty smutty face that she kept hidden under her blank skin.

Who are you? I ask to trace my thoughts.

"I am the sophist-of-the-day for I have won the game. If I touch you with my stick, you're It."

Show me your hands, child.

"But they're empty, sir—I have nothing in my hands to show."

Then where is your stick?

"In the sharp air, sir, you must find it fast."

I know she's lying. I struggle to grasp her hard fingers. She eagerly lets me yank her empty hands into visibility. Her eyes are sweetly glittering. But when I look close I see an ugly gratitude. Can gratitude be defiant? Sophistry's can. Sophistry is now the girl's name. She smiles. I've struggled with her for truth. I've left her triumphant. Damn but she's won the game again. And her stick sprays blood in air. *Yes, you have nothing*, my mind says to hers, *and to have nothing is to be innocent. You can go.* And yet her guilt is as obvious as a piglet's lamb. She curtseys, the practiced bitch.

Do you feel innocent, child?

"I feel nothing."

I feel nothing. I'm riding through the wet and the rain and making fading images of sophistry in the raindrops. I should be paying attention to my passenger. Sophistry is the little girl's name, and sophistry now has a dirty face. It's a song but I'm bored now. Too bored to pursue the intense randomness my mind made up out of rain and memory and the heavy pounding of the horse. And when I return to my thoughts about Ellisand, I have no feelings—only impressions.

And yet Ellisand made my impressions feel. Ellisand made philosophical complications feel like unhealthy obsessions. He made all criticism feel like it masked a dirty secret, made it feel like the secret sin it was. He made monkhood, my monkhood, feel not so much evil as dishonest, which is quite a different thing. And he did this without even trying.

I loved his work. To an artist this is the best and only form of love. Tell an artist to his face he's a rat cud and a bum and a conceited ass and he won't even care as long as you follow your string of insults with the phrase "but I love your work." He'll probably repeat the insults to all and sundry. He'll definitely wave the compliment around in mock-hurt and dismay whenever he wishes to boast. And he'll probably like himself all the better for overpowering someone's personal dislike with his work, for in his own heart he'll feel loved in spite of the insults. Yet tell an artist he's a wonderful person, that you love him for himself and his personality and his deep brown eyes, that you'd die for love of him but that you think his work boring or unskillful or ill done, and I swear he'll never speak to you again. In his heart of hearts he's convinced you despise him. An artist *is* his work. Period. And even Ellisand, for all his nonchalant "professionalism," was no exception. He preferred death to censorship. He would have suffered the cruelest tortures of the damned rather than damn himself to writing to someone else's demands. Rather than give his heart to Cathe and Kursen Monastery and become something he wasn't, he would have willingly died in his elvish dreams.

Unlike me, who had insisted on turning against myself to embrace evil, I thought ruefully.

And so as we cantered along a stretch of road through the rain-sopped woods, I decided the more time I spent with him the more deeply I would regret the path of my own life. There was a time when I would have died *for* a dream—a dream of friendship and liberty and equality and love among a family I once nearly came to regard as my own—

Well, I mean—set it down this way, my lord—a dream of Threle, a dream of myself."

Walworth looked impassive. He was just taking notes and waiting for me to continue. Why pass judgment on a dream?

But I could never die *in* dreams—which is the ultimate triumph and defiance of reality, the ultimate assertion of self and existence. To die in dreams is to enter new worlds. It takes an artist to enter new worlds. It takes a self-belief more relentless than wizard fire and bitter hearts and old obsessive love to die in dreams. All dreams that matter are enclosed in bands of iron, and only the strength of zealots and madmen can keep them close.

Had my dreams ever mattered to me in the way Ellisand's did to him? Perhaps those dangerously beautiful dreams in which Isulde came to me mattered. But it had been awhile since she had graced me with one of those, and I had been so occupied with waking matters I hadn't even remarked on the absence of those dreams until now. And I was always aware that they were Isulde's dreams, not mine. Not mine to die in, anyway.

The first and only dream of myself that ever mattered to me was the dream I found when I first entered Threle. In Threle—in Walworth's household which was so perfectly a microcosm of Threle—I was a dedicated young magician-soldier, sworn to fight and to defend my new country and friends. I was what my young mind had always dreamed I could be—strong and disciplined and willing to die rather than let my comrades be executed on a phony treason charge. And, in the weeks leading up to that horror of a treason trial, I did risk my life, like any hero worthy of the name would, for that haunting dream of eternal friendship. The dream betrayed me. My friends showed their willingness to let me hang instead of them, and so I dedicated myself to evil and coldly let my dreams go dark.

Set this down. I did not die in my dreams. They died in me. By my own hand. And so in this respect I was weaker than Ellisand.

Because of Ellisand's strength, then, I suppose, Cathe would have killed him. Cathe would have been correct to do so in terms of our plans and the state of the world, but Cathe was too enamored of reality to do the killing properly. You don't wall up artists and leave them to die like the decaying vegetables and rotting animal corpses Cathe was so fond of. Cathe was too much the nature lover to love art. He could destroy nature with his words and revel in rotting pumpkins and decaying cockroaches. He could grow hard upon dying lakes and gasping fish. But poetry? Music? That had nothing to do with nature—and the only way Cathe could think of doing art in was by burying it in the earth like fiercely glowing carved and polished bones or poor scraps of worm-eaten silk. He would plow the artist back into the primal seething ooze of nothing. Wall up an artist in the dirt—yes, well, wall up yourself in your own Mother's womb and die. But that one seems to defeat the whole purpose of dying, doesn't it? Suddenly something's—*wrong*. Known *again*, maybe, in exactly the same dark forever way—but still wrong.

You see, destroying an artist is no different than destroying a poem. Killing a poet is literary criticism performed in physical space. Murder is the ultimate commentary. And I'd been trained for years in commentary.

I decided if expediency demanded, I could probably blast Ellisand to his death and not feel any more regret than that which accompanied the failure of any other bad risk. For it was a bad risk to free him—it was a very bad risk to love music beyond sense and wisdom. Hell, it's a very bad risk to love art. Fall in love with art and there's no telling where you'll end up.

"Hey, Lew, think we can get some chaia in the next town? Used to know an old guy there that grew it."

"No. We're not stopping until we reach the border."

"I thought this was the border," announced Ellisand cheerfully.

"Well, it isn't."

"Well, what do I know? Maybe it isn't. But they've got guards and weapons and stopping posts. Just like the real thing."

Damn, he was right. I had been so caught up in the internal border crossing of my reveries that I had failed to notice the world around me. There, at the outskirts of the next Kantish town, was a line of steady commotion that looked for all the world like a border crossing. And we were less than a two-hour ride northwest of Kursen. Medegard was a full day's journey and then some along this road, and I certainly didn't expect to encounter nosy guards until after dark, when Cathe and Kursen would be a good twelve or thirteen hours behind us. I had decided that once we were in the next duchy, it was unlikely that Cathe would do more than grumble to himself about my momentary weakness of reason. We would be too far to follow and he didn't dare send a servant after us. And once in Medegard I would be easy about letting Ellisand perform for lodging and supplies in front of audiences I would screen against illusionists because by the time the rumors got back to Cathe, we'd probably be in Glamisson or Sengan and, well, really at that point what could he do? But here we were still practically in the neighborhood—and even though my papers were in order, to go any farther we would both have to prove who we were. I stopped the horse again to think.

"What's the deal, Lew?"

"There's not supposed to be a border here."

"There was when I came through last Sunreturn. The emperor's been splitting up all the duchies north of Helas."

"Splitting up the duchies?"

"Hey, he's got borders on top of borders in some places. It's wild. There were three crossings in Kant alone last count."

"Then why the hell is Helas clear?" I snapped.

"Damned if I know," Ellisand said easily. "Why ask why? All I do is show my lyre and play a few licks. Musicians get free passage and all that. Guards are usually decent about it."

"You know the guards?" I asked slowly.

"Partied with them on my way down. That's how I met the old guy who grows chaia. His niece works here. Said she'd raid her uncle's garden for me if I let her screw me—"

"And you obliged her no doubt. Damn! Here." I turned. "You keep your face covered." I adjusted the cloak's hood over his features. "And you hold on to me for dear life in case I decide to break the horse into a gallop. The idea is to get some distance between us and Cathe before people recognize you—he's got every reason to kill you, you understand, and he's not a bad aim from a distance. We're still too close for comfort. You stay close against me, you don't move unless I tell you to, and you let me do the talking. If they question you, you don't speak Kantish. Understand?"

"Sure, Lew, whatever you say." He gripped me tight and buried his face in my back.

I maneuvered the horse into a slow walk and rode leisurely toward the guards, where I had to wait for an old woman on an ill-looking donkey to finish cursing them out. Between curses she was giving them her life story. She'd been raised in Shuntan, near Sun-nashiven, and had come to Kant half a century ago with a traveling merchant who married her. I noticed she still carried a trace of a Sunnan accent. She wanted to see her son. She had no papers. The son lived in town. He was a cobbler, the best cobbler in the empire, the best everything in everything until Roguehan's new laws put him out of business. "And I ain't afraid to say it either. And neither is my son. You tell that cud Roguehan from *me* you don't milk the goose dry and expect good eggs. He's turnin' the place into a god-damn Sevalan cud-hole, he is." The guards were smiling. They were used to the old woman. I got the impression this was a daily event for them. "We ain't turncoat Helans up here you tell him—and he's a cud, too. At least Thoren left business alone." She spat. "Roguehan stole our money—and then the cud went and had our duchess exe-cuted—why did he do that, you tell me? She was a good girl, did nothing to him, now I don't get my mail no more. Lousy imperial postal service, that's what it is. Cost a gold piece to mail a letter and it don't even get there. How am I supposed to see my son?"

"You know the reasons." I sensed that the guard had to explain this to her every morning. "No crossing without papers. We all have a social responsibility to our own local communities, and we can't let folks shirk that by going elsewhere. New law for the common good."

"The common *what*?" she spat. "The common nothing. The grand cud sucks it down as soon as it's made. My son was a wealthy man—did something with himself and his life."

"You benefit from your own town, Madam?"

"Look at my donkey, I benefit from my town." She spat again. "My son used to send me piecework to do for a penny—now I scarcely get hay allowance from the goddamn council to feed my poor donkey for the common good—let an old woman starve—for the common good." She lapsed into what sounded like a well-worn speech which the guard chose to ignore in favor of me. He motioned me forward and the old woman tugged her donkey off to the side, where she sat staring at me in bright lumpy misery.

"Good day, good fellow," I said cheerfully, as if I commiserated with him. "Hard show to beat."

"Papers." I felt the old woman staring as I removed my traveling papers from my cloak and handed them over good-naturedly. "Priest of Athena, Kursen Monastery, permission to travel freely throughout the empire," he read aloud. "All right." Guards question clerics lightly, if at all, especially clerics with traveling papers. Actually, there was a time when being a priest of Athena would have given me passage anywhere, but good clerics were now subject to travel restrictions in the new empire. Only musicians and poets were still considered "free." Good thing Roguehan was an art lover. "You taking students down there yet, Brother? Gotta son wants to apply."

"I gotta son," interjected the old woman. "Can't see him, though."

"Not yet," I said quickly, ignoring her. "The high priest is looking for teachers, and most of the qualified good clerics are doing their best to hide right now." The fact was, Cathe wasn't looking too hard. The last thing Cathe needed was a staff of good clerics around him who were capable of determining his true alignment and intentions. His preference was to keep the place basically running but devoid of students until it was time for him to come north to the duchy, at which point he would use his silver tongue to persuade Roguehan to put someone else in charge.

"Guess it's hard to get some people to believe in the new tolerance," said the guard loudly. He intended this as a polite rebuff to the old woman.

"Hard to get some people to *believe* in anything," shouted the woman. "I don't *believe* in nothin' no more. Belief's cheap and dirty, and so's the empire."

"What do you know about the good monastery up in Medegard?" the guard asked me. "My son only speaks Kantish, so he's a little reluctant about applying for permission."

"How's your son going to get permission to go to Medegard when I can't even enter the next town?" the woman called out. "Is that 'cause you got a state job?"

"Don't mind her, Brother." The guard smiled. "She'll be at it all day and tomorrow, too."

"Well, it doesn't hurt to apply," I said quickly, in reference to his son. He had said nothing concerning Ellisand, who had remained tightly huddled against my back the whole time, so I nodded my head and kicked the horse into motion.

"Wait a minute! Wait a minute! What about him?" screeched the woman. "I didn't see no papers from him."

"Yeah, halt!" ordered the guard. I reined in the horse. "Almost forgot." He walked up to Ellisand, who still wasn't moving. "You all right, guy? Need to see your papers."

Silence.

"That a lyre? You a musician?"

Silence.

"Is he OK?" The guard asked me.

"He's all right. Just drunk. He doesn't appear to speak the language. Found him a mile back and picked him up for the Goddess's sake. Think he's a wandering minstrel."

"I don't *believe* him," shouted the woman. "I don't believe *in* him. Looks like a bum to me. Make him show his face." The woman's attitude was a dangerous disaster. I was confident she'd see hands, for my magic and Ellisand's belief were sure and strong. But I realized with horror that she might not hear music. Roguehan had cursed his people with disbelief.

The guard circled to the other side of the horse. "Can't let him through unless he plays something. Music opens borders. Come on, guy, down, give us a few measures of a merry jig and we'll let you through."

Ellisand remained silent and unmoving, while rigidly gripping me. I "translated" for him into Sarana, ordering him to dismount with me and play something. I tried to spring off the horse first, but he was holding me so tight I practically had to fight with him for freedom to move, with the result that he kept gripping me close with his arms and we both toppled into the rain-soaked ground, where he kept gripping me without moving or speaking. I had no idea what his problem was, but I felt very much like breaking his stupid arms and leaving him there. "You can let go now," I hissed. He dropped his arms and sat huddled and immobile in the mud.

"I don't think he really understands you," said the guard. "What language were you speaking?"

I pretended I didn't hear the question. No sense in revealing his northern origins if I didn't have to. "Here—" I unstrapped his lyre from the horse and handed it to him with trembling hands. "—play a quick measure and let's go." He raised his arms to take the instrument. I saw him run his stumps in the air in front of the strings as if his hands were playing. I heard nothing except the old woman, who was covering her ears and screeching for all she was worth, "I don't hear no music. I don't hear nothin'. Nothin' but someone running his hands against the strings at random. Big deal. I could do that and see my son."

"It's gotta be a song, friend," said the guard. "Not a few slapdash chords. Tell him, Brother."

I "translated." "Play a goddamn melody or I'll flag Cathe myself, you miserable minstrel. We don't have time for it." He responded by fiercely and rapidly moving his stumps through the air in front of his instrument. The guard's eyes snapped wide and he began to do a busy, playful dance and howl for joy. All the other guards ran out to join him, dancing and shouting. The old woman was swaying back and forth on her donkey, hell, the donkey seemed to be swaying, and three or four people who were waiting on each side of the border were dancing and shouting in their stirrups. Every few seconds it seemed like more laughing dancing people were being attracted in our direction, and Ellisand, damn him, kept it going for nearly ten minutes while I devoutly wished I could bury both of us in the mud. He finished with a lightning-quick up-and-down movement of his right stump and then his hood fell back, revealing his face to the dancing crowd and cheerful morning sun. "You mean like that?" he smiled at me.

"Ellisand of Gondal," shouted the guard. "Hey, how goes it? Last I heard, you weren't doing too well."

Ellisand looked up at him blankly, looked at me, and said clearly and mechanically in Kantish, "I don't speak Kantish." I decided at that point that I *was* capable of killing him.

"Hey, I know you," shouted the old woman. "You're the boy used to sneak around with my neighbor's granddaughter, down near Kursen Monastery."

"Where?" asked Ellisand. That was the binding spell speaking.

"Kursen Monastery. You know, where they keep all the nuts who destroy things. Where your dippy friend in the mud says he's from."

"Oh," said Ellisand without interest, carrying his lyre to the horse without a problem. I spotted him with wizardry to make sure the lyre got tied back to the saddle the way it should have been. The rope did seem to respond to Ellisand's belief but damn the sun, I wished this was all behind us.

"Don't play dumb with me," lectured the woman to his back. "I know everything what goes on in my street," *I'll bet you do, you old Sunnan busybody* "and I've seen you pawing that girl to pieces for hours at a time up the apple tree, hiding from her father. I told him, you know." The guards were laughing like merry bats, at her more than him. "You're a rough boy, you are."

"How'd you know it was hours at a time?" asked Ellisand conversationally, still in Kantish.

"I watched," she said self-righteously. "It was right in my other neighbor's tree you used to go. And you didn't even kiss her right," she critiqued, obviously pretending to boredom to show her sophisticated superiority to both sex and the "rough boy." "Should lick her breasts *before* you stick your tongue down her mouth—big man ought to go slowly around the nipples, make 'em rise up, give us all a good show." Even though the guards were used to the old woman's name-calling and foul language, no one expected her to get this rude.

Her amusing quirkiness had become poor taste. She was no longer a silly harmless old woman with no claim on life save what she could steal from her son. She was a vampire dragon living and sapping life from wherever life fell around her. There was something ugly and dangerous in her heart. I knew the guards would never laugh at her again. There was a stunned, embarrassed silence all around.

Which Ellisand cheerfully broke. "So go screw your son in a Sunnan latrine." Artists don't like criticism. "And me and my girlfriend will watch."

That silenced her, not least because Ellisand sounded like he would truly like to see such an event. And there wasn't the slightest shade of anger in his voice, just an annoying natural ease that sent the guards laughing to the ground. I helped Ellisand mount and then sprang upon the horse myself when a slightly pudgy guard, whom I took to be Ellisand's "friend" with the chaia-growing uncle, came forward, and asked sweetly, "You in a real hurry?"

"I don't know. Depends on what's real."

"Well, I know you haven't been *through* in a while." She swished her wide hips in a sexual gesture and smiled at her pun, and everyone laughed except the old woman, who studied her in affronted outrage.

"I'd like to *come through* again, Dena," Ellisand grinned. "Slower, next time. But my buddy here's in a hurry. And he can't hold it up much longer. Can you, Lew?"

The guard looked up at me. "I could take him on too. Care to stop awhile, Brother?"

"What the hell? Hey, Lew—" he nudged me. I kicked the horse. The guard grabbed the rein and jerked the horse back.

"Such language!" complained the old woman. "And he gets to go through—they both get to go through." Everyone shrieked with laughter. Except me. "I'm going back now, and I'm telling everyone—I'm telling your girlfriend, and my neighbors, and everyone on my street that *people* like you can travel and decent old women like myself can't see their own sons. I'll go to the council, I'll go everywhere."

"Let's go," I ordered Ellisand, grabbing the rein from the guard and kicking the stallion. The guard grabbed the rein back and jerked the horse to a stop again. I wondered if they'd still let us through if I kicked her.

"How's the chaia supply holding out?" she asked playfully. It was a hint and an offer.

"Actually, I could use some more," said Ellisand.

"*Damn you*, we've got to make distance," I grumbled in Sarana. "The old woman's better than a direct message to Cathe."

"Lew, steady out. She's riding a donkey." He smiled brightly at Dena, who left to go into the guard booth.

"And there's a line of witnesses coming over the border and heading south now. And there's other travelers on the road with horses. And she'll tell her story to each one of them."

"Which'll slow her down."

"And don't you think they all have tongues? Will they slow down? Wise up."

I sat in a state of high annoyance as the guard returned and handed up a rather large herb packet, which I buoyed with wizardry as Ellisand took it and stuffed it in his cloak. "For next time, lover," she sang out for the benefit of her coworkers and everybody else in earshot. It was important to her that everyone in town knew that she'd slept with Ellisand once.

I ordered Ellisand to cover his face and hold on to me tightly as I angrily kicked the horse into a gallop. And I kept galloping through the next three miles of town, and as we left town the horse showed signs of slowing so I kicked him up again, and kept the beast cantering for a good hour until he positively could go no farther and even then I forced him into a brisk walk on penalty of cutting a hole in his side with my anger. We passed a few thin cows huddled near a fence and I slapped the stallion for wanting to stop and inspect them. My slap kept him going at a slow reluctant walk for about a quarter mile. Then he stopped and shuddered, frothing and sweating and bending his head to eat the wild plants at the side of the road. I yanked his head up and held it there to prevent him from slowing himself by eating, but since the horse was frothing and wheezing, I decided there was no help for it but to let him have his rest. So I kicked him into a very slow walk so his muscles wouldn't tighten up on me, and decided I would force him back to a gallop as soon as I felt he could handle it. And that maybe we ought to get a fresh steed at the next town and a proper saddle for two—if I could keep my fool companion quiet about things. And then I decided we'd best not stop yet. There wasn't time to squander.

We jogged along at an excruciatingly slow pace. It was countryside here and late green. The sky was beginning to clear a little. I noticed that many of the fields had not been cultivated this year and that they were filled with hazy long grass. The corn had been harvested early. For the southwest, no doubt, so Roguehan's favored subjects could feast on unripe corn and pretend it was abundance. "How far to the next border crossing?" I asked my companion.

"About twenty miles. Hey, Lew, you think I can let go now?" He was still gripping me tight.

"Shut up. What the hell was that bloody stunt you pulled at the last crossing?"

"What stunt?"

"*What stunt?* Goddamn refusing to let go of me when we dismounted stunt. Goddamn not moving in the mud stunt until *I* was beginning to think your insides had been blasted by Cathe. Goddess-damned miniconcert two hours from Kursen—you better hope to Apollo—"

"Apollo Who?"

"Apollo *Anybody* that Cathe doesn't get wind of that one before we make Medegard—speaking Kantish and not speaking Kantish and goddamn—" The horse halted again. I kicked it and it shot forward at an uneven canter before slowing to a walk. "—Cathe is in his monastery. Monasteries are power places. He can call down Habundia's force with a thought and a wish right now and he can direct the Goddess to find you and strike you dead. Do you have any idea what is at stake for him concerning Kursen's reputation for goodness? Just having locals see you riding around with me could start embarrassing questions."

"So? I thought monks were good at not answering questions."

"Do you have any idea what a high priest of evil can do to you through Habundia Christus?"

"No, Lew, why don't you explain it to me?" he asked politely. I knew he was thinking of his hands and what another high priest of evil had already done.

"Look, until we get into Threle, you don't make a move and you don't say a word unless I tell you to. Cathe could strike you anywhere, but I doubt he'll do anything once enough time and distance have passed. He'll be worrying about whether I have you under control and what's happened and whether blasting you will interfere in my plans and therefore his. He knows enough to not make a move like that if he doesn't know enough—and the farther we get, the less he'll know. But showing off at the border only sends the message that I've got a liability on my hands that he would just as soon relieve me of."

"Why don't you just throw a monk-shield around us? You're the magician and all that."

I kicked the horse again in annoyance. "Magic isn't something you just 'throw around.' There are laws of magic just like laws of physics. The first law is common sense."

"Common what?"

"Common sense." Why was I bothering? "I can't shield us against evil because *I am* evil, you idiot."

"Right. I almost forgot."

"Look—the best I can do is keep you physically close to me. I'm too important to Cathe right now for him to risk harm to me. So hold on. And from now on you only play when I tell you to, you only speak to whomever I tell you to, you eat and sleep when I tell you to, and you keep your face covered at all times! I don't care about your goddamn personal life or how many border guards you've screwed for chaia. As far as I'm concerned, you have no personal life. Your music is all I care about, understand?"

"You mean you now think my music *is* just a job? You disappoint me, Lew. I thought monks were always supposed to be consistent about everything. I was almost beginning to think you were going to insist that I am my music." He was highly amused.

"What *you* are is a regrettable annoyance. But I've dealt with bigger annoyances before. Understand one thing. I'm in charge of your life now, got it? If you want to live to see Threle, you better start listening to me."

"I thought I was."

"Really? I didn't know you could think. Whenever did you think you were listening to me?" I drove my foot into the horse. It walked a little faster, not much.

"At the last border crossing. You told me to hold you for dear life. So I did. You told me not to move without orders. So I didn't. You told me to play a melody. So I did. You told me I don't speak Kantish. So I said I didn't." He was laughing as he spoke. "What the hell, Brother? It's all one to me."

"Did I tell you to wrangle with some bloody idiot of an old woman to give her something to talk about on the road? Did I tell you to flirt with the goddamn guards for chaia?"

"Oh, sorry. I forgot to ask. You want a smoke?"

"No!" I turned and made hard eye contact. "I want you stop taking my words so bloody literally."

"Really, Lew," said the poet, smiling in wide-eyed mock surprise. "I didn't think you were that kind of guy."

I responded by throwing a silencing spell over his tongue. As the spell took, I renewed the binding spell and strengthened the illusion. Then I forced the horse into a wild, no-nonsense canter, and then up into a brisk even gallop for three or four miles, and then down to a canter again. I would get us out of Kant tonight if I had to break the damn horse like a rotten egg. So we sped through neglected fields, past the outskirts of another town, through more miles of farms and woods and wretched cows and dirty yellow sheep. My heart was beating my throat against my skull to make distance, and I prayed fervently to Hecate that we might make Medegard undetected. My prayer went nowhere of course. That is, the Goddess turned it back into myself without comment for my prayer was not motivated by evil or destructive scholarship and so had nothing to do with Her. If I managed to save beauty's source, it would be by chance and accident, and if I lost the source, it would also be by chance and accident.

And all within a mad context of never hearing his music again. I could never make illusion real for me, and until I could find the secret of violating that simple magical law, Ellisand was a worse than useless traveling companion. And honestly, I had no idea what I would do with him once we got into Threle or into the duchy. I supposed I would strengthen the illusion and manage his performances and do my level best to avenge my deepest hurt and in doing so make Cathe, who would have killed the greatest musician in all the worlds, into a god. And this was my life?

I couldn't remember ever acting purely out of impulse, without regard to reason. I couldn't remember myself. Was it me turning years of preparation and study into pure untrammeled absurdity? And I don't know whether I was more afraid of Cathe or my own dizzy irrationality. But the more I thought about the implications of what I'd done that morning, the shakier everything got.

But whenever I probed Ellisand for his emotions, he merely felt bored. He clung to me in a resigned-for-the-moment, why-not sort of way but he would have been perfectly content to dismount, take up his lyre, and go sing for his supper at the nearest farmhouse as a point of entry to the rest of his life. It was as if he'd had his fill of tearing up the countryside with a mad cleric and he just wanted to get on with the business of living. He didn't view Cathe as a threat. He viewed me as a curiosity he was willing to humor for a while, but he was willing to humor me only because underneath all the emotion I dredged through, he was terribly grateful I'd restored his hands and given him freedom. My *act* of healing made me "all right." But he could never know it was an act, or the illusion would fail. He couldn't figure me out, although I felt him trying like hell to do so as we approached the next border crossing and the next. This was the strongest feeling I got—impersonal fascination with the fact that I didn't appear to be "all right" and yet really was. I felt him decide that my whole problem was that I was really all right but that I was too caught up in the "monk thing." He didn't see me as a monk, which I found interesting, but he didn't follow the thought so I have no idea how he saw me. His thinking curved sharply down into resigned impatience with the fact that I only allowed him to speak at the border crossings and magically silenced him again right after.

It might seem cruel to silence a poet, but it did get us into Medegard without further incident. Ellisand behaved himself at the borders and the horse got used to us and made excellent time. I spoke for us in Botha at the Medegardan border, for Botha was the empire's official language, and so once the guard-translator admitted us into the duchy, I decided to let my companion keep his power of speech, although he was still bound against speaking of Kursen. "It's dark. We're long gone from the monastery, and probably fairly safe now. But one stray word from you and I silence you again." The horse was walking through the outskirts of a little merchant town, heading toward the center. It was an hour or two past evening but the streets were devoid of people. "We're going to find a quiet inn that can stable and feed the horse and give us a room. Which won't be easy, travel being as restricted as it is now. I noticed most of the inns in Kant were boarded up, and I expect the same to be true here. But we've got to get you a decent meal and bed after all those months in prison and a day on the road. The trick is, food is horribly expensive now in the duchies and since I carry my own fare, and I'm supposed to be a poor wandering cleric, I didn't budget money for it. You saw the neglected fields in Kant?"

"No, Lew, my face was covered."

"Well, those fields tell me what I already know. Roguehan's army is appropriating whatever crops they can get for themselves and the rest is being shipped southwest. Not to Sunnashiven, or at least, not to the general population in Sunnashiven but to whoever is in favor with the emperor right now. And they're not even waiting for it to ripen—the corn was taken down too early. You see, there's not enough food for the general population. The Kantish are doing something similar to what the south Sunnans did before they rebelled."

"What's that?" He dropped his grip on me and leaned his head heavily into my back as he shifted his weight around. The horse was slow enough, and we were now far enough away from Cathe, for me to be hard-pressed to find a reason to insist that he keep holding. I reinforced the illusion.

"Back before they rebelled, the south Sunnan farmers refused to grow more than they needed for themselves. Pretty much destroyed what was left of the economy but, well, that's all history now. The

Kantish, and presumably the Medegardans as well, are not growing more than they get paid for. They're getting something, which explains the token fields of cow corn. No Threlan would grow even that much extra corn if there weren't pay in it. But judging from the number of fields which have been harvested, Roguehan's quite short on pay. And if he's short on funds and food, he may not be able to hold the Midland cities under siege much longer. And his weakness might be an invitation for more unrest and rebellions down here." *Which means Threle could win after all. Which explains why Roguehan was suddenly agreeable to sending me up north to expedite things for him.*

"The empty fields I can understand. But all the rest sounds like stuff and monkery to me, Lew." Suddenly it started to rain again. Something smelled faintly of smoke but the wind blew it behind us. "Aren't you abstracting oak trees from acorns? How can you tell the course of an entire war from the state of a few Kantish fields?" I felt that he was mildly interested in the answer because critical thinking was sort of novel to him, but mostly he was idly interested in how I would respond. He was also trying to distract me from something. I was about to turn around but my attention was held by lights ahead. We were getting closer to the center of town, and there were little shops along the street, a few of which appeared to still be open. Then I noticed that the "open" shops were devoid of visible merchandise, and that they all contained little clusters of families. The Medegardans were now living in their shops, consolidating and guarding their resources as much as possible, no doubt. One group was huddled in a circle around a little fire and not moving or speaking. They were holding hands and muttering as if they were trying to raise power for something, perhaps they had heard or read of how it was "supposed" to be done. I knew at a glance the only energy present was coming from their frail little fire. They all felt hungry and somewhere beyond their lives. It was profoundly sad.

"You'd be surprised what you can tell about the world if you pay attention to it." The smoky smell got sweeter and stronger. "What the hell—" I turned in the saddle and saw to my dismay that he was holding a burning tube of chaia to his mouth through the strength of his own belief and puffing away. "—Where did you get fire to light that?" was all I could think of saying.

"What fire?" he teased, obviously enjoying my discomfort. "Steady out, Brother. Pretend it's all illusion. Want some? Celebrate our entry into fair Medegard."

I decided it was safe to let him keep smoking, that it would probably help strengthen his already-hard belief. But I didn't want the damn stuff interfering with my concentration. I had still enough residual anxiety to do that job properly, although I was feeling slightly more at ease having made it this far without further incident. At ease enough to use my monastic training to wrench truth out of a poet. I probed and learned that one of the guards at the last border crossing had slipped him more chaia and a piece of burning wood while I was showing my papers. I felt sick as I thanked all the gods that he was able to grasp the gifts. The guard was yet another "lover-friend."

"What's this, minstrel?" I asked, as if his thoughts had been offered in conversation. "Have you screwed everyone in the empire? Or just every bloody guard with an excess of chaia?" I waved the smoke away from my face.

"Well, not everyone. But if a pretty woman likes my music and wants to enhance my dreams, what the hell?"

"How do you manage to stay sober?"

"I don't." He dragged at his chaia. "How do *you* manage not to stay drunk?"

"What does that mean?"

"It means that if I were you, buddy, I'd stop wearing evil around like an illusion. Chaia's better for you." He puffed. I noticed there were people in the streets here but they were wandering aimlessly, going where everyone else went. If a knot of people formed, no one broke away to walk alone. I got an impression that they didn't have anyplace to go. I'd never seen Threlans look so buffeted. Ellisand was still speaking. "You're not in the monastery anymore, and according to you, we should be out of danger from your friend Cathe. You can stop being a monk now. I won't tell."

"Thanks," I said dryly.

We were approaching the lone tree and stone wall that mark the center of all Medegardan towns. Two people, a woman and a much shorter man, were holding candles and giving a speech to an applauding crowd. The woman sounded like she was reading her speech, for she spoke clumsily and mechanically, although Meden, the language of south Medegard, had always sounded clumsy and lispy to my ears the few times I'd ever heard it before. I didn't understand a word of course, but I guessed that the speech had something to do with the empire, for I heard Roguehan's name mentioned by the members of the crowd in disgusted whispers, and occasionally the people broke into angry cheers and applause.

I reined in the horse to see what I could learn. The couple were using their candles to shield their faces, holding the light at a distance from themselves. They probably were speaking out against Roguehan upon peril of their lives, then. I saw a few imperial guards milling in the crowd, but the guards applauded whenever everyone else did and no one appeared to view them as a threat. One guard actually threw a token copper at the tree, to much applause and cheers. Then the rain put out the speakers' candles simultaneously and the man continued to speak in the darkness. In Medegard it is customary to keep a candle burning while speaking by a wall, but there were plenty of candles burning in the crowd now and under the circumstances, no one seemed to be insisting that the speakers relight theirs. The man's voice was easier than the woman's, but there was something hurried about the cadence, and a few seconds after he started speaking, a loud "ooo" from the crowd drowned out his voice altogether. The cries of the crowd were louder and more confident now, so from that point on I ceased to hear him clearly. It had to be an antigovernment speech.

I kicked the horse to move on. Ellisand was quiet until we reached the back of the crowd. Then he said in a voice of amazement, "Hey, you were you right about the fields and the war after all, Brother."

I remained silent for three perfect beats. "Oh, yeah," I said evenly, mocking his usual "so-what" drawl. "How do you know?"

"Yeah, well, I know enough Meden to get something from the speech. Everything you guessed is true out there in the world. That's really cool. And the speakers are trying to incite a local rebellion over it."

"Looks like we're going to miss all the fun."

"Why? I've got a great idea—stop the horse—" He grabbed me and I yanked the reins in surprise. The stallion was so tired it didn't take much to stop him. To my immediate horror, Ellisand started waving his handless arms in the air and hailing the crowd in Meden. He asked something that sounded like a question and got several shouts that sounded like answers. And some helpful soul held up her candle so its light fell across us, making us visible to everyone in the immediate vicinity. I immediately used wizardry to direct the light so it fell low across his raised arm, leaving his stumps in shadow. Then I put the light out as if the rain had done it, but someone else ran forward with a candle and I saw that being speech time in Medegard, the candle supply would be endless and I would have to content myself with keeping Ellisand's hands in shadow and with the thought that no candle was bright enough for the majority of the crowd to see him clearly. Most people were still listening to the speakers, who were in darkness. Ellisand had only caused a local disturbance but the disturbance was quickly growing.

He was making an alarmingly animated speech of his own, in a halting sort of Meden which the crowd appeared to understand. I couldn't probe his mind without dropping my concentration on directing the candlelight. I heard some of the younger members of the crowd chanting his name, and to my intense dismay, the chant appeared to be running back through the crowd and including more people. Then I heard *my* name, "Llewelyn, Stiepsist k'Athena—" and more Meden words, and my name got carried through the crowd as if I too were a celebrity. There was no help for it, Ellisand and I were the center of attention now. I noticed that even the poor speakers had ceased trying to compete. After what felt like an excruciating eternity, long enough for me to consider when and where I would blast him, Ellisand settled down, nudged me, and said in Sarana, "I got us an inn. Two more blocks, then two streets to the left. Man named Liese. Still in business." I was so angry I couldn't move. He kicked the horse into motion. "It's all right. Liese is an old friend. Played there lots of times. He'll take care of us. Old Liese has never been one to turn down business." Ellisand sounded quite proud of himself.

"What the hell did you say to the crowd?" I asked coldly.

"I asked if Liese was still in business. Then I offered them a concert of antigovernment songs—"

"—You *offered them a what?*" I stopped the horse and reeled around angrily, only to see that we were now being followed by a goodly crowd. The crowd was clapping and dancing and calling out his name.

"Antigovernment songs, Lew. The people seem into it." There was no help but to maneuver the horse with the clapping, chanting people. Three people had grabbed the bridle and were steering the horse for me.

"I didn't think your art was political."

"It's not. But hey, whatever sells. We'll ask a copper apiece, they can probably afford that. Liese might even give us a cut for traveling expenses—he owes me for last time. Anyway, I thought up some—well, anti*monk* songs when I was—where I can't say, so why not use them? Church and state, what's the difference? It's all one as far as I can tell."

"You don't think that your 'antimonk' songs would interest Cathe, *when* he hears about them?" I looked at the crowd. "A few love ballads for a small select audience, a room and a meal—not this. You're going to get us both killed."

"Relax, Lew, we're in Medegard, and tomorrow we'll be in Glamisson. And the next day we'll be in Threle or close to it. Besides, I've never used music to touch off a political rebellion before— should be an experience." We were now outside a worn-looking little inn which I took to be Liese's. The crowd was pushing around the horse. Despite my misgivings, I had no choice but to let him perform, because I didn't want to draw more attention to myself by having to explain to the crowd why there suddenly was to be no concert. And I knew there was no way I could silence him while he was onstage without causing further problems, so all I could do was hope he would suddenly acquire the sense to avoid dangerous subjects.

I dismounted and so did Ellisand, and I stood next to him to block his stumps from view and spot him with wizardry as he untied his lyre. A shout of enthusiasm went up from the crowd as he took his lyre down and started toward the inn door. And of course I had to follow him inside, leaving the horse and all my stuff, including my gifts of Venus, untended.

The door closed us into relative quiet, meaning the crowd's chanting was now a little muffled. A very thin young girl with dusty hair and a haggard pointy face was sitting and swinging her legs on a bench which jutted out from the wall. There was a rickety desk and chair in front of us but nobody was sitting at it. To our right, stairs led up to a dark second story that looked closed off. To the left of the desk was a doorway leading to a drinking area. I saw about twenty empty tables and two empty-looking drunks who weren't noticing each other. The girl looked up at us idly. Wizardry told me she'd had nothing to do for hours and that she was too bored to notice the change in the noise level outside. "Herve Liese?" asked Ellisand cheerfully.

"E'n truy sque." She shoved off from her bench.

"She's getting him," Ellisand explained.

"What about our horse?"

"Oh, there's a stable round back. She'll get to it eventually." I opened the door a crack to keep an eye on both the horse and Ellisand. No one seemed to be touching my things. Goddess bless all Threlans. They do tend to respect one's privacy. I strengthened the illusion again, and was relieved to learn I didn't really need to. "If you're worried about the horse, Lew, go tend to it yourself. Liese won't care if you do your own stabling."

"It's my stuff I'm concerned about. Why don't you ask someone to bring it in?"

Ellisand went over to the door and spoke. Three people promptly untied my bags and brought my stuff to me. "Steady out. We're among friends here."

"Look, Ellisand, I don't care what you charge—or what kind of deal you strike with Liese, as long as I screen the audience, got it? And I suggest you keep the performance brief and stay off dangerous topics. What language did you compose your latest work in?"

"Sarana. My own dialect. But your magic will keep most of the words mum. The music will speak for me—unless you want to silence that too." He smiled jauntily.

"Look—just get us a quiet room and yourself a meal—you're still sick, even though you don't act like it."

"That's 'cause I'm high. And I slept a little on the road. Don't be anxious, the sick'll hit me later."

A smiling, paunchy middle-aged man entered the foyer with the sour-faced girl. He spread his arms in a delight which took considerable effort to produce. He was desperate to show cheerfulness. "Ellisand." He tilted his head to the side and spoke a few words of Meden. Ellisand responded and a rapid exchange occurred. I probed Ellisand's mind and he appeared to be saying exactly what I'd told him to, but as he was doing his best to think in Meden, I couldn't be sure if some sort of message wasn't being passed. Ellisand indicated me with his arms, and Liese smiled warmly and nodded in my direction too.

"He doesn't let rooms anymore," Ellisand told me. "But he'll make one up for an hour concert. Liese doesn't like the empire either. And he has a sick son—think you can do something about that, Brother? I told him how good you are at healing."

How the hell can I heal anyone unless my ultimate intent is evil, you stupid jackanapes?

While Ellisand was speaking to me, Liese said something to the girl, who promptly went out the door. "She'll stable the horse. My buddy here will show you upstairs. Take care of him, Lew. Show your heart's all right." Liese started gathering up my things. I took up the rest so Ellisand wouldn't have to lift anything.

"You're coming up with us," I ordered him.

"Gotta tune." He walked jauntily away into the bar.

"Remember, I screen the audience—" I called.

"Right, Lew."

Liese was smiling and nodding toward the stairs. I decided to get my stuff deposited as quickly as possible so I could return to Ellisand. If all he was going to do was tune his lyre, I supposed I could leave him for a minute. But Liese went very slowly up the stairs, bumbling through the dark and making soft jovial exclamations every time he knocked into a wall, as if he were anxious to put me at ease concerning his own clumsiness. I got the impression he was explaining the inn to me, and perhaps apologizing for the lack of light. We deposited our stuff inside the dark doorway of a darker room, and I got another impression that he intended to prepare the room while Ellisand was playing.

I turned to go back downstairs when Liese firmly grabbed me by the arm and steered me in the direction of a faintly glowing light at the end of the hall. The light was creeping and dying out of a cold little room that Liese gingerly pushed me into. I saw a covered lantern on the floor and a bowl of cold stew. There were chunks of beef in the broth, and the sight made me a little queasy, but when my eyes fell on the corner, I gasped back a stronger urge to retch. For there, lying and stinking on a pile of thick blankets, was a young man I took to be Liese's son. His body was white and thin, and his arms and legs were covered with garish purple patches. Some of the patches had burst open and were running. He was in such intense pain that his agony tore along my own back and thighs before I even opened myself to it, and I had to step back into the doorway and steady myself. Liese was covering his own nose and mouth against the odor with a scented cloth and looking at me with quiet desperation.

I knew immediately that the boy was dying. He did not know his father. He only knew the lantern in the way a lizard knows the sun. Something in him stretched to the warmth and comfort of something outside him like light. His body had been born fourteen years ago at noon and his body would die to this queer representation of the noon sun near his dark cold bed. No words but a name—Yolan. And Yolan was only a life force spilling into the flame with each choking breath.

Liese looked appealingly at me and motioned toward his son, then turned his face away to hide his pain. Even if my alignment had been to another deity, or to goodness, I had no idea what I could do for him. If I attempted to heal him through Hecate, I was sure to kill him, for try as I might, I could find no acceptably evil motivation for performing a healing, and to perform a healing through evil is normally to cause damage. And Yolan was in no condition to sustain damage. I knelt by his side in an attitude of prayer while Liese watched me anxiously. *Dear Lady, if my journey to Threle and revenge be easier for preserving the boy's life, please may your power work a healing through me now,* was all I could think to ask. Then I concentrated on my healing as a prelude to working evil on Walworth's household but felt no surge. In truth, it made no difference to my particular evil whether Yolan lived or died, and so Hecate would have nothing to do with my request. I could use mundane methods, but if I kept begging the Goddess to intercede in this act, I risked doing damage to myself. The answer was "no." And in further truth, Yolan was practically dead already. I estimated from the strength of the flame that he wouldn't live until morning. But I did my best. I tried every trick of mind I knew to make my intent evil. I knelt for five minutes twisting and playing with my own thoughts and explanations to convince myself that the powers I served would be pleased to preserve Yolan's life, so I could offer the self-convincing to Hecate for another try. Yet for all my skill, sophistry failed me here, and I realized circumstances were such that I could work nothing.

I stood and touched Liese on the shoulder with my best studied look of support and concern. He touched me back, and wept unashamedly in front of me. "Water," I said in Botha, softly, looking at his son. The innkeeper understood the word and ran to get some. I went through the dark to my room and felt through my traveling bags until I found my supply of chamomile. Caethne had once taught me that chamomile made a good wash for open sores, and it tended to reduce fever and pain, so I carried it with me as an all-purpose healer for the road. It also had the advantage of smelling sweet.

When I returned to Yolan, Liese was already there with a large bowl of water that he pressed into my hands. I warmed the water through wizardry, using more power than I really wanted to spare, and crumbled in the herb, stirring the mixture with my fingers until the scent filled the room. Then I extended my hand for Liese's cloth, which he promptly gave to me, coughing with the sudden strength of the sickbed odors.

The sickness in the room was grinding my senses to the breaking point. I put up my clerical shield against the bodily odors—which I really didn't want to use energy on—and dipped the cloth in the bowl. Then I quickly washed the boy's open sores—to ease the pain and diminish the odor. Yolan did not respond, but his father looked hopeful. Then I held the rest of the mixture to his lips and forced it down his throat, to replace with liquid what the fever had taken and somewhat relieve the internal pain. I knew I couldn't save him. I could only make him more comfortable.

I dropped my shield as soon as I could and the contrast with the sick odors sent me reeling from the room. Liese joined me in the dark. "Stiepsist k'Athena Habundiayne." The words were a profound "thank-you." He was sweating despite the cold, and I felt his gratitude quench the pain which was echoing from Yolan's condition along my back. He was happy we'd met. There was a picture in his mind of him and Yolan waiting on customers and then sharing private jokes about them and about each other in a back room. His son was his best friend. He wanted him to live more than he had ever wanted anything. Then he took me back to the top of the stairs, hugged me, choked the words "k'Athena" again, and sent me down.

Of course I knew this was another lovely disaster in the making. I had no idea how I would explain why my clerisy failed to avert Yolan's death, but I did know his death was inevitable. And under the circumstances, I had no way to communicate to Liese any reasons for refusing to work a healing on his son—even if I could think up anything believable on that score. All I could do was hope that the boy would outlive our stay in the inn. Gave it an even chance.

The inn door was wide-open and the bar and entryway was so full of people I couldn't push my way through the crowd. A young woman was proudly collecting money in her cap, and she waved the cap when she saw me as if she would be happy if I took over. *Damn Ellisand, why didn't he just kill himself now and get the whole miserable business over with?* The best I could do was leap from the stairs to the top of the desk, which commanded enough attention for a few people who recognized me to part and let me through the doorway into the bar.

And there, seated on a low platform, was Ellisand, strumming his stumps in the air in front of his lyre to the rapt attention of a full house. I pushed back to the inn door and closed it to prohibit further entry. There were loud cries of disappointment in the street. Then I went back to the desk where the woman had left the copper-filled cap for Liese and did the only thing I could do in the circumstances. I started checking each person in the crowd for magical ability to see if there were any illusionists present. The entryway crowd seemed to be safe enough, but I was getting exhausted by the time I entered the bar and didn't feel I could check everybody there with any accuracy, so I settled myself quietly in a corner to recover.

The audience inside was all clapping along with whatever

rhythm Ellisand was producing so I decided it was probably all right after all, although I devoutly wished he would finish so I could retreat to the privacy of our room and think about our next move. But he played for two goddamned hours without stopping, except for when he introduced me to the crowd after the first hour, so I would be thoroughly implicated in whatever revolutionary sentiments his music was stirring. Then the woman appeared with the cap again, and I ended up taking the cap and collecting donations. And after the second hour the pointy-faced girl brought him food, and I spotted him with wizardry while he ate and laughed with his many admirers.

It was nearly midnight before we were able to retire, and as I closed the door of our room, I felt far too tired to think clearly about what to do next. I wanted to leave and beat the rumors, if that was possible. I prayed that Roguehan wouldn't hear about me collecting money for seditious music. I prayed that Cathe was still ignorant of Ellisand's escape. Our stuff was still packed, a single candle was lit, there was a single basin of water in the corner, and two beds had been made up. I sat on one bed and looked mournfully at my companion, who was bouncing on the other bed and showing absolutely no signs of exhaustion. Of course, *he* had napped on the road. He felt happy enough now. I felt angry that I was too tired to feel angry. I needed to sleep. I needed to think. We needed to move on. There would be street riots tomorrow. I got up and took some bread out of my satchel and ate it. Then I cupped my hands in the basin and drank water from them. Then I splashed water on my face and eyes, which revived me a little.

There was a timid knock on the door. I motioned Ellisand to stay where he was and I went miserably to open it. A young girl, not more than fifteen years old, looked up at me. "Herve Ellisand?" she asked shyly.

"Go away, he's getting laid," I replied rudely in Botha, not caring whether or not she understood. Then I slammed the door.

"Hey, Lew, what's the deal? She might be fun to know." He got up to open the door. I blasted him back down onto the bed. "You don't make a move without my leave from now on or I'll kill you," I whispered. There were three beats of silence during which I maintained eye contact and slowly built up an excruciating pain in his head, which I then slowly released.

"Hey, it's all right, Lew. It's all right. You're tired, guy." He was convinced I was insane.

"No, it's not all right. But it will be. And I've got no problem killing anyone you talk to without my permission. As far as I'm concerned you're still my prisoner." I walked over and struck his face. Monks can cause a good deal of pain with a single blow, and Ellisand crumpled over like ash in the wind. "You're not a particularly religious person, are you, Ellisand?" I was still whispering so no one would hear. "Are you?"

"No." There was blood running from the side of his mouth. It nauseated me.

"No? Well—" I leaned over and hissed, despite my sickness. "—you damn well better learn to start praying to somebody, because if anything . . . unpleasant . . . occurs to me as a result of anything you've said or done, or will say or do, I'll make you wish you were still in prison without your wretched hands. Remember, what Hecate gives, Hecate takes. You've never experienced the type of physical pain I'm capable of inflicting, and if I have to kill you, I promise I'll make the whole experience last for days." I blasted his head with pain again and then withdrew the pain just before he would have passed out. "And I can keep that melody going for a nice long week."

There was another knock on the door.

"Go away, Ellisand needs his rest," I called in Botha, blasting him again. "We leave in three hours. Until then, you sleep." He was shaking in terror of my anger and power as I started my spell. "Sleep your ease and sleep your heart upon deadening dreams and die in loveliness until I give birth and waking to you again—I'll watch." He was out. Excellent. I could sleep now without worrying about him causing problems. And we'd leave before trouble started in the morning. I lay back on my bed and had just lost consciousness when there was another knock at the door. *Damn everything, would the girl never stop?* I swore, covered Ellisand's stumps with a blanket as a precaution, and got up to answer the knock.

As soon as I put my hand on the door, Liese's son died, for his spirit was sudden and it left a little eddy of light in the air that glanced off the back of my skin. And I heard Liese setting up a cry and a wail in Meden whose tone and sorrow were enough to dampen the light of the spirit which ran past me. And I decided that tired as I was, I had best start putting distance between myself and this popular innkeeper who could claim that his son died after I, a well-known convert to Athena, worked a cure on him. *Lady, what a day and night. Hecate preserve me to work my evil.*

So I decided to send the girl on her way once and for all, and get my stuff ready to take down to the stables before waking Ellisand. I unlocked the door and angrily swung it open. And I immediately—

Lady, what a life—found myself standing face-to-face with—Baniff and Aleta.

They quickly pushed inside the room as I stiffly closed the door again. I stared at the illusionist in disbelief. "Hey, lad," said Baniff, as if we'd last seen each other at breakfast over tea and muffins. "Got a problem. Need yer help." His voice was urgent but not nervous.

"Good thing you knew where to find me," I said lightly, unable to control a hint of sarcasm while thinking *what the hell am I supposed to say after almost four goddamn years?*

"The whole town knows where to find you. It's not hard since you and your friend broke up our speech," offered Aleta. "Hope it was a good show."

"No time," interrupted Baniff. "Ye see, lad, there's been an evil high priest followin' us along the road from Kant. No idea how, why, or who, but there was somethin' wrong about him from a distance—one of Roguehan's people I'm sure. Been keepin' him busy with illusion but I think he's catchin' on now." *Cathe no doubt. He probably thinks the illusion is coming from my ring and mistakes Baniff for me.* "Look, I'll explain everythin' on the road. We need to move fast and we need a good cleric who can shield us into Threle—ye ready?"

Seven

$\mathcal{I}$ stood there considering everything and nothing while Liese's mourning cries filled the room. "I hope nobody died," said Aleta devoutly, looking at Baniff. "What's he saying?"

"Didn't you just give a speech in Meden?" I asked to cover up the cries.

"I read the sounds on paper."

"Based on his cries, he's sayin' somebody died," said the gnome quickly. "Well, lad?" I knew I had to get out of the inn. And I knew it would be impossible not to run into Aleta and Baniff on the road north. And since I had just asked Hecate to preserve me to work my evil, perhaps She was making the decision for me by presenting me with an "in" I couldn't refuse. I glanced at my stuff, still packed in scattered bundles on the floor. Then I glanced at Ellisand with a studied look of concern, wondering how the hell I would keep up the illusion in Baniff's presence. "How's yer friend for travelin'?" he asked.

"He's hurt," I said mournfully. "Bar fight."

"Can ye leave him?"

"No—he needs my care. It's complicated. Clerical duty. Here—" I picked up the bag containing my gifts of Venus and indicated the rest of my stuff with my hand. "—take my things to the stables. Black stallion."

"We know," said Aleta, picking up bags.

"Thanks, lad," said Baniff, picking up the rest and starting after her.

"Uh, Baniff?" He turned in midstep. "Been traveling all day myself and the stallion's exhausted. See if you can wrangle a new horse—and a double saddle. Trade in mine. Ellisand's in no condition to ride alone. And here." I handed over his lyre. "Take this for him. We'll be right down."

"Right. See ye." Baniff hurried out, leaving me alone with my prisoner.

I closed and locked the door. Then I sat on my bed holding my gifts of Venus and failing miserably in my fight against exhaustion. I couldn't work another spell tonight if my life depended on it—and yet my life did depend on it. The Goddess had preserved me to work my evil, but what a thorny road She'd opened toward that fine accomplishment. There was no way I could leave Ellisand—dead or alive. There was no way I could shield Baniff against Cathe even if I were in peak condition. If I could make it obvious to Cathe that he had been following Baniff, not me, I was certain he would quietly retreat in the hope that I had everything under control and in the fear that he might have ruined some grand scheme of mine. But if I made a single error and gave Cathe away, my life was forfeit—from both sides, probably, for my own allegiance to evil would come out and if the Threlans didn't kill me as a spy, Roguehan would certainly kill me for failing in my duty. But if Cathe had heard about last night's concert or Ellisand's antics at the border crossing, perhaps he would assume I had already made too many mistakes to be trusted and—

But there was precious little time to think right now. I had to leave with Ellisand and I had to recover myself before we left. I leaned back and prayed to Hecate a special petition I'd once learned for strength as my mind and body gave out into oblivion with the weight of my own prayer. And I felt my sweet Mother Hecate catch and cradle and comfort me in a strange bright kiss, that is, I felt the kiss and not Her, and a wide drain of exhaustion pulling at the back of my eyes and bursting down through my shoulders and out of my back and into the air between me and what would have been a deep dream had my skill and petition failed. In theory, an initiated cleric can keep awake for days with this trick, but in fact, you have to be careful not to pray the prayer too often. You could literally wear your body out. It's possible to forget that you need repose when you don't feel tired, and it's easy to end up doing awful damage to your physical system. Living for an extended period on one side of the wakefulness cycle is as dangerous as living on any extreme. Extremes come round again to their opposite sooner or later, and they generally come round with a vengeance. So as I sat up sharp with Her strength, Her heart beating mine in full wakefulness, I knew I had to be very careful with my divine reprieve. Come dawn I'd have been awake for twenty-four hours—I could safely give myself another day, or at most a day and a half before my body would tug me down again and that time I'd have to give in to exhaustion. But I couldn't think about that now.

Liese's cries had now become a violent pounding in and through the walls. It sounded like he was fit to smash the inn apart. I also heard the thin screechy wails of a young girl punctuating the pounding. And then loud pitiful sobs. Ellisand could not respond to the noise. He was still firmly under my spell. And he wasn't dreaming, so there was nothing to impede my magic. I leaned down against his ear and concentrated on blocking out the noise as I steadied myself down—down into the sleep I had forced on him. "Remember your binding. No word of Kursen or imprisonment may you speak. We met on the road and I serve Athena. The word 'lyre' renews and strengthens the spell." But there was no need for the renewal, I could feel that the binding still held. "Oh, and about your injuries? If anyone should ask, you were injured in a bar fight, and although you shall certainly remember the pain I can inflict on you, you cannot say that it was I who did it. Again you are bound with 'lyre.' Finally, know that you cannot speak at all, that your tongue must be lax and dumb unless I open your speech with a thought, thus." And I sent the word "speak" into his mind. "And at any time I choose I can close your speech with a thought, thus." And I sent the word "silence" into his mind. I was working the magic through wizardry, lest Baniff or anyone else sense that evil clerical magic had been used on him. Then I renewed the illusion of hands. Then I used a wizard seal to close his sleeves around his "hands." *There, that will serve for now, although I still have to worry about Baniff feeling illusion being passed when I renew the magic again.*

I straightened up. "Wake into new birth, poet." I harshly pulled the sleep out of him like a dagger out of a stuck rabbit. He rolled over and groaned into a bloody sort of wakefulness, his eyes already swollen and discolored from my blow. "Stand up and lean on me. We're going for a ride. No stunts." He slowly and painfully got himself into a sitting position, and then crumpled to the floor as he tried to push himself off the bed with his hands. He lay on the floor staring at his sleeves, which he couldn't open. "We're heading north. I sealed them against the cold to protect your fingers from freezing up. Let's go." I put my arms under his shoulders and helped him to his feet. He swayed heavily and nearly fell a second time. The chaia and the excitement of playing music again had completely worn off. Ellisand was finally confronting his full weakness, reeling with the pain of his recent beating and his own sickness and the effects of his long imprisonment. "Speak." I sent the word rudely into his mind.

He swore at me in Sarana and I felt the words running poison in my gut. So I sent the word "silence" and he stopped his invective. The spell worked, that was all that mattered now.

"Come on. Lean on me and walk." I took up my bag and supported him to the door. He was able to move with me, but his head still hurt him badly and his dizziness caused him to stumble. I had beaten him up much worse than I thought, and I was sorry for it. I remembered how much of a liability I had been when Baniff rescued me from Sunnashiven, and how he hadn't resorted to physical pain to manage me. The self-reproach in my fleeting comparison could have disabled me with guilt, but there were more urgent matters at hand so I couldn't afford to dwell on it. Liese was still wailing storms for his dead son, and I considered cloaking Ellisand and myself in invisibility to avoid a confrontation, but didn't know if one heavy illusion would negate the other. I'd have to take my chances visibly.

As I opened the door, the sound of Liese's cries increased and then the girl wailed something and all sound stopped. Ellisand seemed to become aware of the cries as soon as the silence hit, for he groaned and pulled weakly in the direction of the sickroom. Then there was more pounding and quieter sobs. It was dark in the hall, except for the candlelight I had forgotten to kill that was falling out of our room. Even the sickroom was dark, for the lantern had died with Yolan. Downstairs looked blacker than a new moon. As we haltingly reached the top step, Ellisand threw all his weight away from me and crashed against the wall, crying out in pain. I heard quick footsteps directly behind us and another shriek, the loudest yet. I turned instinctively and there, standing at the edge of the candlelight, stock-still in a look of absolute horror and outrage, was the open-mouthed pointy-faced girl. She was staring at Ellisand's swollen face and gasping. Then she was shouting something and Ellisand was doing his best to break my hold and go to her, but he was far too weak to have any success. As I struggled to pull him back, I saw Liese come slowly out of the doorway behind the girl. The innkeeper's face was an indescribable mess whenever the light licked against it. As I forced Ellisand down the stairs with me, I heard Liese choking out some words to the girl. But neither of them followed us. They were probably afraid to.

As we lurched down into the dark entryway, I released Ellisand's speech and commanded, "Translate."

"She says you've beaten and kidnapped me," he moaned. "Liese told her to get the guards after you. I take it you killed his son—"

Silence, I sent as I forced him toward the inn door. I knew there was a back entrance in the bar that probably led out to the stables, but someone was moving quietly behind us in the dark, for I heard the floor creak slightly near the desk, so I quickly forced Ellisand out the front door and into the street, which was dark and silent and void of people. I kicked the door closed behind us and magically locked it from the outside with a quick invocation. Then I used a clerical spell to throw a lock over every possible entrance to the inn. That should slow down Liese and family. "Stables."

Once in the street, he refused to move. Despite my recent guilt feelings, I could see nothing for it but to change his mind with a jab of pain again, but this time I used enough to frighten rather than really hurt. It worked because he staggered and gestured helplessly toward a little alley which ran between the inn and the next building, some sixty feet to our right. It looked like a darker gap of night against the street, but I decided this had to lead back to the stables. Then a dark noise was swelling out of the distance and there was a smell of burning in the air, first faint and then gone and then less faint and then unmistakable. I hurried us to the alley's entrance but when we got there I discovered that six feet into the alley the passage was bricked over and led nowhere. Ellisand was clearly stalling for time, hoping that someone would come along and notice us. I pulled him to the shadows on the other side of the street and then toward the corner. He wasn't resisting me; perhaps he was saving what little strength he had to try to escape when we reached the corner. I decided the stable entrance must be around that corner to our left, leading to the back of the inn. I saw distant uneven wisps of flame suddenly wink and dart and disappear into the black air, and then steadier fire rising red and full a few streets away, in the direction we were moving toward. I heard an angry chant which included Roguehan's name, and then the steadier flame suddenly burst against the sky into a twisted tower of angry scorching light.

Another sudden tower climbed and exploded at about the same distance behind us as the one before us had. There were shouts hitting us from both ends of the street now and a cluster of people, including three or four guards, ran past the inn, which was completely dark again. More people were spilling into our street with torches, but mostly on the inn side. They seemed to be attracted to something farther up behind us, so no one was stopping near the inn.

A large street lantern suddenly bore down on us from around the corner. I mean first there was light in my eyes, and then there was light gasping from the ground, for the lantern's owner dropped the lamp as soon as he saw us and immediately started to brandish a short sword. His clothes were torn and scorched and he smelled heavily of smoke. He was screaming something in Meden as he threatened us with his sword, the only word of which I caught was *stiepsist*, which I now knew meant priest. I feared blasting him lest the energy of the blast deplete the waking-surge I had drawn from

Hecate back in the inn. Anyway, he lunged at me with his short sword, and as I sidestepped and drew my own dagger, Ellisand took the hit in his upper left arm and fell across some stairs leading up to a balcony while clutching his wound. The assailant decided to follow up by attempting to strike at the weaker party so I placed myself at the bottom of stairs between Ellisand and our attacker, as my stomach pulled inward with the smell of blood.

The man was clearly drunk or crazed. He screamed and attempted to run his sword through my chest as I threw myself under his sword arm and pushed it up to a right angle with the sharp edge of my dagger, making sure to cut into his arm deep and crosswise so the veins would empty of blood faster. The pain I inflicted forced him to drop his weapon but the blood I produced violently increased my own nausea. So as he reeled backward in surprise, I dropped down to a crouch to pick up his sword, swallowing back my sickness and guarding myself with my dagger. He kicked my wrist hard and forced me to drop my weapon, but not before I had sliced open the lower part of his other leg. As he recoiled again, I managed to gather up both weapons in my left hand, for my wrist was clearly broken and I knew my right hand was useless. I couldn't handle both weapons effectively in my left hand, so I dropped my dagger behind me, where I heard Ellisand scramble to grab it, and then I kicked it out of his reach as I rose with my sword arm poised to kill.

My attacker was now trying to strike me with a second weapon, a long dirk which he had apparently produced from under his shirt.

He got the first hit, which grazed off my right shoulder, but I got the second, which cut well into his side below the ribs. But still he continued to fight and I continued to defend myself as best I could. My attacker was trying to lunge at my side and I was successfully beating him off despite my illness, my success due more to the man's tipsiness and clumsiness than my skill. I must have drawn blood again, for a sudden fist of nausea caused me to lose concentration for a beat and he cut me across the thigh. As I staggered backward, he suddenly and incomprehensibly went after Ellisand, who lay there looking terrified as the man ran at him with dirk pointed at his throat. Despite my leg injury and nausea, I forced myself to get behind the attacker and drove my sword into his back just as he would have killed Ellisand. Backstabbing is not the most honorable way to kill someone, but under the circumstances it was the best deal I had. The man turned to me in howling agony and tried one last time to run me through, but I got under his sword arm again and madly carved a long wide line up and down in his body cavity until he and his stinking entrails plopped over dead, my head pounding with violent bursts of pain.

I became aware that somewhere more people were singing and chanting. A shop went up in flames down the street. I was surprised we had attracted no attention, but then there seemed to be plenty of more interesting and popular events occurring in town tonight than our little skirmish.

Baniff would be wondering where I was, but neither Ellisand nor I was in any condition to get to the stables now. Damn the gods but I had to recover and I couldn't recover on the street, not with a mess of entrails in close proximity and the danger of discovery imminent. I averted my face and choked up some vomit as I kicked the corpse back against the dark of the shop wall with my good leg and picked up and sheathed my dagger. I also grabbed the lantern. "Up the stairs," I ordered Ellisand. "Up." He stood trembling, clutching his arm, and then obediently ascended the stairs. I grabbed a railing and dragged my bad leg up behind, using a clerical trick of mind to ignore the pain until we both got to the dark and empty balcony which was enclosed from view of the street.

I didn't have to order Ellisand to lie down. He keeled over as soon as we got to the top. I sat next to him, still ignoring my own injuries, and tore off his sleeve to get a better look at his wound in the light of the lantern, still queasy from his blood, but my stomach no longer had any contents to disgorge. I heard another explosion, closer now. "Speak," I sent, not sure with all my injuries if the command would hold. "What was the guy's problem?"

"He didn't like priests."

"Why did he attack you?"

"He thought I was your friend." Ellisand was bleeding but his wound was a surface hit. He would live. I took the torn piece of sleeve and bound up the wound with my left hand, pulling at the cloth with my teeth. Then I lay down next to him and started to pray myself into a trance. "Mother, heal me," I murmured in a clerical language designed for evil, "for I am hurt and bad."

As my own pain diminished and my own bleeding slowed, Ellisand immediately started screaming in pain. Because we were in such close physical proximity my prayer had pulled Hecate's energy around both of us but because Ellisand was not aligned to evil Her energy was doing damage to him. I released Her force and his screaming stopped, but I could now see that my prayer had torn his wound open, and that he was spurting blood rhythmically through the torn sleeve I had bound it with. He fell into a light swoon as I pressed tightly into his shoulder with my left hand to stop the blood flow with pressure, all the while gagging on the fresh bleeding because I was too weak to form an effective shield against it.

I knew I was done working magic for a while. Any energy I used for magic would tend to deplete the waking-surge I had drawn from Hecate, and there was a limit as to how many of those I could draw. Sure, I could pray the petition again when I felt tired, and it would work a second time, but then I'd be comatose in about twelve hours if I didn't use the prayer yet again, at which point I might have six or eight strong hours left and soon I'd either destroy my body or end up traveling with Baniff in a state of near death from wearing my body out with lack of sleep. And yet it was imperative that I keep Ellisand under close scrutiny, so I needed to remain awake as long and as much as possible during our travel.

Damn! There was no help for it—once his bleeding stopped— and thank Hecate—I mean—thank Anybody—it was slowing now, I'd have to repair the sleeve by conjuring material to fill in where I had ripped it, even though I knew better than to deplete my precious energy by using magic. All right . . . *down, breathe . . . the Amara word for cloth is tol—you can spin tol with wizardry, there's enough for that—yes, got it, got it joined—*I dropped his arm with the effort, but the sleeve was safely repaired, and I noticed the blood flow did not increase as his arm lay flat. That was it—that would have to do.

There was a sound of footsteps near the bottom of the stairs, which was all I needed. I was in no condition to probe, and in no condition to fight another assailant. So I did the next best thing, I resorted to defensive trickery. "Who's there?" I called menacingly in Botha. "Got your swords drawn, boys?" The sudden sound of my voice brought Ellisand out of his swoon. He really did have a strong constitution. I heard another footstep, and I couldn't be sure whether it was ascending or descending, and then I remembered that our visitor might not even understand Botha, although anyone would understand the menace I put into my voice. I heard footsteps withdrawing.

All right, my trick probably scared him off. I forced myself halfway down the stairs so I wouldn't be physically close to Ellisand and prayed for a healing once again. "Mother, heal me. For I am hurt and bad. And ever should my pain be yours, for as I bear your wants you take my pain unto Mother Christus above—" and another exploding building cut off my prayer, but the sound might have been Hecate's, for I felt a swift unexpected lift, like my head had grown lighter and wider and thinner for having been resubmerged in Her womb, like I had jumped off a precipice and risen higher than the world as it is should have allowed, like I had put an angry desperate fist through a brick wall and found the bricks to be paper and old leaves. And I felt a surprising dissatisfaction, for my pain and injuries did not increase into emptiness, they did not push and snap against themselves into the taut hurtful body spasm that usually precedes relief. They pushed against nothing—pushed into space—and suddenly they were just gone, taken back into the infinite.

And I felt a waking-surge so strong and irresistible I was immediately upright and only half-convinced that I wouldn't start floating over the steps and the burning rooftops. Somehow my simple healing petition had pulled another waking-surge into my body, an unplanned, excessive renewal that made standing still a physical effort. But there wasn't time to speculate on Hecate's surprise intervention, and I felt such an unhealthily high energy level pulsing through my mind that I absolutely had to run and move and work magic to bleed off the excess energy or die.

As I bounded back up the stairs to Ellisand, a loud song rose from the cross street as a shop on the corner went up in flames. It was an absolutely lovely melody and in my kinetic frenzy it set me dancing like a storm-sucked willow, and my energy rose unbelievably higher with the song and the fire and the destruction, until I was fit to suck Habundia's own pap in the flesh. It was awful really, like bouncing unwarned through the most joyous moments of one's life and into a mood and peak beyond anything human, into a seething open flare of the source of all uncontrollable emotions. I was surging with the fire as the singing took strength and light from the dying shop. I sang out the tune in Botha, in any words that came to mind, because I could do nothing but sing and throw myself around in the throes of a hypervitality I couldn't control. And then I just sang like a drunk—trying to bleed off whatever I'd brought down into the music, trying to send it up through the fire. Somewhere a building crashed—I wasn't sure if my singing had helped.

Ellisand sat up and pulled himself into the corner of the balcony. He was staring at me in utter revulsion, and staring out at the street. "They're burning their own shops and killing themselves." He was shocked and dazed.

"Yes, the Medegardans are reduced to that. Look at them," I howled, too frenzied not to hurl and scream at the night everything that was bursting in me at once. "*Look at them!* The only freedom they have left is the freedom to destroy everything they've loved and worked for. Fools, don't they know that killing what you love *is* evil—*look at them!* Roguehan's loyal slaves and they don't even know it." A little crowd within the crowd was torching another building across the way. "And some of them are so much their work they choose to die in it. And your music is their accompaniment. They're singing one of your songs." He looked like our assailant had looked when I ripped his insides out. "I'm sure Roguehan would love it. Aren't you? It's exactly what he's fighting for." A shop across the street began to crackle and smoke, "Ooo, yes—here watch. Maybe we'll see another self-immolation or three. Oh, look at that sparkling beauty, would you—how quickly all those years, all those generations of love and work consume themselves into nothing. *Nothing!*"

Glass broke and shattered from a second-floor window in the inn, attracting a large group of people now spilling over from the cross street. The pointy-faced girl leaned out with a candle and started shouting something down to the crowd. I didn't need a translator to tell me she was announcing my "crime" to everyone in the street. So I leveled my gaze at the inn, which was a job considering that my unruly energy was making it near impossible to level anything of myself at anything, and as two more shops went up in music, I brought down Hecate's force through me and blasted the inn and its inhabitants and the crowd beneath the window to silence and ruins. And the sound of destruction silenced the burning music into plain ugly burning, which I still felt going on and on around us. I also felt that Ellisand was now absolutely terrified of my power. I wouldn't need to prod him with pain anymore. Actually, I was rather impressed with the size of my hit myself.

Blasting the inn was probably the best thing I could have done to pull my own energy down to a manageable level, for the death blast did wonders for bleeding off my terrible excess vitality. I could almost breathe and move normally now. But in my heightened state the blast came faster than I expected it to, and its aftermath felt large and sloppy to me, like two giant ocean waves colliding out of phase and dampening each other. But the inn was thoroughly destroyed, and my aim and skill with my deity's force was so exact that the stables behind, which were now visible, were unhit. While the crowd on the corner and Ellisand recoiled in horror, I chanted, "My blast is bound with your imprisonment. Say nothing." And as I forced him down the stairs I continued chanting, "With each step you take you lose what little strength you have, until you sit on horseback and lose it all. You're going back down, down, until I give you birth again.

Come on, walk down with me, step by heavy step, sleepwalk down with me. Move and think and feel but only by my leave."

And I led him through the horror-struck scream-scarred singing on the corner, knowing that in the heat and confusion we weren't likely to be taken particular notice of. I wasn't interested in walking through the corpses and the remnants of the inn, that would verge on the obvious. We were able to move quickly, for Ellisand was too weak and fearful to put up any resistance. And as we walked I renewed the illusion of hands so as to buy myself the longest period of time possible before having to renew the illusion again.

By the time I got him to the stables, where a visibly shaken Baniff and a terrified Aleta were mounted and ready and had a fresh steed and a double saddle waiting for me, I congratulated myself on my sense of magical timing, for Ellisand's strength had dissipated to the point where it was all he could do to silently mount with my help before passing out behind me, which was exactly the way I wanted things. Aleta and Baniff immediately kicked their horses into motion so I did the same. "Your evil priest hit the inn. One of his minions attacked us. Would have hit you if I hadn't shielded and turned the blast," I called curtly, as I kicked my horse up to a gallop.

"Good job, lad. Worth the wait, then," called Baniff, as he and Aleta increased their speed to match mine. Good old practical Baniff—far be it from him to mourn a throng of dead Threlans if he believed his own skin was the price of their destruction.

*N*ever could figure out how you and he got along, my lord."

Walworth smiled faintly. I couldn't decide whether he appreciated my sense of humor or my sense of truth, or both.

*A*nyway, both he and Aleta were most eager to follow me out of the burning town, despite my veering left into the cross street, which had been the main road and was now more like a stony bridge through a fair inferno. But inferno or not, I knew no other way to get north to Glamisson and I had no particular interest in getting us lost on the back roads, which I knew from the sights and sounds around me were just as hazardous as the main way. So the cross street it was, anything to make all possible haste in putting the little town behind us.

The street was not a street. It was an utter impossibility. It was a first-blush faulty strategy for negotiating two yelping walls of flame. There was smoke and stench all over, for all kinds of things were burning in the shops, but worse was the human and animal stench of great roaring crowds running and dancing and crying into the flames. The flames were only kept in check by the stone street, held uneasily by a distant theory that stone doesn't burn. But dancing done in proper measure will burn just about anything, and Threlan dancing will make all theory cringe at the drop of a bright scarf and the kick of a heel. For when Threlans dance they do their best to leave no emotion unrevealed. And when they dance their deaths *en masse*, their flesh and faces burn windows into all their lives. And there's no need to be a cleric to see most of the show, just sensitive. But as a cleric I probably got more details than most. Strangers' lives kept coming at me naked—naked in stench and smoke.

So set this down, my lord. I rode the crest of a rebellion. I saw dancing. And in the dancing I found exceptions to the silly rule that stone doesn't burn. Stone will burn quite beautifully in Threle if one's heart is made out of it and the conditions are just so."

Here in the North Country, stone burns also, I thought, as a wave of sickness passed through me. Here it is all chaos. But that moment in Threle was all chaos, too, I suppose, for hardened as my heart had become against Walworth and his country, I couldn't help but feel pain at the destruction of Medegard, which reminded me of the annihilation of my beloved border town in Helas. I wanted to tell Walworth that even while I was riding to exact vengeance against him, I was moved by the suffering of his people. But for some reason I said nothing.

And so. As I galloped side by side with Aleta, Baniff's pony beating fury at our stallions' heels, I marveled at the conditions Roguehan had created. What an absolute artist the emperor was. I must congratulate him sometime. Along the road was an absolute kaleidoscope of feelings jumping and expiring into smoke before spreading themselves against a dismal groaning sky. I saw and felt and breathed burning stone in all the various deaths.

A gaudily dressed jewel merchant danced joy at freedom as she fiercely waltzed into immolation. Three middle-aged lovers danced misery at saying good-bye. An old candle-maker danced jealousy of himself in a jerky writhey motion that involved throwing his legs over his head and grabbing his ankles in great ungainly hops and jumps—no, it was really jealousy of his own past. He wanted it to be back before the war again and his wanting screamed invectives to the gods. It was a wanting worthy of Habundia Herself, for it actually knocked me slightly off-balance in the eddy of sparks which was now the man's right shoulder blowing over the wind. *Swearing at every god in sight is not the most diplomatic way to cross over,* I thought, but Threlans are usually pretty decent about taking the consequences of their actions so I assumed the man would be patient if it took awhile for a deity to birth him in flesh again. But all around us I felt something worse—hundreds of clumsy faiths in various deities rattling like loose limbs in a storm—faiths not ballasted by knowledge—pathetic fantasies built on hearsay and childhood wishes that for all I knew might lead horribly to Nothing. People really shouldn't throw themselves at deities, in spirit or in flesh, if they don't know what the hell they're doing. It's rather rude, and embarrassing to watch. But I had to admit that their desperate errors lent a devastatingly graceful touch to the destruction, like the delicate outline of wind and feathers one only sees on a second or third inspection of the background of a fantastically painted mural.

As we passed into a more residential section there was a lull in the bright horrors so I glanced at Aleta. She was intent on keeping her own stallion paced evenly with mine, and on avoiding having to look at the sights around us. Her gaze was fixed rigidly between her stallion's ears, except when she occasionally glanced at me to pace herself. Her horse was a lifeline and I was her protection—no telling when another blast might hit. I remembered the first time I had met Aleta, how her youthful bravado and tales of defending County Clio had amused me in the library at Sunnashiven's Wizard School, and how she had gotten me thrown out of the library on that same day, and sought to make it up by arranging for Baniff to help me escape from Sunnashiven before it fell to the peasant rebellion. Now I was helping her to escape from a falling city. I wondered if her father yet lived, or if Aleta were the sole ruler of County Clio now, that strangely independent political entity that belonged to no kingdom. And I wondered what kind of aid she and her people were lending Walworth.

I felt Baniff's pony as close to my steed's heels as it possibly could get. The road was far too fiery and confused for more than two horses to ride abreast. I also felt the pony's fright. The animal was moving on instinct, galloping because my horse was. With Ellisand leaning unconsciously into my back and drawing balance from me through our magical bond, I couldn't turn to look at Baniff, but I guessed he wasn't so much *riding* his horse as holding on. Baniff the Gnome was a highly skilled illusionist who was one of Walworth's closest companions. We used to share private jokes and engage in wild drinking contests. I had once envied Baniff his adventurous life and devoutly wished that my own life resembled his. I used to consider him a friend. But he had left me to rot in Kursen Monastery just like the others had left me. I wondered what he was thinking as we rode out of Medegard.

A quick surface probe of Baniff's mind brought me an impression of a dry hasty nervousness. I kicked my horse harder as we approached a little cluster of burning houses but the animal was already moving at top speed. The road widened enough here for the pony to flank me on my right, and to my surprise Baniff managed to convince the pony to do so. And then, just as we passed the burning cluster three abreast and entered the thinner furor of the little town's last reaches, our horses instinctively pulled up short in front of the most resonant death of all, a death like a spinning stone cliff I'd somehow taken too many steps off of in the heat of a rural noon. I felt Ellisand's weight against me, as I felt a sensation like I was falling and scraping against dirt and pebbles and uprooting the weeds I couldn't grab to stop the falling. And then I was shaking with an age-old adolescent shame that I thought I had long ago learned to hide.

For there, blocking the road before us, were five youths who reeked of parsnips, persimmon, and intense friendship. Four young men and a woman. The woman could have been a twin to one and an elder sister to another of the men and she was wearing a garland of autumn wildflowers, which trailed from her head to her shoulders and wrapped like a garish snake around her too slender waist. But all of them looked half-starved and slender, for food was now scarce and expensive. They held hands in a circle and spun themselves into a frenzy right there in the middle of the road, singing and chanting in Meden. And there was a fire in the middle of their circle, and it grew with their chanting—I knew the woman was using a witchworking to pull the flames higher and higher but yet she was drawing the energy from the chanting of her friends. And the fire was burning rotting parsnips and persimmons, as if in a wretched symbol of starvation, for I could think of no magical reason for burning such an unlikely combination.

I stared distant and bold-faced as the circle broke and a line, led by the woman, danced into fiery bliss and an end. It was a stunning *coup*. They were calling each others' names even after their tongues and throats became ash. And their fused affection was the only sting I felt in all the deaths that night. I felt the friends jelly into runny spirits and experienced their difficulty in separating their identities from each other as they twisted through smoke and flame. I saw where they crossed together into the blackness which bounded my clerical perception. And I sat staring wretchedly at the mark in the air their spirits left, staring hungrily like one of Mother Hecate's dogs waiting for a living heart to feed on.

The suicide of shopkeepers I could understand, for I could understand dying with and for one's work. And I could understand preferring death to slavery as a last-resort affirmation of freedom. But I did not want to understand five friends killing themselves in a circle for each other. I did not want to breathe and swallow and carry in my lungs the smoke of their burnt flesh. It wasn't my sacrifice. I did not want to know about it. And there was an ugly skeletal echo rattling around in my beautiful well-trained mind, asking, "*But isn't art supposed to move?*" I kicked my horse forward to silence the echo, forward over the place of the fire. For the fire had been raised by magic and so it died and grew cold when the friends did.

"I hate witches," murmured Aleta, as we rode on three abreast. There was something deep and devout in her tone, and it wasn't really meant for anyone save the listening air. I wondered what Baniff thought of their deaths, but somehow I didn't want to look at him and then I realized I wasn't probing because I was afraid in my bones to know *what* he was thinking right now. So I just kept riding fast and grim between them, gratefully leaving the burning town for open night.

And the road was dark and clear and fine. I knew from the wind and the dry afterglow of the rain that dawn was coming, but it was still dark enough for the three of us not to really see each other, and so I had time to compose myself and understand my situation. I was fully awake, but my body would have to give out come nightfall unless Hecate worked another intervention. The higher the energy, the sharper and quicker the drop. So I had to plan on securely separating myself and Ellisand from Baniff to preserve the illusion while I was asleep. While we were both asleep, for there was no help for it but to knock Ellisand out first. Which meant I'd best wake him up now and keep him awake all day for his own health's sake. So since the road was straight here and the gallop even, I threw up a wizard shield and plunged quickly into his sleep, kicked him awake with a word, and became aware again a few yards down the road. Ellisand was now moaning out his head pain with each jostle of the horse, but that couldn't be helped.

A few paces down the road, just as I was confident that the dark had masked from Baniff my change to trance, he called unexpectedly,

"Where'd ye go, lad?"

"Praying up the shield," I called back glibly.

"I meant earlier."

I bit my tongue. "So did I."

I pretended to concentrate on the horse. My next consideration was Cathe. I decided the best thing I could do was track Cathe myself and beg Hecate to send a message that all was well and that he should back off. But I needed silence and solitude to pull that sort of thing off. The only link I had to work with besides our deities, which would potentially open anything I sent to any evil cleric in the world, including Roguehan's, was the fact that Cathe was looking for me and fixed on Baniff. Which might not be a bad link, for to track Baniff and combat illusion, Cathe had to be pulling down all kinds of goddess force. It made sense that if he attributed Baniff's illusion spells to me deliberately throwing him off with my ring, he would be more than eager to catch up and get a firsthand look at what was going on. I absolutely had to let him know that he had been following Baniff, but that Baniff and I were now together and that all was well.

But here was a rogue's trick—I could feel for Cathe's energy and give an all's well to carry back to him on the return—but not without going into a longer trance than I cared to under present circumstances. I didn't think Baniff could catch a clerical sending, but he might feel my power being sent out and know it as evil. Hadn't he said the high priest following him was evil? How would he know that, unless he had some way of feeling clerical power and assessing alignments? It couldn't be by sight. Cathe had taken to wearing the dark blue robes of Athena, lined with yellow along the bottom hem to indicate his allegiance to Ceres and the inversion of his previous training in the path of Habundia Christus. He never looked his alignment, so Baniff had to have felt something—and felt something at a distance. And surely he didn't see Cathe up close or he would have recognized him. I congratulated myself on using wizardry on Ellisand. At least that was easily shielded. But I had to know *how* Baniff knew his pursuer was evil.

"Baniff. This high priest. Tell me everything you know about him." My voice was even and perfect. One professional querying another in the interest of doing a better job.

"Saw him twice on a hill at a distance. It was rainin' and foggy. Dark robe, dark horse, hooded face. Seemed to be blessin' the dyin' fields with evil."

"How did you know it was an evil blessing?" I called over the pounding hooves and Ellisand's moans.

"It was too obvious not to be," interrupted Aleta. I winced inwardly. "He reminded me of the clerics in Sunnashiven who used to bless everything in and out of sight just to show off that they could." Sure, and hadn't she once complained about Cathe blessing the plants in the courtyard of the palace in Sunnashiven for show? But perhaps Cathe had been doing his best to be obvious since I didn't seem to respond appropriately to his call. That was a good sign for he might be giving me the benefit of the doubt, thinking that perhaps I was throwing off illusion because I wasn't aware that it was him behind me. And in the fog he could have assumed the two travelers were me and Ellisand.

"What did you feel from him?" I asked Baniff dispassionately.

"The need to make tracks. Confused him into Medegard—saw his back a third time in town after our speech. There's another fine rebellion turned rotgut," he spat.

"I mean did you feel his evil around you?"

"No. I figure that's yer job." The pony tripped over a loose rock and nearly sent Baniff flying directly over its head. Good thing the gnome was gripping the mane. He slapped its neck. "Send ye to a Sunnan potluck, ye miserable—"

"How do you know your new friend's evil?" I called casually.

"Sorry, lad, nothin' personal." He meant the crack about Sunna. "I figure if he's followin' us and blessin' dyin' fields and blastin' inns, he can't be all that believably good."

Excellent! "All right, let me pray about it." I confidently dived into trance and yes, I did feel a faint tingle of evil—Cathe wasn't far behind but he wasn't sending anything in our direction. It felt like he was deliberately keeping his distance behind us—maybe even turning back. Perhaps he'd seen us together and decided to retreat. Since he was close enough to send a message to us directly, using the evil I felt as a fix, I decided to risk an "all's well." There—sent, then nothing. There's one problem licked for now. Cathe was probably retreating to await more detailed word. I came out of my trance and announced cheerily, "Shield's still good."

Problem two. It was clear that Baniff wasn't about to stop anywhere until we made Threle, unless the horses died under us from exhaustion. Well, he'd have to stop if I fell out of the saddle in a dead faint, which according to my sense of my own power would have to happen around sunset or just after if I fought the turning hard enough—but that was not an optimal way to work things. It was imperative that I keep guard over Ellisand at all times. I'd have to strategize a way to stop and get the two of us a separate shelter by nightfall—but come, think—we'd have to change horses by nightfall if we kept to this pace, and surely I could use circumstances for constructing an argument for stopping. We'd have to stop before we made Threle anyway, for it would easily take us all day and part of the night just to make Glamisson, and the better part of two more days to reach the Sengan Mountains, which constituted the present border. Of course, I wasn't taking into account whatever border crossings Roguehan had in store for us. *Border crossings!* There was a tangle, for Ellisand would have to play his lyre, and Baniff would see no hands and hear no music, and—

Baniff suddenly swerved to the side of the road and stopped. I didn't think his pony would keep up to the stallions' pace forever. I stopped too and sent a quick "all's well—go back" for extra security—no sense in waiting for Cathe to catch up to us if he happened to still be traveling in our direction. Aleta joined us, glancing nervously behind, as if she suspected there might be a pursuer back there. Baniff's horse was sweating and panting and coughing up green phlegm. I could feel it throwing off spurs of misery.

"We can make the Sengan range in twelve hours by the forest path," said Baniff. I looked steadily in his direction, not willing to confess my absolute ignorance of how we were to accomplish this feat, or my sheer joy at the idea of avoiding border crossings. "It's a secret path—cuts straight northeast into the mountains where they fall in a due south line. The main road winds through half the small towns and all the border crossin's in the next three duchies. Take us days."

"All right, let's go." I started to kick up my horse.

"Concerned about us bein' alone in the woods—will solitude make us more vulnerable to another blast?"

"Solitude has nothing to do with it. You're either shielded or you're not." Ellisand groaned a little. He was thoroughly conscious, thoroughly in pain, and, thanks to my magic, thoroughly unable to speak.

"How's yer friend holdin' up?"

"As well as he can. But I'll need a separate place to tend to him when we make the border and camp for the night," I added quickly. "And his condition may mean stopping somewhere sooner."

I don't know if Baniff heard me, for he was forcing his reluctant pony into a rough spurt as I spoke. I followed him and Aleta followed me, the three us forming a straight line through the softly lightening woods.

And the autumn dawn came slow and quiet, the way a neglected life comes into old age. But the dawn came and came and seemed to keep coming long past morning. I mean the whole blessed day felt like dawn—or like a day that never quite grew up. The true dawn came dark pink and freshening on the old rain clouds and half-leafed treetops as we rode, and then the pink pushed away the uncertain late-night gray around our heads to make room for the earliest promise of sun. But the sun was just a tease against the morning wind—winking in the morning and fleeing back into dawn, for the sky remained stout with clouds and never really turned itself over to day. And although the woods were full of drizzle sloshing through all the air between the tree trunks and the branches and the silently falling leaves, the sky never turned itself over to rain. It just sat there thick above the woods as we rode. It was the woods which rained and rained as if the trees hadn't noticed that the sky had already stopped. And there was no sound here except the horses beating soft against wet ground and the sound of the moisture sucking at their hooves and slowing our pace.

Yet there was enough slow contrast between true dawn and day for there to be a period of time when my life felt unreal. The unreality started to caress me as the light in the air lifted enough for me to see Baniff's back clearly. For there was no longer any shouted conversation to occupy my thoughts and my immediate problems appeared to have been resolved as much as possible for now. So there was nothing for it but to thoroughly feel the seeming unreality of Baniff once again leading me along a forest path to Threle. This *was* Baniff—this *was* Aleta behind me—I *had* been asked to lend my talents to help Threle—and the whole thing began to feel strangely like the last four years of my life never happened. Like it was right and natural that the three of us should be riding and working together. Like no explanation of time spent during our separation was required or relevant. Like the separation never happened— four years was a mere two days' absence, or a bad afternoon's dream quickly fading. I felt very much like I was *supposed* to be here, and between dawn and day I marveled at how absolutely comfortable I felt, how unexpectedly easy I was with everything. Only once or twice did I catch myself thinking with surprise—*here is Baniff right in front of me and nothing stops me from asking and speaking of our mutual friends*—but the surprise was fleeting and I didn't even really want to talk—just be there like I always was—I mean always wished I was. I was pleased to be trusting to my wish and feeling fine.

Here was an unreality too comfortable to take notice of for long. You feel the fire's warmth most acutely when you first come in out of a storm, but rarely do you mark the point at which you stop feeling it, the point at which the fire becomes an old wish already granted. I felt the strangeness of being there with Baniff and Aleta only until the day came and the light faded back into the dim of its extended dawn. Then comfort was all a grand given. There were even times throughout the journey when I kept forgetting that Kursen had ever existed. But then Ellisand would press into my back and I knew I was older now and on a different mission.

Once it was day and raining, there was another sound besides the sucking plop of hooves in moist ground. For we were riding through the sort of insistent woodland moisture that has a sound. Not that you can hear the wet as itself, but you can feel its sound in the extra time it takes a leaf to fall. You can hear it in the shadows which can't form under gray sky but that would be there if the sun were. You feel the sound in the limbs of trees which are now a scale darker in color than the missing sun would have them. And you hear it in the shade of brightness borne by glistening rosemary bushes— an improbable brightness which comes from the bush itself on such a day—*rosemary is for memory*—shouted a half-remembered line of poetry in my mind, or was that a memory of Caethne teaching me something about herbs?

The day was chill, for the wind was coming down at us from the Sengans even at this distance and had picked up intensity in storms and winter promises over the long cold plains. It was on the cold side of the day that I pictured my map of the world as I knew it and was satisfied that there was a part of Threle that was indeed a day's journey. A largely unpopulated part, I believed, for I knew of no great cities in the southeastern bend and sweep of the plains. But the land beyond the Sengan Mountains was still Threle, inhabited or not. Not that it ever occurred to me that a forest shortcut existed to the mountains, but hey, if there's a direct route anywhere, leave it to a gnome to find it. And thanks be to Hecate for small favors as well.

So I listened hard to the cold and the moisture and was so comfortable I blissfully lost all awareness as time brought us closer to Threle. And sometimes I prayed to Hecate in gratitude and confidence. And I kept sending "all's well—go back" messages in a direct line behind me to satisfy myself that Cathe had indeed retreated for there was never any return sending. And so my sendings were speaking to lonely pines and losing themselves in mist, which I counted as a sort of prayer to the day. And during the afternoon the ground was drying, although the air was not, and so our speed increased. I even once managed to let Baniff ride far ahead enough not to notice me remaining behind with Aleta so I could strengthen Ellisand's illusion safely. And my prisoner's belief still held firm through his pain.

All in all it was a fine smooth journey until I began to feel fatigue flash through my body as we were ascending a brown quiet ridge into evening. The waking-surge I had drawm from Hecate was ending, and now every second between here and rushing oblivion mattered. I felt I had another forty minutes to an hour of consciousness if I fought the inevitable with all my mind—and maybe twenty minutes if I didn't.

I saw a cloud burst orange as the sun tore through its ragged lining and started to slide brilliantly down a sharp peak, tilting into white visibility the under clouds for the first time all day. Dawn into evening. There was a narrow valley here between our ridge and the mountains—perhaps a twenty-minute journey, although the valley was already growing dark. I saw Baniff kick his pony into a gallop on the downhill side of the ridge and so I followed his lead as fuzzy tiredness insisted on washing down through my face.

"Hey, Baniff," I called. "We've got to stop. My friend needs help." To my great relief he jerked his pony to a halt under a dark clump of trees and turned sharply to face the ridge, whose top now bore a soft glow. I turned with him to see Aleta rushing up to us and I followed his gaze to the top of the ridge, where I saw the unmistakable dark outline of a figure in high priest robes sitting on a horse and blessing the valley with evil. I sent another message and the figure started to descend toward us in evening shadows.

"Well, lad? Looks like this one's yers."

Damn Cathe for an idiot. No other word would do. "I'll take care of him," I said grimly, kicking my horse.

Aleta grabbed the bridle. "What about him?" she asked urgently. She meant Ellisand.

"What *about* him?" I wasn't enthusiastic about leaving my prisoner behind, and I decided it couldn't hurt to let Cathe see for himself that Ellisand wasn't a problem.

"You just said he needs help, and you're taking him into a clerical battle?" She was probably more concerned about my success than his well-being, but Ellisand groaned loudly on cue, and so Aleta roughly dismounted and pulled at him to do the same. And of course he needed no further encouragement to dismount. Our double saddle had double stirrups.

As soon as Ellisand touched ground, Baniff slapped my horse into motion. "Go."

Wonderful—so I went, cursing. Like thunder over the Threlan plains, racing the sluggishness in my blood, praying for a thirty-minute reprieve, for the strength to fight to open thirty more minutes of wakefulness. I couldn't see Cathe anymore but as I reached the bottom of the ridge an unmistakable pull called me into a natural rock shelter that I hadn't noticed on the way down. A shelter of night—for as I entered I recognized that night had just arrived here and locked itself in the rocks without intervening dusk. The air was already blacker than my mood, but I sensed the evil and knew that Cathe was waiting—standing calmly and expectantly next to his horse. I angrily dismounted and decided to waste no time. "Really, Cathe, do you take me for as big a bloody fool as yourself that you've got to tail Baniff all the bloody way from Kant as a poor substitute for me? Look—all's fine, except that I'm on the edge of a waking-surge and about to lose it—and even that's not a problem if you go back to Kursen now and wait for word—trust me, I haven't time for details now. Look, Ellisand's my concern—don't worry about him. Worry about Baniff—he knows he's been followed—not by you, but we all saw your outline on the ridge and—we're supposed to be fight-ing—look—send a blast on your way back and make it look good for them and all's done. And wait for word. Perhaps if you haven't screwed up our plans already, the Goddess ought to make you divine Dunce when Caethne works your deification—"

As I began to fall to the ground with exhaustion, I had to stop talking so I could concentrate fully on pushing back the coming faint beyond a few more minutes of wakefulness. I was successful, but as I made what I knew was my last recovery for the day, I realized I wasn't speaking to Cathe. For as I struggled against the coming void, our pursuer lit a candle with goddess force and removed her hood, revealing the most sickeningly serious face I'd ever seen in my life.

I was speaking to Mirra, the student from Kursen Monastery whom El had sent to Sunnashiven to study to become a high priest-ess of Habundia Christus.

Eight

Mirra continued looking feverishly still and fastidiously serious for a full ten seconds before responding. And when she finally spoke, it was in that god-awful, coolly measured, emotionless voice favored by all Sunnashiven high priestesses, that hellishly irritating voice of utter calm which always made me feel like killing something.

"I brought down the surge when you healed yourself after your sword fight. By my estimation you *should* have another night before it breaks." Her "estimation" was a quiet, no-nonsense, you-can't-fool-me reprimand, a placid reprimand uttered without visible agitation. Mistakes in one of her caliber were clearly impossible, and so I wasn't supposed to be clinging to my horse's stirrups and noticeably fighting to keep upright as she spoke. I tried to swallow back tired-ness and failed.

She interpreted my silence as an argument, and a tinge of defensive annoyance did break briefly through her excruciating calm before subsiding again. "I *know* you and Ellisand both heard me in the inn and I *know* you heard me on the stairs before you prayed your healing. I certainly heard you." She said Ellisand's name pointedly, as if discovering me with Ellisand was like discov-ering me in a dirty act of goodness against Habundia Christus Her-self. Other than the fact that she now spoke Botha, and Botha with a horrible Kantish accent I might add, Mirra hadn't changed much. Even her voice of studied calm, which on the tongue of a true high priestess would have sounded tauntingly fair and frightfully rea-sonable, managed to sound gut-wrenchingly self-congratulatory on hers. I don't know who had been wasting her full of praise for the two years since she'd left Kursen, but it was clear that somebody had.

"Feel my head and tell me about another night," I hissed, pulling hard on the stirrup and leaning against my horse for support.

She did so, and looked uncertain for a second before dropping her hand and regaining her composure. "Your healing prayer must have interfered with my work."

"Your damned waking-surge interfered with mine. I'd just

prayed one waking off Hecate and yours came along and damn near killed me."

Her eyes widened a little and her breathing sharpened for one second, but it only took that one second for her to find a new way to insist that my condition was not her fault.

"How was I supposed to know you were already on a surge, Brother? I was only doing my duty in the Goddess. When I saw you leaving the inn with Ellisand after riding all day through Kant, I *assumed* you were dead tired." Ellisand again. But her perfect calm was now marred by the soiled breath of a whine. I almost expected her to add, "it isn't fair." But instead she buried the whine back underground, and said pointlessly, "And in order to get to you I had to break open the clerical lock you put on the inn door. Of course I fixed the lock again." She was justifying her abilities, as if after her years of study, breaking a clerical lock was a divine feat that some-how made up for the rest of her lack of judgment. I swayed a little and forced my eyes open. They had closed themselves without my noticing. "I *tracked* you through Kant," she added, probably because I seemed singularly unimpressed with her lock-breaking.

"Why?"

"I have been asked to spot you for His Highest Excellency the emperor," she replied coldly.

"Why?"

"Because if I keep you safe to carry out your orders, I will receive extra credit toward becoming a high priestess in a few more years."

"Extra credit. Of course." My head dropped in space and I jerked it back upright.

"Spy work is dangerous. I am your backup in case anything goes wrong."

"I see."

"I have special permission to wear the robes of the high clergy as a road disguise. The power in this robe is higher than most priest-esses can handle," she boasted. "So high I had trouble tracking you at first, until I adapted to the higher level through my field-blessings. You and your party were much easier to follow through the forest."

"That's because there's only one trail through the forest, and I was sending calls, you idiot. And you've been tracking Baniff through Kant, not me—"

"Baniff? Is he the little gnome? I have read about gnomes—"

"Never mind." The sleep was punching at my eyes again, but I still had a few minutes. "Mirra, I can't fight the fall much longer. And

I've no strength to pray myself awake—can you bring down another surge—buy me a few hours? It's critical for the cause."

She paused for several seconds, looking hesitant and doubtful as I felt myself growing perceptibly weaker. All her deadly calm had just become dead uncertainty. "I don't think I can."

"I think you'd best." My legs stopped working and I slumped to the ground.

She squatted and peered at me closely, holding her candle in my eyes and dripping hot wax in my face, but my face was growing too numb to really feel anything more than the distant pinging warmth and shrivel of the wax against skin I no longer had anything like a connection to. "I—I can't. It's against the rules."

"Damn the rules, Mirra. You'll do it or I'll tell Roguehan how wonderfully you've screwed things up so far." She didn't like this at all. It took a precious half minute or more for her to think and respond.

"Look, I really can't. Three surges in a twenty-four-hour period will do some damage to you and I cannot damage a brother if I expect to be made high priestess. Habundia wouldn't like it." Then she quoted in a singsong superior fashion, *"'Do not injure your own for Mine is all injury,' saith She Who Harms.* I can't risk it. But is there anything else I can do for you?"

"Yes." My eyes closed beyond my will. I felt that I had perhaps another minute. "You can send a blast to make Baniff think I've destroyed our pursuer."

"All right, that I can do. I can blast the whole ridge. I blasted the inn for you, you know. Your aim was high. It broke into space after *I* did all the damage."

"You did the damage all right," I think I mumbled.

"Yes, it's all right, Brother. Sleep here." The word *sleep* robbed me of twenty seconds. "Trust me. I am sure that Baniff will take care of your precious Ellisand."

"That's what I'm afraid of." I don't know if I said or thought or felt this. There were wet ragged clouds in my face and black heavy mushrooms springing obscurely in my thighs and then the rock beneath my palms felt distant and smooth and gone and I was out.

A dying clutch of afternoon. Red, I think. Coming to sunset on a rainy sleep-washed sail. The sun was pulling me out of the blank. First with warmth in the dark. Then with excessively comfortable light. As I opened my eyes, it was late sea breeze and knowing. Sea pigeons walking kind on the edge of tender waves and flying away into evening. And then seashells smooth and sparkling where the pigeons had been. And an orange cat running out of the waves. I knew without remembering that there had always been wind and light glancing beauty on these rolling dark blue waves. And then I knew that the sand had been cool and pleasing beneath my back and legs. But I was sitting now—sitting with the evening coming soft and long, and my hands were in Isulde's, and she was smiling into me the lovely evening drift.

"Llewelyn," she whispered, and waited warm and perfect while I knew I was with her. "Never have you come to me so deep—to lie for weeks between the sand and the waves—to lie through all the season's sunsets in an evening. I kept seeing you in distance when I filled my baskets with starfish. Sometimes you were dark like the back of a whale, and sometimes you were cold and drawn like the patches of blue water the sun forgets. And sometimes was it you dreaming for days our sun's descent?"

"*Was* I dreaming, Isulde?" I looked steadily into her eyes and loved her. Perhaps I'd gotten myself executed and Hecate no longer wanted me and so this was happily all. "Then perhaps I shall always dream now."

"*Always* dream," she teased. "As if you don't always dream." I held her gently against my chest and she sighed. "My father brought you a bowl of living fish and so I let them go again. And yesterday I brought you bread and vegetables and you ate. Do you remember?"

"No." I smiled over her head at evening sea and sky.

"I cooked them in the broken pot the silly rainbow left last year. I cooked them in the waves."

"Yes." I kissed her. The evening was a strange bright season in our mouths. I wanted so much to be dead, for this to be forever, but I could not remember dying. All memory stopped with Mirra and my swoon. And death would have brought me to Hecate, so I knew I was still unconscious somewhere near the Sengan Mountains. But dream time is different. Here I had lain through an evening which lasted a summer, in a sunset which did not move or swing into night, but was always the moment before the moment the sea and sky showed evening touching at a distance.

But the sunset had its own weeks and days I never felt. She closed my kiss smiling, and gently pulled my left hand's fingers through hers. "Three nights ago your hand lay exposed to the song of the Northern moon and so it froze. And then the sea children came and kept carving their names upon your fingers."

"And what did *you* do?"

"I threw mussels at them. Then I kissed their names away. So you see it is all smooth now." Her smile was another vintage season and we were striding through a little garden with grape trellises and white marble benches and our laughter held the sun still and the evening at bay. And the courtyard was red and glowing before the coming feast. Laughter in a window and we were lovers. But sometimes there was a simple hut of home and grapes like salty crab apples. And the crab apples were wind ripped on a sea cliff over a dark afternoon's storm season, but the season was still our sunset and the gentle waves of light I sat before again. And Isulde asked, "Shall we walk?"

As we rose together from the sand I noticed my hand was indeed smooth, for my illusion ring was missing. And I hoped it was only the nature of the dream—but my dreams with Isulde were real, and when I rubbed my finger and made a wish, my finger vanished but the ring did not appear. But we were walking the sparkling trail the pigeons had left along the waves now, and the orange cat came steady behind us like a drop of sun, and it was only because I felt like speaking and needed something to say after we kissed in the hut and were back again that I showed her my missing finger and asked her for my ring.

"I think the sea children took it," she replied, holding me playfully around the waist. "Else the moon cast a ring into the waves and it was yours. Come." We knelt by the sea and she plunged my hand in the water, water so warm I did not feel it. I mean I felt it warm before I felt it wet. I mean I knew it had to be wet and then I felt it. And when she lightly brought my hand back out my finger was restored but the ring was not. "Alas, your ring is wedded to the moon," she said softly, "but the sea has another gift for you." And as we knelt in water to our waist she bent bare-breasted into the path of light the sunset kept making—a path pink and orange and coral-colored—and she vanished under the waves, and returned quite dry with a large pink-and-white sea conch in her hand, which trailed seaweed from its mouth as she held it earnestly against my ear.

And as I took the conch the water was easily around my neck, only my face was in the sunset where the pigeons had flown, and then I heard the sea surge in the conch, and I was breathing underwater in greens and blues, and I closed my eyes in the warm, where I heard the sounds of setting suns and brown-berried summers juicy and young and thornbushes crowded with apples and white and then midsummer children barefoot and singing rock castles and dropping their pebbles in a new pond and finding rhythms swinging free—

And more rocks, now splitting harder than a dream could hold. A thump and crush of time in the cold and my eyes opening underwater to see what I heard. Another distant crush of rocks coming to focus and the music fled into the conch.

I was awake. My left hand was wringing pain and blood and I knew even before I prayed the healing that made my hand whole again that my horse had crushed my precious illusion ring all to uselessness. And so I sat up mourning in damp choking air. And then I sat up into something like a cave opening into a shower of dirt and rocks and better air. And then a sputtering Aleta, battle-axe in hand, broke through the debris with the pale dawn. "Hecate's heaving hem but it's been a three-wind night!"

"May it be a better morning, my lady," I said gravely. I looked up at her steadily and inscrutably, and then up at the pale dawndark behind her that shaded and softened her features. Aleta had taken a few final swings at some tree branches which were partially blocking the entrance before resting her axe's head on the ground and leaning hard on the handle. She was panting as if her last statement had robbed her of words. I started to probe her mind and faltered the moment I got behind her physical exhaustion and the knowledge that she had been clearing rocks on my behalf all night. I did not want to know what Ellisand might have said if the binding spell had broken in the night, and I did not want to know if my illusion had failed yet. But then I steeled myself and went for the heart, because I couldn't *not* know. But I still came up with nothing more alarming than tired irritation and relief at finishing a hard task.

It took Aleta half a minute to finally ask between gasps, "You mean you *lived*? Horse and all?"

"Praise Athena."

"Why? It wasn't Her fault." I anxiously probed again and still only came up with irritation and relief. Aleta then added, still panting, "Athena didn't move you to dig out your end." She dropped to the ground and closed her eyes, leaning back into the diminished pile of tree branches and twigs that still occupied a corner of the opening, clearly determined to catch breath and strength before speaking again. I decided the best thing I could do was remain sitting and watching her quietly. When she recovered a little breath, she opened her eyes and sat up a little, blurting crossly, "If you can destroy a small hill what in the name of Zeus's zygotes prevented you from blasting open the avalanche that filled the opening?"

"Unconsciousness," I said sternly, with a slight rebuke in my voice. "It takes a lot more than you realize to destroy a member of the high clergy, and in return for the favor, I sustained more damage than was good for me." Then I made eye contact, and said slowly and deliberately, "But you're clear now. Praise Athena."

I was gratified to see Aleta look a little embarrassed over her outburst. She didn't say anything for about a minute, and so I remained silent to increase her chagrin. Finally she spoke. "I'm sorry. I should have thanked you." She paused, then added, "Are you all right?"

"Yes," I lied, thinking of Ellisand and not wanting to appear anxious. "Are you?"

"No. It was Jove's junked job—sorry, Brother, it was the gods' own work clearing the debris and every muscle in my body hurts like Hera's hagged honor." She leaned back again as she said this, closing her eyes, too exhausted to apologize for her second impiety. I chose to ignore it. "Even taking turns to sleep, it was a job," she mumbled. "Because we never really took turns. Baniff hasn't the size for this sort of work, and your traveling companion doesn't seem to have the inclination. He's about as useful as Ceres's hunger at midsummer. Kept pretending he couldn't get his own sleeves off—slept as much as he possibly could. So most of it fell to me. I could use half a day just to rest, and since we're no longer being pursued," she sighed, "I might as well."

"Aleta," I said softly, "thank *you* for your persistence." She waved her hand impatiently and rolled over on the twigs to sleep, as if my words were a nuisance to the moment. But something in the arch of her back bespoke acknowledgment of my gratitude. It was important to Aleta that I consider us even. I did not wake her. I stood quietly, took my stallion's bridle, and led him out into the early-morning side of dawn.

From the opening of the rock shelter I could see where the ridge we had descended last night had been partially destroyed by Mirra's blast, and that a small-sized avalanche had indeed buried the opening. Really there ought to be a rule against clerics having poor aim, for if there was a rule involved, Mirra certainly would have discovered the sense to hit the other side. From the size of the pile of rubble a few feet away I knew that Aleta had to have been working terribly hard and steadily through most of the night to free me.

I looked north across the valley. The sky was clearing violet over the mountains and promising blue over Threle. The path we had been riding led off through the sparse trees in the valley, bending off around the clump of trees where Baniff had stopped last night. I did not see either Baniff or Ellisand, but I saw Baniff's pony and Aleta's stallion tied near the clump. I glanced back at Aleta, who was now blissfully unconscious, and slowly led my horse down the path into the valley, considering the situation I had gotten myself into and the fact that I had no real strategy for getting myself out. Since Aleta had worked all night apart from the others, it was still entirely possible that my game was up, and without my ring, my silly impetuous illusion would flicker and fail. That is, if it hadn't done so already. I had no idea how long the illusion would coast on Ellisand's belief, but I knew with Baniff around that Ellisand's belief wouldn't be coasting for long. I also had no idea if my binding spell still held or if Ellisand was now capable of speaking freely about his imprisonment in Kursen. So I was looking for Baniff and Ellisand.

I didn't see them. I kept walking my horse through the rush and sigh of the falling leaves that skimmed his neck and found the ground, through the sharp pinecone smell of what I knew would be a sharper day, through long morning shadows and wide sun, every step closer to Threle, every thought more open-ended than the last, until at last there were no thoughts, and I was just walking. Walking through all the sensations of morning. Walking in a feeling I can only describe as empty anticipation.

I don't know how much distance from the rock shelter I had covered before I was finally thinking of nothing. One step, then another, and all without thinking I was suddenly taking pleasure in the fancy that the mountains were singing, or that the colors in their peaks were. Another step and there *was* music, I believe. And then another and my heart whipped fear and trembling all under my skin because I knew it was Ellisand's music and I knew that by all the rules of magic I was not supposed to be hearing it and so my instinctive reaction was that something very wrong had happened.

I stopped and listened, wondering irrelevantly why his lyre wasn't tied to my horse, and then remembering that I had handed it to Baniff in the inn. In all the confusion I probably wouldn't have noticed if Baniff had decided to tie the instrument onto his pony or onto Aleta's stallion. Probably Aleta's stallion, I decided, for I had ridden behind the pony yesterday and surely would have noticed it. Ellisand was probably with Baniff now, probably playing to him, probably telling him everything.

I took another few steps before I could tell that the music was coming directly from behind a line of trees which hugged a bend in the path just ahead. So I quickly tied my stallion to one of the trees and approached quietly in the direction of the music. I saw that Ellisand was sitting alone in a morning meadow and playing his lyre to the sun and the mountains. As I walked stealthily up behind him I also saw that he had managed to tear off his sleeves at the shoulder, and that he cringed in pain from his arm wound as he played, but that he did play—beautifully—and that his hands were whole and real as the sun. And he was singing quite clearly of his imprisonment in Kursen Monastery, so I knew that all my binding had broken. I sat on the wet cold ground behind him and waited for him to finish, sure that he was unaware of my presence and not at all sure of what I was going to say. The only thing I found in his thoughts was his music and the pain in his arm, along with an impatience that his wound made playing more difficult. Even as he sang of imprisonment he wasn't thinking of his real experiences in Kursen, only of his music, which was probably more real to him than his life.

Because I also sensed that he was hungry, I manifested a loaf of bread from my own scrip, which was tied to my stallion, and warmed it with a witchworking until it got soft and fresh and the scent of fresh baking spread through the air. Ellisand stopped playing in the middle of a chord and turned suddenly around. Our eyes made a long uncomfortable contact which neither of us cared to break. Then I wordlessly offered him the bread, as if it were an apology.

He took it and ate. "Thanks, Lew." He said this in Sarana, hesitantly, in a voice which lacked its usual ease. He used the word "parana", which usually implies a general "thanks for everything" as opposed to a thanks for a particular action. He finished the entire loaf and started to stretch his arms and back, out of habit, I supposed, for he immediately stopped short, groaning and wincing at the wound he had temporarily forgotten. "Parana," he repeated quietly, as if he were cautiously looking for some cue from me. He was unaccustomed to the feeling of needing to be helped out conversationally.

"Vo keim o anche et mein. You are welcome to all and more." I made the archaic, formal response in a voice of warm generosity because I knew the words wouldn't reveal anything of my anxiety and confusion, and I wished my tone to indicate that I desired him to continue speaking as he would.

He nodded. Apparently my response had cleared something very important between us, for he suddenly seemed to regain some, but not all, of his habitual casualness. That is, his body suddenly seemed looser and so he was able to stretch himself a little now. But he glanced around the meadow, avoiding further eye contact. "Looks like your buddy Baniff made the trip back for naught." Baniff's absence was offered as a safe subject, one that would prevent us from discussing the events in Medegard.

"Where'd he go?" I asked casually.

"To see if Countess Clio was ready to give up and move on." He smiled briefly, but completely. He *was* feeling easier now. "Guess she is." The title reminded me that Aleta could indeed be a countess by now, and sole ruler of County Clio if she and the Threlan army could ever get it back. I hadn't really thought of Aleta as a ruler-in-exile until this moment, and for some reason I took a moment to consider it. My sudden silence seemed to embarrass Ellisand again.

"Hey, Lew, I didn't mean it that way. Baniff wouldn't have just given up—not without trying everything possible to dig you out first, believe me. The poor guy felt really bad about leaving everything in the countess's capable hands—but what can you do when you're three feet tall? I felt bad for the guy—he just sat poking a fire and staring at the stars all night. Least that's what I saw whenever I woke from a muscle ache." He looked chagrined at the unintended reference to our fight, and said quickly, "Anyway, as soon as the sun came up he didn't even take the horse path back but hurried in a straight line because the growth is fairly sparse here and so he said he could get back to the ledge faster." I sat silently, determined now not to help him out, determined to see what I could learn from what he freely chose to offer me. "Too bad you missed each other."

I waited a beat, and said evenly, "Yes, too bad."

Ellisand paused before adding, "Hey, maybe you ought to go back and find him."

"It makes more sense to stay put here and let them find me. Besides, I don't want to be around when he wakes up Aleta. That'll be a swearing match to grace the gods from here to Sunreturn." I laughed a little and so did Ellisand, although not quite as much as I. But he did raise his eyebrows in merry appreciation and surprise at my statement, as if to say, "Yeah, right." For a moment it felt strangely like we were friends. "Anyway, they'll see my—*our* horse in the path when they lead their own mounts back. Then we can all ride on into Threle together." This excuse was the only one I could think of for buying more time alone with him. I was desperate to discover how it was that I could now see Ellisand's hands and hear his music. "And while we're waiting—" I grinned encouragingly. "—I'd really like to hear you play something for me." I leaned back expectantly on my hands.

He flashed the brightest, easiest, sincerest smile I'd ever seen anyone lay claim to, and said lightly, "Anytime, buddy. You got it." Then he picked up his lyre, and played half a minute of exquisitely delicate riffs from a tune he knew was one of my favorites before suddenly stopping and saying, "You know, Lew, there was awhile there, right after your blast, when none of us was even sure who won the fight. But since there was only one blast and no one came after us, we decided that the other cleric lost."

"The other cleric did lose."

"Right. But when they rode back to look for you, they still didn't know who or what they'd find behind the avalanche. I walked back to check for myself and when I got there, I heard Baniff suggest that you and the other monk might have hit each other simultaneously. The countess wasn't interested in a theoretical explanation. She was already chopping rocks. Practical lady."

"Yes, Aleta is the gods' own practical—sometimes."

"Hey, Lew—I—" He paused. "Want some chaia?"

"No. But please, feel free."

He took some chaia out of one of his pockets, lit a roll of it in the embers from what was presumably Baniff's fire, cupped his hand, dragged, and continued. "Anyway, I told them both that I was sure you'd won and that you were in there. That if you can blast an inn, you can blast a ridge, and that I'd seen you blast an inn."

And so that's when the binding broke. Every one of my muscles turned into winter. I could not show the turning. Instead, I said carefully, repeating the story I gave Baniff, "The other cleric blasted the inn. You saw me turn the blast, which would have hit the stables."

"Right. That's what Baniff said. Anyway, we had a long conversation about you while Aleta chopped away and Baniff said that if you had the strength to turn all that energy once, you could certainly turn all that energy again and so perhaps you had been buried alive and were not really dead at all."

This time I paused. "Those were his exact words?"

Ellisand made significant eye contact over his chaia roll and then looked down. "Yeah, Lew, that's what he said to me."

"Well." This time I looked around the meadow, considering. "That's an interesting way for Baniff to put things." And it was, if he were thinking of more than the avalanche. "You must have had quite a conversation."

"We did. Hey, I wanted to help dig but nothing would get my sleeves off, not even Baniff's little knife. Have no idea what you did there, guy. I finally bit them off this morning by tearing through the fabric near the shoulder. Really, Lew, I'm from northern Gondal—what made you think I couldn't handle cold?" Ellisand was clearly trying to change the subject away from his conversation with Baniff, but his question conveyed a puzzling tinge of gratitude and under his light tone there was a very strange sense that he had been thoroughly touched to the heart.

"Don't know," I said helplessly. "I guess I wasn't about to take chances."

"Yeah," he said gently. He wanted to say something very important and couldn't bring himself to do so. So he took a few drags on the chaia as an excuse for not speaking, and then said, as if he meant to change the subject again and couldn't quite bring himself to do that either, "After losing Liese's son I don't blame you. That must have been hard."

"Some things are beyond cure. A cleric learns to accept that." I waited before asking, "So you don't think I killed him anymore?"

"I don't know." He shrugged. "I don't care. Look, Lew—I have to say it, like I said to Baniff. You saved my life—twice."

"I saved your music," I corrected him.

"Same thing," he said quickly, shyly, as if he didn't like saying or admitting it. But since I had finally broached what he'd been struggling to say, there was no going back. "I don't know exactly what it is between you and Cathe, but I do know that whatever it is it's important to you and you jeopardized it—and maybe more—for my music, and I rewarded you by nearly getting us killed. Baniff explained a lot of things to me last night—it's a dangerous world. Monasteries aren't the only places where musicians have to be careful—I saw the destruction in town." He closed his eyes. "Look, I'm not angry. I screwed up. You did what you had to do to get us both out of town in one piece."

"I did what I had to do to save your music."

And thus we both dismissed the beating. I knew it would never be mentioned again, save possibly in jest. "Lew—I *don't* think you killed Yolan."

"I didn't," I said cheerfully. "Yolan posed no threat to your art. And you might say that the only thing I've ever killed for is art."

He nodded. We sat in silence, critic and artist, in the plain good sun near the border of Threle, and we felt no shame. Ellisand grinned. "Hey, Lew, you're all right. Glad you didn't accept my hands were beyond cure when you worked your monk-illusion."

So did he know all along that my prayer to Hecate was only an act to encourage him to believe I was working a powerful healing spell to restore his hands? How could he possibly know that I had actually worked an illusion on him through my ring? And if he did know, how could he have been able to believe that his hands had been healed? How could the illusion have worked?

"*What?* What illusion?" I asked, unwilling to reveal to him the nature of my spell until I knew more. "You know I prayed to Hecate for a healing—"

"Yes, and Hecate has a wonderful reputation for healing artists," he responded with gentle sarcasm. "But thanks, you wanted me to believe in your little prayer act of illusion, so I did—what the hell. I'll believe anything once."

"Is belief a choice?"

"No, it's a job." He was teasing now.

"Ellisand—I don't know how to say this—but to me your hands were invisible—I couldn't see them or even hear your music until now."

"Well, Lew, you're the critic. What do I know? You probably *believed* you couldn't." I considered that. He was right, I obviously believed I couldn't see his hands, because as far as I knew, I had merely worked an illusion and not actually healed them. And since it is a principle of magic that no one who works an illusion spell can experience his own illusion, I certainly didn't expect to see his hands. And so my illusion ring, which I was wearing during our travels, probably strengthened my belief. And it wasn't until I was looking at the mountains, *and thinking of nothing*, that is, until my mind was cleared of belief and my illusion ring was destroyed, that I heard his music, all unaware.

"Ellisand—it's not supposed to happen this way. It's too much to ask the gods."

"Come on, Lew, use common sense. An artist is his work. Therefore, an artist is his illusion, because all art is fantasy, is illusion."

"That's logical."

"Therefore, the illusion of hands you tried to create for me through your phony prayer—"

"—was real. Was real for you. Your music made it real. That is, you believed so thoroughly in my ability to heal your hands that your belief that you could actually play your lyre again transformed itself into your music. And since you are your music, and you are real, your hands . . . could not remain mere illusion, but became real."

"You're the critic. But you healed me through a creative act. You were *acting*, Lew, and I was your captive audience." I stared, incredulous, for some reason touched to the heart as he had been earlier. Ellisand tried to lighten the mood. "Uh, I *believe* that's a pun." He smiled. He *was* teasing me.

"That song you were playing when I came upon you—the one about—" Now I couldn't speak the name. "—Kursen. What is it called?"

" 'The Gift of the Sea.' "

It figured. I just started laughing like a madman, and Ellisand started laughing because I was a madman, and we were actually having a merry time of it when I noticed Baniff and Aleta coming across the meadow, looking glummer than a pair of soggy moon-moths in a weeklong thunderstorm. They had clearly just exchanged a wonderfully heavy package of insults and I couldn't tell who had gotten the worst of it—but as Baniff looked slightly more dour than Aleta, I supposed he had. And since a quick probe brought back extreme suspicion, I knew that Ellisand had told him just about everything there was to tell.

"Hey, buddy," I called out gaily, for some reason feeling totally prepared for whatever was about to fall out between us, "you look a little down. Would a bottle of conjured beer help conjure back your good humor?"

"That's *all* we need now," said Aleta. "Beer and—" She sniffed contemptuously. "—*chana*! See your friend here managed to get his sleeves off for *chana*."

"Hey, Countess, did you say *chana*?" Ellisand was his old self again, and switched easily to bantering in Botha. "Good stuff. Got any? More potent than Kantish homegrown."

"How many languages do you know?" I asked out of curiosity.

"More than a few. It's the elvish blood and constant travel."

"I'd have given a bundle of *chana* for *your* help last night," said Aleta icily. "And the Furies' fifth fever just to be able to sleep the rest of today." This last was said just as icily to Baniff. She threw her riding cloak on the wet ground, plopped down, and closed her eyes. "We ride at noon," she murmured, and passed out, cradling her battle-axe liked a stuffed toy.

"The general's never been much for protocol," I explained to Ellisand.

"General?" he asked, clearly intrigued.

"It's a long story—hey, Baniff." Baniff was looking pale and blank and steadily mistrustful, but somehow my certainty that he now knew I was evil only left me feeling relieved and easy with myself. "Pull up a blade of grass, guy." I conjured three dark thick ales, the best I was capable of, considering the limitations of all conjured food and drink, and passed them around. "And taste a drink to enemy glory."

Ellisand tilted back his head and gulped an appreciative mouthful and I swallowed a little, but Baniff didn't touch his. I probed him again. He knew I was evil, all right. He had been thinking about that single fact all night by his fire. He knew that I had an association with Cathe, for Ellisand had told him, and my probe told me that it had long been no secret to the family that Cathe was evil, despite Cathe's own self-delusion that he was fooling them. But Baniff knew nothing of my mission, because, of course, Ellisand knew nothing of it either.

"Hey, Lew, what's enemy glory?" asked Ellisand. "Is that another monk thing?" So I told the story of the two Habundias with a great deal of relish, of how extremes always meet and come around again to their opposites, of how there is a point at which good births evil and evil births good. Ellisand greatly enjoyed the story, and said it made as much sense as anything did. Baniff kept watching me. Finally, he raised his ale and spoke.

"Here's to blastin' evil clerics." I was determined not to feel the chilling effect of his words, so I drank with him as if his pledge couldn't possibly touch me. He smacked his lips and licked off the ale froth. "Well—" He looked at me intently. "—maybe we got lucky and ye hit Cathe."

"Eh, it wasn't Cathe." I tilted back my head and took one long swallow from my bottle, as if it didn't matter whom I hit, as if I might have just assassinated the emperor himself for all I cared. "Some other spy—I mean former spy—for Roguehan." I laughed. Baniff didn't.

"So whose side are ye on, lad?" he asked quietly.

"My own," I said, suddenly serious, and I kept serious for one deep beat and no longer. Ye gods, this was going to be a delicate business, but words had always been my strength. Then I glanced playfully at Ellisand and shrugged casually. "I play for whoever pays." And we both broke into shrieks and peals of laughter, like we were truly the greatest buddies in all the worlds and shared all sorts of private jokes and could tease each other about all kinds of things—even about our own deaths if we chose. Baniff still didn't laugh. He remained studiously alert.

"So who's payin' ye?"

I decided to include Baniff in the joke. "Here's the guy of glory himself," I said to Ellisand, indicating Baniff easily with my thumb. "Hey, Baniff, remember the first time we met?"

"Aye," he said ruefully, still waiting for me to answer his question.

"Didn't you say to me then, 'I work for myself. That is, for who-ever happens to pay'?"

"Aye, probably. Sort of thing I might say. So?"

"So—what goes around comes around. Look what you got."

"I'm lookin', lad."

"Well, look close. I am a mercenary of morality. Ellisand here is a mercenary of music. You are a mercenary, plain and simple. We all know each other. Besides, you saw me work evil on Threle's behalf once before," I reminded him.

"I didn't account destroyin' an imperial camp as evil. Thought yer heart might be in the right place."

I suddenly lapsed into an absolutely luscious melancholia. "Well, comrade," I murmured softly, "you had the luxury to think that way. It's different when your spirit is held captive by an evil high priest." Then I wrenched my tone, and said harshly, "Do you have any idea what kind of discipline, what hellish tricks of mind, what consum-mate self-torture it takes to dedicate yourself to evil and get away with working good? Yes, look at me, Baniff. Take a good long look." I had him now. Baniff was terrified of both my tone and my words, and I was sure my facial expression was enough to command all his atten-tion and belief. Ellisand was my audience again, interested, attentive, fascinated, believing wholeheartedly in the illusion—but Ellisand was not frightened, for he also believed that he finally understood me. "Do you have any idea what it's like to pray and work magic and risk everything that I am, to wake up and risk eternity every day for years and years—to risk my damnable spirit, which wasn't even my own, for the only friends I ever had? To wear the enemy's glory? *Do you?*"

Baniff swallowed. "Well, lad, what can I say? I don't envy ye yer problems."

"Heart in the right place," I repeated patronizingly and sarcasti-cally, while I built up a good deal of anger. Then I smashed my bottle against the tree, showering everyone with glass shards and ale and causing both of them to jump and Aleta to wake up and curse. "I call it a blessing that after four years in Kursen Monastery I even have a heart I can call my own. Praise Hecate-Athena."

"Has it been four years, lad?"

"Hasn't it?" I made long eye contact and absolutely refused to break it, for I really was angry now.

Baniff looked at the ground first. "When ye have a life that spans centuries," said the gnome, "I guess four years doesn't feel like very much." It sounded like an apology, the way he said it.

"Baniff," I said urgently, "would you understand if I said that I want to be good? If I said that I want to get away from Cathe, and Kursen, and the empire, and all of it?"

"I don't know, lad. I gave up understandin' for drink a long time ago."

Aleta took this opportunity to grumble, "All of you, shut up. The plain fact of it is that none of you is really a mercenary and none of you really understands anything except how to keep me up. Baniff works for Threle because he's a gnome and the south won't tolerate him. Ellisand plays music because it's probably the only thing he's any good at and I suppose he can't do anything else—he sure as hell can't dig rocks. And if I were Llewelyn—and thank the gods I'm not—I'd be on my own side too, by default, because what the hell else is there? Oh, please. Spare me the rest and let me sleep."

"The reality is—we're all Threlans," I said evenly.

"The fact is, none of you are Threlan-born and Threle isn't paying any of you anything," admonished Aleta. "You're all here because you want to be. The only proper *Threlan* in Walworth's inner circle who's fighting for Threle is Walworth himself. That's reality."

"What about Mirand?" I asked.

"Mirand studied in Sunnashiven. Like ye, lad," said Baniff thoughtfully. "Back when Zelar had a post there. Thought you knew that. Why do think he never crosses the Drumuns?"

I could not show that I was stunned. The information made sense, but I had just never thought of Mirand as having southern roots. So I just said quietly and respectfully, "So my old master at one time made his own willing conversion to Threle, and threw off his master's evil to do so. What about Caethne?"

"No one ever accused Caethne of fighting for Threle," said Aleta. "The gods know where her loyalties lie—but it isn't with her country."

"Hey," said Ellisand reasonably, "the three of us are illusionists. We don't let reality control our lives. It's an occupational hazard. So if we *want* to pretend to be mercenaries—" He made eye contact with me. "—what the hell—as long as we know each other."

"Well, Baniff," I said with a hint of a choke, "do we know each other?"

He hesitated. "Ye just destroyed an evil cleric on our behalf. I can't send you back to Cathe."

"I wouldn't go, friend."

He sighed. "I guess we're still a party, then. The general and I are headed up near Disenward—where Walworth's camped and fightin' off a siege. I suppose he won't mind the extra help—wherever it comes from."

"How are the Midland cities holding out?" I asked evenly, as if everything were now settled between us and I just wanted information.

"Not well—but they're holdin'—we were hopin' a few well-placed rebellions in the south would draw Roguehan's attention away from the cities long enough for the Threlan army to bring down more supplies from northern Threle. Ah, look—didn't sleep much myself last night." He rubbed his eyes. Baniff was still overwhelmed with this turn of events and didn't want to keep speaking because he had no idea what to say. "The general's got the right idea—we ride at noon." And with that he rolled over into a rag of sun on the now-drying meadow grass and dozed. I knew it was unlikely that Baniff was completely mollified; but I also knew that Baniff was nothing if not pragmatic, and that he had made an uneasy peace with the situation because he had no other choice.

I quietly checked Ellisand's wound, which was starting to heal, and I fixed his sleeves with wizardry, spinning new material for where he had torn them off near the shoulder. There—good as new. Maybe everything now would be as good as new.

Ellisand silently offered me chaia. This time I took it, giving silent praise to Hecate for my skill with words, and as I smoked I stared steadily toward a thick cluster of bushes where I sensed evil and so knew that Mirra had been listening to my every word all morning. I remember sending "Stay the hell out of sight, get better aim, and don't believe anything you hear" once or twice before I felt her retreat. Then I watched the morning rise and the autumn sun swarm desperate in the grass and thought long and hard about the coming journey through Threle.

Nine

I believe we entered Threle in the cool blaze of an autumn noon, but I didn't really notice the exact moment we crossed into Threlan territory. I was disappointed that I missed noticing the border, for I was sure there would be a change to remark, a difference in the soil or in the clouds, a natural signpost in the tilt and scent of mountain weeds bowing to coming winter. A place between two hoofbeats where nature unmistakably divided itself and where, if I opened myself, I could feel the terrible crawl of the two Habundias smiling at each other's throats.

We rode side by side, Baniff in the middle. For the first day there was little conversation outside necessary communications concerning food and camping. Food was a problem. I was only carrying enough victuals for my own needs, for I had originally planned to travel through the southern duchies where Ellisand could perform for his own supplies. Since the plains are an empty proposition outside of the cities and their associated farmlands, it was likely that we would encounter no one to buy or bargain food from until we reached Walworth's camp near Disenward. My sense of things, which Baniff confirmed, was that the journey would take us a week or more. We were hugging the eastern side of the country and following a route nearly parallel to the one I had once taken to Loudes, since Disenward is almost directly opposite Loudes, separated by miles and miles and more miles of flatly resolute plain. The bread I had given Ellisand that morning represented a significant reduction in my own supplies, for priests of Hecate eat sparingly, and I had counted on that bread lasting me three days. I calculated that even if I gave Ellisand all my food, and did my best to still my own inevitable hunger with prayer and fasting and occasional conjurings, there wasn't enough in my packs to see him through the next week, even if he had grown used to starving in prison.

I said nothing until after we set up camp that night and we were warming ourselves at a noisily cheerful fire, a fire I had graciously created through wizardry so Baniff could feel the warmth too. He and Aleta had been planning to get through the chill nights on blankets and illusion, which meant that he was prepared to freeze and Aleta was prepared to let cold necessity conquer her usual distrust of magic. Aleta had wrapped herself in a pile of Clion army blankets and was sitting as far away from the flames as she possibly could without being completely swallowed in darkness, but as the deep chill of night on the plains narrowed and pierced through blood and muscle, she moved closer to the warmth. I set up a fine wizard shield around the four of us to keep the heat in and the cold out, and once everyone was comfortable and silently determined not to venture back into the cold, I generously offered to leave the little circle and check the horses, which were hitched with ropes to a portable post that Aleta had brought with her and that I had set up in the ground by blasting a little hole.

When I returned with bedding and camping gear, which I promptly set up, Aleta was still buried in her army blankets, despite it now being extremely warm within the shield. Her face was covered with thick tired sweat. I made a flourishing hand motion toward her in fun and she tightened the blankets around her and pulled back from the gesture in annoyance, which told me that she was using the blankets as a physical barrier between herself and the flames produced by what she clearly considered to be my horribly fearsome magic. Baniff was beginning supper preparations. He was putting together a stew of potatoes and jerky in a little pot and cursing the jerky for not softening fast enough in the warming water, so I ventured to ask if he or Aleta would be willing to trade a little of their dried meat for onions. "I didn't carry more food than would get me into Threle, and rescuing Ellisand here was a bit of an afterthought," I explained, not willing to point out that my sparse monk fare would see me easily into the Duchy of Walworth, and entirely confident that neither of them would be able to determine from the amount of my scrip that the duchy had been my original destination.

From the look of dismay on both their faces it was obvious that they had both assumed that Ellisand and I were fully prepared for this journey. Ellisand looked uncomfortably embarrassed under their stare. I felt bad for him because it really wasn't his fault that he had no food and so had to throw himself empty-handed on everyone else's dole.

"Well," said Baniff, grimly giving the pot a stir, "the worst problems always come by way of afterthoughts."

"Haven't you ever traveled the plains before?" Aleta asked Ellisand sharply.

"Sure, General, but not like this." His tone was a respectful tease meant to cover his embarrassment. He wanted to assure Aleta that he respected the gravity of the situation and that he really didn't want anyone to feel uncomfortable on his account. So despite his deep discomfort he managed to sound faintly jocular, because he felt it had fallen upon him to lighten the suddenly dismal mood.

But I also felt under his words a rough thread of self-deprecation. He knew he was traveling with two important personages in the Threlan army and he also knew that neither of them seemed to have any idea who he was. I got the impression that Ellisand wasn't used to dealing with people when he didn't have his musical reputation to stand on, and I wondered if he'd ever spent a significant amount of time with people who really didn't give a damn whether or not he could play a lyre. But be that as it may, I also sensed in him an admirable willingness to embrace this new experience, to see what would happen next.

Aleta, however, was too concerned about the food supply to be cajoled. She stared at him for about half a minute, her eyes wide with angry astonishment, obviously mistaking his light tone for an inappropriate casualness concerning a dire situation. She then repeated his words carefully, as if she couldn't quite believe what she'd just heard. "Not . . . like . . . *this?*"

Baniff looked up from the stew. He knew what was coming and seemed tacitly to approve, for Aleta was about to save him the trouble of even trying to be tactful with this worse-than-useless newcomer.

"I am sooooo very sorry that Master Minstrel here doesn't like our fine accommodations. Do forgive us, please. If we had known we were going to have a bloody *guest* to entertain on our silly little military excursion, why, I'd have brought feather beds and candied yams down from Reathe as well."

"Thanks, Countess, but I can do without Reathen yams for a few days." Ellisand was clearly trying to make a joke at his own expense by pretending he was so extremely and unbelievably spoiled that it was a great sacrifice for him to forgo yams. But the self-parody was lost on his audience, and no one laughed. There was only a deal of silence until Aleta spoke again with an annoyed sigh.

"Look, as far as I'm concerned you'd make a poor excuse for the camp dog, let alone a soldier. *You're* the whole reason we've already delayed our journey by half a day. If you'd seen fit to lower yourself to dig rocks last night, we'd have done the job in half the time."

"Aleta," I remonstrated.

She ignored me. "Can you carry an axe? A sword? If we

encounter a stray band of refugees pillaging whatever food and supplies they can find, can I trust you to fight with me?"

"You can trust me to do my best, General. Lend me your sword and I'll gladly defend your honor." He said this with an easy theatricality.

"*My honor!* We're talking about Threle and my poor county—my honor! Ares's withered arm! Lend you my sword!" She was upset by Ellisand's apparent ignorance of the issue at hand, but she was more upset at the implication that anyone would presume to handle weapons she had spent years training on. "Are you a trained fighter?"

"No."

"I'd just as soon give my precious sword to the enemy as have you drop it in the heat of battle. You don't look strong enough to hold my dagger steady, let alone use my sword correctly. *My sword!*" She looked horrified over at Baniff, who was quietly stirring stew and quite happy to let her continue. "Duke Walworth himself gave me this sword and his master wizard Mirand charged it."

"Really?" I asked. "Can I see it?" She unceremoniously handed her weapon over to me. It was a form of subtle bragging, and a sign to Ellisand that I was at least a useful member of the party. I wanted to feel Mirand's charge in preparation for my love spell. I heard Aleta continuing in fine form.

"What can you do for us? What the hell good are you? And when we get up to Disenward, am I marching with someone who can help our cause or am I carrying some two-bit milk-water dandy who needs to be fed and pampered behind the lines?" Baniff kept looking stolidly at the now-steaming pot. It was painfully obvious to all that he agreed wholeheartedly with Aleta's sentiments and that he was relieved that she had broached the topic first.

"I'm not asking for special favors, Countess."

"Special favors! Athena's angst—sorry, Llewelyn—Apollo's madness!"

"No problem," I said generously, replicating the charge in my mind, softly reacquainting myself with Mirand's special energy.

"Do you know it's war?"

"Of course, General."

"Do you know that I'm responsible for the people in my command? I want to know what you plan to do to help us."

Ellisand glanced around as if to say, "I don't see a lot of people in your command," but he remained silent on the subject.

"Do you know any magic? Are you skilled at healing? Can you

find food for us on the plains? Can you fend off winter storms? Llewelyn, *does* he know any magic?"

"I thought you disapproved of magic."

That quieted her down a little. She pulled her blankets tighter. "Any dog in a storm. I want to know why we're carrying him."

I handed back the sword. "Nice work. Mirand hasn't lost his touch."

"Hey, look," said Ellisand. "I'm here because it happened that way. I guess I don't have to eat." It was the only thing he could think of saying, and he said it in all sincerity. He really didn't want to be a burden. There was another, more deeply embarrassed silence which Ellisand bravely tried to disperse. "I mean, really. Once lived on chaia for two solid days just for the hell of it."

"You smoked *chana* for *days*?"

"And I used to go days without food in Kursen," he tried again.

"No doubt," said Baniff, suddenly looking up at me, sighing, and looking out into the plains' eternal shadows.

Ellisand didn't like the implied accusation concerning his treatment in Kursen. "Hey, it wasn't Lew's fault. He tried to feed me well, but I *chose* to starve—" Baniff and Aleta looked dourly at him. "—*chose* to starve. Uh, well," he faltered, suddenly realizing that he had said something wrong, although he wasn't quite sure what.

"Well," sniffed Aleta, "that's all rather southern of you. I feel so much better knowing that the contribution you wish to make to us is *choosing* to starve. It really bloody helps our efficiency as a fighting force." There was a long, miserable silence, broken only by the crackling flicks of the flame I stoked up, a flame which no longer sounded cheerful. It was like the flame now begrudged all of us its warmth, and we were all silently aware that our fire was just a dot of life on the merciless cold of the plains.

Aleta was again the first to speak and break the silence. Her voice was no longer angry, just resigned and businesslike. She was a responsible commander with a problem to solve. "There's nothing for it but to pool and divide the food supply. What have you got, Llewelyn?" I opened my scrip packs and showed them around. "Seeing as you brought less than a gnome's portion, Brother, we've got exactly enough scrip between the four of us for two full-sized humans to eat semireasonable meals for nearly a week." She glumly pushed the bags aside and stared at the steaming stew, which no one now seemed to want to touch. "It'll be eight days to Disenward," she said mechanically. "Ellisand's too sickly to go without eating, and I insist on leading healthy parties. Who else wants to starve?" She looked at me and then at Baniff. "If there are no volunteers then, as commander of this little unit, I shall." Ellisand looked mortified, not least because he knew there was nothing to say.

"I've lived off scruff grass before," said Baniff dolefully. "The best I can say for it is that it's good enough for the horses."

"Nonsense, buddy. Let me put my monastic training to use. I can fast for days without feeling ill effects." Everyone looked at me, partly alarmed at my casual reference to evil, which seemed to be a subject no one cared to discuss, and partly relieved that there were now only three stomachs to worry about. "Aleta and Ellisand can live off three-quarter portions, which isn't so bad, and the remainder should be adequate for Baniff."

"Are ye sure, lad?" He looked back at the bubbling stew, slightly happier at the prospect of eating, and then back at me.

"Sure as snow," I replied, resolutely turning my face from the pot and looking sweetly toward the north, where we all knew acrid storms were threatening. I saw no sense in reminding them that I wasn't much for meat broth anyway. *Make it look good—make it look like I'd do anything for my friends.* I felt Hecate's approval and so knew that She would keep me through my fast. "And of course I can stretch the food supply with conjurings, although conjured food won't do much besides stop your hunger pains. It's the residual energy of the life that once inhabited the food that nourishes, and no wizardry can create life energy where none existed. But there's always scruff grass and rainwater. Boiled, it makes a brew that's near fit for eating if you're desperate. At least that's what Caethne once told me." My careless mention of Caethne's name caused Aleta to look at me sharply through her mess of blankets. Apparently Caethne was no more acceptable a subject of polite conversation than evil. "Anyway," I continued smoothly, "the broth is quite digestible and will give us all quick energy if we need it, and warmth against the Midland winds. Don't worry, friends, we'll make it to Disenward in decent form."

"Grass broth is great," said Ellisand, trying once again to make things seem better. "I've tried it."

"So have I," said Baniff gloomily, "once't." That single word told Ellisand that he needn't try to put a good face on things. We all knew the next week would be highly uncomfortable, and not just because the rations were poor. Ellisand now knew in no uncertain terms that he was an unwelcome drag to the party and so he didn't speak much to Aleta or Baniff. And neither of them really had much to say to him either, not so much from rudeness but from the fact that there really was nothing left to say. We all knew where we stood with each other. The business at hand was getting to Disenward and that was that. And although my attempts to start conversations with Aleta and Baniff were greeted with decent enough responses, it was always me starting the conversations. No one was in a particularly talkative mood.

I knew from my mind probes that Baniff brooded a lot over the results of the local rebellion he and Aleta had kicked off. I ventured to ask once, during our second or third day of riding the sprawling changeless land, if he thought his rebellion was producing the desired effect of drawing Roguehan's forces back south, and how long Disenward could be expected to hold out. "You said Walworth's got a siege on his hands up there. How do you plan on getting into the city through a circle of imperial troops if they don't take the bait and push off?"

"Invisibly. Same way I always do in such situations." He dourly slapped his pony's neck. "Take each of ye in—one at a time."

"I imagine the general's a lot of fun in an invisible state." I was trying to include Aleta in the conversation, but she wasn't interested in anything except squinting and studying the awful distance. The horizon showed glittery with encroaching frost. The wind was pure chill as we rode.

"Aye," said Baniff absently, after a pause. " 'Cept her state's been invisible fer years now."

"Poor Clio," I breathed solemnly, as if my heart would break for her poor trampled-on little county. "Poor, bleeding land." Aleta bowed her head slightly to acknowledge my words, but kept her gaze fierce upon the horizon, hoping beyond the land's limit to see troops heading south. "How long do you think it will take the emperor's wizards to send word up to Disenward of the fine work you've both done? I'm sure they have the means to track and send messages over great distances."

"Not long." Baniff was thinking about the numberless acts of self-destruction in Medegard. "Was it fine work, lad? Never thought to see the Medegardans—" He stopped.

I wanted him to continue. "It's terrible to see people burning their own lives to shreds," I said softly and encouragingly, as if I too felt all his pain and were capable and willing to carry it. My clerisy worked.

He sighed. " 'Twas never the intent. They were supposed to make things miserable for the guards at all the border crossin's—send the cocked crow's confusion up and down the main road through the duchy as far as possible. But war is a rogue's scandal and who knows it better than a rogue."

"All I know," said Aleta unexpectedly, "is that the only thing I see creeping along the horizon is winter." That sealed the gloom I had tried to destroy, but I made one more attempt to keep communication going.

"It's possible that the troops could be retreating well beyond our line of sight toward the southwest, to reinforce Threlanche or Ignothen while the imperial troops holding those cities rush south."

"Anythin's possible," said the illusionist.

Except further conversation, presumably, for nothing else of note got said and eventually I just gave up trying to speak. And so it was a rather silent journey for the most part, across a land so chill it could freeze frost. Of course I always made our fire. And when Aleta's stallion's cinch broke, I gallantly repaired it with wizardry, despite her protests that she could handle riding in a loose saddle. And I respected the unspoken bounds of conversation—no references to evil, no references to Caethne. I deliberately made myself the most useful member of the party and I did my absolute best to create the illusion of friendship among us all, even as I prayed to Hecate for further guidance through every night of unmoving cold. And I always volunteered to keep guard more than the others during those terrible shivery nights, which was greatly appreciated, although there was really nothing to guard against except Mirra.

But Mirra really was keeping her distance now. You see, the plains are so flat you can see into the next century if you stand still long enough and winter doesn't distract your concentration, so if Mirra had been within a day's journey, it was possible that one of us would have noticed her dark figure crossing the plain. She had heard we were going to Disenward, and so I assumed she had resolved to do her duty and follow, but I was pleasantly surprised to learn that for once she was displaying something like sense by keeping a great distance behind us. It was only through Hecate that I even felt that Mirra was still "spotting" me, for sometimes while I prayed I felt the long low pull of evil tug and rebound south behind me across the plains. And I always took advantage of the rebound to send a "keep distant" message, which seemed to have its effect. But I knew she was out there, all right, just beyond the horizon of sight, moving steadily behind us toward Disenward.

The increasing cold must have suited Ellisand's Gondish blood, for he steadily recovered enough health to contribute to caring for the horses and to setting up camp. It was usually Ellisand's job to keep guard in the early morning, in the dim predawn hours. And although he performed his duties faithfully, and with the skill of one used to travel, he understood that he had no worth as a fighter or a magician and remained in a chastened silence throughout our journey. No one cared to remark upon his contribution as it was the only thing he seemed to have to offer us.

I had been up most of the fourth night of the journey, volunteering to take Baniff's shift as well as my own, for Baniff felt especially tired that day and I wasn't about to miss an opportunity to show my goodwill. And this was the coldest night of all, so I built up our fire to the most heated pitch I could manage and spent most of the night wrapped in warmth and communing with Hecate, thinking about what I would need to do to convince Walworth and Mirand of my friendly intent when we reached Disenward, and asking Hecate if it were at all possible to send Mirra back to Sunnashiven. Anyway, through staring into my own flames and feeding my own thoughts, I went into a more profound trance than I'd planned to and when I came out of it there was a fierce rain threatening to beat through our wizard shield, the fire was practically out, and Ellisand was gone.

And when it rains on the Midland plains it rains forever, and visibility is nonexistent. I knew it was past dawn from the fact that the fire's coals were practically extinguished, but the storm was keeping everything around us fairly dark so I couldn't see Ellisand anywhere. I strengthened our shield and created more fire for light as well as heat. The noise of the suddenly rising flames roused my two companions.

Aleta sat up sharply in her blankets the way she did every morning and quickly began to arm and prepare herself for the journey. Baniff groaned, fell back asleep, smacked his lips, and pulled himself reluctantly toward the flames with outstretched hands, staring through bleary eyes and trying to let the fire's warmth ease the transition to wakefulness. I went out into the cold and rain, called Ellisand several times, got no response, and returned wet and freezing to see my companions sharing some of my dried bread.

"Where'd ye go, lad? Where's yer friend?"

"And how are the horses holding up?" asked Aleta simultaneously.

"The horses are doing as well as can be expected, General. And as to Ellisand, he was gone when I woke up this morning."

"You mean he didn't stand guard through his shift?"

"I have no idea," I had to admit. "But I'd like to shield a torch and take my stallion out to look for him."

"Ye mean ye think he's run off?" asked Baniff.

"I don't know." I looked steadily at Aleta. "What do you think?"

"I think he picked one hell of a nice day for it," said Baniff, looking out at the miserable weather. "Woke up this mornin' and felt like it was a fine hour for a bit of a walkabout myself." He said this without a trace of humor, then he shook his head and stretched.

"I think we don't have enough supplies to delay our journey looking for him," Aleta said. Then she added softly, "I'm sorry, Llewelyn, I know he's your friend, but it's war. I can't let him jeopardize our welfare. Of course, if you wish to look for him, that's your concern, but Baniff and I must move on."

"I'm afraid she's right, lad," echoed Baniff.

As I was considering what to do, we heard one of the horses cough and then Ellisand suddenly emerged out of the rain and into our circle. He was absolutely drenched, and he was completely covered with wet plastered sand, as if he'd been out rolling around on the wet ground. His hair and eyes were matted with wet and there was sand smeared across his mouth and left cheek. You could hear water sloshing in his boots. But he was smiling jauntily as if he were quite proud of himself, and he was carrying one of my scrip bags, the last contents of which had been eaten during the previous night.

"Top o' the mornin' to ye," greeted Baniff. Aleta said nothing. She just kept looking at him and trying very hard to figure out what the hell he was doing. She wasn't the only one.

"Got the best of the morning right here," boasted Ellisand, cheerfully ignoring everyone's stares and indicating his bag.

"Where'd you go?" I asked coldly. "We almost left without you."

"Hunting, Lew. Hunting. Got us some real breakfast—Gondish special, you're going to love this."

"What in the shadow of Artemis's hazy bow is there to hunt in a rainstorm in the plains?" asked Aleta shortly. But I could tell that she was now genuinely intrigued, for clearly there was something in the bag, and perhaps she could learn something useful.

"Got any dried honey left?" asked Ellisand.

"Some. We were going to eat it with our bread."

"I was going to soften it first," I explained, as Ellisand took what remained of the dried honey.

"Do the honors, Lew." I did so. "Excellent. Now give me the pot." Baniff handed the pot to him and Ellisand held it outside the shield where it quickly filled with rainwater. "Now," he said in his best seductive stage voice, "close your eyes and wait."

"Wait for what?" asked Baniff reasonably.

"The best Gondish delicacy *you* ever tasted, guy. Used to love these at Sunreturn when I was a kid."

"Well, be quick about it," said Aleta, closing her eyes.

"Hey, he's only trying to be useful," I whispered.

"That's what I'm afraid of," she replied.

"We're most obliged," said Baniff out loud, both to cover our whispers and to show that he at least appreciated Ellisand's attempt to contribute something to our little gang. I heard Ellisand making noises with the pot and humming happily. He clearly enjoyed concocting whatever it was he was concocting. Then I smelled the broth steaming and knew there was meat involved. I gagged a little.

"Smells good, guy, but a little too heavy for breaking my fast on. I'm afraid I'll have to pass." I really didn't want to make an issue of not eating meat as I didn't want to bring up the subject of my evil.

"Right, Lew, gotcha." I heard him stir the pot a little more. "Almost—there." He dumped water on the ground somewhere. "Now for the honey and we're all set. Beautiful—couldn't have done it better at home. My lady Countess, open your mouth and allow me—"

"Not unless I see what it is first." Aleta opened her eyes. So did I. "Baniff?"

"What the hell," said the gnome. "It's an adventure."

He extended his tongue and Ellisand put a little honey-golden glob of something on it. "Hey, this is great," said Baniff sucking and swallowing. "Sweet and then more sweet—quite tasty."

"They're actually not too bad with southern ale," said Ellisand, "although you wouldn't think so at first."

"Well, pass the Krygon, then," said Baniff. Everyone laughed, and Ellisand placed another glob on his tongue while Baniff sucked and swallowed.

"Glad you like them. They're all for you. They're easier to catch drowned after a good storm. The water fills their burrows and lifts them right out."

Baniff suddenly opened his eyes as Ellisand was lifting a third little glob out of the pot. "Burrows? What do ye call these treats?"

"Candied mice."

The gnome's eyes got bigger than the pot as he ran out of the circle with bulging cheeks. Soon he was upchucking honey and mice all over his feet. I ran to support his shoulders as he threw up into the ground and into the rain. "Baniff, Baniff, c'mon, man, please don't be angry. I'm sure he didn't know—"

"Goddamn—wretched," he sputtered and retched again. "I ought to throw him out in the storm and ride off myself. Turn his wretched tongue to glue and send him beggin' handless again back to Kant—"

"Baniff!" I had to check an impulse to hit him as he emptied himself. "There. Pull yourself tight. Are you with me?" I asked soothingly, chanting, "You're feeling better now." He straightened a little. "We're only halfway to Disenward and we've got to make it together."

"No we don't." Suddenly he looked in the distance, his attention abruptly arrested by a strange line of bobbing lights along the distant horizon. "Put out the fire," he said urgently. I had already done so with a sweep of my hand, but I also made sure the shield was still holding in warmth. When we hurried back into the circle, Aleta and Ellisand were sitting on opposite sides of the ashes. Ellisand had his back to Aleta. He was puffing on chaia and looking as miserable as anyone could look while doing so. Aleta was facing his back. She was huddled over the pot and eating the mice.

"Hey, these aren't too bad," she announced. "I ought to look into getting some for the army."

"I'm glad you kiddies are finally getting along," I said cheerfully.

"Why did you put the fire out? I'm still eating."

"Aleta," said Baniff, "got somethin' for ye to look at." He directed her gaze toward the lights on the western horizon, and as she looked up, a little bit of honey dribbled from her mouth. "What is it?"

Aleta stood and peered over Ellisand's bent head, waving away the clouds of chaia.

"It's Roguehan's army," answered Ellisand unexpectedly. "And it's heading northeast. Toward Disenward. Saw the lights this morning when I went—out." He almost said "hunting." Everyone stared at him.

"Why didn't you tell us?" asked Aleta, voicing everyone's thoughts.

"Because I figured, what can you do? It's there. It's coming." There was a certain logic to this, I had to admit.

"Well, General," said Baniff, "what *can* you do?"

She considered a long time. "Keep pushing on to Disenward and lend our hand to fight off the siege." Aleta suddenly sounded very old. "No change in plans."

"See," said Ellisand. "My point exactly." No one was amused. "Well, hey, what do I know? I thought the rebellion was supposed to attract the army back south and all that."

"My guess is that there is so much utter destruction spreading through the south that Roguehan's army is forced to march north," I said. "The town we left was utterly destroyed, and there's no reason to suspect that the Medegardans' desperate self-destruction didn't spread through the duchies. There may be absolutely no supplies to be had at all from the south now, and so the troops holding the southern Midland cities are forced to take the northern Midland cities. And that tells me the southern cities have just about exhausted their stores. Yes, and they are headed right toward Disenward. I'm sure another line of battalions is moving toward Loudes."

"Well, we'd best get moving," said Aleta grimly. "And no more night fires." So we gathered and packed the rest of our gear and drove our horses hard and silent toward Disenward.

And we saw no more movement along the horizon. Based on our speed, and the fact that we now only stopped at odd intervals to rest the horses and ourselves, I was confident that we had outpaced the army by about a day and a half. I remember nothing but a tense flat hurry through a cold stretch of time, and the terrible large cold sky with a brown smudge for sun. There was no talking, only the heavy thoughts of my companions pinging me like the rain and sleet we rode through, determined thoughts of getting to Disenward and seeing what needed to be done, because to think or speculate on anything deeper was—well, with Medegard for a model, no one cared to pursue the obvious.

But when we reached the sere autumn farmlands which marked the outskirts of Disenward's jurisdiction, all thoughts stopped themselves in apprehension, for there was no movement here either. There was no sign of siege. There was no sign of life within. The city had been visibly brown and square to us for about half a day, and as we sat upon our horses at the edge of the cultivated lands, it was now sharply and clearly brown and square, with black-pointed roofs on rectangular towers, but it was just as dead and distant. I had expected Disenward to contrast with the plains, the way the red towers of Loudes did, but Disenward's structures are mostly square and squat and all of them are nearly the same color as the ground. On a dark day you can be almost upon the farmlands before the city becomes recognizable. The fields were covered by a fragile ice and looked like they had been completely harvested, not burned. As we rode we saw no one, and even our horses instinctively slowed, as if there was something wrong here.

Baniff remarked that we should have reached the camp by now, which had been located as an outpost just beyond the cultivated lands. Walworth had surrounded the fields with his people to keep off attackers while the city dwellers helped the farmers harvest. But now there was absolutely no sign of a camp, as if the camp had never existed, as if everything living had moved off into another life path decades ago. Perhaps Walworth had succeeded in driving off the troops and perhaps Mirand had cleared the land, but still there ought to be some sign or feel of a struggle, I thought. And if Roguehan had taken the city, there ought to be some indication of life within the walls. I wondered if Mirand was in there, in the city, and if he was aware of my presence yet.

Our horses were skittish on the ice we rode over. Not that the ice was slippery, because, strange as this sounds, it wasn't. But it split and cracked into haphazard spidery jags beneath our horses' hooves and the animals became distrustful of their footing and kept refusing to move. The ice didn't break under pressure, it just broke. Long gaping holes appeared if you looked at the ground too long. There were points at which the sun even seemed to break holes, and the horses' breath caused cracks to form. I got the impression that nothing around this city could last, not even ice in bitter cold.

We kept urging our horses toward the city gate, which did not appear to be guarded. We kept gazing up at empty towers. I could feel Aleta quickly formulating what our next move should be and coming up with nothing she could convince herself to speak to us about. But she could see no reason not to approach the walls, and our supplies were nearly depleted, so the city was our last stop by default.

We had gotten within two hundred feet of the gate before it became apparent that someone had seen us, for suddenly a single horse and rider emerged and galloped toward us at breakneck speed. Aleta kicked her steed into a gallop to meet the rider so Baniff and I followed, bounding over the shattering ice and feeling the hardening slap of freezing wind as we rode. The rider pulled short when Aleta reached him and saluted her stiffly. Then he half saluted us by way of acknowledgment. I heard him address Aleta crisply in Botha.

"General." It was Sir Perry. His face and hair had grown thinner but he still carried himself like a soldier. His pride in greeting his commander contrasted sadly with his ill-fitting uniform and the strange silent feel of the city behind him.

Aleta returned his salute. "Captain."

"General." He repeated, saluting back again because Aleta hadn't dropped her salute. The repetition reminded her to drop her hand to her side. "Mr. Baniff." Baniff was too cold to react. Perry then noticed my clerical robe under my riding cloak and said with a hint of puzzle, "Brother." He did not recognize or remember me. He noticed Ellisand sitting behind me and merely nodded, then he sniffed, threw back his shoulders, and looked steadily and alertly at his commander.

"How are my troops holding out, Captain?" she asked.

"Well enough, my lady. We lost three men and a woman to fever last week when the killing frost came. No one else."

"I shall want their names. I shall want their effects saved for their families."

"It is done."

"Isolate all other cases of fever lest it spread."

"It is also done upon General Walworth's orders."

"How are provisions?"

"We can support ourselves for three weeks without reinforcements," said Perry flatly, throwing back his shoulders even farther.

Aleta took this news stoically. "All right, take me to Commander Walworth, that I may give him a full report. And see that my party here gets a good meal. Use my rations if you need to." She looked at me. "Especially the brother. He's gone without the longest."

"General," said Perry with a trace of hesitation that even his soldier's training couldn't completely cover. "We succeeded in driving off our attackers into the west four days ago. But no sooner was victory ours than Master Wizard Mirand learned that a large contingent of Roguehan's troops are heading toward Disenward. That's why we broke camp and went inside the walls. General Walworth has decided to withdraw north, where his army will be closer to the supplies they need, and to leave the food in the city for Roguehan's hungry soldiers. The general hopes that the provisions will delay them here long enough for the army to regroup up north and the civilian inhabitants of Disenward who cannot fight for sickness and wounds to find shelter in Reathe. I have orders from the commander for you to ride up to his duchy and tell the duchess to make preparations for his arrival, as he intends to set up command quarters at home. His soldiers are insisting that he do that, for if he is lost, the war is lost."

The war is lost anyway, I thought.

"General, this horse is prepared and carries enough supplies for you to reach the Duchy of Walworth."

"I won't go," said Aleta. "I belong with my troops, in action, not behind the scenes preparing for action." She really didn't want to be alone with Caethne.

"I know my way to the duchy, and I'm sure I could find the duchess's castle," offered Ellisand, who saw an opportunity to quit the party gracefully and make everyone happier.

"No," said Aleta. "It's too important to risk having you screw up.

You stay here and play marches for the civilians or something, but I don't trust you to carry messages entrusted to me."

Baniff looked at the stallion and said, "I could ride the distance if ye help me mount."

"It's an impractically large steed for you to take on a long journey." Aleta looked at me. "Llewelyn?"

"Guess I'm elected." I felt remiss at leaving Ellisand in the company of the others, especially after all the trouble I'd taken to get him this far, but there was no longer any strategic or magical necessity for keeping together, and I wasn't about to compromise my opportunity to get some time alone with Caethne. That was a fine turn of events. Praise Hecate for that one. Especially if She didn't hold my whimsical act of goodness on Ellisand's account against me. If I was going to be effective in my vengeance, I knew it was best to separate, so I was grateful Aleta forbid him to go, because it prevented me from having to explain to him the real reason we were separating.

"Know the way, lad?"

"Never been up there, but I know there's a main road starts in Reathe and ends in Walworth—and that Reathe is a day's journey north of Disenward."

"You'll see a faint track in the plains north of Disenward that leads straight to the main road in Reathe. Tradin' route. Follow it. Walworth is a four-day ride from Reathe if ye move swiftly. I guess we'll be behind ye."

"Reckon with all the people we're moving out, you'll beat us by a day or two," said Aleta.

"I will do my utmost for the cause." I said devoutly, glad that things were working out this way, not least because I was sure to lose Mirra at Disenward. I could imagine her look of "not fair" when she finally got here and found only Roguehan's army occupying the place. And I could imagine her trying to explain to the emperor how it was she lost track of me and ended up back with him. Maybe he'd let her live. "But I've got to take my own stuff with me," I transferred my gifts of Venus and other traveling supplies to the fresh stallion Perry brought. "And oh, since food is at a premium—" I dug into the new scrip packs and, wincing, removed all the meat, bestowing it on Perry. "—after so much fasting I can go a little easy on eating again." No one argued. I mounted easily. "Give my regards to the chief," I said cheerily, then I looked at Baniff piteously, and said piously, "May goodness prosper," knowing that all my words would get conveyed to Mirand. Then, before he could respond, I kicked the stallion off to circle round the city and head with all speed north.

And so I entered northern Threle alone, with all the rest of Threle falling fast and furious behind me. Fast enough to satisfy the emperor's impatience, presumably. It occurred to me that I was supposed to be influencing Walworth's generals to fight and paw over their own destruction while they thought they were saving Threle. It was supposed to be my mission to push things along, and I wondered what the chances were of convincing Roguehan that I had caused the southern duchies to destroy themselves. For all Roguehan knew, I had influenced Baniff and Aleta to do it up proud down in Medegard. And I could certainly claim that I had calculated the effect of the unfortunate antigovernment concert and decided a few hours of distasteful sentiments were worth all the destruction. Really, for all Roguehan knew, he had my efforts to thank for a quick victory after all. The south Threlans had destroyed themselves, and in doing so had eliminated the seemingly eternal problem of local rebellions. Completely cutting off his soldiers' supply source might not be the way Roguehan had planned on doing things, but the utter self-vanquishment of the southern duchies, supply source or no, was the sort of thing I knew the emperor would appreciate. He might even have been waiting for someone to bring his work to colorful bleeding fruition, to make all the beauties of defeat manifest. And I decided, that since the defeat was arguably grandiose enough to be in my style, that when I saw Roguehan next, I would use the rebellion to my credit. And I also decided that since the emperor seemed bound to win the war, it would behoove me to work with all haste toward Cathe's deification. Hecate might or might not protect me from Roguehan should he discover how little I had really done to help him toward victory, for Roguehan had enough high clergy in his pay to bend Her grace from me. Also, since I had no idea what tricks Zelar knew, and since the price of my revenge was his animosity, the protection of a deified Cathe was a fine thing to have.

So as I left Disenward I decided that circumstances had brought me as close to fulfilling my duty to Roguehan as my own honest efforts would have, and I need concern myself on that account no more. I was riding into northern Threle for purely personal reasons. Any vengeance worth four years of life had best be purely personal; otherwise, you might as well give up and sell yourself smiling into one imprisoned abstraction after another until someday you finally die for real.

I mean—set this down, my lord—as far as vengeance goes, if you can't do it completely for yourself, you have no business doing it at all."

My path was straight and sure, just as Baniff had said it would be. Just a rut wrinkling a sharp hollow through the icy northern plains for another day and then a smooth clear bend into the snowy hills of Reathe. And Reathe is all hills, so when you enter from the plains, all the day's emptiness suddenly rises with you, a quick drift from flat to round, an airy emptiness laden only by sky and snow. Reathe was all white-and-blue perfection, for the sky was clear here and the northern light undulated upon the hills in great golden peals of charm. And in the light I often heard bells ringing, but in Reathe bells are always ringing someplace else—sweet distant sounds keeping comfort as I rode. Reathe is all sheep bells and nodding bleats echoing from unknown sources in the else-quiet hills. And every sound brings imagined warmth under frigid light and air. Winter here is too cold to move. The hills cherish a terrible inward wind which they exhale calmly through rocks and barren trees. And only other trees seem to catch the wind, because it's so very cold here you have to stop your horse and reach down with your senses even to feel the low pervasive freeze. A cold on the dim edge of cold. The effect is that winter is its own business here and not even thoughts can touch it, so you ride like a trespasser in the season, making no mark.

All the northern duchies are snow-soft promises of warm kettles boiling over in valley villages, but the villages are always hidden in another valley and so you never see them. The road wound through Carasag and Glancharg, through valleys where no one lived and over gentle hills overlooking more valleys where no one lived, and I saw a river once or twice, but never any cottages. But the villages had to be somewhere, for something kept causing smoke to rise in the distance. And by the second day my witch sense heard the smoke speaking comfort into the winter winds, and so I knew that there were hidden hearths and hearts somewhere in the silent hills to welcome a winter stranger. For people do live in northern Threle, but you never see them. You just feel eddies of life like old women you'll never meet, women that you know spend their days weaving tea out of herbs and old pots, or bending soap figures out of snowdrifts and yellowed wool. And because it was getting north, some of them might know a star by name, as if a star could be a distant cousin, and up here, of course, it could. And at night the dark is all liquid and pours like an old dry sea over lost jagged lights, and each star a storm coming at you to pierce your heart and pass. The night sky an abyss of cold suns and even the fires I created kept no brightness against the vast still thunder of this passionate tranquility called northern Threle.

And for all I know, I would have hit the Kretch if the road hadn't finally taken me out of hills and into wind-riven fields of deep snow. And the fields kept stretching distance until the snow half hid a sparse cluster of round thatched cottages, with shadows like old trolls moving against windows. And I couldn't help remarking how the cottages pastured all the emptiness around them, how this place made all the rest of Threle seem to absent itself somewhere south beneath the hills.

I supposed I might have stopped and asked the way, but I didn't, for my head was now light with the bone-crunching cold I had forever forgotten to shield myself against, and the frost and the sky kept drawing me on to ride as I pleased. My horse slid through the great northern silence and still I rode, and the brown hills accepted me into their frozen dream of earth and they bound me upward and upward toward a bright crag in the winter sun, like an icy groaning ocean wave to break on a place of wandering mist and dazzling spires of icy light. I was all in light without seeing until I suddenly came upon a brief shadow against the dark.

And in the shadow was a door set deep within a round tower. I dismounted, still dreaming, and left the horse to wander free. Then I opened the door and entered, walking slowly, in trance, up spirals and spirals of stairs. My feet kept walking and the stone stairs kept spiraling and echoing my footsteps into dizzy spasms of cold above and below me. I walked and circled ever higher, through this relentless column of winter that stopped all thought and feeling with ice, until there was another door to push open into light, and life and warmth rushed from a blazing fire to greet me and dispel my trance.

"I thought you'd need help with directions, Brother," Caethne greeted me, smiling as the trance completely lifted. "Pourra told me you were coming." She was stirring a great cauldron and singing a little. The room was warmly decorated with bright rugs and tapestries that glowed in the fiery light, and the sun streamed perfect colors through a beautiful stained-glass window. Pourra, her wood spirit familiar who always assumed the shape of a woodchuck, was napping by the fire. He looked up and yawned as I entered. A stout little woman dressed in dark clothes was watching Caethne intently.

"Put a wren's egg in it, Mistress, and 'tis sure to set the fever right," she said excitedly, peering closely into the cauldron's contents. Then she tested the mixture by sticking in a finger and sucking. Pourra waddled over to her and waved his paws around as if he too wanted a sample.

"I did better than a wren's egg, Inchia, don't you think?" Caethne watched eagerly as the woman sucked her finger and licked her lips. "Nothing stills the fever like cowslip and borage."

"Except death," said Inchia. "But I must admit, it does taste like proper medicine without the egg. Ye want some?" She meant me.

I declined with a wave of my hand.

"Inchia, go tend our guest's horse and bring his things to the room prepared for him. And here, take some of this to your sick baby for your trouble." Caethne ladled a generous amount of sweet-smelling liquid from her cauldron into a large yellow jar.

"My mother's sick too, Mistress."

"Then take two jars," said Caethne sweetly.

"And my dear neighbor Boria and her cow. Been good as a bad harvest what with sendin' all our produce to the Midlands. And my brother's not well. Ye know what they say, Mistress. Bad harvest, good fever."

"I know," said Caethne seriously. "Here." She brought down more jars from a shelf. "Since you know where the sickness lies, take all of it and use it well. It's for you. Twice a day will also ease the colic."

"Thank ye kindly, Mistress." Inchia ignored the jars Caethne had gathered and helped herself to more jars from the shelf, then she swiftly drained the contents of the cauldron by filling all the jars. Caethne promptly poured a basket of pinecones and needles into the cauldron and succeeded in making a mess on the floor, which Pourra amused himself with by sliding around on his stomach and getting tangled up in a rug. He looked fierce when she sent all the needles up in smoke. "Kettle's clean." It was a light and merry dismissal, but Inchia had other ideas.

"Does that mean I might have a spot of tea, Mistress, to get my poor gut through the day?"

"Quickly, Inchia, I have a guest. Is licorice acceptable?"

"My favorite." She sat comfortably on a bearskin rug on the floor and watched Caethne go through the preparations for tea. "Oo, licorice eases my back—and my child's gums too, as he's gettin' teeth."

"Here," Caethne broke off some licorice and gave it to her. As Caethne filled the now-empty cauldron with clean springwater, Inchia wrapped all the jars in an old leather satchel along with the licorice and quickly started toward a door which led into the rest of the castle. "I thought you wanted tea," called Caethne.

"Just the licorice now," said Inchia, heading through the door.

"Servants." Caethne sighed. "And yet she did give more corn than most, and a finer hand in scarcity you'll never find." We were alone now, except for Pourra, who was lying on the window ledge the sun came through. It was warm and warmer. She playfully took my hands in hers and darted her eyes all over my face, smiling her best and brightest big-sister smile. "Come to tea."

I delivered my report coolly, refusing to enter her warmth, refusing to be anything but businesslike. "Walworth is retreating. The southern duchies have fallen and the Midlands are as good as gone. He shall headquarter himself here until the end. He rides a day or two behind me and he asks you to prepare for his arrival." I paused for effect and added in the same cold voice, "Cathe sends me armed with gifts of love."

Bright tears flooded her eyes.

Ten

$\mathcal{A}$s Caethne stood softly stopping her tears, I finished the tea preparations in the way she had once taught me to. As I worked I graciously motioned her to sit at a table near the stained-glass window, a polished oak table brightly laid with the window's falling and stretching colors. She sat watching me in all the late afternoon, smiling approval at my skill with kitchen witchery as I sent the rest of the licorice flavor into the water and wrapped a loaf of bread in a white cloth. I placed the bread directly in the fire under the cauldron, leaning close into the flames.

"I wish I had elderberries for you," she said, alluding to our first meeting. I didn't answer. I increased the heat of the fire so the bread began singing almost immediately. Then I removed the loaf with two sticks and dropped it on the table, where the cloth fell away of itself. "Beautifully done, Brother." She kept looking at the bread admiringly, but she did not touch it.

"So eat it. Habundia." I settled myself across from her and manifested two steaming tea mugs on the table.

She smiled sadly. "Perhaps Inchia—"

"Inchia's busy." I studied her, sipping my tea a little.

" 'Tis better to save for those in need, Llewelyn."

"And the lady of the land has no needs," I said softly, seductively, as if I completely understood her reluctance to eat, as if her reluctance were my own and I really wouldn't press.

She smiled and sighed a loud Caethne-sigh. "Llewelyn, do you really expect the Duchess of Walworth to grow fat on bread while her people give up their harvest for the war?"

"I never expect anything." I broke off a piece of bread and turned around to give it to Pourra, who was happy to emerge from his sun-wrapped nap to eat it. "Or should I say, I no more expect you to refuse my gifts than I expected your brother to feed the enemy to buy a few weeks' safety."

"Well," she said brightly, "it wouldn't be the first time Walworth's fed the enemy." She smiled that familiar seductive we've-got-a-special-secret smile. I returned it with my eyes while keeping the rest of my face studiously impassive. "Anyway, it's well gone from all expectations to see you bearing messages for him . . . again." She added the last word softly.

"I'm not." I refused to let on that I recognized her allusion to Loudes.

Caethne looked puzzled, then she anxiously pushed her tangled hair back from her eyes along with a shaft of colored sun. "I see," she smiled wanly. "And so. You come on behalf of Cathe, for reasons I fear to guess."

"Cathe sent me, as I told you. I came for my own reasons."

She took my hands in hers again and rubbed the backs of my wrists, steadying her gaze into my eyes. "Then why are you here? Surely you didn't make such a winter's journey after so long an absence just to feed an old friend as the world ends?"

"Actually," I said slowly and thoughtfully, "I suppose I did."

Caethne lifted my fingers to her mouth and kissed them. I refused to respond to the gesture. She caught up my palms in hers, pressing our hands together for a second and holding them while she said earnestly, "My long-lost little brother. Do you know I've thought of you every day? Entirely whenever I gathered herbs, or wove charms, or haggled prices with the merchants at market. I missed you most when I read Grima and remembered your stunning reading voice. But of course I missed you whenever I read anything beautiful or interesting." I kept my face expressionless. "Llewelyn—do you know how deeply I thought of you in certain poems—do you know I spread cards for you in the dead of all my nights? I made the moon send you dreams, dreams like a beautiful dark-haired maid." She said this last searchingly. I gave no indication that the moon's dreams were anything to me, and that was hard. "And so often I saw us—two witches—stirring the same cauldron and inventing rhymes and stories and recipes—"

"Lady." I said the word with a Sarana accent, to indicate "liar," but I said it in the most solemn tone of respect I could muster. She dropped my fingers, wincing.

"Do you know there was nothing any of us could have done, Llewelyn? We *all* cared about you, whether or not you choose to believe that. I've always known you were true kin to us, even before the others did, even before you astounded us all with your careless mention of learning Amara from old Grana. I always knew you would find your own way back, with or without our help." I remained stolid and impassive, as if I had more important business to attend to but was too polite to interrupt her speech. She faltered. "I never dreamed our reunion would be like this."

"Baniff told me four years didn't feel like all that much to him." I do not know why I said this.

Caethne nodded and stared gently into the fire for a long time. The flames now shot an old afternoon splendor which intensified the row of copper pots on the mantel. Copper was reflected all over the floor, warmer now than the stained-glass light on the table. Pourra slid down off the window ledge into the copper light and batted the light around as it wavered with the flames. Caethne watched him for a long strange dreamy minute. Then she asked suddenly, "Do you know I had to execute your sister?"

This time I looked briefly at Pourra, making sure to smile softly as if his antics amused me more than following up her question did. My reaction threw her into a deeper puzzle, as I intended it to. Then I looked steadily back at her as if I regarded her question as an irritatingly irrelevant side issue to the business at hand.

"Trenna," said Caethne, as if she were reminding both me and herself. "I had to kill Trenna." She waited for a response.

"I didn't know you knew Trenna that well," I said dryly.

"I didn't—she made herself known. A few weeks after the trial in Loudes she managed to find her way up here from Helas. I suspect she was sent by Roguehan, although I could never really prove it. And I suspect I should have turned her over to Thoren for questioning concerning her relationship with Duke Helas, but I didn't."

"You had your own 'relationships' to worry about."

She ignored my allusion to Zelar, but I could tell from the sting in her eyes that she had considered whether Trenna knew anything of her own dealings with the enemy, and had decided not to risk having her tell Thoren anything compromising. "She said her parents died in Sunna and she mentioned your name a lot and how close you were and how highly you spoke of us and—how you told *everybody* all about us—and for your sake—well," Caethne's voice trailed off. She watched Pourra for a long minute.

"You accepted her into your household." I helped her coldly.

She swallowed. "She claimed protection from my parents on the basis of being related to you. My mother could hardly refuse, for remember you had just saved my brother's life at Loudes and she was more than happy to welcome Trenna for your sake. Insisted on it, actually, and got into quite a tussle with Mirand over the issue. But my mother was duchess and my father was as pleased with your heroism as she was and Mirand, for all his skill, could not persuade a doting mother that her son's savior's sister should be turned out into one of our winters."

"I imagine that was quite an argument."

"It was. Especially since my mother held Mirand accountable for all the trouble in Helas. Threatened to put him on trial again here, and probably would have if there wasn't a war to attend to. The argument went on for days, and by the time it was over, Trenna's presence here was already a fact. I tried to stay out of it, but as I was the only one who both spoke Botha and was willing to at least deal with Trenna, she ended up as my concern. And of course I was kind to her. But really I never liked her either—she was so hard to talk to—having no ideas about anything and a good deal of impatience about everything. The worst of it was that she cast enough doubt on your discretion after the trial, and on the nature of your 'close' relationship, that it seemed the best part of wisdom not to attempt contact with you. And Trenna herself asked me not to mention her presence should I communicate to you for fear of Roguehan's people in Kursen potentially finding out her whereabouts. And as she was under my parents' protection, I could only comply. You remember when I did write I wrote as if I had no idea but that your sister might still be in Hala or elsewhere. And that was a risk, because I wasn't really supposed to communicate with you anyway and the last thing Walworth needed was for Roguehan's people in Kursen to find written documentation of *our* relationship, so it was terribly risky for me to write at all. And what was worse, we all feared greatly for them taking your life."

"They did." I said this without emotion.

"Well." She looked briefly tearful, paused to watch the sun darken the window's colors, and then continued, "It now seems to me that Trenna really feared you might take it upon yourself to come up here and ruin her plans."

"You mean Trenna was smart enough to make plans?"

Caethne swallowed. Whatever was coming was hard to say. "Trenna tried to force Walworth to fall in love with her, to tamper with his judgment, I suppose. By means of a magic not her own. Somehow she had gotten hold of a love ring, designed to hold the force of Aphrodite, and when she washed it properly, she did look rather lovely. Caught the attention of the entire household—excepting my brother and Mirand, who at that point had so much to think about it would be a wonder if they'd have noticed Aphrodite Herself. You know if you wear such a ring three days running and throw it into someone's glass and they drink from it, that someone will love you completely?"

"You mean she pulled it off?" I managed to sound bored, although I was utterly fascinated.

"Yes, she did. For about a minute. Mirand was watching and felt an abnormal pull around my brother after he drank from his glass. There was suddenly a brightness about my brother's heart when he looked at Trenna—a twin feels these things—and then Mirand marched us both out of the room and into his study, where he racked his books looking for a way to disperse the goddess force. We're short on proper clerics up here."

"So how did Mirand disperse the goddess force?" This, of course, was important to know.

"He didn't. It was beyond his skill. But Cathe was here and he chose to make himself useful on the occasion, and when my brother was quite restored to his senses, Mirand sensibly reminded us all that the punishment for treason is death, and interfering with the critical judgment of the commander of the Threlan army in time of war is treason. And so Trenna was arrested. Normally, my parents would have sat in judgment but Mirand seemed to think it would be better if I presided."

I let a shadow of amusement play along my lips. "Was it? Better, I mean?"

"Better than what?" she cried. My clerical sense read incredible pain here. "And of course she was guilty. There was nothing to do but ask if she wished to plea and then pass the sentence. And then *I* had to carry out the execution."

"Did Mirand watch you do it?" I really couldn't help myself. And I had to hand it to my old master—he certainly had an incredible sense of justice.

"No. He was off to Loudes again." She picked up her tea mug in both hands, as if to warm them, and stared into the mug's dark contents as if she were scrying the past. "But before he left he suggested that *I* make her fall in love with something vile, that she might kiss her own desire and die of it." She was crying again. "How do you like that? He said that to *me.*"

"Well, that's Mirand. Coming on the heels of your secret deal with Zelar, that must have felt good, sister."

"Oh, Llewelyn, sometimes—" She angrily pushed her mug away. "—at that point I don't know if I could have remembered to feel anything."

I said nothing, but I made sure to look slightly amused and

clearly sympathetic. Trenna's death and the reported death of my parents did not touch me, but Caethne's story burned beneath my studied clerical demeanor like the damnation I sought to bring them all. Something in me blanched at how far I had come from my early apprenticeship days, and how improbable yet strangely right it was that Caethne, my once-called "sister" of choice, had executed Trenna, my sister by accidental birth, upon my old master's recommendation for a crime that in some respects resembled what I was planning. I felt emptily powerful.

She looked steadily at me. "It was awful. Her face was—well. But then, my poor brother. Which is worse? His heart cared nothing for her. He kept the ring, and gave it to Mirand. And Mirand, who really despises no one, grew close to despising Trenna. She was incessantly dropping your name, and using your accomplishments as her claim on our affection, and that annoyed him to no end. I think the only time he ever bothered to speak to her was to admonish that just because she might or might not be a blood relative to a brilliant young adept at magic, it didn't mean she was a wizard herself. That scared her off Mirand."

"But not enough, presumably."

"No. But you see, after meeting Trenna we were all prepared to believe that you were more kin to us than to your birth family. That we had ties of spirit to you that transcended blood. Mirand thought perhaps you were true kin to Grana, based on your impressive magical ability, but really there wasn't time to speculate. Anyway, a witch knows her own heart when she sees it—child—" She clasped my hands again. "—little brother—almost cousin, I mean—I look at you and I know my own. My heart cries out for knowing."

I removed my hands and sipped my tea, looking coldly unperturbed. "So." With that one word I dismissed her story as if it couldn't touch us. Caethne looked like the ghost of a dull dawn sinking into fathomless night before day could happen. I knew she was speaking truth to me, and that my impassive demeanor was killing her. I also knew it was time to make my business proposition, and in the measured voice of a seasoned trader who knew his customer's every desire and its price, I began anew. "I have brought you your heart's desire, sister. Will you take and eat of it?"

"Eat my own desire," she murmured into her mug. "Llewelyn—you're so—"

"I can force Mirand to love you completely. And I won't get caught."

"How?"

"Through clerisy. I bear the gifts of Venus Whose Beauty Enslaves. I can give you Her blood to spice a witch brew that he might drink of it and love you forever. I can entwine Her blessed hair in yours that you might catch him for eternity in a light embrace. I can dress you in Venus's own girdle, that no man may look at you and refuse his own desire. And I bear the memory and power of Mirand's personal power and charge. I can use my goddess's force to create a conductive path between our minds that no shield or defenses will withstand. I can storm my old master with all the love you seek."

"And your price?" she asked evenly.

"You already know it. Cathe's deification. As you once promised, witch."

"I see." She sighed. "I don't know. It's late," she said wistfully.

"Caethne—it's damn late!" I slammed my fist on the table. "In days or weeks northern Threle will become part of the empire. Roguehan—and Zelar—will find their way here and take all your lives from you—"

"*Our* lives—what about yours, Brother?"

"My life was taken a long time ago. In Kursen." She nodded and cried a little. I wiped her tears with my thumbs, gently and caressingly, but I spoke in a voice of winter. "In a short time you will be dead. Do you wish to leave your life without having experienced the love of the man you love beyond all others?"

"No."

"Perhaps you could have kept waiting through the years for Mirand to attach himself to you, but the years are over. Perhaps your witchcraft could have one day overcome his defenses—but I wouldn't have depended on that either."

Caethne was completely given over to tears now, her messy hair glistered with water, and her body heaved in great sobs. "You tempt me."

"Yes," I said softly, "I tempt you with the finest gift of life. I offer you your soul's desire on the eve of your death. You need only have the courage to claim it."

"To give Cathe what he wants, I should have to kill Walworth."

"Caethne, will Roguehan do any less? It is no longer a question of Walworth's death, but a question of means. Shall your brother be executed by his enemy, or by his loving sister who after all can do so gently, without pain? You know how ingenious Roguehan can be with his executions." She looked steadily at me without tears. "And who knows," I lied, "but that being wife to a god—a *god force*, might spare you and your lover from the wrath of the world, meaning the emperor. I'm sure Cathe would protect you and Mirand for the favor."

Caethne spent a long time considering my words, but as I read her thoughts I knew it was finally the notion of protecting Mirand that seemed to decide things. "It shall be new moon in five days. Should Mirand love me and should Roguehan spare us 'til then—I will do it." She stood and gathered up Pourra in her arms, then walked over to look through the colors in the window. The sun kindled the edges of her tangled hair with brilliant red. "'Haps Cathe will not make the journey from Kant in time?"

"For this?" I asked pleasantly, standing and speaking into her ear, gently holding and relaxing her stiff shoulders. "Once the south fell and the army headed north, you can bet Cathe didn't remain in Kursen waiting for word from me. He knows the calendar, and he knows that the business needs to be done before Roguehan arrives, for the obvious reason that you can't deify him if you're dead. So it wouldn't surprise me if he were on his way now—with all haste." I hadn't felt Cathe, of course, but I supposed if he were on the plains he had heard me calling Mirra and so knew to keep his energy quiet. And if he left when the south fell, meaning the day I left Medegard, and took the main road through the duchies and a straight path over the center of the plains, he could easily arrive within the next four days. Within two or three if he denied himself sleep through an occasional waking surge. "At any rate, five days is all he has—for by the time the moon waxes and wanes again, Roguehan will have you all in the grave. Cathe knows that. And if he doesn't show—nothing lost." I knew he'd show.

"Can you feel him coming?" asked Caethne hesitantly.

I opened myself to Hecate for a few minutes, and then tried to reach beyond Her. "Yes. Three days."

"Then I can make *you* immortal," said Caethne resignedly.

"How?" I glanced down at Pourra, who was snuggled in her arms, and nonchalantly petted his head as if divinity were of merely passing interest to me.

"Same way I'd deify him." Then she suddenly sat back down to avoid looking at me. I sat attentively across from her. "After all, you birthed Cathe from Grana with magic—you stand in a more sympathetic relationship to him than I do. You are kin—I've known that forever, and perhaps *you* could become a force extending divine protection over us."

This was a twist. "Through bathing me in Walworth's blood?" I asked coldly, as if I were giving consideration to a business proposition.

"No. By bathing you in Cathe's."

I had come for vengeance. And now I could become divine if I were to forgo vengeance and become their protector. But the thought of Walworth's household living under my protection, being as beholden to an evil deity as Roguehan's own house was, was pure delight. And it would be a wonderful out from Roguehan's shilly-shallying over whether to give me a duchy, as well as the perfect escape from Zelar's ire. And for an added measure of fun it would certainly give El something to think about, wherever he was now. And as to Cathe, well really, anyone who took the trouble to introduce me to the deathly joys of monastic life deserved a like compliment. I had no personal compunctions concerning Cathe. I liked it. It was a fine idea.

"All right, witch—" I smiled broadly for the first time since entering her household. "—give me eternity."

"All right, Brother," echoed Caethne, sipping her tea. "Welcome home."

𝒥nchia had made up a most comfortable room for me. She had arranged my saddlebags with great care near a large well-stocked hearth, next to a wooden box of candles, a loaf of brown bread, a bowl of incense, and a small jar of Caethne's medicine. I immediately created a rousing fire in the hearth and threw a little incense on it, so the room smelled pleasantly of jasmine and myrtle as I lit the candles and placed them around the room. Once the light was full and perfect I saw how beautifully carved all the furnishings were, with leafy designs like living ivy and gusts of snow swirling in the wood, designs which almost seemed to grow and move as I watched. As soon as I had emptied my bags and arranged my things to my satisfaction, I stripped down and washed myself in agreeably warm water from a low marble basin, water seductively scented with lilacs and rosemary.

Still warm and wet and sky-clad, I reclined easily upon my bed, and stared idly at my silver riding broach as I turned it over and over in the light and thanked dear Hecate for Her providence. I noticed that Inchia had even left a piece of her precious licorice on my pillow, wrapped in a pink ribbon. But I knew that Caethne had also had a hand in the preparations, for my bed smelled deliciously of peonies and snapdragons and musk roses, and the rushes on my floor were fresh and green, and of course only Caethne could have charmed wildflowers out of a northern Threle winter. I just lay comfortable and relaxed for as long as I pleased, and when I rose I took the lazy liberty of donning a thick dark night robe which had clearly been left on the bed for my use. Then I sat softly in the fresh reeds and meditated on the fire.

At some point during my meditation someone brought me mulled wine and soft cheeses and a spiced vegetable sauce for my bread. And when I came out of my trance I was ravenous for fresh food, which I hadn't eaten in nearly two weeks, and so I eagerly ate everything which was spread before me. I had nearly finished eating and drinking when Caethne entered the room and sat softly in the reeds beside me. She threw more incense on the fire.

"Straight from the hands of the fairies." She smiled generously, indicating all the lovely arrangements.

"Best not let a fairy go unanswered for her gifts," I teased seriously, as if we were back in Helas sharing secrets again and all was right with the universe. I stood up and went over to a little painted chest, took out my gifts of Venus, and gave them to her, explaining their uses with much playful solemnity.

And she wove the goddess hair in her tangled locks and donned the girdle loosely. Then she practiced her charms on me until I was satisfied that if I wasn't a priest of Hecate, I would have been completely in love with her myself. But Hecate was with me and Hecate is quite emotionally chaste and so I merely embraced the Venus force and felt Her strength without danger to my heart, and it was no more than one sister kissing another, Hecate to Venus. But we did kiss, and I did let Caethne call me Mirand. And then Pourra was playing in the rushes as we told each other pleasant stories near the fire I had created. And we read shapes into the flames, and sang songs, and remembered old dreams, and spoke at length of the end of Threle. And when Caethne finally took her leave she hugged and kissed me with a fierce sort of embrace and bade me call on her should I need anything in the night. And I squeezed her hand and wished her bright blessings.

But settling back into bed was now like settling into the secluded recesses of a joyous spring, like retreating into the farthest corners of an open season. Before I slept I was dreaming rich earth scents from an insane garden but the garden was really all around me. I closed my eyes in the firelight and smelled lilies. I opened them to a quiet rush of lavender, and closed them again to various suggestions of sudden orchids and the early fragrance of lengthening light.

And how to dream of flowers without Isulde, who ran to me with droves of distant gardens falling through her hands, crying "This is the strange old night when spring turns to winter. The night we run backwards into the sea and skip lightly over spring's pink womb. See where she crushes and grinds in growth—" She covered us in writhing spring garlands. The garlands burned a smooth ridge into my skull as we danced slowly on eastern waves. "—See how growth bursts in glorious tumult," she chanted. "See how my springtide ocean swells." I kissed her hard in greeting as we dived underwater. She gave me a star. The star wriggled into gold and green and then became a glowworm which flew into an evening grown old and thoughtful with flowers. We lay on the beach and a brown bird sang as she stroked my face with a bent reed. "I know the dragon who guards hyacinths for the midmorning sun," she sang.

"Do you now?"

"Now and ever. But mostly I know him under his mountain." She climbed on top of me and kissed me hard. "And sometimes I bring salty ice for his long cold tail, lest it swell and split the world in two." She caressed my thigh as she said this, and I grew so hard I was about to split the world in two myself, but she stopped before I came. Then she just sat in the sand and hugged her knees to her chest as she watched the waves, and her solemn expression reminded me of Caethne looking out the window. "Once in a century he births an old egg, the strange green hen. But still in every spring his hyacinths live and grow an hour, out of his skin and eyes. You know his hyacinths, don't you?"

I made no answer save sitting up to fling my arms around her back and join her in watching the waves. As I held her they pounded through me.

"They come when you greet the coming life of the season—when you sit in the east among your books while tender leaves whisper to you like a snake turning green into gold—" We kissed again and there was love apple on my tongue. "—and then spring fades." She broke the kiss, and gave me her hands. They formed a cup of sand. "So." She smiled. "Eat and be wise like a god." I drank the sand into crushed apples. I drank crushed apples into a city of fragrance. Jeweled birds like nightingales sang in an eastern garden. Somewhere a sad-eyed girl strummed a mandolin and shining rivers promised blooms to the desert which bleated at the city walls. And then there was a grove of pomegranates and eternal delights, where pleasure books summon up hot winds of incense. "So many pretty storms to cull. Which to choose." She looked around at the warm trees and I saw men and women in bright robes discussing all the world's philosophy. Then she broke a branch of pink blossoms that smelled like licorice and gave it to me. We licked the blossoms together and fell kissing each other's tongues, and I closed my eyes into furious garden scents and ran my hand through her cool evening hair and felt a luscious relaxing warmth in my arms before awakening. And when I did awake, opening my eyes in the bed Inchia had prepared for me, I knew Isulde was lying soft against my chest, freshly fallen from her dream. I cried out and grasped her in delight, and we began the day in a long intense kiss.

"Welcome, my heart," I cried again, ecstatically.

"Silly Llewelyn. I am well come. I am here to welcome my love into death. To bring him into the night." She kissed me long and fast.

"Then come, sweet death—" I buried my tongue in her mouth till her body stiffened into orgasm, and mine followed sweetly. "—your love is soon to be a god." She broke away laughing. "A god, Isulde, to chase you through your Northern dreams."

"*Do* gods dream?" she asked, suddenly unhappy.

"Don't you, Isulde?"

"Sometimes I always dream."

"On what?"

"On the name of my love."

"And what be his name?" I asked happily.

"Walworth."

The bed suddenly got colder than a north Threlan winter. Isulde smiled jagged ice storms into me, threw back the covers, and walked easily through the reeds to the hearth, where she brought up a little fire with a gesture of her hand. I sat watching her, unable to speak. "I come to him in dreams," she explained. "And now he comes to me in defeat. Llewelyn, shall I kiss him into death? Or shall I take him North with me for safety's sake?"

I could not recover. "You also come to me in dreams," was the only thing I managed to say.

"And so to others, to poets sometimes, but that is all pretense and fun." She leaped back on the bed. "And you know I cannot take *you* North—"

The door opened without a knock and Inchia bustled in, taking a quiet appraisal of us in all our naked splendor. "Hghm. Our guest is right as relief at home," she greeted us, picking up the jar of medicine.

"Inchia," cried Isulde cheerfully. "Llewelyn is an old friend of mine. The best of all my friends. We run together like fever and flowers in dreams beyond the river Kretch."

"Aye, 'tis a good place to run," said Inchia. "Took my dogs up there once. The mountains turned 'em to sparrows."

Isulde removed the beribboned licorice from her hair. "Here. Eat and grow strong." Inchia took the treat and threw it in the fire as Caethne entered the room. The air smelled like dark lavender. Pourra was with her, and he was squealing like a madman for loss of the candy until Isulde called him and he leapt happily and joyfully into her arms.

"And how are my two fevered flowers?" asked Caethne as Inchia left. "Hungry for porridge?" She was carrying two steaming bowls, which she set on the hearth. Pourra promptly jumped out of Isulde's arms and made himself intimately acquainted with one of the bowls. Then he started on the other. "Ah well." Caethne sighed. "Sweetness went traveling last night and so he's hungry." She looked tenderly at Isulde. "He tells me my brother will arrive near nightfall." Isulde looked tearfully up at Caethne and they held each other in a long embrace while I turned to dress myself, and when I turned to look again, Isulde was wearing a plain linen tunic and Caethne was plaiting her hair. I kept looking at Isulde and knowing that I'd never seen a lovelier woman in my life, that here in the morning of my homecoming was a woman lovely enough to destroy the dreams that had sustained me through my monastic destruction.

The most intense beauty destroys dreams.

And all my dreams were spectres of dead hours, trembling away in an awful waste of memory. Really I had to sit down and suffer.

"We must prepare then, for his arrival," said Isulde finally, turning suddenly to face me. "Llewelyn, you shall help us."

"Of course. As my dear friend wishes."

She ran and hugged me and all trembling ceased. And I kissed her mouth violently and threw her down on the bed, drawing blood by biting her lips as Caethne watched. "Llewelyn," teased Isulde happily, as I rolled off her, "soon we three and more shall all meet in a violent caress."

"Yes," I said happily, stroking her hair. "Violent and sweet as all my dear friends wish."

And the rest of that day was a disordered line. We three were working and preparing toward some goal, and the goal was softly coming, but I could reach nothing of the future in my thoughts. I did not dream. I worked no magic. Caethne took us out into winter, and I believe she and Isulde melted snow for gourds and commanded cranberries from the wind. But I didn't believe much. And yet when Isulde made peaches from snowflakes, I believed in everything until the wind puffed frozen gaps through my skull again. I think they made a snowman out of me, for I stretched my arms upon a stiff white drift and Isulde wrapped strange scarves and hats around my head, and Caethne gave me something comforting to hold like a tired wand. But then Pourra swiped a hole in my snowy stomach and the cold crushed and lashed like a bony serpent as the ice bled. And I was writhing cold and constant between my two ladies as we ran back inside, and Isulde said, "The wind's blowing down from the Drumuns."

There was a large cook area, and the three of us held hands and chanted as we stirred a brew of cranberries and gourds. Caethne added sage and salt, and Isulde gave me a peach and whispered a song to it, and by the time I finished eating the fruit, it was late in the day and darkening. "Soup's on," said Caethne, ladling some in a large spoon. "Taste it, Brother."

"Like liquid ginger," I pronounced, sitting on the floor as Isulde dropped beside me. And there was a black candle burning in her hand as she drank from my lips in a kiss. And somehow we were making love before the cauldron as Caethne stirred in some amber powder and watched smiling as we came. "And now it tastes like the way my head comes apart at the end of a poem," I murmured.

"No, it tastes like the end of all poems," Isulde spoke, caressing my face. "It is a brew to lengthen the night." And now it was night. And the three of us were sitting in a circle we had raised, a circle lined with black candles and in their weak light we held hands and raised a cone of energy and sang to the dark.

> *I want the bird to fly torn from my womb*
> *I want my eggs for the beast of the spring*
> *I want his heat to burst open my eggs*
> *I want the god to say 'now'*

"Now," said Mirand quietly.

"Now," said Isulde in greeting as she faded the dark by killing the candle flames. The cooking area regained its normal luminosity from the hearth fire. I stood between my two witches in the comfortable flickering light, an arm around each of them, and smiled.

"Greetings, Master."

"Greetings." He inclined his head slightly, but made no further acknowledgment of my presence.

Caethne dispersed what was left of our circle. Then she broke away from me and took his hands in hers. "You are most welcome." She sighed. "I have prepared for your arrival. Come and eat."

"Perhaps our old master has important affairs of state to discuss," I suggested.

"No," said Mirand. "We are defeated. What else is there to discuss?"

"Nothing," I easily conceded.

"We might have a go at that soon enough," he replied, walking out of the cooking area.

"Get your things," I ordered Caethne. She was staring at his back, or rather, at the place in the air where his back had been.

"Llewelyn, he's—different now. Like you. Don't you feel that?"

"People get easier when they face death," I replied casually. Isulde nodded in vigorous agreement. "Get your things. Lace his soup with blood. The god said 'now.'"

Caethne gave me a sidelong glance before slipping away.

I extinguished the cooking fire and relit the black candles. Then I held Isulde's hand in my freshly created eeriness and waited. Waited steady until I heard the footsteps of Walworth and his party. And as they entered the room I brought down Hecate's force and took Isulde once again in a terrible long sea-rocking orgasm, which she loved, and which I made sure was evident to all the party as they entered. And so Walworth's homecoming was Isulde moaning and singing and raising a witch storm of reverberations at my command in a circle of black. And I kept the show going for several minutes so everyone could drink their fill of evil's power before I released her.

"Oh, my gods," I heard Aleta exclaim awkwardly.

"Cool," I heard Ellisand comment.

"Welcome home," I said formally to all of them once I had finished. I picked up my black cloak and draped it around my shoulders as Isulde broke from the circle and ran merrily to Walworth.

She threw her arms happily around him and he held her briefly, making eye contact with me before breaking his embrace. "Caethne has been storming a brew for us," she said.

"I see."

"Llewelyn is here for you."

He glanced at me, and back at her. "I know."

"Soon you will be dead, save you come North with me where all healing is." She said this cajolingly and hopefully, and when Walworth did not answer she looked at me. "I should heal Llewelyn there as well, if he could come. For in the North is always an end." And then she faced the rest of the party, which consisted of Aleta, Ellisand, and Baniff. "I should take you all there out of the world."

"There's still a world," said Baniff. "A few days of it, anyway."

"But we witches could slip the days to dreams. Already Caethne softens the edges of time. Come North with me."

"Let us keep the time," said Walworth. "It's all we have."

"Then let us happy few face those final few days out," I said, as Caethne reentered with Pourra. She bid us all enter the dining area to take sup with Mirand. I could feel Venus all over her, and so could Isulde, who ran to embrace and kiss her in play. "Come," I said, as if the castle were my home. "Our dear sister bids us feast." And I ushered everyone into the dining area, where Mirand was now sitting calmly on the floor.

He held out an empty bowl like a beggar to Caethne. She filled it with Venus blood. She poured bright blood from the black vial and she kept her thoughts wide open as nature itself while she did it. Aleta gasped again.

"You're not going to drink blood are you?"

"Silence," ordered Mirand. I was too stunned at Caethne's actions even to attempt to link myself to him and so send the goddess force to his heart through his defenses. So I just sat there trying to understand what was happening and then I knew he had no defenses. And Caethne was hiding nothing from him. She sat on the floor across from him and smiled. No one spoke. The tone of the room was wrong for speaking. "Will you remove your goddess gifts?" he asked Caethne. "Beautiful as you now appear to me, I wish nothing between us for what follows." She flung the locks of hair underfoot.

"You may remove my girdle, Master." I couldn't bloody believe what was happening here. Caethne removed her shift and Mirand gently untied the girdle and let it slip to the ground. She stood before him sky-clad.

"Shall I drink your soft blood, witch?" he asked gently.

" 'Tis the blood of Venus, Master. The blood of a bad moon. 'Tisn't mine."

"Answer my question, student." He raised the bowl to his lips. "I know whose blood it is." I noticed Isulde and Walworth were holding each other and watching. Mirand was oblivious to all save Caethne, but he was cutting her to shreds with his eyes. I wouldn't want that strange intense gaze turned on me, despite all my clerical strength.

"No." Caethne took the bowl from him. She raised it above her head as if she were offering it to her own goddess, stood still in her own breathing, and then brought it to the table. "Perhaps Isulde and Walworth, who already—"

Isulde picked up the bowl and drank the blood, looking intently at me. "It tastes like pearls." Then she turned and kissed Walworth without stopping.

Mirand rose and grasped Caethne tightly around her waist, gently pulled back her head, and kissed her violently on the mouth. It was hideous and gruesome, because she responded with like force, and they were immediately on the floor raising sparks and puffs of fire where their bodies met. Caethne was stiff and sobbing and Mirand was stabbing her with incantations in a magical language I did not recognize. And every word was a shudder and a scream. Mirand was ferocious, and whenever Caethne bit him he bit her back until she bled, and then she drew blood from his chest with her tongue. And then he was inside her, and she was curling and relaxing to his thrusts, as the weird dark energy of their lovemaking sent shocks through the empty air.

Naturally, I just sat there politely, and did my best to look as if this was all a normal pleasant family dinner. I manifested bread and gourd soup for everyone who wasn't sexually preoccupied at the moment. I even conjured up an ale for Baniff but he was too shocked to touch it. So I drank it myself.

Isulde broke off kissing, and then Caethne and Mirand climaxed simultaneously, and then everyone was seated at the table and I was manifesting more food from the cook area.

"I'm glad that's over," announced Aleta.

"Gotta love the North," said Ellisand, who had been thoroughly into the show. "Startin' to feel like home."

"Is this how friends greet the night in Gondal?" I asked him by way of casual conversation.

"Only good friends," he replied. "Everyone else just has sex."

"A toast to civilization's end." I raised my ale, and then conjured more bottles for my friends. Everyone joined except Aleta.

"A toast to you, Brother," said Mirand amiably. "And to your work, which I have followed with interest for years. Well done."

"And to your true love," I added. "Better done than any of us supposed."

"And to Ceres," said Caethne, crying and laughing. "For She told me I am wed in truth away from my cousin."

"And to speaking sense," said Aleta to Caethne. She did not raise her bottle.

"And to centuries of a good life," said Baniff. "To drinkin'."

"To playing," said Ellisand.

"To inspiring," said Isulde.

"To my lady," said Ellisand again, speaking to Isulde.

"To Beauty," I saluted both of them.

"To dreams and death," said Isulde, who once again kissed Walworth.

"To Roguehan's imminent defeat," said Walworth quietly, as the kiss ended, as if he really believed his enemy's defeat was imminent. We all turned to look at him. "May he take Threle and die of it." He drank, and his words ushered a black silence into the company. Everyone except Mirand looked uncomfortable with Walworth's misplaced optimism. "When Lord Roguehan arrives, I bid you do him all honor," the duke continued. "Treat him as you would treat King Thoren himself. Until such time as Roguehan should arrive, Master Mirand and I shall sequester ourselves in my chamber. Do not disturb us, for there still remains much to do." He turned to Aleta. "General Aleta I place in charge of the Threlan army and all military affairs. Aleta—" He withdrew his sword and clapped her on the shoulder. "—in all military concerns your word is law. I hereby abdicate as supreme commander and general. Threle's forces are yours to command."

"My lord." She knelt, awestruck, and rose shaken. "We need you." He turned his face slightly, but his eyes were hard and he ignored her.

"Caethne." Caethne was still shaking and glowing from her lovemaking. A little blood trickled down her neck. "As always, the administrative duties of the duchy are yours. But as I hereby abdicate as duke, the duchy is entirely yours." He leaned over the table and kissed her lightly on the mouth.

"Twin—"

"No longer twin. I give you the land of the Duchy of Walworth, the land which until now I have embodied in my person. Remember, Caethne, that by the ancient Northern blood that runs through both our hearts, you are now 'duke'—you are now the 'lord of the land' and so you now embody the duchy's land in your very person. That means, 'Lord' Caethne, that Mirand is now your 'lady'—in the sense that he, as your lover, now stands in complement to your energy." Walworth said this in a tone of harsh formality, but he softened his voice to add, "You are lovers and true twins now. Reside together that the land itself resides in you."

Really the farther North you go, the more fluid identities seem to get, I thought, trying unsuccessfuly to see Mirand as Caethne's "feminine" complement. I understood the mechanics of this strange transfer of energy, but I had no idea of Walworth's motivation. Mirand sidled over to Caethne and kissed her protests out of her.

"We are wed and so we rule, my sweet lord," Mirand said playfully.

"And should Thoren die at Loudes, as seems likely, Caethne shall be King of Threle while Threle lasts. For it is the Duke of Walworth who stands next in line to the throne, by the king's decree, and Caethne is now, by my decree, the Duke of Walworth."

I had read of such things happening before, way back in Threle's history. Once or twice a woman had ruled as "king" and her male consort as "queen" because of some kind of twisted legality, but it was the gods' own deal why Walworth decided to abdicate in this way. That business finished, he turned to the rest of us. "Baniff."

"My lord." Baniff was looking at him with an expression of sheer incredulity. But then, we all were. Except Caethne, who looked to be in the throes of another orgasm, which Mirand had sent to her with a mind probe and a smile.

"I am now a common citizen, but still I would discharge my debt to you for services rendered."

" 'Tis all right," said the gnome, still wide-eyed. "I discharge ye of all debts to me."

"Then you are free to leave," said Mirand.

"I know," said Baniff, but he made no move to do so. Poor happy Caethne passed out to another one of Mirand's smiles.

"Ellisand," said Mirand smoothly, as Caethne sank sighing to the floor, "nothing binds you to stay with us." By pointedly ignoring Baniff's answer Mirand had expressed an appreciation of loyalty more eloquent than any finely crafted speech. It had always been understood that Baniff would not leave.

"Nothing binds me to leave, either," responded Ellisand. "Unless the new lord and lady prefer it."

"Gondal might be safer for you," said the wizard with slight insistence. The insistence was ostensibly for Ellisand, but it also worked through contrast as more high praise for Baniff's decision.

"Roguehan'll come knocking up to Gondal soon enough," said Ellisand easily. "Besides, I'm not afraid of Roguehan. The emperor and I always got along all right."

"No doubt," said Aleta.

"If you wish to stay, you are welcome," said Mirand kindly. He turned his awful gaze on me. "Llewelyn."

"Yes." I turned my own hardest gaze back, and got the better of him, for he briefly dropped his eyes. Goddess force is near-impossible for nonclerics to combat.

"Threle thanks you for your many gifts." That was all he said. I had hoped he would ask if I wished to stay or leave, because I had a wonderfully cynical speech about unending loyalty and friendship and all that prepared in my head. But since he chose not to make my absence or presence an issue, I said nothing.

Instead, I turned pointedly toward Isulde and sent her a mind-probe orgasm while sipping ale, and she fell back ecstatically into Walworth's arms, moaning and kissing him as he smiled down at her. I made sure Caethne caught part of my force and she shuddered on the floor.

"Happy ladies' night, witch-sisters," I said amiably.

"Stop it, Llewelyn," commanded Aleta. "The whole night's getting too weird to touch." She looked at the floor. "Is Caethne all right?"

"No," said Ellisand. "She's sick and pale with love." He leapt down to the floor and took Caethne's limp body up in his arms. "Shall I sing you elvish songs, child?" He stroked her hair and she sighed and held him like a pleasure-seeking infant.

Walworth spoke. "Isulde." She threw her arms around his neck and looked intently at him without speaking. "I commend you to Llewelyn's protection."

"Why?"

He gently released her hold. "Because Mirand and I must leave you now. And Threle is naught to me should the emperor see your beauty and take it."

"He has. Many times." Something dark and sad passed through Walworth's eyes.

"Inspiration is a starry cloud," said Ellisand lazily. "My lady hovers inconstant through all our dreams. She is known to every star and every shade of light and every storm and every raging moon. She is known to all she chooses to bless." Walworth studied him intently. "She came to me a shadow in my crib. She is Caethne's love for the master here, and Walworth's love for Threle, and Roguehan's love for destruction, and Mirand's love for knowledge, and Baniff's most euphoric drinking state, and Aleta's bravery, and my music, and Lew's love for my music and love for all of you."

Everyone stared at him. Except Isulde, who was once again huddled against Walworth's chest.

"You're doing fine," I said.

"Well—" He shrugged under everyone's scrutiny. "—that's just how I see it. It's why we live to die for her." He started singing softly to Caethne again, then stopped. "I would protect you."

"Oh," said Isulde. "I am witch and wizard and Northern fairy and need no protection."

"You're a regular goddess," said Aleta. There was nothing worshipful in her tone, or even complimentary. She was just stating her honest assessment of the situation. I found Aleta's words moving. So did everyone else.

"Goddess has nothing to do with it," Ellisand corrected her. "Isulde is simply the best." Isulde slid off her chair and went to join Ellisand on the floor with Caethne. Walworth and Mirand rose.

"Take care of the best," said Walworth slowly, as he and Mirand departed for their secret consultations. "That is all."

After they had left, Caethne revived a little and bade us eat as she gushed with her newly requited love. Baniff sipped his ale and told me he'd never had a better brew in centuries, in compliment to my wizardry. Ellisand started a drinking song and we all joined in, including Aleta, who sang cheerfully while she examined her sword. I watched Isulde. She was singing in the hours. And she was weaving rushes in her fingers to speed the time against Walworth's wishes. So when light and dark ran against each other in blocks of a few hours without stopping, I knew that "the best" was moving time like a Northern wind, quietly hastening the end.

Eleven

*A*nd so I was not surprised when somewhere between the increasingly rapid shuffle of darkness and light which Isulde kept spinning out of her song, somewhere within the crush of time she kept carefully drowning us in, Cathe showed up. I have no idea why the rapid succession of the hours didn't leave him cold in the dust of the Midland plains, panting and cursing as the moon shriveled down into yet another newness and so shuddered immortality forever out of his grasp. But I did know that nothing short of the destruction of all the worlds, and maybe not even that, would keep Cathe from the god-appointed hour.

He arrived on a dark crest. He arrived before the moon disappeared. Inchia blandly announced his presence as the light failed for the fourth time, and Isulde immediately stopped singing. And when Isulde stopped, the darkness stopped with her. And the darkness held and collected itself before slowly swaying back into its accustomed pace.

Cathe entered trippingly, staff in hand. "And what a merry ride the time is tonight," he crowed exuberantly as he strode into the dining area. "Such fast and even pulses as the Lady waltzed me here— and then to find all in a dim waking. Ahhh!" He took a deep breath, expanding his chest. "Rather invigorating to slide and slither between such rapid hourly gaps—really the hours pull hard on each other like newly formed scabs."

"I felt for you all along the plains and into the Northern duchies, cousin." I greeted him in a tone of careless accusation. A certain stiffness in his shoulders, a stiffness which perhaps would only be visible to another cleric, betrayed discomfort with my words. "And having felt nothing, I wonder at your arrival, although of course you are welcome."

He was most put out at having to explain himself without knowing what my greeting was intended to imply. "Well," he said mildly, "I suppose the moon brought me in." Isulde giggled. "Well, I suppose she did, you know," he said to her laughter. "Fine waning moon. So fine she lightly burned me as I grappled her and so she pulled me firmly through time." There was a silence circling thickly through the room now, and so Cathe had to speak again. "I—I rode time like a gnat rides dust clouds—swift and easy, and so covered a four—is it four?—a four-day journey in one."

"Well, I suppose you had your reasons for keeping your energy quiet and not returning my sendings." I insisted on making a public issue of having looked for him, just to get him wondering and uneasy about whether my evil alignment was an open secret, and whether he should admit to having felt my evil sendings, being a good priest of Ceres now and all. I did not correct him by telling him I had felt him three days away before Isulde's song blurred and hastened the days, that really he had two solid days to travel the northern duchies in before her song began and it was only one day, his last day, that "the moon" had collapsed into something like hours.

You see, I knew that Cathe was likely to swallow a great deal of discomfort because he had so much at stake, that he would not risk his godhood by asking mutually embarrassing questions. And so I intended to keep him uncomfortable, because his own confusion was sure to weaken his power and concentration. I felt him reach furtively for my thoughts and I blocked the probe with a sending, "Keep low, eavesdroppers." Then I glanced meaningfully at the door as if to say, "Trust me."

He did. Which was an excellent thing, because it's damned near impossible for one evil cleric to shield himself against another. Cathe backed off and decided to subtly insist for his audience that he had been immersed in the novelties of a different, faster order of time and therefore knew nothing of my sending or not sending. "Do you know that the stars ran so fast they clawed deep wrinkles into the old night sky? Really they did, and how—squirmy and trembly and—" He tucked his rod under his arm and fluttered his fingers as if he were most anxious that we all share his deep pleasure.

Then he noticed Ellisand, who was cockily raising an ale bottle to him in salute. Cathe immediately dropped his rod and his jaw. Pourra took up the rod in his teeth and ran off a few paces to play with it, while Cathe did his best to recover from his startled surprise by smoothly addressing Ellisand with a pointed naturalness, as if it were perfectly right and proper that his former prisoner should be here with hands healed. "—or, perhaps I should say, the stars were not so much trembly—but raunchy—and *rhythmic*." Ellisand said nothing, but he was smiling like a well-fed fox at Cathe's discomfort. Cathe hesitantly smacked his lips to cover his embarrassment and turned to Baniff, who was watching him steadily over an ale bottle.

"Or rather—like the death throes of an old donkey. That is—" He hesitated a little under the gnome's gaze. "—when I cared for such things as the death throes of old donkeys."

"Guess it all kind of brings ye back," said Baniff, drinking.

"Yes, well, I suppose it does." He sat at the table. At some point Inchia had cleared the dinner dishes, and at another point a profusion of ale bottles in various states of depletion had appeared, some manifested, some brought out of Caethne's stores through mundane means. Cathe picked up an empty one and examined it. "A fine sloppy absence," he pronounced, setting it back down sharply. "Well. My dears," he addressed all of us at the table, "my sweetling dears." He gasped and took off his traveling cloak, for the room was really quite warm. "Caethne, my special dear." He turned and extended his hand to Caethne, who was lying on her back in the reeds and sucking on an ale bottle which she kept sharing with a delighted Pourra. "Come come come and welcome your dear hus—" Pourra flipped him back his rod so he could continue to devote his full attention to swigging from his witch-mistress's bottle. As Cathe bent down to retrieve his rod, his eyes caught sight of the Venus hair and girdle, which were still lying loosely on the floor, and then his eyes made a rapid questioning glance over to me before returning to Caethne.

"Do you like my pretty things, coz?" asked Caethne languidly. She was smoking some chaia that Ellisand had given her.

Cathe looked at me again before sliding down to sit beside Caethne on the floor. "My cousin-wife," he wheedled, "I love them beyond sense."

"So did Mirand." She chuckled.

"So did Mirand?" he asked pleasantly.

"Yes. Days ago now." She sat up slowly and held out the remainder of her chaia to Ellisand, who took it. " 'Tis wondrous strange to be so loved. Touch me here, cousin." She indicated a spot between her breasts, just over her heart. Cathe touched her lightly, anxiously, and then quickly removed his fingers. "What do you find?" She smiled.

"I—I don't know. To be sure, I don't know." He turned to me again with another questioning glance.

"I don't know either," said Caethne slowly, smiling and stretching and sighing and lazily leaning back. Pourra scampered over her lap and lost himself in a pile of reeds. Caethne sat forward and extended her hands to Cathe, and he took them in his with such a look of utter confusion that everyone except Aleta laughed.

Aleta broke through the laughter by speaking dourly to Cathe's puzzled glance. "Yeah, guy, I know what you mean."

"Well, I—" Cathe looked around at everyone at the table. He was most discomfited.

"He *means* an eternal Nothing," I joked. Cathe did not respond to my comment, because he was trying to figure out Caethne, who with the aid of chaia had enchanted her own thoughts into a random slosh of mazy motion, like slow fat clouds turning over under their own weight, clouds to thicken and kill any foolish wind which tried to penetrate their foggy intimacies. Caethne dropped his hands and picked up the girdle and the hair. She playfully threw the girdle around his neck and tucked the hair over his ear. Her actions only made the general laughter louder, for this time Aleta joined in. I must admit, he did look ridiculous.

"Wife?" he asked politely.

"Wife," Caethne repeated slowly and mysteriously, with a strange touch of wryness. "Wife." She paused. "I'd have blood for you to drink, but alas—" She looked at Isulde. "—it's all gone North."

"Well then, as my lady wishes," said Cathe helplessly. He stood up, looking down at her solicitously. "Where is your brother?"

She hugged her knees and closed her eyes as if in trance. "Closed up with my love and not to be disturbed."

"Ah, yes, but surely I must make report to him on Roguehan's movements. And to you, as duchess. We three must be alone tonight." He spoke urgently.

"And we shall." She opened her eyes from far away. "But Aleta is commander now. You must give report to her. And then you and Llewelyn shall come with me, and I shall call my brother, for the moon awaits us." Cathe looked a little more relaxed at Caethne's reference to the moon. She was aware of the time and the issue at stake after all.

"It'll be fun," I suggested. He seemed to take my words as a hint.

"Of course. Well." He turned to Aleta. "Commander. It is my sad duty to inform you, to inform you all, that the emperor comes quite close upon my heels. I expect him to be upon us rather soon."

"So?" she asked curtly. "Do you also expect us to send out a greeting party and usher him in?"

"No, but I thought, perhaps—"

"There's nothin' to think now," said Baniff. "We'll fight him as we can."

Cathe seemed a little stunned by their matter-of-factness. "Come, coz," said Caethne, rising and extending her hand. "If that is all you have to say, we already know it, and you and I have much more important business to attend to."

"I am yours then," said Cathe, taking her hand to follow.

"*Believe* it." I slapped his shoulder lightly as I exited with them. And as I left I felt Isulde blowing me gardenia-scented kisses all along my back and something in me withered with knowing that every kiss was an explosive fare-thee-well.

The odd thing about the three of us as we climbed through a tower of air and darkness, plodding up stairs which twisted like steep thunderclouds into the highest room in the castle, was our remarkable silence concerning the fast-approaching blessed event. No one was about to acknowledge immortality, although everyone was about to grasp it in one way or another.

Caethne was the easiest among us for she had had her love returned and so could die. She was humming snatches of a wordless little tune and swinging her arms like a boisterous milkmaid testing her strength before a long morning walk. Caethne was our gateway into forever, but our gateway into forever might as well have been strolling out to gather eggs and corn for all the solemnity she wore. Just a poor simple witch off to work another spell. The climb would not even leave her breathless, and the right words would come as easily as "good morning" over breakfast. And ever were her thoughts just trails and dabs of clouds.

I could tell that Caethne's assumed nonchalance was pushing Cathe into a rather superb state of madness. He moved slower than either of us, and leaned heavily on his staff, and trembled in the knees, and stopped frequently, as if at last he hesitated to claim his promise. But for some reason he also hesitated to speak on the issue, as if something in him feared Caethne's response, or feared the words which would make divinity real. Frigid and dark as the air in the tower was, he often complained of sweat burning his forehead and of his eyes hurting. He was constantly wiping his face with a rosemary-scented cloth, and once or twice he gasped uncertainly, "I hope I can make it."

Once he stopped for a full half minute and wheezed and pummeled his chest as if to shake phlegm loose. "Caethne, my dear, my eyes are blinding me—my eyeballs feel like two squishy tadpoles growing soft legs down along my cheeks—no wait, there—" He coughed. "—I peeled one shadow-tadpole off and so I can see—I'm so sorry for the passing of the life but then—I suppose I'm better for it. Yes, the air is quite close here. Llewelyn, please hold your torch a little higher that I might see more."

I gave him the torch. Try as I might to feel some pleasant anticipation of my own immortality, I only felt divinity at a distance. The god I would become was peering through stone-cold fits of dry winter air and sucking meanly at my skin and eyes, but I pushed Him off like an annoying monastic homework assignment or a sluggish beetle clinging to my face. Later I would pin Him to a quiet board for leisured study but not yet, not while there were still minutes of tower to pass through. Eternity was large and cold—and far too clear for mortal thoughts. And the tower was almost as cold as eternity. So cold that my best idea of godhood was never having to suffer winter again.

My thoughts turned like Caethne's clouds, or like the slender white petals a grinning skeletal maiden might pinch from a daisy. *I will become a god. I will not think about it. I will become a god. I will not think about it.*

We reached a closed iron door at the end of my thoughts. Caethne confidently took the torch from Cathe and opened the door with a word. As soon as we crossed the threshold, the door closed behind us, and we stood strangely in a dark silent space as Caethne whispered an incantation and threw the torch under a cauldron. A shallow pit below the cauldron caught the fire and burst into a hole of lurid flames, which made the rough stone floor and walls seem to flutter and writhe in response, as if we three stood in a lonely burning tower at the end of the world. Then I noticed a large hole like a stony portal in the farthest wall. The hole was letting in the night sky.

Caethne sat softly on the floor, gathered her long shift around her, and stared quietly into the night, looking so smugly mysterious that she was beginning to get *me* nervous. She sat all in a perfect stillness, like a living statue, not moving so much as a heartpulse, not showing so much as a winter flush along her skin. And her stillness was terrible, for we could all feel the moon racing down into new, and Caethne's nerve-scraping serenity was an awful indication that she would be pleased to let it. Clearly, Caethne would not begin until one of us asked her to. Clearly, Cathe must speak his needs to her or die.

Cathe paced the floor until at last he couldn't stand it anymore. "Where's Walworth?" he finally allowed himself to ask. He did not look at Caethne as he spoke. He held his back straight and stiff and leaned on his staff while looking out at the night. And he squinted his eyes as if he wished to deflect her words away from him, or disown his.

"He's with Mirand," Caethne replied, in a tone of profound meaning.

"Mirand knows what love is," I said solemnly. Cathe looked at me.

"Well." He sniffed loudly. "Will you call your brother?"

"Come to the night, Brother." She took him by the hand and led him to the hole in the tower wall. He followed her passively, like a little Sunnan schoolchild accustomed to obedience. "See and be dazzled by all the lovely blankness." I knew he was studying the dark through squinted eyes, studying because she wanted him to, and because the moon was falling falling falling and he knew it was now or never. "Will you take eternity?"

"Yes."

"Then love the sky."

Cathe opened his heart. The room got darker. I closed my fist over my dirk.

"Love it louder," coached Caethne. "Or the dying moon won't hear you."

"I am," said Cathe fiercely. He spread his arms, and raised his staff.

"Keep loving. Keep fixed," she commanded. "You are sending yourself into forever. You are falling into the dark." I moved softly. I moved like death. I was death. Caethne's spell was on me too. "Hsst, Brother. Soon, soon your force shall spread a new darkness upon the earth. And for your darkness new worlds shall shudder and die at your command, as many times over as you wish. And I give you the power to end time. You shall become like a star or a tree. Your force is an old star, a dead heart, a tree of dried veins. You shall open your scalloped bones into sea breezes. You shall lie carefully in each wave of thought which drags you under into your own service—*lie* carefully, son and father of evil. Watch your words. Every time you speak, a world dies."

I was closer, with him, hard against his life, no turning back now.

"You are the last glint in a falcon's starving eye. You are the death-mew of the wolf cub as the falcon eats out its life. You are a storm of wolves. You rage in another fall, and the lizard sun licks your deepest summer into dust. You peep cruelly into hidden places, engendering death where you choose, and in death you shall live through all your priests and priestesses, yea even unto the old age of wasted youth."

My blade was out.

"How many lives have you taken?"

"Many."

"Ahh, and how many treasons and turnings have you committed? Against your heart and that of others?"

"Many, for I am evil."

"Do you wish to plea for your goddess?"

"No."

"Then I sentence you to eternity."

I stabbed him once—in the back of his heart—because it seemed like the most appropriate place, and his spirit screamed foul as blood and stagnant water slowly filled and gushed between a rip of black moss that was his lung. And inside the lung was spongy sod which broke sharply and crumbled into soil. Caethne turned the cauldron to catch all the falling. And then we shoved the body into it and I kept helplessly stabbing what was left, pushing and tearing and prying open dead flesh for all the lost years of my life that he had taken from me. Something yellow like blood or insect juice splattered in a thick glob from his other lung and then more stuff just oozed through his organs. But the body was mostly dry. Something like worm-infested pear skin kept flaking off his organs like an old crust of scars.

And because he was evil I was not sickened. On the contrary, I felt rather high about the whole thing, because I was cutting and stabbing and ripping flesh for every poem I never got to write, and for every word I ever loved and murdered on my lips. I was killing the corpse for all my pretty stillborn acts of creation, violent redundancies for all my best magic in ruins. Every loss of my own life was a murderous stab against his. I was singing and chanting all my loss and killing it down for glory, and my sweet sister was chanting it with me, helping me to ease my rage in all the languages we knew. We were two glorious witches together—just as she claimed she had seen in my absence—stirring the same cauldron and calling eternity to settle some ancient personal score.

"Here then—" I slit open his back again, wider this time. "—for all my childhood writings and cravings. And one more slash for killing my glorious friendships. And here—you horrible dead thing—" I separated his back from his spindly legs and ripped it in quarters. "—for killing *all* my loves—for leading me to kill what I love—for the death of my best and brightest self—do you know—*do you know*—I almost heard a flower sing and so you crushed it, you ugly staining viper—may you rot for my curse—may you feed and bloat on the curse of my own evil."

I kept stabbing the body until the meat smelled cold and foul. Caethne echoed every word I said with great energy, screaming all my hatred into the night as if she were the cleansing old Crone aspect of Ceres Herself while the cauldron filled with all the blood and remains and strange old pussy liquids that once constituted Cathe. And blue-black flies kept glistening and swarming out of the roiling brew.

There was a place where our screams pitched and swayed into a tempestuous ragged silence and this was the place where Caethne spoke. "When you bathe in the flies they will eat your flesh and pulverize your bones. Your body will expire piecemeal in the swarm of their bellies, dying a multitude of deaths as your spirit bounds into forever. Intense buzzing pain to part from life, but then—All. Will you have All, little one? Will you give me your hand? Will you crawl quietly into the pot like a nice little boy and let the nicer flies eat you? Will you die for your Mother's dinner?"

She sounded like Grana when she said this, and so I fell on her bosom and called her Grana and Mother and demanded all her childhood promises. "Where is my wizard wand, witch? Where are my bright-painted birds to bring me my sup? Where is my mountain wizard's sword? Where is my elf queen's magic drum? Where is my piece of night sky to wear in my heart—so to tear from my heart—and throw back to you—now—where is the glory of my brilliance and the flower of my promise—Mother, give it back—"

"Give it baaaaaaaaack," shrieked Caethne.

"Take my mutton for your dogs—take back my uses for your dogs of the moon. My birth is cursed and void in you. And all the uses of your words are gone. Your magic cannot touch me. All the uses of my beauty. My blessed beauty—Mother, you destroyer—you broke me—where is the holy moment when I take pen in hand and thrust my life in ink—where is the sacred space between my thoughts and my words—*where am I?*"

"It is now," screamed Caethne. "Give me the knife." I did so as the moon began to hiss into darkness.

First we both held the blade to my neck. Then I released her hand and my lady was holding it. I stretched my neck for the shallow thrust, for some of my blood had to be shed to show the moon I too was dying, to be reborn as she rebounded into her waxing phase, a minute or two away now. We were waiting for the pulse of separation. We were waiting for the gods to say "now."

"You just killed a brethren in evil," Caethne said evenly, pressing the point of my dirk enough to draw blood.

"I know."

"And so when you pass—you must pass from Habundia Christus to Habundia Ceres. For how should Habundia Christus accept the destroyer of Her brood? And shall Ceres send you to Christus? I am Ceres, you know. I am Ceres-Caethne in the heat of my magic. And I, who once loved you, little brother, and having loved you once, do love you forever, do birth you into goodness."

Pass to goodness! What the bloody hell!

"No," shrieked an anxiously imperative voice from the now-open doorway, saving my evil from breaking into destruction against the now-expanding moon. Between my heartthrobs I felt my warm blood trickling down my neck and my dirk clattering hard on the floor.

"Into the pot," Caethne commanded me, ignoring the intruder and speaking like a witch from a Northern folktale, or a half-remembered character from one of Grana's childhood stories. "And I shall eat you into forever—"

"No," shrieked the voice a second time, blasting Caethne backwards with a pulse that also sent me reeling. "His evil is inviolate. He has broken the law of our Lady and so he is ours." The language was Botha. The speaker was Mirra. "And you, Duchess," she intoned impressively, "are under arrest in the name of His Excellency, the Emperor Roguehan." Mirra continued to hold Caethne at bay with her goddess force as she strode peremptorily across the room and spit in the cauldron, destroying forever my path to deification.

Cathe's remains sighed and dried up into a hard brown grunge as two imperial guards led my beloved sister away in chains. And then the room began to stink of Cathe's death. And then the night began to stink. I heard Cathe's spirit screaming as the moon waxed upward.

"I hear you, Brother Cathe," said Mirra piously. "Vengeance is yours."

Mirra was not alone. She was standing next to a quietly intense man in a dark wizard robe whom I took to be Zelar. The folds of his robe swirled with sparks and his eyes spoke memories of dying candles. His eyes were pale gold and deep, but the rest of his face was very dark, and his hair was all shadow gone awry from the light. It was strange, but I was not afraid of Zelar. I just stood looking at him defiantly as my blood crept slowly down my throat. Then I smiled. "Can I help you, Master?"

Mirra spoke. "His Excellency the Emperor has given me authority here to punish you for your crimes against evil."

I started laughing. Zelar interrupted Mirra by speaking to me. "Where is Mirand?"

"Where is Mirand?" I mocked. "Don't you know, Master? He's in love."

Zelar turned to Mirra, who immediately went stiff and self-righteous. "You failed."

Mirra raised her head and I could feel desperate prayers to Habundia Christus pounding thick and furious throughout the room as she spoke. "It wasn't my fault, Master Zelar. I tried my absolute best to kill Llewelyn once, as you know—in an avalanche." She looked at me for confirmation, as if I was supposed to eagerly endorse her excuse.

"I thought you were spotting me for Roguehan," was all I said.

"So you've failed twice." Zelar's voice was perfectly rational and measured, a voice that gusted ghostly logic. I wasn't sure if he was speaking to me or to Mirra, so I looked mildly at Mirra.

"It's not fair," she quavered. "I made the supreme sacrifice for you, striving to kill evil to further the cause of evil. Do you know how much spiritual development I risked for you, Master? How clear I had to make my own motivation to myself and to my goddess? How unalterable my belief had to be that destroying a brother would result in greater evil, lest I slip and condemn myself in Her eyes forever? That alone should count."

"Count? For *me*?" asked the wizard, in a voice which teased lightly like Mirand's sometimes did. Then his voice turned harsh. "Success counts. You were to prevent the spell, Sister. You were to save my student from the anguish of knowing his own love to be the cause of all his own destruction, lest in despair he destroy himself without our guidance. For thus much service rendered I was willing to use my considerable connections to launch you into early high priestesshood."

"Master, it isn't fair. We won anyway. And I understood that my job was—"

"Your job was to prevent this—" he waved a dark-gloved hand toward me "—wildcat operation for immortality concocted between Lord Cathe and the brother here from coming to fruition. I wished to lead Mirand whole and clean into evil. He has now been tainted with love."

"How did you know about our wildcat operation?" I tried once again to enter this amazing exchange.

"I know about want." He said this simply. "Cathe wants forever. Caethne wants love. A fair and proper exchange of need, and," he paused, "a fair and proper time for such an exchange. Of course I used my own usually competent clerics—" He looked at Mirra. "—to research the details for me, but I've dealt with Cathe and Caethne before and so I always knew the general thrust of what was supposed to happen here." Zelar walked solemnly over to the cauldron and looked out through the gap of stones into the night. "So you also sought to be immortal? A god, is it?"

I glanced at the cauldron. "Well, not so much anymore."

"His Excellency shall be fascinated, I'm sure." Zelar softly chuckled.

"Yes," said Mirra self-importantly in an attempt to ingratiate herself with Zelar. "And I shall immediately inform His Excellency of how the brother sought to interfere with the workings of evil by making himself a god."

"No," said Zelar casually. "Llewelyn is useful to me now."

"*What?* Master," she whined, "Brother Llewelyn clearly sought to destroy this household on his own accord, on his own terms. He has taken upon himself the duties of His Excellency, and so is guilty of political treason as well as trying to leap beyond himself into godhood without official clerical sanctification. He's done all this on his own, without consulting *anybody*. Surely you don't mean—"

"—Clearly he did 'consult' Cathe. He was high clergy."

"Cathe." She sighed. "Who knows where Cathe's spiritual loyalties—"

"—Then why are you so keen on exacting vengeance for him, Sister?" Zelar's question silenced Mirra. "Now. I want you to remain silent concerning our arrangement, and to remember how easy it would be for me to implicate you in Llewelyn's . . . unfortunate adventure, should you decide to speak." Zelar said this quietly, without anger, but I thought Mirra was going to shrivel into dust when he said it. "Unless you think the emperor would be pleased to know that you were planning to destroy one of his spies for him, all on *your* own initiative."

I thought Mirra was going to die. Her face and eyes looked like dust as she sank to her knees and looked tearfully up at the wizard. "Master, I did all in obedience to you. I sacrificed all and joined you on your word—your promise—and now—you wouldn't lie about me to make me out to be a traitor, it wouldn't be fair." She choked. "By the Goddess Habundia Christus it wouldn't be fair."

"*Fair*, Sister—" He smiled horribly. "—go, join Roguehan's little clerical coterie and mumble your pretty little chants. And when you finally discover what *is* fair, come and tell me about it." She stood uneasily. "Remain silent on the rest and I shall. And I suggest that you pray long and fervently that I don't change my mind concerning you." She looked at me, bowed to him, and ran off throwing frightened prayers so fast their power slapped my face. I leaned casually against the doorway and glanced coolly at the older wizard. "And now. Llewelyn. My friend, colleague, and inheritor of half my wisdom."

"Yes?"

"I can still persuade Roguehan to spare your life."

"So?"

"So I should like you to remove the Venus force which holds my student bound. Since his love for the duchess hasn't been bought at the price of Walworth's death, disrupting the goddess force won't be as damaging to him as your vengeance had hoped it might be. And while Mirand is imprisoned I suspect that since both you and I can maintain a special link to him, through the path of our common training, we can finally—together—persuade him of the hidden beauties of evil."

I saw no reason to tell him that Mirand's newfound passion was not a result of the Venus gifts or even of Venus at all. Whatever prompted Mirand to finally love Caethne after all these years had nothing to do with me or Venus. But as long as Zelar believed I had something to offer worth my life I could find no reason to introduce reality into the arrangement. "Really, Master." I grinned. "If after all my years of training I can't persuade Mirand of the hidden beauties of evil I might as well cease calling myself a priest of Hecate."

"Well put." He chuckled.

"In fact," I boasted, "I can promise you that Mirand will perform a complete reversal of all things in all respects. That with my help, you will fulfill your own impressive want." Of course I had no idea how I would pull such a feat off, but I did know it was exactly the sort of thing Zelar wanted to hear.

Zelar blanched slightly at my words but recovered into a beatific smile. And when the guards who had taken Caethne away returned, he ordered them to take me too but to treat me gently and with all kindness.

He needn't have bothered. Guards have an inbred way of blurring distinctions, an unerring democratic sense. I was treated no differently than anyone else in Walworth's household. Like Caethne, I was led away in chains, and like the rest of my fine dinner companions, I was shoved and insulted and beaten until we reached the castle's large throne-reception room. And then I was shoved some more and kicked and pushed across the marble floor until my legs collapsed with the blows and I fell panting. I stared at the smooth white floor for a few minutes, not sure whether it was easier to face Roguehan or to face my fellow captives.

When I caught my breath and the pain of my blows subsided somewhat I looked up slowly and the first thing I saw was the back of Mirand's robe. He had a shield up which was wider than winter itself, and from my angle of vision I saw that he had magically broken one of the links in the chain which held his hands, but that the broken link was partially obscured in a fold of his robe. So I shielded myself and magically broke one of my own links. Everyone else's hands appeared to be thoroughly bound, that is, from what I could see as I stood up.

Once standing, I silently remarked how calm and open Mirand's face and eyes were. He was looking brightly and attentively toward

Zelar, as if he were eagerly waiting for his Master's kind instruction. As if he were preparing to take notes and memorize into the rest of his life every chance syllable Zelar let drop. Zelar was lounging on a throne decorated with wildflowers, which I took to be Caethne's, and whispering something to Roguehan, who was stroking a fluffy white cat in his lap and sitting on another throne, which I took to be Walworth's. Both the emperor and his master wizard glanced in my direction, so I knew that Zelar was whispering something about me. I saw that Mirra was also watching this exchange, trying desperately to hear what was being said and trying desperately not to look like she was listening. She was cowering behind one of Roguehan's clerics.

I turned away from the whispered exchange and studied the rest of my fellow prisoners. Aleta stood bravely near the front of our cluster, shoulders back and chest out, a soldier to the end. Her eyes were fixed attentively on the emperor's face and she bravely refused to lower them. Baniff was next to her, sort of. That is, he *was* next to her but then he was sort of wandering through the little space of floor reserved for prisoners. His stride conveyed an easy restlessness, as if he were just waiting to get through whatever there was to get through. On the surface he traipsed around as if he had decided that since there was no longer anything to lose he might as well take a stroll. But prodding through his surface movements there was another walk, a slow mad sort of meander that seemed to be taking place somewhere else. His shoulders twitched with every footfall.

As he paced in back of Caethne he absently brushed against the hem of her shift, and the movement caught my attention so I noticed that Caethne was staring at Zelar with the same intensity as Mirand, and that her eyes were teary but defiant. Baniff's little stroll also caught Roguehan's attention as he trekked past Mirand, and Caethne responded to the emperor's glance by moving to stand in front of her lover. Then I heard Mirand say quietly, "No, stand *by* me, love." She glanced at him and took a step backwards to do so. One of the guards, who had also caught the emperor's glance, started beating poor Baniff roughly with a short club, which effectively put an end to his little walkabout. Walworth just stood and gazed calmly at Roguehan.

Isulde stood a little to Walworth's side, swaying as if in a private, Northern dance. She was smiling merrily at Roguehan, and occasionally the emperor looked up from his whispered consultation to smile sunnily back at her, and once he even kissed the back of his hand to her slowly and respectfully. Of the prisoners only Ellisand was sitting. He looked around the room with an expression of confident curiosity. Pourra was curled in his lap. I didn't see Inchia or any other servant, so I assumed that the servants had either escaped or were being held elsewhere.

As the conversation went on and on, including various guards and clerics that Roguehan motioned over and sent back away, it occurred to me that the emperor had lost no time in settling in. Of course, Walworth had organized no defenses, and had told us specifically to treat the emperor as we would treat King Thoren himself. Maybe Aleta had genially shown him the way to the throne room. And surely Cathe or some other spy had provided Roguehan with a detailed map of the place. But it still seemed incredible that in the space of my recent conversation with Zelar and Mirra, the entire household minus servants would be so neatly rounded up.

Especially since on my way to the throne room I had felt nothing different about the castle, no sense of a foreign presence, no sense of anything being as it shouldn't be, with the exception of the guards. The worst—or best—part of Roguehan's victory was that it felt very much as if he belonged here, as if he'd always been here, as if he were at much at home as if he was Walworth's twin brother. I mean—the castle was already so much his you couldn't even feel a difference. And he had come so quickly. Clearly the emperor hadn't lingered at Disenward, and clearly he hadn't even brought his full army with him. He might have been here for larking for all the military complement I noticed. There were guards for him and chains for us, for guards carry chains and I suppose one must do something to distinguish prisoners, but that was all. Mirand and I could have blasted them all and stood a fair a chance of winning, but Walworth's people were clearly not willing to fight. And so the emperor had a victory, but his victory was a frantically smooth affair that made about as much sense as fairy fun.

I studied Zelar, who was lazily stretching himself as Roguehan held consultation with yet another cleric. Zelar knew his way too. He had had no trouble making a hornet line to the proper tower, although he had to ask me where his former apprentice was. Of course Mirra had probably tracked me, and it would be easy to follow the call of sunrise where the new moon rose and so find the appropriate tower. Sensitive wizards can hear the sun rise, even through stone walls. And Mirand could certainly shield out his master—that didn't surprise me. Turning to goodness was the biggest shield of all. So rather than bumble around after Mirand, Zelar had found it more appropriate to stop the ritual and do his best to interfere with the love spell. His first act was to touch Mirand's life through absence.

So I stood waiting for the show to start. Whatever Roguehan did now was sure to be extempore, sure to be nothing more organized than an ad hoc display of showmanship. He wanted us to admire how swiftly and easily he could act the role of Threlan king, and therefore—damn him—how skillfully he could make his act real. It ought to be the gods' own crime to make one's act real, to make one's fiction real, and then to demand an audience for the event, but, as I've said before, Roguehan was always a bit of a monk. And this hussied-up court was all his sort of thing.

There was more whispering from Zelar and a good deal more cat petting from Roguehan before the emperor finally spoke. "Isulde," he said gently and caressingly, "come to me." She did so. "Remove her chains," Roguehan ordered a guard.

A guard fell over herself trying to get to Isulde to release her, and then fell further into confusion and fumbled and stammered, "Uh, Your Excellency . . . uh . . . it seems my lady here has no chains."

"Never did, never will," chanted Isulde.

"And yet I swear to you we bound all the prisoners, according to your instructions," added the guard desperately.

Roguehan waved the guard away, smiling, as entranced with Isulde as everyone usually was. "Of course. Beauty wears no chains. Come, Dream." He took her hands in his. "Come and pet my cat." Isulde took the animal up in her arms and kissed it. Her kiss turned the cat into a pile of snow which promptly melted into exquisite rainy incense. And then the incense curled around her wrists and formed exquisite silver bracelets while Roguehan's people dutifully applauded his answering gift. "Come upon my lap and kiss me for Beauty's sake."

"Careful, my lord," teased Zelar. "Lest you too become snow."

I couldn't resist watching Walworth's face as Roguehan and Isulde caressed and kissed each other. But then, neither could Roguehan, for despite his joy in Isulde he kept glancing at his fallen enemy. Or maybe he was watching Walworth *because* of his joy in Isulde. But really there was no entertainment for Roguehan there, for Walworth kept his features impassive as their love play concluded in one of Isulde's resounding orgasms.

By the time Isulde emerged from her embrace her bracelets had become bands of delicate snowdrops. She removed them and hung them on Caethne's throne with the rest of the wildflowers. Then she snuggled close into Roguehan's lap.

"I've kissed your dream, Commander," said Roguehan cheerfully to Walworth.

"No. You've kissed everyone's dream," replied Walworth. I supposed it was pointless to correct Roguehan as to who was officially the commander now. I assumed Aleta wasn't too eager to stand on her new title.

"Isulde," said the emperor sweetly, "tell us who you belong to."

"The North." She slid off his lap.

Roguehan did not look perturbed by this unexpected response, but he did not choose to pursue the subject. Instead, he commanded, "Go. Await my pleasure in the hall outside." Isulde did not obey. She glided gracefully to the doorway leading to the hall in question, but instead of leaving she sat on the floor in the entrance and faced the court to watch the rest of the proceedings. The emperor ignored the slight. "Ellisand—" He smiled. "—I am most delighted to find you here and in good health."

"Thanks."

Roguehan turned to the guard who had been confounded by her attempt to free Isulde. "Remove his chains." She did so with all haste. Ellisand remained sitting and the guard made a motion to pull him to his feet as Pourra scampered squealing over to Caethne. "No, leave him." Roguehan commanded. Then he spoke directly to Ellisand. "You are now my chief court musician and poet." Roguehan turned to Walworth again. "I must compliment the king on his musical taste." Walworth did not change his facial expression or acknowledge Roguehan's compliment.

"King?" asked Ellisand. "You mean Threle still *has* a king?" Ellisand sounded honestly confused, like he couldn't for the life of him figure out how that was supposed to work, and his tone completely deflated all the silliness and pomposity of politics, as well as the effect of Roguehan's dark measured courtesy, by eliciting a helpless titter from the guards.

And it was actually a reasonable question, given the strange events of our last supper. As near as I could figure, Caethne was king. That is, if Thoren was dead. But it was the emperor who now ruled Threle, and Roguehan knew nothing of the intricate interchange of power and position Walworth had initiated last night. But Ellisand's question was also an odd one, given the circumstances. Anyone might have expected Ellisand to sob in gratitude over the high honor he had just received, but by appearing utterly unconcerned with his new protected status, he appeared to rebuke the emperor's gift without even really troubling himself to rebuke it. His carelessness reminded me of Isulde turning bracelets into snowdrops, and I wondered if Roguehan was inclined to treat his audacity as kindly as hers.

There was a loud pause filled only with the guards shuffling their feet uncomfortably and hanging their heads. No one wanted to be especially noticed for brashly enjoying the new court poet's first stroke of wit, especially since it was likely that the emperor would see no humor in the remark.

"Thoren's dead," said Roguehan lightly, choosing to make a point of ignoring Ellisand's glaring lack of gratitude. "That makes Duke Walworth king, until I decide to officially assume kingship myself." No one saw fit to correct the emperor's false assumption. "And so," Roguehan addressed his new court poet amiably, "to whom do I owe gratitude for the unexpected but most welcome restoration of your hands?"

"To Llewelyn," said Ellisand truthfully.

Thanks, friend.

"I'm impressed," said Roguehan to me. "Come forward, Brother. Such a gift should earn you a fine reward. I am also pleased with what I hear—" He looked at Zelar. "—of your provocative activities in the south. Rest assured that I am amused with the fall of Threle and inclined to credit you with carrying out my orders. And I thank you for Ellisand. Perhaps I shall make you the next Duke of Walworth." Roguehan glanced at Walworth to see how he was taking this, but Walworth continued impassive as ever.

"Your Excellency—" I stepped forward and made a show of dropping the broken chains completely from my wrists through magic, as if the chains were a silly formality between us and there was really no question but that I was entitled to the same freedom as Ellisand and Isulde. Zelar must have given me one hell of a reference. "—I am happy that my humble act of healing—"

Mirra stepped forward at the same time. She was shaking and she glanced uneasily at Zelar before shrilly interrupting me. "Your Most Highest Excellency—"

"Yes, Sister."

Mirra looked around and shook even more violently with the realization that everyone was now looking at her. Some aspiring high priestess! "My duty impels me to speak what I know of the brother and his—his so-called acts of healing." Zelar's eyes went hard as jade. Mirra swallowed. "I must—I beg to have your protection while I speak, Your Excellency." She breathed hard and murmured in prayer, "Sweet Goddess. I obey."

"Speak," commanded Roguehan impatiently.

"Your Excellency—" She swallowed and coughed. "—Llewelyn is *not* what he appears to be."

"Is anyone?" said Roguehan. All of the emperor's people laughed loudly in appreciation of their dread lord's wit, which more than made up for any lingering chagrin over the subdued titters Ellisand had brought out.

"Yes," said Mirra desperately, "some of us are *really* evil. But Brother Llewelyn is a traitor to both yourself and his fellow clerics. And he has actually murdered a brother in evil, whose spirit even now cries out to me for vengeance. It is his spirit and the will of Habundia Christus which commands me to speak or be damned to Her. And—and—" She glanced fearfully at Zelar. "—I can't bear to be damned to Her." The part about Cathe crying out for vengeance was a lot of cow-wash, as *I* didn't hear anything. By now Cathe was probably trying to wheedle some new deal for an easy birth out of Habundia, so he could come back and screw up someone else's life. "Master Zelar is another traitor." Well and good, she was in it now, goddess or no goddess. Roguehan glanced at his master wizard, who settled back easily in his throne. "Master Zelar wanted me to destroy an imperial spy, meaning Llewelyn here, which is a crime against Your Excellency, the empire, and evil, which of course I didn't do—"

"Which of course wasn't your *fault*, Mirra," I couldn't resist adding. "As far as I'm concerned you should get full *credit* for that one."

Zelar chuckled and explained something in a whisper to Roguehan, and Roguehan broke out into loud peals of laughter. "I am truly sorry I missed that one. Continue, Sister."

Mirra looked mortified but she had no choice except to continue. "Brother Llewelyn sought to destroy the enemy's household to glorify himself into godhood." And she proceeded to recount all the sordid little details of my unclerical behavior, going back to my dreadful "hostility" and "insensitivity" to peacemongers at Kursen Monastery. And I must admit, she had quite a list, even bringing up things that I had forgotten. When she finished, Roguehan looked at Zelar and the wizard shrugged.

"My lord," said Zelar easily, "I freely admit to all she says and more." He stretched and yawned. "You see, the sister had agreed to help me with her—monastic skills in return for my promise to get her initiated into early high priesthood." Several of the clerics that Mirra had earlier taken refuge near looked properly outraged.

"Help you do what?" asked Roguehan.

Zelar explained quite easily about my love spell as a means to revenge and how he sought to stop the destruction I would have wreaked on Mirand. "He is like a son to me, my lord, and I'm sure you will agree that he would be quite an asset to the forces of evil. It was all really my own affair."

"Yes, whatever," said the emperor dismissively. "I give you your wayward child, and let us be done with the issue finally. It is starting to bore me."

"Thank you, my lord."

I assumed I was still safe then, despite Mirra's terrible accusations. Zelar and I would work on Mirand together, just as he had planned.

Roguehan then turned to Mirra. "You, Sister. Since you have such a long litany of complaints against your brother, you may pass clerical judgment upon him."

What! Now I looked at Zelar, who avoided my glance.

Mirra looked calmer now. "My dread lord, I think—" She looked at me. "—I think—it would be fitting to give him to your chief torturer for disposal unto death, where Habundia Christus may judge of his actions."

"Done," said the emperor. "And I now commend you to the judgment of the other court clerics, who have all authority to punish you according to your own crimes against evil." Zelar chuckled and Mirra fell shrieking to her knees. "Take her away," Roguehan ordered, adding generously, "You may use any room in the castle you find appropriate."

"There's a fine empty tower in the east," said Zelar helpfully. "Mirra already knows the way, but—" And he proceeded to give directions, damn him. Cathe's remains were still in the cauldron, and the sight of that mess would bring my fellow clerics to a fine pith of rage against yours truly even if Roguehan weren't about to send me to the chief torturer. Those clerics would surely tear my spirit to shreds at the sight, that is, after they got through with Mirra. Hell, they'd probably send a clerical posse down to stand in line to wait for the honor. Zelar was taking no chances with having to deal with me from the other side.

In fact, as the other clerics dragged Mirra out past Isulde, one cheerful-looking fellow remained behind to plead clerical privilege for disposing of me too. Roguehan cut him off by saying curtly to me, "So. It seems I must thank you for disposing of Cathe." There was a ripple of laughter. "And *I* shall punish you for arranging your own means of destroying the enemy and attempting to deprive me of the pleasures of execution. From duke to traitor. Quite a turn. Have you anything to say, Brother?"

I thought for half a minute. There was nothing to say really, and I noted that the worst part of waiting for my sentence was standing there without words. But as I glanced uncertainly in the direction of the cleric, in the direction of his lean, *serious* face, something spoke out of me slowly and deliberately. "I acted out of love for my friends." This time Mirand chuckled, louder than the circumstances required, I thought.

"Worse and worse. Here," Roguehan called over two guards. "To the chief torturer with him, wherever he's setting up. And if he's not set up yet, find him and escort him to some appropriate room. I don't care where. We'll soon have need of his services."

"My lord, I believe the chief torturer has found a room. I saw him go through the large door at the end of the corridor. No one's seen him come back out."

"Believe it leads down to a wine cellar," said another guard.

"It does," said Baniff helpfully.

"Leads down, anyway, and it smells like wine," said the guard, loath to be outspoken by a prisoner. "I went down looking for prisoners. But it's a fine place to set up for torture, Your Excellency. Cold as the Northlands."

"Excellent. Take him away."

"Your Excellency," spoke up the dour brother as two guards started to lead me out, "perhaps you would prefer *not* to leave someone with magical capabilities in the hands of—guards and—torturers." He spoke with contempt. "His brethren can prevent escape, and under clerical law—"

"His *brethren* have their beloved Sister Mirra to amuse themselves with," snapped Roguehan. "And I'm not concerned with clerical law. He broke *my* law and he's mine."

"Yes, Your Excellency, but perhaps you could best fulfill your own law if you would allow me to give you this, and allow me to beg that you use it." He produced a long black sash, like a swath of dull silk. "I designed this myself as you know. I have always carried it in your service for you have sometimes been pleased to put poor clerics like me in charge of difficult prisoners. Tied around his hands with the appropriate incantations, it will hold all his power sources in check. It will keep him from breaking doors and from not feeling pain."

The cleric gave the sash to Roguehan, who held it out to examine it. It reminded me of the sort of rags the students at Kursen used to use as bookmarks. "Pretty," he pronounced. I also noticed that for a bit of extra cheer the threads formed delicate prayers to Athena. "Come, Brother."

Apparently he meant both of us, for the guards brought me up to the throne, where Roguehan imprisoned my magic with silk as the priest softly chanted the appropriate incantations. And of course, as soon as Roguehan tied the sash I could feel my power dampen and so I knew that it worked quite well in that line.

So I was led out past Isulde, and along the smooth hallway, and through the large door in question, and the air did have an unmistakable viney smell. Then I was pushed and slapped and kicked and pummeled down the winding stairs of a long dark underground tower. I was beaten so badly that I wondered if there would be anything left for the chief torturer to work on. That is, the guard with the torch kept kicking me, and his buddy kept punching me and I kept doing my best to avoid their blows by hurrying down down down the spiraling stairs until I was finally pushed roughly onto a dirt floor and kicked hard in the stomach and dragged into a little stone wine cellar without light. And I just sat there in the frigid icebound air and choked on the scent of wine and listened to the sounds of the guards retreating upward. And then in the resulting silence I listened some more, for surely the silence compelled thought and I wanted to avoid thinking. But it was soon only silence and so thought became inevitable.

My first thought was that if my hands weren't bound I could force myself back up the tower and open the door and try to escape, for I hadn't noticed the door locking. But when I stood on my painful legs I felt the unmistakable tug and pull of the damn scarf bringing me back to the ground, and I knew that damn thing was absorbing my physical energy too, so it was a problem to support my own weight. My second thought was that it was strange to be able to smell so much wine in such frigid air, as if all liquid wouldn't harden and die down here, and then I realized that Caethne had probably once done some witchworking to prevent this wine from freezing in winter storage. And then all that came to me, over and over again, was the sound of Mirand's chuckle and a few sad memories of Helas which I tried to strangle for Hecate's sake. And a certain unexpected joy that Caethne at last had her love returned.

After the chuckle had repeated itself in my head for the fourth time, I heard footsteps and humming approaching from somewhere in the dark cellar, and so I knew I was about to endure some awful long death at the hands of Roguehan's chief torturer. But really, the guards hadn't left him instructions or anything. The whole affair had been rather sloppily performed so far and I wondered if it was going to be up to me to instruct the torturer as to what to do. Then I saw torchlight, or something making the darkness around me pale enough to see in, and I realized I was sitting in a bare stone storage alcove with an open entryway on each side. And as my surroundings got more visible I put my head down, closed my eyes, and did my best to pray, but the scarf was greatly dampening my ability to contact Hecate. I kept pulling at Her energy and I kept only getting trickles in return. Which was awful, because I felt I still had a lot of explaining to do concerning Cathe.

I heard the torturer moving around me, moving loud, with the noise of clinking metal and a great deal of huffing and puffing and groaning, as if moving down here was as much an effort for him as for me. And when I glanced up all prayer wavered at the sight of the gods' own variety of torture instruments hanging from the back of the chief torturer's belt. He not only carried the usual old favorites, pointed and studded with cut glass, but he also had a few whose uses I didn't want to guess at.

He was placing his torch in a holder in the stone wall and cursing the absolute cold in the cell. Then he kicked the wall as if the stones could be blamed for winter and cursed the stones again for hurting his feet. I kept my eyes steady before he turned to me, ready to bravely meet his and do my best to die well, but when our eyes met, my glance stopped him colder than the black ice patch on the wall which now reflected the torchlight. The chief torturer was Devon.

Devon looked at me for several seconds with his mouth open. Then his eyes got terribly big, as if it had taken those several seconds for the sight to impinge on his intelligence. And then his breaths got bigger and louder, as if by noisy gasps he could somehow easier account for my presence. But he made no attempt to speak. He squealed and bounced up and down on his knees, jangling the objects on his belt. Then he stopped bouncing and squealed again as he clutched a knife with horrid incantations engraved on the handle. Then he coughed up phlegm, which I presumed was the knife's doing, for Devon had taken no precautions in grasping the handle even if he had been taught how. Then he choked and snorted to get the phlegm back down his throat in the most disgusting manner possible, so I assumed after all that he was happy to see me.

I waited patiently for him to come to terms with the fact that he was indeed seeing me before I spoke. "Hey, Devon, buddy. How ye doin,' ye old cudcake?"

My voice sent him into further paroxysms of joyous disbelief. "Oh, oh, oh—" He was jiggling up and down again now, not exactly squealing, but too excited to speak. "—Oh, uuuoooo—I—oh, my emperor—O my gods—oh—cud cud cud—" He jumped up to emphasize each word, and then—O blessed gods—insight! "—Luvellun! *Luvelloooon!* It's really you! Oh!" I noticed at this point that he had gotten quite fat since I'd last seen him. His belt was large because his belly was, and his cheeks were now large and red and flaccid. Roguehan certainly made sure to keep his torturers well fed.

"It's really me, Dev." I grinned. "So fine to see you now. What a divine pleasure. Praise Hecate and all concerned."

"Luvelloon—I—" The excitement suddenly stopped, suddenly submerged in a terrible pleading sadness. "Why didn't you come for me?"

Really, where had I heard that before? And Devon's voice was pure torture, for it made me feel like the most heinous murderer. "The emperor wouldn't let me, Dev. You know how he gets."

"Yeah, bad emperor." He looked around, as if he were suddenly afraid of having said it. Then he sat heavily on the ground. His eyes were embarrassingly rich with pain.

"Yes, Dev. The emperor is very bad." I said this loudly, without hesitation, and saw his old accustomed admiration make his pain more intense. I guessed that he hurt most because of all the good times he felt he'd missed with me, because of all the clever brave things I might have said and done that he believed he had missed. In me, he had missed his life. I tried to soften the loss. "But I'm here now. For you."

He nodded solemnly and grinned. "Luvellun, guess what now? I'm the chief torturer. And I'm in charge and can set up anywhere I like."

"Why do you like to work so far underground, in the cold and dark?" I asked. He looked funny, that is, he screwed up his mouth and squeaked and sighed and hunched his shoulders and looked down, as if my question were a hurtful piece of implied criticism. "I mean, Dev," I tried again cheerfully, "don't you think your prisoners would hurt more in warmer air? Doesn't the cold tend to stop and slow their bleeding?"

"Yes," he said dully, as if he liked things that way but was now uncertain as to whether he should, since I seemed to disapprove. Clearly I had broached a bad subject.

"I mean—it's all right. I really don't care. It's your torture chamber, Dev."

"It is." He sniffled. "I want you to like it." He did not look at me.

"I will. I already do."

He wanted desperately to say something. Fear chased this want across his blubbery face.

"Dev?" I managed to say softly. "What is it? You can tell your buddy."

He huddled himself into a fat little ball and gasped. I waited. He was obviously working up the courage to say something of great moment to his life. This was all very difficult for him. Finally, he mumbled, "I like to work in the cold because sometimes—sometimes I think you might come for me. Like when they made me Sun King under the tree in the ice. And you always came in the cold to keep me warm." He sounded sadder than an old fairy's last fluttering fantasy.

"My poor little bird," I said sincerely. "But I have come. In the cold. And if you free me, I'll do my best to keep you warm—"

"Lew—" He uncurled himself again and hugged me. I thought of all the ancient eaten love apples that prompted this hug. "I love you!"

"Yes, Dev, I know. I love you too."

He was all joy again. "Yes! Yes! Yes! Luvellun, guess what else! I get to keep all the people I kill. Wanna see?"

"Are they here?" I tried to sound as enthusiastic as he did.

"Not yet." He said this matter-of-factly, without any enthusiasm or distaste. "But soon they will be. All the prisoners. And I get to kill 'em all. Wanna watch me do it?" He was bright and eager again. "Like bugs, only better."

"Sure, Dev. I'll watch."

"Hooo Uuooh!"

"But why don't you first untie—"

"You do wanna watch me?" He jiggled around, unable to contain his joy. "You wanna help? I'll show you how. It'll be great to make them spread around, you and me."

"Sure, Dev, anything you like. But why don't you see if you can untie this silly scarf and then you can show me where you're setting up shop down here."

"Not much to set up," said Devon proudly. "But you'll see. Just an old board and rope I can tie. And lead spikes with poison for after the ropes. For the prisoners. And everything on my belt is what I need." He hesitated. "Unless there's to be a cleric to help. But usually it's just me. But Luvellun," he crowed, "you can be the cleric to help!"

"Yes, Dev, of course. That's what I'm here for. But you must untie—"

My numerous requests that my torturer free me finally elicited a response.

"Luvellun, I—" He looked at my bound hands. "If you come here bound, it means I'm supposed to kill you. That's how it's always done. Like a sign." He didn't like this. He sighed loudly, and ugly smelly breath from his fat florid face filled the cell. I got the impression from his breath that he had developed a taste for eating his kill, and that was why he had gained so much weight. I choked and gagged on the odor. "Luvellun, this is a sign that I'm definitely supposed to kill you now." He looked around. "Luvellun, what should I do? Tell me what I should do."

"You should kill me, Dev, to show what a true friend you are," I said gravely. "But then I won't be able to help you kill the other prisoners."

"Noooo! But but but—" He looked like he had a sudden idea, bright and eager and proud to show off his thinking ability to me. "If I kill you, I get to keep you, and the emperor can't say nothing. Luvellun, what should I do? Are you a prisoner?" *That was a damn good question actually.*

"Yes, the cud emperor made me a prisoner. And he separated us. I hate him, Dev. Untie me so I can punish him," I commanded. Devon looked scared, torn. I softened my voice. "Please, Dev. I love you."

He did it, and dropped the dark silk on the ground with a look of triumph. "Now, Dev, help me stand." He did so, and after a minute or two I felt all my physical and magical power returning. I moved easily to the entrance of the cell near the stairs, and he followed me.

"Luvellun, I want to come with you. I want—I want to help you punish him." He had absolutely no fear of Roguehan now. He might have been asking to join me in one of our walks around the monastery for all the hesitation he showed.

I stopped and thought a bit and then decided what the hell. I had no real plan beyond getting out of the castle anyway. And there was a slight chance that if the chief torturer and his tools of trade were with me, then my other friends upstairs would have less painful deaths. I would put up with Devon for their sake. "All right, buddy." Devon smiled and hugged me. "Take the torch, and be very quiet, and do as I tell you, all right?"

"Yeah, all right. *All right!*" He was jumping up and down for joy again.

"Follow me. Do everything I tell you."

"Yes." He got so excited he dropped the torch and the fire went out, which was just as well. No need to draw attention to ourselves.

I had no idea what to do next, but I did know I wasn't going to hang around the castle much longer. Perhaps I could get to Gondal, and from Gondal make my way back south and so into the southeast kingdoms. But I couldn't plan that now. The point was getting somewhere. I went as quickly up the stairs as the darkness and winding spirals permitted, using clerisy to ignore the pain of my recent beatings and shielding myself and Devon in warmth for relief against the cold. Devon crept quietly behind me, holding my cloak. When he felt our shield form he squealed with delight and said, "Just like before." I motioned him to be silent and he was, except for his loud breathing and his clanking belt.

When we emerged cautiously into the corridor I saw no one but Isulde, who was still sitting partly in the doorway to the throne room, and whose profile was lit with pale light coming out of the room. All Devon and I needed to do to exit the castle was cross stealthily through a nearby doorway which led into the servants' quarters, and exit through another small doorway near the stables. Then I would steal horses and we'd both ride like hell for Gondal.

But as soon as Devon and I entered the hall, Isulde rose as if to greet us. I motioned her to sit, so no one in the throne room would remark on her attention being drawn in our direction, but she ignored the gesture and moved quietly over to me. Then she held me softly and I stood there holding her and I understood she was offering me comfort as I heard Roguehan sentencing all the people I ever cared about to enough intricate forms of death to keep ten Devons busy for months. The sentencing went on and on and I just kept endangering myself on and on by embracing Isulde when I should have been escaping. And I kept hoping that someone would see us, that Roguehan would see and remember this strange tableau in the long blank corridor. An accidentally evil monk clasping and being clasped by Beauty as the chief torturer impatiently tugs his sleeve. And none of them moving. Title: *Don't You Know That Everything Is Poison?*

Devon spoke as if in answer to my thoughts. "Can we punish him now?"

"Ssh, Dev."

"I'll go listen," he announced importantly, as he destroyed our little set piece by moving heavily toward the open doorway. Roguehan stopped speaking. In the ensuing silence I thought perhaps he would hear the clink of his chief torturer's belt approaching, but he didn't. There was utter quiet from the throne room, then I heard Mirand ask mildly, "By what authority do you mete sentences, Emperor?"

"By my new authority as King of Threle."

"Then do I understand that you have officially assumed the office and function of kingship?"

"Yes," said Roguehan, "by right of conquest I am now King of Threle." There was a significant pause.

"Yes, King," said Mirand, "Then you are lord of all the land, meaning Threle, as well?"

"As King of Threle, I am lord of all the land," said Roguehan succinctly, relishing his new title. "And as lord of the land, I am the land in all its glorious destruction."

"Then you are Threle," said Mirand.

"I am Threle."

"Hold that thought—"

Tender noise like light. A tender chaos I closed my eyes to. Chaos like a Mother Goddess's kiss and better to hold than any thought. In a warm whisper I saw a pale sun vanish into humid beams that drowned the sky with their quavering noise. I mean there was a clamor of shaking light. Then a sudden scream of hot light scraping the sky into thin shades of thunder. And the thunder rippled and lashed open ugly veins and boils in the booming blue air. I was seeing the sky ruined with sonic eruptions along the back of my eyelids, and bright jagged summers rose exploding into thorns of foggy thunder. My eyes were seared closed with the visions and burning themselves blind until Isulde stroked my lids open and ran with me. She was pulling me down the corridor and I was running because she was but I couldn't see because all the light was now too light—I mean, too light to see by, lighter than gusts of hollow birds wearing guesses for feathers. Not birds but living suggestions of failed light floating etherward like sun-flushed ghosts. Then I knew I couldn't see anything because it was all sound where light used to be.

I felt the scar on my left palm open and close. Then the vision ran away, and Isulde and I were running through the servants' quarters, and as we ran the rooms ran and stretched behind us in tatters, and everything seemed to spring and fold backwards, as if reality were waning and waxing like the moon, and we were running along the tenderest edge of change. But we were only moving between clear slow pauses, and we were only able to move because nothing else in the world was.

We did emerge from the castle. Emerging from the castle there was silence. I heard the silence. Then the winter burned before it froze and the wind whispered and howled and there was a dawn along the farthest reach of sky but I knew that neither dawn nor night was moving. Such a strange stroke of time to which Isulde kept chanting, "Go North to die, go North to be healed, come North with me to die, come North to be healed for to die is a healing." And I suppose I was chanting with her for we were running together in an eerie cadence for the stables, and then we were mounting horses and riding out and away from the world, riding from everything in it, riding headlong and hell-bent without help for it, riding obscurely toward the Drumuns.

Twelve

Somewhere indefinable the wind and earth began to feel close and solid again, and the arc of the morning sun steadied into a natural day going its course in natural time. I felt that somewhere long behind us whatever had happened in Walworth's castle was still happening, but coming to its end, and that if I could see back behind the horizon we had fantastically emerged from, there would still be strange reverberations of time and light and sound, but that all was settling out into mundane normality around us.

I of course had no idea of what had happened to Roguehan or to anyone else back in Walworth's castle. I had every reason to assume that Roguehan was now the King of Threle, and I couldn't stop thinking about the horrible deaths I had heard him decree for Walworth and his household, for people I had once felt closer to than to myself. But I could make no sense of those strange inversions of energy we had run through. Did one of Roguehan's magicians cause them? And if so, how, and for what purpose? And now that Roguehan had Threle, what would he do next?

Isulde dismounted and so I did the same. The wind blew ice full and cold around us, and at our feet a slow gray river crawled like an injured serpent. The rising sun dazzled me, as if my rapidly returning sense of reality still bore a touch of hallucination. Isulde's shadow was warm against the winter. I was standing in her shadow and I was facing east into the steadily rising sun, and she was looking at me gravely, and saying with a solemn fairy smile, "And so we have taken a fairy-run out of all the world silliness. Will you then come North with me? To heal and to die? Or shall I stay here with you? Here by the river Kretch, or by this same river with another name?"

I was too empty to answer. I looked north across the river, to shallow sky and mountains, to a rushing season of direction, to an old unknown place that had always been a sucking hole in the bottom of my nightmares. Silver and dull, a sweeping iron lake of land distended distance as I watched. The North Country was out there, beyond the river, beyond the unorganized territory that led to the distant mountains that I knew must be the Drumuns. Even at this distance I could feel the North Country screaming ever so faintly through my ban. If this was the river Kretch, we had to be standing on the absolute northern border of Walworth's duchy, on the absolute northern border of Threle. That is, if Threle as an entity still existed. Or possibly, depending on how far Isulde had led me on her "fairy-run," somewhere in the unorganized territory east of the duchy.

"No, Isulde. I'm not ready to die yet. I'm not ready to enter the North Country with you, although the gods know that death might be the best option I have right now." She pouted a little in response to my words. "I would like to know whatever happened back there, what we rode through, why the world suddenly felt like it was falling apart and coming together again. I would like to know where and how we are."

"Silly Llewelyn, what is to know? We had a hole in space and took the horses on a fairy-run while my other lovers sparred with light. So come home now and believe with me."

"And miss your other lovers?" I asked dryly. "Or are they all dead now and gone North?"

"I am going North. To visit my foster father and catch fish with him and sing him songs. And if you do not come with me, then I shall give other fairy gifts to you. I stole them from the castle, for indeed they are yours." Suddenly, as if we were in one of our dreams together, she held out a torn robe. I had no idea how she produced it, for I felt no magic, but who can question a Northern fairy's tricks?

"This is the robe you wore to be sacrificed in Sunnashiven. You cannot remove it once you wear it. You have so much in your life that you cannot remove." She placed it in my arms. It felt heavy the way a corpse does. "And this is a wizard key that will open anything, even a hardened life." She gave me the key I had once given Baniff in exchange for taking me to Threle. "And this is a Ring of Beauty, sacred to Aphrodite." She placed the ring in my scarred palm, in the center of the waning moon. I recognized it as the same ring Trenna had once possessed. "It shall replace your illusion ring." She giggled. "But now I must leave."

I dropped the sacrificial robe on the ground and placed the key and the ring in my cloak.

Isulde sharply kissed my eyes closed and curtained my neck in brown seaweed. The seaweed was dead and dry. It scratched deep frozen lines in my skin. "To find me you must enter the North alone," she spoke as she stroked the seaweed softly. On her third stroke the lines in my skin opened and bled a little.

"How shall I enter the North and live to find you?"

"Call to the star that is my name, the violent star which dreams disorder."

"How shall I find your star, Isulde? You have so many names. You are so many dreams and disorders."

"Here, listen." She took my hand and gently pressed her palm against mine. "My star beats light inside your pulse." She was right. I did hear light pounding through my blood like the echo of a star. "Follow your life pulse home to healing."

"And when I die, love?"

"When you die I shall be there to heal you," she promised. I tried to hold her but she slipped smiling out of my arms. Then she mounted her horse, rode into the gray water, and was gone.

I stood unsteady in a still wind and watched the frigid river continue unchanged over the place where Isulde had left me. There was nothing to mark her leaving, not even the echo of a sense of anything living having touched the waves. They were old waves, slow and murky. Nothing ever touched them except the slower stain of bad lives and the dust of the world's corpses. And so I lost myself where she left me, lost myself staring softly into the hard gray water, remarking how the river hadn't frozen, how I had once read that the inhabitants of northern Threle liked to say that the Kretch was always too cold to freeze, that its North Country source gave it a quality that defied the natural order.

And I tried to feel and remember the new dream we had been running through as we escaped the castle. But try as I might I could draw nothing into my mind now but quiet river waves, like an earthly river of forgetfulness, and I soon gave up all remembering in bewilderment. I had no idea what had happened back there, but whatever had happened, whatever we had run through, had happened in a life I was breaking from. For obvious reasons I had no intention of returning to a land under Roguehan's rule. I thought of my former friends, but then I stopped thinking because I didn't want to imagine the fates Roguehan had decreed for them, or drive myself insane speculating on whether the cosmic strangeness I escaped through had also provided an escape for them.

I noticed detachedly that my curiosity was growing numb. Then I felt my thoughts grow too numb to care. Then I stopped noticing anything and lost myself in watching. I watched the river for a long time. The river defined the absolute end of Threle. The river defined the absolute end of empire. The river defined the absolute end of everything known.

I was alone.

I made a brief prayer to Hecate and burned the sacrificial robe Isulde had given me, as a sacrifice of my past life, past sacrifices, of the life that had been sacrificed after all to serve the forces of evil. I rededicated to Hecate my learning, my varying skill with the various branches of magic, my role in destroying El, my plotting to kill Walworth, my actual killing of Cathe, my metaphoric killing of myself and my natural inclinations for all those years in Kursen. And despite my destruction of two evil high priests, Hecate was with me, blessing my intent, for it was Her force that lit the flames, as it was always an evil intent that lit my actions. I was still bound to Her as priest. That was all I was certain of.

The fire I had drawn from Hecate died and I watched the cold again. I felt my thoughts become movement. The North was heavy today, so heavy it pulled all my thoughts into itself and let nothing escape. So to steady myself I looked up at the sky again and watched the curve of space, because I could see space curve into the North here. The curve of space is the curve of Habundia's womb. Death and birth are one if you dream it right. The Drumun Mountains displaced my sense of horizon as I watched them too, wide beyond the river, fading in and out of daunting sky. Sometimes they were all sky. And sometimes they had crags like the back of a broken boat against the horizon.

And strange in the silence I heard the jangling of metallic objects, and loud wheezy puffing, and heavy uneven footsteps crunching the snow behind me. I turned, and to my great surprise, there was Devon, who had just dismounted from a horse and was barely able to move for his heavy belt of torture implements and his considerable body weight. He was so breathless he only managed to gasp "Luv . . . ell . . . un" before collapsing in a sweaty heap near the stillglowing ashes of the burnt robe, as if he were yet another sacrifice to Hecate out of the jumble of my life.

I helped him out of the wet snow and waited while he recovered from his exertion, which seemed to take a long time, long enough for the slant of light on the river to change and the ice-wind to grow still. I shielded us in warmth, as much for my comfort as his. He finally caught his breath, leaned without self-consciousness against a large rock as if he simply took it as his due that we would be in each other's company again, and asked, "What happened to the girl? How come we were running so fast? How come it didn't hurt? I saw you go with her, so I grabbed her shift, and then I couldn't help it I was running too, but behind, and then it was like I got dropped. I stole a horse because I saw you did but it took me several tries to mount with all the weight on my belt—I usually get help—and then you and the girl were way ahead in all the confusion so I just kept riding fast in the same direction and then I saw the fire and thought it might be you."

"I suppose in a manner of speaking the fire was me." After all, it was literally an offering of my life, but some things are too difficult to explain, and Devon didn't seem to hear or comprehend my answer.

"The girl. Was she magical like you?"

"No, not like me, Devon. She's a fairy. From the North Country."

"I don't like her," whined Devon.

"So what happened back in the castle, Devon? Do you know?"

"No." And by his manner, he didn't seem to care.

"But it was passing strange, wasn't it?" I tried again.

"I thought maybe you did it."

"You thought wrong, Dev. But I'm—*we're*—out of it now, and the fairy girl has gone back home."

He got all excited. "Great! Let's go adventuring together! Let's go see the world and do magic and scare people and stuff!"

"Late and soon," I said wryly. "I'm not sure what's left of the world to see, or even where we are." The only thing clear to me under the circumstances was that I wouldn't be able to lose Devon easily, if at all, unless I killed him. And I'd really had my fill of killing lately. Also, I had no desire to wreak harm on someone who had just risked his life for mine.

> *I* stopped abruptly in my telling, because speaking of Devon's loyalty naturally made me think again of the intense youthful loyalty I had once held for Walworth, and how I had once risked my life for his. I watched the fire for half a minute, and repeated, "I had no desire to wreak harm on someone who had just risked his life for mine," wondering if my words would make him remember how I had once risked my life for his. "There's something unforgivably cruel about that one, my lord." I thought Walworth blanched a little. But perhaps that was just the fire and moonlight painting shadows in the hovel.

Even if I could lose Devon, I couldn't afford him talking about our escape, since I was now subject to execution by Roguehan should I return, assuming the strangeness we ran through hadn't altered political matters.

I also didn't want to make it obvious to anyone we happened to encounter that I was an evil cleric, because I knew that after all the mischief in the castle, every evil cleric in the world would have a bounty on my head, especially since Cathe had made such a public issue out of me, the famed "beloved of Hecate," converting to the service of Athena. Even though Cathe had his own claims on turncoat status for making his own "conversion" a public matter, I truly had no idea how far that one had gone as Mirra had referred to him as "brother in evil." I did know that Roguehan would now be certain to let my role in El's suicidal conversion be known, as that alone would incite other evil clerics against me. All things considered, it was best to avoid my own kind.

I had to get somewhere where neither the empire nor Threle, if there still was a Threle, had jurisdiction, and somewhere where the clergy hadn't established themselves, preferably somewhere where I knew the language. That is why Gondal seemed like the best choice. They spoke Sarana there and had a reputation of being so politically disorganized that no one really knew if it was properly a kingdom or just a loose confederation of elf colonies and the gods know what else. I had never heard of any monasteries in Gondal, but I had heard that the inhabitants of the region generally had no interest in or history of organized religion and tended to keep to themselves. If I could get to Gondal, I could find a place to think out my next move in relative safety, and even though it was a fairly isolated region, I thought that eventually I would get news of whatever had happened back there in the castle. I had no idea if Roguehan's imperial ambitions thought an outpost like Gondal worth conquering, but I did know he would be busy enough in Threle not to be moving into Gondal anytime soon.

"Do you know where we are?" asked Devon.

"Let me have your dagger, Dev, I'll show you what I think." He obediently handed me a black-handled knife from his belt, and I began to draw a crude map in the snow. "We're on the southern shore of the Kretch. We're either still in Walworth's duchy, or somewhere in the unorganized territory that separates Threle from Gondal in the east." I knew this from maps and books I had read, but I didn't know much more. "We could follow the river east through the unorganized territory and then into Gondal, but there's no way of knowing whether we're hundreds of miles or only a few miles away."

Then I realized there was a deadly problem with that idea. The Kretch had its source in the Drumun Mountains, somewhere up on the North Country side of them, near a place where the Drumuns dropped down into a northern piece of Gondal. If we followed the river far enough to enter Gondal, we would almost immediately have to cross the Drumuns, which was certain death to me. And then I remembered that part of what was generally considered Gondal swept up into the North Country at that point, that there was an area where the mountains dropped down and the two regions fused.

"We need to head southeast, Devon. We need to cross the unorganized territory, which as you can see is a horror of winter right now, and then enter the southern part of Gondal. But we have no traveling supplies and no food. We can't live on conjured food for an extended period of time, there are no edible plants to be found in the winter, I'm not much for hunting and can't eat meat anyway, I have no idea of the way, and by all accounts the unorganized territory is trackless. It will be a miserable journey with no guarantee of getting there alive. You up for it?"

"Why don't we go by the river?"

"Because I could get sick, Devon. Parts of this river don't agree with me."

"Which parts?"

I traced with the knife. "I can't pass the mountains, Dev. We would have to stop before the river comes through. But once we see the river pouring out of the mountains, we'll know we're very close to the border, and from there we can travel south through the country until we find civilization." Or something resembling civilization, I thought, based on what little I knew about the place.

"We have food," said Devon excitedly. "The horses belonged to the emperor's army, and they always carry food and supplies. Always. I'll show you." Devon jumped up from the rock and led me back toward his horse, which was now wandering freely with mine and eating the frozen leaves of a juniper bush that stuck out of the snow. Our heat shield dispersed as we left it and cold wind struck us. Checking the saddlebags, which bore Roguehan's insignia, I discovered that they were loaded with soldiers' rations—enough food to take us for several weeks.

I magically removed Roguehan's mark from the bags. No sense in announcing to anyone we might encounter whose horses they were.

"All right, Devon." I mounted the larger horse and he happily took its smaller companion, although with his heavy belt it took him a couple of tries to mount. "Guess we're a couple of horse thieves stealing the emperor's property and riding into new worlds. The Kretch be our guide."

"All right!" He howled loud excited whoops that echoed strangely in the northern air. Then we kicked into a bright canter and left the world we knew.

*O*ur journey was easier than my recent crossing of the plains. My horse carried sleeping blankets and at night I made fires and shielded us in the heat. When the horses were hungry I used wizardry to produce enough heat to melt snow and expose the scrub grass beneath. I melted snow for water, not being willing to risk drinking from the Kretch with its North Country source. And there was enough bread and dried vegetables in our rations to get me through, while Devon dined happily on dried sides of bacon and whatever river fish he could catch.

I had thought that after so much time in the emperor's service as chief torturer, Devon would have changed, maybe even matured a bit. But now that he was with me it was as if he had never worked for Roguehan. It wasn't that he was naturally reticent about discussing his experiences. He just didn't find them relevant. Just as he didn't seem particularly curious about what we would do in Gondal once we got there. He had implicit faith that I must know what I was doing on that account, and no conception that there could ever be any problems in his life again.

I decided that once we got to Gondal I would not immediately pursue work as a magician as I really needed information on the state of the world before putting myself in a position where another wizard or cleric could find out more about me than I cared to reveal. I knew from my reading and from conversations with Ellisand that most of Gondal was fairly empty but that there were two cities in the south, Anda the capital, and Arula, which was allegedly the capital in ancient times. I had a vague idea that if I could get to one of the cities I could survive in relatively honest fashion as a translator or perhaps as a private tutor of languages since I was fluent in Sarana, Kantish, and Botha. No one need know I also had a working knowledge of Amara as that language was rare enough to potentially identify me. I just needed to bring Devon into my plan.

"Hey, Devon," I said, after he had just finished a dinner of river fish and dried peas by a small fire I created. The horses were tethered to a tree out in the darkness. "Now that you're no longer working for the emperor—"

"I can be your chief torturer!" he proclaimed.

"No, Dev. I don't need a torturer. This will be like a new life. Anything in the past is our secret. Understand?"

"Sure. If that's what you want." He said this earnestly, but he looked a little uncomfortable, as if he sensed for the first time that I wasn't completely easy with his companionship. Then he added with a touch of resentment, "I can act like we just met and I don't really know you." Hurt flashed across his eyes, then it was gone. For some reason he briefly reminded me of myself when, in the days after Walworth's trial, I had to pretend I didn't know him. Devon suddenly grinned and made stabbing motions in the air with one of his torture implements. "We'll be in charge of Gondal in no time."

I grinned back to reassure him. "No telling how our lives will work out there, or if Gondal is even worth being in charge of. But at first, to help things, we'll say you're my apprentice, that you're study-ing languages with me." I had no intention of teaching him any new languages, in the interest of limiting his ability to communicate, but as Devon had never been much of a student, I didn't expect he'd push the issue. He didn't.

"We can say whatever you want." He yawned. "I'm not cuddy Cristo. I can keep a secret. And besides," he added, staring harshly at me over the fire, "if any of the emperor's men find us, it'll be because *you* told them, not me." There was a bottomless anger in his voice that felt like open death in the northern air. "Remember, I've got spe-cial weapons now that can kill with a touch."

I stared back at him through the flames and the lonely northern night, met his empty eyes with mine. Here was my tragic handiwork. The pleasure apples I had fed him for so long had produced a hellish heart that would destroy anything he perceived as displacing his sta-tus with me. I lightly probed his mind and learned he was even liable to destroy me if he thought I was going to abandon him, and that his last sentence was intended as a clumsy, desperate threat along those lines. It was a perversion of friendship and loyalty, and a perversion of what would have been his nature had I not been there to manipu-late it for my own ends several years ago. It was all quite ugly. I mur-mured a heartfelt apology and looked away.

"Why? What are you sorry for, Luvellun? Are you sorry I'm here? Sorry we're riding together?"

"Just sorry, Devon. Sometimes I feel like one of your weapons. Whatever I touch I destroy."

"Maybe that's why you're so good at being evil," he suggested without a trace of irony. "I'm pretty much the same way."

For the rest of the night, and I suppose for the rest of my life, I could parse out no response to that one.

*T*wo days later we rode through a strange, yellow-tipped wind and my chest began to tighten up and sting with pain as I breathed. That is how I knew it was a North Country wind blowing down into the safe side of the mountains, and why I was not surprised to see the Kretch pouring out of the mountains at some distance ahead of us. It was gold and bore touches of living fire as it burst in fury out of the Drumuns, then it quickly turned gray and dull as it reached our side of them. Had I not been experiencing increasing physical discomfort caused by my ban, it would have been dangerously fascinating to watch. I led us south, turning perpendicular to the river and galloping hard until we had covered enough distance to be clear of the wind and I felt clear of my pain. I pulled sharply on my horse's reins and stopped. Devon trotted his horse up alongside mine and stopped as well. The land stretched empty and quiet around us.

"Hey, Luvellun, are we in Gondal now?" Devon asked happily and excitedly.

"By my estimate," I responded easily, although I certainly didn't feel particularly easy about it. We were surrounded by an area that looked exactly like the snowbound unorganized territory we had just crossed, except that without the river to guide us we could only head south by the sun's course and hope to encounter some kind of settlement before our diminishing supplies ran out.

"So where is everybody?" Devon asked expectantly.

"There might not be anybody in these parts, Dev. Gondal's fairly empty, by all accounts. Here, hold these." I passed him my horse's reins and dismounted. "Stay here. I'm going—"

"Then I'm going too. You're not leaving me here," he sullenly demanded, dismounting and dropping both reins.

"Look, Dev, I need to go a short distance away, just enough to be out of sight, to open my senses and see if I can pick up anything magical around here. Where there's magic there's most likely a settlement, and that will tell us where to travel to next. It's the best we can do."

He didn't look convinced. His eyes were arguments against my putting any distance between us. Ever. "Why can't you just do it here?"

"I could do it here, but I'll have the best chance of success if I have a little solitude."

"I want to watch. I don't trust you. You didn't come for me when the emperor took me away."

"And the emperor could take you away again if we aren't very careful, Devon. That's why I need to be alone, to get the most accurate reading I can for us on potential places to go." He started to waver. "You'll see my tracks in the snow. If I don't return in an hour, you'll easily be able to ride after me. You've got the horses."

That seemed to decide matters. He reluctantly agreed to wait, and I strode quickly out in an eastward direction until Devon was hidden from view by a small hillock and I felt utterly isolated. Here there was only empty sky and an emptier winter. The isolation hadn't been strictly necessary, but I wanted to be alone without Devon's possessive energy distracting me, with nothing but sky and earth to open myself against. I wanted to feel for any sense of a passing magical pulse or current, for any indication where there might be a town or a settlement.

But before I opened myself to magical energy I found myself comparing the strange new frozen world I was now traversing with the world I had left. My physical isolation from Devon, who was my only tangible link to the past, intensified the difference between Gondal and Threle. Threle was a land of changes, from the populous mercantile duchies in the south to the large cities and empty plains of the Midlands to the strange hints and promises of comfort and hidden villages in the north. But even northern Threle, with its snow-laden hills, was nothing like the terrifying winter wasteland of Gondal. There was no comfort here. One could live here for centuries and still feel that home was elsewhere.

There was something in the wasteland that impressed upon me in a way that nothing else did—not even my inexplicable escape with Isulde—that I was in an altogether different world now, and therefore in an altogether different life. Except for Devon, I was my only connection to my past. Everybody that wanted to kill me, and everybody I had wanted to destroy, was back in that other world, in Threle or in whatever Roguehan had allowed to remain of it. It was very much like my first entry into Threle so many years ago, when I had broken irrevocably with my past in Sunnashiven. Now I had broken irrevocably with my past again, and there was nothing for it but to enter the rest my life devoid of all familiar contexts, including my yearslong contexts of magical study and revenge.

I opened myself to the north and felt only pain, death, and chaos dancing in the distance, beyond the Drumuns. I opened to the west and felt Devon's impatience blocking anything else in that direction. To the south, where the cities were, I felt nothing but winter, which told me that the cities were still quite far or that they contained nothing magical, which was unlikely. To the east I felt a strange low caustic sort of hum like fire under the earth. Somewhere to our east, within magical shouting distance, there was a power center of magic. I did not wish to encounter whoever's power I was feeling, but there would be no need to if we could only find the outpost of civilization it had to be emanating from, purchase new supplies, see what news was to be had, and move on.

I returned to Devon and told him we were riding east.

"I knew you'd come back," he crowed. "Let's ride for it." He grinned like a sputtering candle and mounted his horse in one try. "East like a beast!"

East it was, through several hours of unchanging frozen landscape and occasional harsh but brief bursts of snowstorms. It was rough on the horses because the terrain was unlike the area around the river and they often had to make their way around snowdrifts that blocked their passage. I opened myself to the power as we rode to help us navigate our course. Although I felt the power source getting stronger as we got closer, I also grew more apprehensive, for I could see no physical signs of a town. There clearly weren't any roads, and there was nothing on the horizon but frozen wasteland. Even when the power grew strong and insistent enough to throw my head for loops when I opened myself to it, which should have indicated that we were immediately in the vicinity of the source, I saw nothing but snow and rocks and barren trees, and heard nothing but silence and the patient plod of our horses.

"Hey, Luvellun," called Devon. "How come you had to go away to feel the magic when you say you can feel it fine right here on your horse?"

"I already explained, Devon. If the magic was far away and weak, I had a better chance of finding it without distractions. But it's strong now, and—" I paused. "Something's wrong." I dismounted and gave him my reins. "Here, you keep a watch around us. I'm going into trance." I called the energies around me into me and within a few seconds determined that the power I was feeling was practically exploding out of a clump of rocks within sight. The rocks formed a cave that reminded me a little of the secret shelter I once shared with Walworth's household back in Threle. So some solitary wizard was down there doing the gods know what. Exactly the sort of encounter I wished to avoid.

"We're heading back west," I told Devon, who had dismounted and tied both horses to a tree while I was in trance. "I was mistaken. There's nothing out here."

"You mean we're lost?" He sounded sort of excited.

"Not exactly. But close. I confused myself, Devon. Which is another reason I sometimes need to be alone. We'll go back the way we came and ride due south until we come across one of the cities. We'll have to start eating smaller rations to make our supplies last."

Something suddenly went dark in the air and spread slowly along the snowbound ground. It wasn't a shadow, and it wasn't a shift in the energy I was feeling. The darkness was more solid than that, as if the darkness was a living creature in its own right. I could see darkness crawling in the angle between the blinding snow and the sun, but if I blinked, the dark would disappear for the space of a few seconds before returning. It was one of the damnedest things I ever saw. Or didn't see.

The darkness filled the silence of the northern wasteland we were standing in with a different kind of silence, one that sounded full against the empty quiet. I would describe the darkness as soundless rather than silent, as pregnant with violence. It charged the air with the same sort of weight I felt just before the peacemongers attacked Roguehan's camp.

Even Devon sensed something had changed and something was wrong, because he grabbed clumsily at one of the torture implements on his belt as if he meant to use it as a weapon, all the while turning to me with an obnoxiously insistent "notice me" smile. But his smile was thin and nervous and betrayed his fear that whatever was happening was beyond his skill to deal with. I instinctively said a brief incantation to Hecate for protection, put up a wizard shield, and put my hand on my dagger, although I had no idea what I was going to do with it.

The darkness floated and thickened and gathered itself and screamed into a sudden fireball of terror exploding the sorry sky directly over our heads into thunderclouds of grinning storms. The force of it shook me even within my wizard shield, and strange to say, I got an impression that my shield was offering me more protection than Hecate was, although there wasn't time to reflect on why that would be so.

The fireball dispersed into ugly thunder that scorched my eyes with a queer sonic brightness before revealing its source to be a black, winged dragon skidding through the air and landing clumsily in front of us. I had seen illustrations and descriptions of dragons in the bestiaries I had read in Kursen's library, and I knew from my reading that they occasionally flew down from the North Country into the empty northern regions of Gondal. But nothing in my reading had prepared me for the experience of actually seeing one.

The dragon had a long pointed face like a piece of solid shadow, and eyes like two black stones. As long as the dragon was in the air it oozed horridly hypnotic serpentine shapes like a living nightmare come to day, and threw lightning from its mouth and tail like jagged curses, but once it touched ground its bulky body dragged awkwardly and it had obvious difficulty maintaining movement and balance. Clearly this was a creature of air and clouds, perhaps even a storm come to take a living form. It did not care for earth.

Devon's eyes got big the way I remembered they used to when he was younger and I had amused him with some minor feat of magic. I could feel an intensity of terror emanate from him. And then, in the time it took me to drop my shield and call down Hecate's power into a blast to annihilate the dragon before it could destroy us, Devon did something I can only call heroic.

In spite of his terror, in spite of his palpable belief that he was risking his life, and most likely because he believed he was saving mine, he charged the dragon. While I had my face covered to focus completely on drawing and aiming the only blast we might have before the dragon chose to attack us again, Devon was blindly and hopelessly stabbing at the creature's underbelly, which was about as useful as stabbing at a thunderstorm in terms of doing any damage. "Cud! Cud! Cud!" he screamed. "Cud you cud—"

At which point my blast hit the dragon and engulfed them both in a killing sheet of flame as I sank in the horror of knowing that I had just inadvertently destroyed Devon. And when I could slowly bring myself to look directly at the damage I had caused, there was nothing but Devon's charred remains on the now-muddy ground.

I retched on the fading energy of what little remained of his corpse for a long time, because despite the physical distress it was causing me, I felt I couldn't just leave it, that the least I could do was blast a small hole in the ground and cover what remained of him in the earth as a show of respect. I did not mourn Devon. I mourned the natural life and affection my magic had robbed him of for years, and I mourned the loss of my own natural life and affections, and of the fact that Devon had died trying to save my life and I stood there knowing that even so, my life would go on just as I had once saved Walworth's life and his went on. I mourned that one most of all, which I suppose *was* mourning for Devon in a higher sense. It's the gods' own bloody damnation when one offers the supreme sacrifice for the noblest of emotions utterly in vain. I suppose it's a sad rite of passage into old age, no matter what age you are when you see it.

"Thank you, Sun King." I murmured in Kantish. "Thanks, Dev, for all your many services. For your friendship, which I took from your heart without earning. Forgive me if you can." I said a prayer for the dead to Hecate and then I kept praying and then I felt strangely clean.

Thirteen

When I looked up from my prayer I noticed that the dragon had left no remains. I thought my blast must have done a spectacularly fine job until I saw that at a small distance from where I expected to find a few steaming dragon bones, there now stood a young woman with dark features and fiery storm-cloud eyes who was partly hidden in shadow near the cave entrance. She had obviously been scrutinizing me, but I had been too far in trance from praying to Hecate to notice her. I slowly stood and cautiously approached her, keeping my wizard shield up. She made no attempt to enter the cave, but neither did she attempt to meet me. She met my gaze with defensive curiosity as the late-day wind blew harshly in the distance over Devon's newly made grave. Then she asked me, in the oddly accented Sarana that Ellisand had taught me to associate with Gondal,

"So how long have *you* been studying with Zelar?"

"Who's Zelar?" I assumed an air of intrigued innocence, the practiced result of my years of clerical training. "Does he live here?" I glanced curiously toward the cave, as if I had no idea who Zelar might be but was politely interested in honoring my new acquaintance's chosen topic of conversation. As if it were all in a blessed day for me to be passing through this northern wasteland and amusing myself by destroying stormdragons and spending a friendly chat with the locals over the grave of my newly dead traveling companion.

My studied courtesy, however, only provoked my mysterious associate into a fine dusty peeve.

"Scorch that goddess-be-damned affected northern Threlan accent and drop your wizard shield! It's offensive. And stop your god-be-damned pretending to innocence! It's even more offensive. Or do you think I can't tell the difference between pretense and reality?"

"Forgive my accent, I'm not from Gondal," I replied, not caring to give even that much information away, but not wanting to antagonize her further in the interest of learning what she knew about Zelar, or whether she was even referring to the same Zelar I knew. Since she could tell I was shielded she clearly had some sensitivity to wizardry so I didn't want to risk probing her mind for details. "And as to my shield, I'm sorry but under the circumstances I consider it a well-earned precaution."

She looked impatient. "I consider it self-righteous cowardice and the gods' own rudeness. And so *what* if you're not from Gondal? Am I supposed to be impressed?"

"I only meant to say that I intend no affectation, and that I'm innocent of—"

"You're 'innocent' of *nothing*! You obviously knew my dragonfire would have killed you if not for your wizard shield, or you wouldn't be bloody shielding yourself at all." She was now beyond annoyed. "Or let me guess. You're one of those would-be adventurer types that needs to make people use semi-intimate phrases like 'would have killed you' to reify your own pathetic lack of self-worth. Pretty damn intimate phrase, isn't it? Ye gods, you infuriate me!"

I was absolutely nonplussed. She was more affronted by her own word choice than by anything that had transpired this afternoon.

"Uh—actually, I'm lost," I responded brightly, not knowing how else to respond to her rant. "And yes, you absolutely would have killed me, so I don't know how else you would put it, if I take your words to mean that you were somehow the stormdragon and that now you are somehow transformed into an angry young woman."

She glared at me with her fiery stormdragon eyes and snapped, "You mean you don't *know* if I'm angry? Or you don't *know* if I'm a dragon turned woman?" She stared at me in utter contempt. "One. There's a stormdragon. You follow that so far? Good. Two. There's a blast to wake the bloody gnomes out of the North Country. Three. Here I am." She sort of sang this last phrase in a voice laden with sarcasm, then continued in a voice meant to mock my accent, "And, uh—no more stormdragon." She then switched back to straightforward yelling. "Hell's bells, what do you think happened? Or *do* you think? *Who* are you? *What* in hell's name are you doing here?"

I had no intention of answering these questions so I tried to throw the discussion in a different direction. "You killed my friend." I made my voice sound slightly accusatory, to induce some guilt and perhaps some mellowness into her tone, guessing that in the confusion of battle and the unruly chaos of her anger, she wouldn't have noticed that it was actually my blast that did the killing. It didn't work.

"Sorry about your bloody friend." She spat the words impatiently. Although she appeared to believe that she was responsible for killing Devon, I could tell she truly wasn't sorry. Not that she was pleased. She just didn't care, or rather, didn't care to be annoyed with any extra work Devon's death could possibly entail for her, even conversationally. She seemed to find it an irksome distraction from more important business, like how irritated she was by me and the phrases she felt compelled to use around me. "Do you think I'm supposed to pay some social obeisance to the loss of your male companion, and maybe weep iron tears composing an epic over the tragic event because *I* happen to be from Gondal?" She made a sarcastic gesture like she was playing an imaginary lyre followed by a second gesture of smashing it. "Grow up."

I kept my expression open and neutral, but I secretly found the tone of her relentless anger darkly fascinating, and I was desperately trying to surmise her story. There was a mystery here, and Zelar was somehow in it, that is, if she was speaking of Roguehan's advisor and not of some other Zelar. But now I was in it too, because the worst thing I could do at this point would be to ride off and risk her being able to relate our encounter to Zelar, if it was Roguehan's advisor she meant. I needed to know her story, and I needed to keep mine from her. Shield up.

She was still ranting. "Let me guess. You and your numskull friend were out on some kind of adventure, risking your lives stirring up angry dragons and single-handedly raiding elf colonies and the gods know what else because it's easier and more enjoyable to fight monsters on the road than the slippery unwinnable daily battles of life in civilization. Zelar's probably paying your expenses for reasons of his own, eh? So what do you care? When the day's done you get to return to society with a claim to adulation and reward because, hey, you killed a dragon. Except you really didn't, but hey—who has to know? You strike me as the type that will cheerfully accept unearned praise."

"Thanks," I responded sarcastically.

Caught up in her speech, she ignored me. "Anyone can fight a dragon. It's a definitive enemy. You blast it, you win. She blasts you, you die. So what? There are a lot of soldiers who conduct themselves with all bravery in battle but choose to live as social outcasts when they return. Do you know why? It isn't war that sent them mad. War enlightened them. It's so much cleaner, and for that reason, so much more humane to fight a stranger who wants to kill you than to navigate the slippery dirty manipulative dealings of society where nobody ever wins or loses."

"I suppose you have a point," I responded agreeably. "But I don't see where you're taking me with it. Are you a former soldier?"

She didn't like my question, or she just didn't like the disruption to her train of words. It was hard to tell. At any rate, she didn't answer it. "Can you forgive an enemy?"

"I have no idea." I thought of Walworth, and then I stopped thinking in favor of trying to follow my interlocutor's circuitous logic or lack thereof.

The violent honesty of her anger continued to intrigue me, although I would have greatly preferred to have been intrigued at a distance. The sadness of this inexplicable encounter was that I found myself experiencing more genuine interest in this dark-tempered stranger in a few minutes than I ever felt toward Devon over the course of years. Life isn't fair. Neither is death.

"So here's another question for you. Truth or truth because you won't dare answer it, I swear you won't dare answer it."

"I've been 'daring' to answer your questions all along," I helplessly objected.

"Are you so bloody brave in front of your parents?"

"As far as I know, my parents are dead." I was roundly confused as to where she was going with this particular non sequitur, or with most of her new rant for that matter, but decided to ride along in case I could learn something.

"So *what*? Aren't you lucky? Think with me, idiot. Because every idiot would-be dragonslayer full-of-refuse self-styled 'hero' I've ever had the displeasure of doing battle with is a phony. Know why? Because they all tighten up into silent emotional cowards in front of their parents. No son ever built a civilization in front of his father. Am I right?"

Again I tried to respond but she was boiling with her topic now and ranted right over me.

"Every man will keep his highest romantic image of himself and his most cherished ambitions under closest guard in front of his birth family. Want to see a hero cry? Seriously? Get him alone in a dragon cave and get him talking about his father." She waited for a reaction, got none, and asked pointedly, "So in what degree are *you* related to Zelar? Bastard son?"

So this was where she was leading. She was trying to prod *me* into revealing something useful about Zelar. Interesting. "I'm not related to him at all," I responded affably. "You haven't even told me who Zelar is."

"Stop *gaming* it with me! The only wizard shield that would have offered protection against my attack was Master Zelar's since it was his magic that fueled my form and fire in the first place. Which obviously you had to know about, despite your claim to being 'lost.' So what the hell are you doing here in the middle of nowhere, just passing through on a jaunt? Nobody comes here by accident. Nobody bloody comes here at all, unless they want to get killed. All right. So Zelar obviously sent you. Why?"

I didn't find it necessary to reveal that I had learned shielding from Mirand, who had learned it from Zelar, which in some sense did make me a kind of "bastard son" although I had never put it in those terms to myself before. More importantly, that piece of information told me that she was indeed talking about Roguehan's Zelar and it explained why my shield seemed to offer more protection against her blast than Hecate did. But whatever dark magic Zelar had used to effect the transformation of this woman into a dragon, and it had to be extremely powerful, however he pulled it off, had been obliterated by my clerisy. That bore further investigation. "So am I to understand that this . . . uh, Zelar fellow imprisoned you in the form of a stormdragon and I inadvertently freed you of the spell?"

She nodded. Stiffly. It was truly a hard admission for her to make, for some reason. She dropped her gaze and stared in melancholy rage at a clump of distant snowbound rocks. My question had shut her up better than a silencing spell.

"Your gratitude is noted," I said dryly.

She glared back at me with immense hostility. "What the hell am I supposed to be 'grateful' for? That your wizardry is so much stronger than mine that you freed me from my dragon form when I couldn't free myself? What the hell am I supposed to say, 'Thank you for impressing my inferiority upon me so I can never forget, for the rest of my bloody life, that I owe my restored humanity to somebody else?' Anything I accomplish in the rest of my life will be predicated on *you* having rescued me? Thanks for ruining my life. There goes any sense of pride I might ever have a chance to feel." If she had still been a dragon, there would have been another fireball, of that I had no doubt. This realization also made me question how much wizardry she actually knew, because had she been capable of blasting me, I was certain she would. Then I remembered she knew I had my shield up and seemed to regard that as an invincible protection against her magic. "And I suppose I'm required to maintain some blood-soaked mask of gracious courtesy for being beholden to you. Obviously you think less of me for freeing me. I know I would," she added with angry illogic.

"Why should I think less of you? All in a day's work."

"All in *whose* day's work?" she screamed. "What makes it *your* day's work? Why aren't *I* off adventuring around saving people?"

"Because until now you were a dragon?"

"Do you *know* who I bloody am?"

"No, not at all. Why don't you introduce yourself?"

She declined.

"Well, actually, it was clerisy, not wizardry that I hit you with. You needn't feel bad for that." I tried to mollify her.

"You mean I'm supposed to be impressed that you know more than one branch of magic? I suppose you're adept with illusion and witchcraft, too."

"Not adept. I've some—I mean extremely limited experience with—both. I wouldn't claim to really know those branches."

"Great, false humility. Now I have to deal with the foolery of 'I'm a great enough magician to free you from Zelar's spell, but I'm soooo damn humble' besides. All right. What does Zelar want to know?"

"Everything that's happened since his last visit." I spoke with cold affectation. Real affectation. Since my first pretense got me nowhere, I decided to give her the performance she seemed to want by pretending that Zelar did indeed send me.

"You mean in the last three bloody years? Tell Zelar that nothing's changed. I've guarded his damn baubles and hunted and gathered my sup and lost three years of life when I could have been telling tales and getting backstabbed by every other bard in Anda."

"I thought you were telling tales."

"*What the hell is that supposed to mean?*" She was screaming so breathlessly loud I could barely understand her words. "Are you trying to insult me by comparing this banal interchange to *my* beautiful stories? Who the hell are you? Do you even *know* my stories? Funny I don't remember you hanging round in wide-eyed wonder the last time I was telling tavern tales."

"You mean your audience is small enough for you to remember everyone?"

That was it. She let loose a blast that tore through the ground like a little earthquake, which seemed to be the extent of her wizardry, as she looked to my experienced eyes to be totally exhausted afterward. Not exhausted enough that she couldn't harangue me with insults for the better part of an hour, though, while I casually made my way to a large sun-splashed rock near the cave entrance and quietly listened, not caring to interrupt her lest she let slip in some valuable information about Zelar. She didn't. It was all attacks on me, my motives, my integrity, my very existence, who did I think I was, what was my point, and anything else she didn't happen to like or that happened to spur her bottomless anger in the moment. I watched the sun go red and fall behind the western horizon, watched the sky grow a pale violet edge and darken, heard the subtle change in the landscape around me as night fell, and still she went on.

The longer I remained silent, the more it seemed to infuriate her, but even a storm can't last forever. There did come a point, not long after sunset when the cold got thicker and barely tolerable, that she had run out of screaming and insults. She crossed her arms on her chest and stared balefully at me, as if she was daring me to speak.

"Are you cold?" I asked politely.

"Is that *all* you can say? You have no other response to make?"

"I mean, if it wouldn't offend you, and I'm not saying this to show off any sense of superiority, but I could shield us both in warmth."

"I am shielded in warmth."

"Then why are you shivering?"

"Because I'm not focused enough to keep it up because you've made me so damn angry with your foolery and no, I don't want your bloody help. I want you to leave. This is *my* cave." She looked more desperate than angry now, like a broken monarch defending her last piece of territory while expecting imminent defeat.

Insight. The only way I was going to be able to befriend and gain the trust of this intriguingly difficult acquaintance of Zelar's and learn what I needed to was to feign helplessness and fuel her pride. "Perhaps you can help me, then," I said with a touch of warm entreaty in my voice, that I thanked my clerical training for. "You're clearly very clever, very intelligent, and I was foolish and direction-less enough to get lost here. Might I spend the night in your fine shelter and have a bit of sup? I will pay coin for the privilege."

"No."

An uncharacteristically brief answer. "I'm in a bad spot," I tried again. "I'm low on supplies and trying to make them last until I reach Anda or Arula."

"Then you should have been smart enough not to get lost in the first place."

I looked dolefully across the rapidly darkening wasteland. "I'm so sorry. Actually, I had thought you could share your beautiful stories with me, as I'm a lover of words."

That sort of, maybe, made her soften for one second, made her look a brighter shade of uncertain, before she grew decidedly harsh again. "Oh, so now you're a 'lover of words.' Since when? First I've heard of it all bloody afternoon. Here's a 'word' for you. Why don't you just do what everyone else does and pretend you can help me?" She stared at me defiantly. "I'll watch."

"I don't know if I can help you as a wordsmith, but . . . well, I would like to know more about you and your life here. For myself, not Zelar. It isn't every day I encounter a hermit, and as I'm a bit of a hermit myself, I'm kind of interested."

"You can stay 'interested' outside." After throwing off this bit of generosity, she stormed into the cave, and I felt her cast a large, very clumsy wizard lock over the entrance, which I easily could have broken. Damn! She wasn't going to break down. Perhaps it was wiser to camp outside and leave at dawn, but since I was this far in it, I knew it was imperative to determine who she was and what she happened to know.

I broke the lock and entered her dwelling.

It was spare. It was creepy with order, which I didn't expect. The entrance opened immediately into a large firelit living area where the stormdragon, now the woman, lived. Perfectly symmetrical casks along one side of the dwelling stored water and dried fruit, and although the casks weren't labeled, it instinctively occurred to me that they were alphabetized by the Sarana name of each fruit. It was obsessively neat. A kind of natural fireplace burned in a perfectly square opening on the opposite wall, emitting smoke through a chimney hidden in the rock. From where I was, the fireplace appeared flat against the wall, with no protruding hearth. Before the fireplace was a dragon-sized, perfectly square, linen mat. The rest of the dwelling was smooth-polished black stone. The back of the area sloped downward into an extended darkness.

My new acquaintance was sitting on her now-too-large sleeping mat and trying to meditate on the fire, but her residual anger was making it impossible for her to work up a trance. It occurred to me that even if she did know wizardry, her skill was limited because her emotions were. The anger of wizards is indeed a byword, but a true wizard needs to be able to master her emotions when working magic. Her blasts would be deadly, that much was clear. Any other working she chose would be hit and miss.

"Forgive the intrusion, Stormdragon, but I didn't get your name," I said by way of greeting.

She stood up as if she was going to attack me physically.

"And I didn't get your story. And it is very much in your—in *both* our interests," I lightly added, "to give it to me."

My chance remark had an effect. She stared at me incredulously, but she didn't seem as eager to attack. "Why? What 'interests' can we possibly have in common?"

"Well, Zelar, for one. It's not in his interest to free you, you know.

I effected that at great risk to myself." Excellent! This tack was getting her attention. Instantly. She didn't even try to argue with me. She looked steadily at me with an impatient "get to the point" expression on her face, but I also knew she was ready to listen to anything I had to say.

"You are far too insightful to fool," I began mournfully, "so you force me to come clean with you."

"Then drop your shield."

"Not yet," I said enigmatically. "You're right in that I was a student of Zelar's, although I never formally became a master wizard. The war interrupted my studies. Zelar mentioned you to me several times, confided in me that he had made you guardian of this fair cave—"

"Of his *name stone*," she interrupted angrily. "You can say it. Name stone. That is, if you're really dropping your pretense to innocence. Or perhaps you're just jealous that not being a master wizard, you don't have one."

So this was the location of Zelar's name stone! That was more than worth the journey to learn! A master wizard's name stone is the source of his power, of his life force, and so all master wizards guard theirs with great care. Caethne had once been able to make use of fragments of Mirand's name stone to bring him back from death. Should I come into possession of Zelar's name stone, I could easily use it to destroy him. Having that kind of power over Roguehan's chief wizard could only be to my advantage. I kept my expression steady and professional, but it was difficult to hide my eagerness to learn more. "Zelar has much confidence in you and your abilities."

She stared at me like I had just hatched from a dragon's egg.

"Zelar *lies*! Or you do. If he mentioned me at all, then you'd know my name and my story, and you'd know how he turned me into a bloody dragon to guard his power objects."

"Zelar was guarded in what he did tell me. I'd like to hear it all from you." I spoke as gently and seductively as my training would allow. "One wizard to another. We can't help each other if we can't be open with each other."

"Help each other do what?" Her tone was angry and hopeless, but quieter than I expected.

I looked solemnly at the fire and gravely back at her, all the while praying lightly to Hecate for words to help me obtain the information I needed, and said, "Perhaps I can help you elicit vengeance against Zelar, and those backstabbing bards in Anda, and anyone else foolish enough to have done you harm."

She seemed to consider. "How can I help you?" She said this with a simple cold sincerity. There was hope in her voice where I expected suspicion.

"Tell me everything you know about Zelar's dealings in Gondal. He kept much of that close, and it would be extremely helpful to me to know about all that from you. I could probe your mind with wizardry, but you could block me with your own. I could use clerisy. But as a sign of respect and of my hope that we might form a mutually beneficial alliance based on trust, why don't you just tell me? I'll regard it as payment for freeing you from Zelar's spell, and you need never feel beholden to me in that regard again."

She didn't respond immediately. She manifested some dried fruit from the containers across the room. She did it clumsily, but she did it. I wisely decided not to risk her wrath by correcting her magical technique. She appeared nervous, and her magical flourish struck me as her way of distracting herself from what she was about to reveal. She fingered a dried pear, motioned me to sit on the linen mat with her, and then threw the pear in the fire, magically causing it to explode with a good deal of noise and violence. I remained patient as the pear-scented smoke cleared.

"I used to tell tavern tales," she began.

"Yes."

She sighed. "Consider what I'm about to tell you a simple tavern tale. You needn't believe a word of it. Even if it is true." She smiled darkly. "It is the tale of my life, oh 'lover of words.' Pass judgment lightly."

"If at all," I responded gently and encouragingly, as she prepared herself to begin the telling.

It wasn't clear whether Walworth considered this reported exchange truth or embellishment.

"You needn't believe a word of my tale, my lord," I quietly suggested, "so long as you transcribe it accurately."

He didn't smile. He did catch the strange doubling. I could sense that much in the subtle change in the cadence of his pen.

"Judge lightly," I lightly suggested.

"Always," he mysteriously replied.

Fourteen

My name is Aeren," she began, speaking more to the fire and to the silent stone walls than to me. "I was born in Anda, the so-called capital of this fair land." She gestured derisively toward the cave entrance. "Most of Gondal looks like the snow-wasted area you've been traveling through. Not much to king it over. But as there's nobody in this empty wasteland to dispute Anda's claim to sovereignty, and as pretending to govern the capital city of a large kingdom is far more fun than actually administering the trivial business of a small city-state, claims to sovereignty get made.

"It is said that in ancient times Arula was the capital, but that's more rumor than history, just like the 'kingdom' of Gondal has always been more wishful thinking than fact. In truth, both cities are run by quasi-democratic Assemblies of self-nominated wealthy citizens who are more concerned with staying in power and preventing a single ruler from emerging than with actually organizing Gondal into anything resembling a kingdom. Neither city even has the power to influence the other, let alone the few elf colonies scattered throughout the rest of the region. So let us begin by saying that Gondal is a semifictional kind of state."

"Maybe that's the best kind," I encouraged her.

"Agreed, eh? To my tale then. Which is truer than my country."

She paused to open herself to the ancient light and shadows that had always inhabited this place, paused to make the space we shared sacred for her tale. When she finally spoke, her voice felt like a cold storm emerging in the form of an unanswerable question. " 'When does a force end?' "

I waited silently for her to speak again. The sound of the fire filled my waiting.

She continued speaking in a voice of unrelenting insistence, "It was Zelar who asked me that question. He was giving me bad figs and old wine. He was teaching me how he thinks. It was a reluctant generosity, his revealing himself in all his dismal brilliance in the questions he wanted me to answer.

"I ate his figs in silence. It was late, and I had been telling tavern tales for hours, although no one, save Zelar, had been listening. I had worked and woven and bled upon those tales for months knowing that nobody would hear them, that nobody would believe in them, that nobody would care. No one had ever been there to hear them.

"Here's a pretty piece of self-delusion. There are many bards who are so full of self-regard that they claim that their life is their art, that they *must* tell their tales or die. They say this to impress, of course, because no one ever died from going into another line of work. But I could not say it. I had no audience for my tales, and so I felt I hadn't earned the right to claim to be so mystically one with my words. The truth was uglier and far more human than that, as the truth usually is.

"The truth, and Zelar knew this, was that I *wanted* to tell my tales despite my lack of audience, but that I had come to want to tell them in the blind, habitual way that old men who are sick of life want to keep living, even if that means living solely to burden the world. Even if that meant telling tales to nothing and nobody. Even if that meant that my life had become a lie that I told myself every day, the lie that what I loved had value, and that it would be evil to destroy it.

"Let me set the scene. I was eating figs in silence, and remembering the night's end, how I came down after a blistering performance given to dust and empty tables and glaring unsold bottles of ale. Zelar had been there, a corner of oppressive attentiveness within an otherwise empty corner of the tavern. He had bought nothing. He would not justify my work. I was also remembering the angry tavern keeper who rudely demanded what little coin I carried to compensate him for the patrons I failed to attract, and how violently confused I felt when Zelar, for reasons I could not fathom, paid the bill.

"I suppose that is why I was now dining with Zelar in his rented rooms. Despite my skill with language, I could not find the proper words to refuse his invitation. And I was flattered out of my habitual bitterness to know that somewhere out of the darkness a stranger emerged and paid ransom for my words. I do not admit this to myself. I had been abused so thoroughly and so often for wanting that particular form of recognition, that I had learned to fear receiving it lest the gift go dark at my touch."

Aeren stopped speaking. She pressed my scarred hand as if she wanted me to know her touch was dark. I did not resist and I did not encourage her sudden intimacy, but I remained shielded against any magical attack. I waited silently for her to continue her tale while she looked hard into my eyes as if I was the living embodiment of everything she had ever learned to hate. It was a strange long silence.

I broke it by asking, "What happened to your tale?"

"This is essential to my tale. Needed background. Revelation of my character and motivation." She paused, uneasily collected herself, and after a long while she whispered urgently, "There was another night that I was helplessly remembering as I ate bad figs with Zelar. On that night I had deliberately gotten drunk in an attempt to burst holes in my inhibitions. I had wanted to say something important to the only person I had ever been foolish enough to trust, the only person who claimed to love my tales, and I needed to loosen my tongue. I said with great difficulty 'Thank you for knowing me in the way I need to be known. Thank you for seeing me in the tales and characters I create. *Thank you for being there.*' I was exquisitely uncomfortable saying this. I had given my friend everything that matters, and I knew how foolish it was to give that to anyone.

"I waited for the warm response that would absolve me of my uncertain revelation, but my waiting was met with dull silence. So I repeated myself, gingerly, and that time my only friend in the lonely world responded, saying, 'You know, I was thinking the other day that you might be a lot happier if you took your tales less seriously. After all, you don't have an audience for them, and there's really no shame in wordsmithing as a hobby.'

"And there, at the bottom of my drink and the bottom of that night, was a new loneliness and a pointed badge of shame. I had presumed that my tales mattered to someone, and I had just learned that they mattered to no one. It broke my heart.

"Anyway, I mention this because Zelar took the memory from me and showed it to me in a wineglass. He commented darkly on the picture. 'No one will love you for being human but for your willingness to pretend to be less. If you know anything, you know this.'"

Aeren dropped her hand from mine and spoke earnestly. "Perhaps for you it was some other betrayal that taught this lesson."

"It was lessons," I answered ruefully, remembering that strange night in Threle when I gave a drunken story to people I trusted, wanting nothing from them in return, and eventually receiving same.

She looked into the fire as if she was reading her tale there, as if she understood what I just told her as well as she understood anything. Then she resumed her tale.

"Zelar repeated his question as if he expected me to take notes. 'When does a force end?' His accent was foreign and so was his air, and that, of course, intrigued me, although I wondered whether his command of Sarana was enough to appreciate all the facets of my tales. I wanted to believe it was. It was all I had.

"Because I did not answer, he answered himself. 'All forces are infinite; all consequences are eternal. If a tale has force, it will never end, but will murmur eternally through the cracks and spaces in the world, through the actions of peasants and statesmen and wizards and priests, through the falling generations in eternal play. If a tale has force, it will write us into its vortex. Do you believe your tales have force?'

"I did not answer. I did not give him the gift of knowing my belief. It would cost more than figs and a stage fee for that. I would not sell him a weapon to wound me with for cheap. He already had the memory he stole in the wineglass, and I did not yet know if he would be kind to that. But I wanted to know his name. I wanted to know who it was that came out of the darkness and paid for my words. I wanted that forever. 'Tell me what you are called, stranger, and where you are from?' I asked hesitantly, lest my question reveal that life had left me enough self-regard to presume to ask.

"'Zelar. I am a master wizard attached to Emperor Roguehan's court.' His self-description was as charming as his accent; it implied so much that I was afraid to question it lest it turn to ashes in my heart. And then, improbably, in a wizard voice that you can't refuse or resist, he said, 'Tell me the tale of your life.'

"I wanted to say that I had nothing to tell that I hadn't told in my tales to the empty tavern. But I did not say that. The last time I said it still hurts, and he knew as much from the memory he stole. So I thanked him kindly for his interest and asked with as much caution as I've ever exercised in my life, 'What would you know, Master?'

"'Everything that matters.'

"Nothing had ever seemed so irresistible to me as this austerely brutal interest. He spoke in his accented Sarana, 'Pretend this is a Threlan court and you are telling me your life for judgment. How would you begin, I wonder? How would you begin to explain why nobody cares for your tales? Why I alone was your audience tonight?'

"I knew nothing of Threlan courts but the picture was charming. And so I consented to defend myself, or what remained of same. Not because it would change anything, but because he was a foreigner who would return to his own land come dawn, and so perhaps I would not see him again. And I began by saying guardedly,

"'Once upon my word, my father accounted himself a merchant prince. That is, on those days when he wasn't a beggar prince. The best I can say for him is that he was as semifictional as Gondal itself. Sometimes he carried gold and rubies in his pockets and on those days his sycophants would kiss his robe and loudly call him "King, King." That is, so long as nobody else was around whose favor they might also need. But as there are always several self-proclaimed "kings" in Anda on any given day harassing the City Assembly for recognition, he often despaired of getting lost in the crowd. So he would take extraordinary measures to put on costly feasts and public festivals.

"'The festivals of Anda are the festivals of lies, and my father's were no exception. He hired bards to lie, that is, to sing and chant of his excellence, while he smiled and drank fruited wine and pretended to know nothing about it. One legend he paid handsomely for was that he was the only living descendant of the last true king of Gondal.

"'There are many legends concerning the last true king of Gondal. In the days when Gondal was a kingdom in fact as well as in name, every claimant to the throne was required to slay a dragon and offer its heart to the sun to prove his fitness to rule. It was believed that only a true king could offer such a dangerous sacrifice without being killed in return, for in those days the king of the land was also the high priest of the land, and skill in battle was accounted equal importance with skill in making sacrifice. Destruction is a sacred act, eh? Anyone can kill, and everyone kills in one way or another, but not everyone can properly sacrifice. Sacrifice makes killing sacred. Sacrifice takes a certain twist of heart.

"'The bards sang that my father was descended from the last Gondish king, a king who so respected and honored the dragon that he killed that he swore upon the blood he shed to befriend all other dragons. He then went off to live among them, ending the monarchy. The bards claimed that a thin shadow of dragon blood, as well as royalty, flowed through my father's veins, and that this heritage accounted for his alleged skill in acquiring wealth. The other legend was that the elves stole and sacrificed a human king to the moon and stars every seven years by leaving him bound in a dragon's cave, and that my father's ancestor escaped those bonds, befriended the dragons, and was never seen again. And in yet another version, this same ancestor sent a goat in royal clothes to be sacrificed in his place, which so delighted the elves that they stopped the sacrifice forever and declared the goat to be king. It is pretty to think that this is truly what ended the monarchy, that our last king disappeared into a joke and that the priesthood went with him.

"'But all of these tales happened so long ago that nobody truly cares for the truth of them, except those who want to be king and can afford to pay the piper to put them in the stories. My father would also attempt to elevate his status by claiming elvish ancestors. Although any elves that currently live in Gondal tend to keep to themselves in the northern wastes and are generally ignored by the city dwellers, those humans who can claim elvish blood are sometimes believed to possess special gifts, although after a generation or two one is hard-pressed to find a correlation. There was nothing obviously elvish about my father except his penchant for telling tales about himself, or paying others to do the same.

" 'But his grandiose tales choked him, because when his pockets went empty and his debts mounted up, his flatterers would mock the stories behind his robe while crowning one of his rivals with their tongues until my father could fill his purse again. And so he learned the truth that, at the end of the day, our lives are worth the gold we carry, notwithstanding our own opinions of the matter.

" 'The only gift my father ever gave me was the following observation, uttered in despair over a pile of bad debts when I happened to be in the room and he uncharacteristically opened himself enough to speak his true thoughts. I had recently told a tale for a small audience at one of his festivals, a tale of my own creation about a dragon and a singing prince, and I had received a good deal of invective from some professional bards for daring to please that same audience. One even threatened to tell my father I shouldn't be performing, for my own good and the good of my father's reputation, because my stories were too wild and might upset somebody. I suspect this bard was more annoyed that my dragon story had the power to draw an audience than he was upset with its content.

" 'Anyway, I was complaining of my treatment to my father and bravely asking him to pay me for my performance as he paid the others. He refused, saying I placed too high a value on my gifts. He said sadly, "Our true value is always determined by others, Aeren, and it is always lower than the value we set on ourselves. None of us can set our own price on our lives, our ambitions, our dreams, on anything that truly matters. That is the first of life's great tragedies. The second is that we are constantly sacrificing our dreams to appease the first. The third is that this is the only kind of sacrifice that makes nothing sacred."

" 'When he said this I felt cold and worthless and forever closed my heart against him. I also thought he was the saddest man who ever lived, and that scared me a little. Now I know he was merely at war with humanity, and had something to prove.' "

Aeren stared darkly into the fire. I wanted to know her thoughts.

"Your father knew much about sacrifice," I interjected thoughtfully.

She nodded slightly and continued the thread of her tale. "Sacrifice and judgment. You tell me what *I* know. My father married seven times, because his wives kept dying. Some said his wives kept dying because he needed money, for each of his brides was wealthier than the last. His first wife was barren, but she brought him a chest of diamonds and so he held her precious until the diamonds ran out and she died. His second wife brought him land. She bore him a child who died shortly after she did. They were buried in that land. His third wife brought him baskets of gold and a son from a previous marriage, a quiet mystical child who went mad from staring at the moon too long. He drowned in a barrel after she died. His next two wives were sisters that he married in rapid succession. They died within a year of each other, which brought him a controlling interest in their family's trading house.

"My father claimed they ate bad fruit from one of his business rival's orchards. He paraded around Anda in mourning clothes and threw gold at influential citizens until he could persuade the City Assembly to grant him those orchards in compensation. He then held a large marriage feast to celebrate his wedding to his chief supporter's daughter. That was my mother, his sixth bride.

"Although she was the only child of one of the wealthiest men in Anda, it so happened that my father did not benefit from her sudden death as he had from the others, because her father had wisely decided to arrange matters so that neither my father nor any of his children could ever inherit any portion of his wealth. My father tried without success for years to change the terms of his marriage contract, but those terms, and the fact that my mother brought him a substantial income while she lived, probably saved her life. For that reason alone I don't believe he was responsible for her death, but when she suddenly took ill and died, all the old rumors about the fate of his other wives were raised like old ghosts, and complete strangers suddenly became quite willing to stop and tell me sordid tales concerning my father's history.

"Especially since my grandfather died shortly after my mother did. His was the sort of death that was so long anticipated that everybody respected it but nobody mourned. Of course there were some whispered speculations about it, but as my father had by then become one of the more powerful Assembly members, and had strings into nearly every major business in Anda, nobody whispered too loudly or long.

"My father cheerfully fanned the rumors by marrying again, this time to a distant kinswoman of my mother. He had made some legal inquiries, and discovered that through some entanglement in the law I don't pretend to understand that this widow-woman now stood to inherit my grandfather's fortune. At least, that is what they easily convinced each other of.

"My father's seventh wife was a pale gossamer moony sort of widow-woman who lived in fear of anyone discovering that she had anything in her character resembling a distinct personality, that is, when she wasn't desperately laying claim to all sorts of nonsensical achievements. It was as if she craved attention for her claims to possessing all sorts of ridiculous rare gifts, but feared being called upon to use her self-proclaimed talents to actually earn a living. You were supposed to respect her on her word, not on anything so pedestrian as an actual achievement.

"She lived in a moss hut where the farmlands fade into the northern wastelands and supported herself and her children as best she could through odd jobs and begging and selling a song for a coin if anyone would listen. She was not charming. She was not even interesting. She was both fiery dragonbird and frightened mouse. Dragonbird when she was safe from being tested on her tales of amazing achievements, mouse when anyone actually questioned her claims.

"My father appeared at her door one day like a hungry whirlwind with a fine story of his own about how she stood to inherit his late wife's father's fortune but only if she married him because of some arcane legal entanglement involving my mother. It was a well-wrought piece of fiction, and she believed him.

"And for her part she earned herself a captive audience for her tall tales. Had she wanted a reputation as a storyteller she might have done well if she hadn't been so desperate to be believed and so eager to demand some special regard for the accident of her elvish features, which were most likely just one of those odd resemblances people occasionally bear to long-dead ancestors. Any elvish blood in my mother's family, and there might be some going way back, would have to be beyond diluted at this point.

"But perhaps because she desperately needed attention as well as gold, she did her best to convince my mercantile-hearted father and anyone else who would listen to her that she was the descendant of an ancient elvish king. She claimed that when the moon was full she could sing straw into gold, that in certain winds and weathers she could shake an old rattle and common dress buttons would become gold pieces, that she had once bathed in a cold gray lake and brushed pearls from her hair. I did not believe her of course, because her poverty spoke loudly against such astounding gifts, and I'm sure my father did not believe her, but he probably pretended to believe whatever he had to in order to make another attempt to marry my grandfather's money. Especially since she encouraged his hopes with many stories of her childhood relationship to my mother, and her determination to claim what she called her 'ancient inheritance' for her children.

"So they convinced each other that their respective fortunes would greatly improve if they married at once, and marry they did, in a well-attended ceremony under a garlanded oak tree in the city square. It was immediately after they concluded publicly pledging their troth, which is how marriages are made in Anda as we no longer have an established clergy, that my father's new bride faced the celebrating crowd and ostentatiously declared, 'I, Ariana Elven-queen, am now the princess of the dead. For here I assume my ancient birthright.' No one understood what she meant, and her strange words and manner caused everybody's carefully crafted smiles to freeze and hold like Gondal's northern wasteland. She smiled like a crazy sword cutting the awkward silence. My father shifted uncomfortably and quickly motioned his hired minstrels to strike up a dance tune.

"And here was the rub. Three weeks later, despite his careful legal inquiries and her eager assurances, the City Assembly uncovered documents that my father had missed, documents that proved that she, like my mother, gave up her claim to inherit my grandfather's wealth upon her first marriage. And so the wealth my father thought he was marrying was confiscated by the Assembly and placed in the city treasury. Worse, my father's new bride decided to become fiery dragonbird for the day and make a public speech to the Assembly outlining the strange, premature deaths of his previous wives, and entreating that if she or her children should follow their example, that detailed inquiries be made. Then she smiled wanly, went home, retired to her sickbed, and demanded to be waited on hand and foot.

"Her children loved her, that I will say, although she had no patience for me. That might have been because she saw me as a rival to her own children, or because I made no secret of the fact that I was completely unimpressed with her irritating airs and eternally unsubstantiated claims to greatness. Sometimes I would sneak by her door and hear her telling stories to her children about their royal elvish heritage and how they were the last remnants of a great and noble race. She told her son Raen that his destiny was to be an elvish king and reclaim the throne of Gondal, and she told her daughter

Eyra that one day she would rule through him. She told me to get lost. Accepting me into her little fantasy was dangerous, because if one were to parse her stories out I could conceivably have a closer relationship to this nonexistent 'throne of Gondal' than her children did, especially if one chose to believe my father's stories about his royal descent.

"When my father discovered that her own claims to my grandfather's inheritance were semifictional, and that she had been as honest with him as he with her, and that he wouldn't be able to free himself of this marriage in his usual way, he roared out in dismay, took to isolation, and died of what I can only call a broken heart. He had lived his life with the single improbable purpose of becoming a celebrated merchant prince in a society with no toleration for princes, and the wide ugly space between his reality and his ideal, an ideal I'm sure he had killed many times for, finally killed him.

"His strange new wife inherited his fortune, which was enough to pay off his debts and leave her and her royal brood as poor as before.

"The result was fairly ugly, as you might predict. Raen got sullen and strange and withdrawn in the way that spoiled children who are raised with the notion that they are the center of the universe get when they encounter real life. Once the debts were paid off he had no money or inheritance to recommend him, but he did have a dangerously deflated sense of expectations coupled with an inflated sense of his own value as the alleged scion of a royal elvish family. Eyra avoided real life and surrounded herself with a shield of fantastic lies like her mother did. And for this reason the three of them remained unusually close, Eyra and her mother always being on hand to bolster Raen's belief in himself. They took poor lodgings in the city. Together they were going to rule the world, I suppose.

"At that point I left my father's house, which had been sold to pay his debts, and began to earn my keep by doing odd jobs for local merchants and telling tavern tales every night I could manage. Sometimes I would tell tales on the street corners for passing coins until some other bard would get threatened and complain to some local authority to break it up so he could have the street corner. Sometimes I'd actually get to tell tales in taverns, and if I did well, whatever better-established bard was threatened by my temporary success would influence the tavern keeper to make sure I didn't get invited back. That was especially humiliating because I would sometimes run across Raen, who frequented the same taverns I did and who lost no opportunity to salvage his own wounds and dashed expectations by telling me how worthless my stories were and who would needle me about some other bard who packed the room. 'What do you have to prove?' he once accosted me in his whiny, threatened-by-life voice. 'Are you so attention-starved that you're desperate enough to throw your lack of talent around to near-empty rooms in the hopes that someone will applaud out of politeness?'

"'Do I know you? Should I?' I responded. 'Are we like related or something?' Of course, my subtle comparison of our respective situations was so much wasted breath. When Raen was in his cups he was the King of Elf Land and none could say him nay. Whatever my state of mind, I was still aware that I was an unsuccessful storyteller. That was the essential difference between us.

"So why was I always performing to empty rooms? I started my tale in response to Master Zelar's question concerning why nobody cares for my tales, and so here I will finish. Anda and Arula are bardic cities. You would look long and hard here to find someone who doesn't claim bardic proclivities. It may be due to our ancient elvish influence, or simply because there's so much of it around that there's always more of it around. All of which makes Anda a particularly miserable city to work in, because when everybody is an artist, nobody is. The rivalry is murderous and the best get out and ply their trade elsewhere as soon as they can. Within Anda itself, you need more than talent to attract an audience. Talent is cheap and easy. You need money, influential friends, an ability to create interest without letting your rivals know you're a threat to their ability to attract an audience. Do you know how difficult it is to perfect your craft while knowing from experience that the very act of doing so will damn you from your craft? It's worse than living in a monastery, from what I hear."

"Perhaps," I interjected, a dark chorus to her passion play.

She didn't appear to hear me. She was speaking to Zelar as if he were present. "And so. Tonight I have told my poor tavern tales to you, Master Zelar, and you have graced me with your presence and asked me to tell you my life." She held silent until the air around us felt like it would break. "And so we sit, we two, at this dark table. I've nothing more to say."

She paused again before speaking in Zelar's voice. "You've told me nothing of your own life and much of events around you."

Then she narrated in her own voice, "Zelar said this without implying he wanted or needed more. It was his only comment. I could not read it. And so I asked bravely, my heart's need screaming through my thin breathless voice, 'And your verdict?'"

" 'I'll pay you to leave Anda and work with me,' Zelar responded flatly. 'You've nothing here. You will apprentice to me and you will tell me stories every night. I've got some influence with the emperor, and as he is always interested in hiring particularly promising bards, it would do me much honor to bring you to his court.' He spoke in a voice so devoid of enthusiasm I had to believe him. I had nothing to lose by believing him. It is what I have always wanted. So much so I was afraid to offend him by asking questions. If he was telling me a mere bard's tale about knowing the emperor, I did not want to know about it, I simply wanted to believe it."

Aeren paused again in her telling. I didn't need magic to read the pain in her eyes. "Have you finished?" I asked respectfully.

"No. There is more. Now there is distance. Zelar brought me north through Gondal's wasteland to this cave. He told me he had business here before making the long journey back to the empire. He regaled me with stories of Roguehan's victories. I was prepared to like the emperor, even prepared to embrace evil for his sake. What did I care for good or evil so long as I could tell my tales? I would of course do anything for the powerful ruler who would make me his royal bard, and I was of course happy to do anything for Zelar who was going to make that possible. So if Zelar needed to ride north into Gondal's wasteland on some crazy errand and wanted me along, who was I to say him nay?

"When we reached this cave his story changed in a way that could only flatter. He said his 'business' was to prepare me to perform for the emperor, and that I must practice my tales every night against meeting him. That he had brought me to this place so we could work without distractions. That he *believed* in me. He said the emperor loved a good story told well, but would be angry if I bored him. And so I told Zelar many tales, old and new ones of my own devising, and I grew to believe they mattered, that my life mattered, and I allowed myself to get positively word-drunk without shame. Here in this cave I felt joy, and started to love my life, because now I could believe in myself as a storyteller. Without reservations. And Zelar would compel this self-belief by chastising me if he thought I wasn't taking what he liked to call my 'gifts' seriously. He was preparing me to meet the emperor, and so nothing less than all high seriousness would do.

"Zelar also taught me magic, not much, but enough to manifest small objects and blast intruders. He said that manifesting small objects would make a charming addition to my performances, and that court life was dangerous and so why not learn how to defend myself? I still can't conjure anything, or manifest more than a small simple object that's relatively physically close. I know now that his point was to force some sort of wizard-apprentice bond between us, to make it easier for him to track me at a distance, and that his blasting techniques were useful for me to know for my future occupation as a dragon guard, an occupation I had no idea was in the planning. Of course his own shielding was proof against any blast I might direct at him or at his magical items.

"How could all this be a lie? Why would Zelar trouble to bring me here if he wasn't serious? Why *wouldn't* I believe I was being prepared to audition for a position as the emperor's court storyteller. It was quickly obvious that Zelar was an extremely powerful wizard, so it was easy to believe that he was attached to somebody's court.

"But there was no emperor, or emperor's court. And no indication that there ever would be. There was only cave. The light outside, meaning Zelar's empty promises, being elsewhere and always.

"To my end. One night, three years ago, there was a winter storm that kept us snowbound for three days. Zelar asked me to tell him the story of the dragon and the singing prince, the same one I had told years ago at my father's festival. I didn't think he even knew of that story, but I had grown so used to Zelar's constant mind probes and of him knowing so much about me, that I didn't find his request startling.

" 'This is my final test of you. To see if you are ready to meet the emperor,' he said in a voice of rare geniality. 'Come here, Aeren, and speak to this mirror. But speak with your whole being, as you have practiced doing every night. Speak not as if you want me to believe every word, or as if you believe every word, but as if you *are* every word. When you speak of the dragon you must *be* the dragon. Your mouth must burn on every word like your language is pure dragonfire. When you speak of the prince you must know yourself as a young prince, as if your young woman's face is bearded and your voice is low and strong. Or what's a story for? Bring forth your other lives, use well the power I've given you. Remember, the emperor will take nothing less from any performer.'

" 'Yes, Master. As you will.' I responded enthusiastically, facing a mirror that was exactly my height, and that hadn't existed before. I assumed Zelar had conjured it or engineered it out of the materials I knew he kept in the lower part of the cave. I studied the glass but I could not find my reflection in it, only shadows reflected from shadows on the cave wall. Zelar stood behind me. I did not see his reflection, either.

"'What do you see, there, Aeren? Whom are you about to tell your tale to?' he asked in what I privately called his spellcasting voice.

"'No one and nothing,' I replied. 'Shadows in the shape of a stormdragon.'

"'Yes,' he agreed. 'As you tell your tale to the storm in the mirror, you are to believe without reservations that you are speaking to yourself, that you are the stormdragon in your tale. Can you do that?'

"'Yes,' I said with all the joy and pride my heart could hold. 'My life goal is to be recognized for being able to call upon such belief at will.' I spoke without shame, without the terrible embarrassed silence on such heartfelt matters that I had tried unsuccessfully to keep that night we first met. My confident voice, my ability to speak those words at all, measured the trust I had gained in Zelar."

Aeren stopped speaking again. Her shame was so palpable I felt embarrassed for her, but I stayed neutral and steady.

"I told my tale to the mirror," she said in an anger so clouded with sadness I didn't know whether to comfort her or strengthen my shield against another blast.

"Let me tell you what it was like to turn dragon," she said, her voice now stiff with anger. "As I told my tale the cave got colder, and the firelight lost its color and went gray. I thought perhaps that Zelar had cast a spell on the place to test my ability to focus on my story despite what was happening around me. So I kept speaking. My voice was mine but it now sounded like a thundercloud speaking my words. I ignored that, too, focusing ever more deeply on becoming the dragon, on being the story. My stomach felt suddenly heavy as if I had eaten too much and it was now sagging with the weight, and my heartbeat grew slow and sluggish as my extremities felt even colder. The mirror grew shorter, that is, I was growing suddenly taller, and soon the mirror completely disappeared. I turned around to see Zelar and it felt like it was taking too long to turn, like a dead-weight kept dragging at my back. And then I was under my own back and my back was stretching longer than I was used to, meaning my limbs were on the floor and my weight was crushing me with surprise, except that something on my back was fluttering and lifting me a little when I breathed. I was so confused and disoriented I kept stopping the story, and starting, and stopping, until I realized that everything in the cave was now gray and blurry, including Zelar. The weight of my own breaths crushed me. My mouth felt too wide. The air around my face felt too warm when I exhaled, as if every time I breathed out I was sticking my face in a candle.

"So I stopped speaking and looked at Zelar with panic. Panic that my confusion was going to cost me my opportunity for a place at the emperor's court, and panic that something horrible had gone wrong with one of Zelar's spells.

"'My voice is strange,' I said in fearful, long, apologetic rolls of thunder.

"'You've become the dragon,' responded Zelar in a voice of fake courtesy. 'You've become your own story.' He spoke as if he was complimenting a recalcitrant child who was complaining about getting something she thought she wanted.

"'Why didn't I become the prince?' was all I could think to ask, while trying desperately not to give in to the sheer terror of knowing that this evil wizard had shapeshifted me into this horror.

"'Because you already were the prince, in a manner of speaking. You are the only true direct descendant of the last true king of Gondal. And now your dragon heritage is manifest. I suppose it is a tribute to the depth of your belief.' He chuckled a little. 'If the emperor were here, he'd find it most entertaining.'

"'Put me back,' I pleaded, frightened because something in his manner told me that wasn't about to happen.

"'I've no intention of putting you back. Not yet, anyway. I'm going to put you to work. Real work.' The way he said 'real work' was a rebuke to all the days and nights I spent practicing and perfecting my storytelling. It hurt worse than the transformation. Without even willing it, my anger exploded out of my mouth in a fireball. Zelar remained unharmed.

"'My shield will always be proof against your outbursts, my dear, for I created your new shape. But I command you to use those blasts against anyone who would trespass into this cave, for here I keep my name stone and my magical items, which are also proof against your blasts for the same reasons. As long as you remain close to this cave, I shall be able to sense you through those items and through our magical bond, for it was I who first taught you magic. Should you be foolish enough to leave the vicinity of this cave, or to allow any of my magical items to be disturbed, the ban you now carry, which I have placed in you with my spell, will kill you. You should be able to hunt your sup within a perfect square mile of this spot and no farther. Those barrels-of-plenty will produce dried fruit such as dragons are fond of.'

"My entrails felt sick, and I screamed thunder with the sickness because its creepy strangeness underscored my new life.

"'Perhaps—someday—at some point in your very long dragon

life, I will return and free you. That is, if the emperor ever finds you of use in your human form. He might decide at some point he needs the support of the heir to Gondal's throne, so he doesn't wish to kill you outright. But he does want you to know the extent of his power, to help ensure your loyalty should that day ever come. Guard well against that day.'

"I guarded well for three years." Aeren ceased speaking in her bardic voice, and offered a short epilogue. "Until this adventure in transformation, I did not believe much in the bardic legends that meant so much to my father. Now I suppose I must confess that they have what Zelar called 'force.' He used my brief belief in myself against me. Perhaps the legend is right about me ruling Gondal some-day, but if that is the case, then the emperor hasn't decided whether I'm more useful to him alive or dead, so he commanded Zelar to keep me in my dragon form. And what's worse than those wasted years is that Zelar never loved my stories. That, more than the rest, makes me feel unclean."

"I like your story. There's a certain charm to the way you tell it. If I were presiding over a Threlan court and listening to you tell me your life, I'd judge in your favor."

"Stop dismissing me with milk-warm praise," she snapped. "If the best I can conjure up is 'a certain charm,' what is the point? Anyone can do that. It doesn't give me the right to call myself a wordsmith in any meaningful sense."

"Maybe you have a right to call yourself Queen of Gondal?" I asked cheerfully.

"Who wants it? I'd rather be a bard than a glorified administrator. I'd give the whole thing to Raen to ease his aching soul if it were truly mine to give. He'd probably volunteer to turn dragon to get it."

"Would you give it to me?"

"I thought my tale was payment for your freeing me of the spell. Besides, our City Assembly would never recognize such a claim, and neither would the people. Gondal needs some central authority, that's for sure, but nobody really wants it unless it's their own authority made central. And Gondal itself really is more of a geo-graphical area than an actual political entity, so what in the gods' name would you do with it?"

"If you don't want the claim, why do you care who gets it or what gets done with it?" I asked nonchalantly. "It wouldn't be your con-cern, and it would relieve you of any further unwanted interest from the emperor."

She considered long and hard. "All right, if you believe in it that much, take it." She spoke harshly and sincerely. "Provided . . . I can be your royal bard?"

"You have my word of honor," I said solemnly. I suppose it was the least I could do. Besides, it sealed the deal.

She took both my hands roughly in hers. "Here, with the fire and the dark for witness, by the dragon blood which squirms and thunders through my veins, I give you my kingdom; if you can find your way to take it."

"And I hereby call Hecate to witness that you are placing your power and birthright in me."

"Yes, call Hecate. Call all the evil deities. If Gondal is mine, Gondal is yours. Unreservedly." She meant it. We could both feel the power shift, and the goddess force was strong around me. Hecate had led me to this cave for a reason. The force and the change dispersed.

"I don't even know your name," she said flatly, as if to emphasize it was truly nothing to her who she gave her birthright to, so long as she could tell her tales.

"It's Llewelyn, my royal bard."

"All right, King Llewelyn," she spoke sarcastically. "What do you plan to do next?"

"Remove your ban and make myself at home with Zelar's treasure chest, oh trusted guard."

"And then?"

"Ride with you to Anda to claim my throne."

For the first time in our long winter night, she smiled.

Fifteen

*T*he next day was slow and strange, burning and drying and passing away long before I began to wake. I had slept far into the morning after spending most of the previous night listening to Aeren's winter's tale, and I roused myself slowly and hesitantly so as not to disturb Aeren any more than necessary. I needn't have bothered, as my hostess was sitting upright and wide-awake on the other side of the mat and staring at me dully through heavy-lidded eyes. At her side were Devon's sleeping blankets, unfolded and unused, which confused me until I came awake enough to remember that I had manifested the blankets from the horses' saddlebags during the night, as I had found the thin mat on the hard cave floor exceedingly uncomfortable and had assumed that in her newly restored human form Aeren did too. I had also manifested firewood from outside the cave because the fire was dying and the air was beginning to get dangerously cold in our little dwelling. I then remembered that Aeren had been sitting in the same position when I did those workings, and that her stiff posture had confirmed my suspicion that she was experiencing discomfort from lying on the mat. But I truly had no idea why she hadn't moved all night or made use of the blankets.

I rolled over onto my back and groaned. "Didn't you get any sleep?"

"No," she said in a tight, slightly rushed voice as if she were defending herself against a criminal accusation.

"Aren't you tired?" I sat up.

"No."

I could tell at a glance she was lying. She looked like a severe Gondish snow figure melting into a summer hell of indeterminable slush. Her skin had a gray sleepless tinge and it sagged dreadfully under her eyes, making her look much older than she had on the previous day. But she was clearly too proud or too scared or some strange combination of both to admit to any weakness in front of me. I decided to ignore her incomprehensible decision to watch the cave all night, but she wouldn't allow me that option for she continued speaking in the dull raspy voice of someone who has clearly been far too wakeful for far too long, "I don't even like the word. It's so personal it's embarrassing."

I rubbed my face to induce more wakefulness. "What's so personal it's embarrassing?"

She looked away and sighed, as if she truly didn't want to say whatever word she so strongly disliked. Then she spoke in an odd thin tone of distasteful distance, "Sleep. Why do you make me say it?" She was annoyed because she seemed to feel I had just intentionally humiliated her.

I decided that she still had a stormdragon's spirit, if not a stormdragon's form, because anything could set her off into one of her opaque rants. It was far too soon after waking to argue with her about my word choice or about anything else, so I assumed a jocular tone in order to deflect the angry storm that I sensed was coming on. "So you find it embarrassing to be human?"

"No, I find it embarrassing to presume so much on life."

"Help me out, Aeren. What does that mean? On whose life did I 'presume' by falling asleep last night?" I laughed indulgently as I said this, both to encourage her to laugh with me and because the concept was so absurd that I couldn't begin to grasp her point. But I was certain nonetheless that somewhere beneath her eternal ire her point was worth grasping, in the way that an odd expression translated from an unknown language was. Not that it would change one's point of view, but it was a valuable intellectual exercise if one had the time for it. Aeren had a good mind, long experience of pain and betrayal, and three years of undistracted solitude for thinking about all sorts of things while held in thrall to a powerful evil wizard. I couldn't begin to claim to understand her, but I did see a lot of myself in her.

Aeren found my friendly laughter annoying. She responded acrimoniously, "Show me one human being, just one, who deserves protection, or any consideration at all, while choosing to sleep. It's mortally presumptuous. The bad taste of it makes my blood crawl into my throat like I swallowed a bitter root. Some things should be private. When people sleep they go ugly, their mouths hang open, they drool and snore and kick and mumble, and they are less aware than a plucked vegetable. Not you perhaps, for you were at least decently buried in your blankets so I couldn't tell, but most people are roundly disgusting in that state."

"You mean it's presumptuous to be disgusting?" I was doing my best to follow her rant, but I wasn't even awake enough yet to think clearly, and her argument was escaping me.

"I mean it's presumptuous to put such nauseating helplessness on display, because it presumes that whoever is present will care to invest time and energy into protecting you while you have chosen to become a disgusting mess."

"You mean my shield didn't hold?" I knew it had, but I couldn't think of anything else to say.

She didn't answer my question. Instead she said resentfully, "Unless you've done something valuable enough with your life to earn that kind of protection, sleeping in front of another implies an incredible sense of unearned entitlement to somebody else's regard. An entitlement I sure as hell haven't earned and wouldn't presume to claim unless and until I accomplish a lot more in my life. I've never felt comfortable even relaxing in front of other people. So I don't."

"Congratulations," I said dryly. "I'm impressed. I guess."

"How did *you* get to be so easy with yourself?" It was strange the way she asked this question, because beneath her angry resentment was a desperately sincere curiosity that came from some horrible depth of pain. I could tell that Aeren truly wanted to be easy with herself, but that some hellish personal terror of revealing her own shortcomings that I could have no idea of without probing her mind prevented her from accomplishing that glorious feat. And yet, despite her self-torturing fears, she had ambitions to be a world-renowned performer, a highly valued storyteller attached to some great ruler's court. I had always assumed that professional entertainers needed a wellspring of self-confidence and self-belief to make a living. Ellisand certainly had the gods' own abundance of those qualities. I knew that Aeren's confidence had certainly been damaged by Zelar as well as by her other experiences. Yet she had managed, despite all, to tell a decent tale on the previous night. Here was another odd color to her character that I would need to be sensitive to, a fascinating psychic crack that I wanted to explore, because not even in El had I encountered such a strange inner inconsistency. She repeated her question impatiently, "Why aren't you answering me? How did you get to be so easy with yourself?"

"I'm really not, but we'll debate that one some other time," I said ruefully, not caring to tell her how uneasy with myself I had always been, precisely because of my own excruciating self-honesty. Aeren, however, was too caught up in her current pique to allow me any space for evasiveness.

"Why not debate it now? What are you trying to avoid? You were certainly comfortable enough with yourself all night long. And comfortable enough with yourself this morning to make infuriatingly cryptic remarks with an air of understated mystery that I'm supposed to be dazzled by." She mocked my accent, "'I'm really not, but we'll debate that one some other time.' Oh, please. If you were truly uncomfortable with yourself, you would have watched all night like me."

I sighed. "And greeted the day with a mind fogged like yours. All right, Aeren, this one is for you. Be gentle with it, if you can. I spent my first night as a wizard's apprentice sitting awake in a chair because I wasn't comfortable enough with myself to ask for a bed. It made about as much impression on my new master as your decision to sacrifice your mind's sharpness for the day to your personal insecurities has made on me. Which is to say it made none."

"I wasn't intending to make an impression. I was intending not to claim a night's consideration from you that I haven't earned. I didn't even touch your blankets." She hesitated a little, and her voice got harshly plaintive. "I—I'm ethical that way. Most people aren't."

"Right. Well, I'm intending to check on the horses. That is, if doing so won't be considered another breach of ethics or unwarranted assumption of self-worth that might offend milady." I said this with a courteous smile and a very slight inclination of my head, as I thought befitted my new position as king. She didn't answer. Her only reaction was a thick, silent impatience for the personal privacy that my temporary absence would afford. I supposed that after having lived alone for three years, she naturally found my presence discomforting, so I decided it wouldn't hurt our new relationship any to give her some solitude.

I left the cave and entered a day that was excruciating in its emptiness. Even the frozen ground felt like it existed apart from my feet, like nothing and no one could ever forge a link with this land. When I came across Devon's grave I stopped and said a brief prayer to Hecate, and took time to drop my shield and open myself to the pale energies of the winter sun. It was colder here than anything I ever remembered, but I didn't care. When I finished I murmured softly into the winter light around me, "The Sun King is dead. Long live the new King of Gondal." I don't know why I felt sad when I said this, but an unexpected hollowness spread through me with these words and entwined itself with the empty landscape and with my thoughts of what had recently taken place in Walworth's castle and with my questions concerning the strangeness I had run through when I escaped with Isulde. My sudden bout of sadness was more profound than the melancholy I had felt over my nonreaction to Devon's death. I had never felt so lonely, not even in Kursen Monastery. There I had revenge to plot and plan, and even in planned vengeance there was an odd strand of comfort, a certain implied promise of a stray ghost of companionship. For in plotting revenge I was still maintaining a relationship with Walworth and his household. Loneliness is incompatible with vindictiveness.

But now, through Hecate's guidance and my own skill, I had a shadowy semilegendary kingship for the taking, but my kingship would be in a life that no longer had reference to anything in my past. I felt blank and strange, as if there was no difference between me and the northern Gondal landscape. *Perhaps I am already the lord of this land,* I mused. Hadn't I symbolically offered my life as a sacrifice when I began this journey by burning the cloak Isulde had given me? And now, by right of both destroying and befriending a dragon, perhaps I had fulfilled the ancient requirement for kingship. The significance of Gondal's ancient kings being also the high priests of the land was not lost on me, either. I was probably more qualified than all the other "kings" making claims in Anda, and with Zelar's magical items at my disposal, I would likely have the power to enforce those claims.

If I could convince what—two City Assemblies, Anda and Arula—that my claim was legitimate, it would be protection against Roguehan, especially since I would have Zelar's name stone in my possession. If the emperor were all that interested in acquiring this northern wasteland, and based on Aeren's tale, he certainly was, then he would be equally interested in making deals with the new king who had his chief wizard's weapons in his possession. And if by some unimaginable means Walworth had been able to defeat Roguehan and reclaim Threle, well, I knew that no Threlan king would even think of asking a foreign leader to extradite himself to stand trial. That would smack too much of interference in a foreign state, and I couldn't conceive that Walworth, with all the work he'd have on his hands restoring his beloved country, would bother. And any of my evil brothers and sisters who thought it was in their spiritual interest to plot some unthinkable vengeance against me for destroying El and Cathe would have to think long and hard about destroying a priest-king who still obviously bore enough favor from his deity to come into rulership of his own country. If Hecate had favored me thus far, Hecate would protect me.

And with Zelar's carefully guarded treasure chest at my disposal and Aeren at my side to substantiate my claim with her story, why wouldn't I be able to make a fine showing? I reminded myself to assume as much deep courtesy and outward respect toward Aeren as I could muster, as I would need her advocacy in Anda to help make my claim stick. She clearly had a difficult personality, but I had become rather skilled in dealing with difficult personalities. I needed Aeren to be well-disposed toward me. I would concentrate all my resources on earning her trust, save forcing her loyalty through magic. I watched the wind blow breaths of dead, distant snow over Devon's grave. "I can't put back your heart the way it naturally was before I forced your affection to help me rule Kursen, Dev," I said quietly, "but I can abstain from forcing Aeren's to help me rule Gondal. And in killing you I did restore her to her natural, human form. In that sense your death has meaning. It is all I can give."

I returned to the cave and entered as quietly and unobtrusively as possible. Despite my best efforts at walking softly, my footfalls woke Aeren, who had dozed off in her sitting position and fallen over on Devon's blankets while I was gone.

Aeren burst into wakefulness like a thundercloud from a storm-dragon's mouth. Her annoyance at getting caught sleeping exploded into a visibly angry embarrassment, which she attempted to cover by manifesting some fruit from the barrels-of-plenty and stretching awkwardly in the heat of the fire while staring pointedly at the flames and stuffing dried pears in her mouth. Presumably it was all right within her moral universe to eat in front of me, just not to sleep. For myself, it was pleasant to walk over and sit easily by the warmth of the fireplace and feel no compulsion to move until it suited me to do so. Even though this was Zelar's cave, and his magical items, which were imbued with his personal power, were somewhere close by, I felt comfortable here. Or perhaps I felt comfortable *because* this was Zelar's cave and it was pulsing with evil power, which suited my personal energy well. I wondered about Aeren in her new human form, though. She knew enough magic to be affected by the ambient power, but she had made no formal alliance to the forces of evil, so it was anybody's guess whether that power was now causing her physical or emotional distress.

"How are you feeling this morning, buddy?" I asked considerately, as if we had not started the morning with a disagreement. "Is it the start of a fine day?"

She responded by rising to walk stiffly to the barrels-of-plenty while remarking with her back to me, "Alas my body aches. I'm not used to feeling human again. Are you?" She asked this in an odd, playful way, as if she was trying to disguise some uncomfortable agenda with a tease, or make up for her strange little morning's outburst. She was keeping her back to me for the same reason she had been staring so focusedly into the flames. She was uncomfortable facing me eye-to-eye with a display of camaraderie. She wasn't insincere in her sudden friendliness, exactly, but she was making the gods' own effort not to be totally discomfited by expressing sensitivity to someone else's pain. In this respect she really did resemble myself in my first days in Threle, poor girl.

"What does that mean? I've never been anything but painfully human," I bantered.

"There's no need to brag. What makes you think you're special in that regard?"

"Everyone suffers in their own way," I responded suavely.

"Suffer me this. I love eating without my food turning to ashes in my mouth." Aeren said this in such an uncharacteristically unguarded way that I was suddenly seized with a sense of charm and found myself smiling indulgently without meaning to. Aeren's mood suddenly seemed lighter. I didn't understand the cause of this sudden shift, but I certainly didn't want to do anything to break it, because I got the impression that such openness was extremely unusual with her, even before her existence as a stormdragon. Perhaps she was suddenly pretending to confidence, as I once had with Mirand, and if so, I had to admire her courage. "Water," she cried enthusiastically while dipping her hands in one of the barrels. "Cool water that doesn't turn to flavorless tepid tea on my tongue!" She took water in her cupped hands and drank long and deeply from them as if she'd never tasted water before, repeating the action several times over. "It is so good to have a real tongue instead of a bed of coals."

"Drink away," I responded as if I were her affable host and she my houseguest. "We'll need your real tongue to tell your tale to the Assembly when we arrive in Anda."

She grinned and flushed a little across her cheeks before responding with what I had learned was one of her characteristic non sequiturs. "Now that you've eaten a dragon's fruit, you shall have to return *here* to live among the dragons one day, my liege," she teased me. It was a harsh, demanding sort of tease, and it masked another sudden, obvious discomfort that I didn't understand the source of. She clearly wanted me to feel comfortable with her, but she was utterly unused to conveying that particular desire through words, and the result of her confusion seemed to be to change the subject without warning. I respected her fear by overlooking her awkwardness with a smile.

"My understanding is it's Zelar's fruit," I said easily. "And since its source is evil and I'm a strict vegetarian because of my own particular evil path, it suits me fine. But I am curious about those barrels.

Do you happen to know how they are able to conjure food you can live on for years?" I asked this lightly, but she turned and stared at me sharply, letting the water spill out of her hands as if I'd just insulted her by not believing in her previous night's tale. "Conjured food can't sustain life, and it wouldn't be practical for Zelar to keep several years' supply of dried fruit near here for the barrels to continually manifest."

"I have no idea," she said a little sharply. "Zelar had all kinds of magical devices at his disposal that I don't pretend to understand. All I know is that he had some sort of magical workshop down in the earth beneath this cave. I was too physically large in my dragonform to negotiate that slender downward arc you can see at the back of my living area that leads to his workshop, and when I was Zelar's apprentice he forbade me to enter that part."

I walked over and inspected the barrels, felt deeply into the magic they contained, but could not find the answer to my question. When I closed my eyes and opened my senses, the barrels felt like old trees eternally giving birth to themselves, although their births felt backward and evil, and so their fruit was dry and dead. The scar on my palm tingled when I touched them. Here was a fascinating magical device but it was beyond my ken to understand how it worked. I focused my attention back on Aeren, who had resumed her place by the fire and was staring at me with a sudden, defensive suspicion.

"About Zelar's workshop." I spoke smoothly, ignoring her expression. "I understand that before I disturb his magical items, I shall have to remove your ban."

Aeren's expression suddenly resembled that of the stormdragon. My comment replaced her defensiveness with anger. "If you know enough wizardry to do that, why don't you just show *me* how it's done and I'll remove my own?" She obviously didn't trust me to work any sort of intimate magic on her. Not that I much blamed her, considering her previous experience with wizards.

"I can't, Aeren," I said uneasily, knowing she was likely to take offense at my response. "Even if I could show you what to do, no one can remove a ban from himself. Ban removal is fairly advanced and fairly delicate, and by your own admission, Zelar never taught you much beyond specific, limited workings. You know how to manifest fruit from across a room or blast an intruder, but you don't know magical theory or why what you do works. And it would take more time to teach you right now than either of us has to give."

She didn't like being reminded of the disparity in our training, and I didn't like reminding her because she took it so badly. Aeren was certainly proud enough to be a queen, although it was a pride based on a wellspring of lifelong hurts, not accomplishments, and it was a pride that sat uneasily alongside her chronic—how can I describe this—fear of herself. She spoke coolly, "Last night you demonstrated an impressive command of clerisy. I know how strong you are in evil because you called Hecate and the shadows changed, and because you once studied extensively with Zelar. I don't care. Evil doesn't bother or frighten me, but I don't trust you with my ban."

"You trusted me with your kingdom."

"I don't care about my kingdom."

"You mean you care about your ban?" I asked in a good-natured teasing tone, and then remembered where I had learned that tone. I learned it when Baniff used to tease me when I was being so self-conscious and so, well, uneasy with myself that I was acting stupid. The difference between me and Aeren is that when Baniff used to tease me under those circumstances, I was utterly chagrined and had to command all my inner resources to pretend to confidence to tease him back. Aeren just got angry and annoyed or closed-up and defensive. Even though she was a storyteller, pretense was not part of the way she dealt with other people. Perhaps there is something honorable about going through life with your worst emotions constantly unmasked, but there is something dangerously vulnerable about it, too. Most people mask their emotions to protect themselves against someone else's reaction, which is why so many conversations never really happen, are not real conversations but intersecting monologues of cowardice. Aeren was not an emotional coward. It was the closest thing I'd found in her to a tragic flaw.

She answered my question by snapping, "No, I care about not subjecting myself to anyone else's magic, good, evil, or indifferent. I've had my fill of that, and I refuse to have any more. Have you ever removed a ban before? Do you know what you're doing?"

"No, I've never removed a ban. But anything a wizard can do a cleric can do better, under the right circumstances, and I'm as confident as Hecate nurses dead scholars that these are the right circumstances. My Goddess will guide me to use my priestly arts to find and destroy it."

"In other words, you're going to guess with my life."

"Pretty damn intimate phrase, isn't it? 'Guess with my life'?" I said this like I was teasing her for yesterday's outburst concerning my similar word choice, and she suddenly looked sweaty and shamefaced at her own. That was not the effect I intended, so I said gently and respectfully, "Well, Aeren, I've been guessing with my own for years. And it will be far less risky if you cooperate with me. Depending on what I'm able to extract, I might even be able to insert your ban into Zelar's name stone, and that would give me all sorts of power over him. Wouldn't you like that? I once did something similar to another wizard."

"What happened?" she asked slowly, still chagrined, still avoiding eye contact.

"It killed him." I didn't think it necessary to tell her the whole story concerning my inadvertently burying my bans with Mirand's name stone, and she didn't seem comfortable enough to display the curiosity to ask, because that would imply the weakness of wanting to know more. She considered my words as if they applied to Zelar, and actually seemed to relax a little, although just a little.

"What do I have to do?" she asked sullenly.

"Trust me. Completely. Be willing to go into trance with me and be willing to let me sense where your ban is. Then I shall call upon Hecate, and ask Her blessing in freeing you. If it works, it will be much more thorough and effective than wizardry. Clerisy usually is."

"And if it doesn't?"

"Then you'll have to spend the rest of your natural life here waiting for Zelar to free you and making sure no one disturbs his items. And when he discovers you've been restored to your natural self, if he hasn't already learned that through some link to you or this place, you know he has little incentive to free you. I hate to say it but I'm the best chance you've got."

This was worse than our friendly discussion about the ethics of sleep. She ranted about all sorts of things I couldn't follow the logic of, but which obviously annoyed her, and once her rant had run its course, I said politely, "A high priest once removed a ban from me. In doing so he brought me to death so that he could initiate me into the priesthood of Hecate. In your case we won't have to do anything nearly so extreme."

She looked at me with an assumed, defensive blankness.

"I mean, I will ask Hecate to enter your heart, and I want you to be prepared for that. Not to make you a priestess but to aid your freedom of movement by destroying your ban, specifically so that you might have the freedom to support my claims to kingship. Motivation is everything in clerical workings. If my Goddess would have me crowned, my Goddess will free you. You will feel Her evil in your veins and in your blood, like an ancient mold decaying the leaves of a long-neglected book some author gave his life for but which nobody ever read." She stiffened so much I couldn't even sense her breathing. *Wrong image*, I thought wryly. "Or the cold in the soul of an old man on his deathbed wheezing with the nightmare knowledge that he killed all the loveliness that was supposed to be his life, and so there is nothing left for him even to die with. But that will be nothing to you having felt your human blood turn dragon. And it will be temporary, unless you wish it to be otherwise. Of course if you were to freely welcome Her, perhaps promise to devote yourself to her worship, all will be even more likely to be better than well, but even that won't be necessary."

"What does a worshiper of Hecate do?" she asked suspiciously.

"Study scholarship without adding anything original. Avoid consuming dead animal life, although that is only really necessary for clergy. Embrace evil. Learn to hate the stars and love the dark around them."

She glared like a dragon. "I'm not about to worship anything. I don't think that way, and neither does anybody else from Gondal. There's no way to worship a goddess without resenting her perfection, unless you become such a skilled cleric that you really can manifest your deity at will. But even if I reached that level, it would be Hecate's power, not mine, so I'd most likely resent it and lose whatever power I had. I'm not much for organized religion."

"On the contrary, you sound like you ought to found your own cult." She looked aghast. I smiled. "That was a joke. It's all right, Aeren. I can work with neutrality." Thank the gods she had no alignment to any good manifestations of Habundia Ceres. That would make things that much smoother. "Here, just make yourself comfor— I mean, please feel free to sit anywhere you choose, and allow me to go to work. I promise I'll stop anytime you give me the command."

She glared at me with intense suspicion and sat in a thoroughly awkward and uncomfortable position in front of the fire. "I'm only doing this to ease the possibility of my vengeance on Zelar," she said. "And to regain my freedom to tell tales."

"Of course. Understood. I'm going to sit behind you."

"Fine." She sounded slightly peeved.

Her back stiffened, but she showed a modicum of trust by keeping her back turned toward me as I sat behind her on the mat, both of us facing the fire. This was all extremely awkward for there was no way to support our backs, but it would have to do, especially since Aeren had one of those odd personalities that seemed to make it a point of honor to resist being too comfortable. "Aeren, I need you to remove your shift. I'm going to put my hands on your bare back. Remember, anytime you want me to stop, just say so." I only said the latter so she would feel a little easier about the process. Once started, I had no intention of stopping. I was too much in need of obtaining her freedom to travel with me to Anda to worry about respecting her rights. After all, this wasn't Threle, and I was king, or soon would be. My training in evil had made me far less queasy about violating other people's personal autonomy than I might have been. "And remember, nothing will fundamentally change except that your ban will be removed. I swear by Hecate."

She nodded assent and took a tense shallow breath as she pulled her shift over her head. She wasn't afraid of the coming spell, she was afraid of both being under someone's else's control and being the center of attention, which she probably regarded as another presumption on her part, and which I noted as another deep contrast with her desire to be a renowned court performer. Well, it was also in my interest to make this process as quick and painless as possible. On that issue we understood each other.

"Breathe with me, Aeren. Deeply if you can."

She tried, but her chest was too tight to allow for deep breathing. Her inefficient shallow breaths would have to do, although they were woefully inadequate for her to enter any sort of trance under her own power. Well, I would have to ensure that her defensiveness wouldn't be an impediment. I'd done more difficult workings.

"Now. I'm going to pray to Hecate. I'm going to call Her. She will come, like last night, but this time you will feel Her enter you, a cold dead sensation. Your wizardry has an evil source, this cave is a place of evil and of learning, thanks to Zelar, so Hecate should come easily to you. There is no need to do anything but welcome Her."

"You needn't speak so soft and spell-like." Her annoyance was tinged with an odd embarrassment.

"Humor me. You needn't respond."

She didn't, unless you count the stiffening and tensing up of her back muscles.

Clerisy is so much cleaner and faster than wizardry, especially when performed under conditions that are conducive to the particular power of your particular deity, for clerics literally draw from the source of divine power, temporarily becoming the deity they draw, whereas wizards merely manipulate the energy inherent in the world at several steps removed from the source. It is the difference between working from inspiration, that is, being breathed into by the deity, and working from theory. The advantage to wizardry is that location is rarely an impediment. Clerical spells depend on conditions being suitable for their deity's presence. I would have much more difficulty calling Hecate in Mirand's library than in Zelar's cave, for Mirand's scholarship was always all to Athena and all to the good. Drawing Hecate's force into Zelar's evil place of study and learning was as easy as drawing Her into Kursen Monastery. A word and a wish and my Goddess and I were one, so much so that there was only a moment of pleasant darkness and I immediately lost myself, for Hecate was speaking through me. Her words came like black waves in my mind in the shuddery cadence of a broken flute.

"I am She who breaks mindful insights into base repetition. I am She who forbids. I am She who banned my darkly beloved priest a second time against entering the North Country and partaking of chaos, for all laws that restrict the spirit are mine, and my clergy shall not cross the Drumuns."

"Welcome, Mother," I responded in my heart.

"I knew your demand even before you dreamed the words to make it. The ban that Aeren carried is now yours to work evil with, my bird. Dark in your hands like a slippery shadow the moon forgot, a lump of old coal for the promise of a fascinating new toy, an empty page for a poem and a spell. For I am She who ransoms desires for curses, I am the hatred that cuts through soft words of praise. And I am She who would have you crowned King of Gondal, that you might spread my law throughout this icebound land. The ban is yours. Use it well."

Aeren squirmed a little. She was self-conscious because from her perspective the cave had grown quiet and cold like a dead thing from Hecate's presence. Hecate's words were in my mind and so Aeren could not hear them. There were black oily rivulets flowing through the pores on her bare shoulders, and as I ran my fingers through the rivulets, they gathered into a sticky black lump. The lump was the physical manifestation of the ban, and it felt like a dead rat stiffening in the ground between its scattered scaly lives.

Hecate spoke, "You may carry it with you with no effect upon yourself. When you will the ban to work to aid you to the throne, it will work. Else it shall be dormant."

"Thank you, Mother. Dark be my heart as Yours is."

I released Hecate's force and the cave regained its normal tone of Zelar's mundane evil. "Get dressed, Aeren. The working was successful. You're free to travel where you will, and we've now got a powerful weapon against your old friend Zelar. Would you like to see it?"

She hunched over in an attitude that was far more protective than modest and wriggled back into her shift, keeping her back to me. Then she turned around to face me. "Sure. Show me my limitations, Llewelyn," she said coldly. "Show me the ban that prevented me from flying where I willed to destroy the emperor for fun, and then from destroying Zelar through his name stone and freeing myself." She examined the ban. "It looks like a greasy lump of coal."

"Some bans do," I said simply, barely repressing a smile.

"What's so funny?"

"The thought of you approaching Roguehan in your dragon form and blasting him into his next nine lifetimes with your dragonfire. The thought of destroying Zelar's name stone, destroying Zelar, and suddenly freeing yourself of the spell and appearing as a demure young woman before Roguehan's astonished court. Maybe you could have ruled the world."

"I'm not demure," she protested.

"I was teasing you, Aeren. Really, I think that would have been one on the emperor but for your ban. But here's one on Zelar. I can now ban him through his name stone, and if he is anywhere outside the square mile surrounding this cave, he loses his power and most likely dies. Elegant, no?"

She looked more closely at the ban. "Elegant. Yes."

"This is also a ban against disturbing his magical items, and I thoroughly intend to disturb them. Straightaway. In theory I could destroy him simply by using it to ban his name stone, as that would create enough disturbance to activate the ban."

"So do it." Her voice conveyed an odd combination of skepticism and hope.

"You say he keeps his magical items in the lower reaches of this cave but that you've never been down there?"

"I told you I was forbidden and that the passageway is too narrow for me to have negotiated in my dragon form."

"No matter. Stay here, Aeren. I have no idea what sorts of defenses Zelar is using, and I'd greatly prefer to encounter them alone."

"Why?" she asked sullenly. "Is that to show you've got more wizardry at your disposal than I have? Or just to forbid me access the way your master did?"

"I do have more wizardry at my disposal than you do. But I have no idea how dangerous it is down there. So your king is giving you an order, bard, stay here. For your own protection."

I thought she was going to continue arguing, but her involuntary smile betrayed that she would respect almost any order given to her as a "bard." I conjured some paper and pen and ink. "Write me a tale. Consider it a command performance." That would keep her busy and out of my way.

"Yes, my liege." She brightened considerably. "As you will."

And so I entered extended darkness. The darkness in the passageway was easeful, and became more so as I descended, for its source was evil. And it was an inescapably familiar darkness, for its energy felt like the inverse of Mirand's, and in a way that was strangely comforting, for in that respect its energy resembled mine. It took the edge off the loneliness I had felt outside by Devon's grave and it surprised me by doing so. I did not navigate my descent by light. The power was so strong as I descended that I just opened myself to what was there and easily made my way down a rough narrow natural opening in the rock that went ever deeper into the frozen ground. Zelar had obviously shielded this place, and there was obviously some device present that made it possible for this shield to continually renew itself, but since my own wizard shield was nearly identical to his, and my own wizard sense ultimately derived from his via Mirand, Zelar's shield was no impediment. Rather, our shields blended and I found myself inside his as well as my own, as securely protected as his magical items were. And the power was warm and warmer as I descended, so much so I began to sweat in my riding cloak, and the waning moon on my palm began to tingle. Dark luck and welladay.

There was light like an underground moon when I reached bottom, and the faint sound of a rush of water like an underground spring, and then a spirit, or rather a tone of feeling of something ancestral and ancient filled the sudden space I was in. Or else I entered the tone and stood there welcoming it until my skin and blood came alive from the energy of the evil around me. Something in this space that wasn't exactly physical and wasn't exactly emotional reminded me of Grana's house. There was a certain tone to Zelar's workplace, and I couldn't avoid recognizing that this tone was what fostered Mirand and his considerable learning and that I had carried it with me into Kursen before I knew how to name and claim my personal alliance to evil. Even the design of a living quarters built into a cave reminded me of Walworth's headquarters in Helas, and I couldn't help thinking that Mirand had learned that trick from his master.

So here was the source of my own wizardry, if not my clerisy. And here, perhaps in a roundabout way I was only just beginning to recognize, was the source of my own journey into evil. This descent into the earth beneath the frozen wastes of Gondal was a descent into myself, a preparation for my dark coronation. And unlike my ascent through the castle tower which resulted in my failed deification to the good side of the universe, this descent would not result in failure to establish my dark rule over Gondal. I would arm myself with my ancestral weapons, my magical birthright. I would be king, crowned by a teller of tales.

I liked it. A lot.

I sat on the ground and pulled my cloak around me for warmth, although it wasn't cold here. The power of the place contained heat like shades from hell. In the moony light I sat in an awful blankness in the center of a sigil carved into the rough rock floor, a sigil which I immediately recognized as sacred to Hecate. I knew from the presence of the sigil that although Zelar was no cleric, he worshiped Hecate with the same intensity Mirand celebrated Athena. And although I was certainly not a master wizard, as Aeren had pointed out, I also knew that because Zelar worshiped Hecate I would have no problem making use of Zelar's tools. Hecate would guide me, as She already had. As far as I was concerned, this wizard workshop and all it contained was now mine.

I took stock of my new armory. Catalog. One Mirror of Transformations, no doubt the same one that had turned Aeren to a dragon. It reflected nothing right now but a dusty evil blank, which was just as well. Three gold tables covered with all manner of crystals and wands in various states of construction. It looked liked Zelar had several projects in process here before he left. I put my scarred hand on several of the crystals, blending my shield with that of the room so as to be undetected should Zelar be able to sense any disturbance. The crystals felt blank with disuse. I couldn't tell if they had once been charged and lost their power, or if Zelar had been planning to charge them and never got around to it. The wands also felt blank and dull, which surprised me. Everything so far was a work in progress. Disappointing, as I'd hoped to get my hands on some firepower for my coming bid for the Gondish monarchy.

Once my eyes had adjusted to the weak light, I noticed a simple wooden cask sitting dull and unobtrusive in a bend of shadow-soaked stone. A protective sigil was carved into the top of the cask with the words "Protected by Hecate." *So am I*, I thought, smiling a little at the irony. The cask was locked, and locked well. Nothing in my wizardry could open it.

Then I remembered the wizard key that Isulde had given to me after all the strangeness that we had run through outside of Walworth's castle, the same key that I had first possessed in Sunnashiven and that broke my life open into a new and unexpected direction. Yes, a wizard key will open anything, even a hardened life. Hadn't Isulde said that? And hadn't Mirand once told me that it was the key that would unlock the cask that holds Zelar's name stone?

I placed the key in the cask's lock and it opened like an old wound at the touch of a searing lance. The top of the cask fell away of itself, and a palpable darkness flowed into the room, obscuring the pale light to the point where I could barely see the cask's contents. I sat quietly in the evil, feeling comforted by the dark of the energy, blessing Hecate for Her guidance and protection. When I felt clear and steady in the thick of the new evil that surrounded me, and the darkness had thinned enough for me to see again, I knelt, peered into the cask, and gently removed a polished black stone that could only be Zelar's name stone.

Bringing the stone up out of the cask was like removing a heart from the split chest of a sacrificial victim that one had previously known under mundane circumstances. I mean I could do it, and do it gently with all the grace and professionalism of my magical training, but I couldn't escape the sensation of being more destructively intimate than I really cared to be, couldn't escape the knowledge that my relationship to Mirand was an unbreakable link to Zelar and that were I to trace the source of my own magical training back behind my clerisy and my wizard lessons with Mirand, it would lead here, to this black stone, this cup of Zelar's soul, this primal object the master wizard kept hidden as the source of his power, and that he had hoped Hecate would protect for him.

I sat cross-legged on the floor and cradled Zelar's name stone, falling into its energy, searching for a pulse, for a life, for the essence of my own early contact with the power of magic. I prayed to Hecate for guidance and slowly opened my heart to whatever secrets this stone contained.

And the secrets were there in a vision, for as I scried the stone my mind entered into a dark place like a prison. There were bars across my vision. I saw a figure sitting on a low wooden bench, his cloak an outline of darkness. At his feet was the complacent ghost of a fading scroll, burning faint like a damned spirit. And then, in his shadows, my heart began to beat with his, locked through the stone. But the beat was sluggish, like the life force was slowly dying, and then the beat got steadily slower until I was in darkness with him. I did not expect such heaviness here. I did not expect to encounter this force like a strange ancestral sorrow.

Before I lost consciousness with the terrifyingly slow beat of my own heart, I released the stone, and concentrated on breathing and dispersing the deathy numbness that had crept through my skin, the slow cool nausea that had taken possession of my blood, the inescapable physical sensation of mourning. It took long moments to feel right again, to draw strength from the pulsing evil around me. The name stone was blank again, and I did not wish to reenter its draining energy. I slowly considered what I saw and felt, played the tone and image over and over in my mind, and decided the image was an unexpectedly quick acknowledgment on Zelar's part that he was utterly in my power. So unexpectedly quick I didn't trust it, although I couldn't ascertain what his ruse might be. Clearly, the figure I saw was Zelar, the energy was too clear and close to being an inverse of Mirand's for me not to recognize it. Clearly, Zelar knew I had possession of his name stone, for our energies had inhabited each other while he was in a state of meditation. I assumed his profound sadness was a ruse, a mask of harmlessness or a way of beseeching me to show him a mercy I could no longer find it in my heart to show anyone. He was my prisoner and he knew it, hence the image he sent.

He and Roguehan may have taken possession of Threle, but I have taken possession of Zelar's power, I thought. *I can destroy Zelar with a word, right now, with an easy blast of his stone, if I found it strategic to do so.* But I didn't. If I blasted Zelar now, Roguehan could easily find a replacement, and I would have no protection from the emperor. But since Zelar had great influence with the emperor, his fear that I could destroy him with a wish would be all the protection I needed. It was far more useful to make Zelar fear my ability to destroy him than to actually do the deed.

I slowly, gently, reentered the dark of the stone and the dark of Zelar's meditation. I closed my eyes into his energy, and there, as my heart began to dangerously slow again, I sent him a message through the stone. "*I have your name stone and all that goes with it. Upon Hecate and all I hold evil, you have nothing to fear from me so long as I have nothing to fear from you. Keep your distance and I shall do the same. Congratulations on your victory, Master.*" At that point I had to jerk myself out of the vision before my pulse went the way of a corpse, but as I did so I saw Zelar make a gesture with his left hand as if to indicate that he had heard me.

And so. That was too easy, but that was that. I wished I had the presence of mind to ask him why his magical items felt so . . . well, useless, and why entering his name stone felt like entering death, but it was just as well that I didn't. Let him guess concerning what I had, what I knew. It was a blessed advantage that communication was so difficult.

I set the name stone gently back in the cask and locked it. As I stood up I noticed some scrolls piled up in an indentation in the cave wall above the cask, and decided they would be worth a read. So I stood in the middle of the sigil on the floor and called down some Goddess fire for better light, and Hecate responded with a perfect reading-quality flame like a cozy hearth in the middle of Her sigil. Then I gathered the scrolls to read.

There were seven of them.

Three were written in a language I didn't recognize.

Two were maps of areas I also didn't recognize. There was no indication of scale or direction, and no writing, just what looked like hastily drawn marks for mountains and rivers and what I assumed were roads. When I held the scrolls next to each other, the marks lined up, so I knew the scrolls constituted one map, although I still didn't recognize the area the map described.

Those five scrolls would take some research to decipher. Later.

The remaining two were written in Botha, in a hand that looked markedly different from the first three. They were a series of disjointed notes on the specific uses of the wands and crystals I saw scattered throughout the workshop. Yes! Dark joy of Hecate! I learned that each item could only be activated by a specific word of power, an Amara word, and that it was possible to use that word to change the charge in each item so that it could only be used by a particular wizard. One of the crystals was the power source of the shield surrounding the cave. Another powered the barrels-of-plenty by sending a backwards energy through the dead trees that the barrels were made of and forcing the dead wood to bear dried fruit. *Ingenious design*, I mused. The rest of the items I saw around me were designed to be destructive devices, some with enough combined power to take out a small town. So this was Zelar's secret armory, or, for all I knew, one of his secret armories. Based on its location, I assumed it was intended for future use against Anda and Arula, just as I assumed that Aeren was somehow intended for future use against those cities, although I had no idea exactly what the emperor and his chief wizard had been intending to do with her.

It occurred to me that it was rather foolish of the master wizard to leave such a clear key to his magical treasures lying around, until

I remembered that the chances of finding this remote location, getting past an angry stormdragon, and breaking through the shield that protected the workshop were near zero. This carefully guarded armory was clearly worth much to Zelar and Roguehan, but before I decided on my next course of action, I needed to determine what these weapons were worth to me.

Highly trained clerics like me have no need of wizard wands that merely emit deadly blasts. I could wreak more destruction with a word and Hecate's consent than with any single one of these weapons. I supposed that if I were to find myself in circumstances in which my Goddess could not be drawn, in which the divine energy stream called Hecate would be decayed and strangled—say I was standing in the middle of a shrine held sacred to Athena or something, which could happen, I'd been in worse places—a deadly wizard wand or three would be of great use. I certainly didn't want to leave this cache here for Zelar unless there was some way I could effectively lock him out of it; but any shield or lock my wizardry could invent he could open, and any clerical lock I placed here would only slow him down as long as it took him to find another evil cleric who could open it. Not that he would dare use weapons against me while I held his name stone, but it seemed fundamentally bad strategy to give Zelar access to anything of power in my kingdom. And this *was* my kingdom. Perhaps I would be able to arm my own master wizards with this stuff when I hired them, or judiciously trade it for weapons of even greater value.

I then decided that I would see if I could lock these items onto my personal energy, and then work in reverse to change their power words so it would be impossible for Zelar to use them. I smiled a little thinking of how Mirand had so generously taught me how to create a magical path between myself and a magical item, how to send a current of my energy along that path to raise the item's energy to match my own, or how to take in energy from the object and disperse it to lower the object's energy to match mine. Considering how close my energy was to Zelar's, this trick should be as easy as moonlight on a blind man's eyes.

But as I carefully took each item and sat within the sigil on the floor, repeating the various power words from the scrolls and steadying my mind to accept and know each word's energy, I discovered that each item did not respond easily to my touch. The energy currents I created were beyond sluggish, like there was some additional magical protection creating a kind of resistance that only allowed a trickle of energy to pass through when I attempted to create a differential. I could change their charges, but it was only with great effort and only because my personal energy while using wizardry was so close to Zelar's I didn't need to make great changes. The latter seemed to be the main factor in my eventual success. By the time I had finished I was convinced that any other wizard who could have by some strange happenstance broken into this place would have been utterly unable to make use of these items, even with access to the scrolls. Even Mirand would have failed, because these weapons were designed to be used by evil wizards, and the intensity of his life-long celebration of Athena would have been an insurmountable stumbling block.

Well, Zelar never counted on his apprentice's apprentice finding his way here. All right. Zelar's weapons could now only be used exclusively by me, but to make assurance double sure, I decided to change the power words to something only I would know, just so Zelar would be unable to change the charges back should he some-how come into possession of the items again. Now that my personal energy was aligned to the charges, changing the words would be easy. The trick would be protecting the new power words so Zelar couldn't take them from my mind and realign himself to these weapons. *How to do that? Think!*

I traced my hands over Hecate's sigil and softly asked Her for inspiration. Before I had finished my prayer I remembered a clerical exercise that El had once taught me. Not a full working, but an exercise for dulling my mind in favor of Hecate's sharpness. It involved offering to Her particular thoughts and words that were associated with things I would sacrifice in Her service, and petitioning Her to keep them that I might never know those things again. The point of the exercise was to help make my mind a receptacle for Her energy, uncompromised by my earlier love of beauty and friendship. I had resisted giving over all pieces of myself as a way to stay strong against El's power, and then Cathe made me a natural priest and so I never had to seriously work that particular exercise. But I did remember how, or else Hecate was making me remember.

And so what would happen if I gave each object a new power word, and then gave that word to my Goddess for safekeeping? I would inscribe it into Her energy stream so that I and only I could retrieve it when I had need, and send it back when I didn't. Zelar could worship Hecate until Threle turned to crows but without any knowledge of clerisy, he would be unable to navigate Her energy and retrieve the word. And searching my mind would be useless. Unless I chose to call down the word from Hecate Herself, I wouldn't even know what it was. Of course it was theoretically possible for Zelar to learn through a mind probe that I had inscribed the words to Hecate and find another priest of Hecate to retrieve the words, but that cleric would only be successful if the Goddess consented. I decided that if Hecate wanted me armed for the throne, my power words would be a divinely kept secret for a very long time.

In fifteen minutes the clerical working was complete. One thing for clerisy, it's there or it isn't, and if it's there, it's there cleanly and quickly without a lot of bother. Perfect. I waited another full fifteen minutes in the moony darkness, grasped one of the deadlier wands, admired its design and felt its blankness, and called the power word down from Hecate. I uttered the word, released it back to my Goddess, and felt the wand surge and hum with energy. *Excellent!* I sat there and felt the wand's energy humming in my hand, enjoying the feeling of power. Then I tried desperately, using every trick of language at my command, to remember the power word, but couldn't. So I called the word back down from Hecate, used it to deactivate the wand, and released the word back to my Goddess as the wand went blank and dull.

Yes, yes, and yes! Hecate be damned to joy! Praise the Goddess, I was now the only person in the world who could make use of these weapons, and not even Zelar himself would be able to reclaim them. For some reason I decided it was all too funny, and found myself laughing uncontrollably. Here was my royal armory. Some of these weapons were worth enough to buy the damn kingdom even if I didn't have a legitimate claim. Here was enough firepower to arm my own chief wizards for my and Gondal's protection. It would now be a simple matter for me to work with another cooperating wizard's energy level to make any of these weapons usable for that wizard, while retaining ultimate control through the words I had passed on to Hecate. It was really too much!

My only concern was how to safely transport the delicate magical weapons. Anda was too far away for me to able to manifest this magical armory to someplace conveniently close when we got there. I had changed the shielding crystal to my own energy so it would keep up my shield around the items, which would be a help. Not that there was much of a practical difference between my shield and Zelar's, but since they were now my weapons, I wanted them to be protected by my shield. It was also a fine thing to have discovered the crystal that forced dried fruit from dead wood, for I could augment our food supply by bringing a few pieces of wood from the barrels. The magical weapons would need to be delicately handled, but that would just take a little consideration and consultation with Aeren.

When I reentered the living quarters, Aeren was finishing writing something on the paper I had conjured for her before I made my descent. She looked up at me in an attitude I can only describe as silently questioning and potentially violent; that is to say, she had settled into her usual cheerful self. "What did you find?" she asked flatly.

"Enough to destroy Zelar six times over if and when we choose," I responded seductively. "Enough for our needs." That raised a smile, so I sat next to her in a friendly attitude, smiling in return with what I hoped was an expression that conveyed a graceful compliment and that would put her at as much ease as she was capable of. "So tell me the tale you've written in my absence, bard."

She smiled and colored slightly as if she couldn't help herself from blushing, and then quenched her show of joy with her usual odd defensiveness. "It isn't a tale. It's a contract. I've written out two copies and before we discuss anything, I want you to sign both of them. In blood. With your Goddess Hecate for witness. King."

It was a contract stating that in return for giving me her throne I was giving her a position as my royal bard for life. I had no idea if it was even enforceable, or how, and decided that I had much to learn concerning Gondish law. But I also knew it was politic to keep Aeren happy and loyal by signing the damn thing because I had already promised her as much and really it was nothing to me if she wanted to be the court storyteller. Every ruler needs a skillful propagandist. I made a show of cutting my arm with my dagger and using wizardry to manifest my blood into words on the paper, signing her contract "Llewelyn, priest, mage, and King of Gondal, by the power of Hecate." I gave both copies back to her with a flourish. "Keep them both, milady, if they will set your oft-betrayed heart at ease. I've no need of a copy. I will keep my word."

Aeren stared incredulously at my bleeding arm and at the bloody writing before she lunged at me and gave me a tight embrace. This unexpected show of affection and gratitude happened and ended so quickly I didn't know what to do with it, so I lightly hugged her in return and did my best to look pleased. "Good. Hecate will heal my scratch and all will be well. Now, the sooner we travel the sooner you will be entertaining important visitors to my hall with your clever winter tales, and the sooner I shall be able to put you up in a fine tower with all the privacy and access to books you need for inspiration to compose more stories. I shall treat you better than well. You shall be one of the brightest treasures in my court." I bowed my head over her hand and kissed it. She was ecstatic. "And since I am a stranger to my new kingdom, and shall need a more thorough understanding of its history and politics, you shall begin your work for me by telling stories of your . . . of *our* . . . fair homeland." When I looked up there were two bright tears running over her smiling face.

"My true liege and lord." She bent her knees a little in a gesture that vaguely resembled a bow. "Together we shall make a little world."

"We will have to prepare for our journey, and I will have to decide the best way to transport Zelar's name stone and provide you with decent traveling clothes, for I suppose you own nothing except your shift." She looked put out at my mention of providing anything for her. "Consider it a gift from your king, bard, and let me take pleasure in providing for you, for a true king supports his people."

"Then I can hardly refuse."

I conjured a good thick traveling cloak that would hold in her body's heat against the cold. She threw it around herself with enthusiasm. "It's perfect," she said enthusiastically.

"And what sort of clothes would milady prefer to wear under her cloak?"

"Dress me as yourself. In male garb." Her voice was a little rushed, as if she feared I might refuse her request.

I did think her request was a bit strange, but I had no intention of arguing with my link to the throne. Male garb. Whatever the lady preferred. "As you will." I conjured a variation of my own clothes to fit her size. She held the bundle in her arms and looked awkwardly at me. "Go on, get dressed. I'll cover my eyes. I'm a gentleman. Let me know when." When I opened my eyes at her word, she had the clothes on, and she was quickly smoothing her thick dark hair with her fingers. I noticed she actually wore the conjured copy of my garb with a certain degree of charm, and I decided that it suited her better than something more overtly feminine. She was one of those rare women who looked more natural, that is, more like herself, in the other sex's attire. *Zelar was right to call her a prince,* I thought, *for that is what she looks like. The image is artful because it is true.* So much so that transforming her from dragon to woman was only a job half-done.

"Do you want a mirror, Brother?" I asked gallantly.

"No." She sounded vaguely insulted, and then I remembered her last experience with a mirror, so I didn't take it personally. "And so I now look the part of a priest of Hecate, though I be none?"

"Not exactly. I wear the clerical garments of Athena. Your clothes resemble mine with enough minor differences so that nobody will mistake you for a cleric. Your riding cloak looks nothing like mine. Evil works best when it isn't overt, so we needn't let anyone know that Hecate is our patroness. That is why I wear a brooch shaped like Her symbol, the waning moon, under my cloak, pinned to the reverse side." I decided I needn't tell her how I had left Kursen Monastery with the intention of passing as a good cleric as a means toward entering the Duke of Walworth's household and killing him.

"I can keep silent for Hecate," she promised. "I can also make sure nobody mistakes me for clergy. Wait." She clumsily summoned power and made more changes to her garb, until she had transformed it into the rough clothes of a traveling bard. It was perfect, in its way. Just as Caethne and Aleta were more like themselves when they covered their aristocratic status in peasant clothes or in the outfit of a simple soldier, Aeren was truly herself when dressed as a male bard. But she still looked like a prince, a disguised prince-in-exile whose nobility showed through despite his best attempts to hide it.

Aeren then made one of her characteristic sudden subject changes. "It's a several weeks' ride south to Anda. I shall tell you everything you need to know on the road."

"Excellent. Your king will be eternally grateful for such kindness." I smiled.

"Eternity is as eternity does," she enigmatically replied.

Sixteen

$\mathcal{T}$ransporting my armory was easier than I had thought it would be. I conjured soft, protective cloths to wrap the crystals and wands with, and thick saddlebags to store them in. Once I showed Aeren what sort of material was needed, she helped me with the conjuring, so the work went fairly quickly. And once we got started, I let her do most of it because she seemed to relish the opportunity to prove herself. Properly packed and stored, my new weapons could all be carried easily by my horse. The scrolls fit inside my riding cloak. Devon's horse, which was now Aeren's, carried all of our supplies, including the food that remained from my earlier trek with Devon. To supplement our food supply the horse also carried a piece of dead wood from the barrels-of-plenty along with the crystal that forced fruit from this wood. I had burned the rest of the barrels in a deadening colorful splendor of smoke and wizard fire because I didn't want to leave anything useful behind us, just on general principles.

The Mirror of Transformations was the only difficulty, both because it was large and bulky and because it was a source of disagreement. Despite my assurance that I alone could summon the power word which was necessary to activate the Mirror, Aeren wanted to leave it behind. "Why do we need to wave around the source of my three-year imprisonment?" she objected as I lashed the securely covered Mirror behind my horse's saddle with some rope I had conjured that morning. "Isn't that the gods' own arrogance, especially since we have no idea how far your claim to kingship will actually go when we get to making it?"

I tested the last knot while valiantly trying to parse out what the hell she meant by that last question. Then I gave up parsing and took what I hoped was the easier path by asking directly, "Why is it arrogant to carry an exquisitely designed magical item that's worth much gold in trade, is at the very least a show of my . . . *our* power and resources, and might very well be required for proof when you tell the story of your imprisonment to the City Assembly?"

"You don't know Anda very well." She sounded deeply frustrated.

"So enlighten me. Is there some local tradition I should know about that reads arrogance into the character of one who enters the city bearing a mirror?" I thought my question was sort of funny, but Aeren was not amused.

"No, but there are so many bards in Anda."

"So?" As used as I was getting to Aeren's odd non sequiturs, I was now completely, utterly lost.

"So?" She had the same odd distasteful look she had when she was reluctantly discussing her aversion to sleeping in front of anyone else. Then she spoke in a rushed voice with her eyes focused steadily on the ground, as if she wanted to quickly finish the subject but couldn't bear to make eye contact with me while she elaborated on her concerns. I remained outwardly bland, listening patiently as she explained, "A lot of the local bards will hold the Mirror against me and consider it in very poor taste for me to show it before the Assembly. A lot of them will secretly wish that Emperor Roguehan's chief wizard had taken enough interest in them to turn them into dragons. I will be roundly criticized for that one." She said the latter in the angry, exasperated tone of voice that I had become familiar with.

I could see that clarity wasn't going to make an entrance anytime soon. "Please grace me with an explanation of your rivals' incomprehensible desires in that regard. Are stormdragons considered high-prestige creatures in Anda? Or just among the bardic set? And why do you care what your rivals think, anyway? I'm not making any of them my royal bard."

"I care because if your claim doesn't stick, I will be back on the street competing with those same bards for tavern space, and they will have reasons beyond mere rivalry to keep me out if they think Emperor Roguehan's chief wizard actually did consider me important enough to keep hostage. None of them will admit it to each other, but all of them will be highly annoyed that they didn't merit that sort of attention. Some will even try to convince me, with varying degrees of hysteria, that it never really happened and that I should just admit that I am making it all up, because an unknown bard like me with no local following couldn't possibly have attracted the emperor's notice. I will hear until there is no end to it that showing the Mirror is a form of subtle bragging that I haven't truly earned the right to, while all the other bards boast and claim that they were nearly charmed into stormdragons themselves under circumstances that will make my experience sound, well, cheap and sordid. It will then be impossible for my stories to get any sort of hearing. I know how the bards in Anda think."

"My claim better stick, then," I responded understandingly. "And having the Mirror with us for show will go a ways toward making that happen." I wasn't attempting to convince her, as the Mirror was coming with us whether she willed or no. I was only making an effort to reconcile her to that fact in the hopes that our journey might be more pleasant.

She stared balefully at the Mirror, glared back at the entrance to the now-empty cave, and then looked hard at nothing in particular. I waited patiently, although I was eager to start on our journey. "You speak truth," she conceded unexpectedly, as if she had just won some deep internal struggle over herself. "Scorch the goddess-be-damned bards, eh? Every last one of them would run screaming from a stormdragon if they ever met a real one." Her expression was so angry and dragonish I could feel her emotions throwing off currents of wrath and heat. She mounted her horse in a quiet sort of fury. "Shall we ride then, my liege?"

"Absolutely," I responded cheerfully. "I thought you'd never ask." I quickly mounted my own steed and merrily gave Aeren a conspiratorial glance, to establish the mood that we were comrades-in-arms and that my claim to kingship was all a great game between us that there was no question but that we would win. "Go forth and lead me to my throne."

*S*he did. Go forth, anyway. It got warm and warmer as we rode south. Not so much as to insist on notice, but enough to remark upon if you made the effort to feel for it. Winter still locked the land, but it did so with a lock that loosened into something less deadly every day. Our pace was slow because we had to make our way over trackless swaths of ice and deep snowfields, and Aeren wasn't always certain of the way, because there really was no definable way to Anda. You point your horse south. You feel through the ether for the energy of a city, for the thrust and pulse of magic in the air. You trust to the wind and the distant northern sun that eventually, if you stay focused and steady, Anda is yours.

Aeren didn't grow comfortable with sleeping in my presence, but she couldn't fight necessity, or rather, she couldn't win this particular fight against necessity, so she liked to hide herself in Devon's blankets on the far side of our heat shield and face in the opposite direction from me at night. But despite her hard protectiveness, or perhaps because of it, she still had much difficulty sleeping, and so she spent many nights staring out into the unbroken dark of northern Gondal until dawn, which tended to dull her mind and increase her general irritation with life on the following day. On those nights that she did manage to sleep a little, her breaths were tense and shallow, as if she was still a stormdragon eternally on guard and not really resting.

I had never known anyone so tense and uneasy in my life, including myself in my younger days. Her self-imposed sleeplessness was like a self-imposed curse against her own mind, because when she had slept she was alert and sharp and had many trenchant observations to make on all sorts of things. She was clearly well-read and very knowledgeable about Gondal's history and politics. But on a day following a wakeful night I might as well have been taking instruction from Cristo for all the useful information I got, except that Aeren wasn't nearly as annoying because there was always a reserve of keen intelligence breaking through even her most incomprehensibly frayed remarks. I just had to fight to get at it.

"Aeren, milady storyteller," I jollied her one night after she had entertained me with a tale about a fox who mistook the full moon for a pie. The fox had starved himself to death because he refused to hunt for his food while his treat waned to nothing beyond his grasp. Aeren thought it was funny, but there was something beyond sad in her tale that prevented me from grasping the joke. My court storyteller was distant in the dark, so much so that her tale had come to me out of the shadows in the form of a pure, bodiless, bardic voice. Since I couldn't see her gestures and facial expressions, I had the solitary pleasure of staring into the campfire I had created and making my own mind pictures out of her words. I would have liked to have seen as well as heard her performance, but as she showed no interest in moving closer, I didn't insist. I had spoken with darker shadows and deeper distances than hers before, and I had long ago learned to respect sacred spaces.

"Yes, my lord king," she responded stonily, but with a sudden touch of uncharacteristic melancholy.

"You said when you told me the tale of your life that Anda is full of self-proclaimed kings making claims for recognition, so much so that your father had much work to do to garner even a modicum of notice for his ambitions. What is the nature of those claims and how are they generally handled? I'm assuming there is some formal procedure for addressing the Assembly."

"There is. But it won't be of much help to you."

"My dear Aeren, nothing in my blessed life has ever been of much to help to me. What will be the nature of the Assembly's particular uselessness?"

"You're not anybody's cousin."

"So?"

"Anda is an extremely insular city, Llewelyn. It's an old city, and it derives a certain sense of civic superiority from its elvish heritage, even though the elves have long since withdrawn to their well-hidden colonies. To most Andans, Anda is the world, and even Arula is credited with no more substance than a believable rumor. Not that my fellow citizens . . . I mean, your subjects . . . are ignorant. Quite the contrary. You'll find a lot of highly educated people there. So highly educated that they all consider themselves quite the business, and, as a consequence, many don't actually see the point of there even being a 'rest of the world' except as a kind of prop to their own exalted pride. It's an embarrassingly rich perverseness, and almost comical in its way, unless you need the endorsement of your fellow Andans to succeed in your ambitions. Which you do. So your first hurdle is that you're not from Anda, and that you're not related to any of the more powerful families. That alone will make it difficult for you to get taken seriously before you even begin the day."

"Your family was busy enough knocking about in influential circles. That gives us something to work with."

"Oh, we'll work with it, although that will hardly carry us, considering the ugly rumors that plagued my father's last years. We'll petition the Assembly to schedule a time for us to speak publicly, and I'll throw my father's and grandfather's names around, and we'll certainly get a hearing. I can't think of anybody ever being refused the right to address the Assembly on any topic, although unlikely and unpopular petitioners are almost always given times when the full Assembly is not scheduled to meet and so nobody is there to hear. I might be telling my story to an empty hall in the middle of the night to one or two old men, but Hecate be blessed, I'm used to that." She said the latter wryly.

I laughed softly to show I appreciated her attempt at self-mockery. "I'm sure we'll be able to persuade our way into a better billing," I reassured her. "So you tell your story and we present my claim. And then?"

"In theory? The Assembly recognizes it and votes to restore the monarchy. In reality? They throw us out. Even if they are convinced that what we say is true, *especially* if they are convinced that what we say is true, they won't vote you in because that would mean voting someone a higher status than themselves. No one is going to warmly welcome a stranger riding down out of the northlands with a north Threlan accent and a believable claim to being the live embodiment of a well-worn Gondish legend. It just isn't done."

"I suppose not," I responded lightly. "But I'm confident through the power of my Goddess that we'll do it."

"You'll need more than confidence. Andans have so much confidence they can't give it away if they paid gold for the privilege."

"Meaning?"

"Meaning that everyone in Anda has delusions of royalty. Everyone secretly wants to be a king, and everyone claims some dubious descent from a past monarch. And please don't get them going on a tale of their children, because every prominent Andan's ill-raised get is a goddess-be-scorched little prince, and woe betide the fool who refuses to recognize it. Ariana's stories to her brood of their royal birthright differed more in degree than in kind from many other people's. The fact is, the primary reason we don't have a real king is that it would destroy too many precious self-images. And that will be your second and more difficult hurdle, claiming the throne without making anybody else feel bad about himself. Don't underestimate the height of that one."

"No, the height of that one I respect." I remembered the resentment my academic successes had caused at Kursen. "I shall be sensitive beyond sensitive concerning same."

"And don't count on popular support, either, even if you could somehow achieve it. The Assembly doesn't answer to the people. Anda's Assembly, Arula's too I suspect, is just an arrangement for wealthy citizens to keep watch on each other and make sure nobody acquires more power than anybody else. If you acquire enough wealth, you get invited to join the Assembly precisely so all your rivals can make certain you don't acquire any more."

"Sounds sensible," I quipped. "What else are governments for?"

"As to kingly claims. Anyone who seriously makes a false claim to the throne gets voted into exile and gets his property confiscated by the Assembly, which is why all the formal claims I know of have come from poor eccentrics with nothing to lose. In private, everyone's a king, or rather, everyone likes to claim royal blood in his ancestry. In public, it has come to be considered socially unacceptable to make a formal claim to the throne, most likely because it is bound to upset one's neighbors. But there are always poor malcontents who make the claim because they're bored and want a little fun. Some just do it to make some political point that nobody cares about except themselves and their friends. Some actually believe they are the legitimate king because it's easier than working a real job."

"Don't the commoners who make the claim risk exile?"

"By strict accord of law, yes. In practice, no. Here's another lesson in Andan culture for you. Exile has connotations of a punishment fit for the better classes, so no commoner with delusions of nobility will ever be 'graced' with such a punishment. He'll get laughed at or ignored, but he won't get taken seriously enough to be exiled. As a result, anyone who makes a formal claim to be king is met with derision, so much so that just making the claim has become quite the joke. Which is just another way Andans have of safeguarding their personal fantasies of royalty, because if you can laugh at someone else's claim to the throne, it means that your own precious delusion may yet prove true, even if you haven't the courage to brave social censure by making it public. So, for the most part, claiming to be king is like claiming . . . I don't know, like claiming that you spent three years in the form of a stormdragon, guarding a cave."

"I see."

"Thought you'd like to know. Anyway, despite all, maybe it could work. Sometimes I think it can be that easy, telling a story for a crown. But nothing in life is ever that charming, eh? I mean, a lot of things could be, but people would only resent it."

"Anda sounds charming." I laughed. "But be that as it isn't, our story is irrefutable so it would be quite embarrassing for the Assembly to reject it."

"The Assembly doesn't know how to be embarrassed; it wouldn't recognize the opportunity for embarrassment if it came wrapped in a royal mantle. But it will take more than a good story, no matter how well substantiated. There will have to be some inarguable advantage to the Assembly to vote to restore the monarchy, and I just don't see what that is."

"Like protection from becoming the next acquisition in the Empire of Roguehan?" I asked coolly.

"Like. Well, that's why it *might* work. Depends if their sense of survival outweighs their pride. And in Anda, the odds are rather even in that way. Which means it could go either way. If it goes at all."

"It will go, Aeren. It will go because assuming the throne through lawful means is only our first strategy. Lovely for all concerned if it works and I devoutly hope that it does. But democracy only works when there's nothing vital at stake. And there is much at stake here for my new subjects because if Roguehan wasn't interested in acquiring Gondal, Zelar wouldn't have bothered acquiring you. I hold Zelar hostage through his name stone, and I alone possess powerful magical weapons that can defend your city against the emperor's forces, weapons that no one can make use of without my leave. Perhaps the wealthy Assembly members with their royal fantasies will resent me for my poor heroic gesture"—*as you resented me for freeing you*, I almost said—"as none of them are equipped to make that gesture themselves, but that is for me to turn around and for Hecate to bless. My Goddess thrives on the energy of such resentment."

"Praise Hecate," said Aeren softly and sarcastically, out of the darkness.

"Ultimately, my poor people have a choice. Slave it for Roguehan where none of them will have the prominence that they crave, or remain in relative freedom to bicker over who's got the most elvish blood, with me on the restored throne not giving a damn who wins."

Aeren laughed darkly. "It is a pretty thought. Perhaps it will even be a true one."

"And perhaps someday you will write my improbable story into one of your tales."

She laughed again. "My pen is at your service, King."

"Which ultimately makes you more powerful than I," I said lightly.

"I know," she replied strangely. "Sometimes I surprise myself. I drive harder bargains than Master Zelar. But in the end I shall burn him with a word, eh?"

*W*e entered Anda under a sweet waning moon, which I took as a divine promise of success and a soft reminder to cover my scar by conjuring fingerless gloves. The city was open to the scarce blue afternoon sky that the moon was waning against, so open it had an air of vulnerability, as if a word or a breeze or the weight of the late thin light itself might crumble the foundations of the old houses and buildings we rode slowly past. Everything in Anda felt late and dull to the eye, and the city was smaller than I had expected it to be, but when I dropped my heat shield and took the raw wind in my skin, the moon felt warm where its dying beams crawled along the city walls and streets, wrapped in cool sunlight. Even through the aging daylight I could feel the waning moonbeams. Hecate was beating and breathing through me, making me exquisitely sensitive to my new home.

"There's tension here," I whispered to Aeren. "Open your wizard senses and you'll feel it in the roofs and in the stones."

"It feels like Anda," said Aeren, lightly rebuking me as if she felt I was sensing more to the city than was really there.

It occurred to me that my companion was so naturally tense that she probably had difficulty sensing the odd discomfort wafting through the cracks of the city, that the energy differential between her heart and our surroundings might not be that large, so I didn't pursue the issue. But I wondered if all Andans were like her: angry, defensive, proud. I kept my magical senses light and open and easily felt unusual stresses and unexpected combinations of personal energy trickling like slow sludge through the streets. The people I saw going about their business looked much like people anywhere, except that many of the older men managed to look both harassed and smug, which is an interesting trick, while their wives were not only quietly pompous but competitively so. And theirs was a remarkable pomposity. Instead of being based on the dully common need to impress, it drew a fierce thorny energy from a deep, eternal annoyance with life. The more they disliked everything else, the better they liked themselves. I had never seen anything like it.

To accurately describe how different the energy of the Andans felt when I first encountered it, I must speak briefly of people in other places, for energy is felt and understood solely through contrasts. I have noticed that elderly people often assume a certain pathetic grandiosity once they've realized that their lives are nearly over and that they haven't accomplished anything worth a damn. In contrast, young people will often swaddle themselves in a clumsily earnest pretentiousness that emerges from a terrible naivete paired with a deep craving for prestige that they haven't learned how to acquire through honest means. Youth boasts, more often than not, because it lacks perspective. It has no idea yet what the competition really is, and so it accounts itself as already having won. Old age boasts because it has gained enough perspective to know how much it can get away with, and with whom, and so it carefully appraises each victim before opening its toothless gums and extending its wizened tongue to suck in unearned esteem. Youth declares, "I can get away with it." Old age whines, "If I can get away with it, why not?" The extremes of life are always ugly with presumption. That is all quite usual.

But the Andan people were not usual in that way. My magical senses told me that the older women were so stunningly disdainful because they resented rather than craved the notice of others. And they resented this notice not out of humility, but out of fear of being found out under close scrutiny to be anything less than they considered themselves to be. That is why they viewed the rest of humanity as a bother at best and as a personal affront at worst. They were defensively in love with themselves, but that didn't make their love any less pure. They simply didn't want to risk their lifelong happy union on any inconvenient facts.

Not everyone had this decidedly unattractive air, and it was less common among the younger people I saw, who all seemed more nervously ambitious and aggressively insecure than anything else, but enough of the elders were dragging around this perverse emotional energy to set an extremely off-putting tone to the city. Yes, my people were generally proud.

What the hell they all had to be proud of was another question, because to my eyes Anda was not a particularly impressive city, and I knew that the rest of the world thought little of it, if it thought of Anda at all. I mean it wasn't a bad city. It certainly wasn't pregnant with decay like Sunnashiven was, but Anda couldn't lay a patch on the charm of even the smaller towns in southern Threle. There were a few attractive areas, and Aeren would occasionally point out an example of elvish-styled architecture on an old building that was worth stopping to admire, but all in all, Anda was rather bland, and well, merely adequate to the task of being a city.

The shops and dwellings all appeared neat and well kept, but some were so pristine that they felt washed of all energy as well as of all dirt. I would describe them as aggressively nonobjectionable, except that being nonobjectionable didn't seem to be the point. It was as if many parts of the city wanted to stay eternally like a piece of blank parchment, because the random touches of spirit that give a place character might just as easily, if a tad out of place, give the eye offense. Everything strove to be perfect in potential without taking the risks that actually grasping for perfection inevitably entails. Nobody wanted to make a mistake. I had no idea that so many Andans were such cowards.

But despite all, Anda definitely felt free, although not in the same way Threle did. Aeren had explained to me that Andans enjoyed the same kinds of liberties she had read that Threlans did, and that the Assembly tended to not interfere with people's personal business. The most striking difference, from what I had learned from her, was that once a commoner managed to earn enough wealth to join the Assembly and become a member of the city's ruling class, he encountered a myriad number of restrictions imposed by his fellows to enforce a sort of wary egalitarianism among the wealthy. The commoners, however, did pretty much as they pleased.

As I was forcing myself to become intimate with Anda, sensing every crack and slant of late-afternoon light, every stiff and ugly attitude, Aeren jerked on her horse's reins and abruptly stopped. The cause of her unexpected decision appeared to be an exceptionally ornate gate that hung at a large entrance in the smoothly polished stone wall that hugged our side of the street. The wall had been too tall to see over as we rode along, but now that we were near the open gate, I got an unobstructed view of a fine, well-maintained horse path that led through a wide snow-covered park and up to the entrance of a large, splendidly tasteless hall. I decided that it was a self-important entrance to what was no doubt a self-important place of business. Crowds of people were flurrying in and out of the hall in a cloud of busy aloofness. "That's where the Assembly meets," explained Aeren, pointing at the imposing building. "It's changed since I was last here. I hadn't planned to stop, but I thought I saw something suddenly blocking our way. I think it was just a sunshadow on the snow blinding my eyes." She looked at me as if she was offering a challenge. "Anyway, in times past, that building was the king's residence."

"It will do," I joked.

She flashed a tight smile and was about to respond when an elderly man with an insistent grin raised his hand and hailed us in a high, querulous voice. The old fellow was lounging on one of the low stone slabs that flanked the gated opening, idly wiggling and stretching his hands around as if he was sifting northern sunlight through his fingers for warmth. Unlike the ever-hurrying, pointedly purposeful Andans I had been observing, he appeared to have absolutely nothing to do. *An old gentleman of leisure*, I thought, *taking in what remains of the day.*

But what he appeared to lack in purpose he instantly made up in desperate self-aggrandizing, so much so that Sarana, which is a truly beautiful language, sounded harsh and wheedling on his tongue and it took me a few seconds to orient myself to his speech. "You see those steps and columns?" As if we could miss them. The entrance to the City Assembly's meeting place was as insistently overembellished as the old man's bearing. "My cousin designed that entrance. It's all new. Thought you gentlemen would like to know," he clucked. "He designed a lot of the better buildings around here, yes he did. That's the best building in the city you're looking at." He nodded toward the hall and nodded up at us with an obnoxious smile that could have been borrowed from a Sunnashiven beggar if it wasn't so heavily self-congratulatory. I half expected him to stick out his hand for money.

"So you've got a skillful cousin," responded Aeren coldly, in a voice that passed for a young man's as easily as her clothes and physical bearing did. "Did *you* design any of the local architecture or do you merely want us to admire you because your cousin achieved some public success with his work?"

Aeren had never been burdened with social graces. In my opinion this was one of her better qualities, although it was a quality I wished she'd been a little less eager to display, as I saw no reason to offend any of my subjects over anything as trivial as vanity. The old fellow was clearly taken aback by her blunt indifference, because he stumbled over his words a little before repeating himself in a more insistent voice, as if perhaps she hadn't heard him the first time. "I said my *cousin*—" He waved his arms around a little. "—designed everything here." He grinned broadly and nodded expectantly up at us. "The whole city you see here wouldn't exist if not for him, no it wouldn't."

"And we should care *why*?" Aeren continued icily, a bit too icily for the occasion, I thought, although I had to admit that the old fellow was rather irritating.

"I just thought you'd like to know," yelled the man up at us in his thinly insistent voice before repeating for the third bloody time, "Everything here is my cousin's design." He nodded again, like he was waiting for his due praise and impatient at not getting it.

"It's all very beautiful," I said gravely, casting a serious look along the street at what to my eyes were a series of nondescript little shops hugging the other side. "I am honored to be in the presence of someone who is so closely related to such a fine architect."

Aeren glared at me, sighed impatiently, and muttered audibly, "Nobody cares."

The man puffed himself up under my praise. "Yes he is. Yes he is. Got another cousin designed all the commons, including the park you're looking at. And then he wrote a book. Best book on gardening ever written. Thought you'd like to know that, too." He smiled and tilted his head back, looking up at me for more praise and simultaneously rebuking Aeren's lack of interest by pointedly ignoring her.

A brief mind probe told me what I already knew, that he was an old fool who merely wanted attention and recognition from us because we had stopped our horses conveniently in his path. I didn't linger to pick up anything deeper than that because he didn't interest me. His need for attention wasn't even that unusual in itself, except that his insistence on fulfilling it was noticeably stronger than most people's. But my light brief probe also told me something strange. The old fellow was positively *threatened* by seeing two strangers stop and admire a building without being aware that his precious self was related to the architect. He was positively *desperate* to set things right on that score, and so he spent a lot of time here letting passing strangers know how important his cousin was.

"Thank you," I said warmly. "If you grace me with his name, I'll be sure to read his book someday." I made a motion to Aeren to start riding again, but I stopped when the man spoke loudly.

"You're not from around here. I can tell from your accent. Northern Threle? Well, we don't get a lot of visitors, especially lately, but isn't it great that someone from Threle can come here and see the new entrance to the City Assembly Hall just like everyone else?" The odd thing was that he did not appear to intend this remark as a put-down. He really thought he was being quite noble and generous, perhaps even hospitable, and that we should admire him for it. "There was a time when all this was closed to outsiders. Hear they've got some pretty good buildings in Threle, so maybe you will learn something here to take home with you."

"Noted," I responded politely. "But we must move on."

"You new in town, gentlemen? You do look travel-weary. Are you looking for lodging?"

"No," said Aeren.

"Yes," I replied, "actually, we would be most obliged if you could recommend a decent inn with stables."

"A decent inn with stables? Inns are hard to come by here as we get so few visitors but my niece lets fine rooms, yes she does. The best in Anda." He grinned and shook his head like he was exceptionally pleased with himself for being able to work another boast into the conversation.

Aeren began swearing under her breath.

The man continued bragging. "My niece's place is the best of the best. It's where all the wealthy citizens rent rooms for privacy and entertain foreign guests when guests happen in. Charges by the month. Here, walk your horses behind me and I'll take you there. Just a short way down the street. Follow me. Follow me."

"We'll find our own lodging," Aeren protested.

"Why find your own lodging when I can get you into the best place in town, sir? Yes I can. I've lived there for years. Just follow me." He quickly got swallowed into the crowded street, although I could still see his gray head bobbing ahead of us. Our horses felt like they were following him of their own accord, which would have struck me as strange except that there was really no other way for them to walk.

As we continued riding down the street, I said to Aeren, with a smile of course, "I picked up waves of hostility emanating from you concerning that old fellow. Is he a friend of yours, guy?"

She smiled ironically at the reference to her male attire. "No, I don't even know him. But I might as well. He's like everybody else in Anda, only slightly more extreme. Everybody in the city is absolutely 'the best' at everything, by their own confession, or related to 'the best' at everything. *Everybody* has a scorched-be-damned cousin. The joke is, *his* cousin is obviously either fictional or dead."

"Why do you say that?" I was curious because nothing in my mind probe had given me that impression.

"Because it's only the dead, or the very young or the very old, that Andans generally praise. You only get bragged about if you're not really a threat to anybody else's ambitions, so it's fairly unusual for Andans to brag about their living, adult relatives, although some people will brag about their adult children as a way of compensating for their own useless lives. It's always easier to brag about a son who designed a prominent building than to design a building yourself, eh? But a cousin? If his cousin was real, our new friend there would more likely view him as competition than use him as a cheap boast. So trust me, the cousin doesn't exist."

"You ought to appreciate a good piece of fiction, then," I teased her.

She drew herself up in thick annoyance. "I've been away for three years and I'm already tired of hearing about how wonderful everybody thinks they are, and how grateful and appreciative I'm supposed to be for the opportunity of being able to listen to someone brag about whoever they claim to be related to. Truth be damned but I really hate Anda."

I laughed. "Well, I checked him out, and he's harmless. Why don't we establish ourselves at some place of your choosing and plan our next move toward supreme bragging rights. That will be one on your fellow citizens."

"Yes, it will, won't it?" Aeren was mocking the old man's voice here, and doing it well enough to amuse me. She then resumed her own. "Well, we could stay there." She pointed out a relatively cheerful-looking building on the other side of the street. "That's where I shared that fateful dinner with Zelar, but I can't hold that against the place. The rooms were comfortable enough. We'll need Andan coins to pay, though."

"Can you conjure some?" I asked. "I don't know what your currency looks like or what it weighs so I wouldn't know how to begin the spell."

"No, all our currency has a peculiar energy and power around it that is designed to make counterfeiting difficult. Gold should be acceptable, though."

I conjured a small pouch of gold. "Done. Shall we take a room?"

A stableboy relieved us of our horses and helped us carry our belongings. When we entered the establishment, the old man was waiting for us like Aeren's fox waiting for the moon to fall into his grasp. It hadn't been our intent to follow him, but there he was, as if this was all in the nature of things. "Yes, I told you, what did I tell you?" he greeted us. "The best inn in Anda." He grinned obnoxiously.

"It's the only inn in this part of Anda," corrected Aeren.

The "inn" was actually a collection of privately rented rooms intended for permanent or semipermanent residence, and, like most of Anda, wasn't particularly inviting or particularly discomfiting. It would do. It would have to. I really didn't care. We needed rooms, and I got the impression that our choices were limited. I paid some gold to a woman whom I presumed was the old man's niece, and who appeared to view him with as much irritation as Aeren did. And for all his boasting, he in turn kept his distance from her.

Neither of them even exchanged greetings, but it wasn't like our hostess had a particularly welcoming personality, even by Andan standards. She was a dour-faced matron who got even more dour-faced when she saw that a foreigner such as myself was able to pay in gold and who assumed a positively hostile demeanor when she saw how much baggage we were carrying. She took my coin, and then felt obligated to establish her superiority by telling me that she once had six foreign guests at once who all paid in gold, and that perhaps someday I would be wealthy enough to have six wealthy gold-laden friends.

"Friendship is overrated," I responded dryly. Aeren giggled.

"That it is," agreed the innkeeper solemnly and unexpectedly, as if we suddenly had much in common, or I had merely said something with which she thought she was supposed to agree.

The old man suddenly decided that he had to help us carry all of our belongings to our rooms, which of course, as he repeated several times over, were "the best" in the city. I didn't refuse his help, even though I had to pay for it by listening to him assure us of how important and instrumental he was in this particular establishment and how he had all kinds of relatives and acquaintances who could get us the best of anything we wanted for a fee.

"Just call me, yes just do. My name is Masgan."

I thanked him, Aeren showed her gratitude by playfully slamming and locking the door in his face, and we were alone.

"What do you think of your subjects so far, King?" Aeren grinned sarcastically.

I smiled and shrugged. "They'll do as subjects. Tomorrow you will petition for a time to speak to the Assembly, and then . . . if all goes as Hecate seems to plan, we'll be taking up residence in that hall." I have to admit I was rather excited about the prospect.

"Or traveling to Arula to get their government's endorsement as well."

"Whatever it takes. Right now I'm going to organize my armory, and then I would like some dark time to pray and organize my thoughts. Here's some gold. Why don't you go buy yourself some better food than dried fruit and obtain whatever other necessaries you want?"

"Because I've no desire to go traipsing through Anda right now. If you need to be alone, why don't you pretend I'm not here?"

"Because pretense has no place in my solitary prayers, bard. Go. I would consider it a courtesy to be left alone."

Aeren left reluctantly, closing the door behind her as if she was angrily closing a rant before she had said everything she wanted to say. No sooner did the door slam shut than I heard the quick shuffle of Masgan's feet as if he was lying in wait somewhere down the hall for us to leave our rooms so that he might throw more unwanted bids for attention in our way. Truly the fellow was a consummate professional as far as that was concerned. Then I heard Aeren's firm heavy step, as if she was doing her best to put distance between herself and this new annoyance before he could accost her.

Too late. Masgan's sententious voice came pattering through my closed door. He greeted Aeren in a tone that was both smug and overly friendly, "Well, hey, there you are, there you are!" He sounded like he hadn't seen her in years. "You look to be such an angry young man, you do"—I could feel her annoyance with Masgan's presumption pounding through the walls, and I wasn't even bothering to open my senses to it—"why are you so angry? Is it your friend? Has he thrown you out? What is he doing in there?" Masgan wasn't just a common braggart, he was a busybody as well, and his voice was so solicitous it cloyed like too much honey in a bombastically sweet wine.

"Communing with his gods," said Aeren, both a touch too dully and a touch too maliciously for the circumstances. "That's what clerics do."

I remembered that Andans had no organized clergy, and I got the impression that the only reason Aeren responded to Masgan at all was to say something that the old fellow might find a bit much for his circumscribed world, despite his eternal boasting. It would be rare indeed if this elderly Andan could claim a cousin who was the "best" cleric in the business, but it would be amusing to hear him try. However, if that was her motivation, it didn't work, because he responded in the same overly solicitous voice, as if he deeply cared for Aeren's welfare, and sincerely wanted to banish whatever problems Aeren was having so that they would no longer be an impediment to her ability to honor him with praise. "Smile. Don't you know there's nothing in life worth getting so dour about, there isn't?"

Aeren responded rudely, "Only if you don't have anything in your life worth caring about."

Masgan wasn't about to let a bit of open honesty stop him. I assumed this was all normal business between two proud Andans and continued listening with some amusement as the old man lectured in an obnoxiously superior voice, "You must be positive like me, you must. Look at me, look at my cousins, look at my niece, we're happy, we believe in ourselves—"

"Positive attitudes are scorched-be-damned excuses for bragging about trivia and extorting praise from everyone else for the same. I don't have a scorched-be-damned positive attitude because *I'm* too busy doing something constructive with my energy." I smiled a little when I heard Aeren say that. When my bard had no use for someone she wasn't shy about letting him know. And I agreed entirely with her sentiments.

"You'd be happier if you had a better attitude, you would."

"Why do I need any kind of attitude and why is it your concern? Why not just take reality on its own terms? Is that so hard? Or can't you endure being seen by the world as an old man with nothing to commend him save some doubtful tales of his family's successes? Does anybody believe in you besides your precious self?"

Masgan gasped a little, as if he wasn't accustomed to such bluntness, and so it was suddenly crucial for him to turn the discussion back against Aeren in order to recover what served him for wits. "Can't you endure being seen by the world as an attractive young lady?" I could practically hear Masgan grinning vindictively through his words. The vindictiveness took me a bit by surprise, as I hadn't sensed that previously in his character. "Why do you wear male garb if you respect reality so much? Why not just be as the gods made you?" It also surprised me that Masgan had clearly seen through Aeren's disguise all along, not because her disguise was impossible to see through but because he had previously addressed her as a gentleman and so I had presumed that her clothes had fooled him. I supposed he wished to be petty. If she refused to grace him with the rapt attention he considered his due, he would refuse to acknowledge her as a fellow man. Perhaps that was supposed to make things even.

Aeren responded curtly and angrily to his question, "Because I *am* a young man. It just doesn't show unless I wear the right clothes."

"It doesn't show anyway," lectured Masgan airily, as if he felt it was all his business to correct her self-image. "It isn't your clothes that make you a man, no it isn't. It's the weak eyes of those who can't see through to what you truly are, it is. But perhaps you are content to pretend to be something you are not, to trick yourself out in a gorgeous lie—"

"I'll tell you what I truly am. *I'm a bard!* I once told a tale about a young man who tells tales and so I decided to become a young man. So what? What better reason to tell tales, eh?"

"Why tell tales if you only want to deal with reality?" responded Masgan in a voice of suddenly assumed reasonableness. "My nephew is a bard, he truly is. He tells stories. True ones. He's really good though, and of course he really is a young man—"

"*Nobody cares!*" Aeren raised her voice to a half scream. I could hear her footsteps stamping loudly and quickly down the hall. She had clearly had enough of old Masgan.

And so had I. I focused my attention on my immediate surroundings. Alone in the space of our gracious and exceptionally well maintained rooms, I leisurely organized my magical weapons, checking for road damage, making an inventory, feeling the surges of magic as I called my power words down from Hecate and released them back into Her. I was pleased that Zelar's name stone was undamaged, although it was so well protected in its thick wrappings I had no real concerns on that score. I uncovered the Mirror of Transformations, which now only reflected the failing light it was given, as I hadn't activated it. Then I watched the sun fade as I looked through our large windows out over the rooftops of Anda and idly opened my heart to the darkness that was beginning its soft entry into our rooms.

When it felt more night than day, I took some plain white candles that had been left for guests, blessed and sanctified them to Hecate, lit them with Her force, and placed them in a protective circle around me. Then I slowly, gently, opened my senses to the city and to my Goddess. While riding through Anda I had used my knowledge of wizardry to sense the random crowd emotions floating around me and to lightly touch old Masgan's mind. Now I wanted to enter oblivion, to kiss Hecate's dark hem, to know intimately the way Her energy flowed in this particular city, in this kingdom whose priest-king I would be.

I extended my arms into Hecate's sweet darkness and studied the way the candles reflected themselves in the Mirror, obscuring the rest of what little light was left for the Mirror to reflect. Then I leaned my attention into the flickering light and sent my prayer to Hecate, whose force was in the flames. I closed my eyes and went into a light trance.

Hecate was with me, and Her shadows gained a sudden unexpected weight and warmth when I felt them, so I had the distant impression that I must have gone deeper than I expected to. But I couldn't have been in that deep, because I remember hearing the door open and close behind me. I quickly shook off my trance, slightly annoyed that Aeren was returning so soon.

Rising in my protective circle to greet her, standing steady in my dispersing goddess energy, I caught the Mirror reflecting the sudden shadowy image of a lean, ascetic-looking man with his face in darkness gliding quietly through the doorway and closing the door behind him. As I turned to face this unexpected intruder, I suddenly felt him lock his clerical power onto mine and draw down such a poisonous blast of good-aligned energy that I nearly left my body for eternity with the discomfiting thought that Athena Herself had taken a divine interest in destroying me. And Athena and Her cleric would have succeeded if sweet Hecate hadn't turned the blinding horror of all that goodness back on my smiling attacker before it could kill me. At least, I believed it was Hecate who came to my defense because I know I didn't react in time. I remember slamming a clerical shield around myself an exploding heartbeat after the blast turned, and only at that point gaining enough sense to fully realize that I was now engaged in a clerical battle. It was some indefinable space of time and strangeness after that when I understood that I was fighting my old master, Brother El.

Seventeen

El drew down another blast that my clerical shield held firm against, although its firmness wasn't absolute because I did clench and sicken a little when it hit. His aim and concentration were impressive, because his blast hit my shield in an odd, unexpected silence without doing damage to anything around me. But my shield was equally impressive because El quickly realized that Hecate Herself had Her arms around my heart and that his attack was futile. We stared at each other across the candles in the darkened room for a long cold minute, stared across the eternal space of good and evil that now separated us.

And then, in formal academic Kantish, I invited him in.

He took up my hospitable offer with a demand shaped like one of his characteristic rhetorical questions. "Drop your shield and die back into your goddess, yes?" He was at the ready to draw another blast.

"Why?" I asked reasonably, wondering how he came to be here at all, how he came to be alive at all. *What had really happened when he turned Kursen Monastery and himself to goodness? This I must know.*

"That I might turn your spirit as it flies to Hecate, and damn you to an eternity of torture in the ever-rising light of Athena's deathless mind and Habundia Ceres's violent abundance. As one day I must die and be damned for my turning, so shall you."

"That's all very . . . *good* of you, Master," I said brightly. "May the forces you now serve—"

"Show me your strength, Luvellun. Show me that you can sacrifice yourself, as you once led me to sacrifice myself. Show me that you are worthy of your calling. *Die!* Die through your own strength of will as I once taught you." He entered my circle and the flames that I had made sacred to Hecate died into eternity. My shield thinned despite the thickness of my prayers. Hecate was with me but Athena was with my opponent in full force. And Her strength was charged with that of Habundia Ceres, for El had been a high priest of Christus, and could now draw upon the highest goddess, the highest energy form, of absolute goodness. It was an abhorrent thought.

The only grace of the candles going out was that we were now in complete darkness. I moved out of the now-despoiled circle, backing toward the Mirror, near which I had placed several wands. I reached behind me for a weapon, any weapon. "Your weapons won't help you, Luvellun. Habundia Ceres and Athena are now shielding me, bless them." He spit the words as if they ran burning poison in his mouth, which, perhaps on one level, they did. I did not question him sensing my action in the dark, or knowing of my weapons. His deities were no doubt whispering revelations to him. Under different circumstances I might have felt pity.

"May they keep you, then," I answered solemnly.

"May they keep us both," he roared. "As it is the duty of goodness to destroy evil, I am fulfilling my calling to Habundia Ceres to destroy you. And by Ceres I will."

I now had a wand in my palm. I had no idea which wand, but I could petition Hecate for the correct power word and the word would come and then I would be armed. A clerical shield is nothing like a wizard shield, which is difficult to send any kind of power through. A clerical shield is a highly concentrated cloak spun with prayer from the energy of one's deity, and so my call, my prayer to Hecate, would easily pass through, although a blast from El would not.

My strategy was to physically extend the wand out of my shield and hope to hell I could break through his, or that he would get careless and let his drop. Until then, we were two powerful shielded clerics doing a serpent dance in the dark. One slip of prayer, of thought, and not just death but damnation from my deity would follow. I remembered the cruelty that El had been capable of when he sent Riven the peacemonger to eternal peace, and I began to get dangerously distracted by my horrid imaginings of the spiritual atrocities that El was no doubt planning for me. I steadied my mind.

We couldn't blast each other through our respective shields, but we both knew that one of our shields would fail first. In theory, meaning in the dark theory that El had once taught me, a cleric can keep his shield up indefinitely. But in reality one of us was bound to lose concentration. If El opened himself first, the wand would let me blast him without dropping my defenses.

Blasting El through my shield was an option but due to simple physics, it carried certain risks. The prayers that form a clerical shield are positively charged to one's deity. A blast is negatively charged to the same. All clerics learn that at the highest level of reality, all deities, even the two Habundias, are pure energies. We perceive them with human attributes because it is easier for us to work with them in that way, not because the deities themselves are limited in form. Each current of divine energy, each deity, runs a positive and negative current within itself, although both of those charges are of course negative or positive to those of a deity of opposing alignment. Sending a negatively charged blast through the positively charged prayers of a shield produces a differential that radically diffuses the energy of both, resulting in a dampened blast and a weakened or destroyed shield. And forget accuracy. What remains of your blast could go anywhere, including harmlessly back to your deity.

So the wand was the best I could do. That, and pray.

I supposed El could attempt a physical attack, that is, if he could find me in the dark. But I didn't fear that, as I suspected he wasn't any more skillful at fighting than I was, and a fight might cause him to drop his shield. I moved silently. I heard him move like a shadow softly stretching to kiss the secret dark of the noontide sun. There was power there.

More power than I was prepared to deal with, because I felt with something approaching terror that my prayers, my energy stream to Hecate, my evil that by all rights should pass through the shield my prayers to my Goddess had formed, were getting choked and strangled in the air. I knew if El could block my prayers, it was only a matter of time, perhaps only seconds, before he could destroy my shield and then do worse than merely kill me. I also knew that if he could block my prayers, his shield was down, because doing so required sending an exquisitely accurate, carefully measured small blast at my prayer stream.

The door was now behind me. I could feel the latch clawing into my stiff back, sticking through the cold nervous sweat which caked my cloak and shirt. I shakily placed the end of the wand outside my shield, summoned enough power to kill without mercy, to kill without hesitation . . . and nothing came because El was skillfully strangling my link to my Goddess. I felt my shield shrivel and give out as El severed my connection with Hecate, and then I felt absolutely powerless to use clerisy, for my link to my Goddess was dead. Then I felt a sickening flood of goodness fill the space around him like a poisoned fountain forcing ill weeds from the bones of an arid waste. He was shielding himself again, taking no chances against my wand or my wizardry. I put up a wizard shield, which was better than nothing, but near useless against a clerical blast. El was enjoying the moment, preparing to blast me into an eternity of agonizing torture.

But he didn't. "Turn, Luvellun," he hissed. "Turn yourself to Habundia Ceres as I once did, and perhaps I will not mutter incantations over your corpse to ensure that you never find your way to Hecate. I might be merciful and let the nature of the gods take its course without interference. Otherwise, I will blast you to an eternity that even the gods themselves would blush in horror to look at—"

As I prepared for my life to close out and explode in a blast, with desperate prayers pounding out of my heart for Hecate to save me, the door behind me banged open, knocking me off-balance and causing me to drop the wand. Aeren stormed into the room carrying a large tray of bright candles for light. El lunged for my wand, and as he grasped it, it blasted him into the wall with enough force to keep him winded while I easily grabbed it and held it against his chest. If he hadn't been shielded, I presumed that the differential between the wand's evil charge and the tragic goodness of his energy would have killed him, but as it was, the blast merely knocked out his shield, which would have surprised me if I had had time to think about it. We were in darkness again, outside of the reach of the light of Aeren's candles. Thankfully, I could sense Hecate's breath returning in my heart.

"Good clerics should never grab evil wands, Master," I lectured. "Do not even think about shielding yourself again because I'll blast you from inside your shield. Do not think about blasting me because Hecate is shielding me again, praise the Lady. Now get up." I kept the wand steady against his chest. "Excellent. Looks like I win."

Aeren had hastily set her tray down on a table to light the room. She had now come forward with a candle, and her voice was full of shock as she asked in loud, rapid Sarana, "Why are you attacking old Masgan? What are you doing?"

As the light fell into my corner of the room, I saw that El was gone and old Masgan was in his place, calling to Aeren in his ugly, whining Sarana, "Help, help, yes please do. I only came to check on the gentleman, yes I did—"

It then occurred to me that something was wrong here, that the wand shouldn't have been charged because I had felt my prayers getting strangled. As soon as I realized this, the candles in my circle appeared to light themselves again. "Get in the circle," I ordered Aeren, because I wanted to get her out of the way. She didn't move, but she didn't make any move to help Masgan either. She kept standing there with the candle, dripping wax on my back and blocking the light from the rest of the room.

I turned back to the old man and hissed in Sarana, "Who are you? Answer or die."

His body collapsed into fullness and strength under my grasp, and a rushed voice answered me in perfect Kantish, "Welm the Illusionist, lad. Same as you once freed from Kursen Monastery, sent there on the emperor's business as a spy."

"Show your true self to my companion," I commanded in Sarana. It wasn't necessary, because I heard Aeren saying incredulously behind me,

"How did you change shape like that? And what language are you speaking?"

"The language of begging for mercy," Welm responded in his ugly Sarana, "as far as that might go with the lad here."

"Beg in Kantish," I ordered. I needed to learn what he had to say before deciding how much of his story, if any, I wanted Aeren to know. Then I commanded Aeren, "Give us room and more light, bard, and make sure nobody disturbs us. I've got a prisoner to interrogate, a powerful illusionist who just tried to kill me."

"Does that make you feel important?" asked Aeren sarcastically. "It's not everyone that nearly gets assassinated by illusion."

"Yes, take it as a compliment, lad," said Welm in hopeful Sarana, as Aeren began to place the candles around the room. When the light was evenly distributed, she positioned herself by the door but I could tell her attention was focused on us rather than on making sure nobody disturbed us.

"Lock the door, bard, and don't answer should anyone knock." I heard her lock it. "Get a chair for our guest and put it in the middle of my circle." Aeren did so, and then returned to take up her position near the door, staring at us all the while. I threatened Welm with another blast in order to encourage him to seat himself in my circle of candles, and then I invoked Hecate to lock the circle in a force that would prevent him from leaving. Once Welm appeared to understand our new relationship, I seated myself comfortably outside the circle and began to think about where to begin, as my would-be assassin was now mine to question and mine to mind-probe.

Mind-probe. Yes, there *was* something wrong there. "You will answer me in Kantish," I said evenly in the same language, "or I will blast you into dear Hecate's womb for eternal torture at Her pleasure. Understood?" Welm nodded eager assent. He also looked understandably frightened, but as he had proven himself to be a consummate actor, I did not place confidence in his expression. "You used illusion to shapeshift yourself into both an old Andan braggart named Masgan and my former high priest and teacher, El of Kursen Monastery."

"Yes."

"I mind-probed Masgan—you—when we first met near the City Assembly Hall. Why didn't I learn who you really were then?" I had no idea if Welm would speak truth, but I didn't trust any mind probe I could work on him now until I knew the answer to that question.

He grinned a little. "I'm a damn good illusionist, lad. The emperor only hires the best." He said this like he was still in character, still bragging like an old Andan, except there was more pride and less desperation in his voice.

"How did you feel my probe? What kind of magical training have you had since our last meeting? Why does Roguehan consider you 'the best'?"

"The emperor has many resources. He found it in his interest to provide me with some very advanced magical training. I can sense a wizard's mind probe, and create thoughts to meet it, especially when I'm conversing with a wizard I'm on guard against. I've learned to create irresistible illusions of clerical blasts of all alignments. I've had advanced linguistic training and probably speak more languages than you do. I've studied with His Excellency's finest court actors to learn how to convincingly mimic any personage I choose to become."

I quickly considered what it would take to hire Welm to work for me and put the thought aside for later consideration. "You overplayed old Masgan. My traveling companion remarked that it was odd for Andans to boast about the accomplishments of a cousin, that it would be more believable had you bragged about an adult son."

"Thanks for the criticism. I'll remember it next time." He gestured gracefully with his hands and shrugged, as if he appreciated the lesson.

"And your Sarana had a strange edge to it, although your Gondish accent was perfect."

"But not so strange an edge that you failed to believe me."

I felt a little chagrined by his pardonable pride in having successfully fooled me, but I didn't let it show. "How did you know we would be riding by that gate at that particular time? How did you even know I would be in Gondal?"

"You sent a convenient message to Zelar via his name stone a few weeks ago. Under the circumstances, it wasn't difficult to guess that you and . . . your new companion . . . would be traveling to Anda."

"I warned Zelar to keep distant."

"He did." Welm smiled broadly. "He sent me instead. I crossed a narrow neck of the unorganized territory near the eastern border of the Duchy of Reathe, and arrived before you did to give you an imperial welcome."

"How did you happen to be at the gate to the City Assembly Hall when we were?"

"That was easy. Anda is small and sees few visitors. I knew approximately when you'd be arriving, kept alert for you, and put myself conveniently in your way. Took some minor illusion to distract your friend into stopping her horse, and to encourage your horses to plod their way to this fair dwelling. Not that there's much choice of inns here."

"So of course you were eager to help us carry our belongings."

"I had hoped to take stock of what you were carrying, lad."

"I suppose you could have used your considerable skill with illusion to help yourself to what we were carrying."

"Yes, but that would have been an easier game . . . later."

"After you'd killed me?"

He nodded. I continued smoothly, as if I was absolutely unaffected by his thwarted assassination plans, "Before we discuss that one, I would like to know about the exchange you had in the hallway with Aeren here." I indicated her with my head. I'm sure if it was possible for her to look more attentive when she heard her name, she would have. She was desperately trying to guess at what we were saying, but it was beyond her skill and she knew it.

"*Aeren* here," said Welm loudly, emphasizing her name, "nearly saw through my disguise in a way it would have been impossible for you to imagine, lad." His voice was both matter-of-fact and slightly arrogant. "She had the wit to ask if anybody actually believed in me. That's a dangerous question to start asking a nervous illusionist with orders to kill, because if she started disbelieving on one level, the trick could be over on any level."

"That's why you cleverly turned her attention back on her disguise and baited her to the point where she was too anger-ridden to think."

"That's why." He spoke like it was all in a day's business.

His strategy worked like a wizard's charm, I had to admit. "You learned from Aeren that I was involved in a clerical ritual, so you entered my room in the shape of El, whom you'd once met under very different circumstances at Kursen." Welm didn't appear to care for the allusion. He remained silent on that score. "And in that shape you were planning to kill me. You could see me grabbing this wand to defend myself with because you couldn't see the illusion of darkness you put on the room, the illusion of my candles going out. That's clear now. What isn't clear is that, now that I think about it, El would have blasted me to divine goodness without hesitation when my shield gave out, but you attempted to persuade me to blast myself to Habundia Ceres. You could have delivered an illusory blast, I would have believed it, and chances are excellent that I would have died and gone to Ceres on the spot on the strength of that belief. You certainly delivered a believable enough blast when you first entered the room—"

"And a believable enough illusion of turning it, yes." Welm smiled a little smile of professional pride.

"All right, I'm impressed with your skill, but my question remains, why didn't you kill me?"

He made cheerful eye contact with me and shrugged easily. "Orders from His Excellency."

"You mean Roguehan doesn't exactly want me dead."

"I mean, Roguehan wanted you to turn yourself to goodness and choose to die doing it, lad. Enemy glory! Like your old master."

I considered. Yes, that was certainly all Roguehan's sort of thing, although something else didn't make sense. "Why wouldn't the emperor want to be on hand to watch? I can't imagine him wanting to miss the aesthetics of that experience."

Welm suddenly looked a little uneasy, but he quickly caught himself back into smooth confidence. I couldn't tell if the confidence was consummate acting on his part, or based on something real, and with his training I wasn't convinced that I would get any definitive answers from a mind probe. "Roguehan wanted it done. That's all anyone in my position needs to be privy to. When the emperor gives an order you don't question it, lad."

Welm smiled hopefully at me as I put away my wand. I stared out the window into Gondal's opaque night, considering, letting Welm feel a spot of relief that my weapon was out of reach and hoping that as a result he would let down his guard a little. Then, without warning, I launched a violent mind probe at Welm, and came back with nothing more rewarding than clouds of whiteness and floating pieces of old children's rhymes. He had received excellent training, that much was certain. Even though I knew his thoughts could be illusory, he was skillful enough to fool me. Despite all, I was intrigued, and I had a sudden, professional interest in how this new kind of magical illusionist shield worked. Welm's smile got cocky.

"How much is Roguehan paying you for this little adventure?" I asked, knowing that as with his other answers, there was no way to verify his response.

"All my traveling expenses, which are as considerable as I care to make them."

I casually picked up the wand again. I could feel that the wand was still charged, and I was fascinated with the unpredictable power of illusion, how Hecate must have been available to me despite my belief that She wasn't, how somehow, without my knowledge, my

Goddess had charged the wand with the power word, or how somehow, I had done so without believing that I had. And how despite all,
I had been unable to make use of my weapon. Welm was the gods'
own magician. As usual, Roguehan had shown excellent judgment in
selecting his people. I made a show of pointing the weapon toward
Welm, ignoring Aeren's involuntary gasp. "No one sets his own price
with Roguehan. How much is he paying you?"

Welm decided to cooperate. "My liege lord has offered to make
me King of Gondal. A king of illusions, if you will."

I had to think this one through. Carefully. My death might be
worth a kingdom to Roguehan because of the power I had to destroy
Zelar, although that price seemed a few shades too high, as Roguehan
was hardly sentimental about his people and Zelar could be replaced.
It wasn't as if Roguehan didn't have access to other highly skilled evil
wizards. And even the crime he had condemned me for back in Walworth's castle hardly added up to a kingdom. This was not a simple
assassination, which would make sense in terms of Roguehan being
able to reclaim Zelar's weapons, which Zelar had no doubt sensed
that I had taken, or reclaim Aeren, the presumed true heir to the
throne. They obviously knew I had gotten past her dragon form or I
wouldn't have been able to send that message through Zelar's name
stone. Did they think I had somehow killed the stormdragon? Or did
they know that Aeren was restored to her human form and was now
traveling with me, and that her claim to the throne was now mine?
That did not explain the horrible spiritual aspect of the death Roguehan required Welm to give me, an aspect that made me feel weak in
my own darkness just thinking about it, but it was something to puzzle over. Welm had shown no interest in killing Aeren, and had intentionally angered her into walking away before he attacked me. Did he
know who she was? Would he tell me the truth if he did?

I slowly repeated the surprising information Welm had just given
me. "And so Roguehan would make you a king of illusions ruling
over an arguably illusory kingdom, which would then become
another of his puppet states."

"Presumably," said Welm evenly. "We illusionists are skilled at
managing puppet states."

"Welm. I do not wish to spar with you and weigh your words.
Remove your illusionist shield and let me into your mind. If you do
so willingly, I won't cause you to drop your shield by creating so
much pain in your head through clerisy that your thoughts will be
mine, anyway."

Welm stiffened a little, and I could feel a hopeless sort of fright around him, although I had no idea if his fright was real. "You can't cause me to drop my shield, lad. I can dress it up in thoughts to fool a probe, but I can't obliterate it through my own doing without destroying all my thoughts and myself along with it. It works like a death charm in that way. The emperor made sure of that."

Here was a fine pass. I had no bloody way to tell if the illusionist was bluffing. I could try to remove his shield and try to determine what had been done, but my theoretical knowledge of illusion was practically nonexistent, and if Welm was telling me the truth, I would be certain to destroy my only source of information on Roguehan, as well as a potentially valuable ally. I gazed back into Gondal's night, my night, which of course yielded no answers. *Damn!* Welm had me there and he knew it.

I had a sudden inspiration. "You have failed in your quest, Welm. The chances of persuading me to destroy myself by turning to goodness are now nonexistent. How will you explain your failure to Roguehan?"

He pursed his lips as if he was slowly adding up an interesting business proposition. "Under torture, I suppose."

I smiled a little at his wit. "You cannot return to your liege lord. Perhaps you will remain here in Gondal, but then it is only a matter of time before he finds you. Perhaps you will go into hiding elsewhere, but again, the emperor has a long reach."

Welm's expression was bright, attentive, and damnably neutral. I glanced at Aeren, who was still desperately and hopelessly focusing on every Kantish word and completely at a loss to understand our discussion. That was just as well for now.

"Welm. If I decide to show you the mercy you desire, to allow you perfect freedom to stay or leave, what would you do?"

He looked around, possibly out of a habit of looking for eavesdroppers when about to say something dangerous, possibly for show, and certainly to take in the weapons I had collected. "Well, lad, I'd suggest we might go partners, if you'll have me. You've got a stash of the emperor's firepower here and enough power over Zelar to make things dicey back home, believe me."

"*Believing* you can be dangerous." Even though I was merely stating a fact, I spoke as if I was giving him a flatly gracious compliment, to encourage him to continue.

"Say we make a joint claim to the Gondish throne."

Too smooth. Welm knew my motives for being here. He had obviously learned them from Zelar and Roguehan, who had clearly made a damn accurate guess. "Say *we* make nothing. Say *I* offer you clemency and protection in Gondal in exchange for your professional services." By speaking in these terms I knew I was admitting that I already considered myself Gondal's rightful king, but Welm showed no surprise at my casual use of royal prerogative.

"Sounds fair," responded Welm decidedly, as if he had anything resembling a choice. "But there is a problem in the making, lad."

"Yes?"

"His Excellency Lord Roguehan already has a puppet king on the throne of Gondal. Been ruling for about a year without incident, though the Assembly would be happy to do without him. It was him whose place I was promised." He held his tongue behind his upper teeth and curled his lips into a stiffly ironic smile. "And he's damn near as well armed as you are."

Of course I wanted to know how Gondal came to have a king, and how Roguehan had a hand in it, but that question would wait. Information is most useful in its proper order. I remained impassive as I asked, "And how was His Excellency planning to replace him with you? Kings don't abandon their thrones quietly. Or did you have orders for a second assassination?"

"It might have come to that, depending on circumstances. It was to start with a contingent of the emperor's people, magically armed with these weapons—" Welm indicated my collection of firepower. "—entering Gondal from the north, marching on Arula, and taking the throne by force."

"So His Majesty of Gondal is in Arula," I mused. "I suppose my ability to destroy Zelar at any time I choose would wreak havoc in Roguehan's battle strategy, as it clearly relies heavily on the magical abilities of his contingent." So that might have increased the price on my life, but it still didn't explain the manner he chose for taking it. "Why would Roguehan find it necessary to take the throne away from his own minion, whom he recently gave it to? And how did that circumstance come about?"

"It came about through the emperor's strongest weapons, words and propaganda. Here's what and all I know about it, lad, and through your skill and mine it may be enough to work with. Get comfortable." He said this in a strangely solicitous tone, a tone that reminded me more of a storyteller about to create a pleasant piece of fiction than an imperial turncoat about to betray his master.

I did not react to his suggestion to "get comfortable," but I did settle my mind to hear and weigh his story.

"Might I speak in Sarana?" He glanced at Aeren, and then back at me. "Your friend will take great interest in this account."

I decided that Aeren's assessment was worth having, so I called her over to us. "Sit, bard," I ordered her in Sarana, but with a much pleasanter lilt to my voice than I had been using with Welm. "My . . . royal illusionist"—Welm made no response to the title I had just given him, but Aeren arched her eyebrows and mouthed the words in surprise—"has an important piece of intelligence for us. As a native citizen of Anda I would like your unreserved evaluation of whatever he is about to tell us."

"My insights are yours," she said in a harsh, wondering simplicity, turning her full attention on Welm.

Welm smiled appeasingly, as if he was determined to smile right through Aeren's cynical demeanor. Then he spoke in a voice that carried a slight resemblance to a Helan merchant bantering for a sale. I congratulated myself on allowing Aeren to hear his story fresh. Her reactions would be invaluable. "His Excellency Emperor Roguehan has long regarded the Kingdom of Gondal, or what passes as the Kingdom of Gondal, as the jewel in his cloak, the ultimate aim and apex of his imperial ambitions."

"Makes sense to me," interrupted Aeren. "It's a snow-fisted wasteland and two small cities' worth of dull arrogance that nobody with anything resembling a life has any business caring about. Kind of place I'd certainly want to rule if my ambitions tended that way." Welm and I laughed a little at her unchecked sarcasm. Our shared amusement felt odd considering the circumstances, and was the measure of Aeren's ability to entertain despite her generally dour outlook. "So, in other words, the emperor is a loser, eh?"

"That's truer than you know." Welm smiled earnestly. "But come home to it, here's what I've gathered though my own observations and through what I've been privy to that accounts for his brilliant little obsession with this cold, forgotten piece of the north, and his erstwhile interest in the lass—lad?—here."

"Lad will do," said Aeren coldly.

"With Aeren," responded Welm agreeably, as if we were suddenly all excellent friends. "The emperor admires Gondal. Gondal is the ancient realm of the elves, and His Excellency fancies to make himself an emperor of the elves with a humble servant king to manage the day-to-day business for him."

"How original," commented Aeren in a voice that sounded so flatly nonimpressed that Welm and I both laughed again. "Imagine that. Somebody wanting to come to Gondal to be the chief honorary elf and rule over everybody else. Now *there's* a new one that nobody in this scorched-be-damned city has ever considered. Another bloody king."

"Well, laddie, it's not purely the romance of crowning himself an elven emperor." Welm laughed bemusedly, running the back of his hand over his mouth. "To understand the emperor, you need to understand this. It's Beauty he craves rule over."

"It's *what*?" asked Aeren incredulously. I couldn't tell whether Aeren was still being sarcastic or if she was genuinely stunned. But I did find the tone of her question highly amusing, considering I hadn't noticed anything particularly beautiful about Anda, leastways anything beautiful enough to attract Roguehan's rarefied sensibilities.

"Beauty," answered Welm smoothly. "The power by which the elves create. Perhaps you know the legends. That in ancient times the elves built Arula out of moonlight and song, that they sang the very rocks and hills of the city into existence and built great lighted towers with the music of their lyres. That they painted cloudy images on the frozen air that held the elvish music, and that those ice images hardened into real streets and dwellings and elegant commons. That in the beginning, Arula had no government save a sweet elvish dance, for the power to organize their society flowed naturally from the elves joining hands and kissing the rhythms of life. And that somewhere in this glorious mist a king emerged, crowned with all the beauteous artifice that the elves could command."

"About that," I asked. "Why did such a free and beautiful society want a king?"

Aeren started to respond to my question. From her manner she appeared to want to tell the rest of what was clearly a well-known Gondish legend, but I commanded her to be silent. I wanted to hear Welm's answer.

"The king wasn't real. Some say that he was an oak tree carved in the image of the most beautiful elf that any of Arula's creators could imagine. Others say that he was a statue wrought of precious metals. Some say that he was ice, and others that he was candle wax spun from pale sun and fiery snow. The king, in his artificial person, was a work of art that embodied the best and choicest attributes of elvenkind and their northern land. He was beauty, grace, wisdom, charisma, and irresistible, terrible power. He was the essence of dark and light. So beautiful was this work of art that the elves worshiped and wept and went cold under the icy enchantment of their own creation. They starved themselves to bring him gifts."

"Like a monastic sacrifice," I commented, almost involuntarily.

"You should know, lad. Except they expected no reward. The elves loved their creation so much they lost the will to do anything but be in its presence. They never built another city. They barely maintained Arula. And then . . . one strange night . . . a stormdragon entered Arula under the dark of the moon on a thin sail of thunder, silent as a frozen planet . . . and . . . snatched away the king."

Aeren smiled a little. Her smiles were so rare I noticed this one, and made a mental note of it.

"The elves wailed piteous crying winds. They screamed out a winter of silver tears, and beat cold earthy moonlight out of their chests. They abandoned their city as they wandered through the wasteland searching for the stormdragon. After years of wandering they found her treasure hoard, but instead of their statue, their love, their life, the power of their creation and Beauty itself made manifest, was a real, living personage. And at his feet lay the stormdragon's frozen body, pierced with an elven sword. The king greeted them kindly."

"Were they disappointed?" For some reason I couldn't even explain to myself, I had to know. "I mean," I asked the illusionist, showing a lamentable weakness merely by the nature of my question, "was the living reality just a dim ghost in the flesh compared to the elves' lovely artifice?"

"Of course it was," responded Aeren. "Reality is never better than fiction. Why should this time be any different?"

"Let Welm answer, bard."

Aeren sighed loudly, but she ceased speaking.

"The laddie here is right. The elves shrieked and panicked and dug great holes in the frozen ground and danced widdershins and brought down storms and cursed the moon and generally had an ill time of it. You see, they had poured the best part of their living essence into that statue, and now that power was alive, and uncontrollable, and so it wasn't theirs anymore. It was a living king.

"Some of the elves stayed in the northlands and formed colonies, swearing upon the moon and stars never to enter the rest of the world again. Some returned heavy-hearted to Arula, led by their living king, who now used his awful elvish grace to set up a throne and rule. They chose to return because they loved the king and they hated him. Loved him for the statue they had once created, hated him for the living flesh he had become. And so the elves, who some say live almost as long as time itself, restored Arula with their king and told each other great tales of his beauteous birth. And over time humans settled in Arula and the elvish inhabitants gradually faded off into the northern colonies, although a few remained in the city for ancient love of what the king once was. And then one fine day the king just left, burst into a storm of eye-searing starlight, or a funny cloud of music, or an enchantment of old autumn leaves. And sometime after that, Arula got a human king, and Anda was built, and the human king moved to Anda, and, well, I'm sure Aeren here knows the rest from the history books."

"That's why to this day Andans see themselves as 'the best' at everything. They've forgotten how far removed from the elves they are." Aeren sounded as if she would like nothing better than to remind them.

"Yes," agreed Welm, eyes bright. "And as I was saying, 'the best' is what attracts the emperor to this part of the world. He believes he can become the rightful ruler of Gondal, and by doing so become invested with the ancient elvish grace and energy. He wishes to own that energy, the energy that once built a real city in the world and that still runs through anything men call beautiful. For that he fights a war. For that he tortures and kills."

"I thought he had some kind of grudge against Threle." I spoke without a trace of irony.

"Threle amuses him. It entertains him to destroy free countries, to demonstrate how . . . well, fictional . . . freedom generally is. When the day is done, lad, nobody is freer than his ability to force the issue at swordpoint on his fellows."

"That's how we are, eh?" Aeren enthusiastically agreed. "The emperor has a point. Every self-proclaimed 'free' individual whose bragging I've ever endured has been utterly dependent on the circumstances that allow him to be free. I haven't yet encountered anybody who's truly earned his freedom, but I've met plenty who boast of it the same as if they'd invented their own lives out of fool's cloth. Is Threle like that?"

"Threle can be like that," I said thoughtfully. "But as to Gondal. As Aeren says, the elves are ancient and gone. And Anda's present citizens don't appear to be particularly worthy, except in their own minds"—Aeren laughed in high amusement—"so what does Roguehan expect to find here? If there is any elvish power left in the world, I'd like to experience it."

"The emperor expects to become in his very person the rightful ruler of this land, which is the only way he can assume and control that ancient elvish power, and thus satisfy his insatiable aesthetic cravings. Essentially, His Excellency wants to become the living embodiment of this land and so become the living embodiment of the elvish energy that once sustained this land and all things beautiful, like that first elvish king."

I couldn't help thinking of Cathe wanting to become a god.

"The puppet king—Raen"—I could tell that as Welm was speaking, he noticed that Aeren glanced sharply at me with an expression that would not have been out of place had she just turned dragon again—"Raen is not rightfully king. The emperor gave him arms to control the people, set him up in an ancient castle in Arula, and gave him powerful servants and all the trappings of royalty. He also gives him exceedingly bad counsel calculated to make him as unpopular with the people as possible. His Excellency never petitioned the Assembly for this king, never gained their consent—"

"Wait. You've now referred twice to the Assembly. Aren't there two? For the two cities?" I was asking both Welm and Aeren.

Welm responded. "There were two. The emperor's people convinced Raen to abolish both of them under threat of arms. A brilliant move on the emperor's part, calculated to cause great outrage among the more prominent and powerful citizens of both cities."

"I presume it was also an illegal move if Raen is not the lawful king."

"The emperor doesn't stand on legal niceties, Llewelyn. That's a Threlan fault. But as I was saying, it was a wonderful strategy on His Excellency's part. Arula's Assembly members left the city in fear for their lives and came here. After Arula was cleared of any meaningful opposition, and fearful sentiment was pitched high and loud in Anda against this pretender to the throne, Roguehan's people convinced Raen that it would increase his popularity if he allowed a single Assembly to meet in Anda, a body politic composed of both former Assemblies. He even provided funding to build a new facade to the City Assembly Hall. His nominal purpose was to have a government to oversee all the mundane business of running the two cities."

"And his actual purpose?"

"Was to create a place where the most important citizens would easily be able to organize opposition to this new 'king' who rose out of the streets of Anda and now rules with a sword and a well-armed regiment of foreign mercenaries."

"I'm trying to follow Roguehan's logic here but I can't find it," complained Aeren. "Why didn't he simply take Gondal by force?"

"Because he wants and needs a lawful, recognized claim. The true descendant of the last true king of Gondal walks upon the earth. Only that descendant has the power and authority to own, and under the right conditons, to embody, the elvish power His Excellency craves."

"But I gave my claim to Llewelyn," started Aeren, without stopping to think about what she was saying. "And I never felt particularly powerful or beautiful when I had it."

I had to laugh again. "And I honestly don't feel I have any power to call down and control the ancient power of the elves," I added. "Perhaps Roguehan is making a grand mistake in his game."

"I can't answer to what you feel or don't feel, lad. All I know is that His Excellency had planned to take the throne by force with the people's consent, so that the people, grateful at having him depose their present tyrant, would legitimately crown him their ruler. He needed a central point of opposition for that, so he convinced Raen to instate the Assembly here in Anda, and invest it with the power to speak for the people. As I said, my job would be to take over the duties of the Assembly in my person, to be the chief administrator of those things the emperor prefers not to be bothered with. I would be the king, but as I would answer to him, he would be the true king of Gondal. Or, more accurately, almost the true king of Gondal."

"Almost?"

"Well, to make the deal stick, he would need to slay a dragon. And that's where the laddie comes in. Not only was Aeren imprisoned as a stormdragon, she was the true king, or queen. Killing her under the proper circumstances would have allowed him to take all that power into his person, and killing her in her dragon form before the people would solidify his claim. But you freed her, lad, and you received her claim, so that put a bit of mud on his plans. Yes, His Excellency knows. Zelar did get a whiff of your power when you made contact."

"So I . . . we . . . shall take a lesson from Roguehan and lead the people against Raen, who as you probably know is Aeren's stepbrother?"

Welm nodded. Aeren looked incredulous, but made no attempt to speak.

"And if your tale be true, we shall be fighting to save more than a mere kingdom."

Welm nodded and airily waved his hand, a serious gesture that was difficult for me to read.

"And by freeing Aeren of her dragon form, I in essence did slay a dragon, so her witness to that deed secures my claim."

"One would think," said Welm. "Kings have been crowned for less."

If the illusionist is speaking truth, my crown will give me the ability to hear the song of the water fairies, to sense the love of invisible fairy flowers, to command all of the secret sources of elvish power to show themselves to me at will! That was worth all. And it was all I could think of and hold to as I graciously dismissed my two chief courtiers for the night.

Eighteen

$\mathcal{I}$n a half-remembered distance still to come and spreading, Isulde was giving me an invisible crown. In a dream still warming, Isulde was giving me an invisible crown. In a half-light still flowing from an early favored tale that drowned a rainy reading corner somewhere in my youth, Isulde was giving me an invisible crown. Three times she crowned me, and three times she laughed her fairy laughter at my clumsy attempts to wear her gift. And whenever I questioned her, she had no words for me, only soft fairy laughter that stung.

Her laughter broke into an open nothing, into the silent thickness of the night that held my rooms, into the darkness like a second face that formed a blind against my own. I was awake and out of my dream now, and doing my best to focus on Aeren, who had been doing her best to focus on waking me while doing me the courtesy of pretending not to notice that I was sleeping.

"King. Liege lord. I want to kill Raen." Aeren was not making a request, or overstating her feelings for dramatic effect, or even sharing a long-cherished ambition with me. She sounded annoyed with herself, and she also sounded as if she devoutly wished that I would be equally annoyed with her. Which I was. But I was also curious, because her words had a strange effect in the darkness and in the silence, not least because it felt as if she suddenly wanted to share some intimate familiarity while obtaining some unimaginable absolution from me for doing so. That, more than anything else, intrigued me.

"Somebody has to kill him," I responded cheerfully, even though my voice was tired. "Why do you believe you're especially qualified?"

"I don't. I don't even truly want to kill him."

"You just woke me up to tell me differently."

"No, I just woke you up to tell you that I think I should want to, but that I can't tolerate the implications of wanting to . . . or of not wanting to."

"You find the whole business too 'intimate' for your delicate taste?"

"*No!*" The word pounced out of her throat like dragonfire, loud enough to wake the entire establishment. "I don't want anything to do with Raen or with the rest of them. But I still feel I have to kill him, even though I'm quite certain that I want nothing to do with him."

I decided I would get the most useful amount of information in the least amount of time if I let Aeren explain her exhausting contradictions in her own way, even if that meant allowing her to keep me up for the rest of the night. I waited impatiently as she paced heavily around the room in severe agitation. After a few minutes of Aeren's pacing and stiff sigh-ridden silence, my impatience got the best of me so I asked her in sharp irritation, "Would you do me the kindness of introducing me to your point, bard? Or did you choose to wake me so I can watch you stormdragon it around the room all night?"

She stopped in midstride and blushed angrily. "Do you know why I hate Raen? Can you even guess?" Her questions were phrased like angry insults to my lamentable lack of insight into her opaquely complex emotions. I let them pass without comment. "Raen has something I would kill to have, something my intelligence and experience prevent me from having more mercilessly than a ban that no wizard can remove. Something he never earned, has no right to, and is too scorched-be-damned ignorant to know he has no right to. Which is why he has it, and which is why I *hate him*!"

"Why he has what?"

"*Self-belief!* Ariana gave him that. Him and his pathetic sister Eyra. A free unearned gift from the 'elven queen' herself. I told you before, Raen is disgustingly talented at living as if he has only crossed paths with reality once or twice in the distant past. He can't keep steady work, he can't keep more than two coins together with which to rub the soles of his feet, he couldn't find Gondal on a map if someone pushed his face through it, and yet, he has no problem believing that he absolutely is an elven king, or the next best thing to it. And he isn't. Except that now apparently he is, thanks to Zelar and friends. And that's the worst part. When ignorance is rewarded with unearned success. He's a pretty mark for your new companion Welm, because Raen is a living illusion. He's a scorched-be-damned beggar riding pilfered dreams for whatever emotional thrills he can steal from unwary strangers. He disgusts me because he never earned his pride."

"Maybe if you believe you are a king, you become one?" I shrugged and grinned as if we were sharing a private joke.

Aeren was not amused. "*Goddess damn it!* Maybe if I believe I'm a successful bard, people will just show up for my stories, Llewelyn? Do you think? Why did I perform for so many empty taverns if all I had to do was . . . hey, *believe* the rooms would be crowded? Why did I need to bother making some divinely witnessed deal with you when it's just as well to *believe* I'm a royal bard in a great court? Why tell tales at all when all I have to do is merely *believe* that I did? Belief is all. Why have ambitions? Or standards? Or anything resembling a life?"

"Because it makes people like us feel better?" I asked seriously.

"I *never* feel better." She said this with a strange sort of pride. "I haven't earned the right to feel better. I'll feel better when my stories have made a real contribution to my audience's dreams. I'll feel better when I've done something to earn my pride."

I was wondering how she was able to craft tales without a measure of the self-delusive belief she condemned, but I didn't have time to pursue that thought. "Unearned pride disgusts me, too, Aeren. My first royal decrees will be laws against same. No one in Gondal will have the right to have any higher self-regard than he has actually earned through real, measurable accomplishments. We'll pillory the self-deluded braggarts like Raen in the public square, and make them justify their self-regard until their dirty little hearts break with the humiliation of being forced to confront how worthless they really are." Aeren looked shocked, but it was the shock of discovering that I understood her sentiments after all, not dismay with my admittedly ludicrous proposition. A small slow smile crept across her usually solemn face, and her fiery eyes softened and widened a little in surprise. "I wonder what sort of society that would result in," I mused.

"A far less annoying one." Aeren spoke definitively, as if she was utterly untroubled by the absurdity of my offer. "If it could be enforced against the right sort. Of course, that would mean just about everybody in Anda would be in for some kind of punishment."

"I wasn't serious, bard. There is no way to enforce such a law, and if there was, everybody . . . except perhaps yourself . . . would be in violation at one time or another. Most people are utterly worthless and are entirely replaceable. Even certain kinds of personalities and energy patterns repeat themselves into divine boredom if you observe enough individuals. But most people are absolutely incapable of getting out of bed in the morning, much less through their lives, if this horrid little fact rises into their minds with any degree of insistence. So they have to lie to themselves to survive, believe in their hearts that they are elven kings, or great magicians, or a hundred other common fantasies that grow like thorns to choke the life out of those few individuals who truly have a claim on greatness. It's admirable that you resist the temptation to lie to yourself, because in my experience that's the hardest temptation to resist, and the rewards for doing so are nonexistent."

My royal bard suddenly looked like she wanted to kill me. "Were you born in splendid ignorance or is that just a result of your clerical education?" Aeren didn't exactly throw this question out in a burst of dragon thunder, but she came as close as was humanly possible. *"I want to lie to myself!* I *want* to have the luxury to believe I'm all sorts of things in the face of the gaping maw of reality, to take out my sword, if I had one, slay the world as it is, and live . . . *be* . . . become my own fantasies."

"Then why don't you?"

"Because I haven't earned it! Because I know better and once you know better, you can't!" She said this so loudly she woke my new illusionist. I now heard him pacing in his own rooms, down the hall from ours. We would all be in fine, sleep-deprived shape on the morrow.

I thought about mentioning that she had no problem attempting to pass herself off as a young man, but I remembered her reaction to Welm on that subject so I decided not to pursue it. Instead, I asked gently, "How will it improve matters if you kill Raen?"

"It will prove a point. It will prove to Raen, and to Ariana, and to anyone else who cares to notice, that pretense is a mortally danger-ous game. The last time I believed in myself, Zelar used that force to turn me into a dragon, remember? Don't you understand? The only time I ever became my own fantasy I got royally punished for it, excuse the pun. But Raen, he gets rewarded. By the same scorched-be-damned emperor."

"So why did you say that you both did and didn't want to kill him?"

"Because I wouldn't want to be killed for becoming my own fan-tasy, even if I could sacrifice my intellect long enough to do so. There is something unforgivably cruel about that. I will never forget turn-ing dragon. But I still think it is a crime against life and humanity to go through life pretending that you are something you're not. There's something unspeakably cruel there, too. If a man tells me he's the most learned wizard in the northern world, he scorched-be-damned better be so. Stealing my respect is worse than stealing my purse."

"Aeren. These are personal matters I cannot help you with, even if I wasn't tired and in need of slee—I mean solitude. You *are* a fan-tasy, if only you would see it, and there is no empty pretense about it.

I can see the dragon in you when you are angry, I felt the elven queen give me her birthright back there in the cave, and I can even see the young man whose pose you adopt in your garb like a prince-in-exile. And whatever happens, you are bard to Gondal's true king, to the only king, who, according to Welm, can embody ancient elvish power and grace. What need fantasies? Or, rather, you've earned your fantasies. Enjoy them with my blessing. They're real."

"Which means nobody will ever bloody recognize them! How real is that?"

"I can't follow you there, Aeren."

"Andans recognize boasting. Andans recognize blaring pretentiousness. Andans wouldn't know reality if it usurped the throne and destroyed them with the spirit-killing glance of an ugly fact. Nothing is real here. Not even Raen, their bloody so-called scorch-be-damned king. Take note, King Llewelyn, nothing is real until it is recognized as such. Not you, not me, not even the gods. I am not a royal bard until the people call me so. I am not even a young man unless perceived as one. Reality is as it is believed in, which is why people such as Raen wear the crown, and why, legitimate as your . . . as our . . . claim might be, you cannot find or feel the source of elvish power that all beautiful things draw their existence from. You will find and claim that when and if you are generally believed to be Gondal's king."

"Yes, bard, and if I can have some bloody rest, that day will come all the sooner."

She paused thoughtfully, as if she respected whatever answer I cared to give to her question. "So do *you* think I should kill Raen?"

"Only if you want to. If it's necessary. I don't care. Just leave me for now."

"As you will, my liege." She said this like she was a monarch dismissing me. Then she left in silent fury.

For the rest of the night I heard Aeren pacing her adjoining room and pounding her fist into the wall, obliterating my own strangely divided dreams.

 It took three days to obtain the promise of a hearing before the Assembly, a hearing that was duly scheduled for the following week. As Aeren had predicted, there wasn't a lot of interest in considering yet another claim to kingship, but there wasn't any interest in denying us the traditional Andan right to speak to the Assembly on any matter, especially since the exercise of such rights had become a point of pride and dull defiance of the new king. Aeren used her family background to wrangle for an afternoon when the full Assembly would be meeting, and Welm made himself useful by shapeshifting into chatty old Masgan and letting everybody in the city know that "the best claim he ever heard for the throne, yes it was" was going to be made. We thought it better if Welm did not appear publicly as himself yet, both because it would avoid premature questions and because old Masgan was free to tell people any number of exciting untruths we wouldn't be held accountable for to help us get a good turnout.

I stayed in the rooms Aeren and I were sharing, practicing with my weapons and preparing speech after speech for what would be one of the most important events of my dark, strange life. I also practiced my speeches with Aeren and Welm, so we would make no mistakes in telling the tale that would earn us a kingdom, or at least the right to lead a revolution against Raen.

One night while Aeren was out storming it around in the marketplace and Welm was in an unusually talkative mood, I paused in our preparations to say to him, "I would be most obliged with a truthful answer, illusionist. When I escaped from the castle in the Duchy of Walworth, I encountered all manner of strangeness. Light like sound, sound like tones of feeling, the world throbbing as if it had turned inside itself. And then the strangeness lost focus and faded into normality. Were you there? Do you know what I experienced?"

Welm scratched at his face and looked up from the speech I had given him to study. I knew that probing his mind was impossible, so I would have to content myself with weighing whatever he chose or didn't choose to tell me. "Yes, lad, I do. Sounds like you escaped through one of your own dreams, or nightmares. But what matter? You escaped."

I studied his face and, despite my knowledge of clerisy, got nowhere beyond his blandly pleasant expression. Welm was always impossible to read, even on the mundane level of his character. "I am not speaking poetry. Nothing in my knowledge of magical theory explains what I experienced. And neither does anything else in my life. Or in my nightmares and dreams, as you suggest."

"Then I can't help you, lad. Your story is your story, as they say in the Threlan courts."

I thought Welm's voice was a shade too smooth and easy, but I couldn't be certain if that was truly so, or merely my own eager curiosity playing havoc with my perceptions. I did know I would get no more information from him, or from anybody else in Anda, for the city was as insulated from the rest of the world as Aeren had told me that it was. I of course had questioned sweet Isulde when she crowned me in my dream, but as I said, her only response to my questions was laughter. Even my Goddess chose not to reveal any answers to me on that score, but as Hecate has nothing to do with fairy magic, Her silence was hardly surprising.

Well, there was much work to be done among the three of us before we addressed the Assembly, so I was not in a position to do much research concerning the manner of my escape. Aeren practiced her part of our story until she practically seemed to live it, Welm agreeably took up his part to my satisfaction, and I coordinated everything we had to say into an irresistible claim on my new people's fealty. I was certain that Raen must know something of our intent, and that Roguehan was not idly awaiting the outcome of my claim, but I was equally certain that my best approach was through the very citizens who resented this unworthy king being forced upon them. Hecate was with me, and so my heart was with Gondal and its crown. Nothing else was relevant.

I can't say I loved Gondal in the way I once loved Threle, my lord, but I can't say that I didn't."

Walworth wrote my line, and waited for me to continue. It was hard to speak my thoughts into the Northern night, but not because of the unmitigated chaos. It was simply difficult to accurately tell the court, to tell my judge, what I needed to say, because I couldn't find the words to say it. I realized that my last sentence was as contradictory as anything Aeren might have said, and I was suddenly startled at the sensation of the Northern night embracing my odd sentiments, at the fisherman unintentionally snoring in tight cadence to my words.

"Set this down. I loved Threle for its freedom, for its unmatched ability to be itself without compromise, for what it was. I loved Gondal for its promise of fairy song and the elvish power that graces all beautiful things, for its history of same, for what I dreamed it would become for me and for what I eagerly imagined it had been in its ancient past. I loved it for what it wasn't. I don't know which love was stronger, or more painful."

I looked up at Walworth, who was thoughtfully contemplating my words. I had thought he might show some reaction to my thoughts on Threle, and I was correct. A barely discernible softening of expression coupled with a hardened distant look in his eyes. For this moment he was not my judge, nor even the king he claimed to be. He was Mirand's student, puzzling out the philosophical implications of what I had just said, and finding them intriguing. He spoke with an uncharacteristic degree of emotion, his neutrality a sacrifice to whatever my words had forced him to contemplate. "Suppose I had the authority to try you under Gondish law. How would you fare?"

"I don't know which law I shall ultimately die for transgressing, or which treason I have committed. That against truth, or that against beauty. But as the poets say, perhaps they are the same. And in truth, your authority does not extend beyond Threle."

Walworth looked as if I had caught him in some painful, internal dilemma. His expression did not last longer than a second or two, but it was impossible for me to miss, and it was equally impossible for me not to relish.

"I forget myself." He was apologizing to me and speaking to himself and to the growling Northern hearth fire all at once. I also sensed that he was speaking to his dreams of Isulde. Dreams that held all answers, and gave none. He reassumed his assumption of neutrality. "You may continue your plea."

*W*e entered the Assembly Hall in an open afternoon, in a day of sharp winter sun and breathless understated promise that the pliant light of spring was gestating somewhere beyond the harshly blue and infinite Northern sky. We waited an hour to be seated before the prominent citizens of Anda and Arula, and before the commoners who crowded every available space and then some inside the large cold hall. Old Masgan, meaning Welm, had done his job better than well. Everyone knew there was going to be a challenge to the throne, and everyone had heard that this challenge had more substance than any other in recent history.

But I felt that there was more resentful anticipation than curiosity throbbing through the crowd. My strongest impression was that Aeren had spoken truth concerning her people. They sincerely wanted somebody to topple Raen, they just didn't want anybody in particular to do so. An imaginary revolutionary leader was all their style. A real leader might be tolerated if there was no other way to get the job done, but a real leader would also be greatly resented and most likely abandoned at the first available opportunity. Well, I would work with it. Hecate be my strength.

"Order down. Order down. Order down the moon and then stand up, oh gentle Assembly of Gondal." A portly elderly man chanted those words in a nasally singsong cadence as he ascended the raised platform near the front of the hall where we were seated and waved an unlit lantern in lazy indeterminable patterns to attract attention. His voice was thin and did not carry well, but the crowd stood up and then sat quietly to hear him. Aeren whispered to me that this was the traditional way to begin meetings of the Andan City Assembly, except that the word "Gondal" was now being substituted for "Anda", no doubt to reflect the combined nature of this new political body.

For someone who made a personal religion out of refusing any comfort she hadn't earned, Aeren seemed unexpectedly at ease here, almost, but not quite, relaxed. Welm, on the other hand, seemed brightly tense. I wasn't surprised so much by his alert discomfort as by his choosing not to mask his unease for the crowd. For myself, I was too intent on making a convincing argument to feel much of anything. I had prayed to Hecate that morning, and felt Her cold divine assurance that my crown was in Her hands. And that was all I cared to feel.

"Gentle Assembly," declaimed the elderly man, who had now abandoned his singsong cadence. "We have several items of business on this afternoon's agenda for your consideration and suffrage." The crowd looked bored, but then so did the speaker. Everyone remained silent, but it was a loudly impatient silence that I found more distracting than chatter. "First, Merry Magweave of All-Fine Linens and Weave seeks license to expand his shop around the corner of its present location. Second, Riana Dema Ryetonge, speaking for the Proud Guild of Andan Bakers and Breadmakers, would like to purchase some city-owned farmland for the guild to grow its own wheat and corn on. Third, we have proposals for entertainers to hire for Anda's Midsummer City Festival."

The crowd made an effort to look as if this last agenda item was no more important to them than selling a field to the local breadmakers, but I knew the looks I saw were lies, for I picked up a strange hodgepodge of anxious thoughts. Some, especially among the commoners, were local bards looking to be hired, and were here solely for that reason. They didn't care who was claiming the crown this week so long as they had a stage to play on. Others, mostly middle-aged women, didn't actually want any entertainers hired lest they compete with their august selves for attention, but they especially didn't want any female entertainers hired, and some were inwardly anxious and a touch spiteful about this. Many of the ladies had once had bardic proclivities that they had abandoned to raise children, and so they did not warmly welcome younger versions of themselves performing. Many of the men were actually a little embarrassed at having to show a preference concerning entertainers, but other men were as quietly resentful as the women. So everyone made a solid effort to appear not to care. Their silent duplicity is what passed for sophistication and class.

The speaker mentioned more business items that I now forget, and concluded by intoning, "And we are bound to hear and suffrage a formal claim to the ancient kingship of Gondal." He didn't even mention our names. I felt a goodly amount of anxious anticipation lurking in the crowd under the sudden burst of short laughs and sneers, but not as much agitation as I had sensed concerning which bards to hire for the festival. I also got the distinct impression that we were slated to speak last because nobody wanted me to confuse getting a hearing with having anything important to say. Anda truly was a strange place, but then, upon close acquaintance, what place isn't?

Merry Magweave was duly introduced and listened to. His proposal was discussed for the better part of an hour, with some Assembly members complaining that his shop was already too large and disparaging his products as "not exceptional" in favor of their own, which were all "the best." Others supported his petition for expansion because he was offering a goodly amount of money for the space. In the end, he got his license. And Riana Dema Ryetonge got her field, although it took another hour to negotiate a price.

All in all, the petitioners did get a fair hearing and, as far I could tell, any Assembly member who wished to speak on their requests was given the opportunity to do so. The commoners, however, were only allowed to observe and quietly comment among themselves. Anda clearly wasn't a dictatorship or anything, and I got no sense of repression, but I did sense that there was no clearly defined charter by which the Assembly governed, or any consistently held view of Anda's so-called traditional speech rights, which appeared to be exercised through rote and sentiment as opposed to through any specific legal guarantees. Whatever the majority of the Assembly voted on any given matter was law until the next matter. I wondered if Raen had any authority in these proceedings, but after observing for a few hours I got the impression that this Assembly's function was to dispose of business that was too trivial to bother him with.

After the guild mistress concluded her petition, the people were getting restless, but the elderly speaker mentioned that the issue of selecting bards was now at hand and that got everybody's flagging attention. The emotional undercurrent I felt with my wizard senses was exceedingly ugly, and almost worthy of the monks in Kursen Monastery. The speaker quickly read a list of about fifteen names that were greeted with either derisive hoots or subdued approval by the contingent of commoners. The Assembly itself remained aloof and neutral, and the female members in particular arched their necks and pointed their elegant noses toward the ceiling as if they were so compelled by whatever was out in distant space that they had no real interest in hearing the list.

Aeren nudged me and whispered cynically, "Here it comes."

The speaker concluded his presentation of the list, there was a tense space of silence, and a well-dressed middle-aged woman stood up to be recognized. No sooner did she have the floor than she began to whine angrily, "Who compiled that list? *I* don't recognize any of those names and *I* won't pass suffrage on someone that *I've* never heard of before." I knew from her thoughts that she had heard of most the names on the list and merely wanted to discredit the candidates, or the listmaker, or both. She was one of those who was secretly hoping that nobody would perform. There were plenty of nods of agreement, but there were also a few quick flashes of anger directed at her.

One of the flashes of anger had emanated from another well-dressed woman who stood and swayed her heavy weight around while bellowing for recognition. She was in such a hurry to speak, her words felt like a series of flung stones in the heat of battle. "My son, who is a *very* gifted storyteller, is a candidate on that list, and if my gentle colleague had any acquaintance with *any* local performers, she would have heard of him. His name is Dri Den Drien and he always fills a tavern."

Aeren rolled her eyes in annoyance as a man stood up and spoke loudly without bothering to ask to be recognized, "He always fills a tavern because *you* let him perform in yours on nights when there's a walk-in crowd anyway, and people get used to seeing him. Put him in a public commons, or in a tavern on an off-night, and he doesn't draw flame from a candle in his own right. No offense to Madam." Madam was already gasping and bobbing her head in offense, but the loud man kept speaking. "I propose we choose on merit and not on who has the advantage of being related to a tavern owner. Now I submit we choose Bara—"

Dri Den Dien's battle-ready mother interrupted without ceremony, "My *son* is very talented and everybody says so and other bards need to earn the right to perform before a crowd—"

"—How did your son earn it?" shouted another member. "People frequent your place for drinks on certain nights and you throw your boy up to a ready-made audience. Why don't we audition the applicants for the festival?"

Loud sighs from the rest of the Assembly. It was clear that nobody wanted to take the time to actually audition any of the bards in question, and so the decision would be based on factors that were far less time-consuming to evaluate than anyone's actual performance skills.

A truly obnoxious woman, who wore a thin, wary expression across her fat face, stood for recognition. "Why don't we hire someone who can entertain the chyuldruuuuuun?" She drew out the last word in an exceptionally smug tone of voice and waved her hands around, as if bringing children into the discussion was supposed to trump all other concerns. "It would be nice to do something for them." From my open wizard senses I could tell that she didn't give a good "scorch-be-damn," to quote one of Aeren's favorite expressions, about the children. She wholeheartedly regretted having burdened herself with offspring, and greatly resented the freedom her non-childed peers still had. She thought she might be able to curtail the prospects of the bards who wished to perform and undermine some of the adult merriment of the festival if she could convince the Assembly to turn it into a noisy, raucous children's event. "After all, isn't the festival supposed to be for the children?"

The elderly speaker on the platform answered her dryly. "Traditionally, the Midsummer City Festival is about honoring Anda's history." He suspected what she was up to and wanted no part of it.

She smiled patronizingly and bleated, "But *shouldn't* it be for the chyuldruuuun?"

Another woman stood up and repeated the question as if she considered herself exceptionally clever for doing so. Her agenda, best as I could read her passing thoughts, also had nothing to do with Anda's children and everything to do with undermining the bards. She was thinking that a children's entertainer would not be taken seriously by the other adults, and so hiring one would effectively prevent the lucky performing bard from getting too much praise and attention from anyone who mattered.

Her protests went nowhere, though, because another Assembly member suggested that no one should perform as it was too much trouble, and others argued that their sons and daughters were all very talented and no trouble at all, and some threatened to hold their own private festivals to compete with the city's, and others sought to sabotage anyone with a claim on talent by declaring that everyone who wanted to perform should be allowed to, and on and on and on until I began to feel heartily bad for Aeren and to sympathize with her explosive antagonism toward this city. I also remembered that Ellisand was from an elvish area of northern Gondal, and instantly understood why he rarely spoke of Gondal's cities and preferred to perform in Threle.

The discussion . . . I mean the broadly angry pride-fueled arguments, continued until after nightfall with no resolution except to table the issue until next time. At that point many of the commoners left, and an Assembly member proposed continuing business on the following afternoon. As there was scattered agreement to this proposal, the Assembly quickly recessed for the night.

"I'm not surprised," declared Aeren as we ambled back to our rooms. "They will delay consideration of your claim for as long as they possibly can, and when it does come up, we'll be lucky if there are three Assembly members awake enough to hear it."

Welm just cheerfully shrugged. It was odd how my illusionist and my bard usually had very little to say to each other, and had fallen into the habit of communicating through me. There was no antagonism between them, but it was always as if there was nothing else between them either.

"It will come up and the full Assembly will hear it," I responded confidently. "And I fully expect that it will cause as much havoc as choosing a bard for the festival."

I wasn't disappointed, and neither was Aeren. The hall was just as crowded and the people were just as anxious on the following afternoon. The discussion was just as heatedly petty concerning the bardic applicants for the festival because everyone was now fresh. But since no resolution was forthcoming, that item got tabled for discussion on yet another day.

"Given the time they devoted to arguing, they could have just held auditions after all," I whispered to Aeren.

"What? And actually have to pay attention to someone besides themselves?"

The remaining business items were "given suffrage," as they put it, relatively quickly, but there were so many of them that night was falling and people were quickly drifting away by the time they were all disposed of. I felt there was still general interest in hearing my claim, but this particular session had lasted two days now and many of the Assembly members had personal business to attend to, as did the commoners. Enthusiasm had waned with the afternoon light. There was a brief recess for people to take their sup before we were finally called up to the platform to speak, at which point only a dozen or so Assembly members remained, along with an equal number of commoners.

"Well, it's better than the audience of three you predicted," I said encouragingly to Aeren. She responded with a glowering dragon look as she took a seat behind me. Welm smiled and waved and put it on as if the hall was full of cheering supporters, and continued to make occasional friendly gestures from his chair next to Aeren.

I remained standing, and quickly surveyed my subjects. Two of the Assembly members were dozing. The rest looked like they wanted to do the same. About half of those were struggling against exhaustion and boredom to give me a fair hearing because they felt it was the right thing to do, while the others looked like they were only there because it was easier than getting up to go home. The commoners who remained were there for similar reasons.

So I was not to be taken seriously. So be it.

"Gentle Assembly of Gondal." I began my claim in a voice that was both entreating and respectful, as if I had nothing but their interests at heart. I noticed a supercilious-looking man raise his eyebrows and glance at a fellow Assembly member when he heard my accent, as if he found it most unfortunate. I didn't care.

"My name is Llewelyn. I am a priest of Athena, formally trained in Kursen Monastery in Kant, a duchy of Threle, after that formerly evil monastery was turned to goodness by its late high priest, El." My introduction made no impact. These events had not occurred in Anda, so nobody cared to understand them. "I have come to claim the ancient throne of Gondal, and to serve you by deposing the present puppet king and by restoring Gondal to its ancient splendor as a realm of elvish grace and power."

I felt a thrill of embarrassment when I said this, because it all sounded so grandiose. My supercilious listener looked blankly sarcastic, which elicited a few laughs from my tired audience. "To begin my tale at the beginning, I present Aeren here to you all. Aeren, whose father and grandfather many of you will remember as prominent Andan citizens, has convinced me through many proofs that her birthright was the Gondish throne. She will tell you how she freely gave that birthright to me." I smiled warmly at Aeren, who was understandably nervous about her part in the telling of the tale. As she rose to speak, I said, "And after Aeren has finished her tale, I shall have more to say concerning my claim."

Poor Aeren. As she took her place before the Assembly, the predominant impression I got from the members was a sense of impatient, high ridiculousness. They would listen to her tale because now they were bound to, but no one was willing to consider it carefully. They had already made up their minds in our disfavor.

Aeren drew a breath to speak and was rudely interrupted by a laughing Assembly member who stood for recognition. "Young lady," he said, "why are you dressed in male clothes like a wandering street performer? Is that part of your claim on the throne?"

The entire crowd, commoners included, exploded in derisive laughter. Aeren was not amused, but to her credit she conducted herself with a great deal of dignity. "I am a wandering street performer, and these clothes are my badge of office. I wear them because it amuses me to do so."

"It amuses us, too," jested the wit, who was greeted with howls of laughter.

"Why wasn't *your* name on the bardic list?" called out a brightly sarcastic woman. "I would think that if you were any good, *you* would be considered for the festival."

"As the new king's royal bard I would be delighted to perform at the festival," responded Aeren gravely. Her determinedly dignified response got more chuckles. "But now, gentle Assembly, I shall tell you a tale for judgment. Many of you knew my father, who had many wives and who was a member of Anda's Assembly for many years. Unlike those cowards who publicly pretend indifference to their heart's desire—" The crowd did not like the implication that they were cowards, and so their laughter dried up like a blasted fig. "—my father made no secret of his ambition to rule the city. I once considered his stories of his royal elvish heritage merely fiction to learn my craft from, but three years ago I was cruelly surprised . . ."

Aeren told her entire story without flinching, and with such bardic charm that the crowd was listening in spite of the lateness of the hour and their tired minds. They found her entertaining, but they didn't believe a word she said, and they shook their heads and laughed when she described having been turned into a dragon as if they considered it all a very good joke. I couldn't exactly blame them on that one, so I was content that they allowed her to finish speaking without further interruption. She finished her tale by proclaiming, "And so I freely gave my claim to Llewelyn in exchange for a position as his royal bard for life. If you find my claim was true, you are bound to accept him as your king."

The elderly speaker thanked her for her story and asked if I would speak again. I assented, and felt the energy in the room dropping as I stood to address my reluctant people. They clearly didn't expect that I would be as entertaining as Aeren had been.

"As my bard has told you, the goddess I serve endorsed the transfer of Aeren's birthright to me. But my bard didn't tell you that Athena led me to a secret armory that Aeren's captor, Master Wizard

Zelar, had stored against the day when he and Emperor Roguehan planned to invade Gondal by force. . . ." And so I told the Assembly the rest of my story, including how I had suspected that those weapons were intended for use against Gondal's cities and how I had magically rendered them useless to anyone besides myself, omitting the details of how I actually did it. I sensed that the Assembly found this interesting but not convincing. I had their attention but not their belief.

I silently congratulated myself that at least no one was laughing at my story, and then I invited Welm to speak of what he knew. Welm instantly held their attention by revealing that Roguehan himself had supported Raen's usurpation of the throne, which was a piece of information that none of them had any idea of until this moment. I could tell that many of them believed Welm on this score simply because they wanted to believe anything that would discredit Raen, but since they had all expressed such merry disbelief early on concerning myself and Aeren, no one was about to publicly admit that they believed Welm.

My illusionist concluded speaking and resumed his seat. The Assembly was quietly thoughtful, more thoughtful than any one member cared to be. Everyone was torn between wanting to make a joke about our story and wanting to believe that Raen was Roguehan's puppet that they now had a viable way to depose.

The speaker asked if any of the gentle members of the Assembly wished to speak. The supercilious man stood and asked for recognition.

"Let us assume that your tale be true," he said grandly, "just for the sake of argument." He was smiling sarcastically for the other Assembly members, who seemed relieved that he was taking the lead on this discussion, but at the same time he was seriously curious about Roguehan's relationship to Raen. "If this quorum was to vote to restore the monarchy with you on the throne . . . Llewelyn is it? . . . then how do you and your . . . friends here . . . propose to lead us against the forces of this . . . Emperor Roguehan? We have heard a little of him even here. Does he not have powerful armies and weapons? What can you do, no matter how well armed, against such a warlord?"

The Assembly was smiling because of course I look nothing like a seasoned fighter, and because my interlocutor had managed to make what he inwardly regarded as a serious question sound like a humorous insult. It didn't matter. I spoke confidently, "As I explained in the course of my story, my goddess has blessed me with access to

Master Wizard Zelar's name stone. I hold immense power over Roguehan's chief wizard, perhaps enough to dissuade him from attempting a magical war against Gondal. And if this gentle Assembly can provide me with the best magicians that Anda and Arula have to offer, I can defeat Raen's armed contingent by magically training our own forces in the use of my weapons."

"Which you claim to control through your alleged goddess, Athena," someone shouted like an accusation. "Why topple one despot only to put another on the throne, and a religious zealot at that? If you had our interests at heart, you would offer to democratically share the power you claim to have. Why not donate this wizard name stone to the city so we can all hold Zelar hostage?"

Ignoring the laughter that greeted her witticism, I gazed at her with the most gentle, concerned, respectful, courteous expression I could muster, all the while wanting to smash her bloody Andan pride to Hecate. "Gentle Madam, I fear that a war cannot be fought democratically. You, and this beautiful, this *best* of all cities, are in mortal danger of losing your enviable way of life to Emperor Roguehan. Welm here explained to you his plan to forcibly take the throne from his puppet king with the consent of this Assembly so that he might embody, in his very person, all of the ancient elvish power that resides in this land. He explained how Roguehan was instrumental in persuading Raen to create this joint Assembly specifically as a potential, organized point of opposition so that, unknown to Raen, the emperor could use it to ensure that his claim was lawful and recognized by the people. For only under such circumstances, the circumstances of legitimately owning the Gondish throne, would the power of this land reside in him."

"Yes, and what the scorch are *you* doing?" called out one of the other Assembly members. "If what you say be true, you're as good as acting the emperor's part." Everyone laughed and nodded vigorously as if they had me on that one.

Well, they certainly had a point. I prayed to Hecate to bless my tongue with the right words, and words came from my Lady in a surprising stream of passion. "Because Roguehan's allegiance is to evil." *Yes, as if mine wasn't, but I trusted Hecate to lead me here.* "I have had dealings with this emperor, and I can promise you that he will lay waste to the ancient spirit and loveliness of this land. Do you love stories? Music? Paintings? A well-wrought dance?"

They didn't. They loved the prestige and attention such things brought.

I ignored what my wizard senses were telling me and kept speaking. "The power, the attraction, the energy in any well-executed . . . I mean well-done . . . work of art has its source in the power that the elves once brought forth here in Gondal. The elves, your ancient forebears, left this spirit of attraction as a parting gift before they withdrew to their colonies, and every tale your bardic children tell, every work of human hands and mind that attracts the human heart, draws power from this gift. Even a lowly woodcarver at the far end of the world, if his art has charm, is channeling the energy the elves once blessed this land with. In Threle, where I have spent considerable years of my life, there is a proverb: 'Beauty is eternally Gondal's gift.' It is often the only thing Threlans know about Gondal."

The Assembly was quiet. I knew they were flattered, and that they were reacting to the novelty of hearing what foreigners thought of them.

"Roguehan knows this about Gondal, too. He knows this in his darkest dreams, and in the shadows of what passes for his heart. He knows that if he was to legitimately become king, become the true, lawfully recognized lord of this land, he would encompass the power source of all beautiful things in his very person. With the aid of his highly trained and extremely powerful wizards and clerics, he will plunge the world into ugliness, into a plain, awkward hell. And then, he alone will have access to that elvish energy, to create for himself whatever he pleases, to compel worship of himself, perhaps to create a new world in his own image, a world in which he alone controls all that makes life worth living, in which he would control the source of your every pleasure."

It was hard for me to articulate, even to myself, why the Andans should care, or why anybody should. All I know is that I did care. For the same reasons that I had always longed to hear the song of the water fairies, and loved the dreams Isulde sent me, and had taken a risk in saving Ellisand solely that he might play music again.

"Imagine with me a world in which an all-powerful, evil ruler will hold your very hearts hostage to whatever number of wasted years and lives he demands for his amusement. I would say you will live and die in slavery, except none of you will ever truly live under his rule. The world as we know it is at stake here, gentle Assembly, and you, should you pass suffrage to accept my claim, will be known as the heroes that saved that world."

This promise appealed to my audience for all of the ten seconds it took them to realize that being part of a collective of heroes brought no individual glory, and keeping the world free for this ancient elvish power to run where it willed might result in someone else getting individual glory for being able to channel that power into a great work of art. This was a cross and difficult group to persuade.

"The emperor will take joy in owning your considerable talents, and in drinking up your collective misery as you helplessly watch him destroy those same talents. None of you, none of your gifted and beautiful sons and daughters, will be able to tell stories or sing songs or weave great tapestries save in his court for his pleasure."

Wrong approach again! Aeren had warned me about that. My wizard senses now told me that every last member of the Assembly was now hoping that the emperor would arrive quickly and designate them and their children as one of the few who were worthy and talented enough to be valued in his court, "sharing the power" be damned. Being an imperial singer in a world of destruction greatly appealed to their strange fantasies of themselves, even though most of them had long given up their artistic proclivities in favor of running businesses and living through their children's accomplishments. They all thought they would make the cut because they were related to the right families, and that their true value and long-neglected talents would be known at last. One woman was daydreaming about how impressed her neighbors would be.

"But it won't be any of you that Roguehan keeps. He will bring his own people, and you will be treated as less than slaves. None of you will matter in the empire."

They weren't convinced. They were too much in love with the part about a new order coming in and lifting one of them above their fellows. This wasn't working. And yet this was clearly what Hecate wanted me to say, and so I had to trust Her.

Aeren rose and began to speak without ceremony. "Listen to Llewelyn. Roguehan will not honor or elevate any of you, no matter how exceptional you consider your own long-buried gifts." Leave it to Aeren to be blunt. "Remember how his wizard turned me into a dragon, how he flattered and used my ambitions, ambitions which many of you share for yourselves, to attempt to destroy me."

"So you've said," called out the sarcastic woman. "If you've nothing more to say, then sit down." If anyone believed Aeren, and best as I could tell none actually did because none actually wanted to, they didn't believe such a fate would befall them. They actually thought their neglected talents would save them, and many of them couldn't wait.

Hecate was around me, prodding me to speak again. I opened myself to the Goddess's inspiration. "As you have pointed out, I stand here before you with seemingly no different a motivation than

Roguehan himself. All you have are my words to judge me on, and your own experience of Raen's rule. But I promise you this. If you make me your king, we will overthrow Raen, and we will success-fully keep Roguehan out of Gondal. And I swear by this land and by my Goddess that I will give my life and power to protect *your* dreams, to protect Gondal's ancient heritage, the heritage that is and rightly should be the envy of the world. That is the only thing I can promise you. It is for you to decide if it matters."

They all considered this, but not with any degree of seriousness. Aeren spoke again. "If Roguehan invades Gondal, he might choose one among you as an honored favorite, or he might not. But he won't chose all of you. How lucky do you feel?"

I wished she would stop baiting the Assembly, but her honest haranguing had the unexpected effect of making them all suddenly nervous about themselves and their prospects. Aeren had them wor-ried that the emperor might favor a rival after all, and I immediately sensed that none of them would stand for that. A few people wavered briefly in our favor, or to be more accurate, in favor of keep-ing their own prospects as bright and open as possible. A few.

The sarcastic woman spoke up. "I understand your claim that by freeing this young woman of her alleged dragon form, you in effect killed a dragon, which in ancient times was required of our kings. A requirement I might add that Raen never fulfilled." There were many nods here. "But there were no witnesses to this event, and her story is difficult to believe. We see the weapons you brought with you for show and understand that you claim to have others. Perhaps . . . Welm is it? . . . speaks truth about the manner of Raen's, I refuse to call him king, dubious ascent to the throne and the source of his army's funding. It explains much. But my first question remains. Why replace one king with another? If . . . Llewelyn is it? . . . if you are sin-cere in your protestations of saving Gondal, of fighting to keep our ancient elvish heritage alive, of saving the world, as you put it, then why don't you just do it?"

"What? While the rest of you just watch?" complained Aeren.

The entire Assembly erupted into shouts of approval that drowned out Aeren's remark, which was just as well. Their gentle colleague had found a potential way to depose Raen without risk to themselves or to their obsessive concerns with status. Emboldened by public approval, the woman continued speaking through a broad, self-congratulatory smile. "It would be a service to Gondal to remove Raen from power. That is something nobody would dispute. He has used the magical forces at his command through his mercenary army to destroy the most powerful of Anda's and Arula's wizards so that we have no experienced magicians to stand against him. His forces then slaughtered those who offered protest." Everyone looked grim. "He claims to own our very businesses in name, and to have the power to change at whim anything that this Assembly passes suffrage on. He compels us to show reverence for his very person, contrary to our tradition that all who earn a place in the Assembly are of equal value."

"Equal value to what?" called out a commoner unexpectedly. The Assembly looked highly annoyed, but they ignored the disruption.

The woman continued. "I propose that we, as a quorum that represents the will of the people of Gondal, give suffrage in favor of allowing Llewelyn full freedom to depose Raen without interference on our part."

What? These jackanape Andans are willing to watch me depose their tyrant for them so long as they don't have to get involved?

"Should he be successful, then I propose we invite him to take his place alongside of us in this democratic Assembly."

Everyone loved this idea. Many were hoping that I did indeed have the firepower to take down Raen and his forces and thought that this was an excellent way for that to happen with minimal risk to themselves. *These people deserve their tyrant,* I thought as the Assembly unanimously voted not to stand in my way, congratulated themselves on their magnanimity, and formally closed the session by walking out.

"Don't look so surprised," lectured Aeren, as I incredulously watched the hall empty. "The more you want to save Gondal for the right reasons, the less likely you are to get support from anybody who matters. But that's true of most things, eh?"

"So what's plan two, lad?" asked Welm reasonably.

I thought about the strange, unexpected argument that Hecate had given me and that hadn't worked. I shrugged. "We save Gondal."

Welm laughed dryly. He appeared to be about as convinced as the Assembly was, meaning he seemed to very much want it to happen but wasn't sure how it could.

I packed up the wands I had brought for show, and said, "We have the people's authority, so to speak. But as it's now late, we are going back to our rooms and getting rest. That means you, too, Aeren. Tomorrow we strategize plan two and I'd like you to be thinking clearly."

"That could be dangerous." She grinned proudly.

When we left the hall, the city was as still and as dark as I'd ever seen it, and so quiet that our footsteps sounded like those of a small army as we walked the horse path that led from the entrance of the hall to the gate that opened on to the street. So when a shrill, panicked voice from somewhere behind us called out, "King, King," it startled me into suddenly turning and activating one of my wands as a precaution. "Get behind me," I softly ordered my companions, an order that neither of them saw fit to respect.

As the voice's owner approached through the darkness, I could see that he had absolutely no idea that I had a magical weapon under my cloak that was trained on him. I also ascertained that he was the same commoner who had annoyed the Assembly, and that he was so breathlessly eager to speak with us that it wouldn't matter to him if he did know he was a potential target. "King," he panted as he drew up to us. "If you want to overthrow Raen, then scorch to the seven darknesses the god-be-damned Assembly and I'll bring you to meet some people who'll support you in a thunderbeat. You've got weapons—" He could scarcely catch his breath. "—as viable a claim to the throne as any I've heard, and you're *not* related to any part of the goddess-be-damned Assembly, which is right by my heart." I said nothing as he choked on the cold air, but I kept my weapon at the ready. My mind probe told me he was unarmed and speaking truth, but I was remembering how Welm had fooled me concerning mind probes so I remained cautious. "We need weapons."

"Doesn't everybody?" I asked mildly.

The stranger smiled, which further delayed his ability to catch his breath, and sent him coughing again. I sensed that he was so fixated on whatever he needed to say that he had no idea of how to deal with breathing except as a physical impediment. But he finally recovered enough to say, "I am part of a large, organized resistance of Gondish commoners who would just as soon see Raen and the Assembly abolished in favor of restoring the Gondal of ancient times. Raen, the pretender, murdered my brother for protesting his rule. The Assembly is a joke. It legislates whatever it can to keep the wealthy in power and block the ascent of everyone else. To safeguard its own status it'll sell out our traditional rights and freedoms in a thunderbeat."

"What makes you think I wouldn't?" I don't know why I asked this, except that I was curious to see his reaction.

"Your open reverence for all things elvish. The way you taught the Assembly about the need to protect the sources of the ancient elvish power that still runs through our land. Fell on stone ears there because, frankly, all the bards in Anda pretty much suck the dragon egg dry when it comes to doing anything beautiful or worth hearing. Anyone with any real talent leaves this city, and what's left wouldn't know talent if their precious offspring and themselves were embarrassed with it. Now my brother was a real bard—"

"—Yes, I'm sure," I interrupted hurriedly, to avoid having to hear a lengthy brag. "Tell me about your fellow would-be revolutionaries."

"Reactionaries," he corrected me. "We want to restore Gondal to its ancient glory, under a real king. We are a Northern people and we value freedom. Even the Assembly honors our tradition of freedom in their awkward, inexpert way. In some ways. They respect speech rights, I'll give them that. But the ancient kings, they ruled to ensure that everybody had complete freedom. They put their power and resources into ensuring that nobody interfered with Gondal's citizens, as opposed to themselves interfering with their subjects' natural rights to keep in power. They slew dragons, and had close relationships to the gods, and they did embody the land."

"So I've heard."

"You've got the right words and if you truly have the right weapons, I've got the right fighters. Raen didn't get all the magicians. Besides, I happen to know that it was our power that helped you track your way down here through the wasteland."

That intrigued me. "All right—"

"—Ygresan D'an Fen." The man nodded. More times than was necessary, I thought. Being Andan, he was probably unused to making obeisance and so he overplayed it like he was flush with the discovery of a fun new game. He also thought it was radical and daring.

"All right, Ygresan. You've said enough to interest me, but I would prefer it if you continued to interest me back in our rooms, where it is more comfortable and private and conducive for planning revolutions."

"I should be most honored and pleased. King."

And so the four of us quickly made our way down the street and entered the inn. The woman who kept the place had retired for the night, and as we approached the stairs that led up to our rooms, the entire building felt emptier and quieter than the city had felt, as if the night's silence had taken a dive into whatever exists below silence. Something was wrong here, so wrong that even our new companion showed a sudden uneasiness. And then I felt a tug of magic against my chest, so strong and unmistakable that I stopped and whispered harshly to my companions, "Stay here."

To my surprise and relief, none of them offered resistance, and I got the sense that whatever I was picking up, Aeren was, too.

"Welm," I whispered. "Throw some illusion on me. Make me invisible."

He accommodated, which greatly impressed Ygresan, who opened his mouth and stared as I faded from sight. Aeren showed no reaction because she was now rigid with the recognition of whose magic she was feeling. I wizard-shielded myself and cautiously ascended the stairs alone. And there, down the hall, his concentration completely focused on how to puzzle through the triple clerical locks I had thrown across the door to my rooms, was Zelar himself.

Of course, you want your name stone and you want your weapons, I thought. I readied my wand, the one I had activated earlier as a precaution against Ygresan. It would be difficult to blast Zelar through my shield, even though the shield was somewhat weakened due to the illusion spell Welm had cast. I also wasn't certain to what extent my wizard shield would hold against Zelar if he knew of my presence, since I was the next best thing to a former apprentice. I drew a clerical shield around me as well, on the chance it would offer me some additional protection against his wizardry, although it was hard to say how much protection it might afford. I could now easily extend my wand outside of my shields and blast him. I had considered using a clerical blast, but I feared that it would also do damage to the building, and from the standpoint of pure aesthetics I wanted to kill this master wizard with what was essentially his own wizardry, passed through Mirand to me. It was sort of a gesture of respect. I confidently felt the power surging through the wand, hot and deadly. I knew that the instant I extended my weapon outside of my shields, it would gain visibility, so I was acutely aware that once I had made that decision, I would have to kill Zelar without hesitation.

And here I was, hesitating. For no good goddess-damned reason except that it was important to me to understand the implications of the murder I was about to commit. To that extent I was still Mirand's student. I coldly watched Zelar attempt to break my clerical locks, and fully felt the oddness that it was Mirand who linked us in a strange magical intimacy that neither of us sought. The irony that Mirand truly celebrated Athena and that here I was, a priest of Hecate, wearing Athena's robes for show, and readying myself to kill my master's teacher, also played briefly through my mind. Mirand's words came to me out of the past, out of the argument that we had once had concerning whether and how to kill Master Wizard Grendel: *Are you suggesting that "we" collaborate to send a fellow wizard to his death? What has he done to deserve your sentence?*

Grendel had invaded Threle with hostile intent, just as Zelar had established an armory in the Northern wastes with the hostile intent of invading Gondal. Zelar had wreaked a nightmarelike sentence on Aeren by using her talent and self-belief against her, an assault I considered no different in kind than Kursen's assault against Ellisand. He had probably had a hand in torturing and killing my . . . uh, one-time friends—although I didn't care to pursue how I felt about that one just at the moment.

I watched Zelar work his spells for what seemed like a long time. I was confident of his inability to detect me and of the impossibility of him breaking my clerical locks, so confident that I felt no need to rush my deliberations. He was a fellow wizard. He was evil like me, and we worshiped the same goddess. He clearly had regarded Mirand with some affection, for it was out of this affection that Zelar had wanted him on our side of the universe, had wanted to force him into an evil alignment. I could not destroy Zelar without fully recognizing that there had been a time in my life when I would have given anything for Mirand to regard me as such a favored apprentice, and how Mirand and I had first begun to grow distant over the issue of killing another evil wizard.

I would kill Zelar, that much I knew, but I would also know what I was killing, and why. And in fairness, in justice, so would he, or there would be something vital missing in the act of this particular murder that would torture me for the rest of my life. Because he had been Mirand's master, because we were colleagues of a sort, because his spirit would go to Hecate as mine one day would, because I had sensed in the cave that my magic started with him, I felt compelled to give him the opportunity to, in the end, understand his own demise.

I withdrew softly down the stairs and approached Welm with my finger to my lips. He of course could see me. The others saw his expression and quickly realized that I was back. I dropped both shields. "Welm," I whispered urgently, "drop the illusion and make me visible."

"You sure, lad?" He was whispering because I was.

Aeren went so quiet and tense when she heard my request that she was scarcely breathing. Ygresan looked confused, but he remained quiet because he sensed the tension in the air.

I nodded agreement to Welm's question. He looked puzzled, but he complied.

"Stay here and keep quiet," I whispered again, and returned slowly to the stairs, both of my shields back in place.

My mouth dry, my chest tighter than Aeren's eternal discomfort, my head buzzing louder than my memories of my apprenticeship and conversion to Hecate, my body heavy in my own evil, I slowly and quietly climbed to the top of stairs, caught sight of Zelar, and suddenly strode with loud heavy footsteps toward him to attract his attention. He saw that my wand was focused on him, so he instantly shielded himself and focused his wand on me. I was expecting him to do so.

"Are you looking for this by any chance?" I asked coldly in Botha as I pulled a conjured replica of his name stone out of my cloak. I had wanted to manifest the real name stone from out of my rooms, but using wizardry to do that through my own clerical lock and my shields was damn near impossible. In fact, that was the point of the clerical lock around my rooms, so Zelar couldn't simply manifest the stone himself should he attempt to get close enough to try. And since I was in such close physical proximity to the real stone, it would be impossible for him to determine that there was no power in the replica, even if I wasn't shielded. As it was, he would assume that he was feeling the power from his real stone, which was actually pulsating in my rooms, through my wizard shield because we were magically related and our shields were nearly open to each other. And since he knew no clerisy, he could have no idea that my clerical shield was also up. That was important, because a clerical shield might act to radically dampen a real name stone's energy, and that would cause Zelar to question why he could still feel the stone's vibrations, and then perhaps to determine that I only had a replica.

"No defenses, Master," I ordered. "Drop your shield and drop your wand. If you blast me, you blast your stone. And if I sense a feather's breath of magic around you, I'll blast your stone." I hoped between my threat and my shields that I would be able to avoid a mind probe.

Since I was shielded I wasn't certain as to whether Zelar actually did drop his shield, but as he gingerly laid his wand on the floor and gave it a light conciliatory push toward me, I had to assume that he had followed my other suggestion as well. He certainly seemed suddenly acquiescent enough for me to assume that he believed that he was utterly at my mercy, of which I had none. I moved close enough to him to roughly kick his wand out of the way, and it shattered into smoke and light and noise against the wall. "Excellent." I stepped back again, never once removing my gaze or the focus of my wand. I put the replica back in my cloak.

"What do you want?" asked Zelar nervously, although he was

making an admirable attempt to sound like he was in a position to make a deal. "You know there is much I could do for you if I chose—"

"—I want you to understand why I, Llewelyn, King of Gondal, sentence you to death. And I want that for myself, not for you. I want you to understand that you will not die for invading my country, although it is within my right to kill you for that."

"You're mad. But if you fancy yourself a king, perhaps I can arrange—"

"—I want you to know that I watched you for minutes, that I was obscured by invisibility as you struggled against my locks, and that I freely chose not to kill you without warning. I want you to consider that, and then to consider, in your last minutes of life, with all the strength of learning you've acquired through your lifelong study of wizardry, whether I was merciful."

"I would consider it merciful if you dropped your wand. There is of course much we might accomplish—"

"Silence!" I gestured a little with my wand and he stopped speaking. Then I called loudly, in Sarana, in a voice to wrench the dead to life, "*Aeren! Aeren, come to me now by order of your king! Now!*"

Zelar looked incredulous as he heard loud footsteps clumsily and slowly ascending the stairs, and even more so as Aeren herself came into view. But he didn't look as incredulous and scared as she did. She was so nerve-ridden at the sight of me holding Zelar captive that she could barely stay balanced as she gingerly walked toward me. She was obviously afraid of Zelar, and she seemed terrified that he might somehow escape and wreak damage on her.

"Aeren." I smiled encouragingly, and continued to speak in Sarana. "Royal bard of Gondal. Chief storyteller of my kingdom. Come here, bard. I have a gift for you. A token of my royal esteem."

She drew up next to me in great hesitation.

Zelar attempted to flatter her through a smile that was difficult for him keep up. "My onetime apprentice and bard—"

"—*Silence!* I don't want your words. I want hers. And I know you know enough Sarana to understand them."

Aeren was now utterly nerve-wrecked. I wanted her to be steady, but there was nothing that I could do under the circumstances to calm her, and I remembered the vow I had made to myself to honor Devon by never forcing Aeren's emotions against their own inclinations. If she was going to be terrified, well, that was understandable.

I took Aeren's cold, sweaty hand in my firm, dry one and placed it on the wand. "My bard, as you were once Master Zelar's apprentice, your magic has an evil source. You may never choose to embrace evil, or adopt an evil alignment, but you do have the ability to handle an evil wand without doing damage to yourself, especially since I am here to guide you. Have you ever used a wand before?"

She shook her head no.

"Yes, well, it is time for another lesson in wizardry then," I said grandly. "After all, we are all part of the same magical family here, so to speak." Zelar was now as visibly nervous as Aeren. "Breathe with me, Aeren, do you feel how I'm helping you to adjust your energy level to the wand's?" She nodded in the affirmative. "Good. Don't fight me, bard. Let me help you relax. Trust that I'm with you, locking your energy into this wand through mine. Feel that?" I dropped my shields to make things easier, and because they weren't necessary anymore.

"Yes," she said. Aeren was so tense it was difficult for me to solidify our connection, but after a minute or so I was successful.

"Now, I want you to feel something else. When you send your will through this magical weapon, you will be able to destroy whatever you choose. You will be freely choosing to kill whatever is in its path. Do you feel and understand that?"

She nodded in the affirmative.

"In your heart, bard?"

She nodded again.

Zelar was praying. It was almost funny. I interrupted him to say, "Master Zelar, I leave it entirely to my bard, whose life and creative energies you deliberately wasted for years, whose beautiful stories you fashioned into a curse against her very own life, to decide whether to execute you or to show you mercy. That is what my own sense of justice demands. And Aeren, in this matter I am your servant. If you send your will to blast him, I will assist."

"I always loved your stories, Aeren," said Zelar hopefully. "I can still help you—"

Aeren blasted him, and blasted him, and blasted him until I had to drop the wand and still she blasted him. His body jerked around and erupted in oozy holes and his spirit fled to Hecate and still she blasted him until the wand lost its charge. I was retching and shuddering with the death that was all around me, and so sick from being in close proximity to Zelar's corpse that I could barely see, but I think I somehow sensed that Welm and Ygresan had now entered the hall. I didn't care. The corpse's open wounds made me too sick to care, and it took some effort to struggle to my feet and make my way to the stairs in order to put distance between myself and the body that was lying like a mess of horror before the door to my rooms.

Aeren ran over to me before I could descend and looked me full in the face, appreciating that her execution of Zelar had somehow caused my sudden illness but not understanding why or how. There was a brightness in her eyes like a dragon's tears. I wiped one of her tears away with my thumb. For that moment we knew that we understood each other, and I knew that Aeren now sensed that my life had been as wasted as hers, and that she understood it so deeply that there would never be a need to speak of it. And from that knowledge, I also knew that someday she would heal me with her stories, that she alone of all bards had lived and earned the words that would reach into my pain. And then I silently remarked on how we physically resembled each other, on how she had deliberately based her bardic clothes on my Athenic disguise, how the male garb that she claimed revealed her true self reflected the clerical robes that I deliberately wore as a fiction to obscure mine.

She stared intently into the moment's intimacy before saying simply, "Thank you, my liege. Of such dark blessings is eternal friendship made."

Nineteen

Since travelers are rare in Anda, and we were the only guests in the inn, I wasn't particularly concerned about being discovered with Zelar's corpse, especially since I practically had a charter from the Assembly to engage in such revolutionary acts as killing Raen's supporters. But I was concerned about making the best use of this particular act, and I needed time to think before having to make explanations, especially since I hadn't yet decided on what sort of explanation to make, if any. Still gagging from my sickness, I broke from Aeren, dispersed the clerical locks on our rooms, and gratefully shielded myself with clerisy against all the death that was around me.

Welm made a gesture as if to ask whether I wanted him to drag the corpse inside, and I indicated that he should drag it into his own rooms. Ygresan made no move to help as he was clearly too unsettled to make a move to do anything, but as Welm managed the business all right on his own, it didn't matter. Aeren stayed close to me, avoiding the corpse and looking almost as uneasy as Ygresan, but for different, more self-reflective reasons.

Against my inclinations, I dropped my shield long enough to probe Ygresan's mind lightly and learn that the only reason he hadn't run away from us was that he was terrified that if he did so, I would either implicate him in Zelar's murder or kill him myself to prevent him from going to the authorities. I also discovered that he was extremely excited upon seeing my display of power, and that despite his fear, he was congratulating himself on having formed an alliance with me. Then I started getting queasy again with the death energy that was still dispersing through the hall, so I put my shield back up, recovered somewhat, and used my skill with clerisy to calm my frightened new companion.

"Ygresan." I spoke in an edgy voice meant to mirror his fears, as if I shared with him his horror of this situation and completely understood his discomfort. "Please." I gestured toward the open door to the rooms I shared with Aeren. "We have much of serious import to discuss concerning Raen and the future of Gondal. There is extensive assistance that you can give me . . . give us."

He stared hard at me and swallowed nervously. It was difficult for him to speak, and so he avoided having to respond to me by shifting his gaze toward Welm, who was now returning through the hall with a light bounce to his step as if he had just deposited nothing more gruesome than a sack of wheat.

"Your comrades." I kept my voice both respectful and urgent because I wanted to encourage Ygresan to feel important. There is nothing like suddenly feeling consequential to banish uncertainty. I also knew that his Andan pride would find the promise of self-importance so irresistible that it would transform his paralyzing fear into sensible caution, which would be far easier for me to work with. "Your fellow reactionary rebels. We need to discuss how much is prudent to tell them about this little adventure. Your advice is essential in this matter. I will hold it in the highest regard."

"*My* advice?" Ygresan sounded aghast, and his voice was as thin and breathless as a broken pan pipe. He clearly had no idea what to think or to do. He wanted to run. He wanted to stay. He was terrified of both options.

"That dead man you saw Welm here drag away," I said softly to calm him as much as possible, "was Emperor Roguehan's chief wizard, Zelar, his most important magical advisor." Ygresan glanced at Welm as if he could ascertain the truth of my words from him. Welm merely looked pleasantly solemn. "As I mentioned earlier, Roguehan is the real power behind Raen." Ygresan suddenly looked quietly excited, although he was obviously still unsure of himself and of me. I realized from his uncertainty that when it came to the blood and dirt of real revolutions, he was too far beyond himself to be useful. He believed in his cause, but he was splendidly unenlightened concerning the actual cost of his beliefs, and without realizing it he had, until now, regarded deposing a king as a sort of theoretical exercise. I hoped his fellow would-be fighters weren't equally confused by real life. I continued in my attempt to flatter and reassure him. "So please. Please come in. I'm sure you can understand that the four of us have much to consider."

"Unless you only want to play at leading a revolution while pretending that you are working to avenge your brother," interrupted Aeren coldly. "In which truth, you might as well go home now. Nobody cares."

Ygresan was utterly chagrined by Aeren's reproach, but he caught himself admirably, and said shakily, turning to me, "I'm yours, King. I'm yours." He was clearly more afraid of Aeren than of me. Then I realized that when he had ascended the stairs, he would have

seen Aeren blasting Zelar to eternity while I was temporarily incapacitated on the other side of the hall. That was just as well, as it
allowed me to assume a reassuring mask of reasonableness against
what he perceived as Aeren's dangerous instability. It was something
to work with.

In the relative darkness of the rooms I shared with Aeren, by the
light of a few candles that I lit with Hecate's force that I might know
the Goddess's presence during our discussion, we plotted how to
take the throne of Gondal and save the power that the elves once
graced its land with from Roguehan.

Welm spoke first and earnestly. "We've got a problem, lad. As you
told the Assembly, and as you've been telling us, one of your best
strategies at keeping the emperor out of Gondal was the ability you
had to threaten to destroy Zelar through his name stone. Now that,
not to put too fine a point upon it, you've lost your threat's effective-
ness, what do you suppose we can do to keep His Excellency out?"

Until that moment I hadn't considered this difficulty. Welm had
an excellent point, and by my measure it was nowhere near "too
fine." I dropped my shield, as it was no longer necessary, and took in
some long, slow, serious Goddess energy from the candles. Hecate
felt slightly warm to me tonight, which was unusual. I silently
blessed Her and silently considered Welm's question while my companions waited for me to speak. "As Roguehan needs the people to
lawfully recognize him as their king in order to make Gondal worth
his while, and as I've effectively prevented that by unknowingly
carrying out his plan and obtaining the people's consent, via the
Assembly, to dethrone Raen, perhaps it's a knave's question now as
to whether the emperor would come here. He's lost his opportunity
to become 'lord of the land' and take the ancient elvish power he
craves." I smiled confidently to encourage confidence in the others,
although I wasn't at all sure of my argument. It was something to say
for discussion's sake, to elicit useful responses.

"The people don't necessarily consider the Assembly to have the
authority to give consent in such matters," spoke Ygresan in a sincere attempt to helpful. He still sounded nervous, but I sensed that
he was also highly motivated to make himself useful, and that he
wanted my approval as a form of reassurance that he was throwing
his support to the right quarters. "Just so you know."

"And remember, lad, even the Assembly doesn't recognize your
claim. They merely promised you membership among their ranks,
should you be successful in overthrowing Raen."

"Is it a negotiable promise?" I wondered, looking to Ygresan.

"You can count on them keeping it, if that's what you mean." He responded eagerly because he thought that this was a subject he was uniquely qualified to help me on. Aeren nodded in quick agreement. "I have no doubt that should we overthrow Raen, the Assembly will honor its word. Our prominent citizens would much rather see you 'passing suffrage' among them than ruling over them."

"Point of cosmic order," I said easily, so as not to let on how utterly unable I was to address Welm's first question. "Aeren gave her claim to me, blessed by my Goddess, which in effect makes me king, makes me lord of this land. Welm here told me that Zelar would have been able to sense this power through his name stone when we made contact back in Aeren's cave. And yet, without the consent and validation of Gondal's people, a validation that Roguehan also seeks, I don't feel this power in myself. Nor did Aeren feel it in herself when she had it, by her own admission."

"That's the way of it, lad," said Welm cheerfully. "Think of it as a word game. Gondal has been a fictional kingdom for centuries, an illusion, if you will. As lord of the land, yes, you embody the land and Zelar sensed that because you and Aeren have wizard apprenticeship bonds to him. It wasn't hard for him to guess what had happened once you made that contact. However, for you, or the emperor, or even Aeren to truly be able to feel and make use of that power, the people of Gondal have to believe in it. But that belief need only be earned once. Once the people believe in you, the kingdom will exist, the monarchy will be restored, and the true king of Gondal will exist in every sense. You can't make an illusory kingdom real without that belief. That's why Raen has no real power beyond his little army."

I wondered why Welm now had a lengthy explanation for my near-royal condition, because the last time I had asked him about not feeling anything concerning the kingship, he had said he couldn't answer to it. I also thought that his careless mention of my apprenticeship bond with Zelar was sure to reveal to Ygresan that I was evil, but Ygresan looked deeply sympathetic, almost shocked on my behalf, when Welm said this.

"How terrible. How terrible for you, I'm sure. So Roguehan's chief wizard forced you into apprenticeship, as he did Aeren? It's no scorched wonder you . . . you . . ." He couldn't bring himself to say "wanted him killed." I noticed for the first time that Ygresan had innocent, naively kind eyes. "Well. I'm sure you're very grateful that you were not also made over into a dragon."

"Yes," I responded solemnly. "But my previous relationship with him is ancient and gone, and I have chosen another path."

Ygresan nodded as if to say he understood. I knew he didn't really understand, and was only trying to be kind, but I was grateful that he didn't suspect I was evil.

Aeren spoke unexpectedly and without a trace of her usual cynicism. "It's as I told you before, Llewelyn, nothing is real until it is recognized as such. Welm is right. Gondal is a scorched-be-damned word game, and there isn't a sharper light to put it in than that." She sounded like this was a sudden metaphor that she didn't want to let go of until she had played it through because she found it so perfect and right. Even Ygresan appeared to agree quietly with Welm's explanation as Aeren continued to elaborate on her thoughts.

"Here's how I see the word game, Llewelyn. Let's say you are the greatest storyteller in all the worlds. Let's say that characters live through you, worlds get birthed and burn in still air through the power of your words, and that there are moments when you feel you have no body because you have become pure language. But if you are unknown, very few people will listen to your tales, and none of them will believe in you. At best you will confuse them, because they've been told throughout their lives that only famous bards are truly skillful, and that all skillful bards acquire fame. As if no one deserving could ever get overlooked, or be unsuccessful at acquiring a reputation. At worst they will denigrate you for being both unknown and talented, disbelieving that a nobody like you could be that good, fearing that a nobody like you might show them up. And so are you truly a storyteller, or just another pretender to bardic talent? Because Beauty exists only when the beholder believes it does, not when the bard insists, no matter how skillful the bard.

"Now let's say you have no skill with words at all. But if your uncle owns a tavern and throws you to a ready-made audience, and people see you in the context of playing to a crowd, then you will be believed in as a storyteller even if you can barely string a plot together. And the energy of that belief will give you the power to perform better and the authority to call yourself a teller of tales. That is why the bard that wins a city award will have light in his step and in his eyes, and will glad-hand it around to all he meets, because the energy of that collective belief gives him the power to do so.

"The cruelty is when people confuse cause and effect and insist that the joyful bard won through being confident in himself, when the fact is that he's egregiously confident because he won. It's cruel because if you try to believe in yourself and conduct yourself like you are a serious bard when nobody believes in you, when you haven't got some popular tavern's seal of approval, *everybody* and their long-dead relatives are immediately on hand to remind you that you have no right to be a bard because they haven't heard of you before. Your stories and skill don't matter. The skill might be there, the talent might be exquisite, but you are not a bard in every sense until your society says you are. Not fair? Cruel? Scorch-be-damn right it's not fair but it's truth, and truth is seldom fair. 'Fair' happens when people bend truth to suit their own weaknesses. So right now you are king, but you are like a skillful bard telling stories to empty taverns. Of course it will be the same stories and the same skill when the people believe in you, but only then will you have full power from that belief."

Welm spoke again, as if he was making a serious endorsement of Aeren's extended metaphor. "And of course such collective belief would have been strengthened and consolidated for His Excellency if he had the opportunity to slay a dragon before the people, and of course the kingship requires more than just being believed. Taking Aeren's power by killing her would have been necessary. But as you've taken, been given, her power by killing her dragon form, you've fulfilled that necessity. And you are a priest, like the ancient kings, which the emperor of course is not. All that remains for you is the belief. Earn that and the crown is yours in all respects, lad."

"Depose Raen and you'll earn it," Ygresan assured me, in a voice that still begged approval.

"It seems to me that Roguehan has no way to earn that now," I mused. "So I wonder why Zelar was here?"

"You wonder?" asked Welm in uncharacteristic amazement before I had barely finished my question. "If I had to guess, I'd say Zelar was here on his own business, attempting to take back his name stone. Hard to say whether the emperor cared about that one way or another, but Zelar himself certainly knew it was in his inter- est to retrieve it whether or not His Excellency had plans to move against you. It's certain that the emperor knew you were going to address the Assembly, and he might even have had spies there, but the fact that he did nothing to prevent it tells me that there's nothing he can do, especially since you've now made it clear as to who put Raen on the throne. But as to my first concern. I suppose if you were to forgo your revolution, His Excellency might be able to undo the damage you've done. After all, he had plans to solidly counteract Raen's inevitable claims as to who put him power. If you were to step aside, lad, Gondal might yet belong to the empire. To keep the emperor out, you must dethrone Raen."

"All the more reason not to waver," I said. "Especially since once

I am king in every sense, I shall embody the very thing Roguehan wants more than anything. Better than possessing his chief wizard's name stone." Welm smiled broadly. So did I. Roguehan was practically defeated already, even if he did already own half the world. And there was no way I would cede to him the elvish power that was the source of the world's beauty and joy. There was more than personal ambition involved in my ascent to the throne. There was something merely personal, and therefore harder to abandon. "Even if Roguehan had proceeded according to his original plan, I doubt that he would get much farther than obtaining the dubious promise of an Assembly seat."

"True," responded the illusionist slowly. "You've got what he's worked and plotted his life for, lad, barring the people's consent. The power of the land is in you now, you just can't use it until the people of Gondal give their belief to the same, for Gondal is currently an illusory country. But should you overthrow their tyrant, you're likely to get that, too, the Assembly notwithstanding."

"The people would acknowledge you in a thunderbeat," agreed Ygresan, nodding vigorously.

"Roguehan won't get that belief if he invades Gondal without the excuse of overthrowing Raen. He would just be another pretender with no real claim on embodying the power of the land. He won't even have the true prince to kill in the form of a dragon to take power from."

"Yes," said Welm, "you've certainly put more mud in his plans, lad. His Excellency knows who now stands to be the real king of Gondal."

Then Hecate had blessed me indeed.

"Ygresan, how many fighters, and how many willing magicians, can you provide?"

"Tomorrow I can take you to our headquarters. Several hundred trusted men and women, perhaps more. Arula has a population of thousands, but most of them despise Raen and would welcome us. Some have escaped to join our resistance." He got greatly excited.

"Escaped?"

"Raen has Arula surrounded with his troops. He's turned a formerly free city into an armed fortress. Business gets conducted as usual inside the city walls, but the walls are guarded."

I looked at Welm for an explanation.

"As I explained, His Excellency did his best to make Raen unpopular. He didn't want anyone else leading a revolution against him until he was ready, and once he was ready he wanted to make it look good, like he was fighting hard to free Arula."

"So this should be an easy force to defeat?"

"With your armory it should be easy. A good fight, but easy," said Ygresan. "If we destroy the encampments outside of the walls, Arula will fall, the city will be grateful, and Raen will be deposed. The people of Anda and Arula, the real people, not the Assembly, will recognize you."

"Next order of business. Disposing of Zelar's body. Which reminds me—" I retrieved his name stone, which was now cracked and dead. The power source had died when the wizard did. "—since he came for this, he may have it." I spoke as if this was a solemn point of honor, a sadly necessary sign of respect given by a courteous victor to a worthy foe. Then I thought briefly of Mirand having learned wizardry from Zelar and realized that I was only feigning what I truly felt. It was strange to suddenly, without effort, find myself pretending to be what I truly was, but I had no time to dwell on that psychic curiosity. "It won't be long before one of Roguehan's people is able to search for this stone through a crystal and determine that Zelar is no more. Not that it should concern us."

"It would be a fair deal if we could remove the remains from my sleeping quarters soon," suggested Welm.

"Of course. I suppose we could show the Assembly what we've accomplished so far, but I suspect that won't be of much benefit in terms of gaining additional support. I could easily blast the corpse to nothing but there's chance that I'd end up doing collateral damage to your rooms, and there's no reason to make a mess." I smiled a jaunty little victory smile, as if we were all sharing a fine and private joke, and to my inward relief Ygresan smiled a little in return. "I suggest that you cloak the remains in invisibility. You and Aeren will carry them outside the city, I'll accompany you and blast a hole in the frozen ground for burial, and there an end." I thought it best not to volunteer Ygresan to handle the corpse, as he was only beginning to get used to the situation he had impetuously thrust himself in. "Ygresan may come or stay here as he pleases."

"I'd like to come," he said hesitantly. "I'd like to help if I can."

"I know a place where they bury pigs," said Aeren brightly.

"Excellent. Then we'll take a little night jaunt, return here, sleep if we can, and Ygresan will lead us to his troops on the morrow, fresh from the victory of this, our first battle."

I felt Hecate's lovely waning energy caress my spirit through the burning candles as all assented to my plan.

---

*E*pitaph. One of those candles was burning in the frozen ground, shedding pale Hecate's flame in distorted veins of light that webbed the snow and rocks and icebound trees. Burning with evil like a funny old star over the place where I had blasted a hole for the others to put the dead wizard in. Burning where I had placed his dead name stone. Burning where I had blasted the wounded dirt and ice to cover over the still invisible body of my dead ancestor. Burning and softly laughing to my spirit as I solemnly thanked Welm and Ygresan for their help and sent them back to the inn.

The candle was my touch, my show of oblique respect. I had buried fistfuls of moonlight in that grave, and ribbons of ice-covered tree shadow, and tattered pieces of words from old wizard spells that Mirand had once taught me. And I had prayed a silent prayer for the dead to Hecate, acknowledging that Zelar was one of Her own and commending his spirit to Her. But I felt nothing of his spirit. I sensed neither forgiveness nor vengeance nor even a distant neutrality. I only knew that he was dead.

Aeren and I remained alone in the shuddering pulsing candlelight that was Hecate's watchful presence. I heard an owl cry. *Athena's bird,* I thought ruefully, wondering if there was any spiritual significance to its presence or if it was merely an unintended act of nature.

Then I quenched the candle flame and there, in the chastity of the ensuing darkness, with only the moon and the dead trees for witness, Aeren and I kissed lightly.

*O*n the following day Ygresan eagerly took me to meet a morosely busy farmer named Relyr Ean Gransag, who ran a good-sized farmstead just north of the city and who didn't care to disguise the fact that he had no use for Ygresan. Ygresan zealously followed Relyr around his large property, enthusiastically chatting to the farmer's broad back as Relyr grunted responses and quietly focused on his winter tasks. I didn't need to use magic to sense that Relyr's busy demeanor was intended to show Ygresan that he had work to do and didn't care to be bothered in the middle of his day. Ygresan also sensed Relyr's busy diffidence, but that only made him nervously talk all the faster, as if he could make himself welcome and charm some friendliness into the farmer's disposition by increasing the cadence of his speech.

"So I came here in a thunderbeat, in less than a thunderbeat, as soon as I could, really, because I knew you would want to be the first—"

"—Fence needs repair," muttered Relyr, turning in midsentence to stride over to a small structure where he kept some building tools.

Ygresan ambled directly behind him. "You know it's really fine to be out here. Your place looks better than a newly washed egg, it does. So . . . are you planning another barley crop this year?" Ygresan was appeasingly polite, but he was also genuinely respectful. He wanted something, that was beyond obvious, but he was far more uneasy than manipulative about it.

"Haven't planted barley since Raen stole the throne," rebuked Relyr, surveying his snow-covered fields as if he was considering more essential matters. "Been busy."

"Yes, yes, by thunder you have," agreed Ygresan voraciously, nodding and increasing his pace to keep up with the farmer, who was now returning to work on his broken fence. Relyr had shown no curiosity concerning who I was, probably because he was truly too preoccupied to care. His indifference didn't bother me, but I could see that it was making Ygresan uncomfortable, and as a result, Ygresan was taking a goodly amount of time to make friendly chatter in the hope of smoothing his way before introducing me. But once he realized that his loquaciousness wasn't going to ease Relyr's manner, Ygresan swallowed hard, deliberately avoided my glance, and awkwardly introduced me as the new King of Gondal. Then he hesitantly asked for the use of one of the farmer's fields. "I don't suppose you have much need for it in the winter?"

Relyr kept hammering at a fence post as he responded curtly, "That last fellow you brought here, that fighter from Arula who claimed to have all sorts of weapons and expertise, was a drunkard and a liar." He tested the post and turned toward us. "And that strange woman who kept claiming direct royal elvish heritage was another. Greetings—" The farmer nodded curtly in my direction and then focused his complaints back on Ygresan. "—and then there was the scorched-off fool that got hold of some kind of wizard wand and took out himself, the wand, and a herd of goats."

Ygresan smiled in embarrassment. He had had previous adventures in reestablishing the monarchy.

"And now you've found this fellow from Threle says he can take out Raen's army." The man nodded in mock consideration. Given Ygresan's record, I couldn't exactly blame Relyr for having a few doubts.

"Not exactly," I corrected. "I've got the weapons. Supply me with the fighters and a few well-trained wizards and together we'll take down Raen and reestablish the rightful throne." I took out the wand I was carrying, quickly activated it, and blasted a clump of trees into a delicate storm of sparks. Relyr was suddenly dazzled, but being Andan, he didn't wish to let on that he was impressed with anything anybody else could do, so he deliberately looked away from the colorful swirls of destruction, adopted an overly casual tone of voice as if he saw this sort of thing all the time, and asked, as if he had any real power in the matter, "Why should we put you on the throne in Raen's place?"

"Because if Llewelyn delivers what he's promised, he's the only choice we've got," answered Ygresan before I could respond. Ygresan then eagerly related my speech before the Assembly and the nature of my claim to the throne, concluding his story by saying, "And the Assembly gave him complete authority to destroy Raen. I was there. So Llewelyn here will help legitimize our endeavors."

"What needs to be legitimized?" Relyr carped. "The Assembly knows about us. Raen has to know about us, too, how could he not? Everybody and their grandam's cow knows. Nobody takes us seriously enough to care to interfere." He made the latter remark a bit pointedly to Ygresan, as if he wanted to say that Ygresan wasn't much to take seriously. It surprised me that Relyr had nothing to say about the improbability of the stormdragon part of the story, but I sensed that he had heard so many improbabilities from Ygresan that he didn't care to chew over this one. His primary concern was Ygresan's inability to produce anything resembling a real rebellion. Whether I'd actually earned my claim to the crown by killing a stormdragon was nothing to him.

I produced the written charter that I had collected in the City Assembly Hall that morning on our way to this meeting. Relyr read it, and then said sanctimoniously, "Well. *If* you win against Raen, this paper merely guarantees you a seat in the Assembly with the rest of the dolts and dunderheads, which I suppose is nice and everything, but it's not the same as receiving the scorched-be-damned crown. Do you understand that?" The question was irritatingly condescending, mostly because he was pretending to be experienced in real politics but really knew nothing about them and because he felt a need to pretend that, despite my firepower, he was in a position to give me orders.

"*When* I win I won't need the Assembly's permission to take the crown." I grinned, aimed my wand at another distant clump of trees, and skillfully negated its existence. "Do you understand *that*?" I waved my hand toward the sparks and newly blackened stumps. "If the Gondish people would have the true monarchy restored, what care anybody for the bloody Assembly?"

Relyr had nothing to say.

"So we'd like to use your field as a training ground," explained Ygresan excitedly.

Relyr rubbed the stubble on his face and tried desperately to find a reason to refuse us. My mind probe told me that his strongest fear was that we might actually win the throne. He was afraid that he might have to conduct his farming business differently under a new regime, even though he genuinely wanted a new regime. Then I learned that he was basically just afraid that things would be generally different under a new king, even though he seriously wanted a new king. His thoughts contained almost as many non sequiturs as Aeren's, and I began to wonder if that was a common Andan trait. He liked supporting Ygresan's acquaintances because it put him in the center of a large social group that talked up his farm and bought his produce, he just didn't want to have to actually get too involved because he was also afraid that it might get found out that he didn't know anything about revolutions. He also, from what I could determine, considered Ygresan and his fellow reactionaries tolerably amusing and eccentric enough to break up his day, but had many reservations about their ability actually to manage a government if they ever stumbled their way into power. In other words, like all cowards, he thought too much about consequences to make decisions easily.

"You won't be obligated to do anything," I said earnestly. "Just let me train a few handpicked magical warriors, allow me to set up a command quarters, and I'll reward you handsomely when I take the throne. I'll pay rent for the privilege in gold." I showed him a few of my conjured coins.

That sealed the deal. None of Ygresan's friends had ever had the decency to offer him payment, much less gold. He took the coins. "You can use this field and that empty barn." He looked involuntarily at my wand. "That is, if you don't destroy it. If I get any complaints from the authorities, the deal's off."

"Thank you kindly," I responded, smiling.

"Thank you. Thank you. Thank you." Ygresan chorused. "See," he bragged to me as Relyr went off to work on another fence post, "I told you we'd get support. I told you we would." He sounded so thrilled and relieved that I didn't need a mind probe to tell me that Ygresan had been carrying serious doubts concerning whether Relyr would choose to cooperate. "Now wait until you meet the rebel army."

*T*he rebel army was both fictional and real. That is to say, it was never clear how much of it actually existed and how much of it was merely insisted upon by Ygresan and his friends, but it was obvious that the whole affair had more than a touch of Northern chaos about it.

Despite Ygresan's eager offer to take me to their "headquarters," there was no recognizably central location for the would-be rebel leaders to meet in and strategize. There weren't even recognizable leaders. Anyone who happened to experience a passing fit of ambition between breakfast and dinner might get his friends together to practice maneuvers in one of Relyr's fields, which was why Ygresan had taken me there in the first place. Relyr, despite his lack of active participation in various reactionary schemes, was viewed as a more or less central figure in the "Restoration" as it was called. But his fields were about as central as anything got.

The Restoration "forces" appeared to consist mainly of various informal groups that met in private dwellings whenever the mood hit to argue with each other about everything from the history of Andan coins to who knew the most words in ancient elvish. Everybody had an opinion on the meaning of the symbols that were allegedly engraved in the first king's crown and had spent copious amounts of time learning outdated methods of clothes- and weapon-making so that they could dress in ancient Gondish costumes and throw parties and claim to be monarchists, but nobody had any idea of the practicalities involved with actually restoring the monarchy, and few cared to know. Most of them viewed real life with strategic contempt. A few considered it an exciting new prospect.

I sometimes got the impression that the reactionaries would argue arcane matters so furiously only because they didn't know how to have real conversations, or because starting a heated intellectual debate with a stranger was considered a form of polite greeting. But I mostly sensed that every new conversation was considered a competitive event that took so much energy to win that there was none left for planning a real Restoration. Most of the reactionaries seemed to be more familiar and passionate about books and bards than about who was actually running the government, although there was no lack of opinions on the latter. But their garishly insistent passion for the arts took second position to their costumed exhibition of their personal fantasies. What need for tales of the elvish past when you and your friends can arbitrarily charm yourselves into believing that you *are* elves? And then get into excruciating arguments about it?

In fairness, it wasn't as if my new forces were effectively armed, so there wasn't a lot they could have done to attack Raen's defenses, but I had expected that there would be some focus on actually attaining their alleged goal. Many were in it merely because there was nothing better to do. Others disliked the Assembly even more than they disliked Raen, although when put to it, their reasons came down to disliking the attitude of certain Assembly members, and not necessarily the concept of having an Assembly to deal with civic concerns. But no one actually resented the Assembly enough to want to be part of it. They mostly just wanted to dress up in outdated clothes and play "Restore the King."

Of course, Roguehan's forces in Helas had merely been playing soldier, too, but these Gondish would-be rebels couldn't even get that far because nobody could agree on what a soldier actually was, and whether someone who had the poor taste to wear pieces of costumed clothing from different historical eras qualified to be in the game.

Aeren heartily despised them all. It took much work on my part to persuade her to keep her opinions of her countrymen a cherished secret between us.

Welm offered no opinion on the reactionaries, except to occasionally remark that illusion is illusion wherever you find it. It was hard to know what he thought. People generally liked him because he appeared to take them seriously. What is more irresistible than a stranger's endorsement?

Ygresan lived in a constant state of excitement and very much enjoyed the status of having discovered me "first," although he sometimes seemed embarrassed by the insistently rigid decadence of his comrades and would sometimes apologize to me for perceived excesses.

The only way I was able to maintain a suggestion of organization among my new forces was to appeal to their Andan pride whenever and wherever possible. I consoled. I flattered. I pretended to carry a foreigner's humility concerning all things Gondish. I used mind probes to ascertain people's strongest desires, and clerisy to get key individuals to bond with me whenever necessary. If a repulsive woman insisted she was a North Country fairy, I gallantly treated her as such and claimed that her beauty blinded my eyes. If a desperately incompetent tailor's son claimed that his dreams told him that he spent other lives winning important battles, I cheerfully called him "General" and pretended to value his opinions. I mentioned once that I had spent considerable time in Sunnashiven and in what was once the Duchy of Helas, which encouraged several people to brag to me in clumsily memorized, simple textbook sentences that they spoke fluent Botha. So I always made sure to converse with them in my native language and to tell them how well they spoke, even if their accents often made me wince. And of course anyone with artistic pretensions got as much empty praise from me as a false god might get from an aspiring dedicant to priesthood, even if it meant staying up until midnight to verbally caress some young reactionary's unimpressive sketchbook.

I understood that the only way my people would believe in me, would crown me king, was if they discovered that they could become their own fantastic versions of themselves in my presence, was if they knew that I would feed and clothe them in their fantasies like fine-spun gold out of ancient elvish dreams. Nobody, except maybe tortured-to-the-core cynics like Aeren, can resist someone who pretends to see them as they wish to be seen. If done right, it usually pays for any resentment that accompanies a perceived difference in status.

And so my first practical adventure in statecraft was obtaining my new people's passionate loyalty under false pretenses, under a mundane form of illusion, if you will.

And they loved me for it. Genuinely loved me for it. Loved me for my lies.

And I had no guilt.

This illusory bonding was more important than I first realized. Raen, or more likely Roguehan's people, had killed so many wizards that very few remained in Anda, and those I met were not particularly powerful or competent. None were recognizably evil. Since my weapons could be used only by evil wizards, or by apprentices like Aeren whose magic had an evil source, I had reason to believe that it would be the gods' own difficulty working out a way to arm my magical warriors. Gaining some trust and affection from them was therefore becoming vitally important, because it might be a useful step in addressing this problem.

I was discussing this matter with Aeren and Welm one night in Relyr's barn, which I had formally dubbed my "command quarters." As Relyr used this barn to house his temporary help during harvest season, the interior was a large, decently furnished living quarters that made the outside seem like a shabby, worn-out mask in need of repair. But then, there was a stroke of fantasy in most of the hidden corners of Gondal. I had learned to see fantasy lurking impatiently behind the fearful scratching-for-perfection neutrality that shrouded most of the buildings in Anda, so the barn's distinct duality felt more natural than surprising. Ygresan had been extremely helpful in getting the three of us settled, and in making sure that anybody who had anything to do with the Restoration had been introduced to me and given an opportunity to brag, boast, and share whatever useful information he or she had about Raen and his army. Now that I had spent a few weeks gathering as much intelligence as there was to gather, it was time to caucus with Aeren and Welm about strategy. And since my evil alignment and the use of my weapons was one of the issues that needed discussion, I had waited until Ygresan retired to his home for the night to call this meeting with my advisors.

I adopted a tone of resolute confidence. "From the intelligence I've received so far, I'm convinced that we can free Arula with half a dozen well-armed wizard warriors. Our soldiers, such as they are, should then have nothing more difficult on their hands than cleaning up the carnage. If they can manage that without undue debate," I added wryly.

Aeren laughed darkly.

"Of course, selecting half a dozen Andan wizards with an allegiance to evil who can safely use my weapons is our first order of business."

"And our last," said Welm. "Unless your confidence in the Restoration forces exceeds mine."

Welm looked both decidedly cynical and absolutely open to whatever would come. His eternal neutrality vexed me, but there was nothing I could do about it. His mind was still thoroughly locked against my probes. I knew that, because I had quietly attempted several mind probes during the course of our acquaintance, with no success. I had even prayed to Hecate about it, but my Lady gave me no answers, which led me to believe that there weren't any answers to give, and so to hope that I was vexed for nothing.

I spoke again, in words that came out of my monastic training and sounded strange in the mouth of a would-be military commander. "I suppose there is a certain aesthetic rightness in leading a 'play army' to restore an illusory kingdom like Gondal. The Restoration forces aren't much, but perhaps they are consummately right for the job."

Welm gracefully shrugged and briefly curled his lip into a half smile before looking considerately serious again.

"But of the dozen or so self-styled 'wizards' we've met, none of them impress me as having any actual magical competence. Collectively they are able to raise a good deal of power, which was a help to

Aeren and me when we rode across the wasteland to Anda, although I'm convinced that the magic I felt existed as a fortuitous accident and not as an intentional flag to us. It was too unstable to be useful for anything. We were probably tracking some group's private brag session. None of the wizards I met have undergone any disciplined formal training."

Aeren spoke up. "Well, Gondal is so isolated it isn't as if there's a run on master wizards, and it's clear that anyone with real skill was executed by Raen's people."

"Some of whom would have had to be magical adepts themselves, to pull that off." It was vital to know what kind of magical forces Rogeuhan had provided Raen with.

I glanced questioningly at Welm, who flashed me a tight smile, and said, "You can count on Roguehan providing the best people for the job, lad. That's all I can say."

Aeren spoke again. "Here's what I know about our local practitioners of magic. Some are, or were before the purge, quite skilled. But all are self-taught. No Gondish wizard would sully his pride by having to claim that he ever apprenticed with anybody. Magic forbid, eh?"

I considered. More Northern chaos, wrecked up with Andan pride. How to use it to my advantage?

Aeren kept speaking. "For that reason it's a darkly burnt guess how much power Roguehan's formally trained wizards would have needed to use against Anda's blustering dilettantes. My guess is not much."

"The laddie speaks truth," added Welm slowly. "I suspect that most of Anda's and Arula's wizards were easily dispatched with."

"Despite the fact that they all like to imply that they were born knowing magic," Aeren couldn't resist adding. "Like that woman we interviewed yesterday who kept claiming that she was reading symbols and solving complex mathematical problems when she was less than a year old. Please! That fool of a girl didn't know any more about magic than I do, but she sure knew how to boast about it, eh?"

"Yes," I responded impatiently, "but her attitude is irrelevant. We need to consider how to best use what abilities she and the others do have, and what sort of abilities we are up against."

Aeren sighed loudly. "Attitude, hers and everybody else's, *is* everything. And that's the major problem with Gondal, or don't you see that? Gondal is nothing but a scorched-be-damned attitude. Nothing is real here. The so-called wizards around here are all happy to cat about each other behind their fancy robes and demand praise for their intellectual abilities while whining to the Assembly for special jobs and favors, but none of them have the discipline or inclination to undergo rigorous magical training from anybody else. That's why there are plenty of low-level magicians in Gondal, because everybody feels entitled to read a few books, make up their own systems, and run with the brag for the rest of their defiantly tawdry lives. But nobody has a name stone, or a magical lineage, or a recognizable claim on being a true master, so it's a scorched-be-damned job determining what anybody really *can* do."

"Well, I only have one out of those three qualifications," I offered cheerfully. "I can't condemn anyone for working outside the system, or I'd have to condemn the entire Restoration." I smiled, and Welm laughed softly and unexpectedly at my joke. "But what do you think of this? There is no organized religion in Gondal, not since the last priest-king abandoned the throne. Private worship is practically nonexistent—"

"—*is* nonexistent," interrupted Aeren. "Andans have read all about the gods, and claim to know everything about them in the same way that they claim to know everything about everything. But Andans don't think in terms of worship for the same reasons that Andan wizards don't apprentice with a master who might know more than they do. Worshiping perfection is a blow to one's pride, if you think about it. And believe me, Andans will think about it. Constantly."

"So you'd be hard-pressed to find a wizard or anybody else with a special relationship to any deity, good or evil?" I already knew the answer to this but confirmation couldn't hurt.

Aeren nodded.

"Well, then, that's a help to us. It means that no one is capable of determining that I'm evil."

"Probably not," conceded Aeren. "Although I'm not sure if anybody around here would necessarily care."

"The wizards I spoke with had the gods' own need of formal training." I considered this fact for a space before continuing. "In any other context, in any other country, I'd hesitate to even call most of them wizards, for that reason. The oddness of it is that I would have thought there would be more fear and hesitancy to openly call yourself a wizard *after* Raen's little purge. But that only seems to have attracted more pretenders to the profession. And since Raen only wanted to destroy the best and brightest, what does that make those who were left out of the bloodshed?"

"Indignant," said Aeren.

"Exactly. Most of them were more than eager to let me know

how they were almost killed too, or would have been killed if they had been home that day. Everybody greatly resents the dead. The fact is, none of the self-proclaimed wizards I met were powerful enough to be worth killing. A few have natural power, but none know what to do with it beyond memorizing some formulas out of books as a basis for playing around with magic. They confuse technique with theory."

"So does everyone else in Gondal. The Assembly doesn't even have a consistent legal theory it governs by. It applies the traditional rights because they are traditional, not because anybody has a moon's old dream as to how and where those rights derive from. The wizards are no different when they apply magic."

"Yes. So here's my proposal. Call it my blood coin to the screaming pride of those who were not worth an assassin's attention. Perhaps the half dozen magically weakest and least focused 'wizards' would do well as our . . . inner guard. An elite magical force specially trained to take down Raen's army. And as . . . shall we say . . . a special initiation into our secret training, let's say I wrench the weak sources of their weak power over to my side of the universe, and then personally train each one of them to safely destroy the pretender king's forces with my weapons. Would they even be able to tell what had been done to them?" I deliberated on this question. "Would my new apprentices recognize evil if it embraced them unawares?"

"*Can* you be evil without knowing it, lad?" Welm sounded uncharacteristically curious, almost tense.

I looked at the waning moon scarred in my palm, the mark that had prophesied my career long before I had become acquainted with anything that was to matter in my life. "Yes. I believe you can."

"But can *you* train someone to be evil without them knowing it? You never took a name stone or became a master of wizardry. You're not much better than self-taught in that branch of magic yourself. Not that I'm doubting your abilities, lad." Welm's voice was nevertheless smoothly weighted with doubt, which had the effect of causing me to feel a little uncertain. "I'm just playing my role of loyal advisor and making sure you don't overestimate your limits."

"Noted. Of course a cleric has to choose freely to become evil. There is no other way. But wizardry is different. Wizardry is manipulating energy as it is manifested here in the world, removed from its divine source, the gods themselves. Anyone with ability can be trained to draw consistently from evil energies, from the universal backward current that washes out of Habundia Christus's womb and into the mundane world. I'm confident that I can teach them to shape that eternal decay, to convert that infinite downward spiral into their own personal power, and so to align themselves with evil and safely wield my weapons."

Welm looked solidly unconvinced. "That will be the gods' own work, lad, but perhaps you know best." The uncertainty in his voice caused Aeren to look doubtfully at me.

"Do you have a better suggestion?" I asked cheerfully, hoping that he did.

Welm paused, pursing his lips as if he was deeply considering all aspects of my proposal. "No," he said simply, but in a tone that implied that he lacked confidence in the viability of my plan. "But if you think our best option is to put our magically weakest comrades in essential positions, perhaps you would consider it a necessary advantage to send someone, say myself, to get a firsthand look at what's guarding Arula right now? I could slip in invisibly, do some eavesdropping, bring back what's useful?"

I considered. Welm's proposal made sense, and under the circumstances, we certainly needed every potential advantage, but I would have no way to verify his report. I thought of sending Aeren with him, but I needed her here to train with my new apprentices. Yet a fresh report on Arula's defenses, especially on the magical ones, would be invaluable. "Agreed. But bring Ygresan with you. You can cloak him in invisibility too, and I'd like to have the perspective of someone from this area. I'll need Aeren to stay here and assist me."

"Sensible," commented Welm. "That will certainly help matters." He sounded a shade or two less doubtful.

I dismissed them both to their private areas of the barn. Welm immediately retired to his and closed his door but Aeren ignored my command. She strode across the living area, sat by a small window, and stared balefully out at the Gondish darkness.

"Let me guess, bard." I put a wide generosity in my voice. "You still want to kill Raen."

She shrugged tensely. "I want to kill everybody. Now that you've met a fair number of Gondish people, King, tell me again why this place is worth saving."

I laughed. "Why are your tales worth telling? Why is a fairy song worth fighting for?"

She stared out at the darkness and sighed. "My tales. Everybody in Anda, everybody in Gondal, tells tales and makes music. Returning here and meeting so many of my fellow Andans has been a scorching reminder of how little anybody's tales do matter. Tales are cheap and plentiful, and why anybody who spends more than two days here thinks telling them is a special talent worth gold and acclaim is beyond my understanding." She jumped up from her seat by the window and faced me like a harsh accusation. "Why aren't you embarrassed? I am."

"Embarrassed by what?"

"Look around, King. The biggest threat to the source of elvish power, to the ancient energy of this land, isn't Roguehan. It's the Gondish people themselves, who practice a legal system by rote, and magic by the book, and pride themselves on an isolationist chauvinism based on an elvish heritage that disappeared into the Northern wastes centuries ago! And look at how they've debased what beauty and art might occasionally get created by sacrificing it all to their ravenously empty pride. It's beyond insane. Here's how much your subjects 'love' the arts, and care about defending the ancient source of inspiration that this land holds. At one point in ancient history, all of the creative endeavors, singing and storytelling and whatnot, belonged to the elves. And then to a few humans, who got a certain status out of it for its rarity. And then everybody wanted the status, and everybody discovered that creating stuff isn't all that hard. You don't need a license or anything, and most people can't tell quality work from hack jobs. Worse, most find quality work boring if it demands too much thought. So everybody and their ugly get are now bards, but nobody wants to give up the need for status. How do you give status to someone who does the same damn thing everybody else does? Well, you decide who's related to the most powerful families, who's got the most gold to finance themselves with, whatever. So status now has only an accidental relationship with talent. Sometimes talented people get recognized and sometimes they don't. But as nobody can admit this, those that don't get recognized live in quiet little hells, rightfully resenting the world."

"But Aeren, one could argue that *is* the world, and not just Gondal. Anybody who believes hard work and talent is always rewarded isn't paying attention. But to your first point. Why do you think I should be embarrassed?"

"Because by your indiscriminate praise of everybody that waves a sketchbook or a lute in front of your cloak, you encourage the confusion."

"Aeren, you do understand how that praise is merely strategic?"

"I understand how that 'strategy' as you call it helps to weaken the elvish power you claim to want to save. If some goddess-awful half-articulate 'bard' earns your respect, however feigned, what's left for someone with real talent? What does being your royal bard mean? Every time you bob your head to one of these oafs and carve praise into a gilded monument to their failed lives, you do Roguehan's job for him. You wield flattery like a double-edge sword. Even if you are just acting."

"Do you think I'll get the throne with the people's endorsement if I don't praise all the oafs, as you put it? No matter how skillful a ruler I might be, skill alone won't get me farther than your stories got you. Nobody crowns kings for skill."

"I think it was Zelar's 'strategic' praise of my tales, and my desperation at not seeing any way to achieve success through the political morass of Anda, that nearly destroyed me in the first place. Zelar strategically praised me to help Roguehan to Gondal's throne. When you're throwing your strategic praise around the neighborhood, remember that."

"Yes, Aeren." I sighed. "I'm sure you won't let me forget. I suppose I am cheapening the meaning of elvish power, but sometimes it's necessary to destroy in order to save."

"Spoken like a true devotee of Hecate." She got off the window seat and stormed off to her private area, slamming the door.

I remained behind, meditating on the hearth fire, considering the wavering shadows and uneasy firelight in my command quarters and sifting through the private implications of my current status. I was the almost-King of Gondal, the would-be protector of the ancient grace and light of the elves. Out of deference to my having inadvertently killed Devon, whose affections I had forced as surely as I was forcing the Gondish people's, I had made a solemn vow to refuse to force Aeren's. And as a result of this vow, I had also decided not to probe her mind or work magic on her without her consent. That was true respect, not flattery, although Aeren was in no position to know that. And of course I was unable to read Welm, my illusionist, no matter how hard I tried. So I needed to make strategic decisions based on guesses, on my own best-thought-out illusions. So what if I found it expedient to insist that awkwardness was grace?

All right. Aeren had a point, but I didn't care to pursue it. I remained alone in light and shadow, praying to Hecate for guidance. There had to be a poem, a meaning, an importance in that somewhere, but I'll be blessed if I knew what it was.

T chose my new apprentices based on their lack of ability. They did not know that, of course. I devised a point system which allowed marginally competent wizards to make the grade if their competence was mitigated by an especially overweening pride that I could flatter into submission. But what I generally found was that the least competent individuals invariably had the highest self-regard, so I ended up selecting the magically weakest ones anyway.

On the morning following my discussion with Aeren, I took a leisurely, solitary tea and compiled my list of losers. Then I strolled around the city and personally invited each one of my new candidates for glory to attend an exclusive, private, evening reception with me in Relyr's barn. I mean, in my command quarters.

That evening, before my unsuspecting new pets arrived, I uncovered and activated the Mirror of Transformations. Its polished surface was glowing a little in the low firelight, like a suggestion of rainbow against a rainy sky when you sense, rather than see, a brightness against infinite dark space. I waited, feeling my power, my wizardry, running through me like a darker space. It was both an act of blessed remembrance and an act of focusing my power. For this evening I would limit myself to the mundane manifestations of divine energy, to the world energies that are the province of wizardry. Hecate would not, and could not, be my guide.

I was grateful to be alone. I wasn't entirely certain that my wizardry was up to my intent, and so it was vital to be able to concentrate without the distractions of Aeren's verbal jabs and Welm's disconcerting neutrality. Welm had left that morning to find Ygresan and do reconnaissance in Arula. Aeren had chosen to remain by herself in her private area, as she did not wish to be present when I flattered and wrenched my new students into a permanent relationship with evil. She said my tactics reminded her too much of Zelar's.

As each of my honored guests straggled in, I rose and offered pleasant greetings, which were invariably returned with a self-conscious stare and a loud, deep-voiced complaint concerning how far it was to walk to Relyr's farm and how difficult I had made things by issuing invitations at such short notice. They all had very important things that they needed to be doing, excruciatingly magical lives that I was of course imposing upon, but they all showed up flushed with the flattery of having been personally invited to the would-be king's living quarters, and they all found the air of secrecy I had set up surrounding this meeting irresistible. I knew that none of them would miss it for all the gold they couldn't conjure.

I also knew that their complaints weren't exactly complaints in the straight sense so much as beggar's greetings, twisted acting meant to con as much respect out of me as the moment would bear. My guests were complaining to show that they felt familiar enough with me to favor me with tales of their alleged distress, and because they thought I would be impressed. Basically, they all liked me. Maybe on some deep level they even needed me, because I had been so exquisitely effective in my feigned respect for their limited abilities. It was sad in its way, but around me they felt and believed themselves to be powerful. And that was how I wanted it. That piece of mundane illusion was more important than anything else in the awful magic I was planning to work that night, and more powerful than any magical illusion that Welm could have cast.

I greeted the women with light, friendly hugs, and the men with firmly friendly words. "Welcome and be blessed! Welcome, welcome all! Be your blessings dark or bright, you are most welcome! Please, please be comfortable. Thank you, thank you, for attending my little gathering."

"So," breathed a smiling woman with a deep voice and an annoying air of knowing all about whatever I was going to say before I even thought to say it, "why are we here, Llewelyn?"

I adopted a very serious, semientreating expression, as if my guests were the keepers of all magical knowledge and were doing me the greatest service by merely showing up at my humble abode. "Because the Restoration depends on you. Because I have made it my business to evaluate everyone in Anda with any magical experience, and it is beyond clear that you are the best magicians in Gondal. I am so grateful to my Goddess Athena that She has led me to choose such impressive magical warriors. I am so blessed." I really put it on for them, and they eagerly swallowed the whole performance goose, feathers, and bone, especially since my special relationship with "Athena" was considered something of an exciting exoticism in these parts. It is easy to persuade people of things beyond their understanding, especially people whose opinion of their own intelligence surpasses understanding.

"Magical warriors?" bellowed the woman through a deep, proud smile.

"Yes," I responded seriously, gently surveying my prizes with a doleful, tortured expression, as if I was thoroughly humbled by my need for their assistance. I explained how I had selected them to play the most important and vital role in the Restoration, to receive secret training from me in employing high-powered magical weapons to destroy Raen's encampments and free Arula. "After the Restoration, you will be the chief wizards of the new kingdom, known to all as the king's best. You will of course be remembered in Gondish history." I said this last sentence quietly and matter-of-factly, as if it was nothing to me and I merely wanted to make sure they understood the ramifications of their contributions in case any of them should object to becoming important personages.

None did. They all glanced at each other with suitably smug expressions, the sort of smug expressions that reeked of the headiness that comes with having illegitimate power over others. They were all quite taken with themselves, and couldn't wait to cause resentment among their friends by boasting that they were "special" and "chosen" to be in the new king's "elite magical corps" and that they were now privy to all sorts of arcane magical secrets that they couldn't discuss with mere citizens.

"To business, then," I continued smoothly. "Because you are so gifted, it was necessary for me to call this meeting with such short notice, to help maintain secrecy and to protect your power from those who would take it from you. You are so important, so essential, that there are many people, even your own friends, who are seeking to sabotage you. For the welfare of Gondal, trust no one. I would go so far as to suggest that you have a *duty* to trust no one."

They all loved this image of themselves, especially since they all knew that the wizards who had been killed by Raen's people were easily their betters. My words made up for them still being alive.

"And so. To place you under my magical protection, I would like your permission to perform a protection ritual over each of you. Privately."

They all became thickly solemn and happily secretive. This intrigue was all to their taste.

"The fate of Gondal might depend upon it."

They glanced at each other. Someone said, "sure," as if he

thought he was granting me my dearest wish and the rest nodded in condescending agreement. I, of course, had no concern that anyone would refuse.

Then they all tried to impress me with pointless monologues on how many wizards they had read, and with who could spit out the most names the fastest. It was very much like Kursen, only it was far more ignorant and annoying. At least Kursen, at its core, had something resembling an actual academic curriculum, even though it had reached the point of empty parody during my studies there. These folks never had anything to parody in the first place. I would call it empty imitation, except that these people were so isolated from the rest of the world that they had no idea of how to begin to imitate it. They were too busy frantically pretending that they already knew all about it, and didn't need it. And since they were terrified to the ghosts of their ancestors' bones that I might point out that they could benefit from some knowledge of the world outside Anda, they were doing their pathetic best to preempt me with their personal reading lists.

Oh well. All the better to manipulate.

I silenced the hubbub by choosing the least competent among them, a young woman who could barely manifest misspelled snatches of words on blank parchment, but who liked to refer to herself as "practically a master." Then I showed the others to an unused private room in the back of the living quarters and asked them to honor me by waiting.

As soon as I returned to my first sacrifice, I took her pudgy hand in mine and went into a light open trance, speaking softly. "Come, Yoa Elin Fraen. No defenses. No shields. Let me feel your power and know in my heart the sources of your wizardry. Come, wizard, open your heart to me."

She looked solemnly into my eyes as if she was capable of feeling whatever I felt. I knew she was barely capable of feeling anything that mattered. Even her solemnity was a bad imitation. My wizard senses told me that she was actually feeling excited and curious, but that she wanted to appear cool and professional, as if she was all quite used to this sort of magic. Her power was barely discernible, a suggestion of surges between her heartbeats, a magic that was more guess than skill. I really had to reach to find it. Perfect. My wizardry wasn't nearly as strong as a true master wizard's, but it was stronger than hers, and that was all that mattered.

"How did you come by your wizardry?" I asked softly.

"Books," she answered proudly. "Teaching myself. In a way, I've always known magic, and most of my learning has been more like remembering. I'm sure I had this skill in another life. I have dreams."

"That's obvious," I responded without a hint of irony. It was an effort not to show my annoyance, but I managed admirably. "Excellent. A natural talent. Now, come, focus your power, focus your wizardly discernment, on this mirror. I know you can. Touch the mirror, touch your mirrored image, and know that your power is merging into the glow, know that you are your own reflection." I placed her hand on her reflection, near where her reflection's heart would be. She was breathing heavily and looking pale now, although I was certain that much of that was merely for show. Then I gently felt for her thoughts and was surprised to learn that she truly was feeling a little faint. I focused on feeling her frail power through her inexplicable throbs of weakness.

"Work some magic for me," I whispered.

She tried to work some kind of spell, but it wasn't clear what. All I felt was a weak fluttery surge of power, bounding and rebounding from the mirror. But I felt enough to know for sure that when she worked with mundane energies, she didn't stay focused on one side of the universal flow or the other. Whichever direction the world energy around her flowed, her magic floated in, like a dead fish in an indifferent stream. This would be easy.

I took her hands in mine and sent a power surge through her body, easily forcing what little power she had to bond with mine.

"Now. Know that you are your own inversion. Know that you are bonded to me, and to Gondal through me. You are my apprentice. When you work magic, your energy shall be as mine is, following in the same flow and direction."

She closed her eyes and shuddered and gagged a little.

"Know that your reflection is disappearing into your heart. And so you are inverted. And so you are one with me." The Mirror of Transformations went dull and blank, as did Yoa's chubby face. I lightly shook my new apprentice to get her attention back on me, and smiled encouragingly. "How do you feel, Yoa?"

"Stronger?" she said this uncertainly, as if she was asking me whether this was the correct answer. She squinted. "And a little nauseous. But not too bad."

"Let's see how much stronger." I placed my hand over her heart and felt nothing. No energy. No magic. Just a surprisingly uneven pulse of life and a dull blank where her power should have been. I did not even sense an apprenticeship bond. "Here." I grabbed some parchment and placed it in her hands. "Grace me with a spell. Manifest some words, manifest your name, show me what you can do."

She tried. She worked up a sweat trying. There was no power. There were no words.

Damn! I had only succeeded in killing what little magic she was capable of! I tried to remain cool while I considered what had happened. She smiled uncertainly. I placed my hands in hers and sent a surge of thoughts at the parchment, manifesting her name. She seemed surprised, but she quickly tried to cover her surprise by pretending she had intended those words all along. She clearly had no idea that it was my spell, not hers.

"Wizard," I said gravely, "you are now protected against anyone sabotaging your magic." I suppose I was speaking truth, considering that she no longer had any magic to get sabotaged. But I was also beginning to panic a little, as I had only intended to make her power flow in the direction of decay, to be aligned to evil, so she could safely use my weapons. I did not mean to destroy it completely. *What did I do wrong?*

While I was considering what to do next, Yoa suddenly sat down, her body trembling uncontrollably, so uncontrollably that I now knew she had been having difficulty standing. I half knelt, half crouched beside her and put my arms around her shoulders as her eyes teared up and she began violently coughing and rocking back and forth. Something was seriously wrong here, and I had no idea where to begin to tease it out. I briefly considered asking Hecate to heal whatever was suddenly ailing Yoa, but I knew that if Yoa was not securely aligned to evil, I would only do more damage to her if I worked a clerical healing. And from her alarming physical reactions and absence of power, it wasn't clear to me what her magical condition was, although I now felt unmistakable surges of evil power throughout the room, power that was beyond my skill to shape and control. I wondered why I hadn't noticed these surges earlier and decided it must have been because I was so focused on working with my new apprentice that I wasn't paying attention to the ambient energy around me. Then I thought ruefully that no master wizard would have been that unobservant, and that maybe Welm had been right to question my estimation of my own abilities with wizardry. Maybe I was as self-deluded as my Andan guests.

And then I stopped thinking, because Yoa's physical condition was getting alarmingly worse. She slid off the chair and onto the floor, holding her stomach as if she was in violent pain, and gagging and crying and shuddering and clawing the air as if she was suffocating.

Don't die on me! I thought in absolute panic. *Please don't die on me!*

"*She won't die,*" responded a lightly terse voice in response to my thoughts. The words were in Sarana with a heavy Sunnan accent. They had been sent directly into my mind.

I looked up from Yoa, who was turning blue and writhing and gasping terrifyingly useless breaths of air, and saw that the speaker was a severe-looking wizard about ten years my senior, who had emerged out of invisibility with Welm. I knew immediately that he was evil and that it was his power that I had sensed pulsing in the room. I also knew that he was causing Yoa's sudden torment. I started to angrily demand that he stop, when Welm made a motion for me to be quiet and urgently mouthed the words, "Trust me, lad."

Yoa was now regaining a little flesh color. A little. She was still suffocating, but not as much. I took that to mean that Welm's new friend didn't want her dead yet. Or that he wanted to torture the poor girl into a slower death for the gods know what reason.

The older wizard sent a magical pass to open the door to the room where my other guests were waiting. "Come, come out," he said in quick, commanding, heavily accented Sarana. "We're under attack."

My guests hurried out and stopped in horror when they saw Yoa writhing and jerking as if she couldn't breathe. Aeren, attracted by the commotion, had joined them. Yoa's torturer turned to me and spoke quickly and decisively. "A true king is a healer. Put your hand on her heart, my lord, and ask the power of the land to protect this young lady."

I took the cue and placed my hand firmly and confidently on her sweat-soaked chest. The wizard stopped torturing her, and she shuddered once, relaxed her obese body into a dead, disgusting limpness, and began to breathe rapidly and regain her natural color. After a minute or so, she was even able to get up and join the rest of the group, who were all extremely curious. Except for Aeren, who quietly withdrew to a corner of the room.

Not that anyone paid much attention to Aeren. They were too busy showcasing their self-importance to Welm and his companion by snubbing them in favor of asking me loud senseless questions that I had no idea how to answer. My silence didn't matter, however, because their questions quickly exploded into splendidly preposterous explanations that just as quickly trailed off into disgusting bids for attention. Because now that Yoa had thoroughly recovered, everyone had to loudly claim that they also suffered from the same condition and could therefore really empathize with her, and wasn't it just so tragic that highly creative magicians of their caliber were so vulnerable to such attacks which were so obviously the result of being physically sensitive to so many things, and how careful they should all be to safeguard their precious selves, and on and on until even poor Yoa looked roundly embarrassed.

I had had about enough, but I decided to wait for another cue from Welm's buddy before speaking again, because I wanted to know what his game was, so I contented myself with merely looking concerned. Fortunately, the wizard had had about enough too, because he disrupted the confusion with a harsh speech that instantly got everybody's attention.

"Yoa wasn't ill. Yoa was suffering a magical attack from one of Raen's wizards. The pretender king knows about you, knows how important you all are. It took the touch of the true king, King Llewelyn, to heal this poor girl. It could have been any one of you in such need."

Everyone looked thoroughly impressed. After all, since it could have been any one of them who had been singled out for attack, they now all felt exceptionally important. Everyone in Anda would hear about this tomorrow, of that I was sure. I decided to let the wizard continue his propaganda speech, but as he was now shielded against a mind probe, I had no way to confirm his true thoughts.

"Who are you?" someone asked, a bit rudely.

"An advisor to the king. The true king." He bowed slightly to me and I nodded noncommittally in return. "My name is Master Cwiven. Unfortunately, because Raen's intelligence-gathering abilities are so keen, I must advise my lord, for the protection of these highly skilled magicians, to forgo their services. At least for now. King Llewelyn—" He bowed again. "—if you insist on using these Andans, highly skilled as they are, Raen will destroy them all. You can't heal them all from the results of every magical attack and lead the Restoration."

"Your advice is appreciated." I responded only because Cwiven had stopped speaking, and it seemed necessary to say something to maintain an air of authority. All the while I was wondering what the hell was going on.

"So for your own safety, you should all go home now." The wizard spoke urgently to the group. "Go home and live to make your important and brilliant contributions to the new kingdom."

I decided to play along. I could always reverse their sudden dismissal, and I was much more curious about this strange interloper who clearly wanted to speak to me alone than I was eager to keep the locals around. "Yes, and please help Yoa home safely," I added. "Go with my deepest gratitude. My advisors and I now have much to discuss in private."

"Of course," a few murmured reluctantly, although nobody seemed in much hurry to leave.

"You are all too important to me to place in such danger," I said with as much quiet courtesy as I could muster. "If I should need you, I will certainly remember your willingness to offer your services."

Some looked a little disappointed, but as none could find a reason to linger, they all began to make motions to leave. One of them kissed my hand to show the others how dedicated she was, and because it was considered dramatic and daring to make reactionary gestures like that. Even though the gesture was more about her than about me, I solemnly squeezed her hand in return, thanked her, thanked the others, and dismissed everybody for the third time.

They left. Slowly.

When I was finally alone with Welm and Cwiven, who of course had remained shielded, I asked coldly, "What the hell are you doing?"

"Getting you a line on some real fighters, lad," responded my illusionist. "The lot you chose has never seen a real battle, and it would be Lord Luck on a flayed goat if any of them could be depended upon, even with the benefit of your fine training."

"I depended on you to bring back intelligence from Arula. What are you doing here?"

"Bringing you something better than intelligence, lad. Master Cwiven here knows some real wizards, with evil alignments and a grudge against Roguehan bigger than yours. Every last one of them is willing to help you take down Raen. I suggest you avail yourself of the help."

I turned to Cwiven. "So you nearly killed Yoa to break up my plan?"

"I nearly killed Yoa and let you appear to heal her to help float another story about your fitness for kingship," responded Cwiven slowly. "And to ensure that you don't sabotage your own revolution by working with inferior magicians."

"Kind of you to care."

"At your service," he responded blandly. "I trust I'm qualified."

"You do excellent work," I admitted. "Where did you study?"

"Sunnashiven. Then I went to work for Roguehan. Been a master wizard for about five years." He was making sure I knew about the difference in our relative status. As if I could somehow miss it.

"Still carry bans?" I asked nonchalantly, basically to show that I knew something of Sunnashiven's wizard school.

"No." He flashed a self-satisfied grin. "Roguehan's people removed them when he hired me. But I still carry an allegiance to evil. It's not as easy to change an alignment as you might think, especially for us mages. No offense, but your strategy with the Mirror was unworkable. At least coming from a wizard with your moderate level of training. Stick to clerisy. I hear you're *good* at it." He chuckled a little at what I assumed was supposed to be a joke.

I pointedly ignored his slight. "So what's your price? Besides clubbing it to Roguehan, I mean."

"When you are king, you will provide places at court for me and my associates, which means lifetime protection from Roguehan, as he has no intention of taking this kingdom from you under the present circumstances. He can't do so without destroying his chances of wielding the elvish power he's fought so many years to possess, because he knows if he invades now, nobody will believe in his claim to the throne. Without that belief, he might as well stay home." He smiled respectfully, but there was a shadow of mockery in his smile. I couldn't decide if the mockery was meant for me or for Roguehan. Then I wasn't even entirely sure it was there.

"One wonders why you and your associates don't make your own bid for the crown?"

"Because we want to practice magic, not fussy up our time with statecraft. Arguing with the Assembly and having veto power over who gets to buy the biggest goat pasture doesn't interest us. That's your job. We'll fight Arula's weak defenses with your weapons, put you on the throne, and the deal's done."

"What do you know of Arula's defenses?"

"I was stationed there. As were my colleagues. I was one of the wizards responsible for the recent purge."

"I'm impressed," I said dryly.

"We left Arula because we heard about you and thought the time was right to offer our services."

Welm broke in eagerly. "As luck would have it, Master Cwiven approached me this morning as I was preparing to leave Anda with Ygresan. We spoke privately, and I decided to bring him here to observe."

"Yes, thanks for the warning."

"Well, a warning wasn't possible. But I recommend you make use of these seasoned, practiced warriors. Trust me, lad, it's the best deal we've got."

I felt slightly uncomfortable with the way Welm was rushing matters, and wished it was possible to probe both his mind and Cwiven's. But I also felt exhilarated, because if Cwiven was telling me the truth, it would eliminate the problem of getting decent work out of the local dolts. However, I mostly felt like things were suddenly moving out of my control, and that made me uneasy.

"Perhaps Aeren would also do well with a weapon. She's already proven herself." I said this because including Aeren was a way of staying partly on semifamiliar ground.

"Yes, great job on Zelar," said Cwiven sincerely, turning to Aeren, who had remained quietly in the corner. "I heard all about that. Wish I had seen it." Cwiven smiled in pleasure, a smile that told me that he really hated Zelar and that he highly approved of our little escapade. I smiled in return. Really I had no idea what to think of this turn of events. Neither did Aeren. She glared suspiciously at him, but made no response.

"Drop your shield," I ordered Cwiven.

"Trust me," responded Cwiven. "I was unshielded long enough to wreak havoc on Yoa. I prefer not to open myself to magical attacks from other sources. The results are too painful."

I couldn't tell if he was being ironic or just wittily letting me know that he was well guarded against me. But the latter possibility made no sense, because if he would have me crowned king, why wouldn't he trust me? I felt a momentary standoff between us, then the feeling faded.

"Aeren might make a good fighter with some training," Welm responded reasonably, as if he wanted to change the subject. "But does it make sense to delay?"

I tried to come up with an argument that would buy me a little time to consider. I turned to Cwiven. "How soon can you and your fellows be ready to attack?"

"Say the word, King." He made a gesture of mock grace and power that was impossible to read.

"Two weeks? That will give me time to organize some Andans to move in behind you, to make plans." And give me time to study Cwiven, and to think through what was happening here. But time was something that Cwiven wasn't eager to give me.

"Your Andans are useless, King. We all know that. You need their approval, their formal recognition, their unmitigated belief. You don't need their ability as soldiers because, frankly, they have none. Gather enough commoners to make the trek at our backs and join the grateful Arulans in welcoming you to the restored throne. That's all that matters in the cosmic scheme of things. Besides, according to what Welm has told me, you've got weapons here so powerful that cleanup work won't be necessary."

"What kind of magical defenses does Arula have?"

"You're looking at him, King." Cwiven playfully bowed. "Arula's defenses were me and my fellow wizards putting on a show. Pity we're sick of dancing. There's a group of toy soldiers camped outside the city that Roguehan found unworthy of his real army. But without us, they have no defenses against a magical attack."

"What's your grudge against Roguehan?"

"Does it matter?"

"I have no bloody idea if it matters. But I would like to know what is motivating you to be so . . . cooperative."

"Maybe you can understand this, Llewelyn, but it doesn't matter if you can't." His voice was easy, almost collegial. He leaned forward over his thighs as if he was going to share some painful secret with me. "Years of training in Sunnashiven. A city not known for its comforts. I gird myself to the task, and finally, after years of study, earn the status of master wizard. Credentialed. Experienced. Every one of my spells worth its results in the gods' gold and then some. I've worked like Hecate's dogs to earn my honors. I've played the politics and flattered the right people. So do I get assigned to court? Am I given interesting espionage work? Weapons development? A prestigious teaching position? Leisure time to explore theories and write books? Am I given anything resembling a career in the magical arts? No, I get to guard Arula, and toady to the less-qualified wizards Roguehan surrounds himself with. Why? Who knows? At one point, back in the day, I was actually friendly with His Excellency the Emperor of Broken Words." He spat. "He used to tell me I was brilliant for magic, used to encourage me to study. He paid my way through school. Then he gave me low-level assignment after low-level assignment, culminating in being a glorified guard for his puppet king Raen."

"Why did you work for him for so long?"

"I had thought perhaps my loyalty might one day earn me a position as Gondal's chief wizard. But now that you are in a better position than His Excellency to grant me that, I say why not serve a young warlord such as yourself? It's nothing to me who I work spells for."

"So Roguehan encouraged your ambitions only to thwart them.

What can I say to it? Seems like there's a lot of that going around."

Cwiven suddenly got harsh and impatient. "Here's your choice, Llewelyn. We're going to take down Arula. You want the throne or don't you?"

"You *do* want the throne, don't you, lad?" Welm sounded uncharacteristically nervous. I knew he was also frightened of Roguehan executing some kind of vengeance and that he considered my kingship his best protection, but something in his tone struck me as false. It was as if he felt it oddly necessary to put his nerves on display.

"Of course." I smiled generously, as if I had no inward reservations. "I just didn't expect to take it with the help of Roguehan's former friends."

"Arula is a three-day ride west of here. I respectfully suggest that you put Welm in charge of gathering your backup forces and that we leave as soon as possible. Ride with us. I understand you've used some kind of clerical technique to control the use of Zelar's weapons. That's clever of you, my lord. Genuinely impressive. Leave them locked into uselessness until we need to employ them. It's safer that way."

"When did you last communicate with Roguehan?"

"I haven't had direct communication in months. I assume that means he has no intention of invading Gondal."

"So I've heard." I looked at Welm, who nodded as if he vigorously agreed with Cwiven's assessment.

"Shall I marshal your forces, lad?" asked Welm lightly.

I stood up and paced across the room with my back to the others to gain a modicum of privacy. I sent a brief prayer to Hecate. It rebounded with silence, and then I heard Her voice between my heartbeats saying, "The crown is yours. Take my gift."

When I turned back to face my advisors, Welm was staring at me intently. "Well, lad?"

I returned his stare with equal intensity, weighing my decision. Hecate was with me on this one. Even if there was something odd about my companions, I knew that I had a duty to trust to Her. After all, wasn't this all for Hecate's glory?

"Yes, marshal whomever you can. With all due speed." I agreed reluctantly despite my discomfort with the suddeness of this turn of events. "Ygresan may be of help to you there."

Cwiven and Welm quickly rose. "My liege lord," intoned Cwiven, bowing very low, "you have made the best and wisest choice. As soon as it is in my power to do so, I will make you a king in every sense."

"I am grateful," I responded gravely. "And shall reward you properly. But please leave me now." Really I just wanted to be alone to think.

No sooner did Cwiven leave than Welm began urgently to assure me that I was making the most expedient choice. "It's better than we could have hoped for, lad. Who would have thought that—"

"—Silence!" I turned to Aeren, who had listened intensely to this entire exchange. "What do you think, bard?"

"I think they're both lying." She spoke without hesitation.

"Why would we lie? For what purpose?" Welm asked with a wide-eyed shrug.

She ignored him. "But despite my misgivings, I also think it's a better option than working with the locals. But it's too neat, too coincidental that Cwiven would happen to meet up with Welm today. Especially since I'm sure I saw him a few days ago. He didn't just arrive from Arula, as he claims. Burn darkly for the truth of anything else he said, but he lied at least once."

"Well, what and if he has been here longer than he claims?" asked Welm. "Can you fault his caution in approaching me first?"

"If he came to find Llewelyn, what took him so long? Everyone in Anda knows where we are, and yet he approached you first? Just happened to find you, and find you alone? Where was Ygresan?"

"Ygresan was there, laddie. I sent him off on some errands because I didn't think he needed to hear what Cwiven was going to say."

"So why all the secrecy? The invisibility? The spying? The high drama of surprise magical attacks and fictional royal healings that shouldn't have efficacy until Llewelyn truly takes the crown and embodies the power of Gondal in himself? Why didn't you just invite Cwiven over for a friendly discussion of strategy instead of waylaying Llewelyn into rushing into this decision? It's obvious to me that you didn't want to leave him any option other than to willingly adopt your proposal, which tells me there's something highly suspect in it."

"I didn't think it in our interest to scorch our own revolution with the help of what passes for the local mages. I brought us certain victory, and some very helpful propaganda to help intensify popular belief in the lad. All of which was Cwiven's idea, to give proper credit. Are you suggesting we can't trust him, laddie? Would you prefer to take a city with Yoa and her friends?"

There was really no answer to this.

"Welm," I said. "This turn of events is certainly too good for the gods' own truth, but it nevertheless seems best to me to follow it.

With due caution. But Aeren's questions still deserve responses. Why didn't you and Cwiven see fit to present this plan to me without wrapping it up in all the high intrigue?"

"I already told you. By the time Cwiven had spoken to me, you had already arranged for tonight's little festivities. Cwiven convinced me that we needed to wreak some friendly sabotage in order to ensure that you didn't involve these inferior wizards so deeply that you couldn't easily rid yourself of the burden later. I agreed that it was all for the good of Gondal—something that is of vital importance to former imperial magicians like Cwiven and me. His Excellency might keep an unhappy distance from this land as long as you are on the throne, but that doesn't mean some of us aren't vulnerable to individual acts of vengeance."

"Yes, of course," I said quickly and understandingly. Perhaps this unexpected turn would be all right. It made sense that both Welm and Cwiven feared that Roguehan would destroy them as turncoats, and that fear alone would go some way toward explaining why they seemed so anxious to rid Arula of Roguehan's puppet king and see me on the throne. But what weighed against my unease the most was that Hecate Herself was blessing Cwiven's offer. "Leave me for now."

"As you will, lad," said Welm easily, heading for his private area. "I'll begin work tomorrow."

After he left, I turned to Aeren. "Bard. You will accompany me and the other wizards. I shall teach you to use a suitable weapon without guidance, and you may fight as you will. But your primary responsibility is to listen and observe our new comrades, and to tell me everything you think."

She nodded agreement. Then she said, "Since you are king, or close to it, and Cwiven apparently needs you as much as you need him, why did you agree to his proposal without giving yourself a chance to investigate it?"

"I prayed to Hecate when I turned my back and I felt Her blessing."

"Are you certain it was Hecate?" asked Aeren strangely.

"Certain as I'm king," I teased. "Why?"

"Because I'm certain Welm did some kind of working when you prayed. I watched his face, and he was watching your back far too intently for the circumstances. But then, what do I know? It's not like you can expect to verify anything he says or does. And all things considered, Cwiven and his associates would make much better wizard-soldiers than the alternative."

"Which is another reason for working with them. Yes, it's all rather unexpected, and their approach is rather off-putting, but I do understand how former imperial loyalists would be loath to take a chance on refusal. As to whether Welm worked up an illusion on me, I'll pray later on that one. Thanks for the observation."

"Then tomorrow you'll teach me how to kill?" She smiled charmingly.

"You've already mastered that. But yes, tomorrow I'll teach you how to . . . shall we say, refine what you already know. Try to get some sleep so you are alert for the lesson."

She sighed and stared out of the window, arching her back in annoyance.

"You want help?"

"No."

I retired to my room.

And as I prayed to my Goddess, asking whether I had made the right choice, asking whether She or Welm's illusions had answered me earlier, I received a vision for answer. I saw a dark wind full of dirt and refuse and foul smoke. The wind was pushing a crown along barren ground, and the crown kept banging and clattering against sharp rocks. I grasped the crown before the wind could break it. The crown turned into a beautiful songbird. Then I watched the wind devour the bird while my fingers bled.

"Was it illusion I heard earlier, Mother, or is this the path that makes the crown mine?"

"The crown is yours, my bird," my Goddess answered.

Darkly I slept.

Twenty-one

*T*he ride to the city was uncomfortably easy.

Welm had gathered half the citizens of Anda at our backs, or so it seemed, and it felt more like I was leading a grand, colorful pageant than a viable revolutionary force. The Andan people had turned this affair into a boisterous traveling party, as if they were expecting to participate in a city festival rather than in a bloody battle. I have no idea what Welm went around telling people to elicit such astonishing hilarity, or what he was doing to provoke all the merriment back where he rode among the people. The only thing clear was that Aeren wasn't the only one who wanted to kill Raen. It seemed like everybody in Anda wanted to do the same, so long as they were safely at my back and could make up songs about it. Some of the aching fools even brought tambourines and were dancing and singing along the muddy roads behind us.

"Wherever there's a crowd there's an Andan who needs to perform," Aeren complained dourly. "Congratulations, King. You've provided your people with their dearest wish—a traveling audience. Freeing their sister city and themselves from a tyrant is nothing to it."

Aeren and I were riding ahead of the colorful madness with Cwiven and his associates, most of whom were nearly as dour as Aeren concerning the Andan people. Cwiven's fellow wizards were all from Sunna and Sevalas. As southwesterners of a privileged class, they had no use for the Andan people's proclivity for mixing personal pride and provincial incompetence up in everything they did, and so they spent a good deal of time complaining about it.

"You'd think they'd invented the concept of revolution," sneered one wizard. "And that they've had so much experience toppling governments that they needn't bother to learn how it's done. A song and a dance and an anxious jig and the crown comes tumbling down."

"Yes, listen to the bloody fools chatter and chant as if it is all quite natural to them to destroy an encampment. They'll all be crediting themselves with our work before they can make the return trip to Anda."

"Which is all the better for us and the new king," responded

Cwiven grandly. "There's nothing easier to rule than ignorance. If the Andans believe that this is truly their victory, they'll be that much more likely to believe in King Llewelyn." Cwiven bowed and offered me a bottle of fresh ale. "My lord."

I declined, even though I felt a little rude in doing so. There was something indefinably *wrong* about Cwiven and his companions, beyond their understandably hard-featured attitude concerning the Gondish people, but damn-the-gods if I was able to articulate to myself what it was. Aeren's insights were useless on that score, because the wizards preferred to speak Botha among themselves and with me, so she couldn't make the fine observations I had counted on. Anything I told her was secondhand, and as I couldn't even explain to myself why I felt something was awry here, I couldn't begin to explain it to her. And since the wizards all kept themselves shielded, I had no way to ascertain their true thoughts.

So even though Welm and Cwiven had fairly plausible explanations for everything they did, I remained wary. The only reason I had consented to cooperate with their plan at all, under such rushed circumstances, was that I knew that Hecate willed me to take this path. I had prayed to Her several times before we left Anda and I was satisfied that Her blessing was not Welm's illusion, as Aeren had feared.

Which didn't mean Welm was trustworthy. It also didn't preclude me from traveling armed with one of Zelar's wands, and making attempts to probe the minds of the wizards I was traveling with. Their shields were solid so my probes always came up empty. That is what bothered me the most, but I couldn't argue with the precaution of their remaining shielded in case Roguehan should have his people around. Had I been in their position, I would have done the same. In fact, I was doing the same.

Had I been of a more poetic turn of mind, I would have been struck by the irony of assuming the throne of Gondal and power over the untrammeled wildness and freedom of ancient elvish power while speaking Botha, the language of the empire and of Sunnashiven, the oppressive city of my youth. But I had more important concerns, like maintaining an image of leadership under circumstances that were not of my planning. Although my new wizard-warriors treated me with all due deference, there was something thin about it, as if their professed respect were all in the way of merely doing a job.

But if I hadn't been Sunnan by birth, and intimately aware of how class distinctions are literally beaten into people from that part of the world, I might not have noticed the way their words and smiles occasionally shaded into something resembling insincerity. It was that subtle and that ephemeral. I expected a degree of hypocrisy such as one always finds in intelligent, ambitious assistants who know they can do your job better than you can and naturally resent the difference in status that forces them to bow and scrape. I didn't expect to get an occasional, disturbing impression of studied pretense in the intonation of a word or to catch an occasional ferociously blank stare behind a perfectly obsequious smile.

But these shaded surprises were never strong enough to question without appearing uncertain and weak. That was the problem. I sensed only that the wizards were both a shade too diffident and a shade too friendly around me, as if they weren't sure whether to keep entirely to themselves or include me in every private joke. And for all I knew they were merely reacting to my having been born a commoner in their part of the world.

Only Cwiven, whom the others respected as a leader, was unfailingly solicitous and amicable. So I pretty much confined my conversation to him, playing it in grand southwestern style as if we alone ranked above the others. While making a virtue of quiet wariness, of course.

Aeren pretty much ignored everyone, partly because she didn't understand Botha and partly because she wanted the business to be finished. On the day before we were to attack the city, I secretly sent her to spy out the encampments and to bring me word if things were not as Cwiven had described them.

She did not return to my tent as I had expected her to, but that night I found her sitting alone outside of our camp on the gnarled roots of an old oak tree, shivering with cold and contemplating the sky.

"I'm nearly as bad as you for not sleeping," I said to her by way of greeting as I leaned against the tree, not caring to comment on her unexplained absence and possibly provoking an unnecessary rant.

"You've got a ways to go for that," she responded flatly. Her silence was troubled. I waited while the wind creaked through the branches above us, branches laden with the energy of early spring. Winter was retreating from the land, but its breath still hung heavy in the night.

I threw a shield around us for heat, without bothering to ask why Aeren hadn't done the same for herself because I assumed she had some convoluted argument for refusing physical comfort. Despite the cold, the night and the relative solitude were comfortable and I didn't wish to mar them by arguing with Aeren. Below us opened a wide dark valley where we could see the lights of Arula. Strange towers rose from the city to sparkle and catch brilliant star beams from the night sky. Arula, unlike Anda, bore a ghost of the elvish power that had once built it, and I could feel that power in my blood. I glanced down at Aeren, who looked like a prince. A melancholy prince contemplating his city. Knowing how much our similar garb and dark hair made us resemble each other, I assumed that I too looked like a young ruler, had anybody been there to see.

"Tomorrow I shall be king, bard, and you shall have your place at court."

She shrugged unhappily.

"What kind of tale will you tell at my coronation, bard? Your audience shall be as large as my kingdom, for all will hear of it. I will dress your stage for you by listening attentively, and so everyone else will have to pay you attention, if only to please the king."

She picked up a dried acorn and threw it carelessly toward the valley.

"I thought you'd be happy, or at least at peace with yourself over the prospect."

"There's Arula," she answered dully.

"Yes?" I waited for her to make her point. "Beautiful city by moonlight."

"I've been watching the city since sunset, King. Beautiful it is. When the wind blows, the towers sing. But there's something missing."

"You mean besides your usual good cheer?"

Her voice turned harsh and hopelessly sad. "Where are the guards? Where's the encampment? Where's the easy resistance we're supposed to fight like heroes against? I thought tomorrow's battle was all in the way of a good show for the Gondish people, to cause more excitement and belief among the masses who will have you crowned king. Where are the supporting players in our little shadow game?"

I could see she was right. Arula looked utterly defenseless. "Raen surely knows of our approach. Perhaps he has withdrawn his forces within the walls."

"He hasn't," responded Aeren sourly. "I entered the city this afternoon, when I went to spy out the encampment as you told me to. Nobody stopped me. Nobody questioned me. I walked freely about in the streets and asked people about Raen, about the encampment. I said that I was surprised at how free and open the city was because in Anda we had heard that the pretender king was keeping Arula under close guard."

"And?"

"He was. But several days ago the encampment, Roguehan's mercenary soldiers, just packed up their tents and left. By my estimate that would have happened about the same time that you decided to join forces with Cwiven, or shortly before. No public explanation. Life goes on."

"Strange."

"It gets stranger. Welm rode ahead of us and entered the city yesterday."

"I didn't know about that."

"I know. Everyone in Arula is now joyfully expecting your arrival, thanks to Welm. The entire city knows we're here. They've got banners all over the streets and shops to welcome your royal entrance."

"And Raen's just sitting there, unguarded, watching the preparations?"

"I assume so." She picked up a small stone and threw it in the direction of the acorn. "Hecate only knows what Raen's deal is. I hear he's still in residence, playing king-of-the-castle with his mother Ariana and his sister Eyra. They didn't leave with the guards."

"It's beyond my skill to read this, bard."

"Mine too."

"What are the Arulan people saying?"

"That you are the true king, here to liberate them from Raen. Some say your weapons are so powerful that Raen's mercenaries went home out of fear of you, although I'm certain that's a rumor that Welm started."

I considered. "Yes, it's all very strange, and because it's so strange I'm not entirely comfortable with it either, but I've no idea what to object to. Taking the throne gets easier and easier all the time, and to say I wish there was more struggle and bloodshed and destruction sounds, well, beyond silly. From what you've told me, I suppose we can lead our little battalion here peacefully through the city, knock on the castle door, and ask Raen for the keys. But since everything so far has felt like a play revolution to save an imaginary kingdom, perhaps that's as it should be."

"It will be interesting to hear what Cwiven has to say on the morrow, eh?" answered Aeren.

"Perhaps I should send for Welm tonight and see what he has to say."

"Why bother? Welm has already told you everything you need to know by not informing you of his visit to the city. Think with me, King. Why wouldn't Welm and Cwiven have told you about this? It's clear to me that the Arulans have known of our approach for quite some time, even before Welm's secret visit. Why wouldn't you have been informed that Arula is now free and open and has no need of military intervention? I mean, you're obviously meant to see all that for yourself on the morrow, so this unexpected accessibility was hardly meant to be a long-term secret."

"They're good questions, bard. Do you have answers?"

"No."

"That's the problem. There's an oddness in this whole situation, but there's nothing definitive to question. Shall I complain to Cwiven about not having to go to war to earn a hero's welcome?"

She sighed. "You don't know Raen. I can't imagine him and Ariana just waiting there, just doing nothing while you walk up and take his crown."

"Perhaps there's nothing he can do. He no longer has a fighting force. It's possible that whatever coin he was getting from Roguehan ran out and so the soldiers all went home."

"It's possible." She didn't sound convinced. "Here's my advice. Welm and Cwiven obviously want you to be surprised by your warm welcome into the city. So act surprised, but stay alert for any dark-nesses the surprises mask. Keep your thoughts shielded as you always do. If they think you aren't suspicious, you'll have a slight advantage because you'll be preparing yourself against the unex-pected contrary to their suppositions. It's all you can do."

"Agreed."

There was a long dark silence between us. The lights of the city glinted and sparkled in elvish colors. I felt those lights, owned them in my heart, wore a crown of them in my mind. Perhaps my corona-tion was too easy to believe, but I couldn't deny how powerfully inti-mate I suddenly felt with this unknown ancient city. Even now I suppose I had the power to walk away, but the thought of Roguehan being able to take this land in the absence of a true king sickened me. I trusted that Hecate was guiding matters, and that this inexplicable ease of ascension was Her doing.

"I worked some magic earlier this evening, King. As the sun set. Tell me what you think."

"You want my advice on magic, bard?" This truly was unex-pected, coming from Aeren.

"No, just your opinion. Before I ceded my birthright to you, this city, those lights, were mine by right, even though I haven't looked upon them until now. My ancestry, back centuries ago, was elvish. I know that now. Even though I'm dark-haired and look nothing like an elf, the blood is there. And the love of beautiful things. I don't experience that love much. Something about my bardic experiences did much to kill that. And now I'm too self-reflective to care. But . . . here . . . now . . . I . . . I was thinking about dragons tonight, and what it was to be one, to be an exiled prince and not know it. To tell tales nobody hears. Well, this odd situation is like a tale nobody hears, but we both know there's a story in there, only neither of us can find it for all our skill with words.

"So I summed up the pieces of this broken tale in my mind, letting myself trance a little against the city as the lights grew brighter against the failing sky. I felt the power here, the elvish power that will be yours to command. I knew how the true king of Gondal would be able to command the choicest stories and songs with a word, the most brilliantly crafted jewels with a sigh, and be able to carry this power in his heart and to assign it to anyone he chose. I stared at the light and felt in my blood how true kings are made, and what a fine thing it would be to own the elvish power that once created Beauty. How in some respects it is the only thing. I understood Roguehan.

"And then, with all the pieces of this untold story in my mind, I summed them into a tale of my own making, an unfinished tale whose end I couldn't find, and I sent it through space, through the elvish lights and elvish power like a tired dream slowly winging its way back to a dragon's cave at dawn. I sent it to my dead father, whom I never loved but who, I now know, was denied his dream and right to the kingdom, to my ancestors, to the elvish kings I never knew."

She stopped speaking for a long time.

"And did you get an answer?" I asked reasonably enough.

"No. Arula's lights remained beautiful in themselves. I don't even know if my sending had the power to go anywhere. It was an elvish sending, something primal in me called out to the land. Perhaps only the land heard. And now you've heard, King. So what do you think?"

"That there are worse ways to spend an hour of contemplation."

She rose. "Tomorrow we enter the city."

I glanced at the lights and the gleaming towers. "And tonight the city has entered us."

"May you guard it well, King. Like a scorching stormdragon."

I didn't care to interpret what she meant by this curious remark, so I said nothing. Not that there was anything more to say. We watched the lights for a long time. Then we silently returned to camp.

The next morning I nonchalantly asked Cwiven for his assessment on how close we should get to the encampment before I activated the weapons. He replied that we'd know when we got there, but that he suspected there wasn't much of an encampment to worry about. When I started to question him further, he abruptly excused himself to make preparations for our approach. I didn't pursue the issue, because I considered it better strategy not to appear as wary as I actually was. All in all, there were only two possible decisions. Enter Arula with Cwiven as planned, or leave. And I wasn't about to leave based on mere feelings that something was out of place. Better to keep aware and to let the story unfold as it would.

The story. We entered Arula the way one enters a dream. That is to say, it was never clear at what point we ceased to approach the city and actually entered it, because cheering crowds ran to greet us with starry incense and bright welcoming chants of "King, King" before we arrived at the gates, and so the city literally embraced us before we were properly introduced. Welm had ridden up to join us at the head of the Andans, and was looking convincingly surprised by our easy reception, as if he had no idea about expecting all this. *Why was he acting?* Neither he nor Cwiven offered any explanation for our curious welcome, and in the noise and generous hubbub, it was easy for them to feign distraction and avoid having to make explanations to me.

I assumed a regal attitude, and smiled and waved to my people, stopping frequently to lean down from my horse and kiss the hands of pretty girls or ostentatiously admire the gifts that were getting tossed at me and my entourage. Aeren looked quietly annoyed by the attention because she was as thoroughly confused as I was, and her obvious discomfort increased when the crowd began to clap and chant, "Kill Raen! Kill the pretender king!" Much as she claimed she wanted to kill Raen, she clearly didn't expect a screaming audience for her desires.

The crowd swept us and the Andans who rode behind us into a city of terrible charm. Grace in the sky. Towers and edifices of rare device that arrested the heart and eye and held them like a perfect minute holds a blessed shade of eternity. Streets so alluring you wanted to ride them forever, into forever. Arula was a city like a vibrant pulsing dream with real lives moving through it, or like a story one could actually enter and live inside. Even time felt slightly different here, weaker, slower, as if everything was young and ancient at the same time. Sunlight was whiter and purer and more insistent than the first light you opened your eyes to at birth. The air sharpened perceptions and thoughts. Arula was beautiful in all the ways Anda pretended to be, and I was damn glad that I had decided to put my reservations aside and enter the city, that Roguehan would have no piece of it.

My smiling fellow wizards, who still hadn't offered any explanation for the lack of an encampment to do battle with, offered no resistance to the welcoming crowd. So I had little choice but to ride with my entourage in the direction where we were clearly meant to go, admiring everything around me, and silently thanking Hecate for Her gift.

Eventually we approached a castle on a large hill that felt markedly still and silent compared to the excitement exploding in the rest of the city. We stopped. The merry crowd fell suddenly quiet around us, as if they were waiting for me to do something.

I glanced at Cwiven as if to ask *now what?* and he responded with a smile and an easy shrug, and then motioned toward a man on horseback who was now advancing toward us from one of the castle's entrances. I watched the man ride slowly in our direction, heard the crowd behind me erupt into ugly catcalls and jeers, and raised my hand for silence as he came within earshot and began to address me.

"My liege lord. King Raen of Gondal—" There were more jeers from the crowd. I raised my hand again for silence. "—*King* Raen invites you and your courtiers to a private audience within his castle, that the crown of Gondal might be peacefully transferred to its rightful owner."

The crowd erupted into loud cheers and cries of "Kill Raen" and "Long die the pretender king."

"His Lordship accepts," responded Cwiven quickly in his heavily accented Sarana, kicking his horse to follow the rider back toward the castle. The other wizards also kicked their steeds to follow, and so Aeren, Welm, and I were riding toward the entrance in the midst of my entourage, with loud cries of "King, King" at our backs.

Really there was nothing else to do. Why argue with fate?

Castle. Imagine a palace of starshine and subtlety. No. Imagine a palace where every room is a different emotion, where all the secret longings of your heart are reflected in barely discerned differences in tone that only you can sense. The air sparkles and cracks, to breathe is to become blessedly drunk, to go into trance is all but unavoidable. This ancient elvish castle is like solidified light, and you are like light. One step, one breath, one word and you never want to leave. Touch the walls and you are wed.

Raen's servants settled us all into our separate quarters. Aeren insisted on sharing rooms with me because she didn't wish to be alone until it was obvious to her what was happening, and as I shared her caution despite my delight in these new surroundings, I didn't object. I could tell from the stiff way she held her head and avoided gazing at the paintings and statues that lined the walls of our living quarters like captured samples of divinity that she was making a physical effort to resist the strange, almost-overwhelming attraction of this place.

"How do you find your new home, bard?" I asked her.

"I hate it."

"You appear to be making a heroic effort in that direction, but surely you can't deny the considerable charms of this place. Even Welm was impressed beyond himself, and could barely move or speak when we passed the fountains in the entranceway. I've never seen such colors, like life itself transformed to splashing sun and burning water and purified joy. Cwiven and the other wizards showed more genuine respect to the dust motes on the floor than they've yet shown to themselves. They were silenced by the beauty here. Silenced. And you hate it?"

"That just shows I'm stronger than Welm, Cwiven, and your near-royal self. Yes, it would be easy to succumb to the elvish power that built this palace. But everything you profess admiration for reveals your own inclinations and weaknesses, the cracks and fissures of your mind and personality for all to see. I refuse to be that publicly intimate."

"Does that mean that you don't want to tell tales publicly?" It was times like this that I realized that I really didn't understand Aeren at all.

She drew herself up in high annoyance. "It means that I absolutely refuse to display the weakness of being emotionally moved by anything Raen is associated with. It's like helplessly admitting that his possessions have emotional power over me, and I can't think of anything more disgusting! Even if they aren't really his possessions."

"Well, you needn't be so Andan about it."

"Let someone else weep for his statues. I refuse to make obeisance to a pretend 'king' who merely got lucky."

"One could argue that I'm a pretend king who merely got lucky."

A servant knocked on the door and interrupted our pleasant chat to say that Raen had sent for me. I quickly took leave of Aeren, fully shielded and armed myself, and, in a state of eager curiosity, let the servant take me to meet the king whom everybody wanted me to kill.

Raen was the strangest, loneliest, most inexplicable man I had ever met. The pretender king was seated near a crystalline window in a sumptuously appointed meeting room, staring at a vista of city towers and distant yellow-and-white mountains. He did not acknowledge my presence. I studied his back for a full five minutes before he turned to contemplate the hearth fire that was burning in a diamond-studded fireplace in the opposite wall. Raen was fair-haired and had vaguely elvish features, but not so definitively elvish that I would have noted it if Aeren hadn't told me how much his mother Ariana resembled her ancestors. His presence made the room feel empty.

I could hear the crowd chanting "Kill Raen" in the streets below, but I gave no indication that the mob's demands were anything to me, or that I was even listening, despite their voices being the only sound in the room except for the soft crack and whistle of the fire. Raen turned his back to me again and resumed staring through the window, not down toward the angry people but up at the open sky and clouds and glinting tower roofs. I stood in his odd silence and found myself likewise admiring the towers. Then I felt a strange old longing to bury myself in beautiful books, to live in one of those towers with nothing but sky and birds and a private library for my companions. That would be Cwiven's life, I supposed a little sadly. His price for the crown. Then I wondered what Raen saw in those towers, what they meant to him, so I took a chance on dropping my shields and probing his mind.

What I found there shocked and nauseated me.

I have seen evil, worshiped evil, become evil. I have killed when necessary and witnessed killings without a pang of conscience. I know how to hate, to hurt, to torture and destroy, and I accept that the universal waning energy that powers those actions is as necessary as the opposing energy that powers healing. But I did not know how to respond to what stretched and rebounded before me in Raen's heart and mind.

Raen simply didn't exist. Whatever he once was or might have been appeared to my wizard senses as a clutch of dust and ashes. My mind felt dirty looking at it. Anda had been full of people living lives of desperate pretentiousness, of weird self-devouring energies like fat snakes gorging themselves on their own tails. But Raen's self, if you could call it that, was like a snake that had already eaten itself and disappeared into some plane of nonexistence that no theology I had ever studied could account for. I had never met a man like a living, gaping hole before and I was sickened and fascinated.

I was probing into a dancing phantasmagoria of brittle images that passed for something like a unified life. The pretender king was nothing. I sifted deeper into the ashes and learned that Ariana had made it so.

Like faint impressions in the dust of what once was, I saw Raen as a young boy in a moss hut who had a talent for bird catching and nutting and who loved to roam the Northern forests. Ariana routinely made him kill and eat the colorful birds he brought home for pets because she considered his trapping skills unworthy of his royal elvish heritage. He was meant to learn the secret language of the deer, of the ancient forests, and if he heard a trace of the cadence of those natural tongues in an old Gondish story and loved the story without understanding why, Ariana would change it into something ugly and tell it to him over and over. He was to love only her stories about his destiny, not choose tales of his own to one day grow into. But mostly I saw that over his first years of life, Raen the Hunter, Raen the Woodsman, Raen who-was-meant-to-be, simply dried up and went away to wherever tortured little boys go.

Ariana had done worse than kill him. She had turned him into somebody else, as surely as Zelar had once turned Aeren into a stormdragon. *There were kings in his ancestry, too,* I remembered, but his mother was so fixated on the Gondish notion that elves were superior to the world that she couldn't acknowledge the mystical bond that the elvish kings had to the common land.

He drank a lot. Not because he hurt, but because he felt nothing, and sometimes drink opened him into feeling something, although he couldn't name what he felt and he wasn't always sure he liked it. Tragically, he was sure he loved Ariana. She had so unfitted him for life, for his life, that he had become utterly dependent on her, needed her, required her.

Aeren was wrong about him. The pretender king had nothing in him resembling the self-belief she so envied. He had no real self and so he had no sense of failure or inferiority. If Ariana told him he was a king, well then, by all the gods he didn't know how to believe in, he was.

But now Ariana was telling him he wasn't and that he must give his crown up to me. He didn't even know how to hurt, or that he was hurting.

As I said, he didn't exist. His mother had destroyed him years ago and built an empty shrine to her pride on the remains. Really she should have been clergy. El would have appreciated her work.

I seated myself next to him, and said by way of greeting, in my most sympathetic clerical voice, "From what I hear, everybody wants to kill you. Congratulations. That's quite an accomplishment."

"Are you going to kill me?" He sounded like he was asking for directions.

"I've no intention of killing you. Why should I be like everybody else?"

The question threw him. "My mother sent for you. Then she left. I don't know what she wanted." He looked around emptily. "She told me about Aeren and the crown. She must have known that my stepsister was the true 'prince' so to speak, but this was the first I had heard of it."

That was interesting but I didn't comment on it. Instead, I said, "Raen, what would you like from me? Safe escort to another country? Coin? Both? I don't have any personal quarrel with you, and I'm certain we would both like a bloodless transition."

"The people never believed in me. The power of this land was never mine. My mother the elf queen said I should be able to command great paintings and statues to appear with the wave of my hands, but I waved my hands and dreamt hard and they never appeared. But I am an elven king. I am. So why doesn't my power work? Why doesn't anybody believe in me? Do you know how to make people believe?"

I wanted to say something dignified, something befitting my new position, but there was something so . . . well . . . haplessly fictional about the persona before me that I decided to counter the living fabrication by speaking the not-so-simple truth. "Why aren't you a true king in every sense? Because you don't exist in every sense. Roguehan knew you were the perfect 'king' for a kingdom that didn't yet exist in every sense either, so he arranged for you to hold a place for him. He forced you to enforce policies that were designed to make you unpopular with the people so he could overthrow you and by doing so, gain the people's belief and support. He didn't anticipate that I would usurp his plans."

Raen was uncomprehending. I could tell that political intrigue was really quite beyond him. So was political philosophy. I absolutely had to admire Roguehan's brilliance. It had obviously been easier than summer rain for the emperor to encourage this puppet, this straw doll of a king, to commit any number of atrocities against the Gondish people. Against my people.

Raen spoke unexpectedly. "My mother says I am no longer to consider myself the king of Elf Land."

"Consider yourself overthrown. But that's all the damage I plan to do to you." Really, Ariana had already done quite enough. I wondered why she wasn't present at this pointless meeting that she had arranged.

Raen stared back out the window. The crowd was still calling for his death.

"Something in me loves the sky," he said haplessly.

"You used to love birds."

He had forgotten why his heart sometimes opened to the spaces in the Gondish sky. He had forgotten the birds, or perhaps I should say, he no longer had them. "The something in you that loves the sky is a ghost of what you were born to be. What 'you' now are is a binding costume, a heavy mask that Ariana found pleasing to herself. So she devoured your true self, day by horrible day, and you grew into an extension of her pride. It's like you were once a young willow tree, and some troll came along and clothed you in a pile of mud bricks, and so you rotted into the bricks, leaving only a faint impression of what you once were."

He squinted his eyes in noncomprehension. Or perhaps it was half-understanding.

"It's just what I see," I said helplessly. "Maybe I'm wrong. But king or no, I've got to decide what to do with you. And with your mother and sister. Your people . . . *my* people . . . want your head."

He responded with a non sequitur worthy of Aeren. "Can you make me exist in every sense?"

"I have no idea. I've never worked a resurrection before. Who's asking?"

He looked at the sky again, missing the subtle wit of my question. "They want to kill me. Make me somebody else. Somebody my mother can't take away. Somebody they can't kill."

I wasn't sure if he meant the king persona his mother had now destroyed, or whether he somehow knew that he had once been somebody else. Then he surprised me with a rant worthy of Aeren.

"Everybody wants to kill me. Kill me for believing I was a king. Kill me for daring to believe I was better than I really am. That is truly my crime against the world, that is what really earned me the death penalty. Nobody cares that I killed the wizards, or disbanded the two Assemblies and cobbled together a new one, or that I had anybody who complained about it killed. Nobody cares about such small matters, do they? People care that I had common birth and came from nowhere and became a king. They care that I believed in myself. *They want me to die for daring to believe in myself! Even though you come here to tell me it was never myself I believed in!*"

I didn't tell him I had a common birth and was here to become a king. I didn't tell him about the broken promises of magic and beauty that Grana had broken me with in my youth, and how they resembled the false promises Ariana made concerning his kingship. I didn't mention that I had grown into something that stood darkly against my real self. I didn't even mention that I too was wearing a mask to no purpose, for I was a priest of Hecate who wore Athena's robes lest anyone object to having an openly evil king. But it was all of those reasons that prompted me to say, "Come with me, Raen. A true king is a healer. Perhaps we can find you again."

And strange as it sounds, without further speech, he immediately went with me back to my rooms.

But when we entered my rooms, it was even stranger. Aeren looked startled at our entrance, recovered herself, and grabbed one of my wands. Not that she could have done any damage with it, as it wasn't activated, but I was surprised that she was willing to take such decisive action on her rhetoric about wanting to kill Raen, especially since Raen clearly wasn't a threat to either of us.

He looked blankly in her direction.

"Aeren," I said generously, "I am going to kill Raen. But not in the way you think. I am going to kill the pretender, and resurrect someone you should have known."

"I'm not even going to pretend I understand what that means." She spoke while deliberately refusing to look in Raen's direction.

"Then watch and be satisfied, bard. Raen, I am going to kill you into a new birth. Come before this mirror." I led him before the Mirror of Transformations, which I had set up earlier in a corner. He moved dully. I activated the Mirror, and willed to show him sky and birds like the heavens he had gazed upon in the meeting room. And then I took an image of his youth, a beloved forest path, and placed it under the sky in the Mirror, so he was gazing at a representation of one of his earliest memories.

"I am the King of Gondal and this is my first act of healing. Go back to the land. Go back and serve it well. Enter this path in your mind and heart and go back the way you were meant. I'm destroying you. I'm healing you."

Raen went rigid with rage. So rigid his anger caused a storm to appear in the landscape I had created. The storm was hungry and swallowed everything else in the image and I could feel myself losing control over my resurrection of Raen's true self. Raen was screaming for the years Ariana had cost him, and he was smashing the Mirror of Transformations in a rage. Aeren retreated quickly into a corner and watched in fascination. I shielded myself because his emotions had such fury they were causing my head to ache.

And then Ariana and a young woman I took to be Raen's sister Eyra entered the room. Eyra looked pale and scared at the sight of her brother's rage, but Ariana had a stiff, self-righteous smugness about her that seemed out of place. I assumed that they had heard from the servants that Raen was with me. Cwiven was behind them, ushering them into the room.

Raen stood screaming invective at the smashed pieces of glass, crying for the childhood memory he had destroyed in his fury. He now had a long, jagged piece of glass in his hand and was moving to attack Ariana, while Eyra froze like a frightened deer. "I'm going hunting, Mother. I'm hunting for what you destroyed. *Where are my birds?*"

Ariana smiled mysteriously, as if this outburst were nothing to her. Cwiven quietly closed the door. I saw him remove a wand I didn't recognize from his robe.

And then . . . he coolly blasted all three of them to their deaths.

Aeren and I stared at the mess. I had no idea what to think, except that it was a fine thing that I had shielded myself before this unexpected piece of business. "Pity about the Mirror," said Cwiven before he opened the door behind him and called loudly to the group of his fellow wizards who had assembled outside, "Our king was treacherously attacked by the pretender, and so the pretender and his family have been executed. Long live King Llewelyn. Take these bodies to the balcony on the far end of this hall and throw them to the crowds."

After the wizards had dragged the corpses out of my rooms and we were alone, Cwiven made an ornately obnoxious bow.

"Was that necessary?" I asked coldly.

"Yes, my lord. Your people demand no less from you."

"This is the second time you've disrupted my work with the Mirror."

"Regretful." He picked up the piece of shattered glass that Raen had attempted to use as a weapon and examined it. "What were you working, my lord?"

I couldn't begin to explain and I wasn't sure I wanted to. "I was working a whim. I was trying to heal . . . to restore Raen to something like his true self. As a true king, my healing should have worked."

"Well, perhaps it almost worked. Very close. As you are very close to true kingship." He set the pointed glass down near Aeren. "Zelar's Mirror is useless now. Ah, well. Come to the balcony, speak to your people who are probably tearing apart the pretender king's body limb from limb, and accept your crown. The time and circumstances are now proper for you to come into your power." Cwiven produced a thin gold circlet. "I took the liberty of stealing this. I think, under the circumstances, it would be most appropriate if your bard placed it on your head, as she originally ceded this crown to you, and what could be finer and more appropriate than your royal bard finishing the story of your ascension to the throne by publicly crowning you? At that point the people's belief, and all the power in this land, will reside in you."

"Go, King," said Aeren breathlessly. "I'm eager to play my part." She took the crown and picked up the piece of glass. "And I shall keep this as a remembrance of how we smashed Zelar and Roguehan, eh?"

Cwiven nodded solemnly, and then turned back to me. "Shall I take you to your people, my lord?"

I didn't care for the sense I had of being pulled by events of Cwiven's making rather than claiming my throne on my own terms. "Let my people anticipate my appearance awhile longer. Leave me here with Aeren."

My new chief wizard didn't care for taking orders from his king. "Your people are gathered now, my lord. They are in a frenzy for you. Surely there is no reason to delay."

"And surely there is no reason to hurry. Leave me time to pray before I take the crown." I stared him down. He returned my stare, slightly inclined his head, and slowly left.

"Why the hesitancy, Llewelyn?" asked Aeren. "We're here. Gondal is yours."

"I want Cwiven to know who's king. I don't want him to think he makes the decisions."

Aeren nodded. "Of course."

I tied the wand I had been carrying on our march to the outside of my robe. "I'd like to remind my court wizards that I too am a practitioner of magic. And that I'll authorize any further executions in this kingdom." I selected another wand, a shorter one, and hid it under my robe. "Old trick." I smiled. "A king can't be too careful, especially around his courtiers. And now, I really must pray."

I dropped my shield, went into trance, and made sure both wands were activated. Then I shielded myself with both wizardry and clerisy. Since Cwiven was so quick to blast Raen and his family to further his agenda of having me crowned and believed in by the people, I wanted to be sure that I was protected against blasts from other wizards who might not share Cwiven's professed loyalty. I knew enough about court intrigue at this point in my life to make a virtue out of suspicion. I was wondering if part of his and Welm's motivation for seeming to force matters, besides their understandable fear of being vulnerable to Roguehan should they fail, was a fear that not everyone in their party was equally committed to my rule. That would explain much.

"And now, my bard," I said cheerfully, "let us go greet our people."

I threw a clerical lock over our rooms, since my weapons were now stored there, and called for Cwiven, who was waiting nearby with several other wizards.

Cwiven led us down the hall to a very long balcony, most of which was hidden from view from the entrance which opened out to it. He remained behind in the hall with the wizards while Aeren and I went to greet the Gondish people.

I stood underneath the cool and brilliant sky that Raen had so loved. I watched a bird sail into the distance. The bird was oblivious to the spectacle of the city in an orgy of violence below, where I knew they were ripping and tearing at the corpse of the king who never really existed and at the self-proclaimed elf queen and her unlucky daughter.

I raised my hand and a shout went through the crowd, through the city. "Long live good King Llewelyn. Long live the crown."

Aeren unceremoniously plopped the crown on my head and took a clumsy step back. Then she smiled a little like maybe, for the moment, she was sincerely happy with herself and with the world.

The crowd exploded into cries and cheers of "King, King."

And somewhere I felt the land move, felt elvish power throb through my blood, as if my shields didn't exist. I extended my arms to my people and smiled. I commanded colors like singing rivers out of the air and the wind and they came, through the power of my will and the people's belief in me. I commanded the colors to play across the city towers and they did, weaving and dancing with the early spring sunlight. It was intoxicating. It was beyond rapturous. The crowd appreciated the display and began to cheer and clap.

"So now you are king," said Cwiven gravely. He had entered the balcony behind me.

"Now I am king."

"Now you are lord of the land."

"Now I am lord of the land. King of Gondal."

I watched my city in sheer joy for a long time. Then I made a theatrical bow to my people and retreated back into the hall, leaving Aeren, who was standing in the far corner of the balcony in the wind and the sun, to enjoy the moment and to do as she willed.

Light and joy.

Peace.

And a laughing voice of rough amusement falling like a shadow on the dawn of my bright new monarchy as I entered the hallway and my court wizards surrounded me.

"Kill him. In the proper place with the proper magic. Now that we have a true king whom the people believe in, the power of the land exists in a living man, and that power will now be magically transferred to me."

The voice was Roguehan's.

I instinctively started to call down a clerical blast but nothing happened. Then I remembered I had shielded myself, and realized that my own shield had neutralized my blast so both had dissipated, as sometimes happens when a cleric tries to blast through his own shield. That mistake bought enough time for one of the wizards to press his wand against my chest, well within my wizard shield, and hold me captive while the others tightly bound my hands with the same damned scarf that had kept my power sources in check in Walworth's castle. A cleric in the group pushed forward and uttered the appropriate incantations to activate the scarf. Then someone relieved me of the wand I had tied to the outside of my robe. My magic was now useless.

"And bring the 'royal bard,'" the emperor ordered. "Welm informed me of her role in killing my chief wizard."

As they led me away I could not see Aeren. But off through the door that opened onto the balcony, I heard my people's cheers turn to screams and I saw Roguehan's troops, the mercenary soldiers that had no doubt formerly comprised the encampment, entering the city.

Twenty-two

The same wizards who had so recently pledged loyalty to me took me swiftly to an empty room at the top of a tower, locked the door, and left me alone with my thoughts. So Cwiven and Welm had retained their loyalty to Roguehan all along, and led me on a fine illusion to become king so that the emperor might have a definitive source to steal elvish power from and so embody the ancient grace and mystery of this land in his person after all. That was clear now. And all more obvious in hindsight than I cared to admit.

The screams of Arula decorated my mind with pain the way a sanctified dagger in the hands of a skilled priest might decorate a sacrificial victim with wounds before delivering the killing cut. So this is what it meant to be a king? To bleed when your people bleed? I had of course read of such things but had always dismissed them as a poetic conceit. And I didn't even particularly care for the Gondish people I had met, who were so horribly debased from their glorious past. Yet something in me cried out in pain for that past. Perhaps it was my own lifelong passion for music and poetry, for anything beautiful that ran bright with ancient elvish power, that cried out in pain for the land, the land whose power I had so recently played with before my new people.

The scarf was absorbing my physical as well as my magical power, so I stood unsteadily before a vertical slit in the bare tower, leaning my weight against the wall as I surveyed my city. It was rapidly falling into night, and with the rising darkness the screams dissipated into an eerie silence. I could faintly hear the voices of Roguehan's soldiers shouting in Botha cadences, but the voices were too far away for me to make out individual words. There were no other city sounds. I watched the last brilliant trails of sunlight vanish and the sky go black, and then I saw that there were no lights except the stars. Arula itself was dark. A cold northern wind whistled through the thin opening, and when I put my face to the opening, I smelled no smoke and sickened on no death.

Roguehan's troops had easily taken the defenseless city, but they weren't burning or otherwise destroying anything. That made sense.

Roguehan wanted to own the sources of elvish power, and Arula, a city built on those sources, was no doubt destined to become his private pleasure palace. Any soldier who defaced the city could confidently expect to be rewarded with death.

It wasn't long after darkness, perhaps an hour or so, when I heard the door open behind me. Turning slowly away from my view of the stars and the night, I saw Welm and Cwiven enter. Cwiven was carrying a candle, which shed very little light, and which he placed on the floor to avoid the drafts from the slit which had afforded me a view of Arula.

While he was bent over the candle, I attempted to kick in his head.

But the scarf was making me so weak and unsteady by dampening my physical strength that before my foot could make contact with his skull, Cwiven countered with a mild wizard blast that sent me reeling to the floor against the far wall, and from which it took me several minutes to recover.

"Would you like the master here to conjure up a chair, lad?" asked Welm.

"Never fight wizardry with physical force," said Cwiven cheerfully, "especially if you're not much of a fighter to begin with."

I turned to Welm, and asked conversationally, "Your loyalty to the emperor is impressive, but how were you acting in Roguehan's interest when you did nothing to stop us from killing Zelar?" I didn't know if Roguehan knew about Welm's contributions to that incident, about how Welm had willingly cloaked me in invisibility, but I did know Cwiven was now certain to make it known. I hoped it would be to my advantage to create distrust between my guards.

I was wrong.

"Under the circumstances there was nothing I could have done without giving away the game, which was to encourage you to take the crown," Welm replied easily. "His Excellency understands that. Master Zelar was looking for his name stone without the emperor's knowledge. Fear and panic got the better of him, and so he refused to wait for me to find an opportunity to steal it back. His death was accounted collateral damage."

"For which I suppose I owe you thanks, my lord," added Cwiven, "as his unexpected passing opened up his position to me."

"You're welcome," I said dryly.

"Now that you've earned the people's belief," explained the illusionist, "the monarchy is restored, the true king of Gondal exists in every sense, and Roguehan need only destroy you with the appropriate magic in order to take your power."

"So what is he waiting for?"

"Information. His Excellency needs your help, lad."

I started laughing.

Cwiven spoke slowly and earnestly, as if he was merely one professional consulting another. "I am prepared to, shall we say, *orchestrate* the transfer of power, but to ensure that it's done properly, Aeren must be present. She was the true prince, the true heir to the throne before she ceded it to you, and so her blood is royal. It is both of your deaths that the emperor requires, because there is of course always the chance that upon your death, the power of the land would revert to her."

"Or even to Ariana and her children," I mused. "Which is why you killed them. But why did Ariana summon me to a private audience with Raen and then leave before I got there? I probed his mind and learned that she was encouraging him to give the throne to me, that Roguehan wanted it that way."

"Yes, lad," answered Welm quickly. "Since you made it impossible for the emperor to become the true king through his earning the people's belief by overthrowing Raen, His Excellency thought it best to help you become that king. Now that you have the people's belief, and the power of this land resides in you, the emperor can take that power from you and so become the true king himself regardless of who believes in him. All he needed was to create a proper vessel to siphon that power from. And so he strongly . . . encouraged Ariana to motivate Raen to give you his crown. The emperor has always preferred propaganda to bloodshed in these kinds of affairs. What matter now?"

I stood up with great difficulty and dragged myself over to the narrow opening in the tower, keeping my back turned on Welm and Cwiven for answer. All I could see through the slit were storm clouds devouring the northern stars.

Cwiven spoke in a matter-of-fact voice as if we were still face-to-face. "So the information we came for is Aeren's whereabouts. You can understand why we can't proceed without her."

"I thought *you* had her. I thought the other wizards took her." I stared into the night as if Aeren's whereabouts were nothing to me, even though I was suddenly mad with curiosity. The last I knew, she was on the far side of the balcony, which would have been death to jump from. I also knew her wizardry wasn't close to being advanced enough to fight off Roguehan's wizards. I wondered if Cwiven was lying and, if so, what his motivation was.

"The other wizards were surprisingly unsuccessful." Cwiven spoke in a tone of cool assessment. "So you'll tell us what you know about her apparent escape, or I'll take it from your mind."

I turned from the window and smiled darkly. "Take it from my mind, Master."

"As you will." I felt Cwiven's sudden probe, which was of course impossible to block with a shield because of the scarf that bound my hands and damped my power. The probe was so smooth that under normal circumstances I might not have felt it, but as it was, I felt Cwiven's energy slapping around in my head, and then I felt Cwiven's profound frustration when he realized that I had no idea where Aeren was or how she had escaped.

Cwiven wasn't lying. Which was all to my advantage.

After Cwiven withdrew his mind probe, I said carelessly, "I don't suppose that Roguehan's new chief wizard looks forward to admitting that he was unsuccessful in interrogating a helpless prisoner." I used the same irritating matter-of-fact tone that Cwiven had been using with me. Welm looked quizzically at Cwiven, realizing from the wizard's reaction to my words that Cwiven had been unsuccessful. I waited a few seconds for Cwiven's discomfort to get the better of him. "But perhaps I can help you."

"Help me how?" Cwiven was understandably cautious. He greatly feared failing Roguehan but he had no reason to trust me.

"Aeren has developed an apprenticeship bond to me." That wasn't strictly true, but it was true enough for my strategy. "It was easy and natural for her to do so because, as you probably know, she first learned magic from Zelar, and I first learned magic from his student, Mirand. That means, Master, as you no doubt also know, I might be able to find out where Aeren is if you permit me to send a calling. But unfortunately, I can't send anything with my power dampened. So if you'll oblige me by untying my hands, I'll oblige you by sending for Aeren."

"Why do you want to oblige us, lad?" asked Welm uneasily.

"Because Aeren somehow escaped, and so I believe she is somehow responsible for me being here." Actually, I didn't believe this at all. But it was a new thought, and my best hope was that since Cwiven had just thoroughly rummaged through my mind, he wouldn't bother to do so again and see through my ruse. As a precaution I did my best to force my thoughts and attitudes into something resembling anger toward Aeren, but it was thin work and I wasn't convinced it would hold up to a skillful probe. "Under the circumstances I'm not in the mood to lose my life and everything else I've worked for to Roguehan, knowing that Aeren won't have to do the same."

Cwiven tested my mind enough to feel my anger but, thankfully, he went no further. "You still think like a Sunnan." The wizard smiled appreciatively, and magically loosened my bond a little. I could feel my strength returning. I also knew that he was poised to magically tighten the knot at the first hint of trouble, which meant that his shield was still down from when he was probing my mind. Not that a wizard shield was much protection against clerisy. "You should have enough power now. Make your call and let us know where she is." He watched me intently, preparing himself to listen to whatever calling I sent.

What he wasn't prepared for was the sudden, clerical blast I drew that transformed him and Welm into a pile of charred bones and ashes. Clerical force is clean like that, and too sudden to anticipate. The deity is there. Or not. One second I was under the direct guard of two of Roguehan's most highly trained magical lackeys, and the next, well, there wasn't even flesh left on their bones to sicken me.

All that expensive training.

Praise Hecate! I pocketed the scarf as a useful magical item and considered whether to send a call to Aeren, wherever she was, on the chance that she could hear it. But there were so many wizards about, I decided it was better not to risk my call being picked up, especially since it was probable that some of them would have a magical bond to Zelar, and therefore to us.

But *damn*, I wondered how the hell she had escaped!

I thought about my next move. Roguehan had his troops all over my city. When I had entered Arula, only my wizards ... I mean Roguehan's provocateurs ... had been armed, and so there was nothing my fine Andan "troops" could do against the present invasion, even if any of them knew how.

Essentially, I was a king with no army, surrounded by the army of a hostile force.

But Roguehan could do nothing with that force unless he killed me for my power. If I were to leave the city, the Gondish people would never accept or believe in him and he would be just like Raen, a king in name only. I now had in my blood, in my connection to the land, in my confirmed kingship, what he wanted, what he had devoted his life to obtaining. And he couldn't easily assassinate me, because he and Cwiven had made it clear that there was some proper magical way to destroy me for my power, and Cwiven had apparently done the training and preparation to play that role. With his new chief wizard's regrettable passing, I assumed it would take Rogue-han some time to find another wizard with the required capabilities. He couldn't kill me during that time, and with the people's current mood, it would be difficult to keep me prisoner. And he'd have to find Aeren to ensure that the transfer of power actually worked in his favor.

So what do you do if you are the most powerful ruler in the world, your army has surrounded and taken a defenseless city, and you still can't take the crown from the reigning king?

I supposed Roguehan would have to answer that question. It was clear that he had no easy alternatives.

Which was exactly why I suspected that Roguehan might be in a mood to make deals, and that I had little to fear by boldly strolling through my castle and requesting . . . nay, *commanding*, a personal audience with him.

Then another thought occurred to me. All of the wizards who had ridden with me into Arula had been carrying unactivated wands from my royal armory. All of them were loyal to Roguehan, that is to say, all of them were enemy soldiers invading my territory with hostile intent. My judgment and sentence? Death. I threw a clerical lock over the tower door for security and spread my arms to the night sky, which was completely clouded over, hurling myself into Hecate's energy, into a trance so heavy I wouldn't have noticed it if Roguehan himself had broken through the door and stuck me with a sword.

"Mother Hecate. Give me back the words I need to activate my magical weapons. Let me hold them all in my mind."

The words came. The trance lifted. Harshly. So harshly it felt like my body had been slapped.

I sat quietly on the floor in the dim light of the candle Cwiven had brought, slowly recovering, and feeling through the recovered words for the location of each of my weapons. The weapons I had left in my rooms were still undisturbed, so I worked carefully to create new shields and magical locks around them and on the door. Then I keyed those locks to new words that I gave up to Hecate and promptly forgot, along with the words needed to activate those weapons. No one would be able to get into my cache without my willing assistance. Even though those weapons were useless to the enemy, they still had use for me, so there was no reason to leave them unguarded for the enemy to destroy.

I extinguished Cwiven's candle so that I might better feel the night around me, better taste the lovely darkness licking into my tight breaths.

Light trance. I focused my power on deftly activating each of the wands that were still on the person of the wizards I had ridden with.

And with a wrench of magic and concentration worthy of Zelar himself, I blasted each of those wizards to death with a force calculated to destroy each wand's carrier but nothing else. It was beautiful. I could hear explosions and shrieks and commotion rising all through my castle as I shielded myself in both wizardry and clerisy, magically transformed my Athenic garb into the simple black attire of a priest of Hecate in order to proudly proclaim what I truly was, unlocked the tower door, and boldly descended to meet Roguehan.

After all, if I was a king going to my first meeting of heads of state, I might as well do it in style.

I strolled easily through the chaos I had created, through groups of running imperial guards and scared servants, and nobody attempted to stop me. It wasn't even clear that anybody recognized me, and my sudden change of clothes probably confused those few servants who had seen me earlier into thinking that I was somebody else. It was easy to find Roguehan. I just stopped a panicked guard, told him I had business with His Excellency, and asked where I might find him. The fellow accommodated by giving me helpful directions to the rooms Roguehan had taken as his personal headquarters. I gave him a piece of gold.

There was of course a flurry of people entering and exiting the emperor's quarters with reports of the recent massacre, so I entered without ceremony and found Roguehan engrossed in serious conversation with the cleric who had waylaid me outside the balcony, who appeared to be a high priest of Habundia Christus, and with a master wizard whom I did not recognize. Other hangers-on were also present. To my delight, I heard Roguehan saying, "So it seems that besides Welm and Master Cwiven, you are my sole remaining magicians."

"Greetings, Emperor." I interrupted their conversation, focusing all the attention in the room on me. "I have come to personally invite you to a private audience." I smiled mockingly at my fellow cleric while continuing to address Roguehan. "Send your people to play elsewhere."

Roguehan looked slightly but genuinely surprised. However, he kept silent and quickly recovered his composure as the high priest fussily demanded, "Who are you and why are you bothering us?"

"I am the King of Gondal," I responded pleasantly. "And as this is my castle, you are greatly bothering me. We Gondish consider it rude to come calling without an invitation. But since you've already done so, I would consider it a great service if you and your associates—" I indicated the other people in the room. "—got lost while Roguehan and I discuss matters of state."

My deliberate use of Roguehan's proper name without any honorifics greatly annoyed the high priest, as did my implication that the cleric was on an equal level with the rest of the hangers-on, but it seemed to quietly amuse the emperor.

"Leave us," commanded Roguehan. "But leave me shielded and remain within call." His magical retainers made deep, crisp, slightly angry bows as the rest of the people in the room filed out. To adjust and strengthen Roguehan's shields, they had to drop their own, and so, with my heart in my mouth, I dropped mine.

Not that it much mattered as far as the high priest was concerned. We could certainly dampen each other's blasts with our respective shields, but it was our deities' own guess how much protection, if any, that would afford. Evil clerics cannot effectively shield themselves against each other, but then, under most circumstances there isn't any need to do so, as any evil cleric who kills a brother in evil, except under highly unusual circumstances and with the absolutely correct motivation, risks eternal damnation from his deity. That was better protection than any shield.

I was more concerned about dropping my wizard shield, but I was also fairly confident that no one would attack me without Roguehan's orders, and that Roguehan now needed me alive. So the instant his magicians were open and vulnerable to magical attack, I used wizardry to send the scarf to tie them together and render them useless, just as the scarf had earlier been sent to me. That was a risk—as I had to trust to my memory of the clerical incantation that activated the scarf—an incantation I had now heard twice—but Hecate was with me and so my spell worked. That would give me time to consider whether it was in my spiritual interest to blast another evil priest and to determine if Roguehan's magicians had any useful information.

As the wizard and the cleric struggled and protested, their strength drained by the scarf, I easily pushed them away from Roguehan.

And then, without hesitation, I drew down Hecate's force and blasted Roguehan.

Nothing happened.

My blast dissipated into dirty light and dull air, like a novice's. By all rights, at that close a range, I should have obliterated his wizard shield and passed enough energy through his clerical shield, dampened or not, to kill him. That shield, however, appeared to devour and destroy my blast.

"You don't have the skill to get through my defenses," boasted the cleric. "There's a current from Habundia Ceres, from the source of good itself, running through that shield. Priests of Hecate use a similar inversion technique to be able to occasionally eat meat without sickening on it. That shield will withstand any clerical blast, good or evil."

I was impressed with the fellow's skill. I doubted that even El could have pulled that off. Roguehan did indeed only hire the best. However, as the magicians who created the shields were incapacitated, I knew that I only needed to wait long enough and those shields would dissipate.

Roguehan made a motion for the cleric to be silent with an irritated wave of his hand. He and I coolly faced each other. The emperor was clearly assessing me and waiting for me to speak first. His shields prevented me from reading his thoughts.

I lounged sloppily on a divan that was covered with exquisitely embroidered cushions and put my feet up on a flawlessly carved table as if neither piece of elvish furniture was of any particular value to me, and as if it was nothing to me whether my blasts were effectual or not. Roguehan winced a little when my shoes thudded on the table. Then I manifested a goblet from a stand near Roguehan, a glorious goblet that blinked and glowed with elvish light like a little piece of carved sun, and made a show of gulping its wine too quickly and exhaling loudly, as if I had no intention of appreciating the craftsmanship that had created either the wine or the goblet. Then I spat some wine on the beautifully polished floor for effect.

"Condolences."

"For what?" asked Roguehan with a thinly assumed indifference.

"For losing. You will remove yourself and your troops from my city at dawn, and from my country before the end of the week." I drank more wine and studied him earnestly.

Roguehan chuckled.

"You will not make a move toward freeing your magicians or I will blast them the way I just blasted Welm, Cwiven, and your other wizards. As these are your only remaining magicians, I'm sure you would hate to lose them. You travel dangerously light, my lord."

Roguehan stopped chuckling. He had no idea that I had taken out Welm and Cwiven, but he knew that the fact that we were having this conversation made it likely. For my part, I decided my best strategy was to remain unshielded so I could blast them without hesitation should I need to. They clearly couldn't attack me magically, and I knew from Roguehan referring to them as his "sole remaining magicians" that I needn't worry about magical attacks from other quarters.

"I've already destroyed two high priests of evil alignment, so what's a third between me and my Goddess?" I smiled softly. Actually I had no idea if destroying this high priest under these circumstances would earn me damnation. But making the threat earned me instant respect from all concerned.

"But here's the crux of the matter. I have enough firepower in my rooms to destroy us, this castle, and a good portion of Arula. You can't access it, as it's magically locked. And even if one of your lackeys here was to escape and somehow find his way through my locks, my weapons would be useless to you because I alone can activate them." And I explained in general terms what I had done, and how I had been able to destroy the other wizards. Roguehan listened with fiercely attentive curiosity.

"So it's really quite simple. I remain king without interference from you or anyone else, or I destroy what remains of elvish power in the land and in the world."

"And yourself along with it."

"The skirts of Mother Hecate are soft. I'm not afraid to die. My Goddess will receive my spirit and someday She will send it back again."

Roguehan considered. "You're good," he responded, in a tone of dark appreciation.

"No, I'm evil." I paused and added, "I'm good at what I do."

Roguehan spoke again, much more confidently than the situation warranted, I thought. "But you are rather new at this, aren't you? Allow me to give you a lesson in statecraft, 'King.' Your threat of mutual destruction—"

I dropped the exquisitely crafted goblet so it smashed to ugly bits on the floor while I smiled in the face of Roguehan's obvious dismay.

"Is real," I assured him.

"Making your marks on carved tables and smashing goblets doesn't fool me into thinking you've no love for what this land is."

"It wouldn't be the first city I've loved and destroyed."

"Ah yes, the Helan border town." Roguehan almost sounded nostalgic. "So many years ago. Although according to my recollection, you are in no position to take credit for that one."

"I was thinking of a certain Helan military camp."

The high priest spoke up. "Now I know who you are. Llewelyn who destroyed Lord Cathe and Brother El of Kursen Monastery. You really are the king and not some crazed impostor come to cause trouble. Do you now expect blessed Hecate to welcome a priest who destroys Her own clerics?"

"Yes. My beloved divine Mother promised me this crown and this kingdom *after* I committed those acts. She knew my intent and did not hold those acts against me, or else I would not now be king through Her blessing and favor. In point of evil, Hecate Herself presided over Aeren's transfer of her birthright to me," I added triumphantly. "So I've nothing to fear from my Goddess."

"So you consider this country to be a divine gift from Hecate? Will your Goddess be pleased to welcome you if you destroy Her gift?"

"Excellent point," said Roguehan smoothly. "But it won't come to that." He stood up and spoke with unexpected cordiality. "Take the throne and get comfortable on it, my lord. I and my army have no intention of leaving your fair country just as I'm certain you've no intention of destroying your city, despite your ostentatious shows of barbarity. Issue whatever commands you will, but know that nothing will get enforced without my approval. And so . . . who then becomes the real power behind the crown? Who then becomes the true king?" Roguehan extended his hand. "Come with me, King. Your emperor is giving you your first order."

"Scorch off."

I noted with satisfaction that the high priest was looking especially sick and pale, almost green. I didn't think the scarf had made me look nearly dead when I was bound by it, it merely drained my energy to the point where I had difficulty standing and moving. Its effect on the high priest, however, appeared to be savage and severe. I wondered if I had erred in my incantation in such a way as to make the scarf's power especially strong. I almost wanted to kill the fellow just to put him out of his obvious misery.

While I was contemplating the extreme effect the scarf was having on the high priest, the door burst open and a breathless guard entered and made a deep bow.

"Your Excellency," said the guard, "Arula is secured, and we await your orders to begin . . . sacrificing the people."

Roguehan smiled cockily at me. "My orders are to wait until dawn, which is an efficacious time for sacrifice. Our new 'king' desires to have an unimpeded view of the proceedings when he gives me his crown, and, as uninvited guests, we must make up for the inconvenience of our arrival by not disappointing our host."

"My orders are for you to leave my city now," I said evenly.

"My army doesn't take orders from you, King. First lesson in statecraft. He who has the biggest army and the will to use it gives the orders."

The guard bowed and left.

"Rescind the order."

"Or you'll what? Destroy the city? Ah, yes, I almost forgot. But by the time you unshield and unlock your rooms, and call down the words you need to activate *all* of your weapons, my magicians—"

To my complete dismay, the goddess-be-damned scarf was now tightly binding my wrists as the cleric breathlessly uttered the incantation that made it impossible for me to work magic. *How?*

"—will have sent your spirit back to Lady Hecate in proper fashion."

The high priest, who was now regaining stamina, began to boast again. "Not only were you unable to blast through the shield I invoked around His Excellency, you clearly don't understand how that scarf works. It's designed to incapacitate one magician, not two. And only those with evil alignments. It only dampened half of our power."

I was beginning to understand what had happened.

"I nearly killed myself trying to work an inversion with half my power so my energy temporarily ran to good," he continued to boast, "but I managed it long enough to be able to loosen the bonds magically. My colleague was then able to perform the manifestation."

The wizard bowed his head in Roguehan's direction for acknowledgment.

Roguehan smiled. "I have always been impressed with your capabilities, Brother."

So was I, I had to admit. *This was certainly an unexpected pass. Hecate be my guide.*

"Well," continued Roguehan smoothly, "now that we've had our private audience, I suppose there isn't much left to do except wait for dawn, give the brother here a chance to fully recover from his feat, and enjoy what's left of the wine."

He poured more wine into a goblet. "Condolences."

"Have you been able to locate Aeren?" I asked as if my question was merely a social nicety.

Roguehan smiled a little into his goblet. "Aeren. The former princess. Or is that prince?"

"My royal bard." I let out a friendly sigh. "It would be a pleasant way to pass the time if she was here to regale us with a bright tale or two. I do wonder where she went." My comments annoyed Roguehan, as they were intended to. "Of course, she could be entering my rooms right now, as I've trusted her with the means to activate my weapons—"

"—In which case you would hardly be giving her away."

I felt the wizard probing my mind. "He doesn't know where she is, Your Excellency."

"What do you hope to accomplish by killing the Gondish people?" I asked.

"They annoy me," said Roguehan lightly. He sort of had a point there, but after the laughter in the room died down, he spoke seriously. "And now that their collective belief has endowed you with the powers of kingship, I've no need of the Gondish people. *You* are the lord of the land, King. You are the land. You will die as your people die. My magicians will transform the energy of that collective sacrifice to take the power of this land from you and bestow it upon me."

"Without Cwiven's help?"

"Cwiven isn't necessary. My other magicians are just as skilled."

Considering the cleric's considerable skill with shielding and inversion spells, that was no doubt true.

"How do you intend to kill all of the people?"

"I don't," replied Roguehan easily. "We only need to kill enough of them to create enough energy—dark, fearful energy—to wrench the power of this land from you and bestow it on me. Unfortunately, my advisors tell me there is no other way to do it. The energy of this land cannot be separated from the true king without sacrificing his people."

"Or the city itself, Your Excellency," added the cleric, who was quite full of himself in the wake of his recent feat.

"The city is mine. Those exquisite elvish buildings, the power that created them, is worth the deaths of any number of the Gondish people. People are common and easily replaced. The elvish artistry that built this city from ancient light is not. If the price of one of those glorious murals is the death of a dozen mediocre commoners who are worth nothing to anyone besides themselves, then I say kill the commoners."

"Are your magicians skilled enough to ensure that Aeren does not end up with *her* heart beating the power of this land? Cwiven made it clear that her presence was necessary. You sent him to interrogate me on that score."

"Her presence would be a great convenience. But *if* it happens that my magicians' work should result in the bard being all that stands between me and the power of this land, I am confident that we will find the bard, and with far greater ease than now, because we will be plagued with fewer distractions."

"You once ordered Welm to fool me into willingly embracing goodness and so to die damned to Hecate. It's a provocative trick."

"It was a brilliant trick," corrected Roguehan.

"But it failed, obviously." I turned to the cleric, my head spinning a little from the weakness induced by the scarf. "Satisfy my curiosity, Brother. What would my eternal damnation accomplish that my simple death wouldn't?"

"Speaking for myself—" He glanced at Roguehan. "—it would have been vengeance for turning your master, El."

Roguehan admired his goblet. "Which I accounted a less-than-adequate night's entertainment. But that is past. Speaking for *myself*, it was an attempt to turn this land through you. You were nearly a true king at that point. You had the power of the land, you just couldn't use it. My advisors had suggested that if you turned against your goddess, who had given you this land, that you and Gondal would be bane to Her, and therefore open for somebody else to take."

"I still have Hecate's blessing."

"Hecate is a lower manifestation of Habundia Christus," said the high priest. "There are promises and there are promises."

"Meaning?"

"Meaning, I suspect, that my prayers are differently weighted than yours. Not that your prayers are going anywhere . . . helpful right now."

Everyone laughed. The moment of merriment was disrupted by the return of the same guard who had left the room earlier, accompanied by another guard.

"It is dawn, Your Excellency."

"Then begin the sacrifice."

The first guard bowed and left.

Roguehan set down his goblet. "Come to the balcony where you first received your people's belief, King, and witness your people's demise. It promises to be an excellent show. Here's your escort."

I was so physically weak that standing was difficult, so it was easy for the second guard to "escort" me through the castle and out onto the balcony where I had last seen Aeren. Roguehan and his magicians followed.

Dawn was only partly there, no more than a promise in patches of sky that were slightly less dark than others, and in a suggestion of coming light in the wind that gently gasped and waned on my cold face. I felt for elvish power, for Arula, for my people and for the land. As in the tower, the scarf had no effect on my ability to feel elvish power, but of course I had no way to use that power to my advantage. Roguehan had won Threle, and now he would win Gondal, and there was precious little I could do but watch.

I heard a scream rising out of the early morning darkness that still obscured the city, and then I heard another. The screaming confused me because it sounded nothing like death shrieks, nothing like victims languishing under the sword or being forced to watch their friends do the same. These were surprisingly aggressive, almost nonhuman-sounding howls and cries that terrified even as their sources took the sword thrusts I couldn't see. Then I heard Roguehan's wizard mumbling incantations in a language I didn't recognize and I noticed that he had dropped himself into trance, no doubt as a preparation to work with the energy that the coming mass slaughter would begin to release.

The screams suddenly crested into an impossible mountain of sonic shrillness that sounded like Gondal itself was being tortured on the rack, when something bright and deadly shot up out of the darkness and pierced the master wizard through the throat. Magical shields being no protection against mundane physical attacks, Roguehan quickly removed himself into the castle while shouting orders to bring me inside as another bright arrow—I could now see it was an arrow, and an exquisitely crafted one at that—pierced the air where he had been standing, bounced off the castle wall, and landed near me. Another struck the cleric in the back as he too tried to exit. A fourth arrow neatly struck the guard in his chest.

The guard fell screaming as I strategically slumped to the floor, grateful that the scarf's physical effect made my ruse easy to pull off. I was now out of sight from the ground and therefore somewhat protected against further attacks, although the sharpshooter with the demonstrably keen night vision could still attempt to rain arrows randomly down on the balcony.

Sickness crawled and convulsed through me as the wizard, the cleric, and the guard writhed and jerked violently into death. From the physical agitations of their dying bodies, I knew that the arrows were poisoned.

Sick, weak, and trembling though I was, I managed to slowly and painstakingly retrieve the fallen arrow that had missed Roguehan, and to work through my bonds enough to carefully manipulate the point of the arrow to cut through the scarf without scratching my skin. With a little work I was able to free myself, but the scarf was ruined and magically useless. I carefully pocketed the arrow.

The next impediment I needed to overcome was my horrible sickness in the presence of the dead bodies. I saw no more missiles coming over the balcony wall, but as I had no intention of showing myself and becoming a potential target to whatever was attacking the castle, I crawled into the far corner of the balcony, felt my power return on every level, and shielded myself while waiting in the rapidly thinning dark until I felt fully recovered. Roguehan did not return, and the battle screams I heard from below repeatedly rose and fell like my strange fortunes that night. Not even the peacemongers I had once led into battle could scream for Ares like that.

The screams from below sounded both terrifying and joyful, and I also heard the rumbling of a large crowd. As I was considering the safest way to look over the balcony and ascertain what was going on before entering the castle and potentially meeting up with Roguehan and his cleric, I saw a burst of shadow in the early morning sky accompanied by tones of bell-like thunder, and high-pitched cries like laughing screams.

And there, circling above the castle like a mad cyclone, was a stormdragon.

The dragon was hissing and spitting lightning as it descended. As I lost sight of it because of the balcony wall, I took a chance, stood up, and grabbed a glance at the city. And there . . . cheering the dragon's arrival and thronging the city streets in full battle array that spun tears of light from the rising sun . . . was an army of elves.

I stared. Fair-haired, graceful warrior-dancers drunk on bloodlust. It made sense that those exquisite arrows were of elvish make, and that the archer with such devastating aim in near darkness had been an elf, for elves are often said to have the gods' own vision, to not merely see in darkness, but to see through it. I had no idea there were so many of them left in the world, having heard that only a few still existed in the Northern colonies. And yet here they were, defending Arula.

And fighting with a terrible grace and intensity that Roguehan's forces were no match for. The emperor's mercenary soldiers fought, but they lacked will, and I noticed small groups bolting here and there, and trying unsuccessfully to hide from the deadly accuracy of the elvish arrows. Each time an imperial soldier took a hit, even if it wasn't in a vital spot, he shuddered so horribly with poison that his frightened fellows ran for cover. And every time a group of imperial soldiers formed and tried to fight, a group of elves formed around them and shot them down.

And what the elves didn't kill, the stormdragon killed for them. The dragon's aim was just as unerring as the elvish archers' but it had the further advantage of a skyview of the city, and those soldiers who managed to hide from the archers were helpless against the dragon. And those who bolted were invariably pummeled with fire and lightning.

It took less time than it took the sun to rise past the tops of Arula's tallest towers for the battle to end. The elves retreated as quickly as they came, and the dragon thinned out as it landed, becoming hazier and hazier until it seemed to disappear into thin ribbons of shadow that got swallowed up by the whooping, cheering crowd.

So the elves had defeated Roguehan.

But what had happened to Roguehan?

I slowly entered the elvish castle feeling wonder but no triumph, knowing that nothing I had done had directly resulted in saving Gondal. I wondered if Roguehan had escaped when he saw the elvish army, but I had no idea how he would be able to break through their lines. And then I wondered how the elves even knew to come down from their colonies and fight and whether they would believe in my kingship as easily as the people had.

I encountered none of Roguehan's people as I walked through the castle, or should I say, as I walked through the living elvish dream, feeling splendidly unworthy now of its magnificence. I activated the wand I had hidden under my robe on the previous day when I first left my rooms to greet the Gondish people, and then I shielded myself. I considered what to do next. There were no answers. There was only silence, and the company of exquisite works of elvish art that became more beautiful every time I saw them, and my memories of the terrible killing grace of the elvish army.

And then, at the opposite end of a long hall, I suddenly spied a dark, melancholy figure silently admiring a large painting. It was Roguehan!

I focused my wand on him and studied him for a long time, as I had once studied Zelar when he tried to break into my rooms in Anda. It did not seem odd to me that this defeated warlord was simply standing defenseless before a work of elvish art. He had no soldiers, no magicians, no defenses. And Arula was so thoroughly overrun with the elvish fighters that escape was clearly impossible.

Roguehan was utterly taken by the painting, so much so that I had no idea if he was aware of my presence. His was the darkest enchantment I had ever witnessed. It was as if he had no natural emotions, not even concerning his soldiers' unexpected defeat, and the only way he could feel was through the intense experience of elvish art.

I dropped my shields and tried to probe his mind, but came back with nothing. The shields his magicians had created for him had dissipated, but his mind was shielded in the same inscrutable way Welm's had been so I could not read his thoughts.

This is the man who made me king so that he could destroy me, I thought, *who crowned me with the elvish power that would allow me to command the energy that makes that painting beautiful, to command the song of the water fairies.* But what I mostly thought was that we both loved this land enough to kill for it and that there was something sad and humbling about that, as if the land owned us.

I shielded myself again and walked over and stood before the painting. He gave no indication that he cared, although he clearly knew that my weapon was trained on him.

"And so Gondal is yours," he said lightly. "Are you going to thank me or kill me?"

"What's your preference?" I asked, as if it mattered.

He smiled sadly and turned away from me to kiss his hand to the painting. "Like melted light from the first idea of stars," he half whispered his commentary. "Who wouldn't sell the world . . . destroy the world . . . kill . . . torture . . . to see this painting for one blessed minute in a dark life? To see and hear the other delights this castle holds? Is not such beauty the only thing that matters?"

He didn't want me to answer. The splendor around us was answer enough.

"I have not decided on how, or if, I'm going to execute you." I said this with a courtesy that surprised me, that was as much a reflection of the strange place we both existed in as anything else. He gracefully waved his hand, as if my decision was nothing to him. We both knew I had no reason to let him live. "There is much you can tell me. About Threle, which I understand you now rule by right of conquest." I felt strange and twisted inside for what I was about to ask, but I couldn't help myself. "I escaped the execution you sentenced me to there, but I should like to know what happened to . . . the others. And what those instabilities of light and sound were that I experienced during my escape."

I steadied myself for his response. It took him a long time to answer.

"Threle." Roguehan looked beyond me, into a distance that was present elsewhere, perhaps in his past. Then he looked directly at me again. "The world is dirty, Brother. Only the gifts of the elves are clean." He smiled sadly.

"Meaning?"

"Meaning . . . that is all I care to say." He opened his arms from his sides while keeping a steady and earnest gaze on me, as if to let me know that he was prepared for me to blast him. "I prefer to die here, in this palace, than to live anywhere else in the world."

I knew what he meant. I put my wand in my robe. "I'm not going to blast you, my lord."

Roguehan looked at me quizzically. There was a dark hope clouding his eyes, delicately balanced against a dark calculation.

I smiled generously. "Look at the painting again." It didn't take any convincing for him to do so. "Let your heart drink deeply from its power. I'm giving you a gift from the elves." Then I quietly took the elvish arrow I had picked up on the balcony and, while he was in raptures over the painting, stabbed him in the back. It seemed more just and appropriate to kill him with something elvish and beautiful. Roguehan fell shuddering and writhing with poison. I watched him die as he tried to embrace the unspeakable beauty around him, my shields keeping the death energy from sickening me.

"Condolences, my lord." The strange thing is, I sort of meant it this time.

I walked somberly down the corridor, and then down another. I dropped my shields.

I sat on the floor before a column that looked and felt like a block of fire and starlight molded out of the days of some ancient joyous week that wouldn't die with the passing of time. Perhaps some ancient elvish love affair had wound happily through that week, and the energy of its rapture had burst into the exhilaration that still pulsed through the pillar before me. I relaxed into the wonder of the column, opened my heart like a new ground for the captured fire and starlight to shine upon, and asked for the ability to read the meaning of my relationship with this castle, with this land.

Then I stretched my hands and called upon the power of Gondal to create a beautiful poem. I asked the land to conjure the words and to let me hear them spoken out of the sacred air around me, to let me know if I was still worthy to rule.

And something very like a poem came out of the air. Light foot-steps strolling through the empty hall and a shadow obscuring my supplicating hands.

"Hey, Lew! What's the deal? I hear you're the King of Gondal now? We'll have to smoke some chaia while you tell me how that came about. Thought I was on the weed when I first heard you were leading some kind of revolution—" The speaker was Ellisand. He was carrying a bow over his shoulder where I was used to seeing him carry a lyre. Aeren was with him.

I was nearly as taken aback as when I saw the elvish army.

"The dragon here—" Ellisand motioned easily to Aeren "—let me crash the gate to see you."

"Royal bard," reprimanded Aeren.

"Uh, yeah, sure, if that's how Lew's partitioning the important jobs." He said this a little heatedly while I tried to collect my thoughts. "Didn't know there was an opening."

"We've got a signed contract," Aeren informed him smugly. "Signed in blood and witnessed by his goddess."

Bloody fine. The battle was barely over and I now had two sensitive Gondish bards on my hands.

"The crown is damn glad to see both of you," I said warmly. "How did you come to be here?" The question was for both of them and so they started speaking at once. I raised my hand to end the confusion. "Wait. One at one moment. Aeren, how did you escape from Rogue-han's wizards? And then, Ellisand, my friend, how did you find your way back here to your homeland? Just before I escaped from Threle I thought you had accepted a position in Roguehan's court."

Ellisand spoke first. "Well, the offer was made, but then Rogue-han left Threle, as I'm sure you've heard." He was teasing me the way he used to.

"And came here," I responded ruefully. "Yes, I've heard."

Ellisand laughed. "Well, after that business I went back to north-ern Gondal, to the elf colony I was raised in. You know I'm half-elven?"

"No." I was teasing him in turn, and we both laughed again.

"So I learned, or should I say relearned, a little archery because everyone was discussing the possibility of Roguehan invading. You're a monk, Lew. I mean—" He made a mock theatrical bow. "—a priest-king. You know what they say about the lyre being Apollo's bow. Well, one is a natural transition to the other, with a little work. Aleta would have been impressed with the hits I made on the balcony this morning."

"That was you? You damn near killed me."

"I freed you for the people's belief." There was so much meaning in that line we both fell helplessly silent.

"*I* freed the people," corrected Aeren, who was clearly impatient with having been silent throughout our exchange. "Remember the call I sent to the stars and to my ancestors on the night before we entered the city? Well, the elves heard it, and since they knew Roguehan was waiting in secret near Arula, something we didn't know, they began to march. When Roguehan's wizards took you, something happened to me. I grasped the shard from the broken Mirror of Transformations that I had taken, and I wished for your safety and for Roguehan's defeat—"

"—But not for Gondal's victory?"

"Scorch Gondal. I went dark. I became a shadow, a thickness in the air, a storm cloud at sunset, and by the time I knew I had blown out of the city, a stormdragon. And in my dragon form, not knowing if I could ever put myself back, I flew instinctively toward the elves, through the bond of our common ancestry. I led them into the city at dawn, helping to destroy Roguehan's army with my fire."

"Defending Arula like you were once supposed to defend Zelar's cave and the weapons that were meant to be used against Gondal's cities."

"Yes. And I actually had fun."

"That must have been a new experience for you."

She looked a little exasperated, but only a little. "And when the battle turned in our favor, which didn't take long, I became cloud and shadow and human again. It was strange and wonderful and I think I really do have a taste for killing things."

"Maybe Aleta would have been impressed with that too." I regretted saying this not just because it was as awkward a change in subject as any of Aeren's habitual non sequiturs, but because I wanted to ask Ellisand what Roguehan had done with Aleta and with everybody else in Walworth's castle, and whether he knew anything about the confusion of light and sound I experienced when I left. But as those events did not concern Aeren, I wanted to hear of them in private and so I quickly changed the subject again by telling Ellisand to make himself at home and requesting Aeren to leave me undisturbed in our rooms while I prayed.

I unlocked and unshielded my rooms because the extra protection was no longer necessary, deactivated the wand I was carrying, and placed it with the rest of my cache. And there, amidst the weapons that had been useless in Gondal's defense, I opened myself in prayer to Mother Hecate.

And like a vision of all the gaping hells of my childhood spewing open their sore vistas of pain, Mother Hecate took me into Herself.

And so I am a black croaking bird in the blank expanse of Hecate's palm.

And my croaks are the blood of the Goddess as Her moon wanes into the words my tongue can't form.

And Her voice is ugly.

"Gondal is yours, my priest, and so it is mine. The land is now bound to me as you are. Sacrifice your pretty land for Mother Hecate. Break your brave new toy. I am the Goddess who restricts the mind and destroys creativity. I require sacrifice. And I require justice.

My priests destroy beauty, my priests destroy what they love. I made you one with the land of Gondal so that I might require of you a sacrifice profound enough to cleanse the murder of two high priests of Habundia Christus, my highest and purest form. My favor was not a sign that I justified your actions, it was the path I tricked out for you that you might make sufficient sacrifice.

Here is your sacrifice. You will take the Beauty and power of this land and turn this land to ruin in my name. You will destroy this castle and all you love in my honor, and you will purge the world of elvish Beauty.

I will blight this land through you and through your rule.

But as this sacrifice means nothing if not freely given, Mother Hecate gives her ugly, croaking, wordless bird a choice.

You can prevent my destruction of Gondal and elvish Beauty only if you ride to the North Country and die there damned to me and so in torture for eternity.

Choose well, my little bird.

*T*he vision faded.

The castle was still beautiful, but its beauty to me was as a poisoned elvish arrow. The paintings and statues in my rooms were still as sacred and compelling as my Goddess's command, but they now existed in a sacred space that was bane to me. I sat in the kind of quiet that often rises through the spaces between the words of the last line of a solemn poem, and drank in the peace and joy of this place like a condemned man attempting to cheat the executioner by drinking venom.

I had done my best to save Gondal because I loved the things Hecate wanted me to destroy. Roguehan would have kept the power of this land for himself and for his pleasure. To uncreate the world. I would never hear the song of the water fairies, but I would have the power and obligation to silence it.

And then?

I thought of Isulde, who had once told me to come to the North Country with her and who had promised me that "when you die, I shall be there to heal you." Isulde, the inspiration of the world. The best dream. The fairy lover of kings and poets and fighters and the gods' knew who else. Isulde, who brought fairy gifts to play with like irresistible embodiments of the best version of yourself, who kissed you like your earliest and strongest ambitions, who came in dreams.

I could go to her now. I could find her North Country home, and risk damning myself to eternity to save what the elves had given the world. Perhaps Isulde would be there in the North Country to heal me, but if she wasn't, I would accept an eternity of torture like another broken promise and call it justice.

Aeren and Ellisand were catfighting outside of my rooms. I listened to them attempt to out-boast each other in Gondish fashion. And yet wasn't that perfect and right? That Gondal would be saved by a minstrel and a storyteller competing over whose work was most beautiful?

My turn. What goes, comes. Enemy glory.

Ellisand noticed me standing there first. "Hey, Lew, are you seeing a ghost?"

"Maybe."

"Hey, *Lew*," cajoled Aeren, mocking Ellisand's nickname for me, "give us your first command."

"My first command is for you to take this ring, bard." I pulled the Ring of Beauty that Isulde had given me out of my cloak, explaining briefly to Aeren what it was and how it worked. "It belongs here, with you."

"Why?"

"Because my second command is that you are to rule as Gondal's rightful queen. Or king, if you prefer the fiction of your male clothes, and this ring might prove useful."

She glowered at me. "Is this some kind of joke? Is this why you've changed the fiction of your Athenic garb back to what it was? So that after all I've gone through, you think to stick me with the throne?"

"Does this mean the royal bard position is now open?" asked Ellisand quickly.

"You saved the city," I said to Aeren. "You earned the crown when you made the decision to become the hated dragon, not knowing if you would get your form back."

"It wasn't a decision. It was the elves and it just sort of happened. If I had to decide, I can't say I would have done it. Why don't you want it?"

"I have a spiritual pilgrimage to make."

"Already?" asked Ellisand. "What do I know? Being a priest-king sounds like a hell of a game, Lew. Where to?"

"The North Country."

Neither of them understood what it would mean for me to go to the North Country, and I didn't feel obligated to explain it to them. As Aeren launched herself into a rant about her aversion to ruling anything and how scorch-be-damned unfair I was to spit on our agreement and how we had a blood contract that I should honor, I politely took leave of the new queen.

Then I requisitioned a well-provisioned horse and rode north across the Gondish wastelands to find Isulde or eternal damnation.

Twenty-three

I rode with the Gondish sun screaming northern poems at my back. At least, that is what I dreamed when I broke my journey each night. By day the sun was silent. It gave nothing. The wastelands were stranger and lonelier than I remembered them, but then, so was I.

I was not part of nature. I was not even part of my own nature.

When I reached the river Kretch, I could see it bursting through the Drumun Mountains with the fury of the falling, screaming sun that I had been dreaming. I sat still on my horse for a long time, watching the water going gray, watching the cold without feeling it. I watched the cold sear sluggish light into the depths of the sluggish water. Then I watched the water destroy the light. This river—here— had always killed light. No—never the same water twice. Never before *this* river and never *this* river again. Always now and nothing.

"Call to the star that is my name. The violent star which dreams disorder." Isulde had said these words to me after she had helped me escape from Walworth's castle. She had placed her "star" in me as we stood together near the river Kretch at the end of our fairy-run, when she was cajoling me to go North with her. And so here I was again at the Kretch, remembering to listen for the light, for the fairy star, pounding through my blood like a fairy song. And yes, it was there, pulsing against my ban. Isulde had said that the star was to be my guide to her "healing" should I ever enter the North Country. I did not know then that I would one day risk eternity on a fairy promise.

There was a brevity of wasteland on the other side of the river before the Drumuns marked the beginning of the North Country, and the mountains shimmered in and out of sight as I crossed the Kretch. It was a solemn crossing. Nothing in the water sang. The farther shore was flat and dull with old sun, and I remember feeling the unclaimed land retreating fast behind me as I urged my horse forward over the last portion of land in the world that was clean for me.

The Drumuns will thin and fade if you think about them too much, and they will move, so once I had crossed the river, there was no way to tell how far they were or where they began. I think I rode for days, and that the mountains sent grave songs all through my riding. I don't know when I finally entered the mountains, because the harder I tried to find them, the less I knew them. And once you enter the range, you don't see mountains at all, just shadows like valleys and pieces of sky blocked out. So there came a day of shadows, and then another, and on the third day I knew from the shadows that I was riding through invisible mountain passes, but how long and how far the days were now, I did not know.

And so I kept expecting death while invisible mountains crushed me fiercely with their voices. No telling where I would cross over and die. I might enter the North Country in hundreds of miles or minutes or in the space of one more half-silent hoofbeat.

When a sharp line of agony suddenly slashed and shivered through my body and my mind, I knew I had entered the North Country, and that live as I might, for as long as I might, I would live only through Isulde's star. I dismounted and leaned against my horse in an emptiness of agony, retching as I felt death press against my ban. I prayed that I might die there, but being North and damned to Hecate, my prayer had nowhere to go but here. Then I rode hard by the grace of the fairy star in my blood and the fairy star in my blood sustained me.

And a sudden sunshine murmured and fell gently from a full moon, a moon so far and high it appeared to be a circle of black surrounding blue against blue. The moon's phases are different in the North than in the rest of the world, and completely unpredictable. In the blink of the pulse of a fairy star, the Northern moon can wax into two disks or wane and thin into a joyous summer sky thick with azure. But then, in that moment, the moon was exuberant and full and the star kept my ban in balance and so there was a break in my sickness for a fairy dream.

It was a fairy dream of words, my words. My words kept manifesting themselves on a scroll formed out of a bright splurge of lunar sunlight. And I opened the scroll and read a stunning tale of love and beauty and thwarted desire, a high tragicomedy of laughter and grief and kings and peasants and mighty armies and victories and death. The words sang right off of the scroll and onto my tongue as I read to sky and earth and lovely moon. But the moment I loved and blessed the tale before me, the Northern moon waned and the words on the scroll became a bone-crunching clerical commentary and my words were no more substantial than dust running wild through my hands. Then my sickness returned with a slam and a wallop.

I rode, doubled over in pain. In doubling, I imagined both Habundias.

Only the star would sustain me home.

By following the star in my blood, I rode into a long dusk where I could no longer feel my heart beat—only the ban and the star pulsing in fierce synchronicity. I had no words save my strangling body's contortions.

Then the dusk vanished into night and I rode where sky was dark and violet, under an orange crying sun surrounded by an eternal glare of black. There were golden lights like stars. Every star wept spears of pain like frost. Starlight glowed into celestial poisons that bled colors that ran agonies through my blood. I wanted to beseech the stars to stop hurting me, but stars are different in the North. They retreat and fade to black whenever you look at them. Deep stars. Broken lights.

I saw random constellations, whole and brilliant as they whirled and disappeared. And then a winter of darkness was all around me but somehow it all came from me too, in puffs of snow and storm clouds and somber moonlight without a moon. My horse kicked up moonlight from the ground, in whispered echoes of something like a poem. I was drowning in a North Country blizzard of darkness. I was sailing into unplumbed night, trackless and fine as a young god's dream.

*H*ave you finished your plea?" asked Walworth evenly. I saw that Walworth had been writing my words all night. He was still slightly feverish. Soon my life would only exist on paper, like a draft of a fictional character. Soon I would die into my own fiction. I did not answer him immediately. I slowly turned my head and gazed beyond him to see that it was early dawn in the hovel. Early dawn in this patch of North Country that Walworth had claimed for Threle. But it might be night or day again in the space of a breath or the thrust of a sword. The fisherman was snoring. The yellow candle on the pine table no longer existed. It had burned itself out. Gull feathers had fallen out of the eastern wall and were waddling around the hovel in the back of a gray-brown gull. The southern fire had died but the scent of sage and lemon grass remained on the old man's breath as he coughed and hooted in his sleep. The water spray on Isulde's altar had dried but the air was heavy with moisture. I heard water waves sighing outside the door. I could drown here. I stared into the hole in the stone, the ambiguous opening in the side of the altar which faced me. The hole hadn't changed. It was still birth canal and grave, still a Northern fit of eternity. "No, I have not finished."

He waited like light and dark.

"I wish to add a question to my plea that it may be duly recorded in the court record." He kept waiting. "How did you come to regain your title as King of Threle? I thought Roguehan won the war."

He was silent before he answered. Then he said without expression, "Mirand deconstructed our defeat."

I waited for an explanation. While waiting I became aware that the muscles in my arms and legs had already died and my ban was pulsing me erratically toward death.

"When I abdicated my lands and titles to my twin sister on the eve of the Roguehan's arrival, Caethne became Duke and Duchess of Walworth in her very person, taking in my position and power by default. Caethne was therefore both 'lord' and lady of the duchy's land. She was also, without knowing it, the 'King' of Threle, for King Thoren had entailed the kingship of Threle to the 'Duke of Walworth' and Thoren was dead."

"And so?"

"And so. When Mirand embraced Caethne, calling on his love for Threle to sincerely make love to the woman who now embodied Threle in her person, he took into himself half of her power, that is, half of the power of the land. In essence, then, Mirand became 'King' Caethne's consort, which made him her 'queen.' In sense of poetry and power, Mirand was, at that moment, the 'lady' of all the land, embodying its feminine power in much the same way a male priest embodies the feminine power of his goddess. And so, when Roguehan claimed that he was now 'lord of the land,' Mirand stood in exact opposition to him."

"What a complicated word game." I managed a smile.

"Precisely. You brought us a Wand of Surprises once. You might recall that Mirand determined that the wand was designed to deconstruct the component elements of objects. He was able to engineer it to work on the component elements of the world order."

"Yes."

"Mirand kept that wand and when Roguehan finally assumed his identity as 'lord of the land,' Mirand, as 'lady of the land,' that is, as his opposition . . . used that wand to reverse the order of things, at least in terms of the war between Threle and the empire, for it was the energy of Threle he was working with. Defeat became victory. The moment Roguehan made his claim to be lord of the land, he embodied Threle. Mirand wrenched that energy from him, and restored it to me. Of course that caused havoc in the world order and reverberations backwards in time. You ran through the results when you escaped from my castle and encountered all those inversions of sound and light. The battles he had won, or barely won, were now lost, and he was now in my castle as a prisoner, not as a conquering warlord. The rest of the story was a simple matter of reclaiming our original identities."

"Poor Caethne," I managed to tease. "So she became Duchess of Walworth again, that is, the lady of the duchy's land, and you became duke—which meant, according to Thoren's will, that you became King of Threle." I smiled again. "Congratulations."

He smiled, but his smile quickly faded. "I do not know if it should have been within our power to change history. It was an act for the gods, not us, and Mirand fears he lost Athena's favor through his action. As he is not a cleric, his loss does not have the ramifications that your decision to accept eternal damnation from Hecate does. But he celebrated Athena through his life and learning, and so he feels that he sacrificed much to save the land he loved. As you did."

"What happened to the wand?"

"It was destroyed by the blast. Perhaps that is best."

"And after you turned Roguehan's victory to defeat, what did Roguehan do?"

"We imprisoned him and Zelar. When you contacted Zelar through his name stone and saw those bars across your vision, you were seeing him in a cell in my castle. But he and Roguehan managed to escape. From what you have told me, it's clear that Roguehan also managed to bring a remnant of his army to Gondal, which he used to augment the mercenaries he had placed around Raen years earlier when he made him a king after Zelar turned Aeren into a dragon."

I gasped under crushing of waves of pain.

"Have you finished your plea now?" Walworth asked gravely.

"Yes."

"You stand accused of high treason. You stand accused of aiding Roguehan our enemy, of using priestly arts to influence my critical judgment and that of my generals, and of the death of my cousin, Lord Cathe." He glanced at the unconscious fisherman, who was muttering and smacking his lips, clamping his mouth like a fish on a fly. "It seems I must render judgment. Of aiding Roguehan, I find you innocent. Whatever your intent at various points of your life, you clearly did not succeed in aiding the enemy. He lost the war, and his victories did not depend on your efforts. Of influencing the critical judgment of myself and my generals, I likewise find you innocent. Your minstrel friend Ellisand made your allegiance to evil clear to all, and so no matter what you intended, your truth was made manifest and my generals' judgment was their own."

So I was innocent through no fault of my own. But innocence was small comfort. I wanted Isulde. I was dying fast, and I wanted to see her and hear her sing the song of flowers and water fairies to me once— just once, before Hecate silenced all my feeling in wrinkled parchment and eternal damnation and dust. "Come soon," I murmured half-aloud.

"As to the death of Cathe, I find you guilty." He put his hand on the pommel of his sword. He lifted his sword out of the sand and placed it across his lap.

"My lord," I choked out the best argument I could find, "I am guilty of murder, then, not treason. Your cousin was evil, and a double spy and a traitor himself. Surely I did both Threle and the empire a favor there."

"Cathe had not stood trial for his crimes. And he posed no imminent threat to your life." Walworth spoke without expression, but he looked like he wanted me to continue arguing. His sentence was a hint for me to speak. He raised his sword and thrust its power deep into my chest, keeping death at bay a little longer.

I looked up the blade directly into his hard eyes. "Cathe was my life's opposition. He never threatened my life. He destroyed my life. When I killed him, I killed my own evil, for that is what he was to me. Caethne recognized that by trying to swerve me over to goodness. By offering me new life and birth. A second Grana," I mused, then faltered.

"Speak. You may still have a new birth." He held the sword steady but we both knew death was imminent. I could hear the shadow of Hecate's gate creak open.

"By killing him, I killed my own evil. By killing *my* own evil, I committed treason against myself. My lord, I am guilty of treason after all."

"And so you shall die for your treason, but not at my hands. Under Threlan law, it is my right to sentence you to whatever method of execution I choose. As you have chosen to die in such a manner as to risk eternal damnation from your goddess so that you might save your country, I refuse to interfere. I would like to think I would have had the strength of heart to risk as much for Threle." He sounded respectful. "My choice. I sentence you to death by exposure to the North Country. Under the circumstances, I also account it a hero's death."

"Friend." I might have said this. I might have only thought it as the door to the hovel opened and sweet cloudy Isulde tripped in with the dawn in her eyes. Isulde was breathing songs of spring lilies and meadowlarks. She held a star in her hand like the star in my blood. The star melted and she washed away Walworth's fever with a palmful of water. Then she set a basket of shells and flowers at my feet and I died.

That is, I heard a raven croaking like the sound of Mother Hecate swishing Her skirt and closing Her gate and so I knew that She would not accept me into Herself and that my damnation, my eternal torture, was now to begin.

But it didn't. Fairies speak easily to the dead, and sing even more easily. Isulde sang to my spirit a long time before she spoke. And in her singing I'm sure I heard the song of the water fairies. And the songs kept coming as I lingered in spirit like a new dream on her breath. And then her songs became half-singing, beautiful speech. "Llewelyn." She wove my name into her half-singing when she spoke. "You can plan your own birth now."

"I know." My spirit voice surprised me. It was so light that the air and her breath seemed to muffle it. It sounded vaguely like the echo of a voice of a hidden bird.

"Where would you go?" she asked.

So sensuous her eyes and mouth. I kissed them in my spirit and she briefly became my kiss. And then, in spirit, I was rising toward the hovel's ceiling.

I was rising into light and morning, rising as the roof which covered my body pulled gently below me and vanished into the surrounding sand. Then I rose higher on the strength of my own thoughts, giddy to see the other shore of the lake dropping far away below me with the rest of the world.

I lingered for a while in a warm breeze and saw birds skimming through sunlight. And white sparkling wave froth kept merging into lovely randomness on the lake as I rose farther with each feeling of joy. And I would never reach the sky because there was all pure light where sky should be. I rose beautifully and peacefully out of the world, rose laughing through a fresh new morning of love and light and joy and quiet splendor until a new energy pulled and snapped and I fell screaming into the top of a black burning sky.

There are no easy births. A line between the worlds had broken and I had fallen through like a burning comet. Angry lightning buzzed and spiraled around my arms. Clouds just slid under my feet and I kept plummeting into heavier and heavier air, air heavier than anything I'd ever touched. And then I was all fire because I was falling so fast and the energy here was so harsh and heavy it burned anything that fell. And because I was spirit I burned and couldn't die.

And then I was back in my body again.

And very much alive.

Dawn in the North Country.

"You saved Gondal with a sacrifice and yourself with a story," said Walworth. "In my judgment, all debts are paid."

"Stay here with me," giggled Isulde, as if saving me from eternal damnation was just another spot of fairy fun. "Or go to Gondal and we will make poems and songs with the elves."

"Threle is also open to you. There is much work to be done there."

Beauty or freedom. Gondal or Threle. Every choice is life and death.

I sat up slowly and looked at the old fisherman, who was joyfully motioning to embrace Isulde and now had eyes for nothing else. She sat on his lap and pulled his beard, laughing.

"Before I choose, my lord, tell me why you followed me here?"

"I arrived in Arula after you had left, thinking to defeat Roguehan's much-attenuated forces in the wasteland, and not knowing that Gondal had become truly a sovereign country. There I learned from your friend Aeren that you had come here. Isulde showed me the way in a dream."

"That is the how, not the why."

"The why. I also learned from Aeren that you had become King of Gondal. The last I had heard about your adventures was when your former colleague Mirra recounted as we all stood in chains before Roguehan how you had planned to destroy me and my household to glorify yourself into godhood. I knew that you had been banned against entering the North Country, but I didn't know whether you had been able to remove that ban. I had to assume you would only have entered this region for a profound and dark purpose."

"You assumed correctly," I said lightly and pointedly. *I mean really, what could I say?*

"Well." He paused a little before continuing. "I did not consider it in Threle's or in my own interest to merely speculate on your motives. So I came here to gather intelligence, to discover if you were a threat to Threle, and to learn what you knew about past events that might have use for me. I knew that encouraging you to tell your life story might stave off your death long enough for me to record a good amount of useful information. Words are sacred to you. And of course my trial satisfied my sense of justice, which is sacred to me." He continued matter-of-factly, "Should you agree to work magic for me again, clerisy or wizardry, I would not have it said that I've taken into my protection someone who has not been cleared of his crimes against my country."

I didn't respond right away to his implied offer. There was too much to consider. I thought briefly of Walworth's love of Threlan law, and then of how Hecate held sacred all laws that restricted growth. I had once loved Threle, too, in my way, but Threle had betrayed me. I knew that Walworth wanted me to work for him so he could better ensure that I wasn't a threat, just as he had once taken me into his household in Helas for similar reasons. And then I thought ruefully that what had hurt me the most about Helas was that I had loved my life there.

My judgment on his strategic offer of friendship?

"I've no idea if I still have a relationship with Hecate," I responded coolly. "I'll have to enter the world again to determine that."

I turned to watch Isulde playing with the old fisherman. She was biting his skin and he was howling as his blood ran. The fairy of the world. Beauty is always deadly capricious, destroying even as it caresses. Enemy glory.

"My decision is to wander freely with allegiance to none." I sat up in my stained cloak, felt the Northern energies swirling and pounding around me, and knew that I would carry the strangeness of this night and this makeshift trial for the rest of my life.

"So be it." Walworth sounded resigned, but his love of justice meant that he had to respect my decision. I heard him sheathe his sword.

Then I walked out of the hovel into a North Country day. I didn't think as I rose. My body was walking itself and I was just going along with it because I was there.

The lake outside was pretending to be a sea. The day was all blue. Even the sun was blue, or rather, it burned more blue into the sky than the sky already had. Isulde's scarefisher still creaked and wove wind shadows in his lap, but mostly it was all warm outside. All sun. All enchantment.